THE
JENSEN
DYNASTY

Look for these exciting Western series
from bestselling authors
William W. Johnstone and J.A. Johnstone

The Mountain Man

Preacher: The First Mountain Man

Luke Jensen: Bounty Hunter

Those Jensen Boys!

The Jensen Brand

MacCallister

The Red Ryan Westerns

Perley Gates

Have Brides, Will Travel

Will Tanner, Deputy U.S. Marshall

Shotgun Johnny

The Chuckwagon Trail

The Jackals

The Slash and Pecos Westerns

The Texas Moonshiners

Stoneface Finnegan Westerns

Ben Savage: Saloon Ranger

The Buck Trammel Westerns

The Death and Texas Westerns

The Hunter Buchanon Westerns

THE
JENSEN
DYNASTY

WILLIAM W. JOHNSTONE
AND
J.A. JOHNSTONE

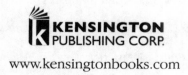

KENSINGTON
PUBLISHING CORP.

www.kensingtonbooks.com

KENSINGTON BOOKS are published by

Kensington Publishing Corp.
119 West 40th Street
New York, NY 10018

PUBLISHER'S NOTE
Following the death of William W. Johnstone, the Johnstone family is working with a carefully selected writer to organize and complete Mr. Johnstone's outlines and many unfinished manuscripts to create additional novels in all of his series like The Last Gunfighter, Mountain Man, and Eagles, among others. This novel was inspired by Mr. Johnstone's superb storytelling.

ISBN-13: 978-1-4967-3623-9
ISBN-10: 1-4967-3623-0
First Kensington Hardcover Edition: June 2021

10 9 8 7 6 5 4 3 2 1

Printed in the United States of America

A BRIEF INTRODUCTION

In November of 1985, Zebra Books published the first in what has proven to be currently the most successful Western series of all time, William W. Johnstone's *The Last Mountain Man*, featuring the adventures, hardships, and bloodshed of frontiersman Smoke Jensen.

Now, almost 37 years and fifty books later, the saga of Smoke Jensen, the Last Mountain Man, continues. The readers, though, wanted more stories about the Jensen family and friends. In December of 1991 came *The First Mountain Man*, later known simply as *Preacher*. Though not related to Smoke Jensen, Preacher was like a second father to Smoke. And continues to be after 32 years and 27 novels.

Still not enough—readers wanted more.

So, in September of 2007, Smoke adopted an abused orphan he named Matthew, or Matt Jensen, who would go on being featured in eleven western adventures of his own. Though not a Jensen at birth, Matt has taken on all the fine attributes of the Jensen family—honesty, decency, morality, and he's pretty handy with a gun when evil rides into town.

Still not enough—readers wanted even more.

Smoke had an older brother, Luke, supposedly killed in the Civil War. Being a Jensen, however, Luke wasn't going to let any war bring him down. In September of 2012, Luke Jensen, Bounty Hunter rode out of obscurity, and by 2022, he will have ten Western adventures of his own, becoming a bounty hunter who gives no quarter and usually brings the bad guys back alive. Though not always—some law-breaking hardcases just don't go down as easily as others.

In this volume, we proudly present for the first time three Jensen family epics: *Smoke Jensen: The Beginning*, *Matt Jensen: The Last Mountain Man*, and *Luke Jensen: Bounty Hunter*.

Enjoy. And God bless.

—J.A. Johnstone
May 2021

CONTENTS

PART ONE
SMOKE JENSEN:
THE BEGINNING

CHAPTER 1

Early October, Stone County, Missouri

Election season of 1860 was the most contentious election season in the history of the United States. Newspaper editorials and campaign speeches suggested that there would be major consequences, depending upon the results. Four candidates were running for President, the major two being Abraham Lincoln as a Republican and John Breckenridge as a Southern Democrat. In addition, two other candidates were in the race. Stephen Douglas was a Democrat and John Bell was running on the Constitutional Union ticket.

Several of the Southern states had already made the threat to secede if Lincoln won, and tensions were running high.

Missouri was a slave state with almost 120,000 slaves, but as of the latest count, only sixteen resided in all of Stone County. Emmett Jensen didn't have any slaves, but he did own a forty-acre farm of loam and rock adjacent to Shoal Creek. The farm required a great deal of work just to make it productive enough to feed a family of five. At twelve years old, Kirby was the youngest of Emmett and Pearl Jensen's three children. Janey was fourteen and Luke was eighteen.

The institution of slavery had an effect on the lives of almost everyone in Missouri and Kansas, a free state. The question of slave or free had gone far beyond mere debate, erupting into actual fighting between armed partisans of the two states.

The guerrillas from Kansas called themselves Jayhawkers. Their counterparts in Missouri were known as Bushwhackers, and for some time, shooting had been taking place between the groups. Led by Asa Briggs, the Missouri Bushwhackers called themselves the

Ghost Riders. The Jayhawkers from southeast Kansas were led by Angus Shardeen.

Shardeen once rode with John Brown, and personally took part in the Pottawatomie Massacre in which several pro-slave sympathizers were murdered. Since John Brown's death, Shardeen had started his own group, and was making his presence known by burning homes and killing innocents in southwest Missouri, all in the name of abolition.

"There's a big war acomin,'" Tom Byrd told Emmett the afternoon he went to Byrd's farm to retrieve the two mules he had rented to his neighbor for the afternoon. "You mark my words. It's acomin'."

"Maybe not," Emmett replied, his response motivated more by hope than reason. "Maybe cooler heads will prevail."

"No, they won't. The Republican, Abraham Lincoln, is going to be elected, 'n that's all it's agoin' to take. Once that ape becomes president, there's going to be war sure as a gun is iron."

Emmett shared some of the conversation with Pearl and the rest of his family over supper that night.

"If war does come, Pa, which way do you think Missouri is goin' to go?" Luke asked.

"Well, seein' as Missouri is a slave state, I don't see it goin' any other way except for the South."

"Yes, sir. That's what I was athinkin' too," Luke said.

"But Pa, you said many times, that you don't hold with ownin' slaves," Kirby said.

"I don't hold with anyone holdin' another man like that, be the man black or white. But that ain't the only thing that's causin' the trouble. People ought to have the right to say what goes on in their state, and the federal government's got no right stickin' its nose into our business. I reckon if it comes to it, 'n all my friends and neighbors go off to join up with the South, why then that's the way I'll have to go."

"That's sort of what I was figurin' too," Kirby said. "If war comes, we'll be fighting for the South."

"There is no *we* about it, boy. You're too young to even be thinking about such things."

"I ain't always goin' to be too young," Kirby said.

"Well, you are too young now."

"Maybe Kirby is, but I ain't," Luke said. "If war comes, I'll be ridin' off to join up with the South. You can bet on that."

"I'm so tired of hearing everyone talkin' about the war," Pearl said. "Can't we at least talk about somethin' else here in our own home?"

"I hear what you're sayin', Pearl. But let's hope that it don't get no further than just talkin' about," Emmett said.

When Emmett first built the house back in 1841, it had only two bedrooms, one for him and Pearl, and one for the child he was sure they would have. Luke came along the first year, then four years later Janey was born, so Emmett put up a wall right down through the middle of the room, dividing it into two cubicles, each barely large enough to hold a bed. That arrangement gave Luke and Janey their privacy. Kirby came along two years after Janey. There was no place to put him, so Emmett built a small shelf just under the eaves of the house in order to make a sleeping loft.

It was a long time before Kirby was able to go to sleep that night. He was thinking too much about the supper conversation. Was it actually going to come to a war? Some might have said the skirmishes between the Bushwhackers and the Jayhawkers meant a war was already occurring, but that wasn't the kind of war he was wondering about. He was thinking of a real war, like the kind he had read about in books.

He knew about the Revolutionary War, the War of 1812, and the two Mexican Wars. The man that owned the leather store in town, Marvin Butrum, had been in both of the Mexican wars. He was with Sam Houston at San Jacinto during the Texas Revolution, and he had been with Robert E. Lee in the Mexican American War.

Kirby wondered what it would be like to be in a war. He pictured himself in a uniform astride a white horse, holding his saber high, and leading men into battle.

Well, it probably wouldn't really be like that. He was pretty sure that a twelve-year-old would not be entrusted to actually command an army. That realization caused the image he had projected in his mind to fade away.

He rolled over. But wait. The battle was in his imagination! While in his imagination, he could be anything he wanted, including a captain or a general or a sergeant; he wasn't sure enough about ranks to know what he wanted to be. But, whatever he was, he smiled as he remounted the white horse, lifted the saber, and gave the order to charge.

* * *

The next morning, Kirby and Janey went out to the barn to milk the two cows.

"You should be the one that does all the milkin'," Kirby complained.

"Why?"

"Because you're a girl, and milkin' cows is girl's work."

"What makes you think it's girl's work?"

"Pa don't never milk a cow, 'n neither does Luke. They plow and plant and harvest, but they don't milk cows."

"No, and they don't gather eggs either, but you do. Let's face it, Kirby. Pa prob'ly thinks you are a girl." Janey laughed at him.

"Yeah? Well, would a girl do this?" Kirby picked up a double handful of straw and dumped it on her.

"Don't do that! You'll get straw all in my hair."

Kirby laughed.

The cows, Ada and Bridget, were back to back in a stall, waiting to be milked. Kirby and Janey put the milk stools in place, then sat down to milk.

"I bet I finish first," Kirby said.

"It isn't a contest, Kirby," Janey replied.

Kirby did finish first, then he got an idea. He had been milking Ada while Janey was with Bridget. Reaching over to grab Bridget's tail, he lifted it up, then did the same thing with Ada's tail. Using the hairy twitches at the ends of their tails, he tied them together.

Janey had been concentrating so much on the milking that she didn't notice what he had done.

"Want me to carry your bucket for you?" Kirby asked, diverting her attention.

"Well, that's very nice of you," Janey said, handing the bucket of milk to him.

They started back toward the house when the two cows began bellowing behind them.

"What in the world is wrong with those two?" Janey turned around. The two cows were trying to go in opposite directions, but couldn't because their tails were tied together. "Kirby! What did you do?"

"I don't know how it happened, Pa," Kirby tried to explain a while later. "As near as I can figure, they was just swattin' at flies 'n their tails musta got tangled up somehow. That's all I can figure."

"Are you trying to tell me they tied their own tails together?"

"Think about it, Pa. I mean, here are these two cows, just standin' there gettin' milked 'n all, and they sort of start swingin' their tails back and forth, not payin' no attention to each other. The next thing you know, why, their twitches has got all tangled up. Don't you think maybe it coulda happened that way?"

"I tell you what, Kirby. You go paint the barn, and while you're painting it, you might just come up with a lot better explanation than that cock and bull story you just tried to pass off on me."

"I thought you wasn't goin' to paint the barn till next summer."

"I changed my mind."

"All right, Pa."

Janey stuck her tongue out at Kirby.

Emmett watched his youngest son leave the house, and not until he was sure Kirby was well out of earshot did he turn to Luke. "Who would ever think to tie a couple cows together by their tails?" he asked, laughing.

"Nobody but my little brother, I'm thinking," Luke answered, laughing as well.

McMullen School was a one-room school accommodating twenty-two students in grades one through eight. Kirby was in the sixth grade. He was naturally a big boy, bigger than anyone else in the school, including the two boys in the seventh, and the one boy in the eighth grade. In addition to his natural size, hard work on the family farm had made him strong.

In the eighth grade, Janey was a beautiful girl with black hair, dark brown eyes, full lips, and prominent cheekbones. But it didn't stop there. Her body was already fully matured to the point that visitors to the school sometimes mistakenly assumed that she was the teacher. Aware that her looks and body had an effect on men, Janey wasn't above being a sexual tease when she could do so to her benefit.

After completing the fifth grade several years ago, Luke had left school to help his father work the farm. After he completed the fifth grade last spring, Kirby had petitioned his father to let him do the same thing.

On the crisp fall day, Kirby was recalling that conversation as he sat at his desk, staring through the window.

"I can already read, write, and cipher," Kirby told his father and

older brother. "I don't see any sense in me staying in school any longer, when I could be helping out on the farm."

"You are going to stay in school," Emmett insisted.

Kirby continued staring at a distant flight of geese. Very high in the sky, the geese were maintaining a perfect V formation as they headed south for the coming winter. He imagined himself down at Shoal Creek with a shotgun. He could bring home a goose, and his mother could—

"Kirby? Kirby, have you suddenly gone deaf?"

The others in the classroom laughed, and it wasn't until that moment that Kirby was even aware he was being spoken to by his teacher.

"I beg your pardon, Miss Margrabe?"

"I just gave you an assignment. From the *McGuffey Reader*, I want you to spell, define, and tell what part of speech is the word *fluctuate*."

"*F-L-U-C-T-U-A-T-E*," Kirby said, spelling the word carefully.

"Very good, Kirby. And it means?"

"It means somethin' is moving back and forth, but it can also mean that somebody can't make up their mind about somethin', like if I'm tryin' to decide whether I want a piece of cherry pie or apple pie."

"And what part of speech is it?"

"It's an intransitive verb."

Miss Margrabe smiled and nodded. "Very good, Kirby. You were paying attention after all."

"Yes, ma'am," Kirby said.

"All right, children, I'm going to be working with the first and second graders now. The rest of you know what your assignments are, so please study at your desks."

The assigned work for the sixth grade was math, and Kirby was working on a problem of long division. He hated long division, particularly when the answer never came out even. The lesson was that it had to be carried out at least four decimal points. Kirby found such problems frustrating, and he was still working on them when Miss Margrabe stopped by his desk to look at his work.

"Very good, Kirby. You wouldn't happen to know if . . . uh . . . Luke might be—" Miss Margrabe stopped in mid-sentence, then gave what could only be described as a self-deprecating chuckle.

"Might be what?"

"Never mind. It was quite inappropriate of me to ask. Keep up the good work; you have an excellent math paper here."

"Thank you." Kirby smiled as Miss Margrabe walked away. He and Janey knew that their teacher liked Luke. Kirby would never say a word about it, but Janey wasn't above teasing her brother.

Returning to his work, Kirby finished the last problem, then turned his attention outside again. A group of riders were coming toward the school, riding fast and all bunched up. That alone was enough to arouse his curiosity, but one of the men was carrying a flaming torch. Because it was the middle of the day, that made their approach even more curious.

As they drew closer, the rumble of hoofbeats became a thunder and soon everyone in the school was aware of the galloping band of horses. They looked at each other in confusion, and Kirby got up from his seat and moved to the window.

"Kirby, take your seat, please," Miss Margrabe said.

"Somethin' ain't right," Kirby said.

"*Isn't* right," Miss Margrabe corrected automatically.

The riders came within twenty yards of the school building, then stopped. The leader of the band had red hair, a red beard, and a very prominent purple scar on his face. His description was well-known. It was Angus Shardeen.

"It's Jayhawkers!" Kirby shouted.

Several of the riders began shooting toward the school, and the bullets crashed through the windows. The students started screaming.

"Get down on the floor!" Kirby shouted as he ran to his sister and pulled her down, just as a bullet slammed into the desk where she had been sitting.

"Don't they know this is a schoolhouse?" Miss Margrabe cried.

"Miss Margrabe, no! You'll get killed!" Kirby shouted. Leaving Janey lying on the floor, he ran to his teacher and pulled her down as well, though not in time to keep her from being shot in the shoulder.

"Burn in hell!" someone shouted from outside. A second later a flaming torch came in through one of the windows that had been shot out. The other students screamed and shouted and ran away from the flames. Only Kirby had the presence of mind to grab the pail of drinking water and toss the water onto the torch, extinguishing it.

"They're leavin'!" a seventh-grade boy shouted. "They're ridin' away!"

With the fire under control, Kirby hurried over to Miss Margrabe, who was on the floor, leaning up against the wall under the blackboard. She was holding her hand over the shoulder wound, and blood was coming between her fingers, though she wasn't bleeding profusely.

"Janey, come look at this, will you?" Kirby called. When Janey didn't respond right away, he called again. "Come here and take a look at Miss Margrabe's shoulder. You can get up now. The Jayhawkers is gone."

"Are gone," Miss Margrabe corrected through clenched teeth.

"Yes'm they surely are."

Janey went over to them, then knelt beside the teacher and examined the bloody wound. The bullet hadn't actually hit her shoulder, but high up on her right arm.

"Kirby, use your knife to cut the sleeve off," Janey said.

"Must I bare my arm?" Miss Margrabe asked.

Janey nodded. "Yes'm. I'm afraid you're going to have to."

Kirby took a jackknife from his pocket and cut away the sleeve. He pulled the severed sleeve down across the teacher's hand, giving Janey an unrestricted view of the wound.

"It looks like it just cut a ridge in your arm, but I don't think the bullet is still there. Kenny, bring me some coal oil," Janey ordered one of the seventh grade boys. Boldly, she pulled up her skirt.

"Kirby, cut off enough of my chemise to make a bandage."

"Janey, that'll leave your legs bare," Kirby replied.

"Either cut enough for me to use as a bandage and bare my legs, or I'll take the whole thing off and bare my butt," Janey said. "Now do it."

Kirby took the bottom of Janey's chemise in his hands, but before he began to cut, he looked at the other boys in the room, all of whom had come closer for a look. "Every boy in here turn around, right now. If I catch any of you lookin' at my sister, I'll black your eye, and that's for sure and certain."

Reluctantly the boys turned away.

"Here's the coal oil," Kenny said, handing the can to Janey.

"You turn around, too," Kirby ordered.

A moment later, Kirby had cut a two-inch strip from all the way around the bottom of Janey's chemise.

"Now, cut a little piece off the end, so I can use it as a wiping cloth," Janey ordered.

After Kirby did so, Janey soaked the cloth in kerosene and used it to clean the wound. Then, pouring a little more kerosene over the wound, she made a bandage by wrapping the rest of the material around the teacher's arm, and tying it in place.

The sheriff and at least half a dozen other men came dashing into the school. Their sudden entrance frightened some of the other students until they realized who it was.

"We heard shooting!" the sheriff said. "What happened here?"

"It was Jayhawkers, Sheriff," one of the students said.

"Any of the kids hurt? We brought Doc Blanchard with us."

"Ain't none of the kids hurt, but they shot Miss Margrabe," Kenny said.

"*There aren't any children* hurt," Miss Margrabe corrected.

"Doc, get over here 'n look at the teacher, will you?" the sheriff asked.

"I'm real proud of both of you," Emmett said at supper that evening. "Kirby, the sheriff says that if you hadn't acted real quick, the whole school could have burned down. And Janey, Doc Blanchard said all he had to do was change the bandage. You did a fine job of nursin' Miss Margrabe."

"I stopped by to see Lettie," Luke said, speaking of Miss Margrabe. "Your teacher had nothin' but praise for the two of you."

"Praises for us, and kisses for you, I bet," Janey teased.

Luke smirked. "That's for me to know, and you to find out."

"I can't imagine any group of men so evil as to do something like that," Kirby's mother said.

"Never underestimate a man's capacity for cruelty," Emmett said.

"That's some real elegant words, Pa. Where'd you come up with 'em?" Kirby asked.

Emmett grinned. "I heard Governor Price say 'em durin' some of his speechifyin'."

"Pa, they's some fellas I know that's plannin' on joinin' up with Asa Briggs and ridin' over into Kansas to set things right," Luke said. "And I aim to go with 'em."

"No, you ain't," Emmett said.

"Pa, we can't just let 'em get away with somethin' like this."

"You ain't goin'," Emmett said again.

"It ain't like I'm plannin' on defyin' you or anythin' like that, but

I'm full growed, Pa. And I reckon if I was to really take a mind to do it, there wouldn't be nothin' you could actual do about it."

"And I reckon you're right. But I would sure hope you wouldn't. It ain't our fight, boy."

"The hell it ain't! They attacked the school where Janey 'n Kirby was. They're family. They also shot Lettie. To my way of thinkin', it just don't seem right lettin' them Jayhawkers get away with doin' what they done."

"Thanks to your brother and sister, they didn't do much of anything. Kirby kept the schoolhouse from burnin' down, 'n Janey kept Miss Margrabe's wound from gettin' any worse. No need for you to be goin' over to Kansas with anyone when I need you here on the farm. Besides that, what do you mean when you say you plan to 'make things right'?"

"Just what it sounds like. Give 'em a taste of their own medicine," Luke said.

"You mean you plan to do the same thing to innocent folks over there that the Jayhawkers have been doin' over here? Are you goin' to burn a few houses, and maybe shoot some women and kids? Because it's for damn certain that you won't be runnin' into any of the ones who actually done this."

"It just don't seem right, Pa, to let 'em get away with it and do nothin' at all."

"Two wrongs don't make a right, son, and if you'll think about it, you'll see what I mean."

"All right, Pa."

"I tell you what. If you're all that anxious to shoot somethin', there's a covey o' quail down in the south pasture. I thought maybe me, you, 'n Kirby could go down there just after dawn tomorrow mornin' and shoot a few of 'em. I'd love nothin' better 'n a mess o' fried quail, gravy, and biscuits. That is, if Pearl 'n Janey would cook 'em up for us." Emmett winked at his wife.

"I'm not a very good cook, Pa. You know that," Janey complained.

"It's 'bout time you learned, don't you think? You're 'most a woman now, 'n you'll be takin' on a husband afore you know it. When you do, you're goin' to have to cook for 'im."

"I'm not ever goin' to have a husband, because I'm not ever goin' to get married," Janey said.

"Why not?"

"I have no intention of being a farmer's wife."

"What's wrong with being a farmer's wife?" Pearl asked sharply.

"Nothin' at all is wrong with it, Ma, if all you want to do is stay home, cook for your husband, and raise a passel of brats. But no, ma'am. That just ain't somethin' I want to do. I don't plan on staying around here. I'm goin' somewhere exciting, like New Orleans, or St. Louis, or maybe even Chicago."

"Well, right now you are in Stone County, Missouri," Emmett said. "And, whether you ever get married or not, you're goin' to learn to cook, if for no other reason than I told you to. And you can start to-morrow."

"What makes you think you'll get anything, anyway? Arnold Parker and a couple of others from school went quail hunting last week, and they didn't get anything."

"They aren't Jensens," Emmett said easily.

The Ozark Mountains could have been an artist's palette, alive as they were with color—yellow, orange, red, green, and brown. A crisp coolness to the morning could be felt as Kirby, his father, and brother walked across a recently harvested cornfield. Somewhere a wood-pecker drummed against a tree, the rapid staccato beat of its beak echoing through the woods.

Suddenly, a brace of quail flew up in front of them, filling the air with the loud flutter of their wings. Quickly and smoothly, Kirby brought the double-barrel twelve-gauge shotgun to his shoulder and pulled first one trigger, then the other.

The double boom of the exploding cartridges caused the sounds of nature to pale in comparison. Feathers flew from two birds as they tumbled from the sky.

"Good shooting, Kirby!" Emmett shouted as the boy started for-ward to retrieve his two birds.

An hour later, the Jensens returned to the house with nine quail, more than enough to make a fine meal. They cleaned the birds and turned them over to Pearl and Janey to prepare.

"While your ma and sister are cookin' our dinner, how about you two boys come on out to the front porch for a few minutes," Emmett suggested.

Once they stepped out onto the porch, Emmett and Luke filled their pipes.

"Boys, we had us a real good corn crop this year. We made sixty bushels an acre, which means we've got about twenty-four hunnert bushels gathered." Emmett sucked on the pipe until the tobacco caught and a cloud of smoke wreathed. "Last I checked, we can get fifty-nine cents a bushel in Galena, which would bring in around fourteen hunnert dollars. That ain't bad for forty acres and a team of mules."

"I'll say!" Luke said enthusiastically.

"Pa, what about the seed corn for next year?" Kirby asked.

Emmett reached out and ran his hand through Kirby's hair. "Good for you, son, for thinkin' of that. I've already took out twenty bushels of the best lookin' seed corn."

"Seein' as we got only one wagon, it's goin' to take us three trips into town to get the corn delivered," Luke said.

"No it won't. Tom Byrd will rent us two wagons and two teams for ten dollars," Emmett replied.

"That still leaves us short one driver."

"Oh, I think Kirby could miss a day of school to drive one of the wagons." Smiling, Emmett looked over at Kirby. "That is, if you don't mind."

"Ha!" Kirby said with a huge grin. "I don't mind at all!"

"I didn't think you would."

"You men come on in for your dinner," Pearl called.

"There's only two men out there, Ma. Kirby's still a boy, remember." Janey smiled as she teased her younger brother.

"He does a man's work, and that makes him a man in my book," Emmett said.

"I hope you like the biscuits, Pa, because I made them," Janey said proudly.

Kirby picked one up and took a bite, even before the rest of the food was on the table. "Umm, umm. You did a great job! Yes sir, you're goin' to make some farmer a fine wife."

"You'll never see it!" Janey said, grabbing the biscuit from a laughing Kirby and throwing it at him.

CHAPTER 2

"How are you doing, Miss Margrabe?" Janey asked when she went to school Monday morning.

"Well, I'm doing just fine, dear, thanks to you and your brother," Lettie replied. She looked around. "By the way, where is Kirby?"

"Him 'n Luke 'n Pa went to Galena to sell some corn," Janey said.

"He and Luke, dear."

"He and Luke," Janey said, correcting herself.

"I don't know if you know it or not, but Luke came by to see how I was doing. Wasn't that sweet of him?"

"Yes ma'am. But, seeing as he is sweet on you, I'd expect him to come calling on you," Janey said.

"Hush, now. You shouldn't be saying such things." Lettie smiled around a blush.

"I'm just saying what's true, is all."

"Well, as much as I'm enjoying our conversation, we do need to get class started." Lettie saw one of the boys standing near the window. "Kenny, would you ring the bell, please?"

"Yes, ma'am."

"I make it two thousand, five hundred, and seventeen bushels," Fred Matthews said after the corn was unloaded and counted. "At sixty-six cents a bushel that would be—"

"Sixty-six cents?" Emmett said.

"Accordin' to the telegraph sent out by the Chicago Board of Trade ever' day, corn's tradin' at seventy-eight cents today." Matthews pointed to a sign on the wall behind him. "Like the sign says, we pay eighty-five percent of the price set in Chicago."

Emmett, Luke, and Kirby smiled at each other.

"It looks like we chose a good time to sell our corn," Emmett said.

Matthews grinned. "Yes, sir, I'd say you did. Twenty-five hundred and seventeen bushels at sixty-six cents a bushel comes to sixteen hundred and sixty-one dollars, and twenty-two cents. Do you want that in cash or by bank draft?"

"Cash, if you don't mind," Emmett replied. "I don't have a bank account, and the banks charge too much when they cash a draft."

"All right. Come on into the office and I'll count it out for you," Matthews offered.

Standing close by was a man named Roy Joiner, supposedly examining a wagon wheel. In truth, he was there to overhear conversations between the farmers who were selling their crops and the broker, hoping to happen upon an opportunity to put the information to good use.

Hearing the talk between the Jensens and Matthews was exactly the kind of information he was looking for. He watched the men enter the office, then hurried away.

"He's a dirt farmer," Joiner told Pogue Mason a few minutes later. "Him and his two sons, one of 'em nothin' more 'n a boy. Hell, just the sight of a gun would probably scare 'em so much they'd piss in their pants."

"How much money did you say they would be carryin'?" Pogue asked.

"Over sixteen hunnert dollars. And it's all in cash. We'll hold 'em up out on the road. It'll be like takin' candy from a baby."

"Let's do it," Pogue said with a wide, nearly toothless grin.

About two miles north of Galena, Emmett, Luke, and Kirby rode in three empty wagons. Emmett was leading the little convoy, while Kirby was bringing up the rear. Aware that they were about to be overtaken by two men on horseback and thinking nothing was unusual about that, Kirby pulled over to one side of the road to give them room to pass.

They didn't pass. One of the men jumped into the wagon and put his gun against Kirby's head. "Call out to your pa, boy."

"What for?"

The man cocked the pistol, the hammer making a loud, double-clicking sound as it engaged the cylinder. "Do it, boy, or I'll blow your brains out. Maybe your brother will have more sense."

"Pa?" Kirby called. "Pa, we got a problem!"

Emmett and Luke stopped their teams and turned to look back toward Kirby. They saw the two men, one of them in the wagon with Kirby.

"Mister, if you don't want to see your boy killed, you'd best do what we tell you," ordered the man on horseback.

Setting the brake on his wagon, Emmett climbed down and started back toward Kirby. "Luke, you be ready to act if you get the chance," he said under his breath as he passed the second wagon. "Don't hurt my boy!" Emmett pleaded, making his voice sound frightened.

"Just give us the money you got from sellin' your corn, 'n ever'thing will be just fine," stated the mounted robber.

"Pa, you want me to get the money and give it to 'em?" Kirby asked.

"You may as well." Emmett kept his voice as if he was resigned.

Kirby stood up.

"Here, what are you doin'?" the man in the wagon asked.

"I'm goin' for the money. Ain't that what you said you wanted?" Kirby replied.

The two robbers were looking directly at Kirby, which meant they had taken their eyes off Emmett. Suddenly, Kirby jumped off the side of the wagon, then quickly rolled beneath it. His action left the two would-be robbers totally confused.

That was all Emmett and Luke needed. Both men drew their pistols and fired, and the two outlaws went down.

Luke jumped down from his wagon and, with his gun drawn, hurried back to where the two outlaws lay on the ground. Emmett gave both men a hard kick, but neither responded.

"Kirby, you all right?" Emmett called.

"Yeah, Pa. I'm all right."

"Come on out, then. These two ain't goin' to do you no harm now."

Kirby crawled out from beneath the wagon, then looked down at the two men his father and brother had just shot. "That's the first time I've ever seen anyone get killed," he said in awe.

"The way things is in this world, it ain't likely to be the last time you'll see it," Emmett said.

"What are we goin' to do with 'em, Pa?" Luke asked.

"Let's throw 'em in your wagon and you take 'em back into town.

Me 'n Kirby will take Tom Byrd's wagons and teams back to him, then you can pick us up on your way back home."

"Take 'em to the undertaker?" Luke asked.

"No, take 'em to the sheriff. Let the county bury 'em. Besides, it's more'n likely that these two have dodgers out on 'em."

"What's a dodger?" Kirby asked.

"A reward poster. I suspect these two men may be wanted, and if they are, we'll collect some reward. And we'll split the reward money three ways." Emmett smiled. "You done real good, Kirby. I'm proud of the way you kept your head."

"Yeah," Luke added with a smile. "For a young whippersnapper who don't have no more sense than to tie a couple cows together by their tails, you just done real good."

Kirby beamed under the praise.

A reward of three hundred dollars on each of the two men was offered and Emmett, true to his promise, gave Kirby and Luke two hundred dollars apiece. It was the most money Kirby had ever had in his entire life.

Long after midnight, Kirby heard a rider galloping toward the house, shouting at the top of his voice.

"Jensen! Jensen! Turn out! Turn out! It's Gimlin's place! They've set fire to it!"

Emmett stepped out onto the front porch, wearing his long handle underwear. "What is it, George? What's goin' on?"

"Jayhawkers, Emmett. They've set fire to Gimlin's barn and house! I'm callin' folks to go give 'em a hand."

"Good for you. On your way, then. We'll be there," Emmett promised.

Fifteen minutes later, the entire Jensen family was in a wagon headed for the Gimlin farm three miles away. They could see the glow of the fire long before they reached the farm. By the time they arrived, the house that had been home to Marvin and Gail Gimlin, and their two young children, was completely engulfed in flames. Several neighbors were gathered around, but all they could do was watch the house burn.

Standing in the yard, five-year-old Mollie was crying and shivering. Janey went to her, carrying one of the blankets she and her mother had brought from home. "Here Mollie, wrap this around you," she said, comforting the little girl.

"Janey, why did they do this? Why did those men come burn down our house?" Mollie asked between sobs.

"Because they are evil," Janey said. "Some people are just meaner than snakes."

"My doll got all burned up."

Janey put her arms around the little girl and pulled her close for a moment. "Wait here. I have a surprise for you."

"What?"

"Well, if I told you, it wouldn't be a surprise, would it?"

Janey walked back to their wagon where blankets, quilts, cooking utensils, and extra clothing were piled, just in case the Gimlins would have need of them. Thinking of Mollie, Janey had included the doll that had been hers when she was much younger.

She took it to the little girl. "You can have my doll," Janey said, handing a China doll to the little girl.

Mollie's eyes grew big. "I can have it?"

"Yes, I don't play with her anymore, and I think she misses having someone to play with."

"I'll play with her." Mollie held the doll in a close embrace.

"That was real nice, what you done," Kirby said when Janey joined the rest of her family in front of the smoldering house.

She shrugged. "It's just an old doll. I was goin' to throw it away some day, anyway."

"Still, he's right. It was good of you to give your doll to the little Gimlin girl." Emmett walked over to Gimlin, and put his hand on the man's shoulder. "I'm real sorry about this, Dewey."

"At least we all got out without any of us gettin' hurt," Gimlin replied. "But we ain't got a thing left to our name. No furniture, no clothes, no dishes, nothin'. And no house to put it in, if we did have them things."

"You will, and soon." Emmett turned to the friends and neighbors who had gathered and held up both arms. "Folks!" he called. "Let me tell you what we're goin' to do."

He pointed to what was left of the house which was nothing but glowing embers and fire-blackened wood. Though the flames were mostly gone, a great deal of smoke was still pouring from it and its heat could still be felt.

"As soon as that pile of burnt wood is cool enough for us to work with it, we're goin' to clear it all out. Then we're goin' to build another house for the Gimlins just like the house that the Jayhawkers burnt down. No, we'll build it even better."

"Yeah!" one of the other men shouted. "By damn, that's exactly what we're goin' to do."

"And ladies?" Pearl called out, stepping up beside her husband. "While our men folk are rebuilding the house, we're goin' to refurnish it. I know that between us, we can come up with furniture, clothes, blankets, quilts, and whatever it takes to get the kitchen put together again."

"Looks like we won't need a cookin' stove," one of the women said, pointing to the rubble of the house. "The one they had come through just fine. All we got to do is clean it up a bit."

By mid-afternoon, a large gathering of wagons was parked at the Gimlin farm. At least fifteen families had come to help. The men were constructing a new house. Three sides of framework were already up, and they were about to put the final side into place. Kirby, doing the work of a man, scurried up one of the ladders, then got into position. Half a dozen ropes were thrown to the men on top of the frame, and Kirby grabbed one of them, pulling with the others as the end frame was raised into position.

With so many men working, the framework of the house was in place with amazing speed. After the siding and roofing was completed, everyone grabbed a brush and bucket of paint and, before supper, the house had been erected and painted, and all the furniture moved in.

The stove had been cleaned but not moved, and even before the house was completed, some of the women had started cooking. A temporary table, long enough to feed forty people, had been put together using boards and sawhorses. By the time construction clutter had all been picked up, the meal was ready and the Gimlins, Jensens, and neighbors sat on make-do benches for supper.

Kirby was watching his sister. Merlin Lewis, who had left school three years earlier, was sitting beside Janey, and it was obvious that she not only welcomed Merlin's attention, she was inviting it. Kirby couldn't help but marvel at how easy it was for her to control Lewis.

The twelve-year-old glanced over at his brother to see if he saw what was going on, but Luke was lost in his own world. Lettie Margrabe was doing the same thing to him that Janey was doing to Merlin Lewis. Kirby laughed.

"What are you laughin' at?" Emmett asked.

"Nothin', Pa. I was just laughin' is all," Kirby said as he reached for another piece of fried chicken.

"Careful, boy. Someone's goin' to see you laughin' at nothin' someday 'n they're goin' to think you've gone crazy."

Kirby turned his attention to another conversation going on near him.

"What I plan to do, 'n what I'm invitin' the rest of you to do, most especially the ones of you that ain't got a family to look after, is to join up with George Clark." The speaker was Lee Willoughby, a man who was the same age as Luke.

"Clark ain't nothin' but a murderer and an outlaw," someone said.

"That may be so, but he don't do none of his outlawin' in Missouri," Willoughby replied. "He does all of it over in Kansas. Luke, what do you say? Me 'n you was talkin' 'bout this the other day."

"We was talkin' about Asa Briggs, not George Clark."

"Briggs is an old woman compared to Clark. You want to come with me?"

Luke glanced over toward Emmett for just a moment before he replied. "I reckon not."

"Why not? You gone scared on me, have you?"

Luke stood up and glared. "Would you like to put that proposition to a test, Willoughby?"

A bit startled by Luke's response, Willoughby blinked his eyes and licked his lips for a few seconds before he responded. "No, no, I didn't mean nothin' by what I said. I don't want to fight you. I don't want to fight nobody from Missouri. All I'm lookin' to do is make things right. You folks has seen what kind of men the Jayhawkers are. They attacked the school, they come in the middle of the night to burn Mr. Gimlin and his whole family out of his house. Like I said, all I'm lookin' to do is set things right."

"I don't hardly see it as right, ridin' into Kansas and burnin' some farmer and his family out, like was done to me," Gimlin said. "I expect most folks over there are just like us. No line drawed on a map, especially one that you cain't even see, would make it right to go over there 'n start burnin' and shootin' and such."

"Yeah, well, a war's acomin', 'n I don't plan on missin' out on it," Willoughby said.

"If war comes, I expect a lot of us will get caught up in it," Emmett said. "And, in this state, I expect some, even some of us here, will choose up different sides."

"Which side would you choose, Jensen?" Willoughby asked.

"Well, sir, I don't have any slaves, 'n I don't hold with the idea of keepin' any. Besides which, I got a brother who lives up in Iowa, and he'll for sure be fightin' for the North. But the truth is, I can't see as the federal government's got 'ny right to tell a state what it can or can't do. I figure if it comes to it, I'll be pitchin' in with the South."

Emmett was normally a man of few words, and Kirby believed that may well have been the longest speech he had ever heard his father make.

Willoughby smiled. "Well now, that's good to know. I've always looked up to you, Mr. Jensen, 'n I've always figured Luke to be my friend. I'm for sure goin' to fight for the South and I wouldn't want us to wind up bein' enemies."

"I don't consider anybody here my enemy," Emmett said, "whether they wind up fightin' for the North or the South."

One month after Gimlin's house was burned and rebuilt, Abraham Lincoln was elected President of the United States. As a result, South Carolina seceded from the Union, claiming independence. Six Southern states soon followed, eventually creating the Confederate States of America.

April 1861

A garrison of Union troops occupied Ft. Sumter in Charleston Harbor. South Carolina demanded that the troops be withdrawn, but the federal government refused to do so.

On April 10, Brigadier General Beauregard, in command of the provisional Confederate forces at Charleston, demanded the surrender of the Union garrison. Major Robert Anderson, the Union commander of Ft. Sumter, refused.

On April 12, Confederate batteries opened fire on the fort. Designed to repel invaders from the sea, Ft. Sumter was unable to withstand an effective defense against an attack from the land side.

At 2:30 PM the next day, Major Anderson surrendered and was allowed to evacuate the garrison on the following day. Not until then were there any casualties, as a Union artillerist was killed and three wounded when a cannon exploded prematurely when firing a salute during the evacuation.

Immediately after that incident, Lincoln called for 75,000 troops to be drawn from every state that had not seceded. That action caused four more states to secede. The Confederate government matched Lincoln's move by calling for 75,000 troops of its own.

Lee Willoughby came by the Jensen farm not long after that, wearing the gray uniform of a Confederate lieutenant. "Iffen you had come with me when I asked last fall, more 'n likely you'd be an officer, too," he said to Luke. "Now, if you come in, you'll have to come in as a private. There ain't nothin' I can do for you, 'cause it's too late."

"Privates'll be fightin' the war same as officers, won't they?" Luke asked.

"Well, yes. Of course they will."

"Then the way I look at it, it don't really matter all that much whether I'm a private or an officer. Fightin' is fightin', 'n now that the war has started, I reckon I'll get into it so's I can do my part."

"When you plannin' on comin' in?" Willoughby asked.

"Right away," Luke answered. "No, wait. Give me till tomorrow. I want to tell Lettie good-bye."

"We're gettin' up a wagon to carry men to the recruitin' office in Springfield. It'll be leavin' Galena long about noon tomorrow. If you're comin' with us, be to the courthouse before the wagon leaves." Willoughby slapped his legs against the sides of his horse and rode off.

Luke looked at his father. "What about you, Pa? What are you goin' to do?"

"I don't plan to rush into anything," Emmett said. "I plan to take the night thinkin' on it. I don't like the idea of the people in Washington sendin' seventy-five thousand troops into various states to tell the folks what they can and can't do. So, if I'm bein' truthful with you, I'd say I'm leanin' hard on goin' with you." As fate would have it, he did just that.

Lettie Margrabe lay naked in bed, staring at the leaf patterns the sun was projecting onto her bedroom wall. She had slept that way for the very first time. It was also the first time she had ever slept with a man.

Lying beside her, breathing the soft, rhythmic breath of sleep, was Luke Jensen. He was also nude.

Lettie had lost her virginity.

She was in love with Luke, and what they had done was no different from what lovers had been doing since the beginning of time. He had come to tell her good-bye, to tell her that he would be leaving for the war. It was Lettie who had asked him to stay, and not until he was sure that it was truly something that she wanted, did he agree.

As she lay in bed that morning she could still feel the exquisite pleasure of the night of passion they had shared. That sensual gratification, however, was tempered by the fact that she knew that if anyone ever found out about it she would lose her teaching position. Such exposure would mean she would leave the county, and maybe even the state, in disgrace. Despite that possibility, she had no regrets about what they had done.

They had made love several times during the night, and Lettie intended to do so at least once more before she let him leave.

Emmett did not own a horse, so he hooked the team of mules up to the wagon. The entire family rode into town with him to say good-bye. When they reached the courthouse, they were surprised to see so many men were going to Springfield to join up with the Confederate army, that it took three wagons. Like the Jensen family, other families were there as well to say good-bye to their husbands, fathers, sons, and brothers.

"Pa, I don't see why I can't go with you," Kirby complained. "I've read that both armies is takin' folks my age and some even younger. Drummer boys they'll be."

"Both armies, Kirby? Are you tellin' me that if I don't approve of you joinin' with the Gray, that you'd be willin' to join the Blue? You'd fight against me 'n your brother?" Emmett was not amused.

"No, sir. I ain't atellin' you that. I'm just sayin', I don't think I'm too young to go. You said yourself that I can do a man's work."

"That is exactly what I said, and that is exactly why you need to stay here. You'll be runnin' the farm, Kirby. The responsibility of the whole thing is goin' to be on your shoulders. You're goin' to have to get the crops put in and tend to 'em. Then you're goin' to have to get 'em out and get 'em to market. I don't want to come back home to a farm that's gone and a family that's most starved 'cause nobody was takin' care of 'em. I'm countin' on you, boy. So is you ma and your sister."

Kirby didn't reply. He knew that his father was correct. Someone would need to keep the farm going. With his father and brother gone to war, he was the only one who could do it. "All right, Pa. I'll do what you say."

Emmett was not a demonstrative man. The closest thing to affection he showed was to reach out and take Kirby's hand in a firm handshake. "I know you will, son. That knowledge is what I'll keep with me the whole time I'm away."

"How long do you expect that to be, Pa?"

Emmett grunted and shook his head. "Truth is, this whole war is a foolish thing, us fightin' against each other. I expect the people in charge will come to their senses sooner than later. I'm bettin' we'll be back in time to help get the crops out, come fall."

"Emmett, you look after Luke now, you hear?" Pearl said. "He's my firstborn. It wouldn't sit good with me, if somethin' was to happen to him."

Emmett looked around. "Where is Luke?"

"He's over there, Pa," Janey said, pointing. "You didn't expect him to leave without sayin' good-bye to his woman, did you?"

Luke and Lettie were standing close together, and though they weren't touching, the expressions on both their faces all but gave away to the discerning what had gone on between them during the night.

"I thought he told her good-bye last night," Emmett said.

"If they really are sweet on each other like Janey says, you'd expect 'em to tell each other good-bye again this mornin', wouldn't you?" Pearl said with a smile.

"I reckon so."

"Recruits!" Lee Willoughby shouted then. "Load up into these here three wagons! It's time we was leavin'!"

"Boy," Emmett said before starting toward the three wagons. "Remember what we talked about. You take care of your ma and sister while I'm gone."

"All right, Pa. I will."

Kirby had no idea how long it would be before he saw his father and brother again, or even if he ever would see them again. He could see tears in the eyes of his mother and sister and felt a lump in his throat.

But he would be damned if he would cry. He had just taken on the responsibility of a full grown man.

Two months later, Kirby had the crops planted and was watching them carefully, taking pride in what he had accomplished in such a short time. On a trip to the barn to get a new bridle for the mule called Ange, he heard a sound coming from behind a pile of hay. Not sure what it was, he looked around for a weapon of some sort, and saw an axe handle without its head. Grabbing the handle, he approached the stack.

"No. Merlin, I said no." That was Janey's voice.

"Come on, Janey. You've let me get this far. You can't stop now!" Merlin Lewis's voice was demanding and edgy.

Kirby stepped around to the other side of the stack of hay and saw his sister lying on the ground with the top of her dress and camisole pulled down so her breasts were exposed. Merlin was pulling on the dress, trying to take it all the way off.

"She said no!" Kirby said firmly.

"What the hell?" Merlin gasped, jumping up quickly. "Where did you come from? Get the hell out of here!"

Kirby drew back the axe handle. "No, Lewis. You get the hell out of here . . . before I bash your head in."

"You talk big with an axe handle in your hand." Merlin sneered.

Kirby tossed the axe handle into the hay stack, then doubled his fists and raised them. "I don't have an axe handle now."

Although Merlin was three years older, Kirby was every bit as tall and a little more muscular.

Merlin looked at him for a moment, then waved his hand dismissively. "Nah, I ain't goin' to fight you. Your sister's nothin' but a slattern anyway." Merlin turned to leave.

"Lewis?" Kirby called to him.

Merlin stopped, but he didn't turn around.

"I don't want to see you on my farm anymore."

"Your farm?"

"Yes, my farm. I'm the one living here. I'm the one working it. Don't come back."

Kirby followed Merlin out of the barn and watched to make sure that he left. He also wanted to give his sister time to cover herself up. He had never seen her like that before and was embarrassed by what he had happened on to.

"Kirby?" Janey's voice was small and frightened.

"Are you decent?" Kirby called back.

Janey was always aware that she was older and a bit more sophisticated than Kirby was, and most times she didn't mind making him aware of that fact. Her voice sounded different from normal. "Yes."

Kirby turned and saw her standing a few feet behind him. He had never seen such an expression on her face before. It showed nothing of that self-confidence. On the contrary, it was an expression of contriteness and fear.

"What was that all about?" he asked.

"I told him to stop, and he wouldn't do it. I'm just thankful that you came along when you did. If you hadn't . . . I don't know what would have happened."

"Janey, I've never been around a girl . . . like that . . . so I'm not real sure how things like what I saw here could happen. But it seems to me like it wouldn't have got that far if you hadn't let it."

"I admit I was . . . teasing him," Janey said. "But I thought I could control it. I thought that if I told him to stop, he would."

"Like I said, I ain't got that kind of experience, but I've heard enough talk to know that it don't always happen like that. You had to know that he's a lot stronger than you. You was playin' with fire."

"I was. I admit it now." She went over to Kirby and put her hand on his arm, then fixed him with a pleading gaze. "I don't know how to thank you. You came along just in time to save me. There's no telling what would have happened."

"Janey, Pa told me to look out after you 'n Ma. I'm goin' to ask you, please, don't be doin' nothin' like this again. You could get yourself in some serious trouble. And I don't know if I could even face Pa then."

"I promise I will be much more careful in the future. I've always had it in mind that I could control boys. Now I see that it isn't as easy as I thought."

"You can control boys. But you're of an age now, Janey that"— Kirby took in Janey's body with a wave of his hand—"it ain't boys you have to worry about. It's men. And you can't control men."

"You're right," Janey said contritely.

"Why don't you go on back to the house now?"

"Kirby?"

"What?"

"You won't tell Ma nothin' about this, will you?"

"I ain't goin' to say a word about it," Kirby promised.

The worry left Janey's face, and she kissed her brother on the cheek.

"Thank you, Kirby. Thank you for everything."

CHAPTER 3

Belle Robb was someone that the people of Galena euphemistically referred to as "a painted woman." She advertised her services by the very method that gave her the sobriquet by which she was called. Her red hair came from a bottle, her lips and cheeks from a paint pot. She wore fine, but revealing dresses and travelled around town in an elegant carriage driven by a free black man. She was the wealthiest person—man or woman—in the entire county.

Strange as it might seem, Belle and Lettie had developed a friendship when Belle began paying Lettie a great deal of money for private tutoring. For the last two years, Belle had been coming to the school on Saturday and Sunday afternoons for the lessons.

On this particular Saturday afternoon, Lettie was waiting most anxiously for her.

"Say, that *Pride and Prejudice* is one fine book," Belle said, returning the book to Lettie. "Thank you very much for lending it to me."

"I'm glad you enjoyed it," Lettie said, though her words were without animation.

"Lettie, what is it? What's wrong?"

"Oh, Belle, I'm so frightened. I . . . I have done something awful, and you are the only one I can talk to."

Belle reached out to put her hand on the teacher's shoulder. "Lettie, I know you, and I know that you can't do anything awful. Now, tell me what is bothering you."

"My womanly time . . . is late. I didn't worry too much about it, but . . . now I have missed it a second time. I'm two months behind, and it could only mean one thing."

"You're pregnant," Belle said matter-of-factly.

The way Belle spoke the words gave Lettie a sinking feeling. She had hoped someone like Belle might be able to come up with another reason. To hear her fears confirmed was devastating. "That's what I was afraid of."

"Does the baby's father know about it?"

"No, and I've no intention of telling him, nor anyone else."

"What are you going to do?"

"I . . . I've heard that there are ways of terminating a pregnancy," Lettie said. "I was wondering if you know anything about it. I mean, how would one go about obtaining such a thing?"

Belle shook her head. "I have known girls who did this, and I would advise against it."

"Why?"

"Because two of the girls I knew died undergoing the process. I wouldn't want to see anything like that happen to you."

"If . . . if the father was here, I would go to him and tell him. I'm sure he would marry me. But he isn't here, and I don't know when he will return, or if he ever will return."

"He has gone to war?"

"Yes. If I have the child, and he doesn't come back for a few years, how could I ever convince him that the baby is his?"

"That could be a problem," Belle agreed.

"Oh, Belle, what will I do? What is left for me besides disgrace? I'll no longer be able to hold my head up among people who had once been my friends . . . among people who respected me."

"You can leave," Belle suggested.

"Leave and go where?"

"I have a friend, a gambler, who lives in Denver. I'll write a letter for you to give him. I'll tell him that your husband was killed, and you want to get away from sad memories. He'll do right by you."

"Oh, Belle," Lettie said, her eyes filling with tears. "Thank you. From the bottom of my heart, thank you."

It was only a matter of a few weeks after Emmett and Luke joined the First Missouri State Guard Infantry, a Confederate company, that they were involved in their first battle. Union troops, under command of Brigadier General Nathaniel Lyon's Army of the West, were camped at Springfield. The Confederate troops, under the command of Brigadier General Ben McCulloch, formulated attack plans.

At 5:00 AM on the morning of August 10, the two forces met at Wilson's Creek about twelve miles southwest of the city. Rebel cavalry received the first blow and fell back, away from Bloody Hill. Confederate forces soon rushed up and stabilized their positions, attacking the Union forces. Three times they attacked that day but failed to break through the Union line.

The Union troops received a heavy blow when General Lyon was killed during the battle. Major Samuel D. Sturgis replaced him.

Meanwhile, Confederates routed Colonel Franz Sigel's column south of Skegg's Branch. Following the third Confederate attack, which ended at 11:00 AM, Sturgis ordered a retreat to Springfield. The Confederate victory buoyed Southern sympathizers in Missouri, giving the Confederates control of southwestern Missouri.

It was shortly after that battle that Emmett and Luke were split up. Emmett protested at first, but a colonel pointed something out to him that seemed to make good sense. "Suppose you and your son were in the same company. And suppose that company was engaged by such superior forces that virtually the entire company was killed. Your wife would lose a husband and a son, and your children, still at home, would lose a father and a brother. Wouldn't it be best for you to be separated, to lessen the chances of both of you being killed at the same time?"

Emmett nodded. "I reckon you're right, Colonel."

CHAPTER 4

Spring 1862

Kirby had been plowing for two weeks, averaging an acre and a half per day. By the middle of May he had the ground broken in twenty-one acres, which was just over half of the farm. What he would plant was entirely up to him, and he planned to do twenty acres of corn, ten of wheat, and ten of oats. He had already spoken with Mr. Matthews, who'd agreed to take his crops as soon as he could get them out.

"Truth is, they ought to bring a premium this year," Matthews had said. "What with the war goin' on an' all, there's a demand for the produce, and with so many men bein' off to do the fightin', not as much will be grown as in years past. It'll be a sellers' market, that's for sure."

Kirby had done some figuring and thought the chances were good that he would be able to bring in at least fifteen hundred dollars. He planned to save as much of it as he could to have for his father and brother when they came back home.

If they came back home.

Reports had already been received from a battle that happened in April at a place called Shiloh. Kirby had never heard of Shiloh, and he didn't know if his pa or Luke had fought in that battle or not. If so, he was reasonably sure that they hadn't been killed. The casualties for Stone County, including names from both participating armies, had been posted on the door of the courthouse in Galena. Neither Emmett's nor Luke's name was on the list, but Lee Willoughby's name was.

So far, the family had received only two letters from Emmett. In one of them, he told them that he and Luke had been split up, and he had no idea where Luke was. They hadn't heard from Luke.

Kirby was thinking about this when he got the whiff of an awful smell.

"Hell's bells, Ange!" he swore at the mule. "Ain't you got no better sense than to fart in a man's face? Damn. You are the fartin'ess mule I've ever seen. Why ain't you more like Rhoda? She don't hardly ever fart. I guess she's more of a lady than you are a gentleman." Kirby picked up a clod of dirt and threw it at the offending animal.

He was just reaching the end of a row when he saw Janey approaching. "Whoa," he called.

Janey was carrying a canvas bag.

"Hi, sis. You're bringing water, I hope."

Janey smiled. "No. I brought you something better." She reached into the bag and pulled out a jar of tea. "It's sweetened," she said as she handed it to him.

Kirby had worked up quite a thirst during the plowing and he took the sweetened tea with grateful hands, then took several, deep, Adam's apple bobbing swallows, until more than half of it was gone. Finally, he pulled the jar away, wiped his mouth with the back of his hand, and smiled at Janey. "Damn, that was good. If you weren't my sister, I'd marry you," he teased.

"I told you. I'm never goin' to get married. And I wouldn't marry you, even if you weren't my brother. You're too onery."

Kirby drank the rest of the tea, but saved the last mouthful, and spit it out toward his sister.

"Kirby!" Janey complained to his laughter.

"That's what you get for calling me onery." He handed the empty jar back to her. "What's Ma cookin' for supper?"

"What difference does it make? You'll gobble it down like a hog. You always do."

Ange chose that precise moment to let go another fart.

"Oh, what is that awful smell?" Janey screwed up her face and waved her hand back and forth in front of her nose.

"You ain't plowed behind a team of mules a whole lot, have you?" Kirby asked, laughing again. He slapped the reins against the back of the team. "Gee!" he called, and the team turned to the right.

* * *

Janey stood at the edge of the field, watching as Kirby started back across the field. She was thankful to him for keeping secret the incident he had happened upon between her and Merlin Lewis. She also realized that he was faithfully fulfilling his promise to their pa to "be the man of the place." She couldn't help but feel a little guilty as she lay in bed every morning when, while still dark, Kirby would go out to harness Ange and Rhoda, then start a full day of plowing. If he found the work too strenuous, he never complained. If he ever had the urge to leave the farm, he never spoke of it.

Janey wanted nothing more in the world than to leave the farm. She hated farming and everything about it. The only reason she was still there was because she felt a sense of obligation to her mother and to Kirby.

She was sixteen but could easily pass for twenty. If she left home now, that's the age she would assume. She was fully developed by the time she was twelve. Although some of the other girls had envied her, it wasn't necessarily a good thing. She sometimes felt as if she were a full grown woman trapped in a young girl's body. She began to have fewer and fewer friends because the things that most interested them seemed childish to her.

The woman she most admired in town was Belle Robb.

She had never spoken to Belle. She knew that her ma would be mortified if she did. But she had watched the woman riding by in the back of a carriage, glancing neither left nor right, either oblivious of, or unconcerned about, the stares and gossip.

What would it be like to have so much money that she didn't care what others thought? Janey wondered.

She also wondered what it would be like to be with a man . . . not a boy like Merlin Lewis, but a real man.

As Kirby started back toward the house that evening with thoughts of supper on his mind, he was surprised to see three mounted riders out front. The riders were wearing military uniforms . . . and the uniforms were blue.

"What's this about?" He hurried, not bothering to take the team to the barn, but going directly to the house. His ma and sister were standing on the porch, talking to the soldiers.

"Ma, what's going on?" he asked.

"Nothin' you have to be concerned about," Pearl replied. "They've come to try 'n take you into the army."

"Wouldn't you like to serve your country, boy?" asked the soldier who had three stripes on his sleeve.

"His father and his older brother are already serving," Pearl said. "Kirby is only fourteen years old. Is the government drafting fourteen-year-olds now?"

"Beggin' your pardon, ma'am, but he sure don't look like no fourteen-year-old."

"Can you read, Sergeant?" Pearl asked.

"Yes, I can read."

"I got his name wrote in the Bible, along with his sister's and older brother's names. That tells when they was born. If you can read and cipher, you can figure out for yourself how old he is. Do you want to see the Bible?"

"How would I know you didn't just put down when he was born so's to keep him from gettin' took into the army?" the sergeant asked. "Is that true, boy? Are you only fourteen?"

Kirby looked the soldier in the eye. "You ain't callin' my ma a liar, are you, mister? 'Cause I don't think I'd take too kindly to that."

"Feisty, ain't he?" the sergeant said to the two soldiers with him. They laughed.

"All right, boy. We'll take your ma's word for it. But if this war's still goin' on when you come of age, you need to think about your duty and come join up with us. Come on, men, we're gettin' nothin' done here."

Kirby watched the men ride away.

"You didn't tell 'em Pa and Luke had joined up with the Gray, did you, Ma?"

Pearl shook her head. "I thought it would be best not to. Supper will be ready soon."

"I'll be in soon as I put the mules away."

Supper was pork chops, poke salad, and corn bread. As Janey had predicted, Kirby ate heartily.

The little town of Lamar, Missouri, was sleeping when Angus Shardeen approached it on the July morning. He held his hand up to stop the thirty-six men riding with him.

"What do we hit first, Angus?" Billy Bartell, Angus's second in command, asked.

"Start by burnin' the houses," Shardeen said. "That'll get ever'one drawn out to put out the fires and save the citizens, then we'll be able to ride on into town without much opposition, I'm thinkin'."

Bartell stood in his stirrups, then looked back toward the other riders. "All right men, get them torches lit!" he shouted.

A match was struck to light one torch, then it was used to pass the light on down until twenty torches were aflame.

"Let's go, men! Burn the town!" Shardeen shouted.

The group rode into town at a gallop. As they encountered the first houses, they tossed the torches toward them. Citizens ran out into the street and were shot down without regard to age or sex. By the time Shardeen's men reached the middle of town, at least eight houses were burning and sixteen men, women, and children had been shot down.

The Jayhawkers stopped in front of the town's only hotel.

"Bartell," Shardeen ordered. "Take five men down to the marshal's office and kill anyone you find there."

"What if somebody's in jail?"

"Kill them, too," Shardeen ordered. "Tompkins, find the newspaper editor and bring him to me."

One hour later, ten women and girls were being held in one of the Lamar Hotel rooms. Shardeen was in the dining room, enjoying the breakfast he had forced the cook to prepare for him. He looked at the emergency broadsheet he had forced the newspaper to print.

PEOPLE OF LAMAR

YOUR TOWN HAS BEEN CAPTURED BY THE SHARDEEN RAIDERS. TEN OF YOUR WOMEN ARE BEING HELD PRISONER. THE TOWN IS BEING CHARGED A RANSOM OF FIVE THOUSAND DOLLARS FOR THEIR RELEASE. IF THE MONEY HAS NOT BEEN COLLECTED BY THREE O'CLOCK THIS AFTERNOON, THE WOMEN WILL BE KILLED.

BY ORDER OF COLONEL ANGUS SHARDEEN,
COMMANDING OFFICER

"Yes," Shardeen said after reading the paper. He smiled and handed it back. "This is exactly what I want. Now, print enough copies so everyone in town will be sure to see it."

"Don't hurt the women, please," the newspaper editor begged.

"If you do your job, and if the town responds, none of the women will be killed."

"Bartell?" Shardeen said after the editor left.

"Yeah?"

"Which one of the women is the best lookin' one?"

"Well, the best lookin' one would be the mayor's daughter. But you almost couldn't call her a woman, seein' as I don't think she's much over fourteen or fifteen."

"Then she's woman enough. I'm goin' upstairs to find me a room. Bring 'er to me."

"All right if I take 'er after you get 'er broke in?"

"Fine with me."

One hour later, Brenda Tadlock, fourteen-year-old daughter of the mayor of Lamar, lay dead in the alley behind the hotel. Bartell never got his chance at her. Brenda had jumped out of the window as soon as Shardeen left her alone in the room.

News of the Shardeen raid on Lamar spread throughout southwest Missouri. Small communities held meetings to discuss the possible organization of a militia to defend themselves should such an attack occur against their town.

"What good would a militia do?" Tom Byrd asked in Galena. "Most of the fightin' age men are already gone. The rest of us is on farms outside of town. Why, by the time you got us mobilized, it would be too late."

"Tom's right," another said.

After an hour of discussion, it was finally decided that raising a city militia would not be possible. The meeting disbanded without any action.

Kirby had come to town, hoping that some sort of militia would be formed, because he was sure that they would take him. He was disappointed with the results of the meeting.

Janey had come with him and, as the meeting was being conducted, had gone to Bloomberg's Mercantile to buy some jars for canning. She was surprised to see Belle Robb there. It was the first time she had ever seen the woman anywhere but riding in her carriage. Looking around to make certain that she wasn't being observed, Janey mustered up the courage to approach the notorious madam. "Hello, Miss Robb."

Belle glanced up, obviously surprised at being addressed by a local citizen. When she saw that it was a young and very beautiful girl who had spoken, and not one of the matriarchs of the town, she smiled. "Hello, dear. Can I help you with something?"

"No, I just wanted to say hello."

"How nice of you."

"Also, I was wondering how . . . I mean, suppose someone wanted to do what you do, how would—" Janey stopped in mid-sentence. "Uh, never mind. I have no right to bother you."

"What is it, exactly, that you think I do, dear?"

"I don't know, exactly, what you do," Janey admitted. "All I know is that you are the most beautiful woman I have ever seen. And you seem to be rich."

Belle laughed. "Oh, believe me, I am rich, Miss . . . what is your name?"

"Janey. Janey . . ." She started to tell her last name but at the last minute thought better of it. "Just Janey."

"Well, 'just Janey,' not everyone can do what I do."

"I suppose not. I'm sure that someone would have to be very beautiful."

"Don't you worry about that. You are certainly beautiful enough. But it takes more than beauty. It takes someone who has the ability to put aside what others may think or say about her. Do you think you could do that?"

"I . . . I don't know. I've never actually thought about it."

"But you are thinking about it now?"

"Maybe."

"Why?"

"The farm," Janey said with a dismissive wave of her hand. "You don't know what it's like. It's nothing but work and drudgery from dawn to dusk. And the thought of marrying a farmer and living the rest of my life that way is almost more than I can take."

"You're wrong, honey. I know exactly what it's like. I was raised on a farm near New Madrid, Missouri. Not a large plantation with slaves to do our every bidding, mind you, but a small pig farm. I couldn't wait to get out of there."

"Then you *do* understand," Janey said with a broad smile.

"Oh, yes. I understand all right. How old are you, Janey?"

"I'm . . . uh . . . eighteen."

Belle smiled. "How old are you, really?"

"Seventeen," Janey lied.

"I'll tell you what. Wait a year. When you're eighteen, come visit me and we'll have a long talk."

"A talk about what?"

"Why, Janey, we'll talk about anything you want to talk about," Belle said.

"All right, and thanks. I'm sorry I bothered you."

"Oh, honey, you have been nothing but nice to me. How could that possibly be a bother?"

Later, as Janey was loading her purchases into the buckboard, a man approached her. She thought he might be the most handsome man she had ever met. His dark hair was perfectly combed, he had a neatly trimmed moustache, and he was wearing a dark green jacket with mustard-colored pants which were tucked down into highly polished boots. The vest was white, and a pearl pin was stuck in the red ascot at his throat.

"May I be of assistance, Janey?"

"Thank you, I— How do you know my name?"

"I heard you give your name to Belle."

"You . . . were listening to our conversation? Sir, you should have made your presence known."

"I feared that to do so might cause you some embarrassment. Please forgive me if I erred."

"What is your name?"

"Paul Garner at your service." He lifted his finger to his eyebrow.

"Mr. Garner . . ."

"Please, it is Paul."

"Paul, how is it that you aren't away at war?"

Garner laughed. "You do get right to the point, don't you?"

"My pa, my brother, so many of the county men are at war. I was just wondering why you weren't, is all."

"Do you believe in this war, Janey?"

"I've never given any thought to whether I believe in it or not."

"Well, I *don't* believe in it. I don't believe in the concept of holding men and women as slaves. I don't own any myself, nor have I ever, and I won't fight a war so those who do own slaves can keep them.

"On the other hand, I think if some states want to break away and go out on their own, they certainly should have the right to do so. I won't fight for an army that would force a state to belong to a union to which it no longer wishes to belong.

"So, as you see, Janey, I see nothing noble or uplifting about either belligerent party in this war. Were I to go, I would have no idea which side to support. Therefore, I have made the conscious choice to remain neutral."

"I've never heard anyone talk like you do," Janey said.

"You mean in my observation of the futility of the war?"

"No. Yes, but I mean, I've never heard anyone use pretty words the way you do. Not even my teacher talked like that. That is, when I had a teacher. She's gone now. Besides, it's been a long time since I was a schoolgirl. Are you an educated man, Paul?"

"Yes. I attended school at Westminster College in Fulton," Paul said.

"What do you do for a living?"

"I'm a peddler."

"A peddler? You mean like Mr. Gray, who goes about in a wagon selling pots, pans, notions, and the like?"

"Not exactly. I sell money."

"Money? How do you sell money?"

"I deal in investments. People invest in me and I make money for them. When I make money for them, I also make money for myself."

"I've never heard of such a thing."

"It can be quite lucrative," Paul said with a broad smile.

She tried not to smile back. "I must get back home," Janey said.

Again, Paul touched his eyebrow. "It has been a most pleasant few minutes, Janey. I do hope we see each other again."

They did see each other again, several times, at first meeting "by chance" in town, until finally, Garner took the bold step of going to the farm where Janey introduced him to her mother and brother.

"I don't like him," Kirby said after a few visits.

"He seems like a nice enough young man," Pearl said.

"I can't help but feel like he has somethin' up his sleeve. Ma, he has to be twenty-three or -four, or somethin' like that. And Janey's only sixteen. What's he doin' hangin' around her? Don't you think she's too young for him?"

"Kirby, you know that Janey ain't none like you or Luke. Ever since she was a little girl, she's been more like a feral cat than a tame kitten. Your pa and I have worried a lot about that girl, wonderin' what is going to become of her. It could be that this feller, Paul Garner, is just what Janey needs. And I warn't but seventeen when I was married."

"I hope so, Ma. But I don't mind tellin' you, he seems a bit uppity to me. I'll keep quiet about it, though. Who am I to tell Janey who she should or shouldn't like?"

"I would appreciate you doin' that," Pearl said.

Frequent and nourishing rains throughout the long summer ensured a bumper crop and, as Fred Matthews had suggested, it was a sellers' market when Kirby took his harvest in to peddle. He was paid $2,088, which was the biggest single year, ever, for the little farm.

"What are you plannin' on doin' with that two thousand dollars you made from selling your crops?" Paul Garner asked during one of his frequent visits.

"What makes you think I made two thousand dollars?" Kirby asked, obviously irritated by the question.

"Why, Janey told me."

"She had no business telling you."

"Janey and I have no secrets between us," Garner said.

"Yeah, well this ain't just between you 'n Janey. This is the whole family, and as far as I'm concerned, you got no business knowin' anything about it."

"I can understand your concern, but my interest is more than mere curiosity. The reason I asked, is because if you will trust me, I can double your money for you in no time."

"How?"

"As I explained to your sister, I deal in money. My profession is to invest money in certain mathematical probabilities, doing so in such a way as to maximize the return."

"Sounds to me like you're usin' big words to say that you are a gamblin' man."

Garner laughed out loud. "Yes, in any investment transaction there is a degree of risk, so, I suppose you could call it gambling. But the degree of risk is inversely proportional to the skill with which the transaction is handled."

"Garner, you can use all the big words you want, I'll not be trusting you with money that I broke my back for most a year to earn. Except for what it takes my ma, my sister, 'n me to live on, I'm puttin' the rest of the money away so that when Pa comes back home, we'll have a good stake to start with."

"Have you not read the Bible?" Garner asked. "Are you not aware of the parable of the talents?"

"I don't know what you are talking about."

"In the Book of Matthew, it tells of a wealthy master who left money with three of his servants. Two of his servants invested the money so they could give even more of it to the master when he returned. But the third buried the money he was given, and when the master returned, that servant gave him only what had been left with him. 'You wicked, lazy servant! You should have put my money on deposit with the bankers, so that when I returned I would have received it back with interest.' Is that how you want to face your father when he returns, not with an increase, but only with what he left?"

"That don't apply to me," Kirby said. "Pa didn't leave me any money. He left me only a team of mules and forty acres of rock and dirt. I wasn't given the money I'm holdin' for him. I earned it."

"Yes, and you are to be commended for it," Garner said. "I only wanted to help, is all. Of course, it is your money and you should do with it as you wish."

"You were rude to Paul," Janey said to Kirby later that evening after Garner left.

"I wasn't rude. I was honest with him. He has no business bein' concerned with how much money we have, and you had no business tellin' him."

"Why not?"

"Janey, I'm going to have to agree with your brother on this," Pearl said. "Your pa always said it's best that not ever'one knows our business."

"I'm sorry," Janey said. "I didn't mean nothin' by it. I was just bragging on you, Kirby. I'm real proud of what you have done."

"I'm just askin' you not to share all our business with him. Sometimes it's good to keep secrets."

The expression on Kirby's face reminded Janey that he had kept a secret for her, and she understood exactly what he was saying. "All right, Kirby. I won't say anything else about it. Please don't be mad at me."

Kirby smiled, and kissed his sister on the cheek. "I'm not mad at you, Janey. I just want you to be careful, that's all."

*   *   *

After their initial meeting in Bloomberg's Mercantile, Janey had become more bold, frequently visiting Belle in her place of business. On one of her visits, one of the customers—Belle referred to them as "guests"—mistook Janey for one of the girls who worked there.

"She is not on the line," Belle said. "And I'll expect you to honor the code that we all follow here. Just as the visits of my guests are kept secret, so too shall the presence of my friend be kept secret. If I ever hear anything spoken about her, I will hold you responsible, and the consequences will be grave."

Belle's admonition to her clients had been heeded, and men that Janey recognized—married men and officials of the town—were confident that knowledge of their visits would not go beyond Belle's establishment. Janey was equally confident that her secret was safe, and she and Belle's clients developed a symbiotic relationship.

"It's called a rubber," Belle said, showing it to Janey.

She had asked how it was that the girls who worked for her didn't get pregnant.

"After it is used, it must be washed very thoroughly to make certain that nothing is left in it. Then it should be lubricated and put back into its box."

"And that will keep me, uh, I mean the girl from getting—?"

Belle looked at Janey knowingly. She nodded. "Yes. It will. I've made every man I've ever been with use it before I will let him lie with me, and I've never gotten pregnant. You are asking about this for yourself, aren't you?"

"Yes," Janey replied rather sheepishly.

"Paul Garner?"

"Yes. I've been lucky so far but every time, I'm frightened as to what would happen if I got pregnant. How would I face my Ma and Pa?"

"It's probably smart of you to have him wear this."

"What will I say to him to make him use it?"

"All you have to do is ask him. He has used it before. Many times, I suspect. I see no reason why he wouldn't use it with you."

"He has?"

Belle put her hand on Janey's shoulder. "Honey, you didn't think you were getting a virgin, did you?"

"No. No, I guess not."

CHAPTER 5

April 1863

The day was unseasonably warm. Kirby was walking behind the plow being pulled by the two mules, Ange and Rhoda, opening the ground to plant this year's corn. He was at the far end of a row when he heard a scream coming from the house. He didn't know if the scream came from his mother or his sister, but it didn't matter. It was a scream of absolute terror. He dropped the reins and started for the house on a dead run.

He heard another scream and saw smoke curling up into the sky. Reaching the fence, he saw at least a dozen men carrying hams and sides of bacon, taken from the smokehouse before it had been set afire.

Jayhawkers!

Janey was on the ground naked. Her clothes had been torn off.

"Spread 'er legs out, boys. I'm goin' to have me a little of this." The raider was a big ugly man with only half of one ear.

"Get away from her!" Pearl attacked the man.

Their leader was standing off to one side, watching it all. He had red hair, a red beard, and a scar that started at the corner of his mouth, then zigzagged like a lightning bolt up the side of his face, ending with a deformed eye. The horse next to him had a dark blue saddle blanket. In a corner was the silver eagle insignia of a colonel outlined in gold.

Kirby knew the man was Angus Shardeen!

"What the hell, Bartell? Can't you handle a young girl and an old woman?" Shardeen asked with a demonic laugh. He raised his gun and shot Kirby's mother in the chest. She flew backwards as if being yanked violently by an invisible rope, then fell and was dead before she even hit the ground.

"Ma!" Kirby shouted as he ran toward her fallen form. Before he reached her, Shardeen brought the butt of his gun down on Kirby's head, and he went down as well.

Kirby came to lying on the ground. For a long moment, he tried to understand what he was doing there. He turned his head, saw his mother lying nearby, and knew that she was dead. In that moment, he remembered what happened.

"I see you aren't dead." The words came from his sister, and they were spoken in a flat and totally unemotional tone of voice.

Looking toward her, Kirby saw that she was sitting on the front porch. She was dressed, and there was a bag sitting beside her.

"Janey." He sat up and felt a sharp pain in the back of his head. Reaching up, he felt blood.

"I didn't know if you was dead or alive," Janey said.

"I reckon I'm alive. How are you?"

"What do you mean, how am I? You know how I am. You seen me lyin' on the ground, bein' used by all of them."

Kirby was surprised to see that, rather than crying uncontrollably, she seemed to express only anger. He was oddly proud of her for showing such gumption.

"I'm sorry I didn't get here in time to stop them." Gingerly, Kirby stood up.

"What could you have done? If you woulda got here any earlier, you'd more 'n like be lyin' there dead, like Ma."

Kirby walked slowly to the porch and sat on the step. "Janey, let's don't tell Pa how Ma died. He don't need to know that while he was off fightin' in the war 'n all, that Shardeen's Raiders come here and killed her. Let's tell him that she died peacefully in her sleep. I think he'll take it somewhat easier, that way."

Janey shrugged. "You can tell him anythin' you want. I won't be here."

"What do you mean, you won't be here?"

"Paul's been tryin' to get me to run off with 'im. The only reason I ain't done so before now is because of Ma. But what with she bein' dead 'n all, I don't see nothin' to keep me here any longer."

"You can't go, Janey. You're my sister. With Ma gone, I need to look after you."

"Yeah, and you did such a good job of it, didn't you?" Janey asked sarcastically.

"I—" Kirby hung his head. "I'm sorry. You're right. I didn't do such a good job of it, did I?"

"It wasn't your fault. Like I said, there wasn't nothin' you coulda done, anyhow."

"But what will I tell Pa when he comes back and finds you're gone?"

"Tell him anything. Tell him I ran off with a peddler."

"Will you at least stay here till I get Ma buried?" Kirby asked.

"Where you goin' to bury her?"

"Up on the hill, I reckon," Kirby said, pointing. "She always liked it up there. She'd go up there to watch the sunsets."

"All right. You go dig her grave, and I'll get her changed into her best dress. I wouldn't want to see her buried in that old work dress."

"Thanks."

"Soon as she's buried, I'm leavin'. I'd like you to drive me into town, but if you don't, I'll walk. 'Cause believe me, brother, I am leaving."

It took Kirby the better part of an hour to dig the grave, but he threw himself into the work to keep from being overwhelmed by grief. He tried to hold back the tears that welled up in his eyes. His father would not have cried. Kirby would not, either. Still, he could not get the horrific image out of his mind of his mother being slaughtered. The woman had given him life, had loved him and his brother and sister with all her heart.

Halfway through the digging, Janey came up to stand beside him. She was still in a state of shock, Kirby knew.

"I got her nice dress on her, but I was thinkin' that if we don't have a box to put her in, the dress will get all messed up when you start throwin' the dirt back into the hole."

"I was thinkin' about that as well, and I got it all figured out," Kirby said.

"What are you goin' to do?"

"The trough we put the hay in to feed the mules is big enough for her. I'll put her in that, then I'll find somethin' to close off the top. It won't be nothin' fancy, but it'll make a passable coffin."

Janey nodded. "Yes. Yes, it will. But, once we get Ma in it, how will we get it up here? I think it'll be too heavy, even for the both of us to handle."

"Soon as I get her into it, I'll hook Ange up to it and let him pull her uphill."

"That's a good idea."

Kirby saw tears in Janey's eyes.

Forty-five minutes later, the feeding-trough-cum-coffin, its top closed with a door from the tack room, had been dragged up the hill, lowered in the grave, and covered.

"All right. Let's go," Janey said.

Kirby raised a hand. "Hold on a moment. Don't you think we ought to say a few words?"

"What for? There ain't neither one of us preachers."

"No, but she was our ma. Seems to me, the least we could do is say a few words over her grave."

"You're right. I'm sorry. Go ahead. Say somethin'."

Kirby took off the hat he'd been wearing to protect him from the sun and held it in front of him as he looked down at the grave. "You was a good ma. You done what you could with us, and I appreciate it, an' loved you for it. I know that I didn't tell you that I loved you as much as I should have, but I never was much for speakin' a lot of words. I reckon I just thought that you always knew.

"Listen, Ma. I ain't goin' to tell Pa how it is that you died. I mean, gettin' killed 'n all. I don't figure it's somethin' he needs to know right away. The time's goin' to come when you 'n him will be together again an' I reckon if you want to, you can tell 'im then, how it was that you died."

Kirby quit speaking, and after a moment of silence, he glanced across the grave at Janey. Tears were rolling down her face.

"You goin' to say somethin'?"

Janey nodded. "Ma, I don't know as I'll ever have any children. I know that I don't want to . . . 'cause I could never be as good a ma as you was. I know I was always a big disappointment to you, and I reckon that while you'll be lookin' down on me, I'll be even more of a disappointment. But, all I can say about that is that I'm sorry." Janey grew quiet then.

Kirby waited for a moment before he spoke again. "That was real good, Janey. I know Ma heard you."

"Will you take me into town now?"

Kirby nodded. "Yeah, I'll take you to town."

It was as if Janey had dropped off the face of the earth. Kirby never heard another word from her, and when he checked on Paul Garner, he learned that he was gone, too. He didn't want to ask around town about his sister, figuring it was nobody else's business that he had lost track of her.

With his mother dead and his sister gone, Kirby was all alone. That didn't actually bother him all that much. On the contrary, he learned to appreciate the solitude.

As he was sitting out on the front porch one day, wondering if he should get a dog, he heard the sound of galloping horses. His first thought was to hide, but he decided not to. It was his farm, and he'd be damned if he would be run off his own property.

Twelve mounted men followed a rider carrying a dark blue flag— the Kansas state flag. Kirby had seen it when the Jayhawkers killed his ma. The riders didn't stop, but continued on at a full gallop.

As it turned out, they were being pursued. No more than fifteen minutes later, another group came riding through, carrying a black flag with a blood red cross. Kirby knew they were part of Bloody Bill Anderson's group.

They stopped when they saw Kirby standing on his front porch. Three of the riders rode toward him. One was wearing a hat with a long, sweeping feather, one was in buckskins, and the third was a young rider who couldn't have been more than a year older than Kirby.

"Boy, did you see a bunch of riders comin' this way?" Anderson asked.

"Fifteen, maybe twenty minutes ago. Headin' west, they were," Kirby replied.

"Jayhawkers?"

"That's what I figure."

"Where's your pa?"

"He's away fightin'. Him 'n my brother."

"Which side is he fightin' for?"

"They's fightin' for the Gray. Same as you."

"What about your ma?"

"She was killed by Angus Shardeen."

"You're runnin' this place all by yourself, are you?"

"Yeah."

"That's quite a responsibility for a boy no older 'n you," said the one in buckskins.

Kirby stood tall. "I'm old enough."

Anderson chuckled. "He's got you there, Gleason."

"I reckon he does, seein' as he's doin' it. Tell me, boy, is it all right if we water our horses here?"

"Sure. Go right ahead."

Anderson and Gleason went back to water their horses, but the young man who had ridden up with them hung back. He spoke for the first time. "What's your name?"

"Jensen. Kirby Jensen."

"You got a gun, Jensen?"

"I got a shotgun."

"That ain't good enough. You need a gun you can tote." The young man had two pistols, one in a holster, and a second stuck down in his belt. He pulled the gun from his belt, and tossed it down to Kirby. Then, reaching into his pocket, he grabbed an extra cylinder and tossed it down to him, as well.

"The gun and the cylinder are already loaded. When it comes time for you to have more ammunition, it takes a .36 caliber. You think you can remember that?"

Kirby held out the pistol to examine it. The initials *JJ* were carved into the handle.

"I reckon I can remember that. You're givin' me this pistol, are you?"

"I am."

"These initials, *JJ*. What do they stand for?"

"They stand for my name. Jesse James."

"Dingus, get on back over here 'n get your horse watered. We ain't goin' to spend the night here," another man called, only slightly older than Jesse.

"Dingus?" Kirby asked.

"That's my brother, Frank. He took to callin' me that when we was kids, and it sort of stuck."

With a nod of his head, Jesse James rode over to the nearby stream to water his horse.

Kirby watched them ride off. He looked at the pistol for a moment longer, then he aimed it at a nearby tree and pulled the trigger. The pistol boomed, he felt the recoil, and he saw a chip of bark fly away. He had hit his target.

*   *   *

When Janey left Missouri with Paul Garner, she thought she knew him. She found out quickly that she knew virtually nothing about him. The investments and the financial risks he spoke of were nothing but wagers. Paul Garner was a gambler . . . a card shark.

"This"—he smiled a huge smile, holding up the two thousand dollars Janey had given him to invest—"is going to make us very rich."

"Not just us," Janey replied. "As soon as we can, I want to replace that money. Kirby doesn't know I took it. He doesn't even know that I knew where he had hidden it."

She'd also expected Garner to marry her, but it hadn't happened.

"You'll be a lot more valuable to me if we aren't married," Garner had said.

"What does that mean?"

"Well, just think about it, Janey. If you are my wife, nobody is going to want to flirt with you. But if you aren't married, why every drover, driver, clerk, and soldier will think you are fair game, and they'll all believe they have a chance to crawl into bed with you. And that's going to make us a lot of money."

"Paul! Are you telling me that you want me to be a prostitute for you?"

"No, you don't understand. You won't have to lie with any man. In fact, I don't want you to." Garner had reached out to put his fingers on her cheek. "You're my woman, and I don't want to share you with anyone else. I just want you to make the others *think* you are available."

Garner gave her lessons on how to act as a distraction. She would wait for his signal and then, at an opportune time, approach a table, making certain that the player Garner had picked out would be paying more attention to her than to the game at hand.

The dresses she wore were cut so low that they left little to the imagination and though she had made friends with some of the bar girls, she wasn't one of them. At first, the other girls were a little resentful, but when they learned that she wasn't in competition with them in any way, they actually welcomed her presence. Having one more, very seductively dressed girl in the saloon increased the business traffic for all of them. They also learned that she had her own reason for being there, dressed as she was.

Neither Janey nor the others knew that Garner wasn't using her just to prevent a man from playing his best game. He was using her as a diversion in order to allow him to cheat his mark. The best plans often went awry, however. Despite Janey's most seductive attire and actions, the two thousand dollar poke they had was steadily diminishing.

"I thought you said you could double the money!" Janey had cried, concerned at how fast the money was dwindling. "We've got less than a thousand dollars left! I have to get this money back. Don't you understand? I stole it from my own father and brothers!"

Garner had been unconcerned. "Relax. In any game of chance, you are going to have your ups and downs. The secret to success is not to panic. We'll recover this sooner than you think. Then we can go on to make some real money."

At the moment, Janey was sitting at a table in the back of the Red Bull Saloon, playing a game of solitaire.

A bar girl named Callie approached the table. "Janey, would you be a dear and take this beer to that man sitting by the piano? He just ordered it, but I have to go upstairs for a while."

"Sure, I'll take it to him," Janey replied. Folding up the deck of cards she took the beer to the man Callie had pointed out.

"I was hoping you'd stop by to see me sometime," the man said. "You aren't like the other girls. You don't seem to get around to all the men."

"I don't work here," Janey replied. "I just come here as a customer, the same as you."

"Really? Well that's—"

"You cheatin' son of a—" someone shouted, followed by the sound of a gunshot.

Janey looked toward the table where Garner was playing cards and saw him sitting in his chair with a pained expression on his face. His hands were clasped across his chest and blood was spilling through his fingers.

"Paul!" she shouted, rushing across the room to him.

"Where were you?" Garner asked accusingly. "I gave you the sign and you weren't there. Now I've been—"

He was unable to finish his sentence.

Kirby bought several boxes of .36 caliber cartridges. He didn't have a holster, so he carried the pistol Jesse James had given him stuck into his waistband. With no holster, he wasn't able to practice drawing, but he was able to practice shooting. He quickly became exceptionally adept in the use of a pistol.

He had always been good with a rifle and a shotgun, and had proven that skill as a hunter almost from the time he was five. However, he had no basis of comparison as far as shooting a pistol was concerned. He knew only that he was consistently hitting anything he shot at.

Not long after an afternoon of target practice, he heard the approach of a group of riders, and quickly climbed up into the loft of the barn. He would stay out of sight, but if he was discovered and their intention was hostile, he was determined to shoot as many as he could before they got him.

When he saw that they were carrying a Confederate flag, he called out to them, then climbed down.

"Where is everyone else?" the leader of the group asked.

"There ain't nobody else."

"You're here all alone?"

"My ma was killed by Jayhawkers, my sister run away to I don't know where, and my pa and brother are off fighting in the war."

"For which side?"

Kirby pointed to the flag. "That's the flag they're fightin' for."

The leader nodded. "If your ma was killed by Jayhawkers, that's who I would expect them to be fighting for. The name is Asa Briggs."

Kirby nodded. "I've heard of you, Mr. Briggs, and I thought this might be you."

"I see you've got a pistol. What were you planning on doing with it?"

"If you had been Jayhawkers, I figured to shoot as many as I could before you got me."

Briggs chuckled. "Did you now? Can you shoot?"

"Yes sir."

"How well can you shoot?"

Kirby shrugged. "I don't know. Pretty good, I reckon."

"You want to show me?"

"All right."

Kirby picked up a pecan and handed it to him.

"That's a pretty small target. You sure you don't want to pick something a little larger?"

"No, this is big enough. Put it on that fence post over there."

"Boy, that's got to be more 'n a hundred feet," Briggs said. "You sure you don't want it a little closer?"

"No, put it there."

The other riders realized what was going on, and all conversation and watering stopped as they turned to watch the shooting demonstration.

"I got a dollar says he misses," someone said.

When nobody took the bet, Briggs spoke up. "I'll take the bet." He put the pecan on the post Kirby had pointed out to him.

Kirby raised the pistol to eye level, aimed, and pulled the trigger. Pieces of the pecan flew off the post.

The riders gasped and shouted in disbelief.

"Damn," Briggs said, a wide smile spreading across his face. "Damn! Who taught you to shoot? I ain't never seen nothin' like that."

"I just sort of taught myself," Kirby said, pleased by the accolades.

"Tell me, boy. Do you want to stay here and break dirt, and maybe get burned out again? Or would you like to go after Shardeen and take a little revenge?"

"I can't leave my mules."

"All right."

"But I'm pretty sure Mr. Byrd will look after them for me."

"Then grab your mules, and let's go."

Paul Garner had been caught cheating, so every cent he had on him—five hundred and seventeen dollars—was divided evenly among all the men who had been playing with him at the time he was killed. That represented the rest of the money Janey had brought to their partnership, which meant she was left virtually penniless . . . except for Garner's pearl stick pin and gold money clip, which she took.

She was forced to leave Ft. Worth but had money enough to go only as far as Dallas.

She tried for a little while to earn an honest living, working in a boardinghouse, but the treatment was brutal, and the pay was barely enough to keep body and soul together. Then one day she saw a woman driving a surrey. The woman was attractive, well dressed, and heavily made up. She didn't recognize the woman, but she did recognize the woman's profession.

"They call her Chicago Sue," explained one of the other women

who worked at the boardinghouse. "They say she's a"—in her early
fifties, the speaker was clearly embarrassed by the subject of the conversation, and she lowered her voice before completing her sentence—"an immoral woman. But I think she is somebody that
immoral girls work for. She's very brazen, the way she promenades
around town in her fancy dresses and her surrey. None of the other
girls do that."

"Where does she live? Do you know?"

"Somewhere on Griffin Street, I think. They call it the Palace
Princess Emporium, and it's the biggest and gaudiest house on the
block."

That evening, just before dark, Janey put on one of the dresses
she had worn when she was a *distraction* for Garner, and went to
the Palace Princess Emporium. She knocked on the door.

Chicago Sue answered it. "Who are you?"

"I'm someone who is going to make you a lot of money," Janey
said.

Chicago Sue looked at her and chuckled. "Honey, you just might
at that. Come on in."

Janey followed Chicago Sue into her house, through an attractive
foyer with a Turkish carpet, and into a drawing room. The walls were
covered with a deep crimson wallpaper and the furniture was painted
white with a rich gilding of gold that complemented the damask-
patterned blue area rugs. The divan and the chairs were shades of
greens and blues.

The women sat across from each other and Chicago Sue asked,
"Now, dear, where have you worked before?"

Janey started to say that she had worked for Belle Robb but decided against it. She wouldn't be able to answer any questions if
Chicago Sue started asking questions about the business. Taking a
deep breath, Janey said, "I've never worked anywhere before. At
least, not in a place like this."

Chicago Sue frowned. "Oh? And when you say, a place like this,
what do you mean?"

"A place this elegant."

The frown left Chicago Sue's face, replaced by a smile. "How
sweet of you. Yes, it is elegant, isn't it?"

"Very elegant."

"Have you ever worked as a paid woman before?"

"No."

"Then what brings you to me? It isn't as if you have the usual hard-time story. Not dressed as you are."

"I had a friend who was in the business. I spent some time with her."

"But you didn't go on the line for her? Why not? You obviously have nothing against the concept, or you wouldn't be here."

"I-I guess I just wasn't ready yet."

"But you are now?"

"Yes."

"Please tell me that you aren't a virgin."

"I'm not a virgin."

"Thank God we can get that out of the way then. What is your name?"

"My name is Janey Jensen."

Chicago Sue shook her head. "No, it isn't."

"Of course it is. I know my own name."

"You know it, and now I know it. But I'd strongly advise against using your real name in a business like this. No one does." She smiled. "You don't really think my name is Chicago Sue, do you? It isn't Sue, and hell, I've never even been to Chicago."

Janey laughed. "I didn't think that was your real name."

"Do you want to choose your own name? Or shall I give you a name to use?"

"You give me a name."

"All right." Chicago Sue crossed one arm across her chest and lifted the other to grasp her chin as she studied Janey. "Yes," she finally said. "Yes, it will be perfect for you."

"What will be perfect?"

"Your new name. I've always liked the name Lil. Your new name will be Lil." She shook her head slightly. "No, not just Lil. It will be Fancy Lil."

"Fancy Lil." Janey smiled broadly. "I like it."

"Have you eaten anything?" Chicago Sue asked.

"I had lunch," Janie said.

"Not dinner?"

"No."

"I haven't eaten, either. Come with me. Mrs. Peabody has probably already gone to bed but I'm sure I can rustle us up something."

"Thank you."

"Do you take coffee or tea?"

"Coffee normally, but it seems a little late for that."

Chicago Sue chuckled. "Oh, honey, if you plan to work here, your days and nights will be backward. My girls are just getting started. And a good strong cup of coffee will keep you going."

"All right, coffee then," Janey said.

"Where did you come from?" Sue asked as they walked to the kitchen.

"Fort Worth."

"Nobody comes from Fort Worth. You were somewhere else first. Where is that?"

"Missouri," Janey said without being more specific.

"Something brought you to me, didn't it? I mean, I don't think you grew up thinking that one day you might want to be a soiled dove."

"Soiled dove?"

"It's a rather genteel way we have of referring to ourselves. Other words are so harsh."

"No, I can't say as I grew up wanting to be a soiled dove."

"I wouldn't think so. Are you running from the law or a man?"

"I would say it is more of a situation that I'm running from."

"Are you with child?"

"No."

"That's good. In our business, babies can really complicate things." Chicago Sue took down two cups, then picked up the coffeepot.

"Do you take cream or sugar?"

"I drink it black."

"Smart move," Chicago Sue said as she poured the coffee.

CHAPTER 6

One thing about being with Briggs raiders was that Kirby didn't have to spend all his time with them. The Ghost Riders would take part in an operation or two, then they would disband and he would actually go back home for weeks at a time.

According to Briggs, doing it that way made it less likely that the Yankees would be able to catch up with them.

Late spring, 1864

Kirby returned to Galena, his first time in town in over a month. As he always did when returning home, he checked at the post office, not really expecting to get any mail. To his surprise, he *did* get a letter, but it wasn't from his father, and it was addressed to Mrs. Pearl Jensen. Kirby opened the letter before he even left the post office.

Dear Mrs. Jensen,

It is with much regret that I tell you that your son, Luke Jensen, was killed in battle on Wilderness Creek in Northern Virginia. We didn't find the body, but believe that the Yankees found him on the battlefield and buried him.

Sincerely,
Colonel Edward Willis
12th Georgia, Commanding

Kirby folded the letter up and put it in his pocket, wondering if his pa knew about it. Perhaps not, since the last word he had received from his pa said that he and Luke had been separated.

Back outside, Kirby climbed onto Ange's back. When he was riding with Briggs, he was mounted on a horse, but the horse didn't belong to him.

Briggs had offered to give him one of the Yankee horses, but pointed out that it might be dangerous. "If the Yankee soldiers come through and find you mounted on one of their horses, they'll hang you for being a bushwhacker. If not for that, for horse stealing. On the other hand, if they see you ridin' a mule, they won't give you a second thought."

Briggs had been right. More than once Kirby had encountered Yankee soldiers, but to the soldiers, he was nothing more than a farm boy, riding a mule.

Two events occurred in Missouri that had some bearing on the fate of the war within the state. The first was on October 26 when Yankees located Bloody Bill Anderson just outside Glasgow. Though greatly outnumbered, Anderson and his men charged the Union forces, killing five or six of them before encountering heavy fire. Only Anderson and Elmer Gleason continued the attack, Gleason riding side by side with his leader. The others retreated.

Anderson was hit by a bullet behind his ear and killed instantly. Gleason immediately turned and joined the others in retreat. Four other guerrillas were also killed in the attack, but the rest of the men were able to escape.

The second significant event occurred when General Sterling Price was defeated by General James Blunt's Union cavalry in the battle of Newtonia. Price and his entire corps withdrew, effectively ending any real Confederate presence in Missouri. No longer were any regular Confederate troops in Missouri, but sporadic guerrilla operations continued.

Archie Clement led what had been Bloody Bill's guerrillas for a little while after Anderson's death, but the group splintered by mid-November, and most of the men joined Quantrill, though many, realizing that the war was lost, gave up the battle.

Elmer Gleason was the only man of Anderson's original group to join Asa Briggs. Shortly after he joined Briggs' group, he recognized Kirby by the gun he was carrying. "You're the boy Jesse give one of his guns to, ain't you? It was right after your ma was killed, as I recall."

"I'm the one," Kirby said. "I remember you. You're the one who wondered if I was old enough to run the farm."

"You've got a good memory." Gleason was at least fifteen years older, but he and Kirby became very good friends.

Briggs continued to operate as he always had, uniting his group for a particular undertaking, then having them break up and return to their homes. That ruse worked so well that the participation of most members was unknown, even to their nearest neighbors. From time to time, the men would encounter each other in town or on the road but would make no show of recognition.

The Union Army had no idea who was and who wasn't a member of the group, giving credence to the sobriquet "Ghost Riders."

Kirby's biggest disappointment during his time with Briggs was that they had not encountered Angus Shardeen. They came close once, arriving at a farm just in time to save a farmer and his wife.

Shardeen had been through an hour earlier, robbing the smoke house of the cured hams and bacon. In a macabre joke, he had tied a noose around the woman's neck and thrown the rope over a beam protruding from the hayloft of the barn. He placed her on her husband's shoulders so that she would live only as long as he could stand there supporting her.

The farmer was at the point of exhaustion when the Ghost Riders arrived.

"Kirby! Get up there and cut her down!" Asa Briggs ordered, and Kirby stood on his saddle and pulled himself up into the hayloft. He cut the rope just as her husband collapsed.

They stayed with the couple until both had recovered from the ordeal, spending the night in the barn.

"I'm going to kill him," Kirby told Elmer.

"Yeah, we would all like to get our hands on him before this war ends."

"No, not *like* to kill him. I am *going* to kill him," Kirby said. "I'm going to hunt him down, no matter where he is and no matter how long it takes. I don't care whether the war is still going or whether the war has ended. I am going to dedicate myself to finding him. And when I find him, I'm going to kill him."

January 1865

Briggs' Ghost Riders who had not taken part in the battle for New-tonia found themselves in position to, in Briggs' words, "hit the Yankees a lick." They were going to rob the payroll being transported to the Baxter Springs post.

"The best way to hurt 'em is to take their money," Briggs said. "And that's just what we're agoin' to do."

To that end, the Ghost Riders were waiting in a cornfield alongside the Columbus Road in Cherokee County. It was very cold.

Kirby shivered in the early morning chill.

"Damn. Why couldn't we wait and do this in the summer time?" Elmer Gleason complained.

"I don't know," Kirby said. "Do you think it might be because the payroll is comin' today and not this summer?"

"There you go, gettin' all practical on me," Elmer teased.

"Asa! The coach is acomin'!" one of the others called.

"All right. Get ready."

Kirby crept up to the edge of the cornfield, then lay down where he would have a good view of the road. He could hear the rumble and squeak of the approaching coach, as well as the drum of hoofbeats, not only from the team, but also from the eight men who were riding as escort.

Briggs pulled his pistol. "I'm goin' to shoot one of the coach horses. After that, all hell's goin' to break loose, so get ready."

The coach and outriders were close enough that Kirby could hear the driver's whistles and shouts to the team. He didn't like the idea of shooting an innocent horse but knew that in order for the plan to succeed, it would have to be done.

Briggs fired, and the first, off-side horse stumbled and went down, bringing the coach to an immediate halt.

Within the opening seconds, at least four of the Union soldiers were down. Others tried to return fire, but were unable to find a target. They simply fired wildly into the cornfield.

"Let's get outta here!" one of the soldiers shouted, and the others fled at a gallop.

The Ghost Riders cheered, then ran out onto the road and yelled after the retreating soldiers with cat calls and jeers.

The coach driver had been unarmed and had not taken part in the brief battle. He was still sitting on the high seat with his hands in the air.

"Throw down that strong box," Briggs called.

"What for?" the driver replied. "There ain't nothin' in it."

"What do you mean, there ain't nothin' in it? You went to pick up the payroll, didn't you?"

"Yeah, that's what we went to do all right. But the money wasn't there."

"I don't believe you," Briggs said.

"I'll throw down the strong box 'n let you see for yourself."

"All right. Do it."

The driver reached down between his legs.

Briggs pointed his gun and called out, "No, hold it. Climb down here. I'll get the strong box myself."

Nodding, and obviously frightened, the driver climbed down from the high seat.

Briggs climbed up, retrieved the strong box, then tossed it down onto the road. "Open it up."

"Kirby, you're the best shot among us," Elmer said. "Think you can shoot the lock off?"

Kirby nodded, pulled his pistol, and fired. The bullet cut the hasp.

Elmer opened the lid and looked inside. "It's empty."

"I'll be damned." Briggs jumped down from the coach and ordered, "Cut the team loose and let the horses go."

The driver, who still had his hands raised, protested. "No need for that. All I need to do is cut the dead horse free, then I can go on."

"You can go on, but it's goin' to be afoot," Briggs said. "Now, cut the team loose, unless you want to see 'em burn to death when I set fire to the coach."

"No, I wouldn't want to see no more of the horses killed." The driver set about the task Briggs had set for him.

Half an hour later, with the driver and horses gone, the dozen Ghost Riders stood near the burning coach, enjoying the heat it was putting out.

"Boys," Briggs said. "I reckon this war is all but over. I aim to give it up. You're all free to go wherever you want." He pointed to the coach. "I had planned for this to be the last operation anyway, but I hoped we'd have some Yankee money to divide before we broke up. I'm sorry it didn't work out."

"Hell, Asa, you don't mind if some of us go ahead 'n try 'n get some of that Yankee money, do you?" Elmer asked.

"I don't mind at all, but you're on your own. I'm out of it."

"What are you going to do?" Kirby asked.

"I'm goin' to Texas," Briggs said. "You want to come along?"

"Now, why would he want to do that when he can come with me 'n get some of that Yankee money?" Elmer asked.

Kirby shook his head. "I appreciate the invite from both of you and would be honored to join either one of you, but I reckon my pa will be coming back sometime soon now. I wouldn't want him to come home 'n find nobody waitin' there for him."

"How do you know your pa is still alive?" Elmer asked.

"Truth is, Elmer, I don't know. But if he is, I aim to be there waitin' for him. Most especially since there ain't goin' to be no one else waitin' there for 'im."

Elmer nodded. "I can see that." He stuck his hand out. "Don't know as we'll ever run acrossed each other again, but don't let nobody never call you boy no more. You're a man, Kirby, and you done proved it more 'n once."

Returning to the farm, the first thing Kirby did was dig up the lidded Mason jar he had buried near the corner of the outhouse. It contained the two thousand dollars he'd received from the crops that first year. If his pa came back, he would give him the money. If he didn't come back, Kirby would have that money to start out on his own.

The stench around the outhouse was pretty intense, but it was for precisely that reason he had chosen to bury the money there. He figured nobody would think someone would choose such a place to bury money, and it was unlikely anyone would make any exploratory digs there.

It took only a few minutes to get to the jar, and with a smile, he reached down to retrieve it. The smile faded when he saw that the money was gone, replaced by a note.

Kirby,
I took the money to invest with Paul Garner. I figure half of it is mine anyway, and I'll pay you back your half, with interest.

Janey

"Janey! You sorry-assed hellcat!" Kirby shouted at the top of his voice. He threw the jar against the side of the outhouse and watched it shatter.

By June, six months after Kirby made his last ride with the Ghost Riders, the war had been over and done for better than two months. If his father was coming home, he should be along any time.

Kirby had made the conscious decision not to tell his father about his own experiences during the war. His father had been with the regular army. Kirby wasn't sure how he would take to the idea of his son having been a Bushwhacker. He remembered his father's reaction when Luke had said he wanted to join up with George Clark, who was what his pa had said he was—a murderer and an outlaw. Briggs was an irregular, but he had not killed any innocents, nor burned any private homes or farms. Nevertheless, Kirby decided he would keep his participation in such activity to himself.

The very way Briggs had operated during the war, allowing the men to spend a lot of time at home, would help keep his secret. Tom Byrd knew of Kirby's frequent absences because he kept the mules while Kirby was gone. Kirby had told him that he was earning money by delivering messages and, as far as he knew, Byrd still believed that.

Kirby wondered what his pa would say when he learned his daughter had run off? He wondered, also, if he knew his oldest boy was dead?

Kirby was entertaining all these thoughts as he was busy plowing. Because of his guerrilla activity, he had not put in any crops in the previous two years. He didn't think he needed to; after all, there was no need for him to support anyone but himself. And he'd taken comfort from knowing that he had two thousand dollars set aside for when his pa returned.

Or at least, he thought he did.

As he thought about finding the money gone with only Janey's note in the bottle, he got angry again. Like his mother had said, Janey always was a little wild, but he never would have thought she was a thief. What bothered him more than the thought of her taking the money was her giving it to Paul Garner. It would have been bad enough had she kept it for herself. At least she was family. But to have given it to Paul Garner? That was almost more than Kirby could take.

He would like to run into Garner again, some day. Not as much as he wanted to run into Angus Shardeen, but he would like to encounter him some day, whether Janey was still with him or not.

"Where the hell are you now, Janey?" Kirby asked aloud. "Are you still with that sorry buzzard?"

The plow hit a rock and jolted Kirby out of his musing and back to his surroundings, popping his teeth together and wrenching his arms. "Damn, Ange. Didn't you see that rock?"

Kirby unhooked the plow, running the lines through the eyes of the single tree, and left the plow sitting in the middle of the field. He was late getting the crops in, but no later than anyone else in the hollows and valleys of that part of Missouri. The rains had come and stayed, making fieldwork impossible. But he wanted to get something up before his pa returned. He didn't want his pa to think that he was a wastrel.

Folding and shortening the traces, Kirby jumped onto Ange's back and kicked the mule into movement. He plodded down the turn row on the east side of the field when dust from the road caught his eye. It was one rider, pulling up to the house leading a saddled but riderless horse, a bay.

Wondering who it might be, Kirby touched the smooth butt of the Navy .36, which he now wore in a holster. As Ange plodded closer to the house, Kirby smiled when he made out the figure in the front yard.

It was his pa.

Kirby slid off the mule and walked over to his father.

"Boy," Emmett Jensen said, looking at his son, "I swear you've grown two feet."

"You've been gone for four years, Pa. Someone my age grows a lot in four years." Kirby wanted to throw his arms around his pa, but didn't. His pa didn't hold with a lot of touching between men. He stuck out his hand and Emmett shook it.

"Strong, too," Emmett commented.

"Thank you. Plowin' will do that for you."

"I expect it will. Crops is late, Kirby."

"Yes, sir. Rains come and stayed."

"I wasn't faulting you, boy." Emmett let his eyes sweep the land. He coughed, a dry hacking. "I seen a cross on the hill overlooking the creek. Would that be your ma?"

"Yes, sir."

"When did she pass?"

"Spring, three years ago," Kirby said, remembering Shardeen's raid and thinking with a twinge of regret that all the time he had been with Briggs, they had never encountered Shardeen.

"She go hard?"

She was shot down in front of her kids. Was that hard enough? He wanted to share that with his father, and maybe he would some-day. There was no need to burden him with that now.

"No, sir, it wasn't hard at all. She went in her sleep. I found her the next morning when I took her coffee and grits."

"Good coffee is scarce. What did you do with the coffee?"

"I drank it," Kirby replied.

"Right nice service?"

She's buried in a feeding trough, covered by a door. Only ones here were Janey and me, and I had to talk Janey into staying until I said a few words. Kirby did not vocalize his thoughts. "Real good service. Folks come from all over to see her off."

Emmett cleared his throat and coughed. "Well, I think I'll go up to the hill and sit with your ma for a while. You put up the horses and rub them down. We'll talk over supper. I assume we got somethin' to eat in the house, don't we?"

"We got some greens. I shot 'n cleaned a squirrel no more 'n a couple hours ago. Was plannin' on fryin' it up. I'll make us some cornbread."

"Sounds good to me." Emmett's eyes flicked over the Navy .36 Colt his son was wearing in a holster. If the sight surprised him, he said nothing about it.

"Pa?"

The father looked at his son.

"I'm glad you're back."

What his pa did then couldn't have astonished Kirby any more than if he had suddenly started dancing. Stepping forward, Emmett put his arms around his son and held him. "I'm glad to be back."

Emmett turned and walked up the hill as Kirby tended to the horses.

The cross had been handmade, probably by Kirby, Emmett de-cided. If so, he had done a good job. The particulars were put on the cross with white paint, the words neatly printed.

PEARL VIRGINIA JENSEN
Wife of Emmett Jensen
Oct 13, 1824–April 23, 1862

Emmett wondered why Kirby hadn't mentioned that she was also a mother, but perhaps he felt he wouldn't have room to get it all onto the cross.

He took off his hat and stared down at the grave. Except for the cross, nothing indicated that anyone was buried there. The earth in front of the cross looked no different from the rest of the hill.

"Pearl, I wish I could've been here for you. I don't think this country has ever done anything more foolish than the killin' spree we just come through. I was a part of it when I shoulda been here.

"I don't reckon I need to tell you Luke got hisself killed in this war. An' the reason I don't reckon I need to tell you is, because more 'n likely, you 'n him is together right now." Despite the solemnity of the moment, Emmett smiled. "I hope the first thing you done for 'im when you seen 'im was make him some cornbread so's he could crumble it up in his milk. Lord knows, that boy did like his cornbread 'n milk.

"About Kirby 'n Janey. I didn't do right by them, neither, leavin' 'em here to look after themselves." Emmett looked around the farm. "But truth to tell, I ain't seen hide nor hair of Janey yet. Could be she's fixin' supper, but seein' as how Kirby said he would do it, I think it's more 'n likely that she's gone.

"And speakin' of bein' gone, I ain't told the boy yet, but I plan for me 'n him to get on out of here. Too many memories here. Even the good ones is painful, what with you gone 'n all. It troubles me some to be goin' off 'n leavin' you, but I know that you ain't really here now. You're up in heaven, an' the day'll come when I'll join you. So, I reckon this is the last time I'll be visitin' you like this. I need to get on in with the boy now. We've got some palaverin' to do." Emmett put his hat back on, turned, and walked down the hill.

Over greens, fried squirrel, and corn bread, the father and son ate and talked through the years that they had lost and gained. A few moments of uncomfortable silence came between them occasionally as they adjusted to the time and place, and the fact that their positions had changed.

No change had occurred in the actual relationship; they were still father and son. But Emmett had left a boy; he came home to a man.

"We done our best," Emmett said. "Can't nobody say we didn't. And there ain't nobody got nothin' to be ashamed of."

Kirby hadn't asked him anything about the war, not knowing if he should. He didn't know if his pa wanted to talk about it. But when his pa started talking, Kirby just listened.

"I thought it wrong for the Yankees to burn folks' homes like they done. But it was war, and terrible things happen in war. I didn't know there was that many Yankees in the whole world." Emmett began coughing, a deep, racking cough. It lasted for several seconds before he continued.

"Sometimes when they would come at us, why, we would mow them down like takin' a sickle to wheat. But the Blue bellies just kept on acomin'. You got to give 'em credit for courage. They saw their friends goin' down all around 'em, but they kept on acomin'. Shoot one and five more would take his place."

Emmett was quiet for a moment, and Kirby thought he was finished, but his pa continued. "They weren't near 'bout the riflemen we was, nor the riders neither, but they whupped us fair and square and now it's time to put all that behind us and get on with livin'."

"Yes, sir. That's what I was thinkin'."

Emmett sopped a piece of cornbread through the juice of his greens, and chewed for a time before he spoke again. "You know your brother Luke is dead, don't you?"

"Yes, sir. I didn't know if you knew it or not. I got a letter from a fella named Colonel Willis. He said Luke was killed last year in a place called The Wilderness. Fighting with Lee, wasn't he?"

Emmett nodded, but he was quiet for a moment.

Luke had always been Pa's favorite, or so Kirby had felt.

"We wasn't together, you know. I think I sent your ma a letter tellin' her that we wasn't together no more."

"Yes, sir."

"About the letters." Emmett coughed again. "I know I didn't send many, but it was hard tryin' to find some way to get the mail to go out. How was we to send 'em? The Yankees wouldn't allow any mail to pass through their lines, and they made a point of interrupting our mail as much as they could. I didn't much cotton to the idea of some Yankee reading one of my letters, so I didn't hardly write none at all.

"But, as for Luke gettin' killed, I prob'ly don't know much more 'n you do. From time to time, messengers would get through between our armies. From what I heard, he was tryin' to get back to The Wilderness. Leastwise, that's what I was told."

"Yes, sir."

"I don't see no sign of your sister Janey, and you ain't brought up her name. What are you holdin' back, Kirby?"

It was the moment Kirby had been dreading.

"She's run off, ain't she?"

"She run off with some fella, Pa. Right after Ma died."

"What kind of feller was he?"

"He was a gambler, I'd say."

"Smooth talker, I'd wager."

"Yes, sir."

"What did his hands look like?"

"Soft."

"You're right. More 'n likely was a gambler. You say this was after your ma died?"

"Yes sir."

"Prob'ly just as good. If she had run off before your ma died, it woulda more 'n likely help kill her." Emmett said it flatly, shaking his head, then rose from the table.

"I've ridden a far piece these last few weeks 'cause I wanted to get home. I was hopin' I would be comin' home to Pearl, but what is past is past 'n there's no point in chewin' on it. Now I'm home, and I'm tired. Reckon you are too, son. We'll get some sleep, then we'll have us a talk in the morning. I got a plan." He covered his mouth and coughed.

Breakfast was meager the next morning—grits and coffee that was mostly chicory, along with a piece of leftover cornbread. Kirby knew that his pa was working up to say something, and he was anxious to hear what it was, but he waited.

Finally, washing down the last piece of bread with the last swallow of coffee, Emmett began to speak. "I spent some time talkin' to your ma last night, 'n I'm goin' to tell you what I told her. I don't think it's good to stay here, boy. Too many memories and the land's got too many rocks to farm. You got 'ny money left from four years of farmin' since I been gone? I figure crops prob'ly brought in a fair price, bein' as so many farmers was off fightin' in the war."

Kirby wanted to tell his pa about the two thousand dollars he had been saving, the money that Janey took, but he held his tongue about that. "I . . . uh, ain't got no money at all."

"Ah, don't fret over it. Farmin' is a hard way to make a livin', and truth to tell, I'm proud of you just for supportin' yourself while I was gone.

"We'll sell the mules and milk cows and buy a couple o' good pack horses. The mules is getting too old for where we're goin'. Problem is, they may be too old to even sell. If we can't sell 'em, I'd hate to have to put 'em down."

"We ain't goin' to put Ange and Rhoda down, Pa," Kirby said resolutely. "If that's what it takes for us to go, you just go on without me an' I'll stay here with the mules."

Kirby's response irritated Emmett, but only for a moment, then inexplicably, he smiled. "You got grit, boy. You ain't just growed in body. All right. We'll find somethin' to do with the mules."

"I don't know if Mr. Byrd will buy 'em, but he'd take 'em, and look after 'em. He likes 'em, and the mules like him."

The expression on Emmett's face indicated surprise and curiosity. "How do you know that?"

Kirby wasn't ready to tell his pa just yet about going out with Asa Briggs and leaving the mules with Tom Byrd.

"He, uh, told me one time that if I ever wanted to get rid of the mules that he would take them." That wasn't a complete lie. Byrd had said once that, as often as Kirby brought the team over, he may as well leave them with him.

"All right. We'll leave 'em with Tom," Emmett said. "What day is this, anyway?

"It's Wednesday, Pa."

"How far you been from this holler?"

Kirby thought about his experiences with the Ghost Riders. He had been as far north as Liberty and Glasgow, Missouri, west into Kansas, east to Clark's Mill, Missouri, and south to Cane Hill, Arkansas. He felt bad about deceiving his pa, but again, that wasn't information he was ready to share just yet. "A good piece, Pa. I been to Springfield."

"Then it's about time you got out to see more of this country."

Emmett stuffed his pipe and lit it, then pushed his rawhide-bottomed chair back and looked at his son.

"You got somethin' in mind, don't you, Pa?"

"Toward the end of the war, Kirby, some Texicans and some mountain men joined up with us. Them mountain men had been all the way to the Pacific Ocean, but they talked a lot about a place the Shoshone Indians call Idee ho, or somethin' like that.

"I'd like to see it. Texas too, and some of the rest of the country between here and there, and maybe get all the way out to the Pacific Ocean." Emmett coughed again.

"I seen the Atlantic Ocean, and I tell you boy, you never seen so much water. If I was to see the Pacific Ocean, too, why that would mean I been all the way across this country from east to west. You just got no idea how big this country is. But the West is where all the people seems to be headed now, so I figure we'll just head on out that way, too."

"Pa? How will we know when we get to where it is we're going?"

"We'll know. You got any regrets, Kirby? Leaving this place, I mean."

"Hard work, not always enough food, Jayhawks, Yankees, cold winters, and some bad memories," Kirby replied. "If that's regrets, I'm happy to leave them behind."

Emmett's reply was unusually soft. "You was just a boy when I pulled out with the Grays. I reckon I done you, your sister 'n your ma a disservice, like half a million other men done their loved ones. I didn't leave you no time for youthful foolishness, no time to be a young boy. You had to be a man at an awful young age, and I don't know if I can make up for that, but I aim to try. From now on, son, it'll be you and me."

CHAPTER 7

The Jensens pulled out the following Sunday morning just as the sun was touching the eastern rim of the Ozark Mountains of Missouri. Kirby rode the bay, sitting on a worn-out McClellan saddle, which wasn't the most comfortable saddle ever invented. Emmett had bought it from a down on his luck Confederate soldier trying to get back to Louisiana.

They left the cool valleys and hills of Missouri, with rushing creeks and shade trees, and rode into a hot Kansas summer. The pair rode slowly, the pack horses trailing from lead ropes. The father and son had no deadline to meet and no particular place to go.

They passed a small sign that read BAXTER SPRINGS 2 MILES.

"Boy, what do you say we stop in this little town ahead?"

"Why?"

"Why not? It's been a hot ride and a beer might taste pretty good about now, don't you think?"

Kirby shrugged. "I don't know. I've never drunk a beer."

"You haven't?" Emmett laughed. "I guess not. You were just a boy when I left. Well, as far as I'm concerned, you're a man now, so if you want a beer, this is as good a time and place to start as any."

Baxter Springs was one of the places Kirby had visited when he was riding with Asa Briggs. They had crossed into Kansas looking for Shardeen but didn't find him. By chance, they ran into Quantrill heading south on the Texas Road on his way to winter in Texas. A short time before the two groups met, he had happened upon and killed two Union teamsters who were from a post called Baxter Springs.

Briggs and Quantrill decided to join their bands together for an attack on the post. They encountered Union soldiers, most of whom were black, and chased them back to the earth and log fort.

There, the Rebels attacked, but the garrison, with the help of a howitzer, managed to fight them off. Quantrill decided to move on the post from a different direction, and chanced upon a small Union detachment escorting Major General James G. Blunt and wagons transporting his personal items from his former headquarters in the Department of the Frontier at Fort Scott to his new one at Fort Smith. During the engagement, nearly all of the Union soldiers were killed, though General Blunt and a few mounted men managed to escape.

As a result, what had started as a battle became known as the Baxter Springs Massacre. Neither Briggs, nor any of his men had participated in that part of the fight, but the word *massacre* had been applied to the entire campaign, which, by implication, included Kirby.

Although he had been but one of many who had participated in the fight, he was a little hesitant about going into the settlement again. He took a deep breath, thinking. It had happened almost two years ago. He could be reasonably certain that he wouldn't be recognized as one of the guerrillas who had been there that day.

Kirby nodded his agreement and they approached the little settlement which had grown up around the fort. A small building built of rip-sawed unpainted boards had already weathered gray. The roof sagged, the building leaned, and an extension was obviously newer than the rest of the building. The sign out front read:

MURPHY'S
BEER WHISKEY EATS

Kirby and his pa tied their horses and pack animals off at the hitching rail, then stepped inside. The interior light was dim, filtered as it was through the dirty windows. Beams of light projected through the cracks between the boards, the shining beams alive with hanging dust motes.

The bar, such as it was, consisted of a few boards stretched between barrels. In a white apron and a low-crowned hat, the bartender was wiping glasses and putting them on a shelf behind the bar. Above the glasses, another shelf sported a row of whiskey bottles. A barrel of beer was just to the side.

Four tables with chairs made up the seating, one of them occupied by three men.

"This is a saloon, ain't it, Pa?"

"Not the fanciest I've ever seen, but yes, it's a saloon."

The two stepped up to the bar.

"We'll each have a beer," Emmett ordered, putting a dime down on the plank bar. He started coughing again, a deep and ragged cough.

"That's some cough you got there, mister."

"It's the dust," Emmett said.

The bartender didn't respond, but filled two mugs and set them before Emmett and Kirby. The two took the mugs over to a table and sat down.

"Drink up, boy," Emmett said, holding his mug out across the table toward Kirby.

Kirby took a swallow. It wasn't the best thing he had ever tasted, but on the day of a long, hot ride, it tasted good enough.

"Ha!" Emmett said, slapping his hand on the table. "I was there when you took your first step, I was there when you spoke your first word, and now I'm here for your first beer. It tastes better when it's cold."

"Hey!" called one of the three men sitting at the other table. "Them pants you're wearin' . . . they're Rebel pants, ain't they?"

"They're just trousers," Emmett replied.

"But they're Rebel pants."

"If you don't like my pants, mister, don't look at 'em."

From under the table, the man brought his hand up holding a pistol, pointing it toward Emmett. "Take 'em off. We don't allow Rebels . . . or Rebel pants here."

"I've no intention of takin' 'em off."

"Do you know who I am? My name is Tim Shardeen. I reckon that name means somethin' to you, don't it, Reb?"

Emmett shook his head. "It don't mean a damn thing to me."

"It woulda meant somethin' if we had ever met durin' the war. The outfit I rode with was called Shardeen's Raiders. Angus Shardeen is my brother. That mean anythin' to you now?"

"Only that you was a bunch of murderin' Jayhawkers."

Tim grinned. "Then you know I ain't kiddin' when I tell you that if you don't take off them Rebel pants, I'll shoot you dead 'n take 'em off you myself."

"Let it go, Tim. What are you wantin' to get involved in this for? Hell, him 'n the boy ain't doin' nothin' but drinkin' a beer," one of the others at the table pointed out.

"I don't like Rebs."

"The war's over," said the third man at the table.

"Not for him, it ain't. I'm goin' to count to three 'n if he ain't took off them pants by the time I get to three, I'm goin' to shoot him dead. One—"

A loud boom interrupted the count, and Tim dropped his pistol and grabbed a bloody wound in his wrist. Everyone looked from Tim to Kirby, who was holding a smoking pistol, having drawn it quietly and unobserved.

"Damn! You shot me!" Tim shouted.

"Yeah, I did," Kirby replied.

A pressure bandage was quickly applied to the wound.

"How . . . how the hell did you make a shot like that?" Tim asked through clenched teeth.

Kirby shrugged. "It was an accident."

"An accident?"

"I was tryin' to kill you."

One of Tim's drinking buddies stood up. "We'd better get 'im to Doc Strafford before he bleeds to death."

Still gripping his wrist, Tim headed to the door with his friends.

"Mister?" Kirby called to him.

Tim Shardeen turned with a frown on his face. "Don't waste your time apologizin' to me."

"Oh, I ain't apologizin'. I want you to take a message to your brother for me."

"What would that message be?"

"My name is Kirby Jensen. I want you to tell your brother that if I ever run into him, I plan to kill 'im."

"Ha! You're goin' to kill my brother, are you? How old are you, boy?"

"How old do you have to be to kill a man?" Kirby pointed his pistol at Tim Shardeen again.

"No, no! Don't shoot!"

"You will deliver that message for me, won't you?"

"Yeah, yeah. I'll deliver it."

"Thank you. I appreciate that."

The three men left the saloon.

*   *   *

A few minutes later, Emmett and Kirby rode on, a little wary at first, but the farther away from the town they got, the less concerned they were. By the time they made camp, they were more than thirty miles west of Baxter Springs.

"Are you good enough with that handgun to get us a squirrel for our supper?" Emmett asked.

"I reckon I am, if I see one."

"What about that one?" Emmett asked, pointing to a squirrel halfway up a tree about a hundred feet away.

Kirby pulled his pistol, raised it to eye level, aimed, and fired. The squirrel fell to the ground and he hurried over to retrieve it.

"You clean the squirrel. I'll gather some wood and get us a fire goin'," Emmett said.

Half an hour later, the spitted squirrel was roasting over the fire, coffee was boiling, and the Jensens were sitting nearby.

Emmett looked at Kirby pointedly. "What happened back in the saloon . . . when you shot the gun out of that feller's hand? That warn't no accident, was it?"

"No."

"I didn't think it was." Emmett nodded toward the gun. "I been aimin' to ask you about that pistol. I know you didn't have it when I left home. How did you come by it? And how did you learn to shoot like that?"

"A bunch of Jayhawkers come through the farm one night, headin' back to Kansas like the devil was chasing them, 'n that was just about right 'cause about half an hour later Bloody Bill Anderson and his boys come ridin' up. They stopped to rest and water the horses.

"Turned out this young fellow was with them. He couldn't have been no more 'n a year or so older 'n me. He seen me there alone with nothin' but a shotgun, so he give me this Navy gun and an extra cylinder."

"That seemed like a right nice thing for him to do," Emmett replied.

"Yes, sir. I thought it was. He was nice . . . and soft-spoken, too."

"You seen him since?"

Kirby looked straight ahead. "No, sir."

In fact, he had seen him several times since then, on those occasions when the Ghost Riders and Quantrill's Raiders happened to join up for an operation. He felt bad about lying to his father, but he justified it by telling himself that the day would come when he'd tell everything.

"You thank him proper, did you?"

"Yes, sir."

"Did he tell you his name?"

"He told me. He said it was James. Jesse James. His brother Frank was with the bunch, too. Frank was somewhat older 'n Jesse."

"All right. That tells me how you got the gun. But it don't say nothin' 'bout how come it is you can shoot so well."

Kirby looked at his pa and grinned. "I practiced a lot."

"You musta spent a lot of money for bullets."

"Yes, sir, I reckon I did."

"Well, then, I can see why you didn't have no money left from the farmin', seein' as you spent it all on bullets for practicin'. As things is turnin' out, what with where we're goin' 'n all, bein' able to shoot is goin' to be a lot more important than knowin' how to plow a straight row."

"Yes, sir."

"Tell me about Angus Shardeen."

"Pa, you know about him. He's the one that burned the Gimlin farm, remember?"

Emmett frowned. "That's why you said you wanted to kill 'im?"

"That's not the only reason. He also come through on a raid and kilt Kenny Prosser 'n his ma and his little brother. Kenny was a good friend of mine, if you 'member. 'N he also kilt Merlin Lewis 'n his family."

Kirby was telling the truth. Those two county families had been killed by Angus Shardeen.

"All right. You do know that takin' a blood oath like that, which is pretty much what you just done in tellin' a man that you aim to kill his brother, is puttin' quite a load on your shoulders."

"Yes, sir."

"How fast can you get the gun out of the holster?"

"I don't know," Kirby admitted. "It ain't anythin' I've ever had to do." Being able to shoot straight had been not only a help but a necessity when he was riding the Bushwhacker trail, but a quick draw wasn't.

"If you set yourself the job of findin' someone and killin' 'im, especially someone like Angus Shardeen, bein' able to pull the gun out fast is somethin' that might come in pretty handy, don't you think? It's called a quick draw."

"A quick draw," Kirby repeated.

"Yeah. Stand up there and do a quick draw for me. Let me see what you can do."

Kirby stood up, then made a grab for his pistol. It was awkward and the draw was slow.

Emmett laughed. "Looks like we've got some work to do. You've already showed that you can shoot straight. Now you need to learn how to draw."

"You think I can learn?"

"I don't have no doubt. You have sort of a natural-born smooth-ness about you, so I have a feelin' you're goin' to learn pretty fast how to do a quick draw. With that and accurate shootin', I've no doubt but that you'll wind up bein' a man to be reckoned with."

"Why would I have to be reckoned with?"

"Because where we're goin', you're goin' to have to live by laws that aren't necessarily wrote down anywhere. But just 'cause they ain't wrote down, don't mean they ain't laws that need to be fol-lowed."

"What kind of laws are you talkin' about?"

Emmett had another bout of coughing before he responded. "I'm talkin' 'bout the laws of decency and good sense. Don't take what ain't yours, don't cheat at cards—for that matter, don't cheat at nothin' else, either—don't call a man a liar if he ain't, and don't be afraid to call him one if he is. And if you do, you have to be prepared to back it up."

"Back it up with a gun, you mean?"

"Yes. Where we're goin', the time is more 'n likely goin' to come when no matter how much you try and avoid it, you'll wind up get-tin' pushed into a corner. When that happens, you won't have no choice but to try and defend yourself. If the one who done the evil is faster and better with a gun than the one that got the evil done to him, the wrong man might die."

"I see what you mean."

"I hope you do see what I mean, Kirby, because I'm going to teach you how to make a quick draw."

"Can you do a fast draw, Pa?"

"Fair to middlin'."

"How did you learn?"

Emmett leaned back against a big rock, thinking about what he wanted to say. "Remember me tellin' you 'bout those boys from Texas? They taught me all the skills a person needs, and I can pass those skills on to you. But it takes more than skills. It takes a natural ability like what I was tellin' you about. I've seen you move all your life, Kirby, and you got a natural way of doin' it. Things has always come easy to you, easier than it ever did to your brother. Easier than it ever did to me, easier than it has to anyone else I've ever knowed or even seen. With a little practice, you'll not only be a lot faster 'n me, few—if any—in the country will be able to stand up to you. But that'll come with a sense of responsibility."

"What kind of responsibility?"

"The responsibility to use your gun only when it's right, only to defend yourself or the innocent. Can I count on you to do that?"

"Yes, Pa."

"You promise me?"

"I promise."

"I know you will, son. I only asked you to make the promise so's it'll be somethin' you'll always keep in your mind." Emmett had another coughing spell.

"Pa, you told the bartender that it was the dust makin' you cough. Only, there ain't no dust here now. Besides which, you been acoughin' a lot ever since you got back from the war. Why is it you're coughin' so much? You ain't got what they call the consumption, do you?"

"Where did you hear about consumption?"

"Miss Margrabe said her pa died of the consumption."

"I ain't got the consumption. Now, are you ready for your first lesson?"

"Yes sir, I reckon I am."

"Good. But before I teach you the fast draw, I'm going to have to teach you to shoot."

Kirby chuckled. "Pa, I've already showed you that I can shoot."

"You have, huh?" Emmett pointed to a thumb-sized protrusion from the branch of a nearby cottonwood tree. "Take a shot at that little branch for me."

Kirby raised the pistol to eye-level and fired. His bullet snapped the branch and he turned to his father with a satisfied smile on his face. "I told you I could shoot."

"You aimed, didn't you?"

"Of course I did."

"Why?"

"Why? Because I wanted to hit what I was shootin' at. That's why."

Emmett gave instructions. "Shoot at it again, but don't aim this time."

"What do you mean, don't aim? I don't understand. How am I going to hit it, if I don't aim?"

"You are going to think the bullet onto your target."

"What?"

"Let me show you what I'm talking about." Emmett pulled his own pistol and shot at the part of the branch that was left. He didn't raise the pistol to eye level and aim, he just pulled the trigger and another piece of the branch was shot away.

Kirby's jaw dropped. "How did you do that without aiming?"

"I told you. I just thought the bullet onto the target."

"I don't understand what that means."

"Here's the thing," Emmett said as he put his pistol back in the holster. "There's no sense in drawing really fast if you have to stop and aim. You have to draw, aim, and shoot all at the same time. In order to do that, you have to think the bullet onto the target. Now, you try it."

Kirby pulled the pistol and automatically started to raise it. He stopped himself, then held the gun out in front of his body and fired. He missed.

Emmett stood up. "Here, let me help you out. Turn yourself at an angle, sort of caddy corner, so that you aren't facing the target." He positioned Kirby accordingly. "Now, don't turn your body, but look at the target by turning your head back toward it."

Kirby responded.

"Bring the pistol up to eye level and aim at the target, just as you did before, but don't shoot."

Kirby did.

"Good. Close your eyes and lower your pistol so that it is pointing straight down."

Kirby did as instructed.

"Now, with your eyes closed, aim at it again."

Kirby opened his eyes and looked at his pa. "What do you mean, aim at it again? How am I going to do that if my eyes are closed?"

"Just listen to me, boy. Close your eyes and with them still closed, bring your arm back up, thinking about where the target is. When you think you have it lined up, tell me."

Kirby closed his eyes and brought his arm up until he thought he was aligned with the target.

"Pull the trigger, but don't open your eyes."

Kirby pulled the trigger.

"Now, open your eyes and look."

He did that and saw a white chip had been taken out of the limb, just below the small branch he had been shooting at. It was a miss, but it was a very close miss.

"I almost hit it!" he said excitedly.

"That was pretty good. Now, spread your feet apart about the width of your shoulders. Keep your legs straight, but not stiff. Think you can do that?"

Kirby tried it a few times, then looked at Emmett. "Yes, I can do it."

"What are you going to do with your other arm?" Emmett asked.

Kirby looked down. "I don't know. I hadn't thought about it."

"Good."

"Good?"

"It's good that you hadn't thought about it. As far as you're concerned, the other arm isn't even there.

"Put your pistol back in the holster, then look at your target by turning your head and eyes slightly without moving from the neck down. When you know exactly where the target is, pull the pistol from the holster, but don't raise the gun to eye level. Shoot it as soon as your arm comes level."

Anxious, Kirby asked, "Should I try a quick draw?"

"No. That comes later. First learn to shoot, then learn to draw. Now, pull the gun and shoot it."

Kirby pulled the pistol and fired as soon as it came level. He had no idea where the bullet went.

Fancy Lil was easily the most beautiful dove in the covey of doves Chicago Sue employed at the Palace Princess Emporium. She had managed to avoid the dissipation so prevalent among the others. While most would lay with anywhere from three to five men a night, Fancy Lil rarely shared her bed. The others charged from two dollars to five dollars, depending on the girl and the length of the visit. It cost fifty dollars to visit Fancy Lil for a short while, and one hundred and fifty dollars to spend the night with her.

Her room, in keeping with her station as Chicago Sue's most expensive girl, was attractively furnished with lace curtains on the window and a floral carpet on the floor. The furniture was made of English oak and the headboard featured elaborate carvings.

Her clientele was of a considerably higher caliber than the average visitor to the place. She entertained wealthy cattlemen, high ranking officers who'd been in the Confederate military, and politicians, including a couple Texas state senators.

Her most frequent visitor, and the one she actually enjoyed being with, was a big man, a Confederate veteran who stood six feet seven inches tall, and weighed 330 pounds. He had given only his first name, Ben.

The well-appointed room was redolent with the scent of sex. She and Ben were lying together, naked skin against naked skin.

Though it had become a little more than routine for Janey—an act without feeling, emotionally or physically—it wasn't like that with Ben. With him, she had experienced every sensation.

Their times together were passion-filled, but she also felt a relaxed shared possessiveness between them that she had never felt with anyone else, not even Paul Garner.

She put her head on Ben's shoulder, and he wrapped his arm around her, cupping her breast in his hand. It wasn't sexual. It was comfortable.

"What is your name?" she asked. "I know there has to be more to it than just Ben."

"Some folks call me Big Ben."

Janey chuckled. "*Big* Ben? Yes, I can see that. But am I to believe that's all there is to it?"

"Am I to believe there is no more to your name than Fancy Lil?"

"I can't give my real name," Janey said.

"Why not?"

"Because girls in my . . . profession . . . never give their real names."

Big Ben smiled. "And men like me, who visit girls like you, never give our real names."

"You are a wealthy man, aren't you, Ben?"

"Why do you say that?"

"Because it costs a lot of money to visit me . . . and lately, you have been visiting me more than all my other gentlemen callers combined."

"I enjoy visiting you."

"But you can get the same thing from other girls for a lot less money."

Big Ben shook his head. "No, I can't. Lil, I would have thought that, by now, you understood. It isn't just the time we're in bed together. It's more than that. With you . . . with us . . . it's just . . . more. I thought . . . that is, I hoped . . . that it was a little more for you, as well."

Janey felt her eyes well with tears, and she leaned up to kiss him on his cheek, feeling the stubble of a day's growth of beard. "My name is Janey. Janey Garner."

She'd decided to expose herself to him, but she chose to use Garner's last name, rather than Jensen. She didn't want to bring any more shame to the Jensen name than she already had. Assuming, that is, that there were any Jensens left alive.

Big Ben turned to smile at her. "Conyers. Benjamin R. Conyers."

CHAPTER 8

Millions of soldiers who had worn the blue and the gray had laid down their arms and picked up where they had left off. Families split by the war were reunited. Friendships were renewed, crops were put in, men and women were married, children were born.

But it was not so for all men. For some, the wounds had cut too deeply and the price had been too dear. Families, fortunes, and dreams were consumed in flames and drowned in blood. So it was for Kirby and Emmett. They had only each other, along with their guns and their courage.

After leaving Baxter Springs, they headed west for a bit, then turned south through Indian Territory, heading for Texas.

"Do you think we need to be wary of the Indians, Pa?"

"No need. All the Indians here is civilized. They got their own towns, their own laws. Most even like white men. Lots of 'em even fought 'n the war. It's farther out West that we got to be wary of 'em. Out there, I hear tell that Indians is notional folks. The same bands that would leave you alone today might try to kill you tomorrow."

"Why?"

"I can't say. It's hard for the average white man to understand the Indians' way of life. But I'm sure there are white men livin' in the mountains, prob'ly been there thirty or forty years or more, who can understand them better 'n whites can now, them bein' gone so long from civilization 'n all."

Every night as they camped, Kirby would practice shooting, though he limited his practice to no more than three shots each day. They were a long way from any chance of buying new bullets.

On the seventh day, he fired three shots, *thinking* his bullets into the targets all three times. "Did you see that, Pa?"

"Can you do it again?"

Kirby repeated his performance, again hitting his targets with all three bullets.

"All right. Instead of shooting one at a time, I want you to fire three times, one shot right on top of another, and hit these three targets." Emmett put pine cones on three rocks, the two farthest rocks separated by at least ten yards. He came back to stand beside Kirby.

"Now?" Kirby asked.

"Not yet. I'm going to add something to it." Emmett took a mess skillet from his pack and put it on the ground in front of him, then he picked up a rock. "When I say, 'now,' I want you to start shooting. At the same time, I'll drop this rock, and I want to hear all three shots before the rock hits the skillet. Do you think you can do that?"

"I can get all three shots off, yes sir."

"And hit all three targets," Emmett said.

"I don't know, Pa. That's askin' quite a lot."

"Wrong answer. Do you think you can do that?"

Kirby smiled. "Yes, sir."

Emmett returned the smile. "That's my boy. Now!" he shouted without further notice.

Using his left hand to fan the hammer, Kirby fired three shots so close that it sounded like one. Then *clank*—the rock hit the skillet. All three targets had been hit.

"You didn't give me any warning," Kirby complained.

"I didn't, did I? Well, you don't always get a warning. I think the time has come to teach you the quick draw. And this won't be costin' us any bullets at all."

"I'm ready," Kirby said with a broad smile.

"All right. Empty your pistol before we begin. I wouldn't want the damn thing to go off accidental while you're tryin' to learn."

Kirby pulled his pistol, poked all the shells out of the cylinder, and stuck it back down into the holster.

"Now, look down at the shank of your holster. That's the part that's attached to the belt. It should have a little kink in it, so that it causes the butt of the pistol to stick out just a little. You can adjust it, but we may have to make a little modification later on, so that the pistol sticks out far enough all the time so there won't be anything to get in the way of your draw."

Kirby made a few adjustments to the shank and finally, after examining it closely, Emmett announced that it was ready and continued with his instructions. "Let your arm hang down completely limp and natural along your side. Don't crook the elbow . . . don't stiffen your arm. Don't do nothin' but just let it hang there."

Kirby did as he was instructed.

"Now, without drawing the gun, bend your arm at the elbow until your hand has come up level with the ground. Stick out your trigger finger. Where is it pointing?"

"It's pointing in the same direction as my arm," Kirby said.

"All right, now what I want you to do is, move the gun belt until the gun is exactly under your hand. The butt of the pistol should be poking out away from your body just a little. That was why we adjusted the shank a while ago. Remember?"

Kirby adjusted the holster as directed, and Emmett inspected the position of the gun.

"Yes," he said, smiling. "Just like that. And the holster should be at the same angle as your arm was a while ago when you lifted it. Do that."

Kirby repositioned the holster.

"Move your hips forward real slow and bring your shoulders back, grabbing the gun as your hips and shoulders move. But don't grab it with your whole hand. Curl your middle finger, ring finger, and little finger around the butt of the gun. If you've got your holster positioned right, that will put the gun in your hand before you even start to draw it."

Kirby reacted to the directions, and as Emmett had pointed out, his hand fell naturally to the butt of the pistol. He smiled at the result. "Pa, my hand went right where you said it would."

"Good. That's very good. Keep your holster there, and do it that way every time, so that when the gun comes out of the holster, it will just naturally be pointed in the right direction. Now, when you make the draw, make sure you bring the barrel up level, 'cause if you don't, you'll shoot low ever' time."

Kirby nodded, indicating that he understood the instructions.

"All right. Good. Now, it's time to cock the gun as you draw it. What you want to do is, pull your thumb across the hammer to cock the gun at the same time you are drawing. The thumb should be moving the hammer back all the while you are bringing the gun up. You got that?"

"Yes, Pa. I got it."

Emmett chuckled. "So you say. We'll just see if you listened to anything I said. I want you to draw the gun just the way I told you. But I want you to draw it real slow, so I can see it, and make sure you're doing everything the right way. Go ahead and draw it now."

Kirby made the draw, doing it slowly and exactly as he had been instructed. Emmett smiled.

"How did you like that?" Kirby asked.

"Don't go getting all smug on me now," Emmett said.

"I did it perfectly."

"How do you know you did?"

"Because, if I hadn't done it perfectly, you wouldn't have called me smug," Kirby said with a pleased smile.

"Right. Now . . . pick out something to shoot at and draw as fast as you can."

Kirby frowned. "I don't have any bullets in the gun."

"You don't need any bullets right now. All you need to do is what I told you. Now, I want you to pick out a target."

"What about that leaf there?"

"What leaf? There are hundreds of leaves. How do I know you won't just shoot, then claim the leaf you hit is the one you wanted to hit?"

Kirby walked over to a nearby tree and put his finger on one of the leaves. "This one."

"All right. Draw your pistol as fast as you can and shoot at it."

Still confused, Kirby asked, "How can I shoot if I don't have any bullets?"

"Just do what I tell you, Kirby. If I want questions, I'll ask for them."

Kirby returned to his original position, drew his pistol, thumbed back the hammer, and pulled the trigger. The hammer fell on an empty chamber.

"Did you hit the leaf?" Emmett asked.

Kirby started to ask his father again how he could hit the leaf if he had no bullets in his gun but checked the question and smiled instead. "Yeah, I hit the leaf."

"Good. Now, put some bullets in your gun and do it again."

Kirby loaded the pistol and put it in his holster. He got ready to make his draw—

"Wait." Emmett stopped him. He picked up the rock.

"You're goin' to drop the rock on the skillet again?" Kirby asked.

"No. This time you're goin' to drop the rock. What I want you to do is hold it out in front of you. When I tell you to, drop the rock, draw your pistol, and shoot at that leaf."

Kirby held the rock out in front of him, shoulder high.

"Now!" Emmett shouted.

Kirby dropped the rock, drew his pistol, and fired. Not until after the gun fired, was there the clank of the rock hitting the skillet. The leaf, cut from the tree, fluttered down. Kirby looked over at Emmett and smiled.

"Not bad," Emmett said.

"Not bad? What do you mean, *not bad*?"

"You had your hand shoulder high. I want you to be able to do that when your hand is no higher than this." Emmett demonstrated, holding his hand lower than Kirby's waist.

"Nobody can do that." Kirby shook his head.

"You can," Emmett said. "And better."

"If you think so," Kirby said.

"No, Kirby, it's not what I think. It's what *you* think. Actually, it's not what you think, it's what you *know*. You have to *know* that you can do this."

Kirby picked up the rock and held it just below his waist. Then, with a confident grin, he moved the rock even lower. Taking a deep breath, he dropped the rock, drew the pistol, and fired . . . before the rock clanked against the skillet. And he hit the target.

As Kirby bedded down that night next to glowing embers of the fire that had cooked their supper, he let his mind pass over events that had brought him and his father near the Cherokee town of Tahlequah in the Indian Territory. He had grown up thinking he would be a farmer like his father. Once he and Luke had even discussed buying acreage just across Shoal Creek from the family farm. If they bought 40 acres apiece, they could farm all the land jointly . . . 120 acres, which would make it one of the biggest farms in Stone County. And because all the land had access to a year-round supply of water, it could be the best farm in the county.

But none of that was to be. His mother was dead. Luke was dead. Janey had run off, who knows where, and his pa had come back from the war no longer interested in farming. If Kirby was truthful with himself, he was no longer interested in it, either.

How strange life was that it could start out in one direction, then make a turn in a completely different direction.

Emmett had another bad coughing spell in his sleep.

Kirby sat up and looked over toward him. "Pa?"

Emmett coughed again. "I'm all right, son. I've just got a cough I can't shake, is all. Go back to sleep."

Kirby lay back down. He hadn't been asleep so there was no *going back to sleep*, but as he lay there, his eyelids began to grow heavy, and finally sleep pushed away all the thoughts tumbling through his mind.

Over the next several days Kirby continued to practice. His draw became so fast that it was a blur, too fast for the eye to follow. His shooting was deadly accurate, as well.

Emmett, having handled guns all his life, was a very good shooter. As he watched, he realized that Kirby was exceptionally good—already better than his pa. Emmett smiled, proud.

He had once been the city marshal of a small town in Missouri, and had found it necessary, in defense of his own life, to kill two men during his tenure in office. God alone knew how many more men he had killed during the war.

Emmett was glad that the boy could handle himself. He had not told Kirby everything—that he would have gone West whether Pearl was dead or alive, and whether or not Kirby had come with him; that his journey was not one of pure impulse; that he had given his word to Mosby that if it took him forever, he would find and kill the men who had murdered Luke and stolen the gold he was carrying to the Confederate government in Georgia.

In this, he was like his son. Kirby had taken his own oath to kill someone. Ideally, they would be together when they encountered the men they were after.

Crossing into Texas, they came across a few stage stops and trading posts along the way but didn't ride into any towns until they reached Dallas.

Emmett looked around. "This is it, boy. Dallas, Texas."

"Wow, this is purt' nigh as large as Springfield," Kirby said, taking it all in.

The main street was cut with wheel ruts and hoof marks, and covered with enough horse apples to permeate the air with strong odor. A busy town, it was filled with buckboards, surreys, carriages, and wagons, as well as riders on horseback. Boardwalks ran the entire length of each block and were filled with the citizens of the town, many of them women who walked around holding handkerchiefs to their nose to blot out the smell.

"We might want to stop here, first," Emmett said, pointing to a gun store. "I expect you're about out of ammunition, ain't you?"

"I could sure use some more," Kirby replied.

Tying their four horses off, the two men went inside.

A clerk sitting behind the counter in a wooden chair leaning against the wall was the only person in the store. He stood up when they entered. "Yes, sir, can I help you?"

"I need some thirty-six caliber shells," Kirby said.

"Very good sir. How many do you need?"

"I'd say about two hundred."

The clerk whistled. "Two hundred? My, that's a lot of ammunition. I do hope you aren't planning on restarting the war." He laughed at his own joke.

"Got no intention of doin' that," Kirby said. "But travelin' like we are, you don't always find a place where you can get it."

"I understand." The man took four boxes from a case, then opened one of the boxes. "As you can see there are fifty bullets in each little box. Four times fifty is two hundred."

"Open all four boxes," Emmett said.

"Do you really think that is necessary?"

"Open all four boxes," Emmett said again.

The man started to put one of the boxes back in the case, but Emmett reached out to grab his wrist. "What's wrong with that box?"

"To tell the truth, it felt a little light to me, so I . . ."

Before he could finish his statement, Emmett opened the box. It was only about half full. "A little light, you said?"

"Yes. You did notice that I was putting it back," the clerk said self-righteously. He put four boxes on the counter and opened them. "Two dollars."

Satisfied that the boxes were full, Kirby paid for the ammunition, and he and Emmett went back outside.

"How'd you know he was plannin' to cheat me, Pa?"

Emmett put his finger alongside his nose. "I smelled it."

"You smelled it?" Kirby asked incredulously.

"You don't actually smell it," Emmett explained. "It's just something that you say when you have a feelin' that somethin' ain't quite right. And I had a feelin' that somethin' wasn't quite right."

"How do you learn to have them feelin's?"

"It's not somethin' you learn. It's somethin' that just sort of comes to you as you get older. I expect it'll come over you, too, eventually."

Looking around, they spotted the Lone Star Hotel.

"What do you say we spend the night in a bed instead of on the ground?" Emmett asked.

"Sounds good to me," Kirby agreed.

After checking into the hotel and boarding their horses, they walked up the wide, sunbaked street, hurrying from the shade of one building to the next, taking every opportunity to get out of the sun. After walking a few blocks, they were drenched with sweat, and the cool interior of the Yellow Dog Saloon beckoned them.

Pushing their way through the bat wing doors, they stepped inside and stood in the dark for a moment or two until their eyes adjusted to the dim light. Unlike the rather coarse establishment in Baxter Springs, this place was rather elegant. Made of burnished mahogany, the bar had a highly polished brass foot rail. Crisp, clean white towels hung from hooks on the customers' side of the bar, spaced every four feet. A mirror behind the bar was flanked on each side by a small statue of a nude woman set back in a special niche. A row of whiskey bottles sat in front of the mirror, reflected in the glass so that the row of bottles seemed to be two deep. A bartender with pomaded black hair and a waxed handlebar moustache stood behind the bar. A towel was draped across his shoulders, and his arms were folded across his chest.

"Is the beer cool?" Emmett asked.

"It's cooler than horse piss," he said in a matter-of-fact voice.

Emmett chuckled. "Good enough. We'll have a couple."

The bartender drew the beers and set them in front of Kirby and Emmett.

Kirby picked up the beer and took a drink.

"What do you think?" Emmett asked. "Is the second one better?"

"Yes, sir. It's a lot better."

"It's good to be able to enjoy a beer now 'n again but, what with you just startin' out to drink, I need to tell you to be careful about drinkin'."

"Careful? What do you mean? Why do I have to be careful?"

"I say that 'cause some folks start to likin' their liquor too much, 'n the next thing they know, 'bout the only important things in their life is the next drink 'n where it's comin' from. I sure don't want to see that happen to you."

"I don't neither. I promise you, I will take care." Kirby turned to look around the place. Nearly every table was occupied.

One of the tables was near enough to where they were standing that Emmett could quite easily listen in on the conversation that was taking place between three men.

"Her name is Lil. Fancy Lil," one of the men was saying. "She works down at the Palace Princess Emporium."

"That ain't her real name, is it, Doc?"

"I'm sure that Fancy is not a part of her sobriquet, though Lil might be. Young ladies who find themselves in such occupations, however, rarely use their real names."

"She must be somethin'," said the man in a blue shirt. "I heard that iffen you want to choose her, it's goin' to cost you a hunnert dollars. Maybe even more."

The man with a bushy mustache shook his head. "There ain't no woman worth a hunnert dollars."

"Oh, believe me, this young lady is," replied the one called Doc.

Bushy Mustache couldn't believe it. "Doc, don't tell me you spend a hunnert dollars on her."

"I have not, but only because I don't have a hundred dollars to spare. But if I did, I would do so without a moment's hesitation."

"The Palace Princess Emporium. That's Chicago Sue's place, ain't it?" Blue Shirt asked.

"Yes."

"Yeah, well, mayhaps that's why I ain't never seen this here Fancy Lil that you're talking about. I ain't never been to Chicago Sue's establishment. They ain't any of them at Chicago Sue's place that's cheap."

"Oh, I wouldn't complain. Those at the Palace Princess Emporium are different," Doc said.

"What do you mean, *different?* They's same as saloon girls, ain't they?"

"No, they are ladies that entertain."

"Does it cost money to be entertained?" Bushy Mustache wanted to know.

"Yes."

Blue Shirt wasn't convinced. "And, does that entertainment include sleepin' with 'em?"

"Yes."

Blue Shirt crossed his arms. "If a woman will go to bed with you for money, she's same as a saloon girl, no matter how much it costs."

"I'm sure that as dissipation takes its toll, some of the young ladies who work there will slip down the scale until you can rightly throw them in with saloon girls, but not now. And you certainly can't say that for Fancy Lil. Anyone who can command one hundred dollars for her services is certainly more than a common saloon girl."

Bushy Mustache didn't believe it. "This Fancy Lil must be some kind of woman."

"She is," Doc replied. "Perhaps Christopher Marlowe expressed it best."

"Christopher Marlowe? Hmm, I don't think I know him."

"That wouldn't be likely, since he died almost two hundred years ago," Doc said.

Bushy Mustache was more confused than ever. "What? Then how could he say anything about Fancy Lil?"

"He was actually speaking of Helen of Troy, but it could have been Fancy Lil." Doc cleared his throat, then, in dramatic fashion, said the words, "*Was this the face that launch'd a thousand ships . . . And burnt the topless towers of Ilium? . . . Sweet Helen, make me immortal with a kiss.*"

His table mates were stunned.

Bushy Mustache grinned. "Doc, you're the smartest man I've ever knowed. You must be. Hell, I don't understand half of what you say."

"I have established the idea that this lady, Fancy Lil, is a person of rare beauty, haven't I?"

"Oh, yeah, you've done that all right. Only I'll never get to see her. A hunnert dollars? I ain't never had that much money at one time in my whole life."

"It doesn't cost a hundred dollars just to see her. For five dollars, you can visit the parlor of the Palace Princess Emporium, enjoy food, drink, and conversation with beautiful women and a convivial atmosphere," Doc pointed out.

"Five dollars? But that don't get you no woman, does it?"

"Only in friendly conversation."

Blue Shirt looked at Bushy Mustache. "Will Fancy Lil be there?"

"She often is, when she isn't otherwise engaged."

"You mean with someone?"

"Yes."

"Hmmph. If it cost one hunnert dollars to be with her, I can't imagine she's with someone all that much."

"She is very selective," Doc replied.

* * *

Kirby had been listening intently to the conversation. He turned to Emmett, who was staring into his glass. "You know what, Pa? I'd like to see this woman they're talkin' about."

"Why?"

"You heard what Doc said. That she is the most beautiful woman he had ever seen. Wouldn't you like to see such a woman?"

"Boy, what do you know about such things? Have you ever been to such a place?" Emmett's question was pointed, but not challenging.

Kirby had never been, but he had seen one . . . once. It had been pointed out by Elmer Gleason. He couldn't share that information with his father, though, without sharing that he had ridden with Asa Briggs.

"No, sir, I ain't never been to one. But I know what one is. Some of the other boys in school was talkin' 'bout 'em one day." That was true. The subject had come up, but none of the boys who'd been discussing it knew exactly what went on there.

"Yeah, I reckon there are some things you can learn at school that ain't really all that good."

Kirby chuckled. "I never heard that till I was in the seventh grade. And remember, I wanted to quit soon as I finished the fifth grade."

Emmett chuckled, then took another drink. "Well now, ain't you glad I made you stay?"

At that moment, the back door opened and a tall, broad-shouldered, bearded man wearing a badge stepped through the door and looked around. For a long moment, he scrutinized Kirby and Emmett, obviously aware that they were new in town, then continued his perusal of the room until he saw a man who caught his attention.

"You," he said, pointing. "We got a telegram sayin' you was comin' to Dallas. I didn't think you was actually that dumb, Cox."

The man stood up slowly, then turned to face the lawman. "Yeah? Why shouldn't I come to Dallas? Am I supposed to be afraid of some piss-ant deputy?"

The situation had the look of an impending gunfight. The others at the table stood up and moved out of the way. All other conversation within the saloon ceased.

"Unbuckle your gun belt," the lawman said, making a motion with the gun he was holding. "And do it slow and easy, so's I don't get the idea you're tryin' anything."

Cox shook his head no. "I don't think so, Deputy. I think me an' you's goin' to have to settle this thing, right here and right now."

Kirby had heard stories about deadly gunfights between men, but not in all the time he had been riding with Briggs had he ever seen one. The shooting he had experienced was from a distance, and it was always one group of men against another group. He had never seen a one-on-one confrontation.

"Are you crazy, Cox?" the deputy asked. "I've already got you covered."

"Do you now?" Cox asked with a mysterious smile on his face.

Kirby was watching intently, wondering why the man called Cox didn't seem to be worrying about the gun that was pointing toward him. When he saw a man standing up in the corner, aiming his pistol at the lawman, he shouted, "Deputy, look out! There's a gun behind you!"

The man in the corner turned the pistol toward the Jensens.

Kirby acted instinctively. Dropping his beer, he pulled his pistol and fired just as the man in the corner pulled the trigger on his own gun. The would-be assailant's bullet hit the mirror behind the bar, and it fell with a crash, leaving nothing but a few jagged shards hanging in place to reflect twisting images of the dramatic scene.

Just like in all of his practicing, Kirby's bullet had gone true . . . only his target had been a man . . . who dropped his weapon and grabbed his neck. His eyes rolled up in his head and he fell backward.

The two gunshots had riveted everyone's attention to that exchange. Cox took the opportunity to go for his own gun. Suddenly, the saloon was filled with the roar of another gunshot as he fired at the deputy, whose attention had also been diverted by the gunplay between Kirby and the man in the corner. Cox's bullet struck the deputy in the back of the head.

Making a fatal mistake, Cox swung his pistol toward Kirby.

Emmett's bullet caught Cox in the center of his chest, and he went down. He sat on the floor, leaning back against the table, his gun lying on the floor beside him. "Who . . . who the hell are you?" he asked, gasping out the question. "What did you get involved for?"

"It seemed the thing to do," Emmett said.

One more gasp, and Cox was dead.

CHAPTER 9

"What's goin' on in here?" asked a loud authoritative voice. "Who's doin' all the shootin'?"

Holding smoking guns, Kirby and his pa turned toward the sound of the voice to see a man standing just inside the open door. With the brightness of the light behind him, he could be seen in silhouette only.

"Get out of the light," Emmett said, his voice a low growl.

"You don't tell me what to do, I—"

Click. Emmett pulled the hammer back and his pistol made a deadly metallic sound as the sear engaged the cylinder. "I said get out of the light," he repeated.

The figure moved out of the light. Kirby and Emmett could see that he was wearing a badge and put their pistols away.

"Marshal, I'm glad you come," said one of the men who had been sitting with Cox. "These here fellas just killed your deputy. Then they killed Haggart, 'n Cox, too, 'n they done it all in cold blood."

"That ain't true," Emmett said.

"Julius McCoy wasn't just my deputy, he was also my friend and my sister's husband. I think you two had better come down to the jail with me till I get to the bottom of this."

Although Kirby had already holstered his pistol, it suddenly appeared in his hand again, the draw so fast that it caught everyone in the saloon by surprise. He didn't shoot at the end of his draw. "I don't think we want to do that, Marshal. If you want to get to the bottom of this, you can find out what happened by askin' these people right here. I'm sure some of 'em must be honest."

Emmett had his gun out, as well, and was covering everyone else in the saloon.

"All right," the marshal said. "Let me hear what you have to say."

"I didn't have anything to do with killing your deputy, but I did kill that one." Kirby pointed to the man lying back in the corner.

"What did you shoot him for?" the marshal asked.

"He had a gun pointed at your deputy's back and was about to shoot him."

"Who killed the other two?"

"I killed that one," Emmett admitted, pointing toward Cox's body. "Unfortunately, not before he killed your deputy."

The marshal looked around until he noticed the man who had been speaking so eloquently about a woman named Fancy Lil. "Doc Dunaway, did you see what happened here?"

"I did indeed." Dr. Dunaway pointed to Kirby and Emmett. "These two men are telling the truth, Marshal. Deputy McCoy was trying to arrest Cox, when that unfortunate gentleman"—he pointed to the body lying back in the far corner—"declared his intention of interrupting the operation by pointing a pistol at McCoy. He was about to shoot, but the boy shouted a warning. At that, he turned his weapon toward those two and fired. The broken mirror behind the bar should be all the evidence you need to validate that. It was a misguided move of the part of the would-be assassin, because the young man drew his pistol and returned fire. It was quite a long shot, too.

"While all that was in progress, Cox killed the deputy when McCoy wasn't payin' attention and then he swung his gun around toward these two. By then, the older gentleman had his own pistol out. He shot Cox. If I am asked to testify in court, I will say, emphatically, that he had every right to do so."

"That's true. Ever'thing Doc said is true. That's the feller that's lyin'." Blue Shirt pointed to the man who had been sitting at the table with Cox—the one who had accused Kirby and Emmett of killing all three men.

"I, uh, just told what I thought I seen," the man said nervously.

Dr. Dunaway's testimony opened the floodgate. Nearly everyone else in the saloon began telling their own stories of the incident, and though there were a few slight variations in the telling, one theme was consistent throughout—all but one of the shootings were entirely justified.

The marshal let out a big sigh and waved his hand dismissively. "I reckon you two can put them guns away. What with ever'one in here tellin' the same story, there won't be no need in arrestin' you. But you might want to come down to my office tomorrow, anyway."

"Why would we want to do that?" Emmett asked.

"Because there's a five-hundred-dollar reward out for Cox, and I expect you'll be wantin' to stick around long enough to collect it." The marshal looked over toward the other dead man. "I don't know nothin' about him, but there may be paper on him as well."

Emmett nodded. "I reckon that's reason enough to stay around for a couple days."

"What's your name?" the marshal asked.

"I'm Emmett Jensen. This is my son, Kirby."

"I don't think I've ever heard the names before. Are you new in town?"

"We just arrived today," Emmett said.

"Just passing through, are you?"

"Sort of. Actually, I'm looking for some friends of mine. Wiley Potter, Keith Stratton, and Josh Richards. Perhaps you have run across them."

The marshal shook his head. "Nope. 'Fraid I've never heard of 'em."

"What about Angus Shardeen?" Kirby asked.

The marshal's eyes narrowed. "Would he be a friend as well?"

Kirby shook his head. "Not hardly. I've got a score to settle with him."

"Apparently a lot of people do. He's took to doin' the same he was doin' durin' the war, only now he ain't got the war as an excuse. He's a thief and a murderer."

"Is he anywhere nearby?"

"Not that I know of."

"Boy, you got quite an appetite on you, you know that?" Emmett's comment was made over supper that night at the Rustic Rock restaurant.

Kirby was eating a steak that was so large he needed a second plate for his potatoes and green beans. He had also asked for an extra serving of rolls. "Can you blame me? We ain't had nothin' but squirrel and rabbit and such for near two months. I just figured when I get a chance to eat like this, well, maybe I should."

"I don't reckon I can argue with that. By the way, Kirby, I been wantin' to say somethin' to you. The way you handled yourself today, even the way you handled yourself back in Baxter, was somethin' special. I'm just real proud of you."

"It wasn't all that much," Kirby said, embarrassed by his pa's accolades.

"Don't sell yourself short. I've been in more battles than I can count and I've seen many men get so scared that they could barely breathe when the shootin' starts."

Kirby took a bite of potatoes and nodded. "Sounds like a reasonable thing to do."

"Yes. But you've been in two shootin' scrapes, and you didn't get panicked either time."

"Didn't seem like the time for it," Kirby said.

"Still, I want you to know that I'm proud of you."

"Pa, who are these men you mentioned, Casey, Potter, Stratton, and Richards? I've never heard you mention those names before."

"Why do you ask?"

"I'm just wonderin' is all. You told the marshal they was your friends, but if they are, how come you haven't mentioned them before now?"

The response to Kirby's question was a long silence, then the silence was broken, not by Emmett's answer, but by another coughing attack. Not until the coughing fit stopped, did Emmett speak. "Why are you so interested?"

Kirby put his finger alongside his nose as his father had done back in the gun shop. "Because there's somethin' not quite right here. I can smell it."

Emmett nodded. "You're gettin' a little smarter after all. You're right. They aren't friends at all. What Angus Shardeen is to you, those men are to me. If and when I find 'em, I plan to kill 'em."

"What did they do?"

"They stole some gold that belonged to the Confederate government, and they killed a lot of good men while they was stealing it."

"Pa, the war's over. There ain't no Confederate government no more, which to my thinkin' means there ain't no Confederate gold no more."

"That's true. But it ain't the gold I'm concerned with, Kirby. It's the men they killed while they was comin' by it. One of 'em was your brother."

Kirby got a surprised expression on his face. "Are you sure, Pa?

The letter I got from Colonel Willis said that Luke was killed in battle on Wilderness Creek."

"That's what the report said. But what really happened was that Casey, Potter, Stratton, and Richards shot 'im."

"Colonel Willis said Luke's body wasn't found. He thought that maybe the Yankees found him and buried him."

"I went up to Wilderness Creek lookin' for his body, but I never found it, so it could be that the Yankees did find him and bury him. It's for sure that the men who killed him didn't take the time to give him a proper burial."

"Pa, you're sure that's what happened? That he was shot by those men you mentioned?"

"Yes. I am very sure." Emmett spoke with such absolute authority, that Kirby felt no need to question it any further.

"Do you think those men might be here in Texas?"

"They could be. They might also be in New Mexico, or Colorado, or Idaho."

"Like you said, Pa, this is an awful big country. How do you plan to find them in such wide open spaces? They could be anywhere between here and the Pacific Ocean."

"I told you they stole Confederate gold. They stole a lot of it, Kirby, enough to make all of 'em rich as Croesus. Men with that much money can't hide. They're goin' to be spendin' a lot of it, and that's goin' to get them noticed. All I have to do is live long enough to find 'em."

Kirby chuckled. "Well, that'll be fifty, sixty years. I reckon we'll find 'em all right."

"Maybe not." The tone of Emmett's voice was flat and absolute.

"What are you talkin' about, Pa? What do you mean, maybe not?"

"I mean that, in all likelihood, I don't have that long left to live."

Kirby put his fork down and looked at his pa. "The cough?"

"Yeah, but the cough is the result, not the cause." As if on cue, Emmett coughed again, then he continued with his story. "I caught a ball in the lung, Kirby. Not a lot of men survived a wound like that, and I don't mind tellin' you that it laid me flat on my back for weeks. It got all festered up on me. Then lung fever hit the other lung.

"Maybe, just maybe, if I stayed in a dry climate, I might make it, according to the doctors. But they didn't sound hopeful. They also said that I should rest, and I shouldn't exert myself too much. But I can't do that. I swore I would find those men, and I aim to do it."

"That's why you wanted me to learn the fast draw, and how to shoot without aiming, isn't it?"

"Sort of," Emmett admitted. "If you are with me when I find 'em, you're goin' to just naturally get drawed into it. So, I wanted you to be able to take care of yourself. What happened tonight tells me I'm not going to have to worry."

"Pa . . . we'll find 'em. And if you don't live long enough to find all of 'em, I will. I promise you that. I owe it to you . . . and to Luke."

Emmett reached across the table and squeezed his son's hand. "I knew I could count on you."

"You think they've got dessert in this place?" Kirby asked as he took the last bite of steak, then pushed the plate to one side.

"Lord, boy. You mean you still have room for dessert?"

"Well, not a whole lot of dessert. Just enough to finish out the meal."

"What kind of dessert would you want?"

"Maybe a couple pieces of apple pie, with a slab of cheese melted on top." Kirby smiled. "We can afford it, Pa. We'll be gettin' the reward money tomorrow, don't forget."

Emmett chuckled and shook his head. "You're right. Travelin' around the way we're doin', we won't always have an opportunity to buy pie. I reckon I'll have a piece with you."

"As long as you get your own so I don't have to share," Kirby replied with a smile.

At that same moment, Dr. Tom Dunaway was standing at the buffet in the parlor of the Palace Princess Emporium, perusing the viand that was laid out for the guests—a glistening ham, a roast beef, and fried or baked chicken. In addition, mashed potatoes, baked sweet potatoes, black-eyed peas, fried and boiled okra, baked loaves of bread, rolls, biscuits, and corn bread were spread out on the long table.

Filling his plate, Dr. Dunaway found an overstuffed chair near the fireplace, which had no fire because it was summer. He began to enjoy the food.

"My goodness, Tom," Janey said. "From the looks of your plate, one would think that you hadn't eaten in a month of Sundays."

"What can I say, Lil? I come to the Palace because the food here is better than can be found at any restaurant in town."

"Oh, my. Now you have hurt my feelings. I thought you came here to enjoy my company. But now I learn it is only the food that brings you to the Palace."

"*Au contraire, mon cheri*," Dr. Dunaway said. "It is the lovely *Mademoiselle* Lil that brings me here. *Je viens à vous prélasser dans votre beauté.*"

When it was obvious that Janey had no idea what he had just said, he translated it for her. "I come to bask in your beauty."

"Oh, what a nice thing for you to say, and to say it in such pretty words."

"Yes, French is a beautiful language." Dr. Dunaway nodded toward the plate he was holding. "The food is really a secondary reason." He took a bite of roast beef, then smiled. "But I must admit that it is a strong, secondary reason."

Janey laughed.

"Say, Doc," one of the other guests called out. "Is it true that you were in the Yellow Dog when the shootin' took place this afternoon?"

"Yes, I was there. And I testified to Marshal Wallace that the shooting, at least in two of the cases, was justified."

"McComb seen it, too, 'n he said one of them wasn't no more 'n sixteen or seventeen, and that he was really fast."

"He may have been a little older than that, but not much, I would wager," Dr. Dunaway replied. "And McComb is right, I don't believe I've ever seen anyone extract their weapon with more speed than that young man did."

The parlor was relatively crowded at the moment. Some of the men were waiting for their particular choice in girls; some had already been with a woman and hadn't left yet, while others, like Dr. Dunaway, were just visiting.

Chicago Sue had established her policy that a man could pay five dollars to visit and eat. That was very expensive for a meal that could be had for no more than a dollar at any other restaurant in town, but the food wasn't the only attraction. The five dollars allowed them to fill their plates from the buffet, and also to visit with the women who weren't currently engaged. However, their interaction with the women could go no further than visiting. If they wished to advance the temporary relationship with one of the young ladies, they were charged an additional fee.

Fancy Lil was one of the principal attractions of the parlor because she was an entertaining conversationalist . . . and the men liked being around someone as beautiful as she was. Her presence also provided the catalyst that some might need to engage one of the other girls for a more intimate visit.

"Fancy Lil," Dr. Dunaway said, holding out a wine goblet. "Would you pour me a little more wine?"

"Of course. I would be glad to," Janey replied with a practiced smile. "Red or white?"

"Red wine, of course. White wine is for women and sodomites. It isn't for real men."

Janey smiled. "Well then, by all means, it shall be red wine."

"Say, Doc, what did that feller say the gunmen's names was?" one of the other guests asked.

"I wouldn't call them gunmen," Dr. Dunaway replied. "After all, the word *gunman* has such a negative connotation."

"What would you call them, then?"

"I would call them gentlemen, who, by circumstances not of their own making, were challenged by unexpected events. And they met that challenge, quite admirably."

Janey approached Dr. Dunaway with a bottle of red wine.

"All right, *gentlemen* then. What was their names?"

Janey started to pour the wine.

"Jensen, I think. It was a father and son. Emmett and Kirby Jensen. They were—"

With a gasp, Janey poured wine onto Dr. Dunaway's trousers.

"Lil, watch what you're doing!"

"I'm . . . I'm sorry." She handed Dr. Dunaway the wine bottle, then turned and ran quickly from the parlor.

"Wait, you don't have to run away! I know it was just an accident!"

The other guest frowned. "What did you say to her, Doc?"

"Nothing that would make her run away like that. I don't know what that was all about."

Chicago Sue had never seen Janey act in such a way, so she excused herself and hurried to Janey's room. "Lil?" she called, knocking lightly on the door. She heard nothing from the other side of the door. "Lil, it's me, Sue. Please open the door, dear."

Janey opened the door, then turned and walked back into her room.

Sue followed her inside, then closed the door behind her. "What's wrong, Janey?" she asked, using her real name. "Did Dr. Dunaway do or say something to upset you? If so, I'll make certain that he leaves tonight, and I won't let him come back until you get an apology and a guarantee that he won't do it again."

"No, no, he didn't do anything wrong. It's nothing like that," Janey said, waving her hand.

"Then what is it? What has upset you? Something has, and that's for sure."

"It's them. They are in Dallas. Oh, Sue, they've come for me. I know they have."

"Who? Who has come for you? Janey, are you in trouble with the law?"

"No."

"Then I don't understand. Who has come for you?"

"My father and my brother. I know they have come to take me back to Missouri. Oh, Sue, what can I do? I'll never go back to Missouri. I can't go back!"

"Are they downstairs now? If so, I'll go talk to them."

"No! They aren't downstairs. I'm sure that they don't know that I'm working here. At least not yet."

"Then, how do you know they are here?"

"Did you hear about the shooting in the Yellow Dog Saloon today?"

"Yes, everyone has heard about it. That's all anyone is talking about."

"That was them. The two men all the people are talking about . . . are my father and brother."

"How do you know?"

"Dr. Dunaway said that the shooters' names were Emmett and Kirby Jensen. That can't be a mere coincidence."

"Jensen? I thought your last name was Garner."

Janey sighed. "My last name is Jensen. I left Missouri with a man named Paul Garner, and even though we never got married, I took his name."

"Where is Paul Garner now? Perhaps he is the one who told your family where to find you."

"He's dead. He was caught cheating in a card game and was shot."

"Janey, if you don't want to go back with your father and your brother, there is no need for you to do so. You are certainly old enough to make up your own mind about such things."

"There's more to it than that."

"Oh?"

"Pa was away in the war and Kirby was running the farm all by himself. He did it from the time he was thirteen. And he did a real good job with it, too. He supported my ma and me. He was saving all the money he made to give to Pa when he came home from the war. Two thousand dollars. He hid the money—"

"And you took it." Sue's comment was more matter-of-fact than accusing.

"Yes. Paul talked me into doing it. He told me that he was an investor, and that if I gave him the two thousand dollars he could double it. I didn't really intend to steal it. I thought I would be able to pay the money back, with interest, before Kirby missed it. I even left a note in the empty jar when I took the money, promising to pay it back."

"But Paul didn't double the money, did he?"

"No, he lost it all. Or almost all. He still had some of the money left when he was shot, but the other card players—the ones who had been cheated by him—took the money and divided it."

"Would you like me to talk to your father and brother?"

"No! Please, no! They can't know that I'm in Dallas! And they especially can't know that I'm a . . . that I'm . . . here," she said, taking in her room with a wave of her hand.

Sue reached out to put her hand on Janey's shoulder. "Honey, you aren't the first girl to run away from home, and you aren't the first girl who took money from her family to finance her escape. And you aren't the first girl who ever wound up on the line." She smiled. "But you are the most beautiful of all the girls I have ever known in such a situation."

Janey smiled through her tears.

"Why don't you let me check around a bit? I won't mention you, and I'll see what I can find out. It may be that they are here for an entirely different reason. You didn't let anyone back in Missouri know you were coming to Dallas, did you?"

"No."

"Then, how could they possibly know you are here? I'm sure the fact that they are in Dallas is just a coincidence."

"They must not know about me, Sue," Janey said. "Please, don't say anything that would get them even suspicious."

"I promise, I'll say nothing about you."

*   *   *

Emmett and Kirby were having breakfast in the dining room of the Lone Star Hotel the next morning when Kirby saw a very attractive woman come into the dining room. She spoke briefly to the maître d', who pointed to their table.

Kirby leaned forward and whispered, "Pa, there's a real pretty woman comin' toward our table. I wonder if it's Fancy Lil."

"Who?"

"You know, the woman Doc and them were talkin' about yesterday. The one they said was so pretty."

Emmett chuckled. "What would make Fancy Lil, or any woman for that matter, come to our table?"

"I don't know, but here she comes."

"I'm sure you are just—" Emmett stopped in mid-sentence when it became evident that the woman actually was coming toward them. "Stand up."

"What for?"

"It's what a gentleman does when a lady approaches him . . . if he is sitting." Emmett stood up.

Following his father's example, Kirby stood as well.

"You would be the Jensens?" the woman asked. "Father and son, I believe." She smiled broadly.

"Yes, ma'am," Emmett replied. "What can we do for you?"

"Oh, you have already done it."

"I beg your pardon?"

"I understand that you killed Emerson Cox, yesterday."

"Yes, ma'am. It wasn't by intention. It was something that—"

"From what I hear, you had no choice. It was either kill him or be killed by him."

"Yes, ma'am. Something like that. Oh, would you join us, Miss . . ."

"Sue. Everyone just calls me Sue. Yes, I would have a cup of coffee with you, if you don't mind being seen with me."

"I don't understand. Why should we mind being seen with you?"

"I told you my name is Sue, but I'm better known as Chicago Sue." The woman smiled again. "That isn't my real name, of course. But women in my profession rarely give their real names."

"Oh." Emmett blushed just a little.

"So you can see why you might not want to embarrass yourself by being seen with me. If you wish to withdraw your invitation to sit with you, I will understand and think no ill of you because of it."

"Don't be silly, Miss Sue. The invitation stands." Emmett held the chair as Sue sat at the table, then he raised his hand to signal for a waiter.

"Yes, sir?" the waiter asked, arriving at the table. The expression on his face as he saw Sue indicated that he knew who she was and that he didn't approve of her being there.

"Coffee for the lady."

"Sir, as you are new in town, perhaps you don't know who she is. Are you sure . . ."

"That I want coffee for the lady? Yes, I'm quite sure. Please bring it."

"Yes, sir."

"I'm sorry. I shouldn't have come," Sue said.

"Don't be silly. You are welcome at our table. But I am curious. Why did you come?"

"The man you shot, Mr. Cox, beat up one of the young ladies in my employ recently. I had him arrested, and he swore that he would extract revenge. I can't be sure that is the only reason he returned to Dallas, but neither can I discount it. At any rate, thanks to you, I no longer have to be afraid of him."

"Does Fancy Lil work for you?" Kirby asked impatiently.

Sue gasped. "What? What do you know about Fancy Lil?"

"We know nothing about her," Emmett replied quickly. He smiled and shook his head. "I don't know what got into him for even asking such a thing."

"I know she is beautiful," Kirby said. "I heard someone in the saloon yesterday say that her face was so beautiful it would launch a thousand ships. I don't know what that means, but she must be some kind of beautiful for a man to say a crazy thing like that."

"Yes, Lil is a beautiful young woman, but then all my girls are . . . or they wouldn't be working for me."

Kirby smiled. "I'd sure like to see what she looks like."

"No, you wouldn't," Emmett said resolutely. "And we don't have time for such things."

"Anyway, it wouldn't be possible for you to see her now," Sue said. "She's away on a trip. I'm not sure when she'll be back."

"They asked about me?" Janey frowned.

"Not about you. The young one . . ."

"My brother."

"He asked about Fancy Lil. And he only asked because he heard someone talking about you in the Yellow Dog. Apparently, someone said that you were so beautiful that your face would launch a thousand ships." Sue laughed. "Now, who do you think would say such a thing?"

"Sounds like Dr. Dunaway."

"Of course, it's Dr. Dunaway. Apparently your brother was fascinated by the idea, and wanted to see someone whose face could do such a thing."

"What did you tell them?"

"I told them that you were away on a trip."

Janey twisted her hands in her lap. "Oh, Sue, what if they come here and see me?"

"I don't think they will. Your father strikes me as a bit of a prude."

Despite her concern, Janey laughed. "Yes, he is a prude."

"Do you really think your father would come to a place like this?"

"No, I don't think he would. But Kirby might."

CHAPTER 10

"I may not be here the next time you come," Janey said.

"What?" Big Ben raised himself up on one elbow and looked down at her lying beside him.

The cover came up only to her waist, leaving the rest of her bare body revealed to him. A bar of light slipped in around the edge of the drawn shade, falling upon her right breast and making it gleam in the light.

Ben frowned. "What do you mean you might not be here? Where would you be?"

"I don't know."

"Janey, that doesn't make sense." Since she'd told him her real name, he insisted on using it when they were together. "I mean, how can you say you aren't going to be here, but not have any idea where you will be?"

"It's just that I can't stay here any longer. I can't take the chance. They might find me."

"You can't take a chance on who finding you? Janey, are you in trouble with the law? If you are, I can afford a lawyer. Hell, I can afford an entire army of lawyers. I don't care what you did. I know I can get you out of it."

"No, it isn't that. I'm not in trouble with the law. It's my pa and my brother that I'm afraid of."

"Why are you afraid of them?"

"Ben, do you really think I want them to know that I wound up doing what I do?"

"I don't think of you in that way."

"Of course you do. How else can you think of me?"

"I can think of you as my wife."

Janey sat up in bed and looked at Ben with a surprised expression on her face. "What?" Her voice was so weak that she could barely be heard.

"I said you could be my wife."

Marshal Wallace found the Jensens in the hotel dining room. "If you two will come down to the bank, I'll see to it that you get your reward money. As it turns out, in addition to the five-hundred-dollar reward for Emerson Cox, there was another two hundred dollars bein' offered for Clarence Haggart. So the total comes to seven hundred dollars. That's a pretty good sum of money."

"Yes, sir, it is," Emmett said. "I wouldn't have killed the man for the money, but neither I nor my boy had any choice in the matter. What's done is done, and I have no regrets at taking the money."

Ben Conyers parked the surrey in front of the bank, and set the brake. "Wait here, I've got some business in the bank, but it'll only take a couple minutes," he said with a smile. "Then we'll go out to Live Oaks Ranch."

"Where is Live Oaks?" Janey asked.

"It's just north of Fort Worth. One hundred and twenty thousand acres of the finest land in Texas. You're going to love it there."

"I know that I will." She watched Ben tie off the team, then walk into the bank.

One hundred and twenty thousand acres, he had said. She remembered making the vow never to be the wife of a farmer, but when she'd made that vow she was thinking about the forty acres she had lived on with her family.

The family that she no longer had.

As she was sitting in the carriage she saw the marshal approaching. She knew that, technically, Chicago Sue was violating a city ordinance by running a house of "entertainment," but she knew, too, that the ordinance was aimed at the rowdy, bawdy houses, more than it was at the Palace Princess Emporium, which actually passed itself off as a private club. Fights, stabbings, and even occasional shootings occurred in the bawdy houses. Such a thing had never occurred at the Palace Princess Emporium, and because of that, neither the marshal, nor any of his deputies, had ever made an official visit.

The marshal stopped at the corner and looked back as if waiting for someone. Appearing from behind the building, two other men joined him.

Recognition dawned and Janey drew a quick, alarmed breath. Her pa and brother were headed right past the surrey! No way they would not see her! She looked around in panic. What could she do?

"Marshal Wallace?" someone shouted.

Marshal Wallace held out his hand to stop her pa and her brother, then he turned his attention to the man who had called out to him. So did Emmett and Kirby.

At that moment, Ben came out of the bank, smiling up at Janey. "We're all set."

"Ben, it's them!" Janey hissed.

"What? It's who? What are you talking about?"

"Those two men down there with Marshal Wallace. That's my pa and my brother."

"Have they seen you yet?"

"No."

"Come back into the bank with me until they're gone. No, wait, they might be going to the bank." Looking around, he saw the Elite Dress Shoppe and smiled. "Come." He pulled her from the surrey. "We'll go into the dress shop. It's for sure and certain they won't be going there."

He lifted her down, then put himself between her and the men. "Stay in front of me and keep your head down."

Although it was only a few steps from the surrey to the dress shop, Janey held her breath and clenched her fists, waiting to hear her name called. She breathed a sigh of relief when they went inside.

"Yes, can I help you?" a female clerk asked.

"Do you have any ready-made dresses? Not everyday work dresses, mind you. I want something fine and beautiful, for a beautiful lady."

"Indeed we do, sir," the clerk replied.

"Good, then help her find something, would you? And you can take your time."

In the bank, the chief teller counted out seven hundred dollars and handed the money to Emmett. Emmett turned and gave half the money to Kirby.

"That is a great deal of money to be carrying with you," the bank president said. "I would be very happy to open an account for you."

Emmett nodded. "Thank you, but we won't be staying in town long enough to have an account. We'll be moving on today."

"I don't know where you are bound, but if you are looking for a good place to settle down, you won't find any place any better than Dallas."

"I'm sure Dallas is a nice town. But my son and I have itchy feet. I've seen the Atlantic Ocean. Now I have a hankering to see the Pacific."

The bank president didn't understand. "Why? Once you've seen one ocean, you've seen them all."

"The boy hasn't seen either ocean," Emmett said.

As his pa and the banker were talking, Kirby saw a newspaper lying on a table in the middle of the bank, and he walked over to glance at it.

MISSOURI BUSHWHACKER
TO BE TRIED IN SALCEDO
ELMER GLEASON RODE WITH
BLOODY BILL ANDERSON

Elmer Gleason, who is one of the most malevolent men ever to come out of the late war, has been captured in Salcedo. It is said that when he rode with Quantrill and Bloody Bill Anderson he kept a string of ears severed from the heads of his victims, be they man, woman, or child.

Although those who followed their conscience to fight for the South have been paroled, the villains who rode with Quantrill and Bloody Bill Anderson can never be forgiven. The trespasses of such men are so great that only He, who is the final arbitrator of the transgressions of those who have made their temporary journey upon this mortal coil, will be able to grant them final remission and absolution of their sins.

Trial for Elmer Gleason will commence on the 28th instant.

"Pa?" Kirby asked when they left the bank a few minutes later. "How long would it take for us to get to Salcedo?"

"I don't know. I don't know where Salcedo is or how far it is from here. Why do you ask?"

"We need to go there."

"We need to go to Salcedo? Why?"

"A friend of mine is in trouble there."

Emmett frowned impatiently. "What friend? And how come you're just now tellin' me this?"

"I didn't know about it until just now. I saw it in the paper while we was in the bank. We need to be there by the twenty-eighth of this month."

"You saw in the paper that you have a friend in trouble in Salcedo, and we have to be there by the twenty-eighth? What happens if we don't get there by the twenty-eighth?"

"It's more 'n likely, Elmer will get hung."

"All right. Who is Elmer?"

Kirby figured it was now or never. "Pa, there's somethin' me 'n you need to talk about."

"I'm sure there is." Emmett waited . . . impatiently.

"Well, I reckon it's about as good a time as any to tell you." Kirby took a deep breath. "Pa, the fella I killed yesterday . . . wasn't the first man I ever killed. I've been in some battles, quite a few of 'em, only there wasn't none of 'em big battles like the kind you fought."

Without expanding on his own role in the battles, he told of riding with Asa Briggs and being in fights at such places as Clark's Mill, Hartville, Pilot Knob, Glasgow, Lexington, and Newtonia.

"I was at Baxter Springs, too," Kirby said. "That's why I was a little hesitant about us goin' there. I was afraid someone might recognize me."

Emmett was shocked. "Boy, answer me, and I want you to tell me the truth. Did you burn any private houses or kill any innocent people?"

"No, Pa, we didn't. I will say that the Ghost Riders, that's what those of us who rode with Briggs called ourselves, from time to time joined up with Quantrill for some of the battles. And I've heard of some of the things he done, but Briggs was real particular about not killin' innocent people. And none of that ever happened on those few times Asa Briggs teamed up with Quantrill. Fact is, I don't think I woulda stayed with him if he had done anything like that."

"What you just told me has something to do with your friend Elmer?"

"Yes, sir. His name is Elmer Gleason, 'n he rode some with Quantrill and some with Bloody Bill Anderson. Then, toward the end, he rode with Asa Briggs, 'n that's when he become my friend. But now they got him on trial at Salcedo, on account of he rode with Quantrill and Anderson."

Emmett gave it some thought. "You say you want to go to Salcedo. What do you plan to do?"

"I'm not sure. But if we can figure out how to do it, I'd like to rescue him."

"It would mean violatin' the law."

"That might be true, Pa. But there's also such a thing as honor, ain't there? Seems to me, if I didn't try to save my friend, that would violate my honor."

Emmett looked at Kirby for a long moment, then nodded and put his hand on his son's shoulder. "You're right. There is such a thing as honor. But, I've got a feelin' you ain't told me ever'thing."

"No, sir. I reckon I ain't."

"Is it about your ma and your sister?"

"Yes, sir. You asked me why I wanted to kill Angus Shardeen, and what I told you about him killin' Kenny 'n his family and Merlin 'n his family is true, but that ain't the all of it. Ma didn't die in her sleep like I told you. She was killed by the Jayhawkers. Angus Shardeen is the one that shot her."

"Him in particular? Or one of his men?"

"It was him in particular, Pa, 'cause I seen him do it. I didn't have no gun or nothin', so there wasn't nothin' I could do. The only reason I joined up with Asa Briggs was 'cause I wanted to go after Shardeen. I wanted to find him and kill him. But we never found him. That's why I say that if I find him, I'm goin' to kill 'im."

"Seems reasonable to me," Emmett said. "We'll just add his name to the list of Potter, Stratton, Casey, and Richards."

"Oh, and Pa, about the funeral for Ma? I lied to you about that, too. I told you that folks come from all over, but the truth is that the only funeral was the one that me 'n Janey give her. It was Janey that dressed her in her best dress, and I'm the one that dug the grave. Janey cleaned out the feedin' trough, the one that was used for the milk cows, and that's what we put Ma in. I'm sorry we didn't have somethin' a lot more fine for her."

Emmett nodded. "You know, I have a feelin' that your ma probably appreciated that a lot more 'n she would have if a whole lot of folks had showed up for it."

"Yes, sir. I kinda hope that's the way it is."

"What about Janey? Did she actually run off like you said?"

"Yes, sir, she did. But I can't hardly blame her. The same men that killed Ma used Janey, Pa. They used her bad. She left home right after we buried Ma."

"With the gamblin' fella?"

Kirby nodded. "Yes, sir."

"When you started tellin' the story, I thought it might be somethin' like that. I reckon now I don't hold it ag'in her so much that she left as I did. I reckon she felt like she had a good enough reason."

She might have had a good reason to leave, but she didn't have a good reason to take all our money with her, Kirby thought, but he didn't share that with his pa.

"I wonder where she is now?" Emmett asked. "I wonder if she is alive?"

"Oh, it's beautiful!" Janey was looking at herself in the mirror at the dress shop as she tried on one of the dresses.

Ben sat in a nearby chair. "Would you like it?"

"Oh, Ben, no. I mean yes, of course I like it. But I can't let you buy this for me."

"Why not? It isn't like I can't afford it."

"That's not the point."

"Of course it's the point. You like it, and I like seeing it on you." He looked at the clerk. "We'll take it."

"Wonderful. I'll just go get the ledger book and the cash box."

"They're gone," Ben said quietly after the clerk left.

Janey turned toward him. "How do you know?"

"I saw them leave the bank and walk down to the Lone Star Hotel. As soon as I pay the clerk, we'll leave town in the opposite direction."

"Oh, Ben, are you sure it will be safe? I don't know what I would do if they actually saw me."

"How long has it been since either of them saw you?"

"It's been four years since Pa last saw me, and three years since Kirby saw me."

"What were you wearing, then?"

"What? I don't know. Some sort of plain cotton dress, I think."

"Nothing like this," he said, taking in the dress she was wearing with a wave of his hand.

Janey looked down at the beautiful dress. "No, nothing like this."

Ben saw a hat with a veil, and he smiled and picked it up. "Put this on when we leave. The way you look now, you could bump right into them, and I doubt that either of them would recognize you."

Janey chuckled. "I think you might be right."

Kirby and Emmett rode into Waco on the twenty-seventh and went straight to the livery stable.

"What can I do for you gentlemen?" the liveryman asked, meeting them as they dismounted.

"We need to board our horses," Emmett said. "Is there a place we can leave our things from the pack animals?"

"Yes, sir. We got individual tack rooms you can rent for fifteen cents a night. For an extra nickel, you can rent a lock."

"Good, that's what we'll do."

"You goin' to be here long?"

"We'll be ridin' out tomorrow, but I plan to leave the two pack horses here for a while. Not sure exactly how long."

"Your horses will be a quarter apiece. That includes hay. Thirty cents if you want 'em to have oats."

"We'll want the oats," Emmett said. "How far is Salcedo from here?"

"It's about ten miles. Just follow the railroad south, and you can't miss it. Headin' that way, are you?"

"I thought we might take a look."

"It ain't that pleasant a town to visit if you want to know the truth of it. They's a bunch of Yankee soldiers down there right now reconstructin' us, 'n they've plumb took over the town. The mayor and the city marshal got no say at all. They got a Yankee captain that runs the town 'n a Yankee judge that makes the laws. The people o' the town ain't got nothin' to say about it."

"I thank you for the information."

"But you plannin' on goin' anyway, ain't you?"

"Yeah," Emmett answered. "We'll take the two saddle mounts tomorrow. Here's sixty cents for them."

"What about the pack horses?"

"I'd like to sell 'em, if you know anyone that might be interested."

The liveryman stroked his chin and examined the two pack horses. "I might be. How much would you be askin' for 'em?"

"Fifty dollars apiece."

"I need to make a little money from 'em. I'll give you thirty dollars."

They settled on forty dollars apiece.

The liveryman gave Emmett the money. "I'll look after 'em real good until I sell 'em. Good luck in Salcedo."

Emmett nodded. "Thanks."

"What do you have in mind for tomorrow?" Emmett asked Kirby in their hotel room that night.

"I don't know, exactly, Pa. Maybe I could testify for him or somethin'."

"What would you say?"

"I'd say that I rode with him when I was with the Ghost Riders, and I never saw him do anything bad."

"I doubt that will help."

"Prob'ly not. But, Pa, he's a friend. I can't just turn my back on a friend now, can I?"

"No," Emmett said. "You're right to try and do what you can for a friend."

Emmett and Kirby followed the railroad south from Waco until they came to Salcedo, identified by a sign attached to the end of the depot, a small, red-painted, wooden building. Posted alongside the track was another sign.

CAUTION TO BRAKEMEN
NO SIDE CLEARANCE AHEAD

As they passed the depot they saw another sign that listed the passenger schedule.

NORTHBOUND TRAINS
11 AM 5 PM 11 PM
SOUTHBOUND TRAINS
9 AM 2 PM 9 PM

Leaving the track they had followed from Waco, they rode on into town where they passed a hangman's gallows in the middle of the street. They stopped to read a sign that had been nailed to the gallows.

AT TEN O'CLOCK TOMORROW MORNING
ELMER GLEASON
THE BUSHWHACKER BUTCHER
WILL BE HANGED
ON THESE GALLOWS

"You boys here for the hangin', are you?" asked a toothless old man.

"Have we missed the trial?" Kirby asked. "The paper said the trial was today."

"No, you ain't missed it. They'll be holdin' the trial at one o'clock today."

"I don't understand. This sign says Elmer will be hung tomorrow morning. How can they say that if he hasn't been found guilty."

"Oh, they'll find him guilty all right. They ain't no gettin' around that. You called him Elmer. He a friend o' yours, is he?"

"Elmer is what the name on the sign says, isn't it?" Emmett asked, speaking quickly before his son could reply.

The old-timer nodded. "Yeah, that's what the sign says, all right."

"Then that's why we called him Elmer. Where's the trial to be held?" Emmett asked.

"Onliest place it can be held." The old man pointed toward the largest building in town. "Right down there in the Scalded Cat Saloon. But iffen you're wantin' a drink, you'd best get it before one o'clock, 'cause that Yankee that's been appointed judge won't let Clyde sell any liquor while the trial is goin' on."

"Thank you for the information," Emmett said.

"Sorry 'bout your friend." The old man waved a hand as the two rode farther into town.

They passed the jail. Two armed soldiers were standing out front.

"Pa, do you think they'd let us see Elmer?"

"I don't know. But we won't know unless we try."

Dismounting, the two tied off their horses, then started across the street toward the jail.

One of the soldiers stepped out in front of them. "Where do you think you're goin'?"

"We want to talk to the prisoner," Kirby said.

"Why?"

"That would be between us and the prisoner," Emmett replied.

"Yeah? Well it don't matter what it's about, 'cause you ain't goin' to see 'im."

"Take their guns and let 'em see 'im," said the other soldier, a sergeant. "He'll be dead by a little after three today, anyway, so what's it goin' to hurt?"

"All right, Sarge. If you say so," the private said. "You boys give me your guns, 'n you can go on in."

Emmett and Kirby surrendered their pistols, then stepped into the office. Four men were playing cards around a desk, two civilians wearing badges and two soldiers. One of the soldiers had captain's bars on his shoulder board.

One of the men wearing a badge looked up. "What can I do for you?"

Kirby spoke first. "Marshal, the sergeant out front took our weapons and told us we could visit with the prisoner."

"Yeah? Why do you want to visit with him?"

"We're looking for someone and he might be able to tell us where to find him," Emmett said.

The marshal was quiet for a moment, then he nodded. "All right. Go ahead, but I'll tell you right now, he ain't much of a talker. We've been tryin' to get him to tell us if there's any more of Quantrill or Anderson's men down here, but he ain't told us nothin'."

"You goin' to talk all day or are you goin' to play cards?" one of the others asked. "I've got a good hand here, one that's goin' to get me back even."

"Go on over there and talk to him, if you want," the marshal said, pointing to the single cell at the back of the room.

Kirby walked to the cell. Elmer Gleason was lying on his bunk with his hands laced behind his head, staring up at the ceiling.

"Hi, Elmer," Kirby said.

"Damn, I thought that sounded like your voice." Elmer sat up and threw his legs over the side of his bunk. "What are you doing here?"

"I came to see you."

"Well, that was damn fine of you."

Kirby motioned to his pa. "Elmer, this is my pa."

Elmer walked over to stick his hand through the bars. "It's good to meet the boy's pa after all this time. He's always spoke high of you, but I'm sure you know that."

"He's a good boy," Emmett replied.

"Elmer, how'd you wind up here in jail?" Kirby asked.

"I got drunk."

"Drunk? They put you in jail for bein' drunk?"

"Not exactly just for bein' drunk. What happened was, I was just passin' through town 'n I stopped in at the Scalded Cat for a couple o' drinks. Well, it was a lot of drinks, 'n I got drunk 'n wound up tellin' that I rode with Quantrill. I figured, this bein' a Southern town, there wouldn't be no problem with it. Turned out they was a lot of Yankee soldiers in the saloon alistenin' to me, 'n the next thing I knew, I was arrested and brought here."

"Why would they arrest you for that? There's no paper out on any of the men who rode with Quantrill, is there?" Emmett asked.

"Not that I know of, except maybe Archie Clement," Elmer said. "But I don't think that matters. They want me, and they've got me."

"All right. You've visited with the prisoner long enough," the marshal said. "We've got to get him ready for the trial."

"We'll be at your trial," Kirby said.

"I appreciate it. And it was real nice of you two to drop by."

CHAPTER 11

"Hear ye, hear ye, hear ye! This here trial is about to commence, the honorable Daniel Gilmore, presidin'," the bailiff shouted.

The judge stepped up from the back of the saloon and took his seat behind a table being used as the judge's bench. He adjusted the glasses on the end of his nose, then cleared his throat. "Would the bailiff please bring the accused before the bench?"

The bailiff, who was leaning against the side wall, spit a quid of tobacco into the brass spittoon, then walked over to the table where Elmer was sitting. "Get up, you," he growled. "Present yourself before the judge."

Elmer approached the bench.

"Elmer Gleason, the charge against you is that you rode for that butchering, thieving, raping bushwhacker Quantrill," the judge said. "How do you plead?"

"Quantrill never raped nobody," Elmer said. "It was only them Jayhawkers that ever done any rapin', 'n they done plenty of it, I can tell you."

"You aren't here to make a speech. I'm going to ask you again, how do you plead?"

Keith Davenport, the attorney appointed to represent Elmer, stood up behind the table he'd shared with his defendant. "Your Honor, if it please the court."

"You got somethin' to say to this court, Mr. Davenport?" the judge asked.

"Yes, Your Honor. Quantrill conducted all of his operations in Kansas and Missouri."

"What does that have to do with anything?"

"Well, Your Honor, we are in Texas. Even if Mr. Gleason is guilty of murder and looting, it didn't happen in this state. Either Kansas or Missouri is the state that should be trying this case. We don't have jurisdiction to try it here."

"Your Honor, if I may?" the prosecutor spoke up quickly. "Everybody knows that Quantrill spent a winter right here in Texas. That's all we need to give this court standing."

The judge nodded. "Your point is well taken, Mr. Taylor."

"But Your Honor, these were his own people. Even if he was here, you know that neither Quantrill, nor by extension, my client, would have done any murdering or thieving while they were here."

"None that we know of, Your Honor," Taylor countered. "But that doesn't matter anyway. We're trying this defendant for being one of Quantrill's riders, not for any specific act of murder or robbery he may have done. Therefore, the fact that Quantrill was once in Texas, and that this defendant was with him, is all that is required to put this case under your jurisdiction."

The judge slapped his gavel on the bench again. "You are right, Mr. Prosecutor. Mr. Davenport, your motion for dismissal is denied. This case shall proceed."

"Very well, Your Honor."

"How do you plead?" the judge asked again.

Before Elmer got a word out, his attorney spoke. "Your Honor, my client pleads guilty and throws himself upon the mercy of the court."

"What? Wait a minute!" Elmer shouted. "Judge, I ain't pleadin' guilty to nothin'!"

"You have already confessed your guilt, Mr. Gleason," the judge replied.

"The hell I have. That was my lawyer that just done that. It warn't me."

"I'm not talking about your lawyer's plea. I'm talking about your own declaration of guilt. Did you, or did you not, confess before several assembled men in the Scalded Cat Saloon, that you rode with Quantrill?"

"I wouldn't put it that it was a confession," Elmer said. "It was mostly just me drinkin' 'n tellin' war stories."

"In the telling of those stories, did you say you rode with Quantrill?" the judge asked again.

"I ain't confessin' to nothin'," Elmer said.

"Very well," the judge said. "Clerk, change Mr. Gleason's plea from guilty to not guilty."

"Your Honor, may I have a moment with my client?" Davenport asked.

"You may."

Elmer returned to the table and sat down.

Davenport spoke quietly. "Mr. Gleason, I think you are making a big mistake here. If you plead guilty, the judge might show some mercy in his final decision. On the other, if this goes to trial, and you're found guilty, you'll get none."

"So what if I am found guilty? What's he goin' to do to me, tell me I can't vote or somethin'? Hell, I ain't never voted for nobody nohow. I ain't got no truck with politicians."

"Do you really not know? No, how could you? You have been in jail all this time."

"What is it I don't know?"

"Mr. Gleason, I'm afraid that a gallows has already been constructed. You are scheduled to be hanged at nine o'clock tomorrow morning."

"What? How the hell can they already say I'm goin' to be hung, when I ain't even been tried yet?"

"That's the point I'm trying to make. Don't you understand? This trial is totally immaterial. The judge has already made up his mind to find you guilty. Your only hope is to plead guilty and beg for mercy."

"The hell I will. I ain't beggin' that Yankee judge for nothin'."

"Very well, Mr. Gleason. But don't say I didn't warn you." Davenport looked back toward the bench. "Your honor, the conference with my client is concluded."

"Have you reconsidered your plea, Mr. Gleason?" the judge asked.

"No, I ain't. I said I was not guilty 'n that's what I'm standin' by."

"So you say, and so it shall be. Mr. Prosecutor, are you prepared to make your case?" the judge asked.

"I am, Your Honor."

"You may call your first witness."

"You men over there," the prosecutor said, pointing to three men sitting in the front row. All three were wearing the uniform of the US Army. "You are my witnesses. Stand up and hold up your right hand."

The men did as they were instructed, and the clerk swore them in.

"Now," the prosecutor said. "Did any of you hear this man say that he had ridden for Quantrill?"

The witnesses answered in the affirmative.

"We all heard him say that," added the only sergeant within the group.

The prosecutor turned back toward the judge. "Well, there you go, Your Honor. All three of these men have just sworn that they heard the defendant admit to being one of Quantrill's riders during the war."

"Mr. Davenport, do you wish to question any of these men?" Judge Gilmore asked.

"Yes, Your Honor. You, Sergeant"—Davenport pointed to the soldier who was wearing three stripes on his sleeves—"what, exactly, did you hear my client say?"

"He said that he rode with Quantrill 'n Bloody Bill Anderson, 'n that him 'n others that rode with 'em kilt a bunch of Yankee ba— Aw, Judge, I don't want to say what he called 'em. Not where women might hear."

"I think we can figure it out. He said that?" Judge Gilmore asked.

The sergeant nodded. "Yes, sir. That's what he said."

"You may continue your cross, Mr. Davenport."

Davenport asked the witness, "Did he say, specifically, that he had killed civilians?"

"Like I told you, all he said was that he had kilt a bunch of Yankee . . . you know."

"Sergeant, did you take part in any battles in the late war?" Davenport asked.

"Yes, sir."

"And did you kill anyone?"

The sergeant smiled. "Oh, I reckon I musta kilt me at least five or six of the Secesh sons of bit—" He halted in mid-word, then corrected himself. "Uh, that is, I figure I kilt five or six of the enemy soldiers."

"Five or six, by your own count?"

"Yeah."

"Sergeant, do you consider yourself a murderer?"

"What? No, it was war. If you kill someone in a war, that ain't murder."

"If you kill someone in a war, it isn't murder. Is that what you are saying?"

"You're damn right that's what I'm sayin'."

Davenport looked pointedly at Elmer. "That's good to hear. No further questions."

"Redirect, Mr. Taylor?" the judge asked.

"Sergeant, did you kill any civilians during the war?" Taylor asked.

"No, sir. Ever'one I kilt was a soldier."

"Thank you. I'm through with this witness."

"Does defense wish to call any witnesses?"

"Your Honor, I have no—" Davenport started, but he was interrupted.

The entire court was surprised when Kirby suddenly stood up and shouted, "Me, Your Honor!"

Angrily, the judge rapped his gavel on the table. "Order in the court! Here, what do you mean by interrupting my court in such a way?"

"I'd like to be a witness on behalf of the defendant."

"Do you know anything about this, Counselor?" the judge asked Davenport.

"No, sir."

"Do you have anything that would qualify you to bear witness to this case?" the judge asked Kirby.

"I do, Your Honor."

"Get to the bottom of this, Mr. Davenport," the judge ordered.

The defense attorney walked to where Kirby was still standing. "Young man, do you know the defendant?"

"Yes, sir, I know him."

The marshal waved his hand. "Your Honor, this man came to visit the prisoner in the jail last night."

"Why didn't you say anything about it?" Judge Gilmore asked.

"I didn't say nothin' 'cause I didn't have no idea he was goin' to want to be a witness. He never told me anythin' about that last night. He and another man just visited with the prisoner, is all."

The judge looked at the gallery. "Is the other man who was with him present in this court?"

"Yes, sir. He's sittin' right there beside him." The marshal pointed toward Emmett.

"Is it your wish to be a witness as well?" Judge Gilmore asked.

"No, sir. I never met the man before last night," Emmett replied. "I couldn't say one way or the other whether or not he's guilty."

"You." Gilmore pointed toward Kirby. "Who are you, and what information do you have that you think might be pertinent to this case?"

"My name is Kirby Jensen, Your Honor. And, during the war, I rode with the defendant."

Several gasps of surprise came from those who were present to watch the trial.

The judge rapped his gavel. "Are you telling the court that you rode with Quantrill?"

"I rode with Quantrill, Bloody Bill Anderson, and Asa Briggs," Kirby replied.

"Bailiff, swear this man in," the judge ordered.

The bailiff signaled for Kirby to come forward, then he held forth a Bible. "Do you swear to tell the truth, the whole truth, and nothing but the truth, so help you God?"

"I do."

"Now, Mr. Jensen, I ask you again," Judge Gilmore said. "And this time you are under oath. Did you ride with Quantrill, Anderson, Briggs, and this man, Elmer Gleason?"

Kirby knew that he hadn't ridden with Quantrill or Anderson in the scope of the question as it was being posed by the judge. But at times a merging of the guerrilla groups had occurred, and from that perspective, he could, truthfully, answer the question in the affirmative. "I did, Your Honor."

"Marshal Ferrell, take this man's gun, and place him under arrest."

"I'm not wearin' a gun," Kirby said.

"Make certain," the judge said.

The marshal checked him closely. "He's tellin' the truth, Judge. He ain't got no gun."

"Very well. He may testify as a witness, but he is also a defendant. This has become a double trial. Mr. Jensen is being tried along with Mr. Gleason, and any verdict reached for one shall apply to both. Put him at the defendant's table alongside Gleason."

"Yes, sir," the marshal said.

"Mr. Davenport, you may present your case now," the judge said.

"I call my first witness, Mister—" Davenport looked directly at Kirby. "Excuse me, what did you say your name was?"

"Jensen. Kirby Jensen."

"Would you take the stand, Mr. Jensen?"

As Kirby sat in the witness chair, the judge looked over toward him. "I would remind the witness that you are already sworn in."

"Yes, sir," Kirby replied.

"Mr. Jensen, you have stated that you rode with the Southern guerrillas."

"Yes, sir."

"How old are you?"

"I'm seventeen."

"Seventeen? Isn't that a little young? How old were you when you began riding with the guerrillas?"

"I was fifteen."

"And you have ridden, specifically, with Mr. Gleason?"

"Yes, sir."

"Did you ever see Mr. Gleason kill an innocent civilian, or a woman, or a child?"

"No, sir, I never did."

"Thank you. Your witness, counselor."

Taylor stood up. "Have you ever killed anyone, Jensen?"

"Yes, sir."

"No further questions."

"The witness is dismissed."

Kirby started, "Your Honor, the only ones I ever killed—"

Rap! The judge cut him short with the sharp rap of his gavel. "I said you are dismissed."

"Your Honor, redirect?" Davenport called quickly.

Judge Gilmore sighed audibly. "Very well, Counselor, you may redirect."

Davenport stood in front of Kirby. "You were about to make a statement. You may make it now."

"I was just goin' to say that the only men I've ever killed were trying to kill me," Kirby said.

"Have you ever killed any women or children?"

"No, sir."

"Thank you. No further questions."

"Marshal Ferrell, return this man to the defendant's table," the judge ordered.

The marshal stepped up to Kirby and walked him to the defense table.

"Mr. Davenport, will Mr. Gleason take the stand in his own defense?"

"You're damn right I will," Elmer said.

Davenport sighed. It was obvious that he would have rather his client not take the stand.

"Can I say somethin' before you start askin' questions?" Elmer asked.

"You may."

Elmer pointed to Kirby. "Kirby warn't nothin' but a boy when I first seen 'im. Hell, he ain't more 'n a boy now. But boy or not, he's a good man. I never seen him do nothin' wrong. Even comin' here, he come to help me 'cause he read about it in the paper. That's the kind of person he is. He coulda just kept on agoin', 'n none of you woulda ever even heerd of 'im. So I'm askin' you now, whatever happens to me, I want you to leave the boy out of it. Like I said, he never done nothin' wrong." Elmer nodded at Davenport. "All right, you can ask your questions now."

"Mr. Gleason, why did you ride with such men as Quantrill and Anderson?" Davenport asked.

"We was at war," Elmer said. "And I felt like it was the right thing to do."

"Did you gain personally from riding with the guerrillas? By that, I mean did you enrich yourself by looting and pillaging?"

"I'm not sure what pillagin' means. But if you're askin' did I ever keep any of the money we took from time to time, the answer is no."

"In your mind, would you say that the only reason you participated in the war was from a sense of duty to your state?"

"Yes. I was just a soldier doin' my duty," Elmer said. "I know they was lots of men that rode for the Blue who done just as bad, and some of 'em done worse 'n we did. I ain't holdin' that against 'em, now that all the fightin' is over. It was a war, 'n I reckon they was thinkin' it was their duty, just like them of us that rode with Quantrill or Anderson. But they ain't none of them looked on as criminals like we are, 'n there ain't nothin' right about that. Nothin' at all."

"Thank you, Mr. Gleason. I have no further questions, Your Honor."

"Cross, Mr. Taylor?"

Taylor stood up, then walked over to stand in front of Elmer. He folded his arms across his chest, leaned forward, and stared directly at Elmer. "You were just a soldier doing your duty, you say?" he asked sarcastically.

"Yes, sir. That's what I done, all right. I done my duty."

"Tell me, Mr. Gleason, would you consider the burning and sacking, and the murder of civilians in the town of Lawrence, Kansas, as just doing your duty? You do recall that, don't you?"

Elmer didn't respond.

"Were you present when Quantrill attacked Lawrence?"

Elmer still didn't answer.

Taylor turned to the judge. "Your Honor, I request you order the defendant to answer the question."

The judge nodded. "The defendant will answer the question."

"Were you present on that day, Mr. Gleason?" the prosecutor asked again.

"Yes, sir, I was there," Elmer replied, the words so quiet that they could barely be heard.

"Speak up please. Loudly enough so that everyone can hear you. Were you present for the sacking of Lawrence, Kansas?"

"Yes!" Elmer said loudly.

"Old men and young boys were rounded up and murdered. Houses and businesses were burned," Taylor said. "Is that duty, Mr. Gleason?"

"It was war. I ain't proud of it, but it was war."

"Your Honor, I am finished with this man," Taylor said.

"Redirect, Mr. Davenport?" the judge asked.

"No, Your Honor."

"Then defense may make a closing argument."

"Your Honor, Marshal Ferrell is a Texan. But he's the only person of authority who is a Texan. I know that you and the appointed mayor and the prosecutor, and just about everyone else with any power in this town, in this state, and throughout the South, are Yankees, sent here for reconstruction.

"But if you would just look out into the gallery you'll see men and women who were born and raised here. They are good people, Your Honor, Southerners by birth, and, during the late unpleasantness, they were Southerners by loyalty. If you ask them to pass judgment against these men, simply because they fought for what they believed in, they're goin' to tell you that Mr. Gleason 'n the boy sittin' there beside him, were no more than soldiers doing their duty in a war that, by its very existence, pitted friend against friend, brother against brother, and in some cases, father against son. Because of that, the war was particularly brutal. It's going to take several generations before all hard feelings go away. As you have come to live among us, I ask that you pass judgment on this matter with some feeling for the sensitivities of those who, by appointment and not by election, you now represent."

The gallery broke into cheers and applause.

Judge Gilmore was surprised by the spontaneous reaction of the gallery and, angrily, he banged his gavel until they were quiet.

"You forget, Mr. Davenport, that the state of Texas is in subjugation to the laws of the United States. I do not give a whit about the laws or the sensitivities of the people of Texas. I am here to perform the duty for which I was appointed." He looked over toward the jury. "You gentlemen of the jury. Do you go along with these folks in the gallery? Do you think these men who rode with Quantrill were nothing more than soldiers doing their duty?"

The men of the jury looked at each other, spoke quietly among themselves, then one of them spoke out. "Yes, sir, Your Honor. That's exactly what we think."

"Are you telling me that if I asked this jury for a verdict right now, it would be not guilty?"

"Yes, sir. We've spoke about it, 'n we've already come to a verdict. The verdict is they ain't neither one of 'em guilty."

Again, everyone cheered. Kirby, Elmer, and Davenport smiled broadly.

Judge Gilmore pounded his gavel on the makeshift bench until the gallery was quiet. "Your celebration is premature. I have not called for a verdict, nor shall I call for a verdict. This jury is dismissed," the judge said angrily.

Davenport objected. "Your Honor, if you empanel another jury, and hold this trial again, you are going to get the same result. No jury of this man's peers is going to find him guilty for doing his duty."

"You don't understand, Mr. Davenport," the judge said with an evil grin. "I have no intention of calling another jury. I will make the decision myself."

"What?" Davenport bellowed. "Your Honor, you can't do that! That's not legal."

"I can and I will. I find both defendants guilty as charged. You are free, Mr. Davenport, to appeal my decision, but in all candor I must tell you that an appeal would be nothing but a waste of time, for the sentence will have been long carried out before any decision can be made on the appeal. Elmer Gleason and—" He glanced toward the prosecutor. "What's the boy's name?"

"Jensen, Your Honor. Kirby Jensen," Taylor said.

"Elmer Gleason and Kirby Jensen, please present yourselves before my bench while I administer the sentence."

"Your Honor, we beg for mercy," Davenport said quickly.

"No, we don't, by God!" Elmer said sharply. He glanced over at Kirby. "I don't know about the boy. I'll let him make his own decision."

"I'll not be beggin' for mercy," Kirby said.

Judge Gilmore took off his glasses and began polishing them. He put them back on, hooking them carefully over his ears. He looked at the two defendants standing before him and cleared his throat. "Elmer Gleason and . . ." Again he paused.

"Kirby Jensen," Taylor added quietly.

"Elmer Gleason and Kirby Jensen, you have been tried before me and have been found guilty of the crime of riding with the butcher Quantrill, and aiding and abetting in the atrocities of murder, arson, and robbery that he visited upon innocent people. It is the sentence of this court that you be taken from this courthouse and put in jail where you will spend your last night on this mortal coil. At ten o'clock of the morrow, you will be taken to the gallows already constructed, and there, both of you will be suspended by your necks until you are dead."

"No!" someone in the court shouted. "You can't hang them, you Yankee crook! They ain't guilty of nothin' but bein' soldiers!"

"Marshal" the judge said. "Arrest the man who just made that outburst, and hold him in contempt of court!"

Marshal Ferrell stood and looked out over the gallery. "Arrest which man, Judge? I didn't see who it was."

To a man, every person in the courtroom was quiet.

"Who was it?" the judge asked. "Who made that outburst?"

There was no response to his inquiry.

"All right, all right!" the judge said. "You Rebels think you are putting one over on me, do you? But we'll see who has the last laugh tomorrow when these men are legally executed. Court is adjourned." He rapped the gavel once more.

The judge, the bailiff, and the prosecutor left the saloon by the back door.

"Damn, Marshal Ferrell, you ain't really goin' to hang 'em, are you?" someone called.

"You heard the judge. He give me the order. There ain't nothin' I can do about it."

* * *

"Kirby, what 'n hell did you do that for?" Elmer asked after the two men were taken back to the cell.

"I wanted to do what I could to help."

Elmer shook his head. "Well, you didn't have to go so far. Damn, boy, just showin' up woulda been enough. But what you done is got yourself caught up into the same mess I'm in."

To Elmer's surprise, Kirby flashed a big smile. "Yeah, I did, didn't I?"

Elmer frowned at him. "Boy, have you gone daft on me? Ain't you got no idea as to what's goin' to happen?"

"I know exactly what's going to happen," Kirby said. "That's why I got myself put in here."

"You got yourself put in here? Of a pure purpose?"

Kirby nodded. "Of a pure purpose."

CHAPTER 12

At that same moment, Emmett was at the livery, looking at a horse advertised for sale.

"He's a real good ridin' horse," the liveryman said. "It was rode by one of the officers in John Bell Hood's Division. Iffen you know'd anything about Hood, you know he had only the best horses."

"Yes, I know all about General Hood," Emmett replied. Hood, though an aggressive and effective officer for most of the war, had gotten many of his men slaughtered in an ill-advised frontal attack at Franklin, but Emmett didn't mention it.

"Do you have a saddle for sale as well?"

"I do, sir. I do indeed."

"Saddle him up, then ride him around the corral for me. I'd like to see him work, if you don't mind," Emmett said.

"Yes, sir. I would be happy to."

A few minutes later, the horse was saddled, and the liveryman rode him in compliance with Emmett's request. During the ride, Emmett observed the horse closely, listening to the rhythm of the gait and checking for equal striding in distance and time on the ground. He watched how the horse held his head and observed the footfalls to see if the animal showed any indication of sore feet. The horse passed his rather thorough examination.

Satisfied, Emmett said, "I'll take him. Please have this horse, and the two that I am now boarding with you, saddled and ready for me to pick up by seven o'clock this evening."

"Yes, sir. They'll be ready for you." The liveryman was happy to have made the sale.

"In the meantime, I need to rent a horse and a buckboard for a couple hours."

"All right. I'll get that ready for you right now."

A few minutes later, Emmett drove the buckboard from the livery down to the depot where he examined the rather high growth of weeds along the track. He decided they were in just the right place as they stretched just far enough to be perfect for his purpose.

Checking the time, he saw that it was just before five o'clock, which meant a train would be arriving shortly. He walked onto the depot platform and waited until the northbound train arrived. The arrivals and departures of the trains in the small railroad town of Salcedo caused much excitement and were always well attended. Emmett aroused no attention as he stood in the crowd, watching the disembarking and boarding passengers. Pulling his watch from his pocket again, he timed exactly how long the train stood in the station before it departed.

Four minutes and thirty-five seconds after the train arrived, it was on its way again. That was good. If the train's stay was much shorter, he wouldn't have time to do what he planned to do. Staying any longer would increase the possibility of being discovered.

He would time the nine o'clock train as well, then do an average of the two times, but for now, he had another stop to make.

Returning to the buckboard parked with several others, surreys, and wagons, he drove to the opposite end of town to Sikes' Hardware Store. A small bell attached to the door rang as he pushed it open and entered the store. "What is the longest chain you have?" he asked the clerk who'd hustled over to see what he needed.

"They are all the same length, twenty feet. But it doesn't really matter. You can make the chain as long as you need it to be," the clerk replied. He picked up the end of one of the chains and showed it to Emmett. "There are hooks on each end, so all you have to do is connect them together. How long a chain do you need?"

"I'm going to snake some sunken logs out of the Colorado River, so I'm thinkin' I'm goin' to be needin' at least a hunnert and fifty feet."

"That won't be any problem. I can give you eight, twenty foot lengths. It's going to cost you forty dollars, though. Do you think those sunken logs are worth forty dollars?"

"I know some people up North who'll buy 'em. The lumber from 'em makes real shiny floors."

Emmett made the purchase, then loaded the chains onto the buckboard.

Shortly after nine o'clock, Emmett worked alongside the track in the dark. The train that just left had been in the station for six minutes and ten seconds. He could hear a dog barking. From somewhere a bit more distant, a baby began to cry. The most prominent sounds, however, came from the Scalded Cat Saloon—the tinkling of a piano, the shriek of a woman, followed by the loud guffaw of several men. From the corral of the freight wagon company came the bray of a mule.

A cat came walking up, looking at him curiously, its eyes shining in the dark.

Emmett looked back into the weeds, but could see no evidence of the work he had just done. So far, not one person had seen him and that was very good. He didn't need to be arousing any suspicions.

Once his work was finished, he walked back to the jail and went inside.

One man, a soldier, was sitting at the desk. He looked up from the game of solitaire he was playing. "If you're lookin' for the marshal, he ain't here. Him and the deputy is out makin' the rounds." He wasn't one of the three witnesses at the trial, nor had he been there when Emmett and Kirby had come to see Elmer.

"I'm not here to see him. I'm here to see my son."

"Your son?"

"Kirby Jensen, one of your prisoners, is my son," Emmett said. "I'd like to visit him."

The soldier examined one of the stacks of cards, then turned up a card, and seeing that he could use it, applied it to another stack.

"That's cheatin' you know."

"Yeah, but I ain't cheatin' no one but myself. Leave your gun here 'n go on back. Seein' as he's goin' to get his neck stretched tomorrow, I don't see no reason why you can't tell him good-bye."

"Thanks."

Emmett lay his gun on the desk, then stepped into the back. Elmer was sitting on one of the bunks, and Kirby was on the other. They looked up as Emmett approached the cell.

"Hi, Pa," Kirby said easily.

"Kirby, Elmer, I've got somethin' I'm goin' to need you to do. First of all, make certain that you are awake at eleven o'clock tonight."

"Hell, there ain't goin' to be no problem with that," Elmer said. "If this here is to be my last night on earth, I sure don't plan to be awastin' it by sleepin'."

Emmett chuckled. "This won't be your last night."

"You've got it all worked out?" Kirby asked. "Is it just the way we planned?"

"Yes."

"We'll be ready."

At a quarter till eleven that night, Emmett took the three saddled horses to the back of the apothecary, two buildings down the alley from the jail. From there, he walked out to the track, hoisted one end of the chain he had stretched out along the track two hours earlier, and pulled it over to the back of the jail.

He looked in through the barred window. "Kirby?"

"Yeah, Pa. We're here."

Emmett poked the chain in through the bars. "Take this, wrap it around all four bars, then pass it back out to me."

Kirby did as Emmett instructed, and taking the end his son had given him, Emmett connected the hook through one of the links. "Now, when you hear the train whistle, get over there to the corner, as far away from the wall as you can."

"All right."

With the chain wrapped around the bars, Emmett hurried back to the depot and waited.

He could hear the train before he could see it, first the whistle, then the chugging sound. As it came around the bend, about a quarter mile down the track, he could see the light, the sheltered gas flame set in a polished reflector to cast a beam before the engine. It was little over a minute before the engine reached him, so heavy that the ground shook as it rolled by. Steam was gushing from the drive cylinders and glowing coals were falling from the firebox. The engineer, with a pipe clenched tightly between his teeth, was leaning out of the open window of the cab, staring straight ahead.

After the engine came the tender, the express car, the baggage car, then the four passenger cars, lit from inside. The train squealed and screeched to a stop. It was still, but it wasn't silent as overheated journals snapped and popped, the water in the boiler bubbled, and escaping steam made a quiet hiss.

Grabbing the end of the chain and bending low, Emmett stayed in the shadows as he hurried up to the rear of the train. There, he wrapped the chain through the coupling, connecting it back on itself. That done, he ran back to the apothecary and, untying the horses, held the three sets of reins in his hand and waited.

The engineer gave two short toots on the whistle, and a gush of steam spewed forth as he opened the throttle.

Emmett watched the chain lift from the ground and grow taut. He heard the loud crashing sound as half of the back wall of the jail was pulled down and hurried up the alley with the three horses. "Let's go!" he called, as he saw Kirby and Elmer climbing out through the hole.

"Hey! What's going on back here!" the soldier shouted, coming from the front. Seeing the two men escaping through the collapsed wall, he pulled his gun and fired, but Kirby and Elmer were already out of harm's way.

"Here's your gun." Emmett handed Kirby's pistol and gun belt to him.

"And here's your horse." Emmett handed Elmer a set of reins.

The three men galloped down the alley, onto the main road, and out of town.

"Did you steal this horse?" Elmer asked the next morning. "The reason I ask is, do I need to be worryin' 'bout someone hangin' me for horse stealin'?"

"Here's the bill of sale," Emmett said. "I've already signed it over to you."

Elmer shook his head. "I ain't got no money to pay you for it. Fact is, I ain't got no money at all."

"Here." Emmett gave him fifty dollars in cash.

"No, sir." Elmer shook his head, pushing the money away. "I didn't say that hopin' for some money."

"I know you didn't, Elmer. But the way I look at it, it's my way of sayin' thanks for lookin' after my boy while I was gone."

"It warn't exactly that way. When we was ridin' together, he was lookin' out for me half the time 'n I was lookin' out for him the other half the time."

"All right. Then this is for the times you was lookin' out for him."

Reluctantly, Elmer took the money. "You've kept me from gettin' hung, you've given me a horse, 'n you give me some money. I don't know what to say. Like as not, we ain't never goin' to run into each other again. I don't know how I'm ever goin' to be able to pay you back."

"Then don't try," Emmett said.

Elmer nodded, then got mounted. "I do have a piece of information you might be interested in. I heerd where Shardeen is."

"What?" Kirby asked excitedly. "Where?"

"I only heerd where he is. I cain't say for sure 'cause I didn't see him for my ownself. And I don't know if he's still there or not. But, last I heard, he was in Dorena."

"Pa?"

Emmett nodded. "All right. We'll go to Dorena."

Emmett and Kirby surveyed the town as they rode in. Kirby had seen many small towns like this since he left Missouri. At this point in his life he didn't realize it, but he would see many hundreds more in the years to come.

Dorena wasn't that unlike Salcedo, except there was no railroad. The single street was faced by false-fronted shanties, a few sod buildings, and even a handful of tents, straggling along for nearly a quarter mile. Just as abruptly as the town started, it quit, and nothing but open road and empty prairie existed ahead.

The street was baked hard as a rock from the summer heat. The sun was still yellow and hot in early September. In the winter and spring, the street would be a muddy mire, worked by the horses' hooves and mixed with their droppings so that it became a stinking, sucking pool of ooze.

The biggest and grandest structure in town was a building with a sign stretching across the front that read EL CABALLO Y EL TORO CANTINA. It also had a picture of a beer mug on one end of the sign and a liquor bottle on the other. Across the street from the building, they saw a man leaning up against the post that was supporting the roof of a leather store.

"Tell me, mister," Emmett said, pointing to the building. "Would that be a saloon?"

"It's a cantina," the man said. "That's Mex for a saloon."

"What does the name mean?"

"The horse and the bull."

"Thanks."

They rode over to the cantina, dismounted, and tied their horses off at a hitching rail. The shadows gave an illusion of coolness inside, but it was an illusion only. The dozen and a half drinking customers had to keep their bandanas handy to wipe the sweat from their faces.

Over the last few months, Emmett had taught Kirby how to enter a saloon. "We're lookin' for men we aim to kill," Emmett had explained. "As time goes on 'n more and more people find out what we are about, we're likely to have men looking for us as well, for one reason or another. So you need to know how to enter a saloon, and it needs to become a habit with you so's that you do it without even thinkin' about it."

Following the lesson his pa taught him, Kirby was on the alert as they stepped inside. He and Emmett surveyed the place with such calmness that the average person would think it no more than a glance of idle curiosity. In reality, it was a very thorough appraisal of the room. They checked out who was armed, what type of weapons they were carrying, and if they were wearing their guns in the way that showed they knew how to use them.

Less than half of the drinkers were even wearing guns, though there was a man standing at the other end of the bar who was armed. His gun was in a holster that was kicked-out in the way that indicated he might know how to use it.

The walls of the saloon were decorated with game heads and pictures, including one of a reclining nude woman. Some marksman had improved the painting by putting a single bullet hole in a most appropriate place.

Several large jars of boiled eggs and pickled pigs' feet sat on the bar. A stairway led to an upstairs section at the back. Kirby could see rooms opening off the second-floor landing as he watched a heavily painted saloon girl take a cowboy up the stairs with her.

The upstairs area didn't extend all the way to the front of the building, which meant that the main room of the saloon was big, with exposed rafters below the high, peaked ceiling. Nearly a dozen tables were full of drinking customers.

The piano player wore a small, round derby hat and kept his sleeves up with garters. He was pounding away at the piano, though the music was practically lost amidst the noise of a dozen or more conversations.

"What'll it be, gents?" the barkeep asked as he moved down toward them. He wiped up a spill with a wet, smelly rag before draping the rag over his shoulder.

"A couple beers," Emmett said.

"That'll be ten cents," the bartender said as he put two mugs on the bar before them. Emmett slid a dime across to him.

A bar girl sidled up to Kirby. She was heavily painted and showed the dissipation of her profession. "Oh, honey, you are a sweet one, you are."

He was embarrassed by her attention. It wasn't the first time he had ever been in a saloon, but it was the first time he had ever actually been approached by one of the bar girls.

"Whoa, Becky," said a man at one of the tables. "You sure you know what you're doin' there? You don't want to be robbin' the cradle, do you? Seems to me like you'd be better off goin' after the old one."

Several customers laughed.

"Yeah," one of the others said. "The old one looks like he ain't had a woman in near twenty years, and the young 'un there, why, I bet he ain't never had no woman."

"Would you like a drink?" Kirby asked Becky.

"A drink? Well, yes, honey, I think I would like a drink."

Kirby turned to the bartender. "Sir, would you give the lady whatever it is she would like to drink?"

The bartender took a bottle from beneath the bar and poured it into a short glass. "That'll be a quarter."

"Kirby, it would appear that your lady friend has expensive taste," Emmett said with a smile as Kirby put a quarter on the bar.

Becky picked the glass up and tossed the drink down in one gulp. Then, smiling, she put her hand on Kirby's shoulder. "Why don't you come upstairs with me, honey, and let me make a man out of you?" she suggested.

Kirby had no idea how old she was, but he was sure that she was older than Miss Margrabe would be.

Wherever Miss Margrabe was.

"No, thank you, ma'am," Kirby said. "I bought you a drink because you were being nice to me. But, I don't want to do anything else."

"Now, just a minute here, boy." The man at the other end of the bar stood up straight. "I think you just insulted my woman."

"I'm sorry, ma'am, if I insulted you," Kirby said.

"Honey, you didn't insult me." Becky turned her head back toward the man who had spoken. "And Streeter, I ain't your woman."

"Sure you are," Streeter replied with an evil grin. "You're anybody's woman that pays you. I've paid you, so that makes you my woman."

"Well you ain't payin' me now."

"Are you sassin' me, woman? 'Cause I ain't goin' to stand for no sassin'."

Becky put her hands on her hips. "I'm not sassin' you. I just told you that I'm not your woman, and I'm not."

"I say you're sassin' me, 'n if you don't apologize to me right now, why I might just have to knock some manners into you."

"I'm sorry," Becky said, showing genuine fright.

"You're sorry all right. You are sorry, washed up, and ought to be glad that anyone at all would talk to you."

"Mr. Streeter, why don't you leave the lady alone?" Kirby said. "She told you she's sorry."

"What?" Streeter nearly shouted the word in surprise that the young boy would talk to him like that. "What did you just say to me?"

"I asked you politely to leave the lady alone."

"First of all, she ain't no lady. But I reckon you're too dumb to know the difference." Streeter's tone of voice had gotten very challenging. With such a sharp edge to it, all other conversation in the bar had stopped. Everyone watched to see what was going to happen next.

"Miss Becky, I'd be real pleased if you would have another drink with me." Kirby put another quarter on the bar.

"Boy, you're beginnin' to put a burr under my saddle, you know that? But I'm goin' to let it pass for now. Because you're new in town, maybe you don't know who I am."

"The lady called you Streeter, so I reckon that's your name."

"That's it. Emile Streeter. I reckon you've heard of Emile Streeter."

Kirby shook his head. "No, sir, I can't say as I have."

"Tell 'im who I am, Jake," Streeter said to the bartender.

"Mr. Streeter, why don't you leave him alone. He's just a boy."

"He's a boy with a smart mouth, and he needs to be taught a lesson," Streeter said. "Tell 'im who I am."

"Young man, Mr. Streeter is a man of some notoriety in these parts. He is quite good with a gun." Jake pointed to the nude painting. "You might have noticed the bullet hole between the young lady's legs. Streeter put it there."

"You shoot paintings, do you?" Kirby asked. "Do they ever shoot back?"

"Boy, I've had about enough of you!" Streeter said.

Kirby smiled at the man. "Mr. Streeter, it looks like me 'n you got off on the wrong foot. If I've put a burr under your saddle, I apologize. Bartender, I would like to buy a drink for Mr. Streeter."

"Uh-uh," Streeter said, shaking his head slowly. "This has come too far for you to back out now."

"Streeter, for God's sake, leave him alone. Can't you see he's tryin' to apologize?" the bartender said as he put another whiskey in front of Streeter.

"You stay out of this, Jake, or I'll be settlin' with you after I'm finished with the boy here."

"Streeter, that's enough! What has gotten into you? Leave the boy alone!" Becky turned to Kirby. "Honey, I'm sorry I come up to you like I did. Believe me, I would have never done so, if I had had any idea that this fool was going to carry on like this."

"Well now, boy, ever'one seems awful worried about you, so I tell you what. If you'll get down on your knees and ask me, please, not to shoot you, this can all be over. Otherwise, me 'n you's goin' to have us a little dance." Streeter laughed, a high-pitched, insane sound. "Me 'n you's goin' to dance. I like that."

"Please do it," Becky begged. "He'll kill you."

"Don't worry. He's not going to kill me," Kirby said, his voice flat and amazingly calm.

"You don't understand," Becky said desperately.

Kirby had had just about enough. "No. Streeter doesn't understand. And one of the things he doesn't understand is that I'm not a boy."

"Hey you, old man," Streeter called to Emmett.

For the entire interplay between Streeter and Kirby, Emmett had done nothing but sip his beer and watch, almost dispassionately. He looked Streeter in the eye. "Are you talking to me?"

"Yeah. Looks like me 'n this boy is about to have us that little dance we was talkin' about. And you're in the way."

"I'm not in the way." Emmett coughed.

"What do you mean, you're not in the way? You're standin' right there behind the boy, ain't you?"

"I suppose I am, but it doesn't matter. You heard what he said. He's not a boy. And you won't get a shot off."

"What? What do you mean I won't get a shot off, you old fool?"

"Kirby?" Emmett said.

"Yes, Pa?"

"Pa? You mean this is your boy?" Streeter asked, laughing.

Emmett didn't move. "This bragging fool seems to be pretty proud of what he done to that painting. But it looks to me like there's room for a couple additions."

Kirby glanced up at the painting of the nude woman and smiled. "Yes, sir. I know what you mean."

"Why don't you finish the job he started?"

In a flash, Kirby pulled his pistol, fired twice, and put the pistol back in its holster. Both breasts in the painting had been punched through by perfectly placed bullet holes.

"What the hell?" someone gasped. "I didn't even see him draw!"

"That's impossible!" another said. "There cain't nobody shoot that good and that fast!"

"Now, Streeter—I believe that's what you told me your name was—shall we get this over with?" Kirby asked.

Eyes wide and mouth open, Streeter reached out with a shaking hand, picked up the glass of whiskey still on the bar, and drained it. He put the empty glass down, then turned to look at Kirby.

Kirby smiled at him, but absolutely nothing young nor innocent was in the smile. It was old as time and as dangerous as the open mouth of a hissing rattlesnake.

"I . . . uh . . . I," Streeter stammered. Glancing at the others in the room, his face mirroring his absolute fear, he held an empty hand out toward Kirby. "Don't shoot. Don't shoot." He started toward the door.

"Come back, Streeter. Next time you want to show off!" Becky called to him, and everyone in the saloon laughed.

Streeter pulled his hat down more firmly on his head and pushed through the swinging batwing doors without so much as a look back.

"Lord almighty! I ain't never seen nothin' like that!" someone said.

"I wouldn't be surprised if Streeter don't never come back here," another said.

"If he don't never come back, it'll be the town's gain, and we owe this young fella a vote of thanks." Jake drew two more mugs of beer and set them on the bar. "These are on the house. What brings you two to town?"

Kirby turned back to the bar. "I'm looking for Angus Shardeen."

The smile left the bartender's face. It wasn't only the expression that changed. The tone of his voice changed, as well. "A friend of yours, is he?"

Kirby shook his head. "Believe me, Angus Shardeen is no friend."

Jake relaxed, and the smile returned. "Good. If he was your friend, I'd be thinkin' a lot less of you than I am now."

"Where is he?"

"Nobody knows. He kilt a young cowboy about a month ago, then he skedaddled out of here."

"Most likely, he went back up to Kansas," Becky said. "I believe that's where he come from."

"Yes ma'am. That is where he came from," Kirby said.

"Why are you lookin' for him, if I might ask?" Jake inquired.

"He killed my ma," Kirby replied.

Jake nodded. "I reckon I can see why you're lookin' for him then. How long do you plan to stay in town?"

Emmett answered the question. "Long enough to finish this beer."

Kirby and his father left Texas and rode north through Indian Territory, following the Washita River. Changing colors, it snaked out across the gently undulating prairie before them—shining gold in the setting sun, sometimes white where it broke over rocks, at other times shimmering a deep blue-green in the swirling eddies and trapped pools, and sometimes running red with clay silt.

Late in the afternoon, a rabbit hopped up and bounded down the trail ahead of him.

"There's supper," Emmett said.

Kirby drew his pistol and fired. A puff of fur and spray of blood flew up as the rabbit made a head-first somersault, then lay perfectly still.

They stopped for the day and made camp under a growth of cottonwoods. Emmett started a fire while Kirby skinned and cleaned the rabbit, then skewered it on a green willow branch and suspended it over the fire between two forked limbs.

Except for Emmett's occasional coughing, they were quiet, staring at the cooking rabbit.

Finally, Kirby broke the silence. "Pa, it's been five days, 'n you ain't said nothin' about what happened back there in Dorena with that Streeter fella."

"No, I reckon I haven't," Emmett replied.

"How come you ain't said nothin'?"

Emmett coughed again before he answered. "I thought you were handlin' things pretty well."

"I figured you musta thought that, else you woulda been tellin' me what I shoulda done."

"Kirby, I'm not goin' to be here forever. Fact is, I ain't goin' to be here much longer at all, 'n you're goin' to be on your own. A fella with a skill like yours, word's goin' to get around. When that happens, people will be comin' for you, wantin' to try you out to make a name for killing Kirby Jensen."

"How can that be, Pa? There ain't anybody even knows my name."

"They will know your name, and soon. I pretty much gave you your head back there because you need to know how to handle yourself. And like I said, you did pretty well."

"I woulda killed him if it hadn't been for you comin' up with a way that let me avoid it," Kirby said.

Emmett coughed again, then reached out to turn the skewer, allowing another side of the rabbit to face the fire. The aroma of the cooking meat permeated the campsite.

"I reckon you might have," Emmett said. "And truth to tell, you woulda been justified. But, anytime you can find a way to do what needs to be done without killin', it's best."

"Yeah, I can see that. I'm glad you come up with the idea about shootin' holes in the woman's . . . you know."

Emmett laughed.

"Pa, that woman . . . Becky. She wanted me to go upstairs with her."

"Yes, I heard her ask."

"I thought about it."

"Did you?"

"What would you have said if I had done it?"

"I wouldn'ta said nothin' at all. They's some things so private that nobody else can tell you one way or the other what to do. Why didn't you go upstairs with her?"

"I ain't never been with a woman before," Kirby said. "Leastwise, I ain't never been with a woman in . . . that . . . way . . . the way she wanted to be. I sorta figure that if you're goin' to do somethin' like that with a woman, then maybe it ought to mean somethin'."

"That's a good way of lookin' at it. Rabbit's done." Emmett lifted the golden brown piece of meat off the fire, seasoned it with their dwindling supply of salt, then lay it on a flat rock and split it right down the middle, head to tail. He gave half of it to Kirby.

Kirby began eating, pulling the meat away with his teeth even when it was almost too hot to hold.

After his supper, he stirred the fire, then lay down alongside it, using his saddle as a pillow. He stared into the coals, watching the red sparks ride a heated column of air high up into the night sky. Still glowing red and orange, they joined the jewel-like scattering of stars.

"Pa?"

"Yes, son?"

"Just so you know, when I find Shardeen, I won't be lookin' for a way to avoid it, no more 'n I reckon you'll be lookin' for a way not to kill them men you're after."

"I wouldn't expect you to," Emmett said.

CHAPTER 13

Three months of dusty cow towns and wide open spaces proved fruitless. The Jensens had not found Shardeen, nor had they located any of the men Emmett was looking for. At the moment, they were in the middle of nowhere, with no particular place to go. Well, it wasn't actually *nowhere*. They knew they were somewhere in Kansas. Or at least, they *thought* they were in Kansas.

It was a cold and very gray day.

"Pa, what's the date?"

"I don't rightly know," Emmett admitted. "Late October, early November, maybe?"

"It's got to be later than that. I don't think it would be this cold unless it was at least December."

"Could be that you're right," Emmett agreed. "You know what I'm thinkin'?"

"What's that?"

"I'm thinkin' that the next town we see, we might want to put in for the winter."

Kirby frowned. "You got 'ny idea where that next town might be?"

"Not the slightest. But that fella we run into a couple days ago said the Arkansas River was in front of us, and it can't be more 'n a day's ride away. Once we get to the river, all we'll have to do is follow it. It's goin' to eventually take us to a town."

"All right," Kirby agreed. "Let's find the river."

During the night, snow began to fall. It came down softly, silently. It was quite a surprise when Kirby awoke the next morning to find himself almost completely buried in snow. He looked around for his father but didn't see him.

"Pa?" Kirby called. "Pa? Where are you?"

"Hrmmph!" Emmett grunted and suddenly sat up from under a blanket of snow. The white stuff was in his hair, his eyebrows, and hanging from his beard.

Kirby laughed.

"What's so funny?"

"You look like a snowman."

Emmett looked around. "We had quite a snowfall, didn't we?"

"Yes, sir, I would say that we did."

"Have you checked on the horses?"

"No, sir. Seemed like the first thing I should check on was you."

Emmett chuckled and nodded. "Good idea. Let's find the horses."

Both men stood, stomped and shook the snow from themselves, and dug through the snow to find their saddles. They walked to where the horses stood, knee deep in snow. They looked cold and miserable.

"Wow, these are going to feel awfully cold to the horses when we put them on," Kirby said as he held up the saddle, still dripping with snow.

Emmett laughed. "It's going to be just as cold on our butts."

Kirby laughed as well. "Yeah, I hadn't thought about that."

Big Ben Conyers' ranch, Live Oaks, lay just north of Ft. Worth. The gently rolling grassland and scores of year-round streams and creeks made it ideal for cattle ranching. Two dozen cowboys were part-time employees, and another two dozen were full-time employees. Those who weren't married lived in a couple long, low bunkhouses, white with red roofs. The married couples lived in small houses adjacent to the bunkhouses, all of them painted green with red roofs. A cookhouse large enough to feed all the single men, a barn, a machine shed, a granary, and a large stable were also on the property.

The most dominating feature of the ranch was what the cowboys called "The Big House." A stucco-sided example of Spanish Colonial Revival, it had an arcaded portico on the southeast corner, stained-glass windows, and an elaborate arched entryway.

In the parlor, Ben watched as Janey decorated the Christmas tree, adding gaily colored pine cones to the red and green ribbon laced all through it. The many small candles would be lit once all the decorations were in place.

"I do believe that is the prettiest Christmas tree I have ever seen," Ben said.

Janey turned toward him. "It's easy for me to say that. This is the first Christmas tree I've ever seen, anywhere."

"Well then, I'm glad that your first tree is so fine. It'll be even prettier when all the gifts are under it."

"Ben, please, no gifts for me," Janey said.

"What do you mean, no gifts for you? Of course there will be gifts for you. Why, what is Christmas without the presents?"

"But, I have no present for you."

"You know what I want from you. It would be the most wonderful present I can imagine."

Janey didn't respond.

"Marry me, Janey. I couldn't ask for a greater present than to have you as my bride."

"Ben, I can't."

"Why can't you? You aren't already married, are you?"

"No, I'm not married. But you know why I can't. You are a very important man here. Maybe if we lived somewhere else . . . someplace where there is less a chance that I would be recognized, I could consider it. But you know, without a doubt, that there are people who know who I am . . . and what I am . . . was. If word would get around, it would be terribly embarrassing. I couldn't do that to you."

"Some may recognize you, that is true. But how would they recognize you unless they, too, had visited the Palace Princess Emporium? If that was the case, it would be just as embarrassing to them as it would be to me. At any rate, I assure you, Janey, nobody will ever dare say anything about it to my face, nor would they even take a chance on me learning that they had spoken of it behind my back."

"But what if they do? What would you do? Would you kill them?"

"If I had to."

"That's what I'm afraid of."

Ben walked over to Janey and pulled her to him in an embrace. "I don't want you to ever be afraid of anything. As long as you are with me, you don't have to be. If you don't want to get married yet, I'll just enjoy whatever part of you, you are willing to share. I love you, Janey. I don't care about your background."

"Oh, Ben, why couldn't I have met you before?" Janey asked, her eyes welling with tears.

"Nothing that happened before now matters. Only *now* matters, and we are together now. So we'll just enjoy what we have, and we'll see where it leads. If I'm the luckiest man in the world, it will lead to matrimony."

As Janey lay in bed that night, she thought of their conversation. Ben had told her that he didn't want her to ever be afraid of anything, but she was afraid. She was pregnant. Ben had accepted the idea that it was his baby, but she couldn't be certain. She wasn't sure exactly how long she had been pregnant, but she had been with at least two other men a few days before she had left Dallas with Ben.

That had been in August. If the baby was born any later than April, she would know that it was Ben's. If it was born in April, or earlier, it might not be.

January 1866

Emmett and Kirby were wintering in Delphi, Kansas, a small town on the Arkansas River near the border of Kansas and the territory of Colorado. Although they still had most of the bounty money that had been paid for Cox and Haggart, they opted to take jobs through the winter to preserve what money they had.

Emmett worked for the company that operated the ferry across the river, while Kirby had agreed to become a deputy for City Marshal Darrell Wright.

"We don't have much call for lawin' here," Marshal Wright told him when he was hired. "About all we ever have to do is pick up a drunk now 'n then. Most of the time, the onliest reason we pick 'em up is 'cause they sometimes pass out on the street. In the winter time, they could likely freeze if we didn't bring 'em in."

It was the cold that worried Kirby the most—not for himself, but for his pa, who was exposed to the weather on the ferry boat. He tried to get his father to quit. "It's not costin' us all that much to live. I'm makin' enough as a deputy to pay the boardin'house . . . and the boardin'house is feedin' us. With your lung 'n all, it can't be good for you to be out in the cold all the time."

"I ain't so damn feeble that my own son has to take care of me," Emmett said. "The work ain't hard, 'n I can wrap up in a buffalo robe that keeps me warm. You don't be worryin' about me."

"I just wish you'd quit, is all."

"And do what? Sit around with my thumb up my ass all the time?"

Kirby laughed out loud. "Well, I don't guess I'd want to see you doin' that, exactly."

"I would damn sure hope not. Now, you do your work 'n I'll do mine, if you'll just let me be."

"All right, Pa. But if it gets too much for you, remember, it ain't somethin' you have to do."

The boardinghouse where they stayed was the Homestead House, owned and run by Mrs. Pauline Foley, an attractive widow in her mid-forties.

"I made biscuits this morning, Emmett," she said when Emmett and Kirby came down for breakfast. "I know how you like to sop them through sour cream and sugar."

"You're too kind to me, Mrs. Foley."

"Oh please, won't you call me Pauline?"

"I would be honored to, Pauline. I just don't want to be too for-ward."

"You could never be too forward," she said, smiling as she poured coffee into Emmett's cup.

As they left the boardinghouse to go to their respective jobs, Kirby smiled at his father. "Pa, I think Mrs. Foley likes you."

"She's a business woman. She's just being nice to her customers, that's all."

"Uh-huh. But she's nicer to you than she is to Mrs. Simmons or Mr. Clark."

"Boy, you know what your problem is?"

"What?"

"You see too many things that aren't there."

"She likes you, Pa. You know she does," Kirby said with a broad smile.

Emmett sighed. "She might, but I'm not encouragin' it. We'll be leavin' here, come spring. I don't want to do anythin' that might cause her some hurt. She's a good and decent woman, and she don't fit in with my plans. You do understand that, don't you, boy?"

Kirby nodded. "Yeah Pa, I do."

"Then please, don't do or say anything to her that might give her the wrong idea."

"I won't, Pa."

"I'll see you at supper."

Kirby nodded. "Try 'n stay warm out there on the water today."

One of the advantages of working as a deputy was Kirby's access to WANTED posters. He had mixed feelings about those he had seen on Angus Shardeen. On the one hand, he was glad that Shardeen was being regarded as a wanted outlaw . . . and not a hero as was James Henry Lane. On the other hand, because Shardeen was a wanted man with a price on his head, it was quite possible that someone else might find and kill him before Kirby had the satisfaction of doing so.

As he was looking through the WANTED posters, he was surprised to see his and his father's names, not on a reward poster, but on a document that rescinded their wanted status.

> *Notice is hereby given that the Wanted status of Elmer Gleason, Emmett Jensen, and Kirby Jensen has been withdrawn. Reason for revocation: an appeal filed on their behalf by Keith Davenport has been granted, and Daniel Gilmore has been removed from the federal bench due to malfeasance.*

Kirby smiled as he read the document, and he gave a silent thanks for the honesty and integrity of the lawyer who, even though he would probably never see his clients again, had done the right thing.

On an early spring day, Kirby was in the bank to deposit a county check for the sheriff's office when his landlady came in with two men. "Hello, Mrs. Foley."

As soon as he spoke to her, he saw that the expression on her face was one of terror. He also saw the reason for her terror. Both men who had come into the bank were armed, and one of them had his gun stuck into her back.

"This is a holdup!" shouted one of the two men.

"Here, what are you doing?" the bank teller called. "You let that woman go!"

"We will, soon as you fill this bag with money." The second armed man stepped up to the teller's cage, passing a cloth bag over the counter.

With shaking hands, the teller began taking money from his drawer, and sticking it into the cloth bag.

"Hurry up!" the robber urged.

"There's no need for you to hurry, Mr. Montgomery," Kirby said easily. "These two men are under arrest. I'm going to ask you to let Mrs. Foley go . . . now."

"What did you say?"

"You may have noticed the star on my jacket. I'm the deputy marshal here, and I'm putting both of you under arrest."

The outlaws laughed.

"Are you tryin' to be funny, mister?" one asked.

"No, I'm quite serious."

"You may have a deputy's star, but you ain't got no sense. Maybe you're too dumb to notice, but you don't have a gun in your hand, and we do."

"That's true," Kirby agreed. "But you're pointing your gun at Mrs. Foley, and your friend is pointing his gun at the bank teller. Neither one of you are pointing your guns toward me. And that's where you have made your mistake."

The one holding his gun to Mrs. Foley glanced at his partner. "Can you believe this guy?"

"I'm going to ask you one more time to let Mrs. Foley go," Kirby said, his voice quiet and calm as it was the first time he'd addressed them.

"What the hell! Let's just shoot him and get it over with!" The one holding Mrs. Foley seemed to be the leader.

Kirby was watching both men very carefully. The instant the man holding Mrs. Foley moved his pistol, Kirby drew and fired twice, one on top of the other. Both would-be bank robbers went down, each of them with a bullet in his forehead, dead before realizing they were in danger.

Shocked by the sudden and unexpected turn of events, the scream that Mrs. Foley tried to make died in her throat. By the time she looked toward Kirby, he had already returned his pistol to his holster. The bank teller, with an expression of utter shock on his face, was still holding the half-filled bag of money.

"You can put the money back in the drawer now, Mr. Montgomery," Kirby said. "Oh, and the sheriff would like to deposit this county check."

The two bank robbers were identified as Frank Morris and Seth Crandall, former Jayhawkers. Within a week, word of Kirby Jensen's unbelievable performance had traveled up and down the Arkansas River and beyond.

Some declared the story fanciful since only two eyewitnesses could claim that they had seen it happen. It didn't seem possible that anyone could have actually done what was being told.

"I'm proud of you, son," Emmett said. "You are already getting a taste of what I told you was going to happen. You are beginning to build a name for yourself. I do believe there's goin' to come the time when ever'one in the West knows who you are."

"I'm not sure that's somethin' I want, Pa," Kirby said.

"I'm not goin' to lie to you. It's goin' to be a burden. But as long as you use this skill and talent for the good, you'll go to bed ever' night with a clear conscience."

Had Kirby known how close he was to Angus Shardeen, he would have turned in his badge and gone after him. The raiding Jayhawker was camped less than fifteen miles west of Delphi, just across the line in Colorado.

"Both of them?" Shardeen replied after being told about what had happened in the bank in Delphi. "Morris and Crandall were both killed?"

"Yes," Bartell said. "By that same kid that shot Tim in the hand."

"Why didn't you do somethin'?" Shardeen asked.

"I was outside with the horses. When I heard the shootin' 'n Frank 'n Seth didn't come out, I figured it was best I not give myself away. I just went across the street into the saloon. That's when I heard what happened."

"He said he was comin' for you, Angus," Tim said.

"One man? And a kid at that?"

"Yeah, but he ain't like any other kid I've ever heard of. Frank 'n Seth both had their guns already drawed when they went into the bank," Bartell said. "Jensen shot 'em both."

"A tiny bank in a one-horse town, 'n Morris and Crandall get themselves kilt. Next time I'll send better men."

* * *

Rebecca Jean Conyers was born on April 15, 1866. The date of her birth did not preclude Ben being her father, but neither did it absolutely establish that he was. She had red hair, and Ben was quick to point out that his mother's sister had been redheaded.

Janey promised that she would marry him but asked for a little time to recover from the birth.

On the day that Becca was three months old, Janey was standing in the nursery holding her.

"Do you want me to give the baby a bath?" asked Juanita Gomez, the nanny Ben had hired to look after the baby.

"Not yet," Janey said. "Juanita, I'm going to be gone for a while. I want you to look after Becca while I'm gone."

"*El bebé hermoso que yo velo,*" Juanita said. Then she repeated it in English. "The beautiful baby, I will watch."

"I know you will. Oh, would you have Mr. McNally bring the surrey around? I'm ready to leave."

"*Sí, Señora.*" Juanita knew that Janey and Ben weren't married, but she called her Señora anyway.

Janey waited until Juanita was gone, then she kissed the baby again. Her eyes shining brightly, Becca smiled up at Janey.

"Good-bye, my sweet child. I know you don't understand now, and you may never understand. But what I'm doing is best for you and for your father. I'll never see you again, but I swear to you, I'll never forget you."

Janey put the baby in her crib, then raised up with tears streaming down her cheeks.

When Ben returned later in the day, he went into Rebecca's room, picked her up, and kissed her on the forehead. "If you aren't the most beautiful baby in the entire state of Texas, I'll eat my hat. Without salt," he added with a laugh. He put her back in her crib and looked over toward the nanny. "Juanita, where is Janey?"

"She said she will be gone for *unos pocos días.*"

"She's going to be gone for a few days? Where did she go? Did she say?"

"No, Señor."

"That's damn odd," Ben said.

Puzzled by Janey's strange and unexpected disappearance, Ben went into the parlor. On the fireplace mantel was an envelope that bore his name.

Even more puzzled and a little worried, he hurried over to retrieve the envelope, then tore it open to read it:

Dear Ben,

  Please forgive me, but I cannot stay here. I am afraid that to do so can do nothing but cause you embarrassment and pain. I'm leaving Becca with you. You have enough love and means to give her a wonderful life. I have nothing to offer her but my love, and on the day she learns of my past, my love won't be enough. Then, I will be an embarrassment to her, as well, and I don't think I'd be able to bear that. Tell her that I died, for it would be much better if she grows up believing that.

  I do love you, Ben, but it is a love that cannot be. If you love me, I beg of you, make no effort to find me. Instead, give all your love to our daughter.

Janey

Ben went back into the nursery and picked up the baby again. He took her into the library, locked the door behind him, and walked over to sit in the big leather chair. There, the six-foot-four, 330-pound man held his baby close to him and wept.

The days had grown warmer and it was time to move on. Emmett and Kirby said good-bye to the friends they had made in Delphi.

"I wish you would stay," Pauline said. "You wouldn't have to work on the ferry boat anymore. You could help me run the boarding-house."

Emmett took her hands in his, raised them to his lips, and kissed them. "Pauline, you are a very sweet woman. My son and I were lucky to have met you, and are very grateful for the way you made us feel so welcome. But we can't stay here. We have to go on."

"But why, Emmett?"

"I'm not sure I can answer that. At least, not in the way you could understand."

"Is it because you are dying?"

"What?"

"I've heard that kind of cough before, Emmett. I don't know how much longer you have, but I know I could make you happy in what time you do have left."

"Pauline, you don't know how much I want to do this. But I have sworn to do something, and I must do it. If I stayed here, I wouldn't actually be with you, not really. The part of me that needs to do this thing would take over my heart and soul, and I would have nothing left. You are too good a woman to have to live with that."

With tears in her eyes, Pauline nodded. "I'll always remember you, Emmett. And I'll keep you in my prayers."

"I'm blessed to have met someone like you. It's just too bad that we didn't meet under different circumstances."

"Pa, would you have stayed there?" Kirby asked as they rode out of town. "I mean if you wasn't lookin' for them men, and I wasn't lookin' for Shardeen. Would you have stayed with Mrs. Foley?"

"I don't know, Kirby. I might have," Emmett admitted. "She's a very good woman, and a man can't ask for more than to have a very good woman." He was quiet for a while, then added, "Your ma was a very good woman, too, and I didn't do right by her. I had no business goin' off to war. I was old enough that I didn't really have to go. If I had been home when the Jayhawkers came through—"

"You'd more 'n likely be dead now," Kirby said, interrupting him in mid-sentence. "There were too many of 'em, Pa."

"Maybe. But about Pauline. She deserves a man who will stay with her, and look after her. You 'n I both know that I can't do that. Not with this lung fever I got."

"Maybe when we get farther west and into dry country, it'll get better like the doc said," Kirby suggested.

"Maybe," Emmett said, but there was very little conviction in his voice.

CHAPTER 14

They rode west and north for several days across seemingly end-less plains of tall grass with no sign of human habitation, then they came across a pile of rocks that had not been arranged by nature.

"Pa, look," Kirby said, pointing to the rocks.

They pulled up.

"Some of the mountain men I met told me about them," Emmett said. "That's what I been looking for."

"What's it here for?"

"It's a sign telling travelers that this here is the Santa Fe Trail. North and west of here will be Fort Larned, and north of that will be Pawnee Rock."

"Pawnee Rock? What's that, Pa?"

"Pawnee Rock would be a landmark, Pilgrim." The voice came from behind them.

Turning toward the one who had spoken, Kirby saw, without a doubt, the dirtiest man he had ever seen. The man was dressed en-tirely in buckskin, from the moccasins on his feet to his wide-brimmed leather hat. A white, tobacco-stained beard covered his face. His nose was red and his eyes twinkled with mischief. He was mounted on a spotted pony and had two pack animals with him.

"Ain't no pilgrim, old-timer," Emmett said, low menace in his tone.

"Reckon you're right, at that."

"Where did you come from?" Emmett asked.

"I been watching you two pilgrims from that ravine yonder," he said with a jerk of his head. "You don't know much about traveling in Injun country, do you? It's best to stay off the ridges. You two been standin' out like a third titty." The old mountain man shifted his gaze to Kirby. "What are you staring at, boy?"

The boy leaned forward in his saddle. "Be darned if I rightly know."

The old man laughed. "You got sand to your bottom, all right." He looked at Emmett. "He your'n?"

"My son."

"I'll trade you for 'im," he said, the old eyes sparkling. "Injuns will pay right smart for a strong boy like this 'n."

"My son is not for trade, old-timer."

"Tell you what. I won't call you pilgrim, you don't call me old-timer. Deal?"

Emmett smiled and nodded. "Deal."

"You don't know where you are, do you?"

"Yeah, I know."

"Do you now? And just where would that be?"

"We're somewhere west of the state of Missouri, and east of the Pacific Ocean."

The old man chuckled. "In other words, you're lost as a lizard."

"If you got no particular place to go, you ain't never lost," Emmett said.

Again, the old man laughed. "Well now, you do have a point there. You got names?"

"I'm Emmett. This is my son, Kirby."

"Folks call me Preacher."

"You're a preacher?" Kirby asked, surprised at the response.

"Didn't say I was a preacher. I said that's my handle. That's what folks call me."

Kirby laughed out loud.

"What you laughin' at, boy?"

"I'm laughin' at your name."

"Don't scoff. It ain't nice to scoff at a man's name. If I wasn't a gentle type man, I might let the hairs on my neck get stiff."

"Preacher can't be your real name."

"Well, no, you right about that, but I been called Preacher for so long, that I've near 'bout forgot my Christian name. So, Preacher it'll be. That or nothin'."

"Well, it was nice talkin' with you, but I reckon we'll be goin' on now, Preacher," Emmett said. "Maybe we'll see you again."

Preacher's eyes shifted to the northwest, then narrowed, his lips tightening in a weird smile. "Yep. I reckon you will."

Emmett turned his horse and pointed its nose west-northwest. Kirby reluctantly followed. He would have liked to stay and talk with the old man.

When they were out of earshot, Kirby said, "Pa, that old man was so dirty he smelled."

"He's a mountain man, some away from home base, I'm figuring. More 'n likely trying to get back. Cantankerous old boys, they are. Some of them mean as snakes. I think they get together once a year and bathe."

"But you said you soldiered with some mountain men."

"I did, but they didn't stay that long. They had to get back to the high lonesome."

"Where is the high lonesome?"

"It's more of a condition, than a place. Men like Preacher stay up in the high country for years. Don't do nothing but trap and such. They won't see another human being for a year or more, and not a white man more 'n once ever' two years or so. All they've got is their horses and guns and the whistling wind and the silence of the mountains. They're all alone, and it does something to them. They get notional, funny acting."

"You mean they go crazy?"

"In a way, I'm thinking. I don't know much about them. Nobody does, I don't reckon. But I think maybe that most of the folks who would go off 'n live like that, don't like people all that much to begin with. They crave the lawlessness of open space.

"The mountain men I was with, now, they were some different. They told me about that old man's kind. They're very brave men, son, don't ever doubt that. Probably the bravest in the world. They got to be to live like they do."

Kirby looked behind them. "Pa? That old man is following us, and he's shucked his rifle out of its boot."

Preacher galloped up to the pair, his rifle in his hand. "Don't get nervous. I ain't the one you need to be afeared of, but I do believe we fixin' to get ambushed."

"Ambushed by who?" Emmett asked.

"Kiowa would be my thinkin'. But they could be Pawnee. My eyes ain't as sharp as they once was. But I seen one of 'em stick his head up out of a wash over yonder. He's young or he wouldn't have done that. But that don't mean that the others with him is young."

"How many?"

"Don't know. In this country, one is too many. Do know this—we better be agettin'. If memory serves me, right over yonder, over that ridge, they's a little crick behind the stand of cottonwoods, with a old Buffalo waller in front of it." He looked up, stood up in his stirrups, and cocked his shaggy head. "Here they come, boys. Get agoin'."

Even as he was speaking, the old man slapped Kirby's bay on the rump, and they were galloping off. With the mountain man taking the lead, the three of them rode for the ridge. Cresting the ridge, the riders slid down the incline and galloped into the timber, down into the wallow. Whoops and cries of the Indians were close behind them.

Preacher might well have been past his good years, but the mountain man leaped off his spotted pony, rifle in hand, and was in position and firing as quickly as Emmett and Kirby. Preacher had a Sharps .52. It fired a paper cartridge, but was deadly up to 700 yards or more.

Kirby looked up in time to see a brave fly off his pony, a crimson gash on his naked chest. The Indian hit the ground and didn't move.

Emmett got a buck in the sights, led him on his fast running pony, then fired the Spencer in his hands. The buck was knocked off his pony, bounced once on the ground, then leaped to his feet, dodging for cover. He didn't make it. Preacher shot him in the side and lifted him off his feet, dropping him dead.

Emmett fired six more rounds in a thunderous barrage of black smoke, and the Indians scattered to cover, disappearing behind a ridge, horses and all.

"Scared 'em off," Preacher said. "They ain't used to repeaters. All they know is single shots. Let me get something out of my pack, 'n I'll show you a thing or two."

He went to one of his pack animals, which, along with the other horses, was standing just inside the tree line. He untied one of the side packs and let it fall to the ground, then pulled out the most beautiful rifle Kirby had ever seen.

"Damn!" Emmett said. "The Blue bellies had some of those toward the end of the war. But I never could get my hands on one."

Preacher smiled and pulled another Henry repeating rifle from the pack. Unpredictable as mountain men were, he tossed the second Henry to Emmett, along with a sack of cartridges.

"Now we be friends." Preacher laughed, exposing tobacco-stained stubs of teeth.

"I'll pay you for this," Emmett said, running his hands over the sleek barrel.

"What for? I didn't pay nothin' for either one of 'em," Preacher replied. "I won both of 'em in some shootin'. Besides, somebody's got to look out for the two of you. You're liable to wander around out here and get hurt. It appears to be, you don't neither of you know tip from tat 'bout staying alive in Injun country."

"You may be right," Emmett admitted. He loaded the Henry. "So I thank you kindly."

Preacher looked at Kirby. "Boy, you plannin' on gettin' into this fight? Wait a minute, maybe I better ask you, can you shoot? Iffen you cain't shoot, better stay out of it. Don't want to worry none 'bout you maybe shootin' one of us."

Proud of his son, Emmett answered. "He can shoot. Kirby, pick up the Spencer."

"Better do it quick. Here they come," Preacher said.

"How do you know that, Preacher?" Kirby asked. "I don't see anything."

"Wind just shifted, and I smelled 'em. They close, so get ready."

Kirby wondered how the old man could smell anything over the fumes from his own body.

Emmett, a veteran of four years of continuous war, could not believe an enemy could slip up on him in open daylight. At the sound of Preacher jacking back the hammer of his Henry .44, Emmett saw a big painted up buck almost on top of him. Suddenly, the open meadow was filled with screaming, charging Indians. Emmett brought the buck down with a slug through the chest, flinging the Indian backward, the yelling abruptly cut off in his throat.

The area changed from the peacefulness of summer quiet, to a screaming, gun-smoke-filled hell.

Kirby jerked his gaze to the small creek in front of them. He had seen movement on the right side of the stream. For what seemed an eternity, he watched the young brave, a boy about his own age, leap and thrash through the water. Then he pulled back the hammer of the Spencer, aimed at the brave, and pulled the trigger.

Kirby heard a wild screaming and spun around. His father was locked in hand-to-hand combat with two knife wielding braves. Too close to use the rifle, Kirby jerked the pistol from the holster and fired in one smooth motion. He hit one of the braves in the head, just as his father buried his Arkansas toothpick to the hilt in the chest of the other.

Then as abruptly as they came, the Indians were gone. Two braves lay dead in front of Preacher, two more lay dead in the shallow ravine. The boy Kirby had shot was facedown in the creek, arms outstretched, the waters a deep crimson, the body slowly floating downstream.

A thin finger of smoke lifted from the barrel of the Navy .36 Kirby held in his hand.

Preacher smiled and spat tobacco juice. "You're some swift with that hogleg. Yep. Smoke will suit you just fine. So Smoke it'll be."

"Sir?" Kirby asked.

"Smoke," the old man repeated. "That'll be your name from now on. That's what I aim to call you. Smoke."

Preacher took another .36 Navy Colt from one of the dead Indians, then tossed it to Kirby. "I seen the way you handled that pistol. Ain't never seen no one your age that good with a handgun, and not sure that I've seen anyone full growed who was any better. Now you got yourself two guns."

From another Indian, Preacher took a long-bladed knife in a beaded sheath and handed that to him, as well. "Any man worth his salt out here needs hisself a good knife, too. Most especial someone who calls hisself Smoke."

"I don't call myself Smoke."

"You will."

"Why should I?"

"All famous men needs 'em a moniker, a name other 'n the one they was borned with. I've knowed some right famous men in my day, and Smoke sounds good to me."

"But I ain't famous."

"You're goin' to be, Smoke. Ain't no doubt in my mind. No doubt at all. You're goin' to be a famous man someday, the kind of man folks writes books about."

"I doubt that," Kirby said, but already he was beginning to think of himself as Smoke. He smiled. Yes, he liked that name.

Kirby and Emmett were shocked at what happened next. Preacher scalped the Indians they had killed.

"Good God, man, what are you doing?" Emmett asked.

"What's it look like I'm a' doin'? I'm takin' hair. I know a tradin' post that'll pay a dollar a scalp for ever'one I bring in. I won't do this with a Ute or a Crow. I've lived with them for too long. But I pure dee can't abide a Kiowa or a Pawnee." Carrying the scalps with him, Preacher started back toward the horses. "What we need to do is get out of here now . . . put as much distance between us and the Injuns as we can." He put the scalps into a buckskin bag that hung from one of the pack animals.

"Won't those stink?" Kirby asked.

"They do get ripe," Preacher replied as he mounted his pony.

The three men left the site of the battle at a gallop. Holding the gallop for several miles, they then walked their horses, then galloped them again, then walked them again, so that by late afternoon, Emmett believed they may have ridden as far as thirty miles. They made a quick camp by a creek.

"Get a fire goin'," Preacher said. "I'll get us some grub."

"I'll go hunting if you want," Kirby offered.

"'Preciate the offer, Smoke, but you'd more 'n likely have to shoot our food. Don't know who might be lurkin' around here listenin', so whatever game we take tonight has to be took quiet."

"I guess Smoke's my new name," Kirby said after the old man left the camp afoot. While there was still light, he carefully cleaned and oiled the Navy Colt taken from the dead Indian.

Emmett looked at him. "What do you think about that?"

"You know what? I kinda like it."

They ate an early supper, then doused the fire, carefully checking for any live coals that might touch off a prairie fire, something as feared as any Indian attack, for a racing fire could outrun a galloping horse. They moved on, riding for an hour before pulling into a small stand of timber to make camp for the night.

Preacher spread out his blankets, used his saddle for a pillow, and promptly closed his eyes.

"I'll stand the first watch, *Smoke*," Emmett said, grinning at Kirby. "Then I'll wake Preacher for the second, and you can take the last watch, from two until daylight. Best you go on to sleep now until you're needed."

"All right, Pa."

Just as Kirby was drifting off to sleep, Emmett said, "If you don't like that nickname, son, we can change it."

"It's all right, Pa," the boy murmured, warmed by the wool of the blanket. "Pa? You know what? I kind of like Preacher."

"So do I," Emmett replied.

"That makes both of you good judges of character," the mountain man spoke from his blankets. "Now why don't you two quit all that jawin', 'n let an old man get some rest?"

"Night, Pa, Preacher."

"Night, Smoke," they both replied.

Preacher rolled the boy out of his blankets at two in the morning, into the summer coolness of the plains. The night was hung with the brilliance of a million stars.

"Stay sharp, now, Smoke," Preacher cautioned. "Injuns don't usually attack at night 'cause they think it's bad medicine for them. A brave gets killed at night, his spirit wanders forever, don't never get to the hereafter in peace. But Injuns is notional kind of folk, 'n not all tribes believe the same. Never can tell what they're goin' to do. More 'n likely, if they're out there, they'll hit us at first light, but you don't never know for sure." He rolled over into his blankets and was soon snoring.

The boy poured himself a cup of scalding hot coffee, strong enough to support a horseshoe, then replaced the pot on the rock grate. The fire was fueled by buffalo chips, hot and smokeless, and it couldn't be seen from ten feet away. Preacher had given him a holster for his second weapon and a wide belt from his seemingly never empty packs. Smoke adjusted it so that he was wearing a brace of pistols.

He had no way of knowing—with what had happened in Salcedo and especially in Delphi—that he had already taken the first steps toward creating a legend that would endure as long as writers would write of the West. Men would fear and respect him, women would desire him, children would play games imitating the man called Smoke. Songs would be written and sung about him in the Indian's villages and in the white man's cities.

On this pleasant night, Smoke—he was already thinking of himself as Smoke—was still some time away from being a living legend.

He was just a young man in the middle of a vast open plain watching for savage Indians. He almost dozed off, caught himself, and jerked back awake. He bent forward for another cup of coffee, rubbing his sleepy eyes.

That movement saved his life.

A quivering arrow drove into the tree where, just a second before, he had been resting. Had he not leaned forward *at that precise moment*, the arrow would have driven through his chest.

Smoke drew first the right-hand Colt, then the left-hand gun, his motions almost liquid in their smoothness. The twin Colts were in the hands of one of the few men to whom guns were but an extension of the body. Two Pawnee braves went down under the first two shots. He shifted position. The muzzle flashes were like lightning, and the gunshots like thunder as the Colts roared. Two more bucks were cut down by the .36 caliber balls.

The night, filled with acrid smelling gun smoke, was silent except for the fading sounds of ponies racing away. The Indians wanted no more of that camp. They had lost too many braves.

"I ain't never seen nothing like this!" Preacher explained, walking around the dead and dying Indians. "I knowed Jim Bridger, Kit Carson, Broken Hand Fitzpatrick, uncle Dick Watt, 'n as many as a hunnert other salty old boys, but I ain't never seen nothing to top this here show you just put on. I tell you what, Smoke, you may be a youngster in years, but you'll damn sure do to ride to the river with."

Smoke did not yet know it, but that was the highest compliment a mountain man could ever give to another man.

"Thank you," Smoke said to Preacher as he reloaded the empty cylinders.

July 1867

Early morning, and though most self-respecting roosters had announced the fact long ago, half-a-dozen cocks were still trying to stake a claim on the day. The sun had been up for quite a while but the disc was still hidden by the mountains in the east. The light had already turned from red to white and here and there were signs that Westport Landing was starting another day.

A pump creaked as a housewife began pumping water for her daily chores and somewhere a carpenter was hammering. Janey was awakened by the sounds of commerce. She could scarcely believe that she was living in Kansas, given the hard feelings between Kansas and Missouri during the recent war. But she was in the place that was sometimes called the City of Kansas and sometimes called Kansas City, though it wouldn't acquire that name for a few years to come. It was known as Westport Landing, Kansas.

Getting up, she poured a basin of water and washed her face and hands. She stood by the open window and looked out on the town. She had been there for almost a year. Her baby would be fifteen months old, and she wondered if Becca was speaking. Did Becca know she had a mother? Did she wonder about her mother?

Scarcely a day went by without Janey thinking about Rebecca. Sometimes she considered going back—when she thought she couldn't stand being away any longer—begging Ben for forgiveness and spending time with her daughter. But she never followed through on it. Maybe after the first few weeks, maybe even after the first couple of months, she could have done so. But it was far too late for that.

Westport Landing was considerably more unruly than anyplace she had been. The customers of the house where she worked were rugged men who were more at home in the saddle than in a parlor. Some were hell-raisers when they came to town. Often they let off steam by shooting their guns, if not at each other in some spontaneous fight, then at any target that might catch their fancy.

The most troublesome of all the visitors to the place was a man named Cole Brennen. Twice in the last month, he had abused the woman he was with, and Maggie had told him he wasn't welcome anymore.

As expected, he didn't take that too kindly. He was a member of the city council and threatened Maggie with closure if she ever tried to deny him services.

Maggie Mouchette owned and operated the Pretty Girl and Happy Cowboy House. Janey did not occupy quite as elite a position as she had at the Palace Princess Emporium, but she and Maggie had become very good friends over the past year. As a result, Janey operated as Maggie's second in charge.

As Janey looked outside, a couple freight wagons rolled slowly through the street. The boardwalks were full of people, and a game of horseshoes was being played between two of the buildings on the opposite side of the street.

There was a knock on her door. "Abbigail? Are you ready for some breakfast?" Maggie called.

"Sure, I'll be right down."

Janey had gotten rid of the name Fancy Lil, because just as she didn't want her father or brother to track down Janey Jensen, neither did she want Ben Conyers to find Fancy Lil. She didn't really think there was much chance of him finding her, though. Westport Landing was quite a ways from Dallas.

Most of the citizens of the town had eaten breakfast quite some time ago but, as Maggie said, "The town people have their schedule, we have ours."

The other girls were already sitting at the table when Janey came down. Penelope was holding a cat in her lap.

"Penelope, why do you bring that dirty old cat in here?" one of the girls asked.

"Hortense isn't a dirty cat. He cleans himself all the time," Penelope said. "Don't you, Hortense?"

"That's another thing. If it's a tomcat, why do you call him Hortense?"

"Because I like the name."

"You are a strange person."

An older woman wearing a black dress and a white pinafore came in. "Ladies, breakfast is served."

The days passed leisurely for Maggie's girls. Some napped, some played cards, and some read. Normally Janey was one who enjoyed reading, but she had agreed to go to town with Maggie. When any of the girls went to town, they wore no makeup of any kind and plain dresses, which made them appear no different from any of the other women of the town.

Despite the fact that they purposely dressed down, all the girls were known on sight. When they went somewhere, they were generally shunned, not only by the "good" girls of the town, but quite often by the same men who frequently came calling on them at night.

Not everyone shunned them. One who was always nice to them was Elmer Gleason. He had arrived in town at about the same time Janey did. She heard, once, that he had ridden with Asa Briggs during the war, and though she was not aware that her own brother had ridden with him, she knew that many young men from the county had. It was quite possible that if Elmer Gleason ever learned her real name that he would know who she was. But he would never connect Abbigail Fontaine "from New Orleans" to Janey Jensen.

Elmer was a shotgun guard for the Westport-Landing-to-Wichita stage line, so he was often gone. When he was in town though, he was a frequent guest of the Pretty Girl and Happy Cowboy House, and had even been with Janey a few times.

His visits with her were limited though. Her time didn't cost as much here as it did back in Dallas, but she was still the most expensive girl on the line. As he once said, "In the dark, they all look alike."

Elmer was in the hardware store when Janey and Maggie stepped inside. When he saw them, he smiled, and touched the brim of his hat. Janey smiled back at him. Unfortunately, Elmer wasn't the only one in the store. Cole Brennen was there as well.

"Mr. Deckert," Brennen said to the proprietor of the hardware store. "You do know what these two women are, don't you?"

"As far as I'm concerned, they are customers," Deckert said. "The young women from Miss Mouchette's establishment stop by here from time to time, and they have always been good customers."

"Yes, well, they may not be good customers much longer. I intend to introduce a city ordinance which will close that den of iniquity, once and for all."

"Then where will you go, Brennen?" Elmer asked.

"What? Why you insolent cur! I'll sue you for libel and slander."

"I don't know what them fancy words mean," Elmer said. "But if you're tryin' to say you ain't never before been to Miss Mouchette's place, then I'm callin' you a liar, 'cause I've seen you there."

Brennen wheezed and gasped for breath, then angrily spun around and stomped out of the building.

Maggie laughed. "Elmer, next time you come to my place, I'll set you up for a free drink."

"Just a free drink?" Elmer asked.

"And a visit with one of the girls," Maggie added.

"That's more like it. All right, missy, I'll be by tonight."

CHAPTER 15

Elmer did show up that night, and he had his drink—whiskey—then claimed Penelope for his free visit.

But he wasn't the only one who showed up. Cole Brennen also arrived with another man that neither Janey nor Maggie recognized.

"This here is Marvin Lewis with the Westport Landing City Marshal's office. I've brought him with me to be a witness to what's goin' on here. However, if you treat us right, why, nothin' will happen to you, 'n you can go on doing business just like you always have."

"You are a pathetic excuse of a man, Brennen," Maggie said.

Brennen's malevolent smile stretched the skin tight across his face, giving his head the appearance of a skull. "I may be. But it seems to me like you got no choice but to be nice to us."

By midnight, all the visitors were gone except for Elmer, who had opted to spend the night with Penelope, and Cole Brennen, who was in one of the downstairs rooms with a girl named Louise. Even Marvin Lewis, who had come with Brennen, was gone.

Janey and Maggie were alone in the parlor, sitting in front of the fireplace, drinking a glass of wine.

"I don't usually pry into the past lives of my girls," Maggie said. "Almost all of them have a story as to why they got into this business. Some of them share it and some don't. Before I ask you to share your story, I'll tell you mine.

"I'm the daughter of a preacher man. I married the son of a very rich Boston banker, but he treated me like dirt, so I left him. No divorce. I just left him. Because of who he was, I had to leave Boston."

She smiled. "But I took ten thousand dollars with me when I left. That's how I was able to buy this house and start my business here."

Janey thought of the two thousand dollars she had taken from Kirby, but before she responded, they heard a blood-curdling scream coming from Louise's room.

"What is going on in there?" Maggie asked, jumping up quickly, with an expression of anger and concern on her face. "Louise, what is it? What's happening?"

Maggie ran to Louise's room with Janey close behind her. She opened the door and they saw Brennen, his naked body shining gold in the light of the lamp. He was holding a bloody knife in his hand. Louise had her hand across a bloody cheek.

"He cut me!" Louise cried.

Maggie picked up a vase and held it over her head as she approached Brennen. "Get out of here!" she shouted angrily. "Get out of here now! And don't you ever come back!"

Brennen suddenly thrust his hand forward, burying the knife up to its hilt in Maggie's chest. With an expression of pain and shock on her face, Maggie stepped back from him.

"You've killed her!" Janey screamed.

Brennen turned to face her. He was nearly covered in blood, and the reflected flame in his eyes could have been the fires of hell. The smile was demonic, and he held the knife out toward her. "You're next," he said in a low hiss.

Janey backed away from him, stumbling into the chair where Brennen had put his clothes. She stuck her hand back to keep from falling and felt his pistol!

Instantly and instinctively, she pulled the pistol out of its holster and brought it around, firing just as Brennen lunged for her. The bullet hit him in the chest. The impact knocked him back against the fireplace, and he slid down to the hearth, leaving a smear of blood on the bricks behind him.

Elmer Gleason raced into the room with a gun in his hand. He didn't have to ask what happened. In one all-encompassing look, he took it in. "Girl, throw what clothes together as fast as you can. We're getting out of here."

"I had no choice!" Janey said. "He killed Maggie and he was coming after me."

"That's true," Louise said. "Abbigail didn't have any choice!"

"I believe you, Louise," Elmer said. "I believe both of you. But this feller is on the city council, 'n the man who come here earlier is a deputy marshal. They ain't nobody goin' to believe you. That's why we got to get out of here now."

"Elmer, no. If you run with me, they'll be after you, too."

"I need to get out of here, anyway," Elmer said. "I made a few rides with a feller over in Missouri called Jesse James. So I expect my welcome here is goin' to be wore out pretty quick."

Smoke and Emmett were about to partake in an event that would be one of the last of its kind. It was called Rendezvous, a gathering of the breed of men civilization sometimes raised a dubious head toward and pushed the mountain men into history. The smoke of scores of campfires could be seen from some distance away. As Smoke and his father drew closer, they became aware of the sounds of Rendezvous and the aromas of roasting meat from the many cooking fires.

In the early days of trapping, before the war and the Western migration, Rendezvous would be the biggest city between the Pacific Ocean and St. Louis. Those days were over. The mountain men that remained were, for the most part, advanced in years, heading for the sunset of their lives. They had spent their youth, their best years, and the midpoint of their lives, in elements where one careless move could result in either sudden death or slow torture from hostiles.

Mountain men were not easily impressed, but those gathered were standing and watching as Smoke and his father rode slowly into the ruins of the old post, rifles across their saddles. Preacher had already spread the word about the boy called Smoke.

As did many boys of that hard era, he looked older than his years. His face was deeply tanned. His shoulders and arms were lean, but hard with muscle.

"I don't know. He don't look all that much to me," an aging mountain man said to a friend.

"Neither did Kit Carson if you recall," his friend replied. "Hell, he warn't but four inches over five feet, but he were one hell of a man."

"The boy is faster than a snake, Preacher says."

The mountain man cocked his eye at his friend. "Yeah, but don't forget, Preacher has been known to spin a tall tale ever' now and then, when he thinks it might be a mite more interestin' than tellin' the truth."

172 William W. Johnstone

"Yeah, but not this time, I wager. Look at this kid. He's got a mean look to his eyes."

Smoke and Emmett sat their horses and stared. Neither had ever seen anything like the colorful assemblage. The men, all of whom were over sixty years old, were dressed in wild, bright colors—buckskin breeches and shirts, beaded leggings, wide red, blue, or yellow sashes about their waists. Some were wearing cord trousers with silk shirts shining in a rainbow of colors. All were beaded and booted and bearded. Some held long muzzle-loading Kentucky rifles. A few had lever-action repeating rifles. Many were decorated with colorfully dyed rawhide strings dangling from the barrel, the shot and powder bags decorated with beads.

It would not be the last, but nearly the last great gathering of the magnificent breed of men called mountain men.

When Emmett and Smoke spotted Preacher, they couldn't believe their eyes. They sat on their horses and stared.

He was clean and his beard was well trimmed. He wore new buckskins, new leggings, and a red sash around his waist. His eyes sparkled with a light they had never seen. "Howdy," he called. "Y'all light and sit, boys."

"I don't believe it," Emmett said. "His face is clean."

"There's water to wash in over there," Preacher said, pointing. "Good strong soap, too. But you'd best dump what's in the barrel and refill it. It's got fleas in it along with the ticks."

Elmer took Janey to the one-room cabin where he lived, just on the edge of town. It had been the middle of the night when they left the Pretty Girl and Happy Cowboy House. Nobody had seen him sneak her into his place.

She stayed in the cabin for two weeks, not daring to show herself outside. The wisdom of that decision was borne out when Elmer brought a newspaper by a couple days later.

MURDER SO FOUL

Cole Brennen, a sterling citizen and member of the city council, was murdered on the 19th instant. Brennen and Deputy Marshal Marvin Lewis were investigating a residence on the suspicion that activity of an illicit nature might be taking place there. It had been re-

ported that the owner of the house, Maggie Mouchette, was running not a boarding house for young women as her city license stated, but a bawdy house.

Deputy Lewis reports that, upon confirming that such was true, Brennen informed them that he would be reporting the true nature of the business to the authorities. That was when two of the occupants of the house attacked him. Although Brennen was able to subdue Miss Mouchette, the other woman, Abbigail Fontaine, managed to secure a pistol and shot at him. The ball, thus energized, struck Brennen in the chest, taking terrible effect.

Abbigail Fontaine has since disappeared, and authorities have asked that anyone who can give information as to her location should provide such to Marshal Kilgore.

"Lewis wasn't even there," Janey said after she read the story. "But Penelope was. Why didn't they ask her what happened?"

"I'm sure she did tell them what happened, but bein' as she is what she is, why it's most likely they didn't pay her no never mind," Elmer said.

"Elmer, what am I going to do? I can't stay here in your cabin forever."

"How'd you like to go West?"

"Go West?"

"They's a riverboat leavin' first thing in the mornin', headin' up the Missouri toward a place called Montana. I figure to get us on it."

"How am I going to get to the boat without being seen?"

"You let me worry about that."

When Elmer returned to the cabin that night, he showed Janey the tickets for the riverboat *Cora Two*. "You're Mrs. John Smith. I'm John Smith. I figured maybe we should go up river as husband and wife. Folks that's lookin' for you won't be lookin' for you to be travelin' with a husband. Most especial since we'll be usin' names that ain't our'n."

"And John Smith is so original," Janey said.

"Yeah, I thought it was pretty good my ownself. It was the first name I come up with," Elmer said, failing to catch the sarcasm in Janey's voice.

Janey smiled. Who was she to criticize this man who had made all the arrangements to get her away? And, she was pretty sure that once she was away from Westport Landing, she would be safe. The authorities would be looking for a woman named Abbigail Fontaine from New Orleans. She had never given her real last name to anyone, not even to Maggie, nor had she ever shared with anyone that she had come from Missouri, by way of Texas.

It was after dark when they left Elmer's house, and they reached the river without arousing any suspicion. The *Cora Two* was tied up at the landing, a long, white stern wheeler with three decks and a pilot house. Two chimneys sprouted from just aft of the pilot house.

Once they were aboard, Janey stepped out onto the hurricane deck, which was between the boiler deck and the Texas deck, and looked out over the town of Westport Landing. It was quiet and dark, and she could hear a dog barking way off in the distance. The city was so peaceful at that hour of the night. The loudest sounds were the gentle lapping of the river against the hull and the creaking of the boat at its hawsers as it pulled at the current while at anchor.

She walked forward and stood against the railing to look out over the bow. Down on the boiler deck she could see neat stacks of cargo, ricks of firewood, and the men, women, and even children who held steerage tickets. They would be making the journey on that deck. They had no bunks, and would have to bed down wherever they could find room, unprotected against the weather.

A cool breeze came up and Janey shivered, then hugged herself. She thought of the river they would be following, stretched out before them for many miles. It was, she decided, a metaphor, not only bridging the distance she must travel, but reaching into her future as well. What did lie before her?

Smoke stood in front of the trading post at dawn. His pa was mounted; he wasn't.

"You do understand my ridin' off alone, don't you, boy? I wouldn't be leavin' you, but I've seen you when you was up against it, 'n you come through just fine. You can handle them guns better 'n anyone I ever saw, so I ain't worried none 'bout you bein' able to take care of yourself. But there's some things you're goin' to need to learn 'bout livin' out here. I cain't think of nobody more able to teach you them things than Preacher. Problem is, it's goin' to take you some time to learn all you need to learn, 'n me 'n you know that I don't have that much time left. So, I aim to leave you here to get your learnin' while

I go out lookin' for them men that kilt your brother. You got 'ny problem with that?"

"I reckon not," Smoke replied quietly. "I know you're doin' what you feel you got to do."

"You're a good boy, Kirby. No, you're a good man. I know that when you was growin' up, you might sometimes thought I was favorin' Luke. I warn't. It was just that he was older and a mite easier for me to understand. But there ain't no man ever lived who had himself a son he was more proud of than I am of you. I'm glad the Good Lord give us this time to be together, so's I could find that out.

"Bye, Kirby." Emmett smiled. "I mean, bye, Smoke. That'll be your name from now on."

He turned and rode away. He had taken only a little of the money with him, leaving the rest with Smoke. He rode for some distance, then stopped, turned his horse, and waved at his son. Then he was gone, dipping out of sight, over the rise of a small hill.

Smoke knew, at that moment, that he would never see his father again and tried to swallow the knot that was in his throat.

For the entire time of their good-bye, Preacher had sat on the porch of the trading post, watching, saying nothing.

Smoke turned away from the road and looked up at the man who was to become his mentor. "He won't be back."

Preacher spat a stream of tobacco off the porch and onto the dusty ground. "Some things, Smoke, a man's just got to do before his time on earth slips away. Your pa has things to do. If you're wantin' to cry, I want you to know that there ain't no shame in it."

Smoke squared his shoulders. "I'm a man. I lived alone, I worked the land, and I paid the taxes all by myself. And I haven't cried since Ma died."

"Ain't nobody ever goin' to question whether or not you're a man, Smoke. You're as much a man as anyone I've ever knowed."

Smoke put his foot on the steps. "Let's get outfitted." He climbed the steps and entered the trading post. He bought a new Henry repeating rifle, one hundred rounds of .44 caliber ammunition for it, and an extra cylinder for his left hand .36, then they rode out.

Preacher told him he knew of a friendly band of Indians up north of the post. He'd see to it that Smoke got himself a pair of moccasins and leggings and a buckskin jacket, fancy beaded.

"I ain't got that kind of money to waste, Preacher."

"Ain't going to cost you nothing. I know the lady who will make them for you."

"She must like you pretty well."

Preacher smiled. "She's my daughter."

On board the *Cora Two*, a long, deep throated blast blew from the boat's horn, then the captain stepped out of the pilot house. Lifting a megaphone to his lips, he called forward to the main deck bow. "Lead man!"

"Lead man, aye!" an unseen voice called back from the front of the boat.

"Sound the bottom!"

"Aye, Cap'n!"

"We must be in shallow water," Elmer said.

Janey walked up to the front of the boat. The soundings had been taken frequently during the long journey upriver, and she was familiar with the routine.

"By the mark two!" the lead man called. To make certain that his call was heard in the pilot house, it was repeated by someone up on the Texas Deck.

The lead man continued to call his soundings, which were then echoed, both calls intoned so melodically that it was almost as if the men were singing. Janey had actually grown to appreciate them, and enjoyed listening to the calls as they played against the rhythmic slap of the paddlewheel in the water.

During the trip upriver the boat had to proceed very cautiously because of shallow water. Three times they had encountered sandbars with the water so shallow that it was necessary to "grasshopper" over them with long heavy spars carried vertically on derricks near the bow. The ends of the spars were dropped to the bottom, tops slanted forward, and with block, tackle, cable, and capstan, lifted and pushed the boat forward as if on crutches while the paddle wheel thrashed furiously. After each splash down, the spars were reset for the next "hop," until the boat was free.

At the moment, they seemed to be proceeding upriver at a steady, brisk pace.

Seventy-one days after the *Cora Two* left Westport Landing, Janey stood on the hurricane deck and watched the bluffs slide by on the south bank as the boat worked its way up the Missouri River to Ft. Benton.

Elmer came over to stand beside her. "Well, our long journey is nearly over. The cap'n told me we'd reach Fort Benton today."

"Elmer, I can't thank you enough for helping me out the way you did. I mean, you gave up your job and everything."

Elmer chuckled. "Ridin' shotgun on a stagecoach ain't that much of a job. It was about time I was movin' on."

The *Cora Two* beat its way against the current as it approached around a wide, sweeping bend. Smoke was pouring from the twin chimneys and the engine steam-pipe was booming as loudly as if the town were under a cannonading. With the engine clattering and the paddle wheel slapping at the water, it approached the Ft. Benton landing.

"Deck men, fore and aft, stand by to throw out the lines!" the captain called.

"Aye, Cap'n, standing by!" the first mate called back as two men rushed to the front of the boat and stood side by side, holding the ropes.

At the last minute, the engine was reversed, and the paddle started whirling in the opposite direction, causing the water to froth at the action. The reversing paddle wheel held the speed of the boat until the movement through the water was but a slow, gentle glide up to the dock. Waiting stevedores stood ready to receive the lines.

"Heave out your lines!" the first mate shouted, and both ropes were tossed ashore. One of the men on the boat deck walked his rope back to the stern where he wrapped it securely around a stanchion. The men ashore pulled on the lines—fore and aft—so that the boat was pulled sideways until it was snug up against the dock.

"Well, missy, we're here," Elmer said. "You got 'ny ideas as to what you might do next?"

Janey smiled. "Don't worry about me, Elmer. For the next few years, at least for as long as I can keep my looks, I'll always be able to make a living."

Elmer laughed out loud. "I reckon you will."

Janey checked into the Grand Mountain Hotel. Once she was in her room she went through her dresses and selected one that left little to the imagination. Donning the dress, she got out her powders and paints, and with an artistry developed over the last few years, she transformed her face, combining subtle eye shadows with bold lashes and mascara. A crimson smear across her lips completed the transformation, and when she walked through the lobby of the hotel a short while later, not one person would have connected her with the woman who had registered as Fannie Webber.

Exiting the hotel, Janey made her way to the largest and grandest saloon in town, the Gold Strike. She went inside, strode up to the bar, and ordered a drink.

"What kind of drink?" the bartender asked.

"I expect, if I'm going to be drinking with men all day, you'd better give me something that doesn't make me drunk." Janey fixed him with a penetrating stare.

"Uh . . . drinking with men?" the bartender asked.

The well-dressed man sitting at a table close to the bar got up and walked over to stand beside her. "Henry, I do believe this young lady is applying for a job."

"I might be," Janey replied, turning her charm toward the man. "If so, who should I see?"

"That would be me. The name is Andrew McGhee. And you would be?"

Janey thought for a moment, wondering if she should use the same name she used when she checked into the hotel. "The name I use will depend upon whether or not I can get a room here in the saloon."

McGhee laughed out loud. "For you, my finest room."

Janie's smile broadened, and she stuck out her hand. "It's nice to meet you, Andrew. My name is Fannie Webber."

CHAPTER 16

July 1869

It had been two years since Emmett rode off on his own, and Smoke had not heard anything from him since. He wasn't surprised by that, given that Emmett had written only two letters the whole time he was away fighting the war.

Nothing of the boy was left. Smoke was a man, fully grown and hard in body, face, and eyes. The bay he had ridden west hadn't survived the first year after Emmett left. The horse had fallen on the ice and broken his leg. Smoke had had to put him down, but Preacher found another horse for him, a large, mean-tempered Appaloosa. The Indian had sold him cheap, because he hadn't been able to break him.

Strangely, not only to the Indian who sold him, but to other Indians who knew the animal, the horse seemed to bond immediately with Smoke. He was a stallion, and he was mean, his eyes warning any knowledgeable person away. In addition to its distinctive markings—the mottled hide, vertically striped hooves, and pale eyes—the Appaloosa had a perfectly shaped numeral seven between his eyes. And that became his name—Seven.

"Smoke, I've done learned you about as much as I know how to learn anyone," Preacher said one summer morning. "There ain't no doubt in my mind, but that you could light in the middle of the mountains some'ers and live as good as me or any other mountain man I ever knowed could.

"But truth to tell, the time of the mountain man is gone. There warn't even no Rendezvous this year, 'n I don't know if they'll ever be another 'n. Just be glad you got to see one of 'em when you did."

"I am glad," Smoke said. "If I live to be as old a man as you are, I'll still remember gettin' to go to that Rendezvous."

"Whoa, now! Are you tellin' me that's all you're goin' to remember? That you ain't goin' to 'member nothin' else I learned you in all this time?"

Smoke laughed. "I reckon I'll be rememberin' that, as well."

Shortly after that conversation an old mountain man rode into their camp. "You just as ugly as I remembered, Preacher," he said in the form of greeting.

"I didn't think you was even still alive, Grizzly," Preacher said. "I heard you got eat up by a pack o' wolves. No, wait. That ain't right. Now that I think on it, they said you was so old and dried up that the wolves didn't want nothin' to do with you."

Smoke had already learned that mountain men insulted each other whenever possible. It was their way of showing affection.

"Can I talk in front of the boy?" Grizzly asked.

"Anythin' you can tell me, you can say in front of him," Preacher replied.

Smoke poured himself a cup of coffee and waited.

"A man rode into the Hole about two months ago. All shot up, he was. And 'sides that, he had a bad cough."

"Is he still alive?" Smoke blurted.

The old man turned cold eyes toward him. "Don't ever interrupt a man when he's palaverin'. 'Tain't polite. One thing about Indians, they know manners. They know to allow a man to speak his piece without interrupting."

"Sorry," Smoke said.

"Accepted. No, he's dead. Strange man. Dug his own grave. Come the time, I buried him. He's planted on that there little plain at the base of the high peak east side of the canyon. Zenobia Peak, it's called. You remember it, Preacher?"

Preacher nodded.

The old mountain man reached inside his war bag and pulled out a heavy sack and tossed it to Smoke. "This would be your'n, I reckon. It's from your pa, a right smart amount of gold." Again, he dipped into the war bag and pulled out a rawhide-wrapped flat object. "And this is a piece of paper with words on it. Names, your pa said, of the men who put lead in him. He said you'd know what to do, but for me to tell you, don't do nothing rash."

His business done, the old man rose to his feet. "I done what I give my word I'd do. Now I'll be goin' on."

Smoke had purposely held off reading the letter until he found his pa's grave. When he did find it, he used a rock to chisel his pa's name onto it.

EMMETT JENSEN

BORN 1815 DIED 1869

He wasn't sure that 1815 was correct, but he figured it was close enough, especially since he was the only relative left who would ever see it, or even care about it. He wasn't counting Janey.

With the words chiseled onto the stone, Smoke moved it over to the mound of earth that was the gravesite. The stone was big and hard to move, and he was glad. That meant it would be too heavy for any vandals to mess with it for no reason other than to make mischief.

Not until the tombstone was put into position did Smoke turn his attention to the letter. He opened it and read it by the fading light.

Son,

I found some of the men who killed your brother Luke and stoled the gold that belonged to the Gray. They was more of them than I first thought. I killed two of them but they got lead in me and I had to hightail it out. Ackerman is the man Luke thought was his best friend, and the one that betrade him. He got away.

Came here, but not going to make it. Son, you don't owe nothin' to the cause of the Gray. So don't get it in your mind you do.

I got word that your sis Janey left that gambler. Don't know where she is now, but I wouldn't fret much about her. She is mine, but I think she is trash. Don't know what she got that bad streek from.

I'm gettin' tared and seein is hard. I love you Smoke.

Pa

"You're goin' out after 'em now, ain't you," Preacher said. "The fella that kilt your ma, and the ones that kilt your brother and your pa." It was more a statement than a question.

"Yeah, I am," Smoke said.

"Like I said when your pa left, they's some things a man just has to do."

Over the next couple months, Smoke's justice was thorough and extreme.

Two names he learned about belonged to men who had been complicit in shooting his brother, stealing the Confederate gold, and ultimately killing his pa. Ted Casey was the fourth man who'd stolen the Confederacy gold with Stratton, Richards, and Potter—the men Emmett had set out to find and kill. Ackerman had ridden with Quantrill. Smoke didn't know Ackerman's first name, but he'd learned from someone he met that the Confederate deserter owned a ranch just outside Canon City, Colorado.

"Sounds like all them boys done right good for themselves," Preacher said. "They all come out here and commenced ranchin'."

"They started ranchin' on the gold they stole from the South after shootin' my brother," Smoke said sourly.

Casey's place—TC Ranch—was close by so they headed there first. The shootout was deadly, with the ranch hands putting up quite a fight before they were killed. Casey wasn't among those killed at the ranch, but Smoke found him, then hung him in front of a sheriff and scores of people from the nearby town. Nobody made any real effort to stop him.

"Now," Smoke said. "I'm goin' to Canon City."

"*We're* goin', you mean," Preacher said.

"All right, we're goin' to Canon City."

"Oreodelphia," Preacher said.

"What?"

"That's what they wanted to name it. Oreodelphia, but there couldn't nobody hardly even say it, let alone spell it, so they wound up callin' it Canon City."

Smoke frowned, thinking that was more information than he needed to know at the moment. "Do you know how to get there?"

"I know."

"Then why are we standing here jawboning?"

"Boy, you got to learn patience, you know that?"

"What is his name?" Ackerman asked.

"Smoke."

"Smoke? Somebody named Smoke killed Casey and all his hands?"

"His last name is Jensen. I was told that would mean somethin' to you."

Ackerman smiled. "Luke had a brother 'n a sister he used to talk about some. His sister was named Janey. Accordin' to Luke, she was a real good looker. She must be somethin' by now. His brother was named Kirby. I ain't never heard of anyone named Smoke Jensen."

"Well, from what I've heard, he's Emmett Jensen's son."

"Damn," Ackerman said. "Then it has to be the one Luke said was Kirby. Smoke must just be the name he's took for some reason. And he's comin' here, you say?"

"That's what I've been told."

"All right. We'll just take care of 'im when he gets here. Once we kill him, there won't be nobody left but the sister. An' she ain't likely to go out after nobody."

For two days, Smoke and Preacher waited and relaxed in Canon City, making a special effort to keep out of trouble. Smoke bathed twice behind the barbershop, and Preacher told him if he didn't stop that, he was going to come down with some dreadful illness.

The mountain man and the gunfighter were civil to the men and polite to the ladies. Some of the ladies batted their eyes and swished their bustled fannies as they passed by Smoke, but he paid them no attention.

"You boys are sure taking your time buying supplies," the sheriff noted on the second day.

"We like to think things through before buying," Preacher told him. "Smoke here is a right cautious man when it comes to partin' with the greenback. You might even call him tight."

The sheriff didn't find that amusing. "You boys wouldn't be waiting for Ackerman to make a move, would you?"

"Ackerman?" Smoke looked at the sheriff. "What is an Ackerman?"

The sheriff's smile was grim. "What do you boys do for a living? I have a law on the books about vagrants."

"I'm retired," Preacher told him. "Enjoying the sunset of my years, I am. Smoke here, he runs a string of horses."

"Would you like to buy a horse?" Smoke asked. "I've got some really nice ones, and bein' as you are with the law, I can give you a real good deal."

"I ought to run you both out of this town."

"Why?" Smoke asked. "On what charge? We haven't caused you any trouble."

"Yet." The sheriff's back was stiff with anger as he walked away. The man knew a set up when he saw one.

But his feelings were mixed. Ackerman and his bunch of rowdies were all troublemakers, and he owed them nothing. He swung no wide political loop in this country, and there were persistent rumors that Ackerman had been a thief and a murderer during the war, as well as a deserter. The sheriff could not abide a coward.

He sighed. If he was right in reading the young man called Smoke, Ackerman's future looked very bleak.

A hard ridden horse hammered the street into dust. A cowhand from the Bar X slid to a halt in front of the sheriff's office. "Ackerman and his bunch is ridin' in, Sheriff," the cowhand said, still panting from his ride. "They're huntin' bear. He told me to tell you he's going to kill this kid called Smoke and anyone else that gets in his way."

The sheriff's smile grudgingly filled with admiration. The kid's patience had paid off. Ackerman had made his boast and his threat, which meant that anything the kid did now could only be called self-defense.

The sheriff thanked the cowboy and told him to hunt a hole to hide in. He crossed the street and told his deputy to clear the street from the apothecary to the blacksmith shop.

In five minutes, the main street resembled a ghost town. A yellow dog was the only living thing that had not cleared out. Behind curtains, closed doors, and shuttered windows, men and women watched and waited, anticipating the roar of gunfire from the street.

At the edge of town, Ackerman, a bull of a man with small, mean eyes, stopped for a moment. With a small wave, he started the five cowhands with him down the street, riding slowly, six abreast.

Standing on the porch of the hotel with Smoke, Preacher stuffed his mouth full of chewing tobacco, then they walked out into the street to face the six men.

"I've come for you, kid," said the big man in the center of the riders.

"Oh? Who are you?" Smoke asked.

"You know who I am, kid. I'm Ackerman."

"Ah yes!" Smoke said. "I do know that. You're the man who was supposed to be my brother's best friend, but you helped kill him by shooting him in the back. Then you stole the gold he was guarding."

Inside the hotel, pressed against the wall, the desk clerk listened intently, his mouth open in anticipation of gunfire.

"You're a liar. I didn't shoot your brother. That was Potter and his bunch."

"You stood by and watched it. Then you stole the gold."

"It was war, kid."

"But you were on the same side," Smoke said. "That not only makes you a killer, it makes you a traitor and a coward."

"I'll kill you for saying that!"

"You'll burn in hell a long time before I'm dead," Smoke told him.

Ackerman grabbed for his pistol.

The street exploded in gunfire and black powder fumes. Horses screamed and bucked in fear. One rider was thrown to the dust by his lunging mustang.

Smoke took the men on the left, Preacher the men on the right. The battle lasted no more than ten or twelve seconds. When the noise and the gun smoke cleared, five men lay in the street, two of them dead. Two more would die from their wounds. The one shot in the side would live. Ackerman had been shot three times—once in the belly, once in the chest, and one ball had taken him in the side of the face as the muzzle of the .36 had lifted him with each blast. Dead, he still sat in his saddle. The big man finally leaned to one side and toppled from his horse, one booted foot hanging up in the stirrup. The horse shied, then began walking down the dusty street, dragging Ackerman and leaving a bloody trail on the ground behind him.

The excited clerk ran out the door. "I heard it all! You were right, Mr. Smoke. Yes, sir. Right all the way." He looked at Smoke. "Why, you've been wounded, sir."

A slug had nicked the young man on the cheek, another had punched a hole in the fleshy part of his left arm, high up. Both were minor wounds.

Preacher had been grazed on the leg. He spat into the street. "Damn near swallowed my terbacky."

"I never saw a draw that fast," a man spoke from the storefront. "It was a blur."

The sheriff and the deputy came out of the jail, walking down the bloody, dusty street. Both were carrying Greeners, double-barreled, twelve-gauge shotguns.

"Right down the street," the sheriff said, pointing, "is the doctor's office. Get yourselves patched up and then get out of town. You have one hour."

"Sheriff, it was a fair fight," the desk clerk said. "I seen it."

The sheriff never took his eyes off Smoke. "One hour," he repeated.

"We'll be gone." Smoke wiped a smear of blood from his cheek.

Townspeople began hauling the bodies off. The local photographer set up his cumbersome equipment and began popping flash powder, sealing the gruesome scene for posterity. He also took a picture of Smoke.

The editor of the paper walked up to stand by the sheriff. He watched the old man and the young gun hand walk down the street. He truly had seen it all. The old man had killed one man and wounded another. The young man had killed four. "What's the young man's name?"

"His name is Smoke Jensen. But if you ask me, he's the devil."

"Your pa would be pleased," Preacher said as they rode out of town within the hour assigned by the sheriff. "Do you plan to get the other men he was looking for?"

"Yes, I do. But I'm going after Shardeen first."

"Before you start out, I want you to come to Denver with me. I've got a fella there I'd like for you to meet."

"Somebody who can help me find Shardeen?"

"You might say that," Preacher replied, without being any more specific.

It took them three days to get to Denver.

Preacher led Smoke to a low-lying building made of white limestone. A United States flag flew from the flagpole out front, and as they started into the building, Smoke saw a sign chiseled above the doorway. UNITED STATES FEDERAL OFFICE BUILDING.

"What are we going in here for?"

"You're askin' questions again. Didn't I tell you a long time ago that when words is goin' outta your mouth, nothin' can be comin' in your ears? You learn quicker if you're just quiet and pay attention," Preacher said.

Smoke smiled. "Have you always been such a cantankerous old fart?"

"Pretty much," Preacher said.

Both men were wearing buckskins, and both were a little more gamey than the average citizen of Denver. When Swayne Hodge, the office clerk, looked up and saw the two men coming in, he became a little agitated. "Gentlemen, gentlemen, are you lost?"

"Pilgrim, I been out here more 'n fifty years 'n I ain't never been lost but one time. I cain't say as I was all that lost then, since it didn't take me more 'n a month to find my way back to the trail."

"But you *do* know that this is a federal office building, don't you?"

"I didn't exactly figure it to be a house of ill repute," Preacher said.

"Oh, my," Hodge said, clearly discomforted by the vulgarity.

"Preacher! What are you doing here?" Another voice spoke openly and without reservation.

"Excuse me, Marshal Holloway, do you actually *know* these, uh, gentlemen?" Hodge asked, stumbling over the word *gentlemen*.

"I don't know both of them," the marshal said. "But I certainly know the older gentleman. Preacher, come into my office and introduce me to your young friend."

Hodge remained standing, watching with his mouth agape as Uriah B. Holloway, United States Marshal for the Colorado District, holding his commission by U.S. Senate confirmation since April 10, 1866, led the two unwashed men into his office.

"Have a seat, men," Marshal Holloway offered.

"Thank ye, kindly, Uriah." Preacher held his hand out toward Smoke. "This here is Smoke Jensen."

Holloway frowned. "Smoke? His name is Smoke?"

"It's as much Smoke as my name is Preacher."

The marshal chuckled. "All right, Preacher, I'll go along with that. Smoke, it is good to meet you."

"Marshal," Smoke replied, taking the lawman's extended hand.

"Now, what can I do for you?"

"Have you ever heard of a man named Angus Shardeen?" Preacher asked.

Holloway's eyes narrowed. "Yes, I've heard of him. What about him?"

"First, let me ask what you know about him," Preacher replied.

"He has federal and state arrest warrants out on him," Holloway replied. "He's wanted for murder, robbery, arson, and probably half a dozen other things."

"Do you have any idea where he might be now?"

Holloway shook his head. "I can't say as I do. I do know, however, that he has some bad men with him."

"An army?" Smoke asked.

"You might say that. Angus Shardeen was a colonel in the Union Army during the war . . . though there are some who dispute that. He was actually a Jayhawker, operating at the head of a gang of guerrillas, supposedly riding in support of Union troops. But his tactics were so brutal, and quite frankly, so self-enriching, that if he ever did actually hold a commission, it was probably withdrawn.

"Since the end of the war, he has continued the guerrilla operations using many of the same men, only it is without regard to any cause, other than his own."

"Bein' as you are a U.S. Marshal, would you have the authority to go after 'im, no matter where he is?" Preacher asked.

Holloway nodded. "I would."

"And say there was somebody who was a Deputy U.S. Marshal, say it was someone that you appointed. Would that fella also be able to go after Shardeen, no matter where he might be?"

"Yes, he would. Tell me, Preacher, why are you asking me all these questions? Do you know where Shardeen is?"

"I don't have 'ny idee where he is, but if you was to appoint Smoke as one of your deputies, he'll find 'im for you."

Holloway looked over at Smoke. "Do you have an idea as to where Shardeen might be?"

"No, sir."

"Then what makes you think you'll be able to find him, when I haven't."

"Marshal, you bein' the law for this whole territory, I would expect that you have a lot more things to do than just look for Angus Shardeen, don't you?"

"Well, yes, as a matter of fact, I do."

"I don't and I intend to find him," Smoke replied with grit.

"And you want me to appoint you deputy so that you can?"

"No, sir."

"No?" Holloway looked over at Preacher in surprise. "Look here, isn't this what you just asked me to do?"

"I mean no, sir, I don't want you to appoint me deputy so I can find him," Smoke said. "I intend to find 'im, whether I'm appointed as your deputy or not."

"You did hear me tell you that Shardeen was riding at the head of his own army, didn't you?"

"Yes, sir, I heard you say that."

"Well, here's the thing, Mr. Jensen. I don't have funding for an-other deputy."

Preacher spoke up. "Look here, Uriah. Sometimes when you form a posse to go after someone, don't you appoint them men in the posse as Deputy U.S. Marshals?"

"Yes, I do. But I don't pay them."

"You don't have to pay me," Smoke said.

"Let me get this straight. You are willing to be an unpaid deputy in order to go out, single-handed, to find Angus Shardeen, even though you know there are at least half a dozen with him?"

Smoke nodded. "Yes, sir."

"You will have to function alone. I don't have enough men to as-sign anybody to one specific task."

"That's all right."

Marshal Holloway looked over at Preacher again. "Preacher, you go along with this?"

"I do."

"All right, Smoke Jensen, raise your right hand."

Smoke did as he was directed.

"Now, repeat after me. I Smoke Jensen . . ."

"I Smoke Jensen . . ." He continued with the oath as administered by Marshal Holloway. "Do solemnly swear that I will faithfully execute all lawful precepts, directed to the Marshal of the United States for the District of Colorado, under the authority of the United States, and true returns make, in all things well and truly. And without mal-ice or partiality, perform the duties of Deputy Marshal for the District of Colorado during my continuance in said office, so help me God."

That done, Holloway reached out to shake Smoke's hand. "Congrat-ulations, Smoke. You are now a Deputy U.S. Marshal. That gives you full authority to arrest any fugitive, anywhere within the borders of the United States. That includes all states and territories." Holloway smiled. "But you won't be paid."

"I understand."

"But even though you won't be paid, you still intend to bring him in."

"No."

"I beg your pardon? I thought that was the whole reason for ap-pointing you a Deputy U.S. Marshal."

"I won't be bringing him in," Smoke said cryptically.

* * *

Shortly afterward, Smoke took his hunt for Angus Shardeen public. He had a letter printed in newspapers all over Kansas, Colorado, Idaho, and Wyoming.

> *To the murderer and bandit, Angus Shardeen.*
>
> *You killed many women, children, and old men during the war. You have continued your murdering and killing since the war, having abandoned all pretense of patriotism, and are doing so for selfish reasons.*
>
> *During your murderous spree, one of the women you killed was my mother, Pearl Jensen. I watched you do this, then you clubbed me down and left me for dead. You should have checked me more closely Shardeen, for I was not dead, and now I am coming for you.*
>
> *I'm coming for you for my mother and for the families of all the innocents you have killed, and I am doing this, not for revenge, but for justice. That is because as an official Deputy United States Marshal, I have the power of the law on my side.*
>
> SMOKE JENSEN

"Who in the hell does this arrogant deputy marshal think he is?" Shardeen demanded angrily, after he read the letter in the newspaper.

"He tells us right there who he is," Bartell said. "He is Smoke Jensen."

"Is that name supposed to mean anything to me?"

"From what I've heard, he may be the fastest gun there is," Bartell replied. "And they say he can shoot the eye out of a squirrel from a hundred yards away."

"*They* say? Who says?" Shardeen demanded.

"People who have seen him shoot. He could give us trouble."

"How much trouble can he be if he is dead? I want him dead," Shardeen said. "And I'm willing to pay well for it."

CHAPTER 17

March 1870

In the six months since Smoke had pinned on the star of Deputy U.S. Marshal, he had been wandering around, sometimes chasing a lead, sometimes going from town to town with no particular lead but merely "casting his net," as Preacher described his travels. And like fishermen who cast their nets into the sea, his net came up empty many more times than it provided results.

Even as he rode on, he remembered what he'd learned two months ago in the small town of Sage Creek, Wyoming.

A bartender nervously handed him a piece of paper. "I don't know if you know anything about this, and I want you to know I ain't havin' nothin' to do with it. By that, I mean I ain't handin' these things out to nobody, even though somebody give me near a hunnert of 'em 'n tole me to pass 'em out to any cowboy who might want to make a little money."

"What is it?" Smoke asked, wondering what the mysterious piece of paper might be. He opened it to read.

Five Hundred Dollars
Will Be Paid By
Angus Shardeen
To Anyone Who Kills
Smoke Jensen

Smoke chuckled.
"If you don't mind my sayin' so, Mr. Jensen, that seems like an

odd reaction from someone seein' his name on a flyer that's offerin' five hunnert dollars for his bein' kilt."

"I suppose so. But to me it means that I've finally got his atten- tion. And it isn't as if these are something that's been put out by the law." Smoke folded the paper over.

"Yeah, but to an awful lot of bounty hunters it don't make no dif- ference who is payin' the reward, long as there is one," the bar- tender said.

Smoke nodded. "I guess you have a point there."

Smoke stopped on a ridge just above the road leading into the town of Commerce, Idaho. The cold gray sky was spitting snow, though it wasn't falling heavily. He tried to take a drink of water from his canteen, but it was frozen. He wasn't thirsty enough to start a fire to melt it.

He watched a stagecoach a few minutes as it started down from the pass, making its way into the town. Then, corking the canteen, he put it away, hunkered down inside his buffalo coat, slapped his legs against the side of his horse, and sloped down the long ridge. Al- though he was actually farther away from town than the coach, he would beat it there because he was going by a more direct route.

He stopped beside a small sign just on the edge of town.

COMMERCE
POPULATION 125
A Growing Community

The weathered board and faded letters indicated that it had been there for some time, most likely erected when optimism for the town's future was still prevalent. Smoke doubted there were that many residents in the town, and he was positive the town had no fu- ture.

He continued on into town, checking the corners and rooftops of buildings, doorways, and kiosks . . . any place that might provide concealment for a would-be shooter. His pa had taught him to be cautious. Preacher had suggested that the better he became known, the more cautious he should be. The actual procedure as to when, where, and how to look out for snipers and those who would am- bush him was something he had developed by experience and com- mon sense.

SMOKE JENSEN: THE BEGINNING 193

A moment later, he pulled up in front of the saloon, dismounted, and made a cautious entrance inside. Taking off his hat, he brushed away the snow, then removed his heavy coat and hung it on a stop that protruded from the wall.

He examined the saloon for a moment. Two pot-bellied stoves blazed away with such intensity that they were gleaming red. The heat was disproportional with an area that was too hot close to the stoves . . . and too cold far away, but with a wide comfort zone in between. Most of the bar was within that comfort zone, and Smoke stepped up to it.

"What'll it be?" the bartender asked.

"A beer and maybe a little information," Smoke replied.

"The beer I can supply. Not sure about the information, but you can try."

Smoke waited until the beer mug was put in front of him before he asked, "Does the name Angus Shardeen mean anything to you?"

"I know who he is. I expect just about ever'one in the West knows who he is."

"But do you know where he is?"

"I don't have any idea where he is, 'n I'm not sure I'd tell you where if I knew."

"Why not?"

"If you're plannin' on joinin' up with him, far as I'm concerned, he has enough dregs with him already. And anyone who is plannin' on joinin' up with him is a lowlife."

"And if I'm not plannin' on joinin' him?"

"Then I got two reasons not to tell you nothin'. Number one, I don't want to give you information that could get you kilt. And number two, I don't want it gettin' back to Shardeen that I'm tellin' folks how to find him."

At the opposite end of the bar stood a man wearing a slouch hat above a weather-lined face. Hanging low in a quick-draw holster on the right side of a bullet-studded belt was a silver-plated Colt .44, its grip inlaid with mother-of-pearl.

He had been listening to the conversation and watching Smoke in the mirror. When he'd heard enough, he tossed his drink down and wiped the back of his hand across his mouth. Then he turned to look at Smoke. "Hey, you."

Smoke did not turn.

"I'm talkin' to you, boy."

Smoke looked at him and raised his beer in salute. "Good afternoon." He knew from the tone of the man's voice that it wasn't going to be a simple exchange of pleasantries.

"You're lookin' for Angus Shardeen, are you?"

"I am."

"And would your name be Smoke Jensen?"

"I am."

"You do know, don't you, Mr. Smoke Jensen, Mr. famous . . . gunfighter"—he set the last word apart from the rest of the sentence and said it with a sneer—"that there's reward money out for you."

"How would you know that?" Smoke asked.

"I know that because I'm a bounty hunter, 'n it's my business to know."

"Well, I hate to disappoint you, Bounty Hunter," Smoke said. "But you don't want me. That dodger isn't official. I'm not wanted by the law."

The bounty hunter laughed a harsh and dismissive laugh. "Hell, mister, that don't matter none to me. A reward is a reward, 'n I don't really give a damn who pays it."

"What's your name?"

An evil smile spread across the bounty hunter's face. "The name would be Blackwell. Sledge Blackwell."

Smoke gave a short nod in acknowledgment. "Well, Mr. Blackwell, I would suggest that you not try to collect this particular reward."

"Don't try?" Blackwell replied.

The saloon had grown deathly still as the patrons sat quietly, nervously, and yet titillated by the life and death drama that had suddenly begun to unfold in front of them.

He turned to address the others. "You'd like for me not to try and collect the reward. Is that what you're saying? I suppose you would rather I just walk away, wouldn't you?"

Smoke put the beer down with a tired sigh and turned to face his tormentor. "It would be better for both of us if you would. But you're not going to do that, are you?"

"I can't. Why, this is how I make my livin', boy. I'm sure you've heard of Sledge Blackwell."

"Yeah, I've heard of you." In truth, Smoke had never heard of Blackwell.

"Yeah? What have you heard?" Blackwell asked, the smile on his face broadening.

"I've heard that you are a used-up old man who shoots people in the back because you don't have the guts to face them down."

Smoke's response had just the effect he wanted it to have. The smile on Blackwell's face turned to an angry snarl. "Draw, Jensen!" he shouted, going for his own gun even before he issued the challenge.

Blackwell was fast and had proved his mettle in many gunfights, but midway through his draw, he realized that he had made a big mistake. The arrogant confidence in his eyes was replaced by fear, then acceptance of the fact that he was about to be killed.

The two pistols discharged almost simultaneously, but Smoke had been able to bring his gun to bear and his bullet plunged into Blackwell's chest, while the bounty hunter didn't even get his gun high enough to avoid punching a hole in the floor.

Looking down at himself, Blackwell put his hand over his wound, then pulled it away and examined the blood that had pooled in his palm. When he looked back at Smoke, an almost whimsical smile appeared on his face. "Damn, you're fast. I ain't never seen anyone that . . ." His sentence ended with a cough, then he fell back against the bar, making an attempt to grab onto the bar to keep himself erect. His arm moved across the top of the bar, sweeping away both drinks. His shot glass and Smoke's beer mug wound up on the floor. The slouch hat fell from his head into the half-filled spittoon. The eye-burning, acrid smoke of two discharges hung in a gray-blue cloud just below the ceiling.

Smoke turned back to the bar. "Looks like I'm going to need another beer."

"Yes, sir, another beer, and this one is on the house," the bartender said, holding a new mug under the spigot of the beer barrel.

Behind Smoke, the silence was broken as everyone discussed what they had just seen. He was only halfway through his beer when the town marshal and two of his deputies arrived.

"What happened here?" the marshal asked.

The question wasn't directed to anyone in particular, so everyone started answering at once, availing themselves of the first opportunity to tell a story they would be telling for the rest of their lives.

"Hold it, hold it!" The marshal put up his hands. "Don't everyone talk at once." He looked over toward the bartender. "Ed, did you see what happened?"

"It's this way, Marshal Moore. Blackwell tried to brace this man."

The marshal looked at Smoke. "Blackwell braced you?" the marshal asked.

"Yes."

"Blackwell's a bounty hunter. If he braced you, he must've thought you've got a wanted flyer out on you. Do you, mister?"

Smoke started to reach for his shirt pocket.

"What are you doing?" Marshal Moore demanded anxiously.

"Take it easy, Marshal," Smoke replied. "You asked if I had paper out on me, and I'm about to show it to you."

"You mean to say that you are a wanted man, and you not only admit it, but you are going to prove it?"

Smoke smiled. "Yeah, you might say something like that." He pulled a folded up piece of paper from his pocket and handed it to the marshal.

The marshal unfolded the paper, read it, then looked up at Smoke. "You're Smoke Jensen?"

"Yes, sir."

Moore folded the paper and handed it back. "Did Blackwell realize this wasn't a real reward poster?"

"Oh, it's real all right, Marshal. It just isn't a reward that was put out by the law."

"Evidently, Blackwell didn't care who put out the reward."

"That's right, Marshal," the bartender said. "Why, Blackwell stood right here and said as much."

"I've heard of you, Jensen. But I'm curious as to what brought you to our town?"

Smoke showed the marshal his Deputy U.S. Marshal badge. "I'm looking for Angus Shardeen."

"Alone?"

"Yes. Do you know where he is?"

"I'm sorry. I don't have the slightest idea.'"

"That's too bad. I was hoping you might have some idea."

"Look Jensen, with all the men Shardeen has around him, I hope you're just trying to locate him, and don't have any intention of bringing him in by yourself."

"I have no intention of bringing him in," Smoke said, repeating what he had told Marshal Holloway.

"That's being smart," Marshal Moore said, not understanding the intent of Smoke's reply.

*   *   *

Three hundred miles north of Commerce, the town of Fort Benton sat alongside the completely iced-over Missouri River. Elmer Gleason stopped by the Gold Strike Saloon to see Janey. He had taken a job as deputy city marshal and though he did drop by to see her fairly often, he had never become one of her more intimate customers. For one thing, he couldn't afford her. She was considerably more expensive than any other girl who worked the saloon. But the real reason was more complex than that.

"It's just that I sort of look at you as my sister, Abbigail," Elmer told her as they shared a table, using the name by which he had first known her. "I ain't never had me no sister, but if I did, I sure wouldn't be takin' her to bed."

Janey laughed. "No, I wouldn't think so."

"You got 'ny brothers?"

The smile left Janey's face, and Elmer held up his hand. "Never mind. Hell, I know better 'n to ask a question like that. Forget that I asked."

"No, it's all right," Janey said. "I think I will tell you. It might be nice having a friend who knows something about me. Otherwise, being this far from home, with a name that isn't mine, and with nobody who really knows me, it becomes almost like I don't exist. Do you know what I mean?"

Elmer smiled. "I'm not sure that I do. That kind of talk is sort of hard for me to get aholt of."

"It means I want somebody to know me, to really know who I am. And I'd like for that somebody to be you. That is, if you don't mind listenin' to my story.

Elmer nodded. "I think I'd be plumb honored if you'd tell me."

"To begin with, yes, I do have a brother. I had two brothers, but one of them was killed in the war. And of course, my name isn't really Fannie Webber, nor is it Abbigail Fontaine. My real name is Jane. Janey, my family always called me. Janey Jensen."

Elmer was surprised. "Jensen?"

"Yes. My father is Emmett, and my brother is—"

"Kirby," Elmer said. It wasn't a question, rather a statement of fact.

Janey gasped and put her hand to her mouth. "How long have you known?"

"I didn't know. Not till right now when you told me. But it turns out that I do know your brother. Me 'n him rode together with the Ghost Riders durin' the war."

"I didn't know Kirby had gone off to war. It must've been after I left."

"He was a good man to ride with, one you could count on when things got a little testy. Me 'n him was great friends. He 'n your pa even saved my life once."

"My pa? You also know my pa?"

"I met 'im."

Janey reached across the table and put her hand on Elmer's arm. "Elmer, please, you must swear to me that you will never tell them about me. Don't tell them where I am. Don't even tell them that you know me."

"They are good people, Abbi . . . uh, Janey. Why not tell them?"

"Do you have to ask? You're right. They are good people. But you know me for what I am. Do you really think I could compare the life I have lived with the lives they have lived?"

"Janey, you being what you are don't make you a bad person. Fact is, you're one of the best women I've ever knowed."

"Please, Elmer, if you care anything at all for me, you'll never tell them about me."

"All right. Prob'ly don't matter, anyhow. I don't expect to ever see either one of 'em again. One of the reasons I come by today was to tell you good-bye."

"Good-bye? What do mean, good-bye? Where are you goin'?"

"I've always had me a hankerin' to go sailin' acrossed the ocean so's I could see me some of the rest of the world."

"Will you write me?"

"I ain't never been much for writin'," Elmer said. "Anyhow, I don't even know how I'd go about sendin' you a letter from Australia or Siam or China, or some such place. Besides, you more 'n likely won't be here much longer, anyhow. You damn near got as much of a wan-derin' around itch as I do."

Janey smiled. "I do at that. I reckon I'll leave soon as you're gone. There's bound to be some place that's warmer 'n Fort Benton."

"You got that right."

"I'm goin' to miss you, Elmer. If I never see you again, I'll keep your memory forever in my heart."

Elmer nodded and got a strange, almost yearning look in his eyes. "Abbi . . . I mean, Janey, that thought brings me more comfort than I can say."

The two hugged good-bye.

* * *

"Sally, dear, I'm so happy you decided to come to New York to visit your old aunt."

"Oh, I'd hardly call you old, Aunt Mildred." Sally Reynolds was sitting on the windowsill of the third floor of one of the Greek Revival row houses on the north side of Washington Square. The apartment belonged to her Aunt Mildred, and Sally had come to New York to spend a couple weeks with her. It was a cold and gray day in late March. The steely sunlight illuminated but did not warm the city. Spring had already begun, but the pedestrians walking on the sidewalk below wore heavy coats and scarves. From this elevation, they were a never-ending flow of black figures, rather like a stream of ants on the march.

She heard the distant rumble of an el train and the clatter of an omnibus, and wondered about so many people on the move. Who were they? Where were they going? What lay ahead of them?

What lay ahead for *her*?

Sally had already made the decision for her own future and had announced it to her family with great passion and intensity. She had recently graduated from Mary Woodson Normal College and was a qualified teacher. She was going West to teach school and to see some of the country she had only read about.

Sally's parents were completely opposed to the idea and had sent her to New York on a visit in the hope that she would, in her father's words, "come to her senses."

"Have you given any thought as to what you want for supper?" Aunt Mildred asked. "There are so many nice restaurants close by."

"Could we just have some scrambled eggs and stay home for supper?" Sally asked. "I've something I would like to speak with you about."

"Of course we can. But instead of scrambled eggs, suppose I make us an omelet? If you don't mind a little bragging, I will tell you that I make a wonderful omelet."

"That would be great," Sally replied with a smile.

A short while later, the two sat down at the kitchen table for supper.

"Oh," Sally said after her first bite. "It's not bragging if what you say is true. This really *is* a wonderful omelet."

"Why, thank you, dear. You said you had something you wanted to discuss with me. Would it be your idea about going West to teach school?"

"Oh!" Sally replied with a gasp. "How did you know that?"

"I got a letter from my brother telling me about it. He wants me to talk some sense into you."

"And are you going to try?"

"Yes."

"I see."

Mildred smiled and put her hand across the table. "I'm going to tell you to go where your heart tells you to go."

"What? Oh, Aunt Mildred, I thought . . . that is, I was afraid . . ."

"I know what you thought. You thought I was going to try and talk you out of it. May I share a secret with you?"

"Yes, of course!"

"There was a time when, more than anything else in the world, I wanted to move to San Francisco, to see what was on the other side of this country.

"I didn't go, because my older brother, your father, talked me out of it. I've wondered about that decision for my entire life. I know now that I should have gone. I don't want you to spend the rest of your life wondering. Go, Sally. Follow your heart while you are still young. If you find that you don't like it, you can always come back home, like the prodigal son, or in this case the prodigal daughter." Aunt Mildred chuckled.

"I'm going to do it," Sally said, a broad smile spreading across her face.

"Do you have any idea where you'll wind up?"

"I sent some letters out, and the only place that responded was a town called Bury, Idaho."

One month later, Elmer Gleason was standing on the waterfront in San Francisco. The ship *Pacific Dancer* was tied alongside the dock. The canvas was rolled tight against the yardarms and the lines hung loose, whistling in the breeze. The ship was taking on a cargo of buffalo hides, and it rocked gently in the waves that lapped ashore.

Elmer had just applied for a job as an able-bodied seaman.

"Have you ever sailed before?" the purser asked.

"Cain't say as I have, 'cause I ain't," Elmer said.

"Why should I sign you on, then? More 'n likely you'd wind up doin' nothin' more 'n spendin' all your time pukin' on the deck. The crew will have enough to do without cleanin' up your puke."

"Look, sonny. Sign me up or don't sign me up, I really don't give a damn which one you do. This here ain't the only ship tied up in the bay. If you don't take me on, I don't reckon it's goin' to be all that hard to find me one that will." Elmer turned and started to walk away.

"Wait," the purser called out to him. He chuckled. "It might be good to see you get seasick at that. Could be that it'll take you down a notch or two. Can you sign your name?"

Elmer wrote his name in bold, legible letters.

"Report to the First Mate."

"Who would that be?"

The purser pointed to the gangplank. "Go on aboard and stand there without doin' nothin' for a moment or two. The man that yells at you will be the first mate."

"Where's this ship bound?"

"You mean you signed on without even knowin' where the ship was goin'?"

"Yeah."

"Why would you do that?"

"Because I didn't really care where it was goin'."

"Then why do you care now?"

"'Cause now I'm actual on it," Elmer replied, starting toward the gangplank.

"China," the purser yelled at him. "We're goin' to China."

Elmer lifted his hand in recognition that he had heard, but he didn't turn his head around. He had seen his share of Chinamen. Now, he supposed, he was about to see a whole bunch of them.

The man caught Janey's attention as soon as he got on the train. He was a handsome man, tall, with black hair, dark eyes, a fine nose, and a strong chin. The clothes he was wearing indicated that he must be a wealthy man. He was wearing fawn-colored riding breeches tucked into highly polished calf-high boots, a dark jacket held closed by one brass button, and a vest that matched his trousers, across which was strung a gold watch chain. At his neck he wore a maroon cravat.

He looked as if he might be every bit as wealthy as Big Ben Conyers, but something else about him Janey found even more intriguing. She knew instinctively that he was a man who had few compunctions and little concern about what others might think of him.

She got up from her seat and walked to the front of the car to take a drink of water from the water barrel. She gave him a very close look as she passed him by, then studied him over the brim of the dipper. When she walked back to her seat, she managed to lose her balance just as she drew even with him. "Oh, my!" she exclaimed as she fell into his lap. "Oh, dear. I'm so sorry."

She made an effort to get back on her feet, but she put her hand on the inside of his thigh, then slipped again, causing her hand to slide up his thigh. "Oh! I'm so clumsy. Please forgive me!"

"Nothing to forgive, my dear," the man said, smiling at her. "It can sometimes be difficult walking on a moving train."

"So I see."

"May I suggest that you sit next to me until you have quite recovered."

"Thank you, sir. You are such a gentleman. I don't know how to thank you, mister . . ."

"Richards. Josh Richards."

"I'm Janey Garner."

"It's good to meet you, Miss Garner."

"It's Mrs. Garner."

"Oh, I beg your pardon for the mistake."

Janey smiled. "I assume Mrs. is still appropriate. Poor Paul was killed in . . . a boating accident." She'd started to say, "in the war," but since the war was some five years past, she didn't want to appear old enough to be a war widow.

"Actually, and I do hope you don't think it too forward of me, I would prefer to be called Janey."

"Then Janey it shall be," Richards said.

"Where are you going, Mr. Richards?"

"Please, if I am to call you Janey, you must call me Josh."

"Very well, Josh. Where are you going?" She put her hand across her mouth. "Oh, please, you must forgive me. I have no business in inquiring about such a personal matter."

"No forgiveness is necessary. I don't mind at all telling you where I'm going. I am an owner of the PSR, which is an obscenely large ranch just outside the town of Bury, Idaho."

"Oh! What a coincidence! I, too, am going to Bury," Janey said, making the decision at that very instant. "I am sure that your wife is looking forward quite anxiously to your return."

"I suppose she would be if I had a wife. I'm not married, Janey."

"Well now, that is very nice to know."

CHAPTER 18

Smoke heard the high, keening sound of a steam-powered saw and knew that he was close to a town. If he had followed directions, the town was Buffington. At least, he hoped it was Buffington. A couple weeks ago a man had told him that Angus Shardeen had been seen in the town.

As he rode closer, he smelled meat cooking and bread baking. His stomach churned as those aromas reminded him of just how hungry he was.

Finally, he saw a church steeple through the trees, a tall spire, topped by a brass-plated cross that glistened in the high noon sun. He reached a road running parallel to the railroad tracks and moved onto it, following it the rest of the way into the settlement.

The town impressed him with its bustling activity. In addition to the working sawmill, he saw several other examples of commerce—freight wagons lumbering down the street, carpenters erecting a new building, a store clerk in a white apron sweeping the boardwalk in front of his place of employment. Well-maintained boardwalks ran the length of the town on either side of the street. At the end of each block, planks were laid across the road to allow pedestrians to cross to the other side without having to walk in the dirt or mud.

Smoke stopped his horse and waited patiently at one of the intersections while he watched a woman cross on the plank, daintily holding her skirt up above her ankles to keep the hem from getting soiled. She nodded her appreciation to him as she stepped up onto the boardwalk on the opposite side of the street.

Smoke clucked at Seven, and the Appaloosa stepped across the plank, then headed toward the livery, a little farther down. Smoke dismounted in front of it.

An old man got up from the barrel he had been sitting on and walked, with a limp, over to Smoke. "Boardin' your horse, mister?"

'Yes."

"How long will you be stayin'?" he asked.

"I'm not sure," Smoke said.

"It'll cost you fifteen cents a night."

"Does that include feeding him?"

"Hay, only. Oats'll cost you five cents extra."

Smoke gave the man a silver dollar. "I'll be back before this is worked off."

"Wes," the old man called, and a boy of about fourteen appeared from inside the barn.

"Yes, sir?"

"Take this man's horse."

"Wait a minute," Smoke said.

"Beg your pardon?"

"I need to let Seven know that you've got my permission to be around him. I'd better introduce you."

"Mister, I been handlin' horses since I was ten years old," Wes said. "You don't need to introduce me to your horse."

Smoke smiled and stepped away. "All right, come get him."

The boy started toward the horse, and Seven lowered his head and bared his teeth.

Startled, the boy jumped back. "Uh, maybe you had better introduce us."

"Yeah, it might work out better that way," Smoke said with a smile. He put one hand on the side of the horse's face and the other hand on the boy's shoulder. "Seven, it's all right. This boy's name is Wes, and he's going to take good care of you while I'm gone."

Seven nodded his head, and Smoke reached out to take the boy's hand. He was about to put it on Seven's face, but Wes pulled back.

"It's all right," Smoke said. "Seven's going to treat you fine. Here, give him a couple pats."

Hesitantly, Wes allowed his hand to be put on Seven's face. Only when Seven moved his head against the hand did the boy smile.

"There, now you and my horse are friends. Wes, I'd suggest that before anyone else handles him, you tell Seven it'll be all right."

"You mean he'll listen to me?"

"Sure he will. Like I said, you and Seven are friends now."

The smile broadened, spreading across Wes's face. "Yes, sir, I'll be sure 'n introduce the others to 'im!" he said proudly. "Come on, Seven. Like he said, me 'n you's friends now."

Smoke turned to the livery man. "The name of this town is Buffington, isn't it?"

"Yes, sir, it is." The man extended his hand. "I'm Tony Heckemeyer."

"Smoke Jensen." He examined Heckemeyer's face for any sign of recognition, but he gave none. "This seems like a nice, industrious town."

"Yes, sir. We like it."

Suddenly, several gunshots interrupted their conversation. Looking toward the opposite end of the street, Smoke saw two men backing out of a building.

"That's the bank! They're robbin' the bank!" Heckemeyer said.

A third man suddenly appeared from the alley that ran between the bank and the building next to it. He was mounted and leading two horses. Leaning down, he threw the reins to the two others. Once they mounted, all three began shooting up the town in order to keep people off the street.

Their efforts were effective, in that most people were scurrying to get out of the way. But Smoke saw a little girl not more than five or six years old standing at the edge of the street, obviously in the line of fire from the shooters. She was too frightened and too confused to move.

Dropping his saddlebags, Smoke ran out into the street toward her, scooped her up in his arms, and was about to carry her to safety, but it was too late. The three bank robbers were galloping down the street toward them.

He put the girl down, then stepped out between her and the gunmen. "Stay behind me and don't move!" he shouted at her.

Smoke's initial intention had been no more than to get the little girl to safety, but in so doing he had put himself in the path of the robbers' escape route.

Pulling his pistol, Smoke aimed at the closest rider and fired. Even as that robber was tumbling from his saddle, Smoke knocked a second rider from his horse. The two riderless horses galloped by.

The third robber, suddenly realizing that he was alone, reined in his own horse, tossed his gun down and threw both arms into the air. "No, no!" he shouted. "Don't shoot, don't shoot! I quit, I quit!"

With the surrender, nearly a dozen armed men of the town came running out into the street with their guns aimed at the one remaining robber.

"Get down from there, mister," one of the men shouted in an authoritative voice. His authority, Smoke saw, came from the badge he was wearing on his vest.

A woman came running into the street and picked up the little girl. "Oh, Frances, sweetheart! Are you all right!"

"Did any of the bullets hit her?" Smoke asked anxiously.

"No, no, I don't think so," the woman said. "I don't know how to thank you."

"Just seeing that she wasn't hurt is thanks enough for me," Smoke said.

"Take him to jail," the man with the badge said, referring to the robber who had given up. Two others responded to the order, prodding their prisoner along at gunpoint.

The man with the badge came back to speak to Smoke. He stuck out his hand. "I'm Sheriff Gwaltney. Mister, I want to thank you for what you done. You not only saved the little girl there, you probably saved several others by stoppin' those men before they could shoot up the whole town. Also, because of what you done we got the bank's money back. The whole town owes you for that."

"That was a real brave thing, you standin' out in the middle of the street like that," Heckemeyer said, coming over to join them.

"I didn't have much choice," Smoke said. "I sort of got caught out there."

"You coulda just stayed out of the way."

Smoke looked at the little girl, who was examining him closely with blue eyes that were open wide in wonder. He shook his head. "No, I couldn't."

Even as Smoke and the sheriff were speaking, a man wearing a long black coat came driving up in a wagon. He stopped the wagon between the two men Smoke had shot.

"Doolin, don't you go puttin' them fellas in any of your fancy coffins, thinkin' maybe that the county's goin' to pay for it," Sheriff Gwaltney said. "'Cause I'm tellin' you right now, we ain't agoin' to do it."

"I won't use nothin' but a couple plain pine boxes," Doolin replied.

"Why waste a box? Put both of 'em in the same box," another said, and those gathered laughed rather nervously at the macabre joke.

At that moment, Smoke couldn't help but think of the feeding trough he had used as the coffin to bury his mother.

Sheriff Gwaltney looked back at Smoke. "What's your name, mister?"

"Jensen. Smoke Jensen."

"Smoke Jensen?" Gwaltney replied as a look of recognition passed across his face. He stroked his chin. "Seems to me like I've heard that name before. Do you have any paper out on you?"

"Yeah, I do."

"What?"

As he had done with Marshal Moore, Smoke took out the WANTED poster that Angus Shardeen had circulated.

"Damn. That's purdee advertisin' for someone to murder you," Gwaltney said. "It takes someone evil and arrogant to do somethin' like that. Don't he know that somethin' like this will get the law after him?"

Smoke laughed.

"What's so funny?"

"The law is already after him. What would one more thing matter?"

Sheriff Gwaltney laughed. "I guess you're right. And, to tell you the truth, it wouldn't make no never mind to me whether the law had paper out on you or not. After stoppin' the bank robbery the way you done, you have certainly made some friends in this town. I don't know what brought you here, but I'm sure glad you showed up when you did."

"Mister Jensen, have you had your lunch yet?" asked the mother of the little girl.

"No, I haven't."

"My name's Kathy York. I would love to fix lunch for you."

"Well, I—uh . . ." Smoke stuttered his response.

Kathy chuckled. "It's not what you are thinking, Mr. Jensen." She pointed to a building directly across from them. "That's my café there, Dumplins. You come on over and have lunch, on me."

"Thanks," Smoke said.

While Smoke was having his lunch, several of the townspeople stopped by his table to thank him for what he had done in saving little Frances York, and in stopping the bank robbery.

"Most ever'one in town's got money in that bank. Why, if them men had gotten away with it, there's several of us would've fallen on hard times, and that's for sure," one of the men said.

The accolades were growing so profuse that Smoke was beginning to feel self-conscious about it.

After lunch, Frances came over to Smoke's table, very carefully carrying a small plate. "This is Mama's blackberry cobbler."

Smoke smiled. "Well, thank you." He turned serious. "But I don't know. Is it any good?"

Frances nodded. "Oh, yes. It's very good."

"You know what? When I have something that is very good, like blackberry cobbler, I like to have someone else eat with me. Do you think your mama would let you have a plate of cobbler so you could eat with me?"

"Mama! He wants me to have some, too!" Frances called out happily, and a moment later she was sitting across the table from him as they ate the cobbler together.

Smoke got a sudden image of his sister when she was a little girl. Blackberry cobbler had been her favorite dessert, and he wondered if she still liked it. He wondered, too, where she was, and if he would ever see her again.

She had run away because she obviously wanted to be on her own. If that was really what she wanted, he had no intention of disturbing her.

Smoke walked back down to the sheriff's office.

"Mr. Jensen, what can I do for you?" the sheriff said, greeting him effusively.

"You asked me earlier what brought me here," Smoke said. "It didn't seem the right time or place to tell you then, but I'm looking for a man." Smoke turned his vest out, so the sheriff could see that he was a Deputy U.S. Marshal.

"A Deputy U.S. Marshal, are you? Well, now I can see how you were able to handle those two men so easily. Who are you looking for?"

"Angus Shardeen."

"Angus Shardeen? You mean the one that's put out the reward to have you killed?"

"Yes."

"Well then, with the two of you lookin' for each other, you're bound to meet up with him, don't you think?"

"No, there's a difference. He's not actually looking for me. All he's done is put out Wanted posters promising to reward anyone who can kill me. I'm actually looking for him."

"Do you have a posse with you? Or are you looking for him alone?"

"I have no one with me."

"That's quite a job for one man. I know Marshal Holloway. I can't imagine him sending one man out for Shardeen."

"He didn't send me out," Smoke said. "I volunteered."

"If you're tryin' to make a name for yourself, Jensen, you don't need to go so far as to try and tackle Shardeen all by yourself. Hell, you're already gettin' known around."

"It has nothing to do with making a name for myself," Smoke said. "Truth is, I'd just as soon not have a name. What's between Shardeen and me is personal."

"Yes, but there's the problem you see. It might be personal for you, but it won't be for him. Last I heard, he had at least six or seven men ridin' with him, and maybe even more than that. Here's the thing, most of 'em is the same ones that rode with him durin' the war."

"So I've heard. I also heard that he had been seen here in Buffington."

"That's true. He and his men passed through town one day a few weeks ago. They stocked up at the general store, then rode on. But like I said, there were quite a few of 'em. They didn't give us any trouble, so we didn't give them any trouble."

"You wouldn't have any idea as to where they might be now, would you?"

The sheriff shook his head. "No, I don't know. I'm just telling you that if you go after him alone, you may be takin' on a bigger bite than you can chew."

"You may be right, but I'm determined to find him. By the way, I don't think I saw a hotel when I came into town."

"The reason you didn't see one is because we don't have one. At least, not 'ny more. The one hotel we had burned down last month, and it ain't been built back. But if you're lookin' for a place to stay, you might check in at the Salt Lick Saloon. You can get a room there if they aren't all in use."

The Salt Lick was the most substantial-looking saloon in a row of saloons. A drunk was passed out on the steps in front of the place and Smoke had to step over him in order to go inside.

The chimneys of all the lanterns were soot-covered. Dingy light filtered through drifting smoke. The place smelled of sour whiskey, stale beer, and strong tobacco. The long bar on the left with a large mirror behind it was like everything else about the saloon—so dirty Smoke could scarcely see any images in it. What he could see was distorted by imperfections in the glass.

Eight or ten tables were nearly all occupied. A half-dozen or so bar girls were flitting about, pushing drinks. A few card games were in progress, but most of the patrons were just drinking and talking.

Smoke stepped up to the bar. The bartender was pouring the residue from abandoned whiskey glasses back into a bottle. He pulled a soggy cigar butt from one glass, laid the butt aside, then poured the whiskey back into the bottle without qualms.

One of the other men standing at the bar recognized Smoke. "Hey, you're the man that stopped the bank robbery, ain't you?"

"I was here when it happened," Smoke replied.

"Here? Hell, you was a lot more than just here. Sam, give this feller whatever it is he wants to drink. I'll pay for it."

"Thanks," Smoke said.

"What'll it be?" the bartender asked.

"A beer."

Sam drew a mug of beer, then set it before him.

"I'd also like a room."

"With or without."

That was confusing. "With or without what?"

The bartender looked up in surprise. "Are you kidding me, mister? With or without a woman."

"Without."

"All right. That'll be six bits."

"Six bits? Isn't that a little expensive?"

"If we left the room empty so the girls could use it for their customers, we could make three, maybe four times that," the bartender said. "But since the hotel got burnt down we sometimes take in people who just want a room, so we gotta charge six bits for it. Take it or leave it."

It had been a while since Smoke last slept in a bed, so even though he complained about having to pay seventy-five cents for a room, he considered it well worth it. "Here," he said, slapping the coins on the bar. "Tell your girls and their customers not to come into my room by mistake. If they do, they just might get shot."

"Mister, I don't know who the hell you are, but it ain't healthy to go around making threats you can't back up," the bartender growled. He picked up the silver and took it over to the money box, then reached for a key.

"Sam," someone called from the other end of the bar. "Come here."

The bartender went over to the customer, then leaned over as the customer whispered something in his ear. The bartender looked back toward Smoke, listened a moment longer, then nodded, and hurried back down the bar with the key.

"Mr. Jensen, you don't have to worry none about anyone disturbin' you tonight. I'll make sure you're left in peace."

"I appreciate that, Sam," Smoke replied.

One of the bar girls sidled over to Smoke. Dissipation had not yet taken its toll with her, and she was actually rather attractive. "I heard you say you didn't want to be disturbed tonight," she said as flirtatiously as she could. "I don't blame you. Once you find someone that you want to be with for the rest of the night, the last thing you'd want would be for someone to come bustin' in on you. My name is Gloria, and don't you worry, if you come to my room with me, I'll make certain we aren't disturbed."

Smoke smiled at her. "You know what, Gloria? You could almost tempt me to do just that. But I'm so tired that when I finally do get up there tonight, all I'm going to want to do is sleep."

"All right, honey," Gloria said. "But you don't know what you are missing."

"Oh, I've got a pretty good idea."

"We're losing a player here!" somebody called from one of the tables. "We need another man! Anybody want to get into the game?"

Suddenly Preacher's words came back to Smoke. *You want to get the measure of any place, you get into a friendly card game in one of the local saloons. Men gets to palaverin' in a card game 'n if you keep your mouth shut, and just listen, why you'll learn more in an hour than you could by readin' a month o' newspapers.*

"I'd like to join you, if you don't mind a stranger playing with you," Smoke said.

"You be a stranger do you? Well, tell me, stranger, are you goin' to be playin' with American money?" asked one of the others at the table.

"Yes, but what difference would it make to you whether I'm play-

ing with American money or not? None of you will ever see it. I intend to win all the hands," Smoke teased.

"Ha! Come on in here, stranger, and sit at the table," another player
said. "There ain't nothin' I like better 'n partin' an overconfident fool
from his money. And anyone that thinks they're likely to not lose anythin' at all is just the kind of fool that is goin' to lose."

The others laughed, and Smoke joined them at the table. They
noticed that he did not sit in a way that would compromise his ability
to get to his gun quickly, if he had to.

The other players quickly learned that Smoke was the man who
had stopped the bank robbery, and since all three of them had
money in the bank, they were grateful to him.

One of the players was Robert Vaughan, owner and editor of the
local newspaper. Seeing it as an opportunity to get a story, he began
questioning Smoke rather extensively.

Smoke didn't mind the interrogation as it actually opened up av-
enues for conversation which allowed him to get information, as well
as give it. "I understand that Angus Shardeen was in Buffington a
while ago."

"He was here, all right," Vaughan said.

"I heard some folks say that it was him, but I don't know as that's
true," Rick Adams replied as he picked up his cards.

"It's true, all right." Vaughan looked at the cards he'd been dealt.

"How do you know?" Smoke asked.

The conversation continued between Smoke and the newspaper
editor as he answered, "I know because I recognized two of them.
Their leader had red hair, a red beard, and a scar that runs up the
side of his face and looks like it damn near cuts his eye in two. That,
my friends, could be no one but Angus Shardeen. I also recognized
one of the others. He only has half an ear on the left side of his head.
That could only be Billy Bartell."

"You wouldn't happen to know where they are holed up,
would you?"

"I don't have any idea, but if I had to make an educated guess, I
would say that they are holed up in the mountains where they can
use the rocks and the draws as a fortress. That way they could stand
off an army."

Smoke looked at his cards. "Has anyone actually ever gone into
the mountains to try and find Shardeen and his men?"

"No, and they aren't likely to, either. At least, not anyone who has good sense. Why are you asking so many questions about Shardeen, anyway?"

Smoke chuckled. "I guess you could say I'm one of those people who doesn't have very good sense."

"I'll be damned! Are you planning to go after him?"

"Yes."

"I've heard about you, Smoke Jensen. They say you are quite skilled in the way you employ your pistol, in terms of speed with which you can extract your weapon and the deadly accuracy of your shooting. I also know that the reward being offered for Shardeen has reached a rather substantial amount. But no reward is worth getting yourself killed."

"The reward has nothing to do with it. I have a personal reason for going after Mr. Angus Shardeen."

For the remainder of the game, Smoke explained his personal reasons for going after Shardeen, telling how he had witnessed his mother being murdered, and his sister violated.

"And after I take care of Shardeen I intend to deal with Mr. Billy Bartell. By the way, I raise the bet by five dollars," he added, pushing five more dollars into the pot.

"All I can do is wish you luck," Vaughan said. "And call your bet," he added with a triumphant smile.

When Smoke got up from the table somewhat later, he was down by twenty dollars. "Damn. Maybe I shouldn't have played with American money," he teased, and the others laughed.

After a supper of biscuits, bacon, and beans, which he ate at the saloon, he went up the backstairs to the room the bartender had rented him. Smoke poured water into the bowl, took off his shirt, washed, then turned the covers down and crawled into bed.

He was awakened in the middle of the night by a small clicking sound. Instantly, his hand went to the pistol hanging from the headboard. He slipped out of bed and walked barefoot across the carpet, then stood with his back to the wall just beside the door.

The *click* he had heard was the latch being unlocked. He watched the doorknob turn. Holding his pistol in his right hand, arm crooked at the elbow, and pistol pointing up, he eased back on the hammer, cocking it so slowly it made practically no sound as the sear engaged the cylinder.

The door opened, moving silently on the hinges. A little wedge of light spilled into the room from the hallway, the wedge growing wider as the door opened farther until finally it stretched from the open door all the way to the bed. Every muscle in Smoke's body tensed as he waited for the confrontation.

"Hello?" a woman's voice called quietly. "Is anyone in here?"

Who was this woman, and what was she doing here? With a sigh, Smoke's tension was relieved, and he eased the hammer back down as he lowered his pistol. "I'm here," he said from the darkness behind her.

"Oh!" the woman gasped, startled by the sound from an unexpected direction. She put her hand to her chest. "Don't do that! You could scare a body to death that way."

"You *should* be frightened."

"Who are you?"

"My name is Smoke Jensen. Who are you?"

"Smoke Jensen? You're the one who stopped the bank robbers, aren't you?"

"You didn't answer my question. Who are you, and what do you mean coming into my room in the middle of the night? I could've shot you."

"My name is Ida Jean, and this is my room."

"Ida Jean, is it? Well, Ida Jean, if this really is your room, why did you ask if anyone was in here?"

"Sometimes one of the other girls uses it to entertain one of their gentlemen friends. I didn't want to come bargin' in on something."

Smoke shook his head. "I'm all alone in here."

"You rented the room for the night, did you?"

"Yes."

"You know, you don't have to be all alone."

"Yeah, I do."

"Too bad," Ida Jean said. "All right. I'll go somewhere else."

"No," Smoke offered. "If this really is your room, I'll leave."

"Honey, there's no need for you to do that. I have somewhere else I can go. You don't. Good night . . . and sleep tight."

"Thanks," Smoke said.

Ida Jean left the room and Smoke closed and locked the door. He propped a chair under the doorknob. If the woman who just came in had a key, how many more keys were out there? he wondered.

As Smoke lay in the darkness, he thought about the woman and her offer. He had not yet been with a woman . . . in that way . . . and he sometimes wondered about it. He remembered his conversation with his pa.

"I ain't never been with a woman before. Leastwise, I ain't never been with a woman in . . . that . . . way. The way she wanted to be. And I sorta figure that if you're goin' to do somethin' like that with a woman, then maybe it ought to mean somethin'."

Smoke hadn't changed his mind.

CHAPTER 19

Smoke left the saloon the next morning and headed toward Dumplins for breakfast. He had just crossed the street when he heard a voice call out to him.

"Mr. Jensen, look out!" The warning was shouted by Wes, the boy from the stable.

Almost on top of the warning, Smoke felt a blow to the side of his head. He saw stars, but even as he was being hit, he was reacting to the warning so that, while it didn't prevent the attack, it did prevent him from being knocked down.

When his attacker swung at him a second time, Smoke was able to avoid him. With his fists up, he danced quickly out to the middle of the street, avoiding any more surprises from the shadows. It wasn't until then that he saw his attacker, a large man with heavy brows and a bulbous nose.

Smoke called out, "What are you doing? Why are you attacking me?"

"Mister," the man replied with a low growl, "you kilt my brother a few weeks ago."

Almost instantly, a crowd had gathered around Smoke and the man who had come at him from the shadows. It was still fairly early in the morning. He hadn't seen anyone on the street when he first came out of the saloon. Where had all these people come from? he wondered before calling out, "Who is your brother?"

"Damn. Have you kilt so many men that you can't even keep track? It was Sledge Blackwell."

"I'm sorry about your brother. I didn't have any choice. He drew against me."

"Yeah, well, bein' sorry don't do much for bringin' 'im back, does it?" Blackwell caught up with Smoke in the middle of the street.

"Ever'body knows that Sledge Blackwell wasn't worth a bucket of spit. Why's Bull fightin' for 'im?" someone asked.

"Because Bull ain't got good sense."

Blackwell threw a long wild swing at Smoke, but it was easy for Smoke to slip away from it, then counterpunch with a quick, slashing left to Blackwell's face. It was a well-delivered blow, one that would have dropped most men, but Blackwell barely showed the effects. He laughed a low evil laugh. "That the best you got?"

"Somebody ought to stop this," said a man on the boardwalk. "Bull is almost twice as big as Jensen. He's goin' to beat 'im to death."

"Yeah? Well, Smoke ain't no little man, and what he's got is all muscle. I'm goin' with him."

With an angry roar, Blackwell rushed Smoke again, and Smoke stepped aside, avoiding the rush. The big man slammed into a hitching rail, smashing through it as if it were kindling. He turned and faced Smoke again.

A hush fell over the crowd as they watched the two men, observing the fight with a great deal of interest, wanting to see if this young man could handle Blackwell.

Smoke and Blackwell circled around for a moment, holding their fists doubled in front of them, each trying to test the mettle of the other. Blackwell swung, a club-like swing which Smoke leaned away from. Smoke counterpunched and again he scored well, but again, Blackwell laughed it off.

Smoke hit Blackwell almost at will, and though the big man continued to shrug off the punches, the repeated blows were beginning to take effect. Blackwell's eyes began to puff up, and his lip had a nasty cut.

Smoke saw an opening and was set perfectly to deliver the blow. He sent a long, whistling right into Blackwell's nose and when he felt the nose go under his hand, he knew that he had broken it.

Blackwell's nose bled, the blood ran down across his teeth and chin. The big man continued to throw great swinging blows toward Smoke, but he was getting clumsier and more uncoordinated with each swing.

Growing exhausted from his ineffective efforts, Blackwell quit swinging and started with bull-like charges, all of which Smoke was able to easily avoid. As Blackwell rushed by with his head down, Smoke stepped to one side and sent a powerful right jab to Blackwell's neck, connecting with his Adam's apple. Grabbing his neck, Blackwell went down, gasping for breath.

Smoke stepped up to him and drew his fist back for the final blow, but he stopped when he saw the abject fear in Blackwell's eyes. "You are a lucky man. You came at me with your fists. If you had come after me with a gun, you'd be dead."

As Smoke walked away, he saw Wes standing close by. It was his warning that had enabled Smoke to duck, thus ameliorating Blackwell's first blow. "Thanks, Wes."

"I never thought you could whup him. He's a lot bigger 'n you are."

"Big doesn't always count," Smoke said.

"Yes, sir, I seen that. And I'm goin' to 'member it, too."

"How is Seven doing?"

Wes smiled. "He's a great horse, 'n he won't let anybody aroun' him unless I say it's all right."

"That's because he knows his friends." Smoke flipped a quarter to the boy. "Tell you what. Why don't you give him an extra rubdown today?"

"Yes, sir!" Wes replied enthusiastically.

Smoke stepped into Dumplins a few minutes later.

He was greeted warmly by Kathy. "I hope you like biscuits and gravy, because that's what I've made for breakfast this morning."

"My favorite," Smoke replied with a smile.

After breakfast, Smoke tried to pay for it, but Kathy refused his money.

Smoke shook his head. "No ma'am. You fed me last night. I don't intend you to lose money on me."

"I'm not losing money. Your breakfast has already been paid for."

"What? Who would do that?"

"Mr. Vaughan picked up your bill," Kathy said, pointing to the newspaper publisher.

Smoke walked over to him. "Mr. Vaughan, I want to thank you for buying my breakfast, but there was no need for you to do that."

"It was my pleasure, Smoke." Vaughan chuckled. "Anyway, it isn't costing me anything. I paid for it with money that I won from you yesterday, so you might say that you are paying for it yourself."

"Well, then I don't feel so bad."

"By the way, do make it a point to read the *Delta Metro* today."

"*Delta Metro?*"

"That's my newspaper. The title comes from the delta formed by the confluence of Horse and Coffee creeks," Vaughan explained. "Not quite the Mississippi River Delta, I admit. But then, *metro* isn't any more appropriate than *delta*, so you might call it poetic license."

Later that same day, while sitting at a table in the back of the Salt Lick, Smoke saw his name in print for the very first time.

SMOKE JENSEN, WESTERN HERO

> *Yesterday our fair town of Buffington rang with the sound of gunfire as three outlaws attempted to hold up the bank. They were stopped and economic disaster was prevented by the heroic and timely intervention of Smoke Jensen.*
>
> *Like Leonidas at Thermopylae, Smoke stood his ground, defending a young child as he dispatched two of the would-be robbers and forced the third into an ignominious surrender.*
>
> *It is said that Smoke Jensen is seeking that most perfidious of outlaws, Angus Shardeen, with the intention of bringing him to justice. But Shardeen is a coward who surrounds himself with cowards, believing that there is bravery in numbers. This reporter has taken the measure of Smoke Jensen, and believes that he will find, and bring to justice, Angus Shardeen and his minions. Some may wish to compare Smoke Jensen with Don Quixote, dueling windmills. But I say that if it weren't for the Don Quixotes of the world, we would be overrun with windmills.*

Smoke chose the corner, which not only put his back to the wall, but limited the access to him from either side. One of the bar girls approached him, and he recognized her as the one who had come into his room last night. "Hello, Ida Jean. You aren't planning on coming into my room again tonight, are you?"

"No. You made it pretty clear last night that you aren't really interested in that sort of thing."

"Just because I didn't want to share my bed with you, doesn't mean I won't have a drink with a pretty girl." He gave her some money and she walked back over to the bar to buy the drinks.

As he watched her, Smoke noticed a man standing at the far end of the bar staring at him. The man had only half an ear on the left side of his face, and he was glaring at Smoke. An old memory flashed back.

"Spread 'er legs out, boys, I'm goin' to have me a little of this," one of the men was saying. He was a big ugly man with only half of one of his ears.

"Get away from her!" his ma said. She attacked the man.

"What the hell, Bartell, can't you handle a young girl and an old woman?" Shardeen asked with a demonic laugh.

The man at the bar was Billy Bartell, one of the men he had seen at the farm that day, and one of the men, it was said, who was still riding with Shardeen. Bartell had no way of recognizing Smoke, but must have had Smoke pointed out to him, because suddenly and without warning, Bartell reached for his pistol.

If Smoke had not recognized him, Bartell may have had an insurmountable advantage. As it was, he did have the advantage of drawing first, and his many years on the outlaw trail had made him a formidable man with a gun. He got his pistol out first, and for a brief second Bartell actually thought he had won. He smiled as he brought his pistol up.

It wasn't until then that Smoke drew and fired. The bullet hit Bartell in the chest with the impact of a hammer blow, and he was slammed back against the bar before sliding down. He sat there, leaning back against the bar, his gun hand empty and the unfired gun on the floor beside him. He watched as Smoke approached him.

"There ain't nobody that fast." Bartell coughed, a body-shaking cough.

"Don't die yet, Bartell. I want you to know why I killed you."

"I know you been alookin' for us. I reckon it's for the reward."

"It isn't for the reward. It's for Janey."

"Janey?" Bartell got a puzzled look on his face. "Are you crazy? I don't know nobody named Janey."

"I didn't say you knew her. But not knowing her didn't stop you from raping her when you and Shardeen raided my farm during the war."

"I raped a lot of women durin' the war. Some of 'em even liked it."

"She wasn't a woman. She was just a girl."

"How do you know it was me that done it?"

"Because I was there, and I saw you."

"You was there? You musta been just a kid then. How do you even know what you seen?"

Smoke's eyes glinted with retribution. "I know. Where is Angus Shardeen?"

Bartell coughed again, another body-racking cough, bringing up blood. "You know what? I think I am goin' to tell you where he's at. Only I ain't doin' you no favors, 'cause if you find 'im, he'll kill you."

"Where is he?"

"Rattlesnake Canyon." Bartell tried to laugh, but it turned into another blood-oozing cough. "Yeah, you go on out there . . . 'n after he kills you, me 'n you will be meetin' again . . . 'cause I'm goin' to be waitin' for you in hell."

There was a rattling sound deep in Bartell's throat, then his head fell to one side as his eyes, still open, glazed over.

Smoke called out, "Anybody know where Rattlesnake Canyon is?"

"It's about twenty miles west of here," one of the customers said.

"Thanks."

"Jensen, if that's really where he is, you might want to think twice 'bout goin' out there," the bartender said. "Shardeen has some bad men with 'im. You go out there alone, you'll just be committin' suicide."

"I thank you for your concern." Smoke started toward the door.

"You're goin' out there anyway, ain't you?" the man who had spoken to him earlier asked. "You're goin' out there, knowin' that in them rocks he may as well be in a fort, and knowin' how many men he's got with 'im."

Smoke stopped and turned around. "I've been after him for a long time. If he was on the moon, and there was some way I could get there, I would go after him."

"I know that area. Hell, if Shardeen is up there with his men, an army couldn't get him out of there."

"I won't be going with an army," Smoke said. "It'll just be me."

"All by yourself?"

"Yes. The problem with an army is that many men can't hide or keep quiet. Shardeen and his men would see an army comin', and they would be able get ready for them. But one man travelin' alone would more 'n likely be able slip around the rocks and through the crevices and such so as to be able to sneak up on them."

"Jensen, all I can say is, you got a lot more guts than you got brains."

Smoke left the saloon and went directly to the stable to get his horse.

Heckemeyer came over to talk to him as he was throwing the saddle over Seven. "I heered what you was plannin' on doin'. I mean, goin' after Shardeen 'n all."

"You aren't goin' to try and talk me out of it, are you, Mr. Heckemeyer? Because it won't do you any good. I'm goin'."

"I ain't goin' to try 'n talk you out of it. I just thought I might give you a little advice. When you get out there, they's two trails that go to the top," Heckemeyer said, speaking quietly. "You can stay mounted if you take the lower trail, but you'll have to leave your horse somewhere if you take the upper trail. The upper trail is a lot steeper and harder, but that's the one I'd take if I was you."

Smoke nodded as he tightened the cinch strap.

"Thing is . . . if you take the lower trail, you can be seen for a long way before you get there. You take the upper trail, you'll be on top long afore anyone has any idee that you're there."

"Thanks." Smoke handed Heckemeyer two dollar bills. "Give one of these to Wes. You keep the other one."

"Thank you," Heckemeyer said with a smile.

Smoke swung into the saddle, and with a nod, rode out through the open doors at the front of the stable.

Wes walked over then. "He won't be comin' back, will he?"

Heckemeyer gave Wes one of the two dollar bills. "More 'n likely, he won't even live to see the sun go down. 'N that's too bad. The world could use more men like him."

"He ain't goin' to get kilt," Wes said.

"What makes you so sure?"

"I just know."

Rattlesnake Canyon was unique in that it had so many perfectly formed arches that it almost looked as if they were man-made, rather than a work of nature. The interior was so well concealed by rocks and ridgelines that its entrance couldn't be seen unless someone was specifically looking for it. Inside the canyon was a source of water, which made it an ideal place for an outlaw encampment.

After Smoke dismounted, he let Seven go, but not ground tethered. He was free to graze and water. Remembering what Heckemeyer had told him about the two trails, Smoke took the upper one, staying close to the wall, and taking advantage of the many rocks and protrusions. He passed through apertures when possible, rather than going around or over the long fingers. The climb up to the top of the promontory was easy enough at first with an inclining ledge that allowed him to walk upright. The higher he got, the more narrow the ledge became until finally the only way he could stay on the ledge was by holding on to whatever rocks and protrusions he could grab. Then the ledge disappeared altogether, and at the very end of the climb, he had to go straight up, finding footholds and handholds where he could. Finally he reached the top.

From a concealed position, he saw several men sitting around a campfire about two hundred yards away. They were drinking coffee as casually as if they were in a downtown café, showing no concern about anyone approaching them, and why should they? There were five of them, and they were well fortified. Also, as Heckemeyer had promised, Smoke's approach had been totally unnoticed.

Smoke could see the men, but he couldn't approach them directly. Boulders and draws would provide them cover in any gunfight, but the two hundred yards between him and them were wide open, with very few positions along the way where he might be able to take cover.

Lying on his stomach, Smoke used a looking glass to peruse the campsite. He was able to pick out Shardeen, the prominent scar on his face making him easy to spot. Smoke counted six more men and . . . no. As he studied the faces, he realized there were only five more men. The sixth person was a woman.

At first, he thought she was one of them, then he saw that her arms and legs were bound. Whoever the woman was, she was their prisoner!

Smoke gave some consideration to just shooting Shardeen. After all, the Jayhawker was the one he wanted. If he killed him, he could just leave the others behind, then go after Potter, Stratton, and Richards—the men his pa had been after.

Smoke put the looking glass in his pocket and jacked a round into the Henry, then aimed at Shardeen. His finger rested on the trigger, but he didn't shoot. He couldn't do it. He couldn't just shoot Shardeen and leave. He couldn't leave the woman at the mercy of the others. He was sure they would kill her.

With a sigh of frustration, Smoke kept the Henry cocked, then stood up and walked toward the encampment. For the first twenty-five yards or so, nobody noticed him. Nobody expected anyone to just walk in on them.

"When in the hell is Bartell comin' back? He's s'posed to bring me a bottle of whiskey," one of the men complained.

Smoke recognized him as Tim Shardeen, the man he and his father had encountered a few years ago, when they first started West.

"Hell, Tim. More 'n likely he's took your money and bought his-self a woman," one of the others replied, and they all laughed.

"He better not have done that."

"Bartell's not coming back," Smoke said, his voice startling those gathered around the campfire.

"What the hell?" Tim shouted. "Who the hell are you?"

"I'm the man who killed Bartell."

One of the other men, responding more quickly to the unexpected intrusion, pulled his pistol and fired. Smoke fired back, never lifting the rifle higher than his waist. The man with the pistol went down.

Smoke fired two more times, killing two others. The remaining three men ran behind cover, leaving only the woman exposed.

In the open as he was, Smoke was at a disadvantage. He ran quickly to a small rock that did little to provide cover for him. They began shooting at him, the bullets hitting the rocky ground all around him, whining as they ricocheted away.

A puff of gun smoke hung just over one of the distant boulders, indicating that someone was behind it. Smoke aimed at the corner of the boulder and waited.

A few seconds later, a man's head rose up, just far enough for the man to see where to shoot.

It was all the opening Smoke needed. He squeezed the trigger and watched a little spray of blood and brain detritus fly out from the bullet wound in the outlaw's head.

The shooting stilled. A long period of silence was finally broken by a man's shout. "Shardeen? Shardeen, you yellow belly! Don't you leave me here all alone!"

Was Shardeen really leaving? Or was it merely a ploy? Smoke wondered.

"Shardeen! Come back here, you low-assed chicken!"

After that last shout, Smoke heard the clatter of horseshoes on the rocky surface as a horse galloped away.

The man shouted more obscenities, the tone of his voice betraying his anger and fear.

"Mister, it looks like you've been deserted. There's only one of you left," Smoke called out from behind his scant rock.

"Who the hell are you?" the disembodied voice shouted.

"My name is Smoke Jensen. Who are you?"

"The name is Hanks."

"Hanks? That name doesn't mean anything to me. I didn't come for you, Hanks. I came for Shardeen."

"Yeah, well, you mighta come for Shardeen, but you have near 'bout kilt all of us."

"Come on out into the open, and let me see you," Smoke invited. "I think we can palaver a little, then both of us go on our way."

"I ain't acomin' out lessen you do."

"We can come out at the same time."

Hanks tried a bit of negotiating. "You said you didn't come for me?"

"That's right."

"Then why don't you just ride away?"

"I'm not leavin' the woman here."

"Why not? She ain't nothin' to you."

"I'm not leavin' her here," Smoke said again a bit stronger. "Now, if you want this to end, put your gun in your holster and come on out."

"I'll come out, but I ain't puttin' my gun away."

"All right. Come on. As long you aren't shooting."

"You said we'd come out at the same time," Hanks replied.

"I'll count to three."

Smoke counted. At three, he stepped cautiously out into the open.

A small man with a narrow face and a hook nose came out from behind the boulder across from Smoke, gun in hand, though the gun was pointing down.

Smoke stood up and walked toward him, still holding the rifle. "Do you have any idea where Shardeen might have gone?"

"Why should I tell you?"

"Why shouldn't you? He ran off, didn't he? You don't owe him anything."

Hanks was obstinate. "I don't owe you nothin' neither."

Smoke walked backwards to the woman, keeping his eyes on the outlaw.

Although out in the open during the entire exchange of gunfire, she hadn't been hit, but her eyes were wide open with fear. So far, she had not uttered a sound.

"Let me get you untied. Then we'll get you back home." Smoke put the rifle down and leaned over to untie the woman.

"Look out!" she shouted suddenly.

In one motion, Smoke drew and fired at Hanks, who was raising his pistol and thumbing back the hammer.

With a bullet in his chest, he stumbled back with a look of shock and pain on his face. He dropped his gun, then slapped both hands over the wound. "How did you—?" was as far as he got before tumbling over, dead.

"Chugwater, Wyoming," the woman said as Smoke untied her.

"That's where you live?"

"No. That's where Shardeen will be going."

"How do you know?"

"He has a woman there. Lulu Barton."

"You know this woman?"

"She's my sister."

Sally Reynolds' first day in Bury, Idaho, was nearly her last. Nobody had met her at the train, so leaving her luggage at the depot to be picked up later, she started down the boardwalk toward the address that was on the acceptance letter she held in her hand.

Suddenly, she heard and felt the concussion of something whizzing by her very fast. Concurrent with her hearing the report of a gunshot, a bullet crashed through one of the square panes of the big glass window next to her. Actually, it was two gunshots, one right on top of the other. She turned and looked out into the street. Two men faced each other with smoking guns in their hands. She stared at them in shock for a moment, then one of the two men fell to the dirt.

"Miss!" A very attractive and expensively dressed woman called out to her. "Get in here, off the street! Quickly!"

Sally didn't need a second invitation to hurry into the building, which turned out to be a dress shop.

"There's likely to be more shooting. Clay, the man who was just shot, has a brother," the pretty woman said. "I expect Jeb will be coming out into the street shortly, wanting revenge."

"Heavens," Sally said. "Does this sort of thing go on often?"

"Fairly often."

True to the pretty lady's prediction a second man walked into the street, firing his pistol. The two men continued to shoot at each other until the second man, Sally assumed it was Jeb, went down. The first man put his gun back in the holster, then started toward a nearby saloon as several others rushed forward to congratulate him.

"It's over now," the pretty lady said.

"I must say, this was quite a dramatic welcome to Bury," Sally said.

"Just arrived?"

"Yes, by train a few minutes ago."

"Have you come to work at the Pink House?"

"The Pink House?"

The woman nodded. "For Miss Flora."

Sally shook her head. "I don't know who Miss Flora is." She smiled. "My name is Sally Reynolds, and I'm the new schoolteacher."

"A schoolteacher, are you? Well, Miss Reynolds, it's good to meet you. I'm Janey Garner." Janey remembered Miss Margrabe, and gave a passing wonder as to where she might be.

"Do you work at the Pink House? Whatever that is."

"No, I'm a business manager for PSR," Janey replied.

"PSR?"

"It's a ranch, the Potter, Stratton, and Richards. Only it's not just a ranch, it's a *huge* ranch."

"A lady ranch manager? That's most impressive. You must be as intelligent as you are beautiful."

Janey laughed and extended her hand. "Sally, I think you and I are going to wind up being very good friends."

CHAPTER 20

Smoke had been riding for more than six hours. Behind him, the darker color of hoof-churned earth stood out against the lighter, sunbaked ground. Before him, the desert stretched out in motionless waves, one right after another. As each wave was crested, another was exposed, and beyond that another still.

The only sounds were the jangle of the horse's bit and harness, the squeaking leather as he shifted his weight upon the saddle, and the dull thud of hoofbeats.

He had filled the canteen before he left Rattlesnake Canyon, but that was more than forty miles ago and he had come across no other water since then.

His tongue was swollen with thirst and the canteen was already down by a third, but he was allowing himself no more than one swallow of water per hour. He was also rationing the water for Seven by taking two mouthfuls, then spitting the water into his hat and holding the hat up for Seven to drink.

"I'm sorry, boy. This is all we have," he apologized, feeling sorry for the horse. "I tell you what. I won't be riding you anymore. We'll both walk the rest of the way," he promised.

Smoke had no idea how much farther he would have to go, but he was determined not to burden Seven any longer.

Just before dark, a scattering of adobe buildings rose from the desert floor, wavering in the shimmering heat waves. The buildings so matched the desert in color and texture that Smoke wasn't even sure the town was there. Gathering what strength he had remaining, he started toward it. He had no other choice. If it was real, he and Seven would live. If it was a mirage, they would probably die.

It took at least another hour to reach the town, but within thirty minutes he knew that the town was real. "It's real, Seven!" Smoke exclaimed, his voice hoarse from thirst. "It's a real town! A real town with water!"

At the edge of town he stopped to catch his breath and read the sign.

CHUGWATER, WYOMING
POP. 256
"FRIENDLY PEOPLE"

Smoke limped on into town and, seeing a pump in the town square, hurried toward it. He moved the handle a couple times and was rewarded by seeing a wide, cool stream of water pour from the pump mouth. Holding his hat under the pump, he filled his hat and let Seven drink. Seven finished that hatful and two more before Smoke allowed himself to drink. Putting his left hand in front of the spout, he caused the water to pool and, continuing to pump, drank deeply. Never, in his life, had anything tasted better to him.

With the killing thirst satisfied, Smoke stood up from the pump and patted Seven on his neck. "I'm sorry to have put you through that, Seven, but you were a good horse, and I'm proud of you."

Just down the street a door slammed, and an isinglass shade came down on the upstairs window. A sign creaked in the wind and flies buzzed loudly around a nearby pile of horse manure.

Smoke walked on down the street, leading Seven. He saw three saloons, sure that if Angus Shardeen was there, he would be in one of them.

But which one?

Smoke continued walking as he looked around. A horse in front of a saloon that identified itself as the Ace High caught his attention. Under the saddle was a distinctive saddle blanket—dark blue with a gold band around the outside edge. Nestled in the corner was the silver eagle insignia of a colonel.

He remembered seeing the very saddle blanket on one of the horses when his farm had been raided. He knew that would be Shardeen's horse. Whether he was really a colonel or not, he had passed himself off as such.

After examining the horse, Smoke started toward the saloon door.

A man stepped in front of him. "Where do you think you're goin'?"

The man blocking Smoke's way was thin and muscular, with a moustache that curved up at each end like the horns on a Texas steer. He was wearing a yellow duster, pulled back on one side to expose a Colt sheathed in a man's leg holster that was tied halfway down his leg. He had an angry, evil countenance, and looking directly at him was like staring into the eyes of an angry bull.

"Mister, you're in my way," Smoke said dryly.

"Would your name be Smoke Jensen?"

Smoke was surprised to hear himself addressed by name in a town that he had never visited.

"It is. Why? Do you have a particular interest in me?"

"Yeah, I've got an interest in you." The big man pulled his yellow duster to one side and Smoke saw a peace-officer's badge pinned to his shirt.

"I've got one of those, too." Smoke showed his own Deputy U.S. Marshal's badge. "And my badge outranks yours. Now, step out of the way. I've got business inside."

"Would that business have anything to do with Angus Shardeen?" the lawman asked.

"It would."

The lawman shook his head. "Uh-uh. Not here. Shardeen has been good to this town, so he has sanctuary in Chugwater."

"Mister, if I had to go to hell to get Shardeen, I would do it," Smoke said coldly. "As far as I'm concerned, he doesn't have sanctuary anywhere. Now, get out of my way."

The lawman went for his gun. He was exceptionally fast and his hand moved toward his Colt as quickly as a striking rattlesnake.

Smoke had not expected the lawman to draw on him and didn't even start for his gun until the man's gun was coming out. But if Smoke had been surprised by the lawman's sudden draw, the peace officer was undoubtedly surprised by the speed with which Smoke drew and fired.

The lawman staggered backward, crashing through the batwing doors, and backpedaling into the saloon, landing flat on his back, his unfired gun still in his hand.

Smoke bounded up the steps, onto the porch, then pushed through the batwing doors, following the lawman's body inside. A wisp of smoke curled up from the barrel of the pistol he still held in his hand.

"Mister, you just killed our marshal," said one of the men in the saloon.

"Yeah, I guess I did." Smoke slipped his pistol back into its holster.

"Damn. I never figured anyone would be good enough to beat Coyle."

"He drew first," Smoke said. "I didn't have any choice."

"Uh-huh. He drew first, but you still beat him. Is that what you want us to believe?"

"To tell the truth, I don't care whether any of you believe it or not," Smoke said. "I'm a Deputy United States Marshal, and I've come to arrest Angus Shardeen." He saw the nervous exchanges of glances among the customers in the saloon.

"What makes you think Shardeen is here?"

"His horse is out front." Smoke stood for a moment, studying the layout. To his left was the bar. In front of him were four tables; to the right, a potbellied stove, sitting in a box of sand. Because it was summer, the stove was cold, but the stale, acrid smell of last winter's smoke still hung in the air.

One man was behind the bar, three customers were in front of it, and a heavily painted bar girl was standing at the far end of it. At least six more men sat at the tables.

"I know he's here," Smoke said. "Now, where is he?"

No one answered.

Smoke drew his pistol from its holster. "I asked, where is he?" When still no one answered, he pointed his pistol toward the barkeep and pulled the hammer back. A deadly double *click* sounded as the sear engaged the cylinder. "You want to die protecting a murderer like Shardeen?"

"I don't know where he is, mister," the barkeep answered nervously. "I don't pay no attention to what folks come and go here."

"For God's sake, tell 'im, Gene!" the woman said. "He's right, you know. A man like Shardeen ain't worth dyin' for. Just—"

"Sue Ann, shut your mouth," the bartender ordered in sharp anger, cutting her off in mid-sentence.

"Mister, I think you had better be the one who keeps quiet." Smoke lowered his pistol. "Go ahead, Sue Ann. Where is he?"

She looked nervously toward the bartender.

"Don't be worrying about Gene. If that's all that's keeping you from talking, I'll kill him for you right now." Again, Smoke pointed his pistol toward the bartender.

"Tell 'im, Sue Ann!" Gene shouted nervously. "Tell 'im!"

"He's up there," Sue Ann said, lifting her head toward the landing that looked out over the saloon floor. "First room on the right. He went upstairs with Lulu."

"Thanks." With his pistol still cocked, and holding it in his crooked arm, muzzle point up, Smoke started up the stairs. He had just reached the top step when the bartender shouted a warning.

"Shardeen! Look out! Someone's comin' up for you!"

Surprised that anyone would actually shout a warning, Smoke turned to look back downstairs. Gene was standing at the bottom of the stairs with a double-barrel shotgun pointing up at him.

Smoke managed to jump behind the corner at the top of the stairs, just as Gene fired. The load of buckshot tore a large hole in the door to a room just behind him. Smoke fired back before Gene could get off a second shot. His bullet hit Gene in the forehead, and he dropped the shotgun, then fell heavily to the floor.

At almost the same moment, four shots sounded from inside one of the rooms. Dust and sawdust flew as the bullets punched holes through the door. Smoke flattened himself against the wall, clear of the door. A second later, he heard the sound of crashing window glass.

Smoke ran to the door, kicked it open, and dashed into the room. A naked woman on the bed screamed as he rushed by her to the broken window. He leaned through the shattered glass to look down to the ground below. If Shardeen had jumped through the window, Smoke should still be able to see him.

He wasn't there.

Intuitively, Smoke realized that someone was behind him and he turned, leaping to one side, just as Shardeen, with a broad, triumphant grin on his face, pulled the trigger. The bullet slammed into the wall behind where Smoke had been but a split second earlier.

Smoke fired back. As his bullet struck home, Shardeen's grin of triumph turned to a look of shock and pain.

Shardeen dropped his pistol, put his hands over the wound in his chest, then sank to his knees. He looked up at his shooter. "You must be Smoke Jensen."

"I am."

"Why? Why have you hounded me all these years? I don't even remember you."

"It doesn't matter. I remember you."

* * *

The old mountain man and the gunfighter rode slowly down the main street of Yampa, Colorado, drawing some attention. The sheriff and one of his deputies were among those watching the pair as they reined up in front of the saloon and dismounted.

The sheriff approached them. "Howdy, boys," he greeted.

"Sheriff," Smoke replied.

The lawman looked at the mountain man. "You're the one called Preacher?"

"That's what I'm called."

"And you are the gun hand called Smoke."

"That's what I'm called," Smoke replied, mimicking Preacher's response.

"You boys planning on staying long?"

Smoke turned his dark eyes on the sheriff and let them smolder for a few seconds. "Long enough to do what we plan to do."

"I've been hearing a lot about you, Smoke Jensen," the sheriff said, speaking in low tones. "I've heard how you killed Sledge Blackwell, Billy Bartell, how you wiped Shardeen's band like some one man army, and how you went up to Chugwater, Wyoming, and killed Angus Shardeen his ownself. I hope you ain't lookin' for anyone in this town. Yampa is a nice little place. I wouldn't want to see it turned into a battleground."

Smoke smiled at the sheriff. "You don't mind if we buy some supplies, have a few hot meals, and rest for a day or two, do you, Sheriff? Maybe take a hot bath?"

"Speak for yourself on that last part," Preacher said. "I had me a bath no more 'n a month ago. I don't hold with too much bathin'. It ain't healthy, keepin' your skin all exposed like that."

"Smoke, from ever'thing I've heard, you ain't never kilt nobody that didn't need killin'," the sheriff said. "I'm just sort of hopin' that nothin' like that happens here. If you'll give me your word on it, why, that'll be good enough for me."

"Sheriff, I'm not after anybody in this town. To be truthful with you, my pa is buried at the foot of Zenobia Peak, 'n all I got in mind is just visiting his grave and payin' my respects."

The sheriff nodded. "You got ever' right to do that. I'm sorry if I come off a bit cantankerous there, 'n I hope you don't take offense, but I feel like I owe it to the folks here 'bout to keep the peace as best I can."

"I understand. No offense taken," Smoke said.

"Also, I'm sorry 'bout your pa."

"I appreciate the sentiment," Smoke replied.

The sheriff wasn't the only one who had heard about Smoke single-handedly cleaning out the Angus Shardeen gang. By the time he and Preacher stepped into the saloon, word of their arrival had spread and, in the words of one of the saloon patrons, "Your money is no good here! Anybody that's got rid of a no-account polecat like Angus Shardeen and those scoundrels who rode with him has done a good service to ever'one between St. Louis and the Pacific Ocean."

"What will you have?" the bartender asked.

"Before we get started on the drinkin', don't you think maybe we should get us a bite or two to eat?" Preacher suggested.

"We got food," the bartender said. "Our food is as good as anything you'll get over at the City Pig Café."

"What do you have?"

"Beans cooked with ham, taters, and hot peppers, with a side of turnip greens, and cornbread."

"Sounds good enough," Smoke said.

"You got coffee?" Preacher asked. "I don't mean brown water. I mean real coffee."

"You like it strong, do you?" the bartender asked.

Smoke chuckled. "If it won't float a horseshoe, it's too weak."

"I'll see what I can do."

After the meal, Smoke and Preacher enjoyed a couple beers bought for them by the patrons of the saloon. They could have had as many as they wanted, without having to pay for any, but Smoke knew better than to ever allow himself to get drunk.

"Last thing you need is to be too drunk when some young scoundrel decides to make a name for hisself by shootin' you," Preacher had told him once.

It hadn't been necessary for Preacher to warn him. He had figured that out a long time ago.

In Bury, Idaho, Sally Reynolds was having lunch with Miss Flora. They were dining in Sally's house, because Flora didn't want to embarrass Sally by being seen in public with her.

"Nonsense," Sally said. "Why should I be embarrassed to be seen with you?"

"I'm a lady of the night, honey. I own the Pink House, and the girls who work there, work for me. I don't actually bed with men, but how do you think I got the money to buy the house in the first place?"

"I want to read something to you," Sally said. She stepped over to the buffet to pick up a Bible, turned to the selection she wanted, and began to read. "'And one of the Pharisees desired that he would eat with him. And he went into the Pharisee's house, and sat down to meat. And, behold, a woman in the city, which was a sinner, when she knew that Jesus sat at meat in the Pharisee's house, brought an alabaster box of ointment, and stood at his feet behind him weeping, and began to wash his feet with tears, and did wipe them with the hairs of her head, and kissed his feet, and anointed them with the ointment.

"'Now when the Pharisee which had bidden him saw it, he spake within himself, saying, This man, if he were a prophet, would have known who and what manner of woman this is that toucheth him: for she is a sinner.

"'And Jesus turned to the woman, and said unto Simon, Seest thou this woman? I entered into thine house, thou gavest me no water for my feet: but she hath washed my feet with tears, and wiped them with the hairs of her head. Thou gavest me no kiss: but this woman since the time I came in hath not ceased to kiss my feet. My head with oil thou didst not anoint: but this woman hath anointed my feet with ointment.

"'Wherefore I say unto thee, her sins, which are many, are forgiven; for she loved much: but to whom little is forgiven, the same loveth little.'"

Closing the Bible, Sally smiled at Miss Flora. "You are a *friend*, Flora."

"Janey said you were different from the others," Flora said. "She said you wouldn't judge her."

"You mean because she isn't just a business manager, she is also Josh Richards's mistress? No, I don't judge her at all. She was very nice to me the first day I arrived in town." Sally laughed. "She was more than nice. I'm quite sure that she saved my life."

EPILOGUE

Smoke stood at the grave of his father, holding his hat in his hands. He was pleased to see that the markings he had chiseled in the rock-turned-tombstone were still quite legible. Preacher was standing some distance away, having told Smoke that he needed some private time with his pa.

"Pa, I've settled some accounts. I've killed Billy Bartell. He was the man that raped Janey, and in my way of thinking, is probably the one that sent her down the wrong trail. I don't know where she is now, and to be honest with you, I haven't been lookin' for her. I hope she's alive, and livin' well somewhere, but I figure that's none of my doin' anymore. I set things right for her, by killin' Bartell. What happens to her from now on is up to her.

"I'm happy to say, I also found and killed Angus Shardeen. I told you he's the one that killed Ma.

"I'd like to say that ever'thing is all settled now, but I can't say that just yet. I'm goin' after the ones that killed you and Luke. I killed Ted Casey already. He was one you didn't know about. I know the names of the others—Wiley Potter, Keith Stratton, and Josh Richards. I'm goin' to find 'em, Pa, and I'm goin' to make things right. I give you that promise."

Smoke stood there in silence for another moment, then put his hat on, and started back toward Preacher.

"Got things settled with your pa?" Preacher asked.

"Yeah."

"He was real proud of you, boy. Same as I am."

The lump in Smoke's throat wouldn't let him reply.

PART TWO

MATT JENSEN:
THE LAST
MOUNTAIN MAN

CHAPTER 1

Martin Cavanaugh shifted his position on the saddle to try and find some relief from the bone-deep tired of four long years of war. Although Cavanaugh was mustered out at Jefferson Barracks in St. Louis, he was still wearing the uniform of a captain of the Union Cavalry as he made the long ride back home to Kansas.

Just ahead was an old, weather-beaten building. For a moment, he thought it might be deserted; then he saw a hand-lettered sign nailed to the side.

FOOD—WHISKEY—TERBACKY—GOODS—BEDS

He didn't plan to waste any of his mustering-out money on a bed, but he thought a meal might be good. Also, he could use a drink, and a little tobacco for the trail, so he rode up to the building, dismounting at the hitching rail.

There were two men sitting on the porch. Both were wearing the tattered gray and butternut uniform of the Confederate army. One had sergeant's chevrons, but the tunic was so filthy that they barely showed. He had a puffy scar, starting above his left eye, disfiguring the eye, then streaking down his cheek and jaw like a purple flash of lightning, twisting the left side of his mouth into a sneer. The other man was wearing a bushy black beard, but the most distinctive thing about him was his left ear. Only half of it was there, the earlobe having been shot off in the war. Both men were thin, and they had the look in their eyes and faces of men who had seen a lot of the war.

Warily, Martin nodded at them as he passed by them to go inside the building. The two Rebel soldiers returned the nod, but they never took their eyes off him. One of them spat a stream of tobacco juice in the dirt, but neither of them spoke.

The interior of the inn was a study of shadow and light. Some of the light came through the door and some through windows that were nearly opaque with dirt. Most of it, however, was in the form of gleaming dust motes that hung suspended in the still air, illuminated by the bars of sunbeams that stabbed through the cracks between the boards.

Martin found a table in the back corner of the room, near the stove. Since it was warm outside, the stove wasn't being used, but the smell of burnt wood clung to it like the low-lying, early morning fog on a grassy meadow.

The proprietor of the establishment came over to his table. Picking some sort of bug from his beard, he examined it for a moment, then flicked it away.

"What can I get for you?"

"What do you have to eat?"

"Beans, bacon, biscuits."

"All right, I'll have that. Do you have beer?"

"I've got whiskey."

"A glass of whiskey and some tobacco."

"Chewin' or smokin'?"

"Smoking."

"I've got a woman here iffen you'd like to spend a little time with her. It'll cost you six bits," the proprietor said. He nodded toward a woman who was sitting a few tables away. She smiled a toothless smile at him, and brushed an errant tendril of hair back from her forehead.

"No, thanks," Martin said. "I've got a woman of my own, and two kids, waitin' for me back home."

"Suit yourself," the proprietor said. "I'll get your vittles." He turned away from the table and walked back into what Martin assumed was a kitchen.

Even as he was giving his order to the proprietor, Martin saw the two Confederate soldiers come inside. They sat at a table near the door, but he noticed that both of them sat in such a way as to be facing him. Something about the way they were looking at him made him suspicious, so he eased his pistol out of his holster and held it under the table.

"Cap'n?" one of the men said. This was the one with sergeant's stripes. "You are a Yankee cap'n, ain't you?"

"The war's over, boys," Martin said. "I'm a civilian now, same as you two."

"Ain't quite the same," the sergeant said. "You still got your horse. The Yankees took our horses."

"I'm sorry to hear that."

"The name is Payson. Clyde Payson," the sergeant said. "This here is Garvey Laird. It's like I was tellin' Garvey, we got us a long way to go and the way things is now, 'bout the onliest way we got of gettin' there is by shank's mare."

"Well, Sergeant Payson, I feel for you, I truly do," Martin said. "I've got a long way to go myself, and I'd hate to have to make the whole trip without a horse."

"Yeah, well, here's the point," Payson continued. "Me'n Garvey here was thinkin' on maybe takin' your horse."

"What good would that do you?" Martin asked. "There are two of you, there's only one horse."

"We figure we could double up till we come up on another horse," Payson said.

"Oh, I don't think I would like that," Martin said. "And I know my horse wouldn't like it—being ridden double like that, I mean."

Garvey barked what might have been a laugh. "Well, now, that's real funny," he said. "Specially seein' as the horse ain't goin' have no say-so in the matter. And like you say, there's two of us and only one of you."

Payson and Garvey stood up from their table and made a point of turning to face Martin.

Martin moved the pistol out from under the table and pointed it at them.

The two soldiers, surprised to see that Martin was holding a gun on them, stopped in their tracks.

"Hold on, mister, we didn't mean nothin' like that," Payson said. "We was just goin' to palaver a bit, that's all."

"I'd feel a mite more comfortable if you boys weren't wearin' guns while we were palaverin'," Martin said. "How about comin' over here and droppin' 'em down in the stove?"

"Now why would we want to do a fool thing like that?" Garvey asked.

"Because I'll kill you if you don't," Martin said easily. He punctuated his comment by pulling back the hammer on his pistol. It made a deadly-sounding click as the sear engaged the cylinder. "I killed my share of men wearing that uniform. I wouldn't lose any sleep over killin' two more."

The two Confederate soldiers stared at him for a long moment, but did nothing.

"Use your thumb and finger to pull your guns out, then carry them over here and drop them in the stove," Martin said.

The two did as Martin ordered.

"Now what?" Payson asked.

"How long has it been since you two boys had anything to eat?" Martin asked.

"We had some hardtack yesterday," Garvey said.

"Nothing since?"

Both shook their heads.

"Sit down over there," Martin said, waving his pistol toward one of the tables.

The two complied.

"Innkeeper," Martin called.

"Yes, sir?" the innkeeper replied. It wasn't until then that Martin noticed the innkeeper was standing just inside the door from the kitchen, holding a plate of beans, bacon, and biscuits. He had watched the entire drama unfold.

"How about feeding these two boys?" Martin said. "On me."

"Cap'n, you'd do that for us after we was goin' to steal your horse?" Payson asked.

"Yeah, why not?" Martin answered. "And it isn't captain, it's mister now," Martin said. "Name's Cavanaugh. Like I said, the war's over. No need for us to be killin' each other anymore."

Fellsburg, Kansas

Matt Cavanaugh knocked on the door of the office of the R.D. Clayton Livery Stable.

"Come on in, Matt."

Although only nine years old, Matt was a big boy for his age and had proven to be a good worker for the owner of the livery.

"I'm all finished, Mr. Clayton," Matt said.

"Every stall is mucked out?" Clayton asked.

"Yes, sir, every one," Matt said.

Clayton was in his late sixties, a bald-headed, fat man with chin whiskers.

"Don't think I'm not going to inspect the stalls," Clayton said. "I'm paying you fifty cents a week to keep 'em clean. I don't intend to throw away good money on a bad job."

"You can check, Mr. Clayton," Matt said. "I cleaned them all."

"You wait here till I get back," Clayton said.

"Yes, sir," Matt said.

Matt picked up the newspaper and began reading it as he waited.

FREE LAND IN THE WEST

Reports have reached this city of much free land in the West. With the rebellion now put to rest, the government is anxious to see enterprising citizens occupy land in the more western extremes of the nation, thus expanding the reach of civilization and enterprise.

"Here, boy," Clayton said, returning to the office. "If you want to read the paper, you will have to pay for it the same as I did."

"I'm sorry," Matt said. "I meant no harm."

Clayton ran his hand through his hair, then sighed. "Go ahead, take it," he said. "I have finished with it." He stuck his hand in his pocket and pulled out a coin. "Here is your half-dollar. You did good work."

"Thank you," Matt replied, taking the coin.

Matt's mother, Mary, and his fourteen-year-old sister, Cassie, were hanging clothes on a line. They took in washing while Matt worked at the stables to make enough money to buy food. They were living in an old cabin that was within sight of a burned-out house and barn. The house and barn were part of what had once been a very fine ranch. It had been destroyed by Bushwhackers two years earlier.

"Here's my week's pay, Ma," Matt said, handing the half-dollar to his mother.

"Oh, Matthew," Mary said, putting her arms around her young son and pulling him to her. "You are such a help. I am so proud of you. You work so hard for the money that I just wish you could keep it for yourself."

"Someone's coming up the road, Mama," Cassie said.

"A soldier?" Mary asked.

"It looks like a soldier," Cassie replied.

"No doubt someone going home," Mary said. "We'll have to set an extra plate for supper."

"Mama, why do we have to feed all the strays?" Cassie asked.

"Child, your pa is on the road somewhere, coming home to us," Mary replied. "Wouldn't you like for someone to be feeding him, if he's hungry, or giving him a place to get out of the rain?"

"Yes, ma'am, I reckon you're right," Cassie said.

"You go set the extra plate, I'll invite him," Mary said. "Maybe he knows something about . . ." Mary stopped in mid-sentence and stared long and hard at the approaching rider. "It's him," she said in a small, quiet voice.

"Mama?"

"Praise be to God, it's him!" Mary said, shouting loudly this time. "Children, it's your father, come safely home to us!"

Spreading her arms wide, Mary started running toward the rider. The rider spurred his mount into a gallop, then leaped down from his horse just as Mary reached him. They embraced in the middle of the road.

"Is that Pa?" Matt asked.

"Of course it is," Cassie said. "Don't you remember him?"

"Yeah," Matt said, "I remember him."

Though Matt said the words, he wasn't sure he remembered his father well enough to recognize him. Matt had been five years old when Martin Cavanaugh left home as a lieutenant in the Ninth Cavalry Regiment of Kansas. His memory was hazy, and consisted mostly of seeing a tall man, in uniform, riding away on the horse Buster.

"No, I didn't bring Buster back," Matt's father said over supper that night. "Buster was killed at a place called Pleasant Hill."

"Poor Buster," Mary said. "He was such a good horse."

"Yes, he was," Martin agreed. He got up from the table to pour himself another cup of coffee. Then he stood at the window for a long moment, looking toward the burned-out house and barn.

"When did that happen?" he asked, nodding toward the ruins.

"Three years ago," Mary said. "Bushwhackers came by, burned us out, and took what livestock we had left."

"I'm sorry," Martin said. "Here I go off to fight the war, thinking I'm protecting you, and the war comes here to you."

"It doesn't matter," Mary said. She walked over to put her arms around him. "You are home now. Everything will be fine."

"Mama, what about the bank?" Cassie asked.

"The bank? What about the bank?" Martin asked.

"It's nothing. We can discuss it later."

Martin shook his head. "It won't go away by putting it off, will it?"

Mary sighed. "No, I don't suppose it will," she said.

"What about the bank?"

"I—I'm sorry, Martin. I had no choice, I had to mortgage the place."

"And now the bank wants to foreclose?"

Mary wiped a tear away as she nodded.

"I'm so sorry," she repeated. "I know how important this place was to you."

"Nonsense," Martin said. "This is just a place. I've seen hundreds of places in the last five years. You and the children are all that's important to me now."

"Mama took in laundry and I helped," Cassie said proudly. "And Matt works down at Clayton's Livery."

"I muck out the stalls," Matt said.

"You've taken in your last laundry and you've mucked out your last stall," Martin said.

"But what are we going to do? The bank wants the money and we don't have enough, do we? Did you bring any money home with you?"

"How much do we owe the bank?"

"Five hundred dollars."

Martin shook his head. "I don't have that much. But I have enough for us to start over somewhere else."

"Start over where?" Mary asked.

"Out West!" Matt said excitedly.

"Out West?" Mary chuckled. "Matthew, wherever did you get such an idea?"

"I read about it in the paper in Mr. Clayton's office," Matt said. "There's free land out West for people who want it."

"Free land. I've never heard of such a thing," Mary said.

Martin held up his hand. "No," he said, "I've heard that. I wasn't sure whether or not it was true, but I have heard it." He looked over at Matt. "You say you read this in the paper?"

"Yes, sir, I read it today," he said.

"Free land in the West, huh?"

"Martin, what are you talking about? Surely you don't intend to just leave here, do you?"

"What is there here for us, Mary?" Martin asked. "My parents are dead, your parents are dead. Neither one of us have a brother or sister. What's keeping us here?"

"Well, nothing, I guess," Mary replied. "But how are we going to get there?"

"You let me worry about that," Martin said. "First thing I'm going to do tomorrow is find out how a person gets hold of some of this free land. Then, if I see it's somethin' we can do, I'll figure out a way to get us there."

"All right," Mary said. "Whatever you decide is fine with me."

"It's real good to see you back, Martin," C.D. Folsom said the next morning when Martin rode into town to see him. Folsom was president of the Fellsburg Bank. "Yes, sir, it's good to see all our men back home from that war."

"Not everyone made it back," Martin said.

"No, sir, they didn't and that's a fact," Folsom said. "How many did we lose?"

"Three officers, one hundred ninety-two enlisted men," Martin said.

Folsom shook his head. "Well, now, that is a shame," he said. "That is truly a shame." Folsom cleared his throat. "But I'm sure you came to discuss business, right?"

"I did," Martin said.

"Your note is for $594.60," Folsom said. "I'm sure you will want to pay that off so you can get back to running your ranch."

"Five hundred ninety-four?" Martin said, surprised by the figure.

"And sixty cents," Folsom added.

"I thought the note was for five hundred dollars."

"It was originally. But with compound interest for three years, it comes to $594.60. You do have the money, don't you?"

Martin shook his head. "No," he said. "No, I don't."

Folsom blew air through pursed lips and tapped his fingers on his desk for a moment. "I see," he said. "Uh, Mr. Cavanaugh . . ."

Martin couldn't help but notice that the friendly "Martin" had changed to the more businesslike "Mr. Cavanaugh."

"I hope you weren't counting on the bank extending your note any longer. We extended it once for your wife last year. Of course, I suppose if you could pay just the interest . . ."

"I don't have enough money to pay the interest either," Martin said.

"Then what exactly do you propose?"

"I would sell my ranch to the bank," Martin said. "You can give me the difference between what the ranch is worth and what I owe."

"You have to be joking."

"No, I'm very serious."

"Mr. Cavanaugh, you owe almost six hundred dollars. If the buildings had not been burned out during the war, it might be worth a thousand dollars. But with the buildings gone, it is barely worth what you owe."

"But it is worth what I owe?" Martin asked.

"Barely."

Martin sighed. "If I signed the ranch over to the bank, would it clear the books for me?"

"We are a bank, Mr. Cavanaugh, not a realtor."

"And yet, when you loan money on property, don't you always run that risk?" Martin asked.

Folsom nodded. "We do."

"Then I ask you again. If I sign the ranch over to you, will it clear the books?"

"I hate to see you do that," Folsom said.

"I don't see as I have any choice," Martin said. "Nor you either, for that matter. Because I'm either going to walk away from here after making a deal with you, or I'm simply going to walk away. In either case, you are going to wind up owning the ranch, but in the latter case, you are going to be out the legal expenses of foreclosure."

"I don't like being put over a barrel like this, Cavanaugh," Folsom said. Now, even the "Mr." had been dropped.

"Believe me, Mr. Folsom, I don't like this any more than you do. But I know that my ranch, even without the house and barn, is worth almost a thousand dollars. I figure that, in the long run, you are making out on the deal."

"All right," Folsom finally said after a long moment of contemplation. "I'll have Miss Steward draw up the papers for you to sign."

"Thank you," Martin said.

"Where are you going now?" Folsom asked.

Martin smiled.

"Out West," he said.

CHAPTER 2

With Smoke Jensen

As Matt Cavanaugh and his family prepared to start their trek West, another young man, some eight years older than Matt, was standing in front of a trading post, watching his own father ride away. When he and his father had come West a year earlier, they'd met up with an old mountain man known only as Preacher.

Preacher had befriended the men, taking a special interest in young Kirby Jensen, providing him with an education in survival that was the equal in intensity and thoroughness to a doctorate in any chartered university.

Kirby had already proven his worth in a short, but savage Indian battle and, though he was only seventeen years old, he could hold his own with anyone. Preacher had given him the nickname Smoke, and already, Smoke thought of himself in that way.

"Where's Pa goin', Preacher?" Smoke asked the old mountain man.

Preacher squirted out a stream of tobacco juice, then swiped the back of his hand across his mouth before he answered.

"Your pa ever tell you about a man by the name of Casey? Ted Casey?"

"I've heard the name," Smoke said. "And from the way he said it, I figured there was bad blood between them. But he never told me anything specific."

"I reckon that's because he still sees you as a boy, and not a man," Preacher said. "Maybe a pa always looks at his son that way."

"Pa's goin' to look Casey up?"

Preacher nodded. "He's got some business to take care of with him," the old man answered.

"Killing business?"

Preacher nodded. "I reckon so. Problem is, Casey ain't likely to be alone."

Smoke watched as his father stopped, turned his horse around, and waved. Smoke returned the wave; then his pa was gone, dipping out of sight over the rise of a small hill.

Smoke's pa had taken a few gold coins with him, but he'd left the bulk of his money with his son. Smoke felt the weight of the money in his pouch, then cleared his throat before he spoke. He had to, because he knew that he would have a catch in his throat if he hadn't, and he didn't want to sound like a baby to Preacher.

"He won't be coming back, will he, Preacher?"

"Like as not, he won't," Preacher said. "If you want to cry, Smoke, why, there ain't no shame in it. You could step around behind the trading post and have yourself a good cry all alone."

"I haven't cried since my ma died," Smoke said. "Don't reckon I'll be doin' any cryin' now."

Smoke made a few purchases with the money his father had left him and now, with a new pistol, knife, and Henry rifle in his saddle sheath, he rode with Preacher through the thick timber and up into the high country. It was their way to ride without talking, so Smoke saved all his questions for nighttime, when they were camped by a small fire that popped and snapped and sent sparks up as it cooked the bacon and warmed the coffee.

"How old were you when you come out here, Preacher?"

"Fourteen or so," Preacher said. "I run away from home at twelve, fought in the Battle of New Orleans, cordelled upriver to St. Louis, then found my way out here. Been here ever since."

"You've never been back East?"

"Once, I went to Philadelphia to kill a man that needed killin'," Preacher said matter-of-factly. "But for the most part, I been out here all along."

"You never got married?"

"Injun married," Preacher said.

"You got 'ny kids?"

"You ask a lot of questions."

"How'm I goin' to learn if I don't ask questions?" Smoke replied.

"You'll learn what I want you to learn," Preacher said. "Get some sleep now. We got us a lot of ridin' to do yet."

With Matt Cavanaugh

Matt wondered if this was what it was like to be at sea. For the last two weeks, they had been following a set of wagon tracks that stretched front and back from horizon to horizon, broken here and there by deeply cut gullies and rock outcroppings. The wagon tracks were from the days of the great wagon trains, two decades earlier. Now their wagon was all alone, its movement providing the only animation on the vast, open plain.

Matt and his father were walking alongside the wagon, which was being driven by Matt's mother. Cassie had been walking as well, but a few minutes earlier had climbed up onto the seat to ride beside Mary.

"Pa, what was it like in the war?" Matt asked.

"It was like hell," Martin answered.

"Really? You mean like it says in the Bible, with the Devil and a burning pit of fire?"

"You might say that," Martin said. "There was fire, and there certainly was a Devil, though just who he was depends on the tellin', I reckon."

"Martin," Mary said, calling down from the wagon seat. "Over there."

Martin moved up to the front of the wagon so he could look to the other side, in the direction pointed out by Mary. He saw six riders coming toward them.

"Indians, do you think?"

"No, I don't think so," Martin said. "Not from the way they're riding."

The riders, still about a half mile away, turned toward the wagon, approaching it at a leisurely gait.

"What do you think they want?" Mary asked.

"I don't know," Martin answered.

"Should I stop?" Mary asked.

"I see no need to stop," Martin said. "Just keep on going. I reckon we'll find out what they want when they get here."

The wagon continued to roll across the plains, the wheels creak-

ing, the pots and pans banging back and forth, the tree chains clink-
ing, the horse hooves rising and falling. All the while, Martin kept an
eye on the riders who were coming closer and closer.

"Matt," Martin said. "Move the rifle over to where I can get to it."

"Martin, no," Mary said. "You are just one man. You know you
can't take them all on. And if they see you with a rifle, it might pro-
voke them."

Martin ran his hand over his cheek, then nodded. "You may be
right," he said.

The riders, all of whom were wearing long, tan dusters, came up
to the wagon. Martin recognized two of them. One was the man
with the puffy scar that disfigured his left eye, then streaked down
his cheek and jaw like a purple flash of lightning, twisting the left
side of his mouth into a sneer. One of the others was the man with
half an ear.

"Payson, isn't it?" Martin said as the riders stopped. "Sergeant
Payson?"

"You've got a good memory, Cap'n Cavanaugh," Payson said,
stretching his mouth into what might have been a smile.

"What are you boys doing out here?" Martin asked.

"Just sort of ridin' around, lookin' at the countryside," Payson
replied. He nodded toward the wagon. "Movin', are you?"

"Yeah," Martin said. "Wasn't much left for me when I got home,
I'm afraid."

"So, you're startin' over, are you?"

"You might say that."

"You got 'ny money?" Payson asked.

"I beg your pardon?"

"Money," Payson repeated. "You don't really think you're goin' to
be able to get a fresh start if you don't have no money, do you?"

Martin didn't like the way the conversation was going. "We don't
have any money," he said. "I spent everything I had on the wagon
and things we'd need to make a new start."

Payson turned to the others. "What do you think about this?" he
said. "Here's a man who was smart enough to be a captain in the
Yankee army, but is so dumb that he comes out here with no money."

"Well, hell, Payson, how smart do you have to be to be a cap'n in
the Yankee army?" one of the others said, and they all laughed.

"You!" Mary said to Payson. "You were one of them. And so were
you." She pointed to the bushy-bearded man.

"We was one of who?" Payson asked.

"You were one of the ones who burned our house and barn."

"Could be," Payson agreed with a chuckle. "Garvey and me rode with Bloody Bill Anderson and we burned us up a lot of Yankee houses and barns. But that was war. You see that, don't you, Cap'n?"

"Yes," Martin agreed. "The war's over now, and I figure a lot of us have done things we'd just as soon not remember."

"You don't have any money, huh?"

"No, I don't. And I'd feel a lot better if you folks would just ride on and leave us be."

"What if we don't want to ride on?" Payson asked.

"Then I'd be obliged to make you move on."

"How you goin' to do that? There's only one of you and there are six of us."

"You seem to be the one in charge," Martin said. "I'll kill you."

Payson threw his duster to one side and raised a double-barrel shotgun. Martin snaked his pistol from his holster in a lightning-fast draw. Before Payson could shoot, Martin pulled the trigger. But the hammer made a distinct clicking noise as it misfired.

Payson pulled the trigger on his shotgun and the blast, at nearly point-blank range, opened up Martin's chest, cutting his heart to shreds. He was dead before he hit the ground.

"Martin!" Mary screamed.

"Get the two women down here!" Payson ordered. "If they ain't got no money, we may as well have us some fun."

"Matt, run!" Mary shouted.

Earlier, Matt had moved his father's rifle closer to the edge of the wagon. Now, he grabbed the rifle and darted into the rocks alongside the wagon trail.

"What about the boy?" one of the men shouted.

"You can have 'im if that's your taste," Payson said. "But for me, I'm goin' to have me one of these women."

The others laughed at Payson's comment. Then they grabbed Mary and Cassie and jerked them down from the wagon seat. Mother and daughter fought hard, biting and scratching.

"Damn you!" Payson said, jerking back from Mary. "Be still!"

Mary and Cassie continued to struggle, putting up such a fight that Payson and the bushy-bearded man, who had taken first dibs, couldn't get the job done.

"To hell with it!" Payson said. He took a knife from his belt, then slashed it across Mary's throat. Mary began gurgling as blood spilled onto the dirt.

"Mama!" Cassie shouted.

"Cut the bitch, Garvey!" Payson said, and the bushy-bearded man silenced Cassie.

Payson stood up then, and looked down at the bodies of Mary and Cassie.

"Damn," he said. "Why'd they make us do that? Hell, I don't want 'em now."

"I'll do it," one of the other men said.

"What are you talkin' about, Cooper? They're both dead," Payson said.

"What the hell difference does that make?" Cooper asked. "Hell, all I wanted was a poke. Wasn't aimin' to make her fall in love with me."

The others laughed nervously.

"Anyone else goin' to join in the fun?" Cooper asked as he began unbuttoning his pants.

By the time Matt found a place in the rocks that would let him see what was going on, his mother and sister were already dead. Matt was less than twenty-five yards away from the six men who were standing around his mother and sister. He aimed the rifle at Cooper's head, and pulled the trigger.

The sudden gunshot startled everyone.

"What the hell?" Payson shouted, spinning around. Behind him, Cooper was pitching back with blood and brain matter oozing from the top of his head.

The moment Matt shot, he pulled back from the rock where he had been, and slipped into a very narrow fissure between two large rocks. As a result, Payson didn't see Matt, but he did see a wisp of gun smoke hanging in the air from where Matt had fired.

"It's the kid!" Garvey shouted. "Somehow he's got hold of a rifle."

"Get him!" Payson ordered.

"He went in between them rocks," Garvey said.

"Lucas, you the smallest one of us, see if you can get in there and pull him out," Payson ordered.

Nodding, Lucas ran over to the two rocks, then started squeezing through the narrow opening between them.

"Can you get through?" Payson called.

"Yeah, it's tight but I can do it," Lucas called back as he struggled to work through.

From his position behind another rock, about ten yards beyond the fissure, Matt watched Lucas working hard to squeeze through. He was in a very contorted position when Matt noticed that, while both arms were through, his waist, and consequently his gun, was not.

Matt stood up then and stared pointedly at Lucas.

"Ha!" Lucas called. "Payson, Garvey, come on. We've got his ass now."

"No," Matt said as he raised the rifle to his shoulder. "I've got yours."

"What?" Lucas shouted. In an instant, his sense of triumph turned to terror. "No, kid, no!" he shouted.

Matt pulled the trigger and felt the rifle kick back against his shoulder, watching as a black hole appeared in Lucas's forehead.

Matt had now killed two men in as many minutes.

"What are we going to do, Payson? Just stay around here until the little brat shoots us all, one at a time?" Garvey asked.

"Corey, Taggart, you find anything in the wagon?"

"No money, Payson," one of the men said. "Just some bacon, beans, coffee, flour, and sugar."

"Take the bacon and coffee and let's get out of here," Payson said. "And take the horses."

"What about the brat?"

"Leave him," Payson said. "He's out here in the middle of no-where, all by himself. If Injuns or wolves don't get him, he'll likely starve to death, or . . ." Payson took an ax from the side of the wagon and smashed the water barrel. The water that Matt and his family had been so preciously hoarding spilled to the ground in one quick splash. "Die of thirst," Payson concluded.

"What about Lucas and Cooper?" Taggart asked.

"They're dead."

"I know they're dead. What are we goin' to do about 'em?"

"Leave 'em."

"We can't just leave 'em here."

"Why not?" Payson replied. "It ain't goin' to bother 'em none." Garvey laughed.

"Come on, let's go."

"What about the wagon?"

"Burn it."

* * *

Matt could no longer hear them. He wasn't sure if they had actually left, or if they had just pretended to leave, so he stayed where he was, listening to the sound of burning wood, smelling it, and watching the smoke roil into the sky.

He spent the rest of the day there, then the whole night, then most of the next day. Finally, he decided to take a look, so he came out from the crevice, then climbed up on one of the rocks and looked down at the scene.

There was nothing left of the wagon except blackened residue and the iron bands around what had been the wheels, and the chain of the tree. There were five bodies, his mother, father, and sister, as well as the two he had killed. Four were on the ground; one was still wedged in the crevice between the rocks.

Matt started to climb down when he saw another wagon approaching. This wasn't the kind of wagon he and his family had been traveling in; this wagon was somewhat smaller and squared off with wooden sides. It was making a terrible racket as it rolled across the plains, and as it got closer, he could read the big red sign on the side.

Moe Goodman
Pots– Pans– Knives & Notions

Matt slipped back behind the rock and waited until the wagon approached. He watched as it stopped and the driver stared, in shock, at the carnage.

"Oh, my," he said, shaking his head. "Oh, my, what has happened here?"

The driver set the brake, then climbed down from the wagon and walked over to look at the bodies. He examined Matt's father, then his mother and sister for a long time. Then he walked over to look at Cooper, then took a cursory glance toward Lucas, who was still wedged in the crevice.

Shaking his head sadly, the driver walked back to his wagon, then untied a shovel that hung on the side. He started digging.

Matt continued to watch for several more minutes. Then, deciding that anyone who would take the time to dig a grave for someone he didn't even know must be a good man, he climbed down from the rock. He walked up behind the man, who, because of his digging, didn't notice Matt's approach.

"That's my ma and pa," he said. "And my sister."

Startled by Matt's unexpected appearance, the man jumped and grabbed his chest.

"Sorry," Matt said. "Didn't mean to scare you."

"Well, you did, boy, you like to give me a fit," the man said. His expression softened. "Your ma, pa, and sister, eh?"

"Yes, sir."

"And who might these two be?"

"They're the ones I killed," Matt said.

The man looked shocked. "You killed?"

"Yes, sir. I killed 'em."

"How old are you, boy?"

"I'm nine."

"What's your name?"

"Matt Cavanaugh."

"I'm Moe Goodman," the man said.

"Thanks for buryin' my folks."

"Seems like the only decent thing to do."

"If you've got another shovel, I'll help dig."

"It so happens I do," Moe said, walking back over to his wagon. He opened the back door, reached inside, and pulled one out. "Brand-new," he said, "but I reckon using it one time won't keep me from sellin' it."

Matt took the shovel and, for the next several minutes, the only sound was the sound of the spades turning dirt.

"I'll say this for you, Matt," Moe said, finally breaking the silence.

"What's that?"

"You've got yourself one hell of a start in life."

CHAPTER 3

With Smoke Jensen

Smoke and his mentor, Preacher, ran across another old mountain man named Grizzly. They shared a meal of venison, potatoes mixed with wild onions, and gravy sopped up by a piece of pan bread Smoke had made for them.

The three ate in relative silence. Then Grizzly nodded toward Smoke, but addressed his remark to Preacher.

"All right to talk in front of the boy?"

"Don't ask me," Preacher said. "He's a man, full growed, ask him."

"Boy, uh, Smoke," Grizzly said. "This here is goin' to concern you, and I reckon it ain't goin' to be pleasant."

Smoke steeled himself for the worst. "I'm listenin'," he said.

"Man rode in here about two months ago. He was all shot up. Strange man he was, dug his own grave afore he died. It was like as if he just hung on long enough not to put anyone else out."

"He give you a name?" Smoke asked.

"Yeah. Said his name was Emmett. Emmett Jensen."

Smoke nodded. "That'd be my pa," he said.

"I reckoned it would be," Grizzly said. "He told me he had a boy who would be travelin' with Preacher. And when I seen the two of you, well, I know'd who it was without askin'."

"Where's he buried?" Preacher asked. "Me'n Smoke here might like to visit the grave and pay our respects."

"Like I say, he chose his own spot," Grizzly said. "He's on a little plain at the base of the high peak, east of the canyon. You know where it is?"

"Yeah," Preacher said. "I know where it is."

Grizzly reached into a little bag and pulled out a heavy sack. He tossed the sack over to Smoke.

"This here belongs to you. Right smart amount of gold in there."

"You could've taken it," Smoke said. "You could've taken it and I would've never known anything about it."

"I reckon I could have, but that wouldn't have been the right thing to do now, would it?" Grizzly asked.

Smoke shook his head. "No, sir, it wouldn't have been."

"He left you a letter too," Grizzly said. "Figure you might want it." Grizzly handed Smoke another package, this one flat and wrapped in rawhide to protect it from the elements.

"Thanks."

Grizzly got up from the fire then, wiped off the seat of his pants, then walked over and mounted his pony. Taking the lead to his pack-horses, he rode off without looking back.

When Preacher and Smoke awoke the next morning, Smoke started saddling his horse.

Preacher watched Smoke for a few minutes; then he filled his pipe and lit it from a small burning twig he took from the campfire. He took several puffs, not speaking until the pipe was well lit.

"Looks like you're leavin'," Preacher said.

"Seems right," Smoke replied.

"I wish you all the best."

Smoke mounted his horse before he spoke again. Then he looked down at the old man who had been such an important part of his life for nearly two years now.

"Preacher, you've taught me how to find my way around, how to shoot, what plants I can eat and what I should stay away from," Smoke said. "Fact is, I reckon I wouldn't be alive if it weren't for you."

"You was easy to teach," Preacher said. He pointed to the pistol at Smoke's side. "But one thing I didn't teach, 'cause you just got a God-given natural talent for it. And that's pullin' your gun."

Unconsciously, Smoke put his hand on the handle of his Colt .44.

"I ain't never seen no one who could pull a gun as fast as you, Smoke, or shoot it as well. That's goin' to come in real handy to you, but it's also goin' to be a burden."

"A burden?"

"Aye, boy, a burden," Preacher said. "There will be those who will hear about you, and they'll want to test you. That's where the danger is goin' to lie, 'cause you won't be expectin' it. It won't be anybody you've ever run into before. Like as not, you won't even have words with 'em. They'll know who you are, but you won't know who they are."

"I've thought about that," Smoke said. "I know what you mean."

Preacher nodded. "Uh-huh. I figured you was smart enough to understand it. But I wanted to warn you about it anyway."

Smoke leaned over and patted his horse on the neck. "Preacher, I think the time has come for me to be goin' off on my own now."

"You'll be lookin' for Casey, will you?"

"I reckon so," Smoke replied with a nod.

Preacher nodded. "What's got to be done has to be done," he said. "Don't be a stranger, you hear? Drop in to see an old man from time to time."

"I'll do that," Smoke said, slapping his legs against the sides of his horse.

Two days later, Smoke found his pa's grave. Dismounting, he looked around until he located a rock that was just right; then, using a small hammer and a miner's spike, he chiseled his father's name and the year of his birth, 1815, as well as the year of his death, 1866, then put the rock at the head of the grave. He would have liked to put some sort of message on the headstone, but it was hard enough just to get the name and dates on.

That done, Smoke hung a small coffeepot over the campfire, then found a comfortable place to read the letter his father had left him.

Son,

I found the man who killed your brother, Luke, and stolt the gold that belonged to the Gray. But he had more with him than I thought he would. I killed two of 'em, but they got led in me and I had to hitail it out. I come here to this place, but I'm not goin to make it. Son, you don't have no call to try and settle accounts for me'n your brother, so don't get it in your mind you do. Make yourself a good life.

I'm getting tard and seein is hard. Lite fadin. I love you Kirby-Smoke.

—Pa

With Matt Cavanaugh

His name was Landers, "Brother Charles G. Landers, a simple man of Gawd" was the way he had introduced himself to Moe Goodman.

Goodman had explained how his life as a peddler wouldn't allow him to keep the boy, and he asked Landers if he could find a home for Matt.

"Indeed I can," Landers said. "There are many among my scattered flock who would take great joy in receiving into their bosom a wonderful young man like this."

From the moment he laid eyes on Landers, there was something about him that didn't set well with Matt. He wanted to ask Moe not to give him to the itinerant preacher, wanted to beg to be allowed to stay.

But he said nothing.

Landers was unlike any preacher Matt had ever seen. On the four days they had been on the trail, Landers had cursed, gotten drunk, and once paid an Indian woman to be with her. Matt didn't know what family Landers was going to leave him with, but anything had to be an improvement over the current situation.

On the fifth day, they came into a town, identified by a sign just outside the town as Soda Creek.

Soda Creek had one main street, fronted on both sides by ripsawed, weather-beaten, false-fronted buildings. From what Matt could tell from his position on the horse behind Landers, it consisted mostly of saloons. One building, which didn't have a sign to identify it, had several women sitting out on an upstairs porch. As Landers rode by, a couple of the women stepped up to the railing and looked down.

Matt glanced toward them, then cut his eyes away in quick embarrassment. It looked almost as if the women had come outside in their underwear. The two who leaned over the rail were showing the tops of their breasts.

"Hey, Preacher Man, where'd you come by that little boy?" one of the women asked.

Landers stared straight ahead.

"Why don't you leave him with us?" one of the other women called. "It'd be nice to have a young boy around."

"Yes, we'll raise him right. Why, by the time he gets old enough, he'll know how to treat a woman real good."

262 William W. Johnstone

The other women laughed, though Matt wasn't sure what was so funny.

"Brother Landers, who are those women?" Matt asked.

"Boy, don't you pay them no never-mind," Landers said. "They're nothin' but harlots, the lot of 'em."

"What's a harlot?"

"It's a woman that a man pays to be with," Landers explained.

"Like the Indian woman you were with the other night?"

"Shut up about that, boy," Landers hissed. "Don't you say nothin' to nobody 'bout that. What I was doin' was savin' that poor heathen's eternal soul. Most folks wouldn't understand that, 'cause most folks got dirty minds."

"Yes, sir," Matt said. "Where's the family that's goin' to take me?"

"There ain't no family goin' to take you."

"But you said . . ."

"I know what I said, but it don't work like that," Landers said. "First thing I got to do is get you into the orphanage. They can't nobody take you in 'lessen the law says it's all right, and the law's got to go through the orphanage."

"Oh," Matt said. He had not considered an orphanage, though as he was now an orphan, he supposed that it made sense. "Where is the orphanage?" Matt asked.

"Boy, you ask too many questions," Landers replied. "Things will go a lot better if you just keep your mouth shut and do as you're told."

"Yes, sir," Matt said contritely.

Emanuel Mumford had been elected as captain of the First Idaho Cavalry during the Civil War. The First Idaho was never activated, but Mumford continued to call himself Captain Mumford, and insisted that all who dealt with him refer to him in that way.

Captain Mumford was director of the Soda Creek Home for Wayward Boys and Girls. There had been some who suggested that the term "Wayward" implied that the children had behavioral problems, when most were merely orphans.

However, as Mumford pointed out, several of his residents were children of prostitutes who had died either of disease, or of alcoholism, or even giving birth. "And those children, being issue of wayward women, are by inheritance wayward," he insisted.

When Landers came in to see him, Mumford was going over his

books. He had three ways of supporting the Home. One was a grant from the territorial government in Boise. A second was from generous donations made by the three churches in town. And the third, and most lucrative, was from wages earned by the children Captain Mumford farmed out to the various businesses and individuals in and around the town of Soda Creek.

"Captain Mumford, I wonder if I may have a word with you, sir," Landers asked.

Mumford shook his head. "We have been through all this before, Landers," he said. "I am not going to allow you to conduct a church service in the Home. Why, it would be so disruptive that we would wind up losing at least half a day's earnings, maybe more."

Landers held up his hand and shook his own head. "No, it's nothing like that," he said. "I understand your position and would never try and compromise it."

"Well, I'm glad you see it that way, Landers. Now, what can I do for you?"

"It's more in order of what I can do for you," Landers replied.

Mumford's face brightened. "You have a donation for the Home? How marvelous of you."

"No, no, nothing like that," Landers corrected quickly.

"Oh," Mumford said. He was obviously disappointed.

"What I do have for you is another guest."

"Another mouth to feed? No, impossible. We are overcrowded as it is."

"But this is a fine, strong young boy," Landers pointed out. "I'm sure that you will be able to find a position for him somewhere that will prove to be quite lucrative for you."

Mumford stroked his chin. "You say he's a strong boy?"

"Yes."

"How old is he?"

"I think he is about twelve," Landers lied. He knew that Matt was not yet ten.

"Well, perhaps I could find a place for him," Mumford said. "A young man like that can always bring in enough money to support himself."

"Good, I thought you might see it that way," Landers said. "You can have him for twenty-five dollars."

"What?" Mumford gasped. "Are you out of your mind?"

"Not a bit of it," Landers replied. "If you aren't interested in buying the boy, I can always sell him to some farmer or rancher who lives nearby."

"You aren't going to find anyone who will give you twenty-five dollars for him."

"Then I'll sell him for what I can get."

"I'll give you five dollars."

"Twenty."

They eventually settled on twelve and a half dollars, and after Landers counted and pocketed the money, he went back outside to where Matt was leaning against the hitching post, watching the activity of the town.

"I've got it all set up for you," Landers said. "It's costing me twelve and a half dollars, but I'll have the personal satisfaction of knowing you will be safe."

"Thank you, Brother Landers," Matt said.

"I'm only doing my Christian duty, boy," Landers replied. "You learn from that, so you can grow up to be a decent, God-fearin' man."

"Yes, sir," Matt said.

"You go on in now," Landers said as he swung back into the saddle.

Matt reached for his rifle, but Landers put his hand out to stop him.

"You won't be needin' a gun in a place like this," Landers said.

"But it was my pa's rifle," Matt said.

Landers shook his head. "Let's just say it's you payin' me back for the twelve and a half dollars I just spent on you."

"But . . ."

"You goin' to argue with me, boy?" Landers asked in a sharp voice. "S'posin' I give you your rifle back, what good will that do? They'll take it away from you soon as you go inside. And like as not, it'll wind up gettin' sold and you won't get one penny for it. Leastwise, this way you know it's goin' to someone that was out some considerable money to get you situated."

Matt nodded. "Yes, sir, I guess you're right," he said. "All right, you can keep Pa's rifle."

"I'm glad you come to your senses. Go on in. The man you want to see is Captain Mumford."

Matt's eyes brightened somewhat. "My pa was a captain," he said. "Maybe Captain Mumford knew him."

"Maybe," Landers said. He slapped his legs against the sides of his horse, clicked at it, and rode away.

Matt looked at the front door of the home. He remembered back on the farm in Kansas, how he would sometimes go swimming in the swimming hole. In the late spring the water would still be really cold, and he would have to take a deep breath and get up his courage before jumping in.

For some strange reason, he felt like that now, so taking a deep breath and squaring his shoulders, he walked up the brick walk, then opened the door and went inside.

"Boy, have you no manners?" the man who was inside asked gruffly.

"Sir?"

"You don't walk into someone's home without knocking on the door," he said.

The man was thin and bald except for the sides of his head. And that hair came down in bushy sideburns, though they did not join to make a beard.

"I thought this was the orphanage," Matt said. "Maybe I'm in the wrong place. I'm sorry." He turned and started to leave.

"Did you come with Landers?" the man asked.

"Yes, sir."

"Then I already paid for you. You are in the right place."

"You paid for me?"

"Twelve and a half good dollars," the man said. "You'll be workin' that off."

"But he took my rifle."

"Who took your rifle?"

"Brother Landers. He said he paid you so I could stay here, and he took my rifle to pay him back."

The man chuckled. "Let that be a lesson to you," he said. "Don't trust somebody just because they tell you they are a preacher."

"Isn't he a preacher?"

"He is sometimes, I reckon. What's your name?"

"Matthew Cava . . ."

The man held up his hand. "Your ma and pa alive?"

"No, sir."

"Then you don't have a last name."

"But my last name is . . ."

"You don't have a last name," the man said again. "Do you understand that?"

"Yes, sir."

"Yes, Captain Mumford."

"What?"

"When you talk to me, you will always address me as Captain Mumford."

"Yes, Captain Mumford," Matt said.

"You're awfully small for twelve years old."

"I'm not twelve," Matt said.

Mumford slapped Matt in the face, not hard enough to knock him down, or even bring blood, but hard enough that it stung.

"What did you say?"

"I said I'm not twelve," Matt repeated.

Mumford slapped him again. "You don't learn very well," he said. "Now, I'm going to ask you again. What did you say?"

"I said I'm not twelve—Captain Mumford," Matt said, getting the last part out just before Mumford slapped him again.

Mumford smiled. "Well, maybe you aren't so dumb after all. Not twelve, huh? How old are you?"

"I'm nine, Captain Mumford."

"Nine, huh? Well, you are a big enough boy for nine. I'm sure I can find something for you to do. Connors!" he called loudly.

An older boy came into the office from the back of the house.

"Yes, Captain Mumford?"

"Here is a new boy," Mumford said. "His name is Matthew. Take him into the back and"—Mumford paused for a moment, then smiled, though Matt found the smile frightening, rather than comforting—"break him in."

"Yes, Captain Mumford," Connors said, his own smile as malevolent as that of Mumford.

Connors led Matt through a door and down a hall. Matt saw a room with a lot of bunk beds, and he started toward it.

"Nah, that's for the girls," Connors said. "Boys is this way."

"There are girls in this place?" Matt asked.

"Yeah," Connors said. "But don't get no ideas about any of them. All the girls belong to me'n Simon."

"What do you mean they belong to you and Simon?"

Connors looked at Matt and laughed. "Never mind," he said. "You're too young to know."

CHAPTER 4

The room was long and relatively narrow. The floor was made of wide, unfinished boards and the walls were nothing more than studs and outside planking. There was only one window in the entire room.

The beds that ran in rows down either side of the room were crowded so close together that there was barely room to get between them. Most of the beds looked to be very spartan; small, even for children, with blankets with holes and lumpy cotton mattresses. There were no sheets.

"You'll sleep here," Connors said, pointing to one of the beds. Stuffing was coming from the mattress, and roaches were running across the filthy blanket.

"Where do you put your clothes?" Matt asked.

"You got 'nything other than what you are wearin'?" Connors asked.

"No."

Connors chuckled. "Then don't worry about it."

Glancing toward the far end of the room, under the window, Matt saw two beds that were set aside from the others. These beds were larger, had sheets, pillows, and blankets. There was also a rack and shelf on the wall beside each bed and a trunk between the beds. Several changes of clothes hung from the racks, and boxes were stacked on the shelves.

The open window provided some relief from the sweltering heat outside, though none of that relief reached the rest of the room. There was a stove there too, and though the stove was now cold, it didn't take much thought for Matt to realize that what little warmth it would produce in the wintertime would be confined to the area immediately around it.

"Who sleeps there?" Matt asked, pointing to the two beds.

"The bed on the left is mine," Connors said. He pointed at Matt. "And don't ever let me see you down there. The other bed belongs to my friend, Simon."

"How come you two get the good beds?"

Connors laughed. "You'll find out soon enough," he said.

Matt heard voices from outside.

"The others is comin' back for supper," Connors said. "To show you what a good guy I am, I'm goin' to let you eat with us tonight, even though you ain't done no work yet to earn it."

"You are going to let me eat? I thought Captain Mumford was in charge."

"He is in charge," Connors said. "But you'll mostly be dealin' with me'n Simon." Connors smiled proudly, and hooked his thumbs under his armpits. "Cap'n Mumford says that me'n Simon is his sergeants."

"Am I supposed to call you Sergeant?"

Connors laughed. "You don't even talk to me, boy, unless I talk to you first," Connors said. "I'm just talkin' to you now 'cause you're new and you need to know the rules. Come on, I'll show you where we eat."

The dining room was about the same size as the dormitory. It had two long tables, flanked on either side of the table by a wooden bench. One of the tables appeared to be for the girls, the other for boys. At the back of the room there was one smaller table. Matt didn't have to ask who that table belonged to.

"From here on, you are on your own," Connors said as he walked away.

Matt saw a line of boys and girls and, figuring they were waiting to be fed, he joined them. At nine years old, he decided he was one of the youngest—if not the youngest—but he wasn't the smallest.

Matt had been around other children before, at school and in church, but he had never seen such dispirited expressions as he saw here. Not one person was smiling, there was no animated conversation, and in fact there was very little interaction of any kind. They just stood there in silence until a couple of women came out, carrying a large pot and a plate of bread. The woman carrying the pot was very fat. The one carrying the tray of bread was very skinny.

"Bow your heads!" the fat woman shouted.

Matt bowed his head, but he looked up with his eyes to see what the others were doing.

"Lord, for the blessing of this food, we thank you!" the fat woman shouted.

Once the blessing was given, the atmosphere changed. The boys and girls who were standing in line became much more animated, engaging each other in conversation. The boy just in front of Matt turned to him.

"You just get here today?" he asked.

"Yes."

"My name is Eddie, what's yours?"

"Matt Cavanaugh."

"Shh!" Eddie said, putting his finger across his lips. "Don't let nobody hear you say that."

"Say what?"

"Your last name," Eddie said. "We don't have last names in here. Don't none of us have last names."

"That's right. Captain Mumford told me that."

"It could get you a beatin'," Eddie cautioned.

"I wonder what's for supper," Matt said.

Eddie laughed. "Can sure tell you are new," he said.

"Why is that?"

"'Cause what is for supper is what we have for supper ever' night. Pease porridge. Pease porridge and bread. There's s'posed to be some bacon in the pease porridge, but ain't nobody ever seen none."

"You have that every night?" Matt asked.

"Oatmeal for breakfast ever' mornin' and pease porridge for supper ever' night."

"What about them?" Matt asked, pointing to the table at the back of the room. There he saw Connors and another boy as big as he was. They were eating fried chicken and mashed potatoes, talking and laughing with each other.

"That's Connors and Simon," Eddie said. "They don't count. They're Captain Mumford's toadies," Eddie said.

"Toadies?"

"Yeah, they get the best food, the best clothes, the best everything. Wait until you see where they sleep," Eddie said.

"I did see it. Why do they get such good treatment?"

The boy that was standing just in front of Eddie laughed. "For one thing, they are the oldest. They're both thirteen. And for another, they are tattletales. They tell Captain Mumford everything we do."

"Oh."

"I'm Timmy," the second boy said.

"Matt Cava—uh, Matt," Matt said, remembering to correct himself.

"I'll bet they don't have any friends," Matt said.

"They don't need friends. They've got everything else," Timmy said.

Matt took his bowl of pease porridge and a hunk of bread to the table where he sat with Eddie and Timmy. Eddie introduced him to some of the others, though, for the moment, the names sort of passed him by. He knew that if he stayed here long enough he would eventually learn everyone's name, so he didn't ask anyone to repeat it.

Matt looked down at his pease porridge with obvious distaste. "This is what we have for supper every night?" he asked.

"Every night."

"What do we have for dinner?"

"We don't eat dinner here," Eddie said. "But most of us get lunch from the place where we're workin'. And that's generally the best. Where will you be workin'?"

"I don't know."

"You ever worked anywhere before?"

"I've mucked stable stalls," Matt said.

"Yeah, well, you don't want to have to do that if you can help it. Best thing is to get a job with a café or a saloon. You'll be sweepin' out and washin' dishes, but you get to eat good there."

"How do I get a job there?"

"I'll talk to Mr. McDougal down at the saloon and see if he'll ask for you," Eddie said.

The bread was good and Matt was hungry, not having eaten since the day before when Landers had shared some jerky with him. But not even hunger could make him eat the pease porridge. He took one bite, then pushed the uneaten gruel away.

"If you aren't going to eat that, can I have it?" Timmy asked.

"How can you eat it?" Matt asked.

"After you been here a while, it'll taste just like apple pie to you," Timmy said.

The others at the table laughed. "When have you ever had apple pie?"

"Well, I know it's good because I've heard said it was good," Timmy said.

Matt thought of the last apple pie his mother had made. She had used dried apples and made the pie on the trail for them, just about two days before Payson and the others had attacked them.

Matt's eyes filled, and tears began streaming down his cheeks, but he didn't sob out loud.

Timmy looked at Matt.

"You thinkin' about apple pie your mama made?" he asked.

Matt nodded, but didn't speak.

"I'm sorry I brung up the memory," he said. "Me, I ain't got no memories like that. They say my mama was a whore, but I got no way of knowin' that. I don't even remember her."

Matt slid his bowl of porridge across.

"No," Timmy said, pushing it back. "Even if you don't like it, you better eat it."

"Like you say, there will come a time when I can eat it," Matt said. "But I can't eat it now, so you may as well take it."

"Thanks, Matt. So now you got two friends in here. Me'n Eddie. That's good. Boys that come in here and don't make friends, they are the ones who have it the hardest."

Matt looked back at Connors and Simon, salivating as he saw them eating the fried chicken with such relish.

CHAPTER 5

With Smoke Jensen

The name of the little town was Prosperity, and it sat on the banks of the Cuchara River. Prosperity was a ranching and farming community with a sign posted just outside the town limits with the proud boast:

Come Watch Us Grow
Progress and <u>PROSPERITY</u> in Colorado

The city marshal, having seen Smoke approaching from some distance away, met him just outside of town.

"Welcome to Prosperity, stranger," the marshal said. "The name is Crowell, Marshal Crowell." He put his hand to his badge, even though Smoke had already seen it.

"Marshal," Smoke said, touching the brim of his hat.

"I didn't catch your name," Marshal Crowell said.

"Folks call me Smoke."

"Smoke?" The marshal chuckled, more in dismissal than in humor. "That's it? Smoke? Smoke what?"

"I've been spending some time in the mountains," Smoke said. "One name is all anybody needs up there."

"Well, Smoke, if you're just makin' a friendly visit to my town, then you're welcome," Crowell said. "But if you're comin' here for any other reason, well, I'm goin' to have to ask you to just keep ridin'."

"I'm looking for a man named Casey," Smoke said. "Ted Casey."

"What do you want with him?"

"That's my business."

"I'm the law here'bouts," Crowell said. "I reckon that makes it my business."

"Is that a fact?"

"You know what, mister, I don't much like your attitude," Crowell said. "Why don't I just . . . ?"

That was as far as Crowell got. He was reaching for his gun, but stopped in mid-draw and mid-sentence when he saw the pistol in Smoke's hand.

"What the hell?" Crowell gasped. "I didn't even see you draw!"

"Like I said, where is Casey?" Smoke asked. He neither raised his voice, nor made it more menacing. Ironically, that made his question all the more frightening.

Crowell hesitated for a few seconds. "His ranch is southeast of here, on the flats. You'll cross a little creek before you see the house. I ought to warn you, though, he's got several men workin' for him, and they're all good with a gun. Maybe not as fast as you, but there's only one of you."

"You got an undertaker in this town?" Smoke asked.

"Of course we do. Why would you ask?"

"I'm about to give him some business," Smoke said.

Ten miles out of town, Smoke encountered two rough-looking riders.

"You're on private land," one of the men said. "Turn your horse around and git."

"You're not being very hospitable," Smoke said.

"Don't intend to be. Strangers ain't welcome here."

"I'm looking for Ted Casey."

"You deef or somethin'? I told you to git."

"I'm looking for Ted Casey," Smoke repeated.

"What do you want with Casey?"

"Just to renew an old friendship from the war," Smoke said.

"From the war?" one of the men said with a laugh. "Boy, you're still wet behind the ears. You ain't old enough to have been in the war."

"I'm sorry, I wasn't very clear. I'm actually looking him up for my pa."

"What was your pa's name?"

"Jensen," Smoke said. "Emmett Jensen."

"Jensen?"

"Yeah. You remember him, don't you?" Smoke said. His words were calm and cold.

"Kill 'im!" one of the riders shouted, and both grabbed for their guns.

They were too slow. Smoke had his pistol in his hand and he fired twice, the shots coming so close together that there was no separation between them.

The two riders were dumped from their saddles, one dead, the other dying. The dying rider pulled himself up on one elbow. Blood poured through his chest wound, pink and frothy, indicating that the ball had passed through a lung.

"Figured when we killed your pa that would be the end of it," he said. He forced a laugh, and blood spattered from his lips. "You're good, a hell of a lot better'n your brother. Casey shot him low and in the back. It took him a long time to die too. I enjoyed watchin' him. He was a coward, squealed like a pig and cried like a little girl."

Smoke made no reply.

"So was your pa a coward."

Smoke was quiet.

"What's the matter with you?" the rider asked. "You just goin' to let me talk about your folks like that? You're yellow."

Smoke turned his horse and rode around the two men, following the road in the same direction from which the two riders had come.

"Shoot me!" the rider shouted. "You yellow-bellied coward, don't leave me here to die like this! Shoot me!"

Smoke continued to ride away. Thirty seconds later he heard a gunshot, the sound muffled by the fact that the shooter had put the barrel in his own mouth.

Smoke didn't bother to look around.

Stopping in a copse of trees a short distance from the ranch house, Smoke studied it for a moment or two. The house was built of logs with a sod roof. If it came to it, it would burn easily.

"Casey!" Smoke called. "Casey, come out!"

"Who's callin'?" a voice shouted from within the house.

"Jensen."

"Jensen? I thought we killed you."

"That was my pa. And my brother," Smoke said.

"What do you want?"

"I'm here to settle up."

There was a rifle shot from the house, and though it missed, the bullet came close enough for Smoke to hear it whine.

Smoke took his horse into a ravine that circled the house. Fifty yards behind the house, he dismounted, snaked his rifle from the saddle sheath, then lay against the bank of the arroyo. Inside, he saw an arm on the windowsill. He shattered the arm with one shot from his new Henry. A moment later, he saw someone's outline through one of the other windows and he shot him, hearing a scream of pain.

"You boys in there," Smoke called. "You want to die for Casey, do you? I've already killed two of you back on the road."

"Your daddy ride with Mosby?" someone called from inside.

"That's right."

"You had a brother named Luke?"

"I did."

"Yeah, well, he was shot in the back and the gold he was guardin' was stole. Casey done it, not me! You got no call to come after me."

Smoke fired several more rounds into the house.

"Jensen! The name is Barry! I come from Nevada. Din't have nothin' to do with no war, never been East. They's another fella in here just like me. We herd cattle for wages, we ain't got no stake in this fight."

"Come on out and ride away then," Smoke called. "I won't shoot you."

The cabin door opened and two men came out with their hands up.

"We're just goin' to get our horses," one of them shouted.

"Go ahead."

The two men were moving toward the barn when a couple of shots rang out. Both were shot in the back by someone from within the house.

"What'd you do that for, Casey?" Smoke shouted. "They weren't part of this."

"When I pay men to work for me, I expect loyalty," Casey called back.

Smoke didn't answer. He was quiet for several moments, trying to decide what he should do.

"Jensen? Jensen, you still out there?" Casey called.

Casey's voice was getting nervous.

"Jensen? Come on down. Come out in the open so I can see you and we can talk."

Smoke still didn't answer.

"Jensen, you there?"

"I think he's gone," another voice said.

276 William W. Johnstone

"That's what he wants us to think, you fool," Casey's voice replied.

Smoke followed the arroyo on around to the bunkhouse. In a pile behind the bunkhouse he found a bunch of rags, and in the bunkhouse, a jar of coal oil. He stuck the rags down into the mouth of the coal-oil jar, lit it, then threw it at the ranch house. The jar broke and the fire erupted almost immediately. As the logs burned, they began filling the house with smoke and fumes.

From inside the house, Smoke heard coughing. Then one man broke from the cabin and started running. Smoke cut him down with his rifle. A second began running and Smoke pulled the trigger on the rifle, only to hear the hammer fall on an empty chamber. He pulled his pistol and shot the man once, watching him double over with a slug in his gut.

Casey waited until the last minute before he stumbled out into the yard, his eyes blinded from the smoke and fumes. He fired wildly as he stumbled around, finally pulling the trigger repeatedly on an empty gun.

Smoke walked calmly up to him, even as Casey was trying to reload, and knocked him out.

Just outside the little town of Prosperity, Smoke dumped a bound and gagged Casey onto the ground. Curious about what was going on, several townspeople came forth to watch as Smoke took a rope from the saddle of Casey's horse and began making a noose.

"What do you think you are going to do here?" Marshal Crowell asked.

"Obvious, isn't it?" Smoke replied. "I'm going to hang the son of a bitch who killed my brother and my pa."

"I am an officer of the law. What if I ordered you to stop?" Crowell asked.

"Then I'd just kill you and hang him," Smoke answered.

"But you can't do this," Crowell insisted. "He hasn't been found guilty."

"Yeah, he has. He's already admitted it to me," Smoke said. "I also watched him kill two of his own men. He shot them in the back."

"That doesn't make what you are doing right," Crowell said.

"It's right in my book," Smoke said. He put the noose around Casey's neck, then threw the other end of the rope over a tree limb. "Get up on your horse," he ordered.

"You go to hell," Casey said, spitting at him.

"Have it your way," Smoke said. He tied the end of the rope to the saddle horn, and started to slap the horse on the rump.

"No, wait!" Casey shouted. "Not that way." Casey's hands were tied in front of him, but he put them on the pommel, then swung himself into the saddle.

"You got anything to say before I send you to hell?" Smoke asked.

"Yeah. I already sent your brother and your pa there, and when I get there I'm going to kick them both in the ass. Now, do your damn'dest, you son of a bitch."

Smoke slapped Casey's horse on the rump. With a protesting whinny, it leaped forward and Casey, dying quickly from a broken neck, swung back and forth, the only sound being the creaking of the rope and the cawing of a distant crow.

"I'll be notifying the governor about this," Crowell said.

"You do what you think you need to do," Smoke said. Without looking back, Smoke walked over to his horse, swung into the saddle, and rode away.

"Son of a bitch," someone said, almost reverently. "That's the damn'dest thing I done ever seen."

CHAPTER 6

With Matt Cavanaugh, three years later

True to his promise, Eddie managed to get Matt a job at McDougal's Saloon. There, Matt emptied and shined the spittoons, swept and mopped the floors, washed dishes, chopped wood in the wintertime, and swatted flies in the summertime.

During the school year, they came to work at the saloon for two hours before school opened, then worked from three o'clock until eleven every night. Despite the long hours, the owner of the saloon, Drew McDougal, did treat them fairly, and he did provide them with lunch every day.

For their labors, Matt and Eddie were paid a dollar and a half per week, but the money went to the Home, not to them.

"This money is needed to pay the expenses," Captain Mumford informed them.

As time went by, Matt learned that every penny any of the home residents earned went directly to Captain Mumford. And while he claimed to spend it all on upkeep, there was no one to look over his books but him. Whatever he spent it on, Matt was certain it wasn't spent on food or clothes. He got new clothes only when he outgrew what he was wearing, or when he wore them out.

In Matt's case, it was generally a matter of outgrowing them because he had grown considerably in the three years he had been there. Although there were several kids who were older than his twelve years, only two, Connors and Simon, both of whom were sixteen, were bigger than he. And in their case, they were only marginally bigger.

In the early days of Matt's stay in the Home, Connors and Simon had sometimes taken it upon themselves to punish him for real, or imagined, infractions. But there came a time when Connors told Matt to bend over and grab his ankles so he could swat him.

"Hit me with that paddle one more time and I'll cram it down your throat," Matt responded menacingly.

Startled by Matt's challenge, Connors walked away without administering punishment, and now neither Connors nor Simon was courageous enough to take him on by himself.

Matt's size, courage, and demeanor had made him a popular leader among the others in the Home, and even those who were older than Matt looked up to him.

That is why when Matt told them all to follow his lead and not eat supper one night, no one questioned him as to why they should do such a thing. When they went through the line for supper, they accepted their bowls of pease porridge, then went to their tables. As they looked toward Matt, he reminded them by sign and signal that they were not to eat their porridge.

In the meantime, they watched as Connors and Simon walked confidently back to their table. Unlike the other residents of the home, neither Connors nor Simon had to go through the line. Instead, they were served at their seats.

One of the kitchen workers brought two bowls out to them and set them on the table in front of Connors and Simon.

"Here, hold on!" Simon called out as the woman started back toward the kitchen. "What is this?"

"It's your supper," the woman answered.

"The hell it is. We're having ham tonight."

The kitchen worker shook her head. "No ham," she said.

"What's going on here? What happened to our ham?"

"I haven't seen any ham," the woman answered.

Though none of the other residents laughed out loud, they all repressed giggles and smiles while they watched the frustration of the two oldest of their number as they tried to eat the pease porridge.

"What is this?" Connors shouted in anger. "Nobody can eat this shit!"

Again, there were repressed giggles from the other residents. Then, at a nod from Matt, everyone got up from the table and took their untouched bowls of porridge to the garbage can. There, they dumped the porridge, turned the bowls in, then filed out of the dining room.

"Connors, did you see that?" Simon asked.

"Did I see what?"

"None of them ate."

"Yeah, well, who can blame them?" he replied, looking at his meal with disgust.

"No, you don't understand," Simon said. "None of them ate so much as one bite. They always eat."

"Yeah," Connors said. "Yeah, you're right. I wonder why not. Why don't you follow them, Simon, and see if you can figure out what's going on."

"Yeah," Simon said. "I will."

Simon slipped out of the dining room, then hanging back a little, watched as the others went into the chapel. Curious, he moved up to the door of the chapel, then looked inside. Everyone was sitting quietly in the pews, with their heads bowed and their eyes closed.

"Simon," Matt called, seeing Simon standing at the door. "It's so good to see you here. Come on in."

"What?" Simon asked.

"Why don't you go get Connors and bring him with you? We would love to have you two join us."

"What are you doing?"

"Why, we're having a prayer service, of course," Matt said.

"What do you mean you're having a prayer service? How can you have a prayer service if there ain't no preacher here?"

"You don't need a preacher to have a prayer service," Matt said. "All you need to do is pray. Won't you join us?" He reached out as if to grab Simon and pull him on into the chapel.

Simon held out his hands as if warding Matt off. He shook his head.

"No," he said. "I ain't doin' no prayin'."

"What about Connors? Won't you ask him to join us?"

"You're crazy," Simon said. "There ain't neither one of us goin' to be comin' in here and sayin' a bunch of prayers."

"Then we will pray for you," Matt said.

"You're crazy, I tell you. Every last one of you."

"Oh, Simon?" Matt called as Simon started to leave.

"What?" Simon responded in a belligerent bark.

"Enjoy your pease porridge."

The others laughed out loud.

"You're crazy," Simon repeated.

Matt waited for a moment, then looked over at Eddie. "Make sure he's gone."

Eddie went to the door, looked through it, then turned back. "He's gone," he said.

"Let's eat," Matt said, and with that, everyone crowded up to the altar where, from beneath the pulpit, Matt pulled out a large cooked ham.

"Oh, this looks so delicious," Tamara said. Tamara was two years older than Matt. In the early days, when Matt first came to the home, it had been Tamara who recognized the grief he was suffering, and who had tried, as well as she knew how, to comfort him. "Where did you get it?"

"The ladies of the Episcopal church cooked it especially for us," Matt said. "I just happened to be outside Captain Mumford's office when they brought it. Captain Mumford thanked them for it, then told Connors that he and Simon could both have a little of it before he took it home."

"Took it home? He was going to take it home?" someone asked.

Matt nodded. "Yeah. You think pease porridge is all we ever get? Churches and the like been bringing us food ever since I got here, only we don't ever see any of it," Matt said.

"That ain't right," one of the boys said. He had only been there about six months.

"I agree, Billy, it isn't right, so that's why I decided to do something about it," Matt said.

"Get this ham?"

"Yeah, get this ham. I waited until Captain Mumford stepped out of the office, then I took it and brought it here."

"I wouldn't have had the nerve to do that," one of the others said.

"Sure you would have," Matt said. "All you would have had to do was smell it when you were hungry."

"When is anyone not hungry in here?" one of the other girls asked, and they all laughed.

Timmy carved the ham and several came back for seconds, until everyone had eaten their fill. Now, the only thing remaining was the large ham bone.

"What are you going to do with the ham bone?" Eddie asked.

"My mama always made beans with it," Matt said. "Beans and cornbread."

282 William W. Johnstone

"Oh, beans and cornbread. If I weren't so full right now, that would make me really hungry," Timmy said, and again, everyone laughed.

"Seriously, what are you going to do with it? If you just throw it away and Captain Mumford discovers it, we're all going to get in trouble," Eddie said.

"Yeah," Matt said with a big smile. "If Captain Mumford discovers it, he really will be mad, won't he? I mean, really mad. There's no tellin' what he might do." Matt chuckled.

"I'll say," Eddie started. "He would . . ." Eddie paused in mid-sentence. "Wait a minute! You are up to something, aren't you? What are you going to do?"

"You'll see," Matt said.

"Matt, do be careful," Tamara said.

"I will be," Matt promised.

The next evening, just before supper, Captain Mumford came into the dining room.

"I want all of you to line up!" he shouted. "Boys on the right, girls on the left."

Everyone began to do as he ordered, though nobody had any idea what it was all about. They began talking among themselves, asking questions and speculating as to what this was about.

"Shut up!" Mumford shouted. "All of you, just shut up!"

"Cap'n Mumford, you want me'n Simon to go take care of some of the loudmouths?" Connors asked.

"I do not, sir!" Mumford said in a cold and calculating voice. "I want you two to stand over there with the boys."

"You—you are asking us to stand over there with them?" Connors asked, surprised by the request.

"I'm not asking you anything," Mumford said. If anything, his voice was even colder now than it had been earlier. "I am telling you."

Simon and Connors exchanged worried and confused glances, then walked over to stand against the wall with the others.

Mumford was holding a gunnysack.

"Any time you get several people living together as we do here, the one thing that you must be able to count on is trust," Mumford said. "You must be able to depend upon one another to be loyal, and honest. The worst thing that can happen in a society such as ours is that one might steal from another."

Mumford stuck his hand down into the gunnysack, then pulled out the remnants of the ham the residents had eaten the night before.

"This ham was to have been a gift to you." He took in the residents with a wave of his hand. "To all of you," he continued. "It was provided to us by the ladies of St. Paul's Episcopal Church. I had it on my desk, ready to take back to the kitchen for your supper. I stepped out but for a moment, and when I came back, it was gone."

No one made a sound.

"Stolen!" he shouted loudly.

He looked over at Simon and Connors. "Then, this morning, I found this ham bone in the trunk shared by these two."

"What?" Connors shouted. "Look here, we didn't have nothin' to do with stealin' that ham!"

"I will not tolerate stealing, sir, and I will not tolerate lying," Mumford said coldly.

"But we didn't . . ." Simon said.

"Hush, sir! Hush your foul mouth," Mumford said. "You are both sixteen years old. I have kept you on here out of the goodness of my heart. But I am not required to keep anyone beyond the age of sixteen. So, I am ordering both of you out of here tonight."

"What do you mean out of here? Where are we supposed to go?"

"I don't care where you go," Mumford said. "As long as you aren't here. If I see either of you here ever again, I shall go to the sheriff's office and have you both charged with trespassing."

"I don't know who did this to us," Connors shouted to the boys and girls who were lined up on either side of the dining hall. "But when I find out, I will get you. I will get you for this, I promise!"

"Get out," Mumford said.

Connors and Simon both left, followed by the cheers, jeers, and catcalls of the ones they were leaving behind.

The next day, Mumford asked Matt to come to his office.

"Yes, Captain Mumford?" Matt said.

"I've been watching you, Matt," Mumford said. "And I like the way you handle yourself."

Matt didn't answer, because he had no idea where the discussion was going.

"Connors and Simon served their purpose well, as long as they were here," Mumford continued. "But they outlived their purpose, and it was time for them to go."

"I think everyone was happy to see them go," Matt said.

"Maybe so," Mumford said. "Still, as I say, they did serve their purpose. Matt, when you are in charge of something like this, you need people to help you. Specifically, you need someone who is himself a resident, someone who knows what is going on, who knows what the others are talking about. Someone who can report back when they see misbehavior."

Matt said nothing.

"I'm sure you saw how much better Connors and Simon had it than the rest of you," Mumford said.

"Yes, we all saw that."

"It is a necessary part of the procedure," Mumford said. "I could not expect someone to work for me without some sort of compensation. In the case of Connors and Simon, I compensated them by allowing them to eat better, to have better accommodations. And of course, I will do the same thing for you."

"For me?"

"Yes. Winter is coming on, this will be your third winter. I'm sure you remember how cold and drafty the dormitory is. But if you move down to the end, where Connors and Simon were, you will find it much warmer and much more comfortable."

"Why would I move down there?"

"If you are working for me, then it is your due," Mumford said.

"You want me to do what Connors and Simon did? You want me to spy for you?"

"Yes."

Matt shook his head. "No," he said. "No, I won't do it."

The smile left Mumford's face. "You have no choice," he said. "You will do it because I am ordering you to do it."

CHAPTER 7

"I can't do it," Matt told Tamara later that night. The two were sitting on the back porch of the home, listening to the frogs and the night-calling insects. "I won't do it."

"I thought you said he ordered you to do it," Tamara said.

Matt nodded. "He did order me to do it. But I'm not going to. I can't be like Simon and Connors. I can't turn on the others in here."

Tamara reached up to brush a fall of hair back from Matt's forehead.

"You wouldn't be like them," she said. "You couldn't be like them."

"There might be some who wouldn't understand," Matt said. "They would think I had turned against them."

"There might be some who would think that," Tamara agreed. "But I would know better. So would Eddie, and Timmy, and Billy."

Matt shook his head. "Maybe," he said. "But I'm not going to take that chance."

"What do you mean? What are you going to do?"

"I'm leaving this place."

"Leaving? But where will you go? How will you live?"

"I don't know, but anyplace is better than this."

"When are you going?"

"Tonight," Matt said. "When I know everyone is asleep."

Tamara didn't answer right away, and for a long moment the silence was invaded by the bleat and thrum of the frogs and insects. Finally, she reached over and put her hand on his.

"Matt, take me with you," she said.

"Tamara, I can't," Matt answered. "Like you said, I have no idea where I'm going or what I am going to do. Winter is coming on. I could freeze to death up in the mountains, if I don't starve first."

"I don't care," Tamara said. "I'm willing to take that chance if you are."

"Tamara, I . . ." Matt started.

"Matt, please. I'm fourteen years old now. Next year I'll . . ." She paused in mid-sentence.

"You'll what?"

"Matt, don't you know what Captain Mumford makes the older girls do to earn money?"

"I thought all the older girls worked at Emma Smith's Boarding House."

"And you have no idea what goes on there?"

"Don't you just clean and cook and make up the beds and such?"

"Beds, yes," Tamara said. "Only we don't just make them up."

Suddenly Matt realized what Tamara was talking about.

"Are you saying that Captain Mumford makes you be with men?" he asked.

Tamara nodded, and her eyes brimmed over with tears. One began sliding down her cheek, and she reached up to brush it away with the tip of her finger.

"I didn't know that," Matt said. "I've been here for three years, and I didn't know that."

"Captain Mumford says he will horsewhip any girl who tells," Tamara said. "Besides, it's not something anyone would want to tell anyway."

"Are you . . . ?" Matt began.

"Not yet," Tamara said. "He doesn't make anyone start until they are fifteen."

"I'll take you with me," Matt promised.

"Oh, thank you! Thank you!" Tamara said, spontaneously embracing him and kissing him on the cheek.

"Be ready to go tonight."

"What time?"

"I don't know, after midnight sometime, when everyone else is asleep," Matt said. "You be standing in the door of the girls' room, looking for me. I'm not coming in there."

"I'll be there," Tamara said.

* * *

Matt wasn't sure exactly what time it was when he left. He knew it was late at night because everyone was asleep and he could hear the snores and rhythmic breathing of the others. It was getting colder outside, and he had no overcoat, so he decided to take the blanket off his bed.

He walked down to the hall and stood just outside the girls' dormitory. When Tamara didn't come out, he decided to leave without her, but suddenly she was there.

"When I saw you with the blanket, I thought that might be a pretty good idea," she whispered. "So I went back to get mine."

"All right, let's go, but keep quiet," Matt said.

Leaving the dormitory, Matt and Tamara tiptoed through the darkened building, passing through the dining room, then making their way into the kitchen. There, they found several chunks of stale bread, which they stuck down into their pockets. Then, wrapping themselves in the blankets, they sneaked out through the back.

Once outside, they looked back toward the building that housed the Home for Wayward Boys and Girls. For a moment, Matt almost went back in. It wasn't much, but it was the only home he'd had for the last three years. For some of the residents, it was the only home they had ever known.

"Are you sure you want to go with me?" Matt asked. "I mean, when you think about it, the Home kept us warm in the winter, gave us a place to sleep, and provided meals."

"Such as they were," Tamara said.

"We are giving up a safe haven for the unknown," Matt said.

"Who are you trying to talk out of going? Me or you?" Tamara asked.

"I don't know," Matt answered honestly. "Both of us, I guess." He shook his head. "But I can't stay. I cannot and I will not replace Connors and Simon."

The moon was full and bright, and it lit the path for them. A cool night breeze caused Matt to shiver, though in truth he didn't know if his trembling was entirely from the cold, or from nervousness over his uncertain future. He pulled the blanket around himself, then began walking.

The Home for Wayward Boys and Girls was three blocks from Muddy Creek, and while that had not been a conscious goal, Matt quickly found himself on the bank of the creek, looking down at the water. That's when he saw the boat.

"There," he said excitedly, pointing to the boat. "That's our way out of here!"

"We're going to steal a boat?" Tamara asked.

"Nah, we're not stealing it," Matt said. "We're just borrowing it. You keep a watch out while I untie it."

Scrambling down the creek bank, Matt started untying the boat. That was when he heard the dogs barking.

"Tamara!" he called up the embankment. "Tamara, what is it?"

"Someone's coming," Tamara called down.

"Come on, hurry!"

"No!" Tamara said. "You go ahead. I'll lead them away from the water."

"Tamara, no, come on!" Matt said. "Hurry, we have to go now!"

"You go on!" Tamara called.

Matt saw Tamara turn and run away from the top of the bank.

"Help!" Tamara called. "Help me!"

"What are you doing out here, girl?" a man's voice asked.

"I don't know," Tamara answered. "I think I must have been walking in my sleep, I just woke up out here. I'm lost and frightened. Please, help me get back to the Home."

As Tamara distracted whoever had been alerted by the dogs, Matt stepped into the boat and pushed himself off. Picking up the paddle, he helped the swift-flowing water propel him downstream.

It was five or six miles before the creek was no longer wide enough or deep enough to support the boat. There, Matt abandoned it, and started walking. He stayed close to the creek because it was a source of water and because he had an idea that it might eventually lead him somewhere.

He ate the last of his bread on the third day. On the fourth day he found some wild onions and ate them, though the taste was so bitter that he could barely keep them down.

He had nothing at all to eat on the fifth day, but on the sixth he managed to catch a frog. He remembered eating frog legs back in Kansas, but they were rolled in batter and deep-fried. He had no way of cooking these legs; he had no matches. But he did have a pocket knife and he cut off the legs, skinned them, and ate them raw.

An early snow moved in just before nightfall of the sixth day, and the single blanket Matt had brought with him did little to push away the cold. It was also tiring to try and hold the blanket around him while walking, and he considered cutting a hole in the middle, but decided against it because he thought it would be less warm at night that way.

As the snow continued to fall, it got more and more difficult to walk. At first, it was just slick, and he slipped and fell a couple of times, once barking his shin on a rock so hard that the pain stayed with him for quite a while.

As the snow got deeper, he quit worrying about it being slick, and concerned himself only with the work it took just to keep going. His breath started coming in heaving gasps, sending out clouds of vapor before him. Once he saw a wolf tracking him, and he wished that he had his father's rifle.

He found a limb that was stout and about as thick as three fingers. Using his knife, he trimmed the smaller branches off it, then managed to cut it to just the right size. He was able to use the limb as a cane to help him negotiate the deepening snowdrifts.

Just before dark, he sensed more than heard something behind him and, turning quickly, saw that the wolf, crouched low, had sneaked up right behind him. With a shout, and holding the club in both hands, he swung at the wolf and had the satisfaction of hearing a solid pop as he hit the wolf in the head. The wolf yelped once, then turned and ran away, trailing little bits of blood behind it as it ran.

Matt felt a sense of power and elation over that little encounter. He was sure that the wolf would give him no further trouble.

After the sun set, he found an overhanging rock ledge and got under it, then wrapped himself in the blanket. When night came, he looked up into the dark sky and watched as the huge, white flakes tumbled down. If it weren't for the fact that he was probably going to die in these mountains, he would think the snowfall was beautiful.

"Lord," he said, praying aloud. "I reckon I haven't been all that good at prayin', even though we had a chapel back at the Home. But I know that Mama used to pray to you all the time, and she seemed to take a lot of comfort in it, so if you don't mind hearin' from someone like me, I'm goin' to pray to you now.

"I want you to look out for Eddie and Timmy, and all the other kids back at the Home. Truth is, Lord, I probably shouldn't have left. Without me there to take care of them, there's no tellin' what

Captain Mumford is goin' to put them through. And there's no tellin' who he's goin' to get to take the place of those two no-accounts, Connors and Simon.

"But that's spilt milk, Lord. The Home is back there, and I'm here, and I probably wouldn't live long enough to make it back there even if I tried. I'm probably goin' to die pretty soon now. Of course, I don't reckon I have to tell you the way things are right now. I'm out of food, it's gettin' colder, and the creek has quit so I'm out of water too. I know Mama is up in heaven with you, 'cause she was a very good woman. And Cassie is up there too. And though I didn't know Pa all that well, seein' as he was off to war for most of my life, well, I figure he's probably up there also, 'cause I don't think Mama would've married a bad man.

"But now it comes to me, Lord, and I have to confess that my chances don't look all that good. I killed those two men back at the wagon. Well, I don't have to tell you about it, you saw me do it. I can't rightly say that I shot either one of them to save my family because, as you know, my family was already dead. The only reason I shot 'em is because they needed killin'. And I have to be honest with you, Lord, I aim to hunt down Payson and Garvey and the others who were with them, and kill them as well. So if you let me live through this, then I'm going to take it that it's all right with you. And if it isn't all right with you, Lord, then I hope you just go ahead and take me tonight.

"Amen."

Finishing his prayer, Matt pulled the blanket more securely around him, pulled up his legs, then leaned back against the rock. Strangely, the cold seemed to be less intense and he felt his body warming. He also felt his eyes growing very heavy and he closed them, then drifted off to sleep.

CHAPTER 8

With Smoke Jensen

The sudden snowfall had caught Smoke by surprise. It shouldn't have caught him by surprise. Preacher had taught him well how to gauge the change in weather.

"When the clouds is low in the west and there's these long, scraggily tails hangin' down from 'em, then like as not you'll be gettin' snow soon as they start movin' over the mountains."

Smoke needed to be on the other side of the mountain range, and he was afraid that the snow might be so heavy as to close the pass. So, though every ounce of him wanted to hole up somewhere long enough to ride the storm out, he pushed on through, fighting the cold, stinging snow in his face until he reached the top of the pass. He made it through, and had started looking for a place to spend the night when he saw the boy.

He almost didn't see him; there was a big drift of snow so that only the boy's head and shoulders were sticking out. He was under an overhanging ledge, and his head was back and his eyes were closed.

"Damn, who is that?" he asked aloud. "And what's he doing here?"

Smoke stared in shocked surprise at the young boy. Was he sleeping? Or was he dead?

The boy's face and lips were blue, and there were ice crystals in his eyebrows and hair. The blanket around him, which was his only protection against the cold, was frozen.

It didn't look good.

* * *

"Here, try some of this."

Matt opened his eyes and saw a man sitting on the bed beside him, holding a cup. He took the cup and raised it to his mouth, but jerked it away when it burned his lips.

The man who handed him the cup laughed. "Oh, maybe I should have told you it was hot."

Matt tried again, this time sipping it through extended lips. It was hot, and bracing, and good.

"What is it?" he asked.

"Broth, made from beaver," the man said.

"Don't know that I've ever tasted beaver before," Matt said calmly. Smoke laughed.

"What's so funny?"

"I'll say this for you, boy, you do have sand," Smoke said. "You sure seem to be taking this in stride."

Matt took another swallow, then looked around. He was in a room, or more accurately, a one-room cabin. There was a fireplace on one side in which a fire was burning briskly, putting out enough heat to warm the entire room. The interior walls were made of mud-chinked logs. There was a table and several chairs, a couple of chests, and a wall rack that held three rifles and a shotgun. There were antlers on the wall, and bearskins on the floor. The very bed he was lying on had skins as well as blankets.

"Beaver broth is good," he said.

"I made some biscuits," the man said, handing one to Matt.

Matt took one of the biscuits and began eating it hungrily.

"Whoa, slow down, slow down, you'll make yourself sick," he said. "How long has it been since you ate?"

"I don't know," Matt said. "I don't even know how long I've been here."

"I brought you here night before last," the man said. "You've been asleep for the whole time. In fact, I wasn't sure I'd ever be able to wake you up. I was thinking I would have to bury you out back somewhere."

"Where is here?"

"I'll tell you where here is after you answer some of my questions. Who are you?"

"My name is Matt."

"Matt what?"

"Just Matt."

The man nodded. "All right, Just Matt, that's good enough for me," he said. "My name is Smoke Jensen."

"Smoke? You mean, like smoke from a fire?"

"Yes."

"I've never heard of such a name."

"I've never heard of someone who was just Matt."

"I'm sorry," Matt said. "I guess if your name is Smoke, then that's your name."

"My real name is Kirby. Kirby Jensen. But folks have called me Smoke from the time I was a kid, so it sort of belongs to me now."

"You were going to tell me where I am."

"You are in my cabin in the Gore Range."

"Gore Range? What is the Gore Range?"

"It is a mountain range in Colorado," Smoke explained.

"Oh."

"Are you lost, Matt?"

"No, I'm not lost. I knew I was in Colorado," Matt replied.

Smoke laughed again. "Well, as long as you knew you were in Colorado," he said.

Matt took another swallow of the broth.

"Tell you what, Matt. As soon as you've got your strength, I'll take you back."

"No!" Matt said sharply. "No, I won't go back!" He tried to get up and get out of bed, but he was too weak and he fell back onto the bed.

"Here, hold on, hold on there," Smoke said. "You're too weak to be doin' that."

"I'm not goin' back," Matt said.

"All right, if you don't want to go back, I won't make you," Smoke said. "But don't you think your ma and pa might be worrying about you?"

"My ma and pa are both dead," Matt said. "They've been dead for three years."

"I see," Smoke said. "So, where is it you don't want to go back to? Are you living with relatives or something?"

Matt shook his head and finished the broth. He handed the cup to Smoke. "Is there any more?" he asked.

"Yes, there's more," Smoke replied.

"And another biscuit, please?"

Smoke refilled the cup with broth, then handed it and another biscuit to Matt.

"It's an orphanage," Matt said, answering Smoke's earlier question. "Only it's called the Home for Wayward Boys and Girls. None of us are really wayward, though. The only thing is we're all just orphans."

"So, if it's just an orphanage, why did you run away?"

"You wouldn't understand," Matt said.

"Maybe I wouldn't," Smoke agreed. "But in the meantime, you can put your mind at ease. I'm not going to make you go back."

"I don't want to be a burden on you, so as soon as I get my strength back, I'll be going on," Matt offered. "Just tell me the way to the nearest town so I can find a job somewhere."

"The nearest town is a good fifty or more miles from here," he said. "And even if you knew where it was, you wouldn't be able to make it. Most of the high passes are filled with snow by now. You wouldn't be able to get through."

"Oh."

"So, I'm afraid you are going to have to just stay here with me."

"Stay here? Stay here for how long?"

"Four or five months anyway," Smoke replied. "Until the high passes are open."

"I'm sorry."

"What are you sorry about?" Smoke asked.

"I'm sorry I'm goin' to have to stay here and put you out."

"Well, don't worry about it. In the first place, I could use the company. It gets awfully lonely sometimes, spending a winter in a cabin like this all by yourself. And in the second place, you won't be puttin' me out because I aim to see to it that you earn your keep."

"Yes, sir," Matt said. "I'll do whatever you ask me to do, Mr. Jensen."

"Is that a promise?"

"Yes, sir!"

"Then I'm going to ask you not to call me Mr. Jensen. The name is Smoke. That's what I'll be wanting you to call me."

"All right—Smoke," Matt replied with a big grin.

"First thing we're going to have to do is build you a bed," Smoke said. "The bed you've been sleeping in for the last two days belongs to me, and I don't plan on sharing it."

"I've made my bed, but I don't think I've ever built one before," Matt said.

"Matt, during your stay with me you're going to be doing a lot of things you've never done before," Smoke promised.

CHAPTER 9

"It doesn't make the best coffee," Smoke said as he poured the dark substance into the bottom of a coffeepot. "But if you roast dandelion root, then crush it up and boil it, well, the coffee is passable."

"The meat smells good," Matt said. He was talking about a cut of venison that was cooking in a roaster that was sitting on a rock at the back of the fireplace. Wild carrots and wild leeks surrounded the meat and were now bubbling in the meat juices.

"The meat, carrots, and cattail roots will make us a fine meal," Smoke said. "Afterward, we'll have dessert of wild blueberry pie and coffee."

"I had no idea there were so many things you could eat in the wild," Matt said. "I mean, if you think about it, I nearly starved to death out there and there were all sorts of thing to eat."

"Well, don't feel bad about it," Smoke said. "I wouldn't have known about it either if it hadn't been for Preacher."

"Preacher must be quite a fella," Matt said. "I'd like to meet him someday."

"You will," Smoke promised. "The thing about Preacher is, he likes his time alone."

"Why is that?"

"He's an old-time mountain man," Smoke explained. "One of the originals."

"You're a mountain man too."

"I am," Smoke agreed. "But I don't plan to spend my whole life in the mountains. Truth is, I like civilization too much. One of these days I intend to get myself a ranch and settle down."

"Not me," Matt said.

"You don't want to settle down?"

"No, sir. I want to just wander around from place to place."

"I guess you'll get to see a lot of the country that way," Smoke said.

Matt was quiet for a long moment before he spoke. "After I kill some people," he said.

Smoke didn't reply.

"I reckon you think that's wrong of me, don't you? Saying that I'm going to kill some people."

"Depends on who you are going to kill, and why you are going to kill them," Smoke said.

"I only know the names of two of them," Matt said. "One is Payson and the other is Garvey."

"Are those first names or last?"

"I don't know," Matt said.

"Well, would you know these people if you saw them?"

"Yes, I'd know them. Payson has a long, ugly, purple scar on his face and it's made his eye look funny," Matt said, using his finger to illustrate the scar. "Garvey only has half an ear."

"You said your ma and pa are dead. Did these fellas kill them?"

"Yes, and my big sister too," Matt said. "They were also going to—uh—I mean, with my mom and my sister they were going to—uh—don't know how to say it."

"Rape?"

Matt was quiet for a moment. His eyes brimmed with tears; then they began flowing down his cheeks. He held back his sobs as he brushed the tears away. Finally, he nodded.

"Yes. One of them was going to rape my mom and sister," Matt said. "My mom and sis were already dead, but he was going to do it anyway."

"You said he was going to," Smoke noted. "But he didn't?"

Matt shook his head. "No."

"What stopped him?"

"I—I did," Matt said. "When they shot Pa, I grabbed Pa's rifle and I ran. Like a coward, I ran."

Smoke shook his head. "That wasn't being cowardly, Matt. That was being smart."

"I managed to get behind some rocks and I climbed up so I could

298 William W. Johnstone

see. But by the time I got up there, it was too late. Ma and Cassie were already dead, and one of them was standing over my ma, unbuttoning his pants, getting ready to . . ." He paused for a moment before he continued. "To be honest with you, Smoke, I was nine years old then, so I didn't really know what he was planning to do. I thought maybe he was going to pee on them. So I shot him in the head."

"Good for you," Smoke said.

"After I shot that one, one of the others tried to come after me, but he got wedged in between a couple of rocks and couldn't get to me. So I killed him too."

"How do you feel about that?" Smoke asked.

"What do you mean?"

"Do you think what you did was wrong?"

"I don't know," Matt admitted. "I mean, I know it's wrong to kill people, but I also know that soldiers kill people. My pa was a soldier in the war. He killed people and I know he wasn't a bad man."

"That is something to think about, Matt," Smoke said. "If good men can kill good men during a war, then there can't be anything wrong with a good man killing an evil man."

Matt smiled and nodded. "Yeah," he said. "Yeah, I hadn't thought of it that way before, but I think you are right."

"It smells like supper is ready," Smoke said.

"That's good. I'm starving."

Smoke laughed. "If anyone else told me they were starving, I would figure they didn't know what they were talking about. But seeing as how you actually were starving when I found you, then I guess you don't fall into that category."

Throughout the long winter, Smoke began teaching his young protégé things he needed to know to get by. In the teaching, he felt almost as if he was doing nature's bidding, passing along things he had learned from Preacher. And just as it wasn't a father-son relationship between Smoke and Preacher, neither was this a father-son relationship. But the fact that they didn't share a familial bond didn't mean the relationship wasn't just as strong, nor the continuity as valid as it would have been if they had.

"Just because we're livin' out here in the wilds, doesn't mean we don't have laws that we follow," Smoke said, recalling almost the same conversation he once had with Preacher. "Only out here, it isn't laws that you find written on paper or in books. And it isn't laws that have to have sheriffs enforcing, or judges settling."

"What kind of laws are they?"

"You might say they are the laws of decency and good sense," Smoke explained. "For example, don't go putting your hands on another man's wife, don't steal from him, don't cheat him, and don't call him a liar. Do that, and somebody is going to get killed."

"Somebody? Don't you mean the man that's doing the wrong?" Matt asked.

Smoke shook his head. "Not always. Sometimes the one who is wronged has no choice but to try and defend those laws. But if the one who wronged him is faster and better with a gun, then the wronged man dies."

"I see what you mean."

"I hope you do see what I mean, Matt, because I'm going to teach you how to use a gun. And by the time I get through with you, there will be few, if any, in the country who will be able to stand up to you. But with that comes the responsibility of knighthood."

Matt chuckled. "Knighthood?"

"You've heard about knights, haven't you?"

"Yeah, I've seen pictures. They are the guys who wore the iron suits, right?" Matt asked.

"Right. Those suits were called armor. The knights were appointed by the king, and he made sure that he only appointed the best men for the job. You see, the knights were so strong they could kill anyone they wanted to. But they didn't. They took an oath never to use their power to enrich themselves, but always just to help others."

"Are you a knight, Smoke?"

Smoke nodded. "Yeah," he said. "In a manner of speaking, you might say that I am a knight. I respect the rights of others, and I settle my own accounts without running to the sheriff."

"How do you settle accounts?" Matt asked.

"Say a cougar is sneaking up on my horse," Smoke suggested. "Do you think I should go to a sheriff or a judge to complain?"

"No, sir," Matt replied.

"What would you do?"

"I'd shoot the cougar."

Smoke nodded. "Uh-huh. It's the same with a man, Matt. If a man calls you out, you don't go to the sheriff or a judge, you deal with him, straight and simple."

"Like Payson and Garvey?"

"Like Payson and Garvey," Smoke agreed.

As soon as the streams melted and the water began flowing again, Smoke asked Matt to come down to the creek with him.

"Are we going fishing?" Matt asked.

Smoke chuckled. "Something like that," he said. He handed Matt a pan.

"Hmm. I've never fished with a pan before," Matt said, looking at the pan.

"That's because you've never fished for gold before."

"Gold? You fish for gold?"

"I do," Smoke said.

The walk from the cabin to the creek was about half a mile. There, a wide bed of gravel wound its way through the valley, and in the middle of the bed of gravel was a creek, approximately thirty yards wide. The creek ran cool and clear, except where the whitewater broke over the rocks.

"It's very pretty here," Matt said.

"Yes, it is," Smoke agreed.

"Is this where we are going to fish for gold?"

"Yes, but it isn't called fishing, it's called panning," Smoke said. "Pay attention."

"All right."

"The first thing you have to do is look around for the best location to work. Find yourself a spot where the water is at least six inches deep and flowing just fast enough to keep the muddy water from getting into your pan. Also, it's nice if you can find a rock that will let you sit down."

Smoke continued his lesson, demonstrating as he talked.

"Fill the pan about three-quarters full of gravel, then hold it deep enough so it is just under water. Shake it back and forth and from side to side, but not so hard that you wash anything out of the pan. Keep doing this until everything heavy goes to the bottom of the pan and the lighter stuff comes to the top. Then turn the pan just enough to pour out the lighter rocks," he said, continuing to demonstrate.

"After that, you sort of swirl things around in the pan to look at what you have and . . . ha!" he said, reaching down into the pan. "Here is what we are looking for."

Smoke held a little rock in his hand, not much bigger than a pea.

"That's just a rock," Matt said.

Smoke turned it, and Matt saw a quick flash in the sun.

"Not just a rock," Smoke replied.

"It's gold!" Matt said.

Smoke nodded.

"If there's gold in this creek, why aren't more people up here doing this?"

"Right now only three people know about it," Smoke said. "Preacher, me, and you. I'd like to keep it that way."

"Wow!" Matt said. "This is fun!"

Smoke chuckled. "I'm glad you think so," he said. "Because this is what we are going to be doing all summer."

CHAPTER 10

Cedar Creek

There wasn't much to the little town of Cedar Creek. It was hot, dry, and dusty, out in the middle of nowhere and baking under the blows of the hot September sun. An old yellow dog was asleep under the front porch of the general store, the shade shared by a black-and-white cat.

School had just started, and on the school grounds a group of Miss Miller's second-grade students were laughing and playing during their afternoon recess.

As the children played and the rest of the town went about its business, a drama was taking place inside the Bank of Cedar Creek. Seven men, wearing yellow dusters and brandishing guns, were holding the bank employees and customers at bay. The bank robbers were wearing as masks bandannas tied around their faces. But the leader of the group had a puffy scar, starting above his left eye, disfiguring the eye and streaking down his cheek like a purple flash of lightning, then disappearing under the bandanna.

Even as Payson and his men were robbing the bank, Jason Feeler was coming up the boardwalk, carrying an envelope. The envelope contained twelve dollars and seventy-five cents, a deposit from the livery stable. Jason, who was seventeen, felt pleased that Mr. Hecke-meyer considered him responsible enough to take the overnight receipts to the bank.

As Jason reached the front of the bank, he looked in through the window, then gasped. Mr. Fitzhugh, the bank president, was standing against the wall with his hands in the air. So were several others. Mr. Boykin was on his knees in front of the safe, twisting the dial, while a masked man was standing beside him, holding a gun against his head. There were six other robbers in the bank.

Fitzhugh saw Jason, and made a slight motion with his head. Jason understood, nodded, then left the front of the bank. As soon as he was clear of the bank, he started running. A moment later, he pushed open the door to the marshal's office.

"The bank's bein' robbed, Marshal Cobb!" Jason shouted breathlessly.

"What?"

"They's some men with guns robbin' the bank," Jason said. "They're in there now!"

Marshal Cobb pulled a rifle down from the gun rack and tossed it to Jason; then he pulled another one down for himself.

"Get down to the general store," the marshal ordered. "Tell anyone you find there to get ready. I'm goin' to get some help from the saloon."

Spurred on by the warning and moving quickly and quietly enough to avoid giving the bank robbers any sign of what they were doing, the men blocked off both escape routes out of town. They pushed wagons across the street to use as barricades; then with rifles, pistols, and shotguns, they took up their positions. Armed and ready, they stared back toward the bank, watching and waiting.

Inside the bank, unaware of the ambush being set for them outside, the scar-faced man was holding his gun on the bank teller, who was kneeling in front of the vault door, nervously twisting the combination dial.

"Mister, if you don't have that lock open in thirty seconds, I'm going to blow your brains all over the front of this safe," the scar-faced man said menacingly.

"I'm trying to open it," the trembling teller replied. "But I'm so scared that I keep makin' mistakes."

The scar-faced man cocked his pistol and pressed the barrel against the teller's temple. "Yeah? Well, don't make any more, 'cause the next mistake will be your last one."

The teller began again.

"Garvey, what's it look like outside?" the leader asked.

"Damn, Payson, you said my name," Garvey said.

"Yeah, and you just said mine," Payson replied.

Like Payson, Garvey had a very distinguishing feature. The lobe of his left ear had been shot off, leaving him only half an ear on that side. He moved over to the window and pulled the green curtain aside so he could look out into the street.

"Never mind, what does it look like?"

"It looks quiet," Garvey said.

There was a click as the vault door came unlocked.

"There, that's more like it," Payson said with a wide, evil grin. He pulled a sack from the pocket of his duster and handed it to the teller. "Now, fill it up."

The teller reached for the coin drawer.

"To hell with them coins! I want greenbacks!" Payson ordered, waving his pistol toward the drawer that was full of banded stacks of bills.

"Yes, sir," the teller replied, and with trembling hands he began scooping up the bank-note packages and dropping them into the bag.

"Hurry it up, hurry it up," Payson demanded. "We ain't got all day."

"Marshal, look!" one of the townsmen said, pointing toward the school.

Through all their preparation, no one had thought to warn Miss Miller and her second-grade pupils. The games of recess continued without interruption.

"Somebody needs to get them kids out of there!" another said.

"All right, go down there and . . ." Marshal Cobb began, but before he could finish the sentence, the front door of the bank swung open and seven men dashed toward the horses that were tied at the hitching rail. "No, wait, it's too late now," the marshal said.

Marshal Cobb raised up from his position and called out to the seven robbers.

"You men hold it right there!" he shouted. "You ain't a'goin' nowhere!"

At almost the same time Cobb shouted, he fired. His bullet went through Garvey's hat, knocking it into the dirt.

"What the hell?" Garvey shouted. "Payson, look out! It's a trap!"

"Poke, Syl, Clem, Bart, Pete, get mounted!" Payson shouted to the others. "Let's get out of here! Let's go, let's go!"

The other outlaws also began shooting as they started for their own mounts.

From the front porch of Lambert's Café, a citizen with food stains still on the front of his shirt appeared with a shotgun. He let go a blast, but the range was too great. His pellets peppered the outlaws without penetrating their skin. Another man fired a shotgun from a little closer range, and the front window of the bank came crashing down.

Once the robbers were mounted, they started down the street at a full gallop, while two dozen armed townsmen fired at them from every possible position.

"I'm hit, I'm hit!" one of the outlaws shouted.

"Sonofabitch! They got Pete!" Poke yelled. He reached over to try and steady Pete on his horse, but the outlaw fell. "Payson, Pete's down!"

"Leave 'im!" Payson shouted back.

Payson and his gang reached the end of the street, only to find the barricade that had been erected.

"Damn! They got us blocked off! What'll we do, Payson?" Syl shouted.

"This way!" Payson answered, and leading the way, he started back through the town, riding back in the opposite direction. They were galloping hard when they came up on the barricade that had been erected at the other end of town. They had to pull up short. The horses, now as panic-stricken as the men, twisted around in nervous circles and reared up, anxious to run, but not sure where to go. It was all the riders could do to control them.

"They got us blocked off at both ends!" Clem yelled.

"There!" Bart shouted, pointing toward the school yard. "We can go through there!"

Without answering, Payson veered off the street and headed straight for the school yard, where the kids, who were by now frightened by the exploding gunshots, had gathered around Miss Miller. The teacher was also rooted to the spot by her own terror.

"Hold your fire, men! Hold your fire! We might hit one of the kids!" Marshal Cobb shouted.

With the marshal's order, the fire of the townspeople stopped, giving Payson and his men a chance to get away. When Payson reached the alley behind the school, he and the others turned and fired back though the playground at the townspeople. Then they galloped away, followed by the shouts of anger and frustration from the men of the town. Marshal Cobb led them through the school yard to the alley, where they formed a skirmish line of shooters, firing at the cloud of dust as the riders grew smaller and smaller in the distance.

"Cease fire, cease fire!" the marshal shouted. "We're just wastin' ammunition now. They're well out of range."

"Marshal, you ain't gonna just let them get away, are you?"

"Nothing I can do about it," the marshal said. "They're out of town now, I've got no jurisdiction."

Looking back, they saw one of the outlaws lying dead in the street.

"At least we got one of them," Marshal Cobb said.

"Yeah," one of the others said. "And they got two of us. Look over there."

"My God," Marshal Cobb gasped when, for the first time, he saw that Miss Miller and a little girl were lying on the ground, victims of the outlaws' last fusillade. The fallen figures were surrounded by the other children, who were looking down at their teacher and their friend in shocked silence.

"Somebody get a doctor, quick!" Marshal Cobb called.

"We won't be needin' a doctor, Marshal," one of the men who had walked over to check them said. "What we need is an undertaker. They're both dead."

By now the outlaws were in full gallop, running away from the town. They ran the horses for several minutes before Bart Ebersole called out.

"Payson! If we don't give these horses a blow, they're goin' to drop dead under us!"

"Yeah, all right," Payson answered. "Pull up."

The six outlaws stopped the gallop, then dismounted, walked their horses to let them regain their breath.

"Anyone else hit?" Payson asked. "Garvey, Poke, Syl, Clem, Bart?"

"Nah," Garvey said. "Except for Pete, we come through fine."

Payson laughed. "Damn, boys, that was good. Jesse James don't have a thing on us!"

CHAPTER 11

Matt was standing just outside Smoke's cabin, throwing a knife at a target he had carved on a tree. The hunting knife, a gift from Smoke, was perfectly balanced for throwing, and whenever he had time during the long summer days, Matt would practice.

"Matt," Smoke called from the door of the cabin. "Let's see how good you really are."

Smoke threw his knife, hitting the target dead center.

Smiling, Matt threw his own knife at the target, hitting so close to the one Smoke had thrown that the blades were actually touching.

"Whoa, you've gotten pretty good with that," Smoke said.

"Thanks," Matt said, walking out to the tree and pulling both knives free.

"You remember what I said about going into town when summer was over?" Smoke said.

"I remember."

"Well, summer is over. Why don't you go out to the corral and pick out your horse?"

"*My* horse?"

"Yeah, your horse. A man's got to have a horse."

"Which horse is mine?" Matt asked.

"Why don't you take the best one?" Smoke replied. "Except for that one," Smoke added, pointing to an Appaloosa over in one corner of the corral. "That one is mine."

"Which horse is the best?" Matt asked.

"Uh-uh," Smoke replied, shaking his head. "I'm willing to give you the best horse in my string, but as to which horse that is, well, you're just going to have to figure that out for yourself."

Matt walked out to the small corral that Smoke had built and, leaning on the split-rail fence, looked at the string of seven horses from which he could choose.

After looking them over very carefully, Matt smiled and nodded.

"You've made your choice?" Smoke asked.

"Yes."

"Which one?"

"I want that one," Matt said, pointing to a bay.

"Why not the chestnut?" Smoke asked. "He looks stronger."

"Look at the chestnut's front feet," Matt said. "They are splayed. The bay's feet are just right."

"What about the black one over there?"

"Uh-uh," Matt said. "His back legs are set too far back. I want the bay."

Smoke reached out and ran his hand through Matt's hair.

"You're learning, kid, you're learning," he said. "The bay is yours."

Matt's grin spread from ear to ear. "I've never had a horse before," he said. He jumped down from the rail fence and started toward the horse.

"That's all right, he's never had a rider before," Smoke said.

"What?" Matt asked, jerking around in surprise as he stared at Smoke. "Did you say that he's never been ridden?"

"He's as spirited as he was the day we brought him in."

"How'm I going to ride him if he has never been ridden?"

"Well, I reckon you are just going to have to break him," Smoke said, passing the words off as easily as if he had just suggested that Matt should wear a hat.

"Break him? I can't break a horse!"

"Sure you can. It'll be fun," Smoke suggested.

Smoke showed Matt how to saddle the horse, and gave him some pointers on riding it.

"Now, you don't want to break the horse's spirit," Smoke said. "What you want to do is make him your partner."

"How do I do that?"

"Walk him around for a bit so that he gets used to his saddle, and to you. Then get on."

"He won't throw me then?"

"Oh, he'll still throw you a few times," Smoke said with a little laugh. "But at least he'll know how serious you are."

To Matt's happy surprise, he wasn't thrown even once. The horse did buck a few times, coming down on stiff legs, then sunfishing and,

finally, galloping at full speed around the corral. But after a few minutes he stopped fighting, and Matt leaned over to pat him gently on
the neck.

"Good job, Matt," Smoke said, clapping his hands quietly. "You've
got a real touch with horses. You didn't break him, you trained him,
and that's real good. He's not mean, but he still has spirit."

"Smoke, can I name him?"

"Sure, he's your horse, you can name him anything you want."

Matt continued to pat the horse on the neck as he thought of a
name.

"That's it," he said, smiling broadly. "I've come up with a name."

"What are you going to call him?"

"Spirit."

Smoke nodded. "Spirit. That's a good name. The Indians will like
that name."

"I wonder how long it will take him to learn his name," Matt said.

"Not too long," Smoke replied. "What do you say we get started
into town now?"

"How far is town?" Matt asked.

"About fifty miles north of here," Smoke said. "We'll spend tonight
on the trail, and get there sometime tomorrow."

"Smoke, we're not going to the town of Soda Creek, are we?" Matt
asked.

"Soda Creek? No. Why the concern? Is that where the orphanage was?"

"Yes, and I don't want to go back there. I don't even want to go to
the town."

"Don't worry about it. Soda Creek is south, and we're going
north," Smoke said. "Do you know how to find north?"

"I know the sun rises in the east," Matt said.

"What if it's nighttime, and you can't see the sun?"

"I know about the North Star."

"That's good. Do you know how to find the North Star?"

"The Big Dipper," Matt said. "All you do is line up the two stars on
the cup of the dipper, and you can find the North Star. Pa showed me
how to do that when we were on the trail."

"Good for your pa," Smoke said. "That's a good thing to know. But
what if you are in trees or something so that, for some reason, you
can't see the stars? Did you know that you can also find the north
with the moon?"

Matt shook his head. "No," he said. "I didn't know you could do that."

"On a fairly full moon you can see a crescent of shadows. The finger in the crescent points to the north. When the moon is at a phase where you can see where the shadow starts, you can find north by making an imaginary line from the tip of the shadow to the north."

"That's good to know," Matt said.

Smoke chuckled. "If you can keep a few things like that in mind, you might be able to locate yourself just a little closer than by saying you're in Colorado."

Matt laughed, remembering that he had insisted to Smoke that he wasn't lost because he knew he was in Colorado.

The two men rode on through the afternoon; then Smoke held up his hand as a signal to stop.

"We'll camp here tonight," he said, pointing. "There's water, and it's always good to camp by water, as long as you know the dangers."

"What's dangerous about camping near water?" Matt asked.

"All critters need water," Smoke explained, "squirrels, rabbits, horses, men, dogs, and the like. But so do bears, and mountain lions, and wolves. And some of them are pretty possessive. If they see you around their water hole, they aren't going to like it. So you're going to have to stay alert the whole time you are by a water hole."

Matt remembered his encounter with the wolf when he was on the trail, running away from the Home. "I see," he said.

"Also, the water might be poison."

"Poison? How, why?"

"Don't always know why the water would be poison, but there is bad water out there and you'll run across it from time to time."

"How do you tell if it's poison? By taste?"

Smoke shook his head. "No, that's not good enough. Some bad water tastes pretty good, some good water tastes awfully bad. About the only way you can really tell is to take a look around it. If you see the bones of dead animals real close to a water hole, the chances are they died drinking the water. That's a good sign for you to just keep moving on."

"I'll try to remember that," Matt said.

"You'll try? I hope you remember everything I'm telling you," Smoke said. "Otherwise, I'm just out here batting my gums for nothing."

"I will remember," Matt promised.

Mule Crossing, Colorado

There was no town called Mule Crossing. It was a place about fifteen miles west of Meeker, where the White River could be forded. Here, a man named John Grant had built a saloon and general store.

The man who came into Grant's saloon stood at the door for just a minute, allowing his eyes to adjust to the darkness. He was about average size, with a drawn face, watery-blue eyes, a hooked nose, and a sweeping handle-bar mustache. He wore a low-crown black hat encircled with a silver hatband, from which protruded a small, red feather.

"My name is Amos Bodine," he announced. "And I'm lookin' for a man by the name of Cleo Wright."

There were only six others in the saloon, and Bodine studied each one of them. All but one returned his gaze. The one who did not was making a point of staring at his drink.

"You," Bodine said to the one who hadn't looked up. "What's your name?"

"Smith," the man replied. "John Smith."

Another man came in behind Bodine then, and the fact that Bodine didn't look around indicated that he knew who it was.

"He's lyin', Amos," the new man said. "I seen him at the trial before he broke jail. This here is Cleo Wright."

"Well, Mr. Cleo Wright," Bodine said, a wicked smile spreading across his face. "There's a reward out for you, did you know that?"

With a sigh, and a set of his shoulders, Cleo Wright stepped away from the bar and faced Bodine. "Yeah," he said. "I know that."

"Tell you what," Bodine said. "You pay me the reward money, and I'll let you go."

"I don't have any money," Wright answered.

"Then I guess I'm just going to have to take you in. Unless you can stop me."

"Stop you? How am I supposed to stop you?"

"Well, you could draw against me," Bodine said. "You might get lucky. Or you can just show everyone in here what a sniveling, low-assed coward you are, then get down on your belly and slither out to your horse."

"What?" Wright asked with a gasp. "What are you asking me to do?"

"You heard me," Wright said. "You can either draw against me, or get down on your belly and slither across the floor like the cowardly snake that you are."

"No way in hell am I going to do that, mister!" Cleo said.

The smile had never left Bodine's face. "Then you are going to have to draw against me," he said in a sibilant tone.

The expression on Cleo Wright's face turned from one of anger to fear, then to resignation. With a shout of fury, Wright made a desperate grab for his gun.

Bodine's gun was out and firing before Wright was able to clear leather with his own pistol. Wright went down with a bullet in his heart.

Meeker, Colorado

Two men rode into town. One of the men was leading another horse, and draped across that horse was a body. As they rode down Main Street, several of the townspeople stopped what they were doing to watch, some coming out of the stores and buildings to stand on the side of the street.

The horses' hooves raised little clouds of dust and made hollow clopping sounds that echoed back from the buildings that lined the street.

In Dunnigan's Barber Shop, Ernie Peterson, who was waiting for a shave and a trim, happened to see the rider through the window.

"I'll be damn," Peterson said.

"What is it?" Dunnigan asked as he applied lather to the face of old Gil Tucker. Tucker was a veteran of the War of 1812.

"It's Amos Bodine," Peterson said.

"Bodine? The bounty hunter?"

"That's him all right," Peterson said.

Dunnigan left his customer and walked out onto the front porch, followed by Peterson and Gil Tucker. Tucker, whose face was half-lathered, was still wearing the barber apron Dunnigan had put around him.

"Who's that with him?" Dunnigan asked.

"You mean the one ridin' with him? Or the fella he's bringin' in?" Peterson replied.

"Both."

"I expect the one with him is a fella by the name of Colby. I've heard Colby is his partner. I don't have no idea who the one draped over the horse is," Peterson said.

"Yeah, well, they say that Bodine ain't none too particular," Dunnigan said. "If you're wanted, no matter what the reward is, he'll bring you in. And most of the time when he does bring someone in, he's dead."

When they passed by the saloon, Colby pulled over and dismounted, then tied his horse to the hitching rail.

"I'll be back in a few minutes," Bodine called to him.

"I'll be in the saloon," Colby called back.

By the time Bodine reached the sheriff's office, Sheriff Adams had already heard about his arrival and was standing on the front porch, waiting for him.

Bodine stopped in front, then rode back to the trail horse, leaned over to cut a rope, then gave the body that was draped over the saddle a push. The body landed on the dirt street, faceup, his arms thrown out to either side. His eyes were still open but opaque. His face had a bluish tint.

"Sheriff, I'm . . ." Bodine started, but Sheriff Adams finished for him.

"Amos Bodine. Yeah, I know who you are," Sheriff Adams said. He nodded toward the body on the ground. "Who is that?"

"His name is Wright. Cleo Wright," Bodine said. He pulled a piece of paper from his pocket. "I got a dodger here says he's worth two hundred fifty dollars."

"Did you have to kill him?"

"Read what it says on the paper," Bodine said. "It says dead or alive."

"I'm sure it does," Sheriff Adams said. He sighed. "That's not what I asked. I asked if you had to kill him."

"He drew on me," Bodine said.

"They always draw on you, don't they, Bodine?"

"I reckon they figure that's better'n goin' to jail."

"And it makes it easier for you to bring them in, doesn't it?"

"Some," Bodine admitted.

"How many have you killed, Bodine?"

"Twenty-five or thirty, I reckon," Bodine replied. "I really don't know, but I've never killed anyone that I didn't get paid for killin'."

314 William W. Johnstone

"I'm sure you haven't."

"Speakin' of which, when am I goin' to get paid for this one?" he asked, nodding toward Cleo Wright.

"It'll be a day or two before I can get your money," the sheriff answered.

"That's fine by me, as long as I get it," Bodine said. "My partner, Colby, is already down to the saloon. If you need me, I'll be there. I can wait."

"You've got a partner now?"

"It's come in handy a time or two," Bodine replied. He turned his horse to ride away.

"Bodine?" Sheriff Adams called out.

Bodine turned back.

"Yeah?"

"Bodine, I don't want any trouble in my town," the sheriff said. "Do you hear me? I don't want any trouble in my town."

"Sheriff, let me get this straight. Are you sayin' that if I see a wanted man in Meeker, I can't go after him?"

"Yes—uh, no," Sheriff Adams replied.

"Yes or no what?"

"Just—just don't cause any trouble in my town," Adams repeated.

CHAPTER 12

When they rode into Meeker, Matt had a good look around. It had been several months since Matt had been in any town at all, and he had not really seen that many Western towns, so he had no real way of judging this one.

Someday, such towns would become the means of defining his life. Like mileposts, he would move from one town to another, each with a different name and with different people, but all with the same personality. And in some strange way that he could neither comprehend nor explain, he seemed to sense that even now.

The town was called Meeker, and it sat at the junction of Sulphur Creek and the White River. No railroad served the town, and its few streets were dotted liberally with horse droppings. The buildings of the little town were as washed out and flyblown up close as they had seemed from some distance.

The first building they rode by was a blacksmith's shop, and a tall and muscular man was bent over his anvil, working a piece of metal. The ringing of his hammer on steel was audible above everything else.

They rode by a butcher shop, a general store, a leather goods shop, and an apothecary. Next to the apothecary was a building that had a sign reading:

ASSAY OFFICE

That was where they stopped.

"What is an assay office?" Matt asked.

"You know all the panning we've been doing this summer?" Smoke asked.

"Yes."

"Well, this is where it pays off. This is where we are going to get some money."

Swinging down from his horse, Smoke took the saddlebags down from his horse. "Let's go see how we did."

Matt followed Smoke into the little building. Smoke dumped the contents of his saddlebags out onto a counter. Matt knew that this was only a portion of what they had panned over the last three months. The rest of it was buried in cans around Smoke's cabin, with Smoke being careful to show Matt where each can was buried.

The man behind the counter was wearing a white shirt, buttoned to the neck. He was wearing a collar too, but the collar was askew. He had rimless glasses, which were raised to his forehead, but as he saw the nuggets that were dumped from the saddlebags, he moved the glasses down to his eyes, then positioned them with his forefinger.

"Oh, my," he said as he looked at the display before him. "Oh, my, oh, my, oh, my."

"Is that good, Smoke?" Matt asked. "Why does he keep saying oh, my?"

"You'll see," Smoke said.

The man with the glasses picked up a magnifying glass and looked more closely at the rocks.

"It's going to take me a while to figure how much all this is worth."

"Is it worth enough for you to advance my partner and me forty dollars apiece right now?" Smoke asked.

"Oh, heavens, yes," the assayer said. "It's worth much, much more than that."

"Give me a receipt for the ore, less eighty dollars," Smoke said. "We'll be back for the rest of the money later."

The assayer wrote out a receipt, then handed Smoke four twenty-dollar bills. Smoke gave two of the bills to Matt.

"No," Matt said, shaking his head and handing it back. "This is your money."

"Are you saying you didn't have anything to do with panning it? Are you saying you didn't feed and water the animals, you didn't chop firewood, you didn't bring in water, you didn't do any hunting?"

"Well, yeah, I did all that but . . ."

"No buts," Smoke said. "We're full partners in this operation."

From the assayer's office, they went to a café for lunch. Although he had spent three years eating in a dormitory, this was the first café that Matt had ever been in in his life.

A very large woman, seeing them come in, smiled broadly.

"Smoke Jensen, you old heartbreaker you," she said in greeting. "I see you survived another winter in the mountains."

"That I did, Julie, that I did," Smoke replied.

Julie looked at Matt. "Well, now, either Preacher has found some elixir that made him get really young, or you've got yourself a new partner. This sure don't look like Preacher."

"This is my friend Matt," Smoke said.

"Matt is ever' bit as good-lookin' as you are. You been hidin' somethin' from me, Smoke? Have you gone off and spawned a young'in of your own?"

"Afraid not," Smoke said. "But I wouldn't be ashamed to claim Matt as my own. He is a fine young man."

"I can tell that just by lookin'," Julie said. "Come on in and sit yourself down. What'll you have, Matt?"

"What will I have?"

"To eat," Julie said. "What do you want to eat?"

"I'm not particular," Matt said. "Whatever you've fixed for supper, I'll eat it."

"You have to be more specific than that," Julie said.

"Maybe this will help you," Smoke said, picking up a menu and showing it to Matt. "You can have ham, roast beef, fried chicken, pork chops, meat loaf."

"All that? Who could eat all that?" Matt asked incredulously.

Smoke chuckled. "You've never been in a café before, have you?"

Matt shook his head.

"You don't order all of it. You just order what you want."

"Anything I want?"

"Sure."

"I want fried chicken and apple pie," he said.

"You want potatoes with your chicken?" Julie asked.

Matt shook his head. "All I want is fried chicken and apple pie."

"Hon, that's not a very . . ." Julie began, but Smoke interrupted her.

"You heard him, Julie," Smoke said. "Bring him some fried chicken and apple pie."

At the next table someone got up and, as he was leaving, handed a newspaper to Smoke.

"Here's the latest paper, friend, if you would care to read it," he said.

"Thank you," Smoke replied. He read the paper for a few minutes, then glanced across the table toward Matt.

"The full name of the man you are looking for is Clyde Payson," he said.

"What? How do you know that?" Matt asked. "Is it in the paper?"

"See for yourself."

Smoke handed the paper to Matt.

DASTARDLY DEEDS
IN CEDAR CREEK!

Bank Robbers Kill Teacher
and a Child.

Leave One of Their Own Dead.

On the fifth, ultimate, a band of bank robbers led by desperado Clyde Payson rode into the small town of Cedar Creek, Colorado. In a daring daylight robbery, the robbers relieved the Bank of Cedar Creek of its cash reserves, equaling at the time a little over six thousand dollars.

Told of their presence by an alert citizen, Marshal Jeremiah D. Cobb established wagon barricades at either end of the street, with the intent of preventing the robbers from getting out of town. However, the robbers managed to escape by riding through a school yard, which, at the time, was crowded with children at play.

Miss Margaret Miller, a beloved matron and longtime schoolteacher, as well as little Holly McGee, one of her second-grade students, were both killed in the gun battle that ensued. Also killed was Pete Lew, one of the robbers.

Clyde Payson is described as being a peculiarly ugly man. He is five feet nine inches tall, with a purple scar that starts at his forehead, disfigures the left eye, then proceeds unabated down his cheek and jawline until it pulls the left side of his mouth into a sneer.

One other member of the gang has also been identified as Garvey Laird. Laird is easily identified by the fact that, during the war, a minié ball diminished his left ear by one half. Readers are cautioned not to approach any of these men as they are very dangerous. Should one of them be seen, a county sheriff or United States marshal should be informed of their whereabouts. Marshal Cobb reminds readers not to inform him as he has no jurisdiction beyond the town limits of Cedar Creek.

"That's them!" Matt said, tapping the newspaper article with his fingers. "They are the ones who killed my ma, pa, and sister."

"If they stay this active, you won't have much trouble finding them," Smoke suggested. "Unless somebody else kills them first."

"I don't care who kills them," Matt replied. "As long as they are dead."

After the café meal, they went to a general store, where Matt bought three pair of jeans, three shirts, some underwear, socks, and boots.

"My, what a large purchase," the proprietor said. "It's almost as if you were starting from scratch."

"I am starting from scratch," Matt said without any explanation.

The shopping done, Smoke took Matt into one of the saloons.

"There's a way of entering saloons," Smoke explained. "And though you don't have any need to do so now, the time will come when it will serve you well. So you may as well learn how to do it."

"All right," Matt said.

Following Smoke's lead, Matt went into the saloon, then stepped immediately to one side with his back at the door.

"Always take a good look around," Smoke said, quietly.

"What are we looking for?"

"You'll know it if you see it," Smoke said.

Matt saw it almost as quickly as Smoke. A rather gaunt-looking man with a sweeping handlebar mustache was standing at the far end of the bar. He had seen them both in the mirror. He reached down and slipped his pistol out of his holster, then held it down out of sight, alongside his leg. He did it quietly and unobtrusively, and neither looked around nor made any sign of recognition. Had Smoke and Matt not been making it a point to study everyone in the saloon, neither of them would have seen it.

Because of their diligence, both saw it.

"Smoke," Matt hissed.

"I see it, boy," Smoke answered quietly. "Step away from me, over to the other side of the door. And keep your back to the wall."

Matt had only been with Smoke for about six months now, but he knew enough to do exactly as Smoke asked, doing so without question.

The man at the bar called out without turning toward Smoke.

"Mister, would your name be Jensen? Smoke Jensen?" the man from the bar called.

"That's me," Smoke replied.

"I've seen paper on you," the man said. "The paper says you are a murderer and a low-life son of a bitch."

These were challenging words, words that even Matt knew were killing words. Everyone at the bar knew so as well because, almost as one, they broke away from the bar and scrambled quickly to get out from between the two men.

"Are you the law?" Smoke asked.

"Nah, I ain't the law," the man replied. "The law can't collect rewards."

"I guess that makes you a bounty hunter."

"That's what I am, all right. And you are worth fifteen hundred dollars to me."

"No, I'm not," Smoke said. "The paper on me has been called back, so I'm worth nothing to you. Even if you could take me in."

"I don't plan on takin' you in. I plan on just killin' you right here, and havin' the sheriff vouch for it so's I can collect me that reward."

"What's your name?"

"Bodine," the man answered. "Amos Bodine. I reckon you've heard of me."

"Bodine, we don't have to do this," Smoke said. "You can just walk away now and nobody has to get hurt. I told you there is no reward."

"Well, now, maybe there is a reward and maybe there isn't," Bodine replied. "That still leaves you a murderin' low-life son of a bitch."

"Is there any way I'm going to be able to talk my way out of this?" Smoke asked.

Smoke's question surprised and disappointed Matt. Was Smoke scared? He would never have thought that Smoke would run scared.

Almost as soon as he thought it through, he felt ashamed of himself. Smoke had saved his life, and had kept him alive through the long, cold winter. What's more, Smoke had shared his gold secret with Matt. And right now, Matt still had about thirty dollars in his pocket, more money than he had ever held at any one time in his entire life. What an ingrate he was for questioning anything Smoke did.

At the bar, Bodine just shook his head. He still hadn't turned around to face Smoke.

"You ain't goin' to be able to talk your way out of this one, mister," Bodine said. "The reward says you are worth fifteen hundred dollars dead or alive, and I intend to collect."

"Then I expect it's time the killin' started," Smoke said dryly.

Bodine suddenly swirled away from the bar, his hand already coming up with a cocked pistol.

Smoke, reacting to the bounty-hunter's move, had his own pistol out so fast that it was a blur. He drew, fanned the hammer back, and fired in one fluid motion.

Matt saw Bodine gasp in surprise as the bullet from Smoke's gun plunged into his chest. Bodine staggered backward, then fell flat on his back on the floor of the saloon. His gun arm was thrown to one side, and the still-unfired pistol was in his hand.

Then, even as Bodine was falling, Smoke was firing a second time. Looking up, Matt saw someone tumble over the railing at the top of the stairs. The second man had been holding a rifle and the rifle fell before him, reaching the floor an instant before the man did. Matt had not even seen him until this moment, and he was amazed that Smoke had.

In the close confines of the barroom, the two gunshots were a sustained roar, like a sudden clap of thunder.

Smoke stood in place for a long moment, holding the discharged gun in his hand while a little stream of smoke drifted up from the end of the barrel.

"Holy shit!" someone said. "Did you see that?"

"And I thought Bodine was fast," another said.

"I need a drink," the first man said, and there was a mad rush to the bar.

"Matt, are you all right over there?" Smoke asked quietly.

"Yes, I'm fine," Matt answered in a small, awed voice.

"Get us a table," Smoke said. "I'll get you a sarsaparilla."

"I'd rather have a beer," Matt said.

"You might rather have a beer, but you are getting a sarsaparilla," Smoke said resolutely.

"Yeah, that's what I said. I'd like to have a sarsaparilla."

Smoke smiled. "I thought that was what you said."

Matt found a table and sat down.

"Did you see that?" someone asked at the next table.

"Of course I seen it. I was in here when it happened, wasn't I?"

"He beat Amos Bodine," the first man said, not to be denied telling the story, even though he was telling it to another eyewitness. "I tell you true, I didn't think anyone would ever be able to beat Amos Bodine."

"Hell, he beat Bodine and the man he was ridin' with."

"What's the name of the fella that shot Bodine?" one of the others asked.

"Jensen. Smoke Jensen."

The sheriff was in the saloon almost before the gun smoke drifted away. He saw the two men lying on the floor. Then he looked over at the table where Smoke was just rejoining Matt with a beer in one hand and Matt's pop in the other.

"Hello, Sheriff Adams," Smoke said.

Adams nodded toward the two dead men. "I see you got Bodine and Colby."

"Colby, huh? I was wondering who it was. I never got the chance to ask him his name," Smoke answered matter-of-factly.

Adams stared at Smoke for a moment; then he saw the humor of the statement and he chuckled. "Well, it's too late to make friends now."

"What were they in town for?" Smoke asked. "Surely they weren't here just to kill me?"

Adams shook his head. "He just came in today, bringin' a body for claim. He would'a been gone by tomorrow once the money come in. If you had waited one more day before comin' in, you two wouldn't have run in to each other."

"If not now, later," Smoke said. "People like Bodine don't seem to care much whether the reward poster is still good or not."

"I reckon not," Sheriff Adams said. He looked over at Matt, then stroked his chin as he studied him.

"Who'd you say this young man was?" he asked.

"I didn't say who he was. But he's my partner," Smoke said.

"The reason I asked is, I got a letter from the sheriff in Soda Creek. Seems a boy ran away from the Home up there."

"The Home?"

"The Home for Wayward Boys and Girls," Sheriff Adams said.

"You don't say," Smoke replied. "What about this boy that ran away? What did he do?"

"He ran away."

"No, I mean, why was he in the Home? Had he stolen from someone?"

"Oh, I don't know whether he stole anything or not. The letter didn't say anything about that. It just said that he ran away from the Home."

"You get a name for the boy that ran away?"

"The sheriff said his name is Matt."

Smoke chuckled. "You don't say. Well, now, that is a coincidence. My partner's name is Matt. But he sure doesn't belong in a home for wayward boys and girls."

"No, I reckon not," Sheriff Adams said.

Smoke looked over at the two bodies. By now, Lennie Holman, the town undertaker, had arrived and was looking at the two men, gauging the size of the coffins he would have to make.

"Are you going to need me for a hearing or anything?" Smoke asked.

Sheriff Adams shook his head. "I don't think so. I know Bodine, and there's no doubt in my mind what happened here. Also, there are enough eyewitnesses to give me all the statements I need."

"Well, if you do need me, Matt and I are going to spend today and tomorrow in town."

"Enjoy your stay," the sheriff said. With a final nod, Sheriff Adams left the table, then went over to start talking to the eyewitnesses. There were many who saw it happen, and nearly all were anxious to tell their story.

"I don't mind telling you, I was a little nervous when you told the sheriff that my name was Matt."

"I had to tell him," Smoke said. "Otherwise, I might have tripped up and called you Matt. Best to get that part out in the open."

"And then when you said I didn't come from the home, well, I . . ."

"That's not what I said," Smoke interrupted.

"What?"

"I didn't lie. What I said was, 'My partner's name is Matt. But he sure doesn't *belong* in a home for wayward boys and girls.' I didn't say you didn't come from there."

Matt chuckled. "No, I guess you didn't." Matt turned the sarsaparilla up to his lips, then looked across the table toward Smoke. "You know, someday I hope to be as fast with a gun as you are," he said.

"Why? So you can kill Payson?"

"No," Matt said. "I mean, yes, I am going to kill Payson. But that's not the reason I want to be fast with a gun."

"What is the reason?"

"I don't know exactly. Maybe it is just because I would like to be really good at something."

Smoke smiled at his young friend. "That's a good enough reason," he said.

CHAPTER 13

"And what do you think about this one, young sir?" the gunsmith asked, handing a pistol to Matt. The first place they had gone to after leaving the saloon was a gunsmith shop.

"It's a beauty," Matt said, holding the pistol gingerly in his hand as he looked at it. "What kind is it?"

"It is a Model 1861 Colt, manufactured at the Colt firearm factory in Hartford, Connecticut," the gunsmith replied.

"Take a look at the markings on the gun," Smoke suggested.

Matt studied the markings. On the barrel was stamped: "Address COL. SAML COLT New York U.S. AMERICA." The left front side of the frame was marked: "Colts/patent." The caliber marking, ".36 CAL," was stamped on the left rear side of the trigger guard.

"You like it?" Smoke asked.

"Yes," Matt replied.

"We'll take it," Smoke said to the gunsmith. "And a gun belt and holster rig."

"Yes, sir," the gunsmith said. "Would you like it wrapped, or in a box?"

Smoke looked at Matt and smiled. "I'm sure he would much rather wear it."

"Yes!" Matt said excitedly. "I would rather wear it."

"Then, wear it you shall, young sir," the gunsmith said, selecting a belt and handing it to Matt.

Matt put the belt on, then slipped the gun down into the holster.

"Let's see your draw," Smoke suggested.

Matt drew the pistol as fast as he could, and Smoke laughed.

"What is it?" he asked. "What did I do wrong?"

"Let's start with what you did right," Smoke said.

Matt smiled. "All right, what did I do that was right?"

"You didn't drop it," Smoke said.

"That's it? I didn't drop it?"

"That's it," Smoke said. "Everything else you did was wrong."

"Will you teach me?"

Smoke nodded. "Yeah," he said. "I'll teach you."

Smoke's cabin in the Gore Range of Colorado

"When you shot that bounty hunter, that was the fastest draw I ever saw," Matt said.

"Was it?"

"It sure was," Matt answered enthusiastically.

"How many fast draws have you seen?"

"Well—uh—I guess that is the only one I've ever seen," Matt admitted.

Smoke chuckled. "Then it isn't very hard to be the fastest, is it?"

"Are you the fastest?" Matt asked.

"I don't know," Smoke replied. "There are some out there who are very fast. Wild Bill Hickock, Payson Allison, Ian MacCallister, Angus Boone."

"I've heard of Hickock, Allison, and MacCallster," Matt said. "But I've never heard of Angus Boone. Who is he?"

"Some people call him the Gravedigger," Smoke said.

"Is he fast?"

"Very fast," Smoke said. "And he is one of those rare people who kills for the sake of killing."

"Why would someone do that?"

"Because he likes killing," Smoke said.

"Well, I wouldn't enjoy killing," Matt said. "But I do want to be fast."

"Being fast means nothing if you can't hit what you are shooting at," Smoke explained. "First thing we have to do with you is teach you how to shoot."

"I can shoot," Matt said. "I used to go squirrel hunting back when I was only eight or nine years old. I could hit them too."

"But you were using a rifle then, right? Or maybe a shotgun?"

"A shotgun," Matt admitted sheepishly.

"Well, that's pretty good, but now you have to learn to use a handgun, and that is very different. Are you willing to learn?"

"Yes."

"Good. Take off your holster and give it to me."

"What? Why?"

"Because you don't need it right now, and I don't even want you thinking about it. This is shooting, not fast draw."

"Whatever you say," Matt said, unbuckling his gun belt and handing it to Smoke.

"All right, show me what you can do," Smoke said. Looking around he found a rusty can, then stepped off about thirty yards and placed the can on a rock. "Shoot that can," he said.

Matt pulled the trigger. The pistol boomed and the bullet kicked up dirt well to the side of the rock where the can was sitting. It ricocheted across the meadow, making a loud whine.

"I missed," Matt said.

"Try again."

Matt fired a second time, with the same result.

"Here, let me see what we can do to help," Smoke said. Putting his hands on Matt's shoulders, he turned the boy to a position of about forty-five degrees from the target.

"Now, don't turn your body, but look at the target by turning your head and eyes only."

Matt responded.

"Bring the pistol up to eye level and sight on the target. Then, close your eyes, raise your pistol and arm straight up, and with your eyes still closed, bring your arm back down until it feels to you as if you are lined up with the target."

"Like this?" Matt asked, doing as instructed.

"Yes," Smoke said.

Matt let his arm come back down, then he opened his eyes. He was almost perfectly aligned.

"It's there!" he said excitedly.

"Good," Smoke said. "Now, spread your feet apart about the width of your shoulders. Keep your legs straight, but not stiff. Think you can do that?"

Matt tried it a few times, then looked at Smoke. "Yes, I can do it," he said.

"What are you going to do with your other arm?" Smoke asked.

"I don't know. What should I do?"

"Forget that it is there. It should be totally relaxed."

"All right," Matt said, again responding to Smoke's instruction.

"Now, again, look at your target by turning your head and eyes slightly without moving from the neck down. Once you are looking at it, raise your pistol so you can sight on the target. You should feel that the pistol is hanging from above, and not that you are pushing it up from below."

Again, Matt complied with Smoke's instructions.

"Are you aiming at the target now?"

"Yes."

"Shoot it."

Matt pulled the trigger. Again the pistol boomed and the bullet whined, but this time it knocked the can up into the air with a direct hit.

"Hey!" Matt shouted in excitement. "I did it!"

Smoke made Matt practice shooting every day for the next month. Matt was a natural shooter, and he hit the can so many times that, toward the end of his shooting, rather than reset the can, he just continued to shoot it, knocking it about the meadow.

Then, one day, Smoke came out to watch him. He stood there for a few minutes, nodded, then went back into the cabin. When he returned, he was carrying the pistol belt. He handed the holster rig to Matt.

"Put it on," he said.

"All right!" Matt replied excitedly.

"Empty your gun."

"Empty it?"

"I don't want you to shoot yourself in the leg while you are practicing."

Matt chuckled. "I don't want to shoot myself in the leg either," he said as he poked the cartridges out of the revolver. He put the empty gun back into his holster.

"I'm going to show you a draw," Smoke said. "First, I'll do it fast, then I'll do it slow, so you can see what I'm doing."

Smoke drew his pistol and fired, doing it with such blazing speed that, even though Matt was watching him, he was unable to see the actual draw. He saw only a quick jump.

"Now, I'll do it slow," Smoke said.

Smoke eased the pistol from his holster. As he was doing so, his left hand came across his body to fan back the hammer. He pulled the trigger when the gun came in line with the target. The gun had traveled just enough distance to clear the holster.

"You didn't bring the gun up to aim it," Matt said.

"No, I didn't," Smoke answered. "I aimed before I drew the gun."

Matt thought for a second, then nodded. "Yeah," he said. "Yeah, I know that doesn't sound like it makes sense, but I think I know what you mean."

"Matt, it all comes down to this," Smoke said. "The time is going to come when you will just think the gun into your hand, and the bullet into your target. The arm, the hand, the trigger finger are no longer there. They are just an extension of your mind. You think draw and shoot, and your mind will draw and shoot the gun for you."

"How do you do that?"

"Do you think about breathing?" Smoke asked.

"No, I just breathe."

"Think about breathing."

Matt took a few breaths, then laughed. "It's harder when you think about it."

"When you can draw and shoot a gun the same way you breathe, you'll be ready," Smoke said. "Now, let me show you something."

Smoke emptied Matt's pistol, and handed it to him. Then he emptied his own gun, checking each chamber in the cylinder again. He put his gun back in his holster.

"Point your gun at me," Smoke said. "When you see me start my draw, pull the trigger."

"Ha," Matt said. "Do you think I'm so slow that you have to give me that much of a head start?"

"Just do it," Smoke said.

"All right." Matt raised the pistol and aimed it at Smoke.

Smoke drew his pistol, fanned the hammer, and pulled the trigger before Matt could pull the trigger on his own gun.

"Wait, I wasn't ready," Matt said.

"We'll try it again," Smoke offered.

They did it several times, and Smoke beat Matt every time.

"How did you do that?" Matt asked.

Smoke chuckled. "Don't be so impressed," he said. "It was easy."

"Because I'm so slow?"

"No. You could be faster than I am, and I would still beat you."

Matt shook his head. "Wait a minute, that doesn't make sense. If I was faster than you, how would you beat me?"

"Remember when I said you had to think the gun into your hand?"

"Yes."

"Thinking about it takes longer than actually doing it," Smoke said. "See, when you saw me start my draw, you had to think to pull the trigger. But I had already thought about it. I had already thought the gun into my hand."

"That's amazing," Matt said.

"No, it's just a fact, but it might save your life some day."

"I see."

"All right, put your pistol back in your holster and start working on your draw," Smoke said.

"When can I load my pistol?"

"I'll let you know when."

For two weeks, Matt drew and pulled the trigger to an empty pistol. Then Smoke let him start drawing and shooting.

Before the first snow, Matt was good enough to perform a few shooting tricks. With tin cans put on posts that were set fifty yards apart, Matt stepped halfway between the two. He stood there, his gun in his holster, looking over at Smoke.

"Are you ready?" Smoke asked.

Matt nodded. "I'm ready," he said.

Smoke held a rock out over a pie pan. Matt watched Smoke's hand. When Smoke opened his hand to let the rock fall, Matt drew his pistol, shot the can off the post to the right of him, then whirled and shot the can off the post to the left.

After the sound of the second shot, the sound of the rock hitting the pie plate could be heard.

"You got both shots off in under a second," Smoke said, grinning broadly.

"Is that pretty good?" Matt asked.

Smoke nodded. "Yes," he said. "That's very good."

"How good?"

"What do you mean?"

"How many do you think are faster?"

"It doesn't matter how many are faster," Smoke said.

Matt looked confused. "What do you mean, it doesn't matter how many are faster?"

"It doesn't matter," Smoke repeated. "There may be some who are faster. There probably *are* some who are faster. But you have now reached the point to where the speed of your draw is no longer a consideration."

"What is?"

Smoke sighed, and ran his hand through his hair before he answered.

"I've held this for last, Matt. What I'm about to tell you is the final secret of the gunfighter. And, I'm sorry to say, it is a terrible secret."

"What is the secret?"

"At this level, being fast or accurate is not the differing factor. At this level, everyone is fast and everyone is accurate. But not everyone is willing to kill."

"What?"

"The average man will pause—hesitate for just a heartbeat—before the pull of a trigger that he knows is going to kill," Smoke explained. "In a situation like that, the victory goes to the man who will not hesitate."

"Yes," Matt said. "Yes, I see what you mean."

"I hope you do see," Smoke said. "Because being able to see and understand that will keep you alive."

"How do you overcome it?"

"You have one thing going for you," Smoke said. "You have had it going for you from the beginning, and if you hadn't had it, I don't think I would have taught you how to use a gun at all."

"What? What do I have going for me?"

"You have already killed," Smoke said.

Matt was quiet for a moment before he spoke. "I'm not proud of that, Smoke."

"Nor should you be," Smoke answered. "Matt, the fact that you have killed is not a matter of pride. But it is a matter of survival."

"Survival?"

"Yes. I want you to think about it every day. I want you to know that if you have to do it, you can kill a man without a second thought."

"All right," Matt agreed.

"There's one more thing I want you to remember," Smoke said.

"What is that?"

"Remember our talk about knighthood?"

"Yes, I remember."

"Matt, you now have an awesome power. You have the power of life and death. Only God, and the righteous, should ever have such power.

"You aren't God, so you must be righteous. Be a knight, Matt. Never abuse this power you now have."

"I won't."

"Swear to me, Matt," Smoke said. "Swear on the graves of your ma and pa that you will be a knight."

"I swear to you, Smoke. I will be a knight," Matt said.

CHAPTER 14

Gehenna

The little town was hot, dry, and dusty. It had grown up in the middle of nowhere and now sat baking in the sun like a lizard. To the six riders approaching from the north, the collection of adobe and sun-bleached wooden buildings was so much a part of the land that it looked almost as if the town was the result of some natural phenomenon, rather than the work of man.

Out on the edge of town a sign read:

YOU ARE ENTERING

Gehenna
POPULATION UNKNOWN
The Law Ain't Welcome.
If You Got No Business Here,
GET OUT — OR <u>GET SHOT</u>

On first glance, Gehenna looked like just about any other town in this part of the country, but that was on first glance only. A closer observation showed many differences.

Gehenna was a town that existed, not in spite of having no law, but because it had no law. It was a robber's roost, an outlaw's haven, and Clyde Payson, Garvey Laird, Clem Tyson, Bart Ebersole, Poke Lawson, and Syl Richards were drawn to it for just that reason.

"I'm so thirsty I'm spittin' dust," Clem said. "I aim to get me two beers an' drink 'em both down afore I even take me a breath." Clem smiled. "I aim to get me a good meal and a bottle of whiskey, then the best-lookin' whore in town."

Poke laughed.

"What's so damn funny?" Clem asked.

"There ain't goin' to be no good-lookin' whores in Gehenna."

"Why not?"

"'Cause whores that's still good-lookin' can make a livin' somewhere else. They don't have to come to a place like Gehenna."

"Then what the hell are we comin' here for?" Clem asked.

"We ain't here for the whores," Payson said. "We're here 'cause there's no law here."

"No law a'tall?" Syl asked.

"Only the law that we make," Payson said.

As the six men rode into town, not one person gave them a second look. Stopping in front of the single saloon, they dismounted.

A tall man dressed all in black stepped out onto the front porch and looked down at them.

"You're Payson, ain't you?" he asked. "Clyde Payson?"

"Yeah, you've heard of me?"

"I've heard of you."

Payson smiled and looked at the others. "What do you think, boys? I'm famous," he said.

"You've come here to stay away from the law?"

"That's right," Payson replied. Payson was still standing beside his horse, so that it was between him and the man who was addressing them.

"It'll cost you a hundred dollars to stay here," the man said.

"A hundred dollars? Says who?" Payson asked angrily.

"Says me. You might say I'm the sheriff here. It's my job to collect taxes from those who come to enjoy our hospitality."

"You're the sheriff? I thought there wasn't no law here," Payson said.

The man spat a stream of tobacco, then wiped his lips with the back of his hand.

"Well, now, that ain't entirely true," he said. "We ain't got no courts or judges, or jails or such. But we do have me."

"And who are you?"

"The name is Loomis. Frank Loomis."

Payson was quiet for a moment before he answered. "Loomis. Frank Loomis," he said. "Yeah, I've heard of you. You used to be a sheriff, didn't you? Till you had a run-in with a U.S. marshal. You kilt 'im, I believe, and now you're a wanted man yourself. So, how come you're still sheriffin'?"

"It's a different kind of sheriffin' here," Loomis explained. "And I make a lot more money sheriffin' here than I did back in Colorado."

"Who pays you? The town?"

Loomis laughed. "No, the town don't pay me nothin'. I pay myself."

"I see. So the one hundred dollars you are asking for in tax, that's just to go to you, right?"

"You understand, I'm sure. If I'm going to pay myself to protect the town, then I have to charge a tax. I don't think a hundred dollars is askin' too much."

"What if I say I ain't goin' to pay it?" Payson asked.

"Then you aren't eligible for the protection of the town, so I'll ask you to just move on."

"What if I say I ain't goin' to pay it and I don't plan to move on?"

"If you've heard of me, then you know that I can back up what I say," Loomis said.

Unnoticed by Loomis, Payson had snaked his shotgun from the saddle holster. He now held the gun behind the horse to shield it from Loomis's view.

"Are you sayin' we ain't never goin' to be able to work this out?" Payson asked.

"Not unless you pay the one-hundred-dollar tax," Loomis said. He pushed his coat flap back, exposing his pistol. "Either pay, or git," he said menacingly. "You ain't got no other choice."

"No, I reckon there is another choice," Payson said. In a quick, smooth action, Payson raised the shotgun up, laid the barrel across the saddle, and pulled the trigger.

The gun roared and the horse reared. Loomis was so surprised by the sudden move that he never even touched his own pistol. The impact of a load of double-aught buckshot caught Loomis full in the chest and knocked him back through the batwing doors, taking one of them off the hinges. He wound up lying on the floor with his chest opened up so that his insides could be seen.

"Son of a bitch!" someone shouted from inside.

Payson stepped into the saloon right behind Loomis's body. He was carrying the shotgun with him, and a little curl of smoke was still streaming up from the end of the barrel.

"Anybody else want to talk about me payin' taxes?" Payson asked.

Nobody answered. In fact, nobody even looked at him.

"Yeah, I thought this might be the end of it," Payson said. He set the butt of the shotgun on the bar with the barrel pointed up. "Bartender, what do you have to drink in this place?"

"Beer and whiskey," the bartender answered.

"I'll have it."

"You'll have what, sir?"

"Beer and whiskey," Payson said.

"And we'll have the same," one of the five men who came in with him announced.

"Very good," the bartender said.

A moment later, the bartender returned with six empty whiskey glasses and a bottle of whiskey. He also had six mugs of beer.

"That'll be six dollars and fifty cents," the bartender said.

"Six fifty?" Payson gasped in amazement. "Six fifty for what?"

"Five dollars for the bottle of whiskey, and a quarter apiece for the beer."

"That's outlandish to charge so much," Payson complained. "I can get beer for a nickel anywhere else in the country. Why should I pay you so much for it?"

"Because you ain't anywhere else in the country," the bartender replied. "You're here. And here, beer is twenty-five cents."

Grumbling, Payson pulled enough money from his pocket to pay for the beer and the whiskey.

Payson tossed the whiskey down, then chased it with almost half the beer. He sat the beer glass down as well, and looked toward the body of the man he had just killed.

"What happens to him now? Does he just stay there and rot?"

"No," the bartender replied. "We learned just real quick that in a town like Gehenna we was goin' to need an undertaker. So we went out and hired us one."

"What about whores?" Clem asked. "You got 'ny whores?"

"Hell, yes, we got whores," the bartender said. "What good would a place like this be without whores?"

"Which one is the best-lookin'?" Clem asked.

"Hell, nearly ever' whore in town would make a train take five miles of dirt road," the bartender replied. "But I reckon Jolene is somewhat better-lookin' than most."

"Where's she at?"

The bartender didn't answer, but he pointed to a table in the back of the room.

There was someone sitting there, holding a whiskey bottle in one hand and a glass in the other.

"Jolene," the bartender called. "You got some business."

Jolene filled the glass one more time, then tossed the whiskey down before she walked up to the bar.

"You wantin' to ride me, cowboy?" Jolene asked.

"How much?"

"Two dollars."

"Two dollars? Damn, ain't that a little high?" Clem asked.

Jolene turned to go back to her seat at the back of the room.

"No, wait," Clem called. "I got two dollars."

"In that case, I got me a room upstairs," Jolene said, pointing toward the stairs at the back.

"Wait a minute," Clem said. He turned to the bartender. "Give me a bottle. If I'm goin' to have to pay two dollars, I plan to make it a party."

The bartender gave Clem a bottle in exchange for a five-dollar bill. Then, clutching the bottle by the neck, Clem followed Jolene up the stairs.

"Who's in charge around here?" Payson asked.

"If you mean do we have a mayor or something like that, we ain't," the bartender said.

"But somebody is in charge. Somebody always has to be in charge," Payson said.

"There was somebody in charge," the bartender replied. "But you just kilt him."

"Really," Payson said with a big smile. "Well, I reckon that sort of makes me the headman around here then, doesn't it?"

"I suppose so," the bartender said. "That is, until . . . ."

"Until what?"

"Until the Gravedigger comes back."

"The Gravedigger? You mean Angus Boone? Boone is here?"

"Not all the time," the bartender replied. "But when he is here, he is in charge. Unless you want to challenge him."

"No, that's all right," Payson said. "The Gravedigger can be in charge while he's here, and I'll be in charge while I'm here."

"What if you are both here at the same time?"

"We won't be," Payson said.

CHAPTER 15

Durango, Colorado

Two young men passing through the town stopped in front of the Sundown Saloon. Swinging down from their horses, they patted their dusters down.

"Donnie, you're as full of shit as a Christmas goose," one of them said. "There ain't nobody that lives on the moon."

"How do you know?" Donnie asked. "There ain't nobody ever gone up there to see that there ain't folks up there."

"Yeah, well, that's my point. There ain't nobody up there 'cause there ain't no way to get there."

"How did we get here?" Donnie asked.

"What?"

"How did we get here?"

"What do you mean, how did we get here? We've always been here."

"Well, they've always been there."

"No, they ain't."

"You know your problem, Bobby Joe? Your problem is, you ain't got no imagination."

"Yeah, well, right now I can imagine what a cool beer tastes like. And if we wasn't standin' out here in the road arguin' over whether or not there's people on the moon—which, if you ask me, is about the dumbest thing you can argue about—we'd be drinkin' a beer by now."

"You got that right," Donnie said, laughing. "It don't make no sense to be standin' out here jawin' when we could be inside drinkin'."

The two young men went into the saloon, then stepped up to the bar. The saloon was relatively quiet, with only four men at one table, and a fifth standing down at the far end of the bar. The four at the table were playing cards; the one at the end of the bar was nursing a drink. The man nursing the drink was dressed in black. A turquoise and silver band around his short-crowned black hat provided the only bit of color.

"What'll it be, gents?" the bartender asked.

"I want the coldest beer you've got," Donnie said.

"Every beer I have is the coldest one I have," the bartender replied.

Bobby Joe chuckled. "I'll have the same," he said.

"Two beers it is," the bartender replied. He turned to draw the beers.

"What brings you boys to Durango?" the bartender asked.

"Nothin' in particular," Donnie said. "We're just passin' through."

"We're up from Texas," Bobby Joe said proudly.

The bartender put the beers in front of the two boys and they each picked up one.

"Yes, sir, the great state of Texas," Donnie added.

"Well, welcome to Colorado," the bartender said.

"Nothin' good ever come out of Texas," the man at the end of the bar said.

Using the back of his hand, Donnie wiped beer foam from his mouth. It was obvious that he had been irritated, and for the briefest of moments, that irritation reflected in his face. But he put it aside, then forced a smile.

"Hell, mister, Texas is a big state. You can't say you don't like Texas unless you've seen all of it. And I know you ain't seen all of it, 'cause no one has seen all of it."

"Is that how you get around people tellin' you they don't like your state?" the man in black asked.

Bobby Joe had not been a part of the conversation, but he was listening to it, and now he joined in.

"What the hell, mister? You trying to pick a fight or something?"

"Why?" the man in black asked. "If I was tryin' to pick a fight, would you be obligin' me?"

The way the man in black responded angered Bobby Joe even more.

"Hell, yes, I'd be willin' to oblige you," Bobby Joe said angrily. "Nobody up in these parts knows me, but if they did know me, they'd be quick to tell you that Bobby Joe Brubaker ain't a man you want to get on the wrong side of."

"You don't say," the man in black responded. Although Bobby Joe was getting angrier and angrier, and his voice getting louder and louder, the voice of the man in black was never more than a sibilant sneer.

Donnie recognized the growing danger before Bobby Joe did, and he reached out his hand to try and ease the situation.

"Easy, Bobby Joe. I'm sure he doesn't mean anything personal by that remark. Not everybody likes Texas, nor are they expected to."

"I just don't like being insulted by some son of bitch who doesn't know what he's talking about," Bobby Joe said.

"Let's just have our beers and get on our way," Donnie suggested.

"After you apologize," the man in black said.

"Apologize? You expect me to apologize?" Bobby Joe said, so angry that his face was turning red. "Apologize my ass. What I'm going to do, mister, is wipe up the floor with your sorry ass!" Bobby Joe put up his fists.

The man in black smiled, a smile without mirth. "If we're going to fight, why don't we make it permanent?" he asked. He stepped away from the bar and flipped his jacket back, exposing a pistol that he wore low and kicked out, in the way of a gunfighter.

"Mr. Boone, I'm sure these boys would apologize to you if you would just give them a moment to reconsider," the bartender said. "There's no need to carry this any further."

"My God, Bobby Joe, back off!" Donnie said. "Don't you know who this is? This is the man they call the Gravedigger!"

Bobby Joe realized now that things were beginning to go much further than he had intended, and he opened his fists and held his hands palm out in front of him.

"No, wait a minute!" he said. "We don't need to be doin' this. This is just a little dispute, it ain't worth either one of us dying over."

"Oh, it won't be *either* of us, sonny. It'll just be you," Boone said. "Both of you," he added, looking at Donnie, "for when the shootin' starts, I'm goin' to kill both of you."

"Uh-uh," Donnie said, shaking his head. "Neither Bobby Joe nor I have any intention of drawing on you. So if you shoot us, you are going to have to shoot us in cold blood in front of these witnesses."

"Oh, it ain't goin' to be in cold blood," Boone said. "You'll be drawin' on me. Both of you."

Donnie's knees grew so weak that he could barely stand, and he felt nauseous.

"Please, Mr. Boone, we don't want any trouble," Donnie said. "Why don't you just let us apologize and we'll go on our way?"

Boone shook his head. "I give you boys the chance to apologize. You didn't take it. It's too late now. Pull your guns."

Donnie and Bobby Jo looked at each other, then, with a scream from Donnie, they made ragged, desperate grabs for their pistols. They were slow, so slow that Boone had the luxury of waiting for just a moment to see which of the two offered him the most competition. Deciding it was Donnie, Boone pulled his pistol and shot Donnie first.

Bobby Joe, seeing his friend killed, and knowing that he was about to die, peed in his pants as Boone's second shot hit him in the neck. He pulled the trigger on his pistol, firing a shot into the floor before he collapsed and fell on top of Donnie.

Angus Boone put his pistol back in his holster, and was calmly sipping his whiskey by the time a few of the citizens of the town got up the nerve to look inside.

Smoke's cabin

By the time Matt was eighteen years old, he was six feet tall and strong as an ox. The older Matt got, the narrower the difference between him and Smoke, in size, in quickness and accuracy with a handgun, and in just about any other attribute.

Sometimes, for fun, the two would wrestle, and the winner depended not on strength or skill, but on whoever happened to achieve a temporary advantage in leverage or position.

Also, the age difference between the two seemed less significant now, and the "fatherly" relationship had gradually changed into one of "big brother."

The two had continued to pan the streams and the streams had continued to be productive. For the entire time Matt had been with Smoke, they had buried the gold, each year taking just enough into town to buy goods and supplies for another year. But in the spring of Matt's eighteenth year, they took everything they had into town, having to enlist four pack animals to do so. When they cashed it out, it was worth a little over thirty thousand dollars, which was more money than the local bank had on deposit.

"We can have the money shipped from Denver," the assayer said.

"Can you write us a draft that will allow us to go to Denver to get the money ourselves?" Smoke asked.

"Yes," the assayer said. "Yes, of course I can do that. But you don't have to go to all that trouble. As I say, I can have the money shipped here."

"It's no trouble," Smoke said. "Denver's a big city. I think I'd like to have a look around. How about you, Matt?"

"I've never seen a big city. I'd love to go to Denver," Matt replied enthusiastically.

"Write out the draft," Smoke said.

"Very good, sir. And who shall I make this payable to?"

"Make it out to both of us. Kirby Jensen and Matt . . ." Smoke looked over at Matt. "I've never heard you say your last name."

"Smoke, just make the draft payable to you," Matt said.

"No, what are you talking about? This is your money too. You helped pan every nugget."

"You can pay me my share after you cash the draft."

"It might be easier if it is made to just one man," the assayer said.

Smoke sighed. "All right," he said. "Make it payable to Kirby Jensen."

The assayer wrote out the draft, blew on it to dry the ink, then handed it to Smoke.

DENVER BANK & TRUST

Colorado Gold and Silver
Acceptance Company   *June 19* 18 *74*

PAY TO THE ORDER OF *Kirby Jensen* ——————— $ *32,100* no/100

Thirty-two thousand one hundred & no/100 DOLLARS

Parker Allison ~Assayer

"Here you are, Mr, Jensen," he said. "Just present this to the Denver Bank and Trust, and they will pay you the amount so specified."

Smoke held the bank draft for a moment and looked at it. "Hard to believe this little piece of paper is worth all that money," he said.

"I assure you, sir, it is as good as gold," the assayer promised.

Smoke turned to Matt. "What do you say, Matt. You ready to see Denver?"

"I'm ready!" Matt answered eagerly.

Denver

Although there had been predictions that Denver would reach the magic number of 100,000 inhabitants by 1870, the actual growth of the city had fallen far short of the mark.

William Byers, editor of the *Rocky Mountain News*, wrote an article about what he called the go-backers:

> Because they cannot shovel out nuggets like they have
> been accustomed to digging potatoes, they raise the cry
> that it is all a humbug and take the back track for home,
> where it is to be hoped that they will ever after remain.

Despite Byers's complaint, the city seemed exceptionally crowded on the day that Matt and Smoke arrived. It was certainly larger than any city Matt had ever seen, and as they rode down Wynkoop Street, they actually had to move aside frequently to allow coaches, carriages, and wagons to pass. Men and women walked briskly along the boardwalks on either side of the street, the women carrying parasols against the sun, the men wearing bowler hats and suits.

On one corner, some musicians were playing a fiddle, banjo, and guitar, accompanied by someone blowing into a jug. Several people had gathered around to hear them, and occasionally someone would drop a coin into an upturned hat.

There was a large banner stretched across the street. One corner of the sign had come loose and was flapping in the breeze, but it could still be read.

DENVER WELCOMES
THE DENVER PACIFIC RAILROAD
JUNE 24, 1874

Shortly after they passed under the sign, they saw a building with a new sign proudly proclaiming it as the DENVER PACIFIC DEPOT.

"Have you ever seen a railroad train, Matt?" Smoke asked.

"No, I haven't," Matt said. "Have you?"

"I used to see them back in Missouri when I lived there as a boy during the war," Smoke said. "But I haven't seen one since."

"I'd sure like to see one," Matt said.

"According to the sign, the train will be here tomorrow," Smoke said. "How would you like to come down here tomorrow to watch?"

"Yes! Yes, I'd like to very much!" Matt said.

"Well, then, we'll just do that," Smoke said. "What do you say we go get our money, then get us a hotel room?"

"Sounds good to me," Matt agreed.

The Denver Bank and Trust was on the corner of Market and 17th Streets. Like most of the buildings in Denver, the bank was constructed of brick, and it was positioned in such a way that the entrance was at the corner of the building. Like nearly every other building in town, it was decorated in a festive mode with red, white, and blue bunting draped over the entrance.

Inside the bank, on the left wall, there was a Currier and Ives print. The print was of two trains on parallel tracks. It looked as if the trains were racing each other. Smoke and steam streamed back from the engines and the great drive wheels were blurred in motion. There were people standing alongside the tracks waving at the engineers, who could be seen in the windows of their respective cabs, eyes staring ahead as they drove their iron steeds along the tracks.

Beside the Currier and Ives print was a large, printed sign.

The Denver Bank & Trust
Welcomes

THE DENVER PACIFIC RAILROAD

There were three tellers in the bank, and all three were wearing the caps of railroad conductors, as part of the celebration.

"Yes, sir, what can I do for you?" one of the tellers asked as Smoke stepped up to the window.

"Everyone seems excited about the arrival of the railroad," Smoke said.

"Yes, sir, we are indeed excited about it," the teller said. "By this time tomorrow, Denver will be a part of the railroad age. Why, did you know it will be possible to board a train right here in our own fair town and, within less than one week, be in San Francisco or St. Louis? What's more, it will only take two weeks to travel all the way to New York City."

"That is truly amazing," Smoke said. He took the draft from his pocket and slid it across to the bank teller. "I would like to negotiate this instrument, please," he said.

"Yes, sir, we'll be glad to take care of . . ." The teller stopped in mid-sentence as he looked at the size of the bank draft. "Uh—sir, this is a draft for over $32,000."

"Yes, I'm aware of that."

"But I don't know," the teller said.

"Is the draft not good?" Smoke asked. "Does Colorado Gold and Silver Acceptance Company not have enough money to cover it?"

"Oh, I'm sure they do," the teller said. "But they aren't who I'm worried about."

"Who are you worried about?"

"I don't know if we have that much money in our reserve," the teller said. "Wait here, please. I must talk to the bank manager."

The teller started to walk away with the bank draft in his hand.

"Uh-uh," Smoke said, pointing. "Leave that here."

"But Mr. Flowers will have to see it."

"You bring Mr. Flowers here to see it," Smoke suggested.

"Yes, sir," the teller said, handing the draft back to Smoke.

A few minutes later, the teller returned with a short, rotund man. Mr. Flowers had a flowing mustache that joined with his muttonchop sideburns. He had no chin whiskers.

"Mr. Jensen is it?" Flowers asked.

"Yes."

"This is quite embarrassing," he said. "But at the moment, we don't have enough funds on hand to honor the draft. However, if you will give us twenty-four hours, I believe we will be able to transfer some funds from some of the other banks in town. On the other hand, if you would like to do so, you could open an account in our bank and leave the draft for deposit. I would suggest that as the better solution."

Smoke shook his head. "No, thank you," he said. "You go gather up the money, we'll wait for it."

"Very good, sir. We'll have the money for you by tomorrow."

CHAPTER 16

A long layer of blue tobacco smoke hung just beneath the ceiling of the Lucky Strike Saloon. Normally, there were as many as five or six poker games going on at the same time, but now there was only one. All the other games had stopped and the other players, the bar girls, and even the casual drinkers had been drawn to the action at the remaining game table.

Smoke had three piles of poker chips stacked in front of him, representing over fifteen hundred dollars in cash. He pulled out a long, thin cigar and lit it, examining the man across the table from him. The man had just taken a seat at the table, attracted by the size of the stakes.

"I'm told your name is Smoke Jensen," the man said.

"It is."

"Do you know who I am, Mr. Jensen?"

"Should I?"

"I'm a professional gambler, Mr. Jensen. My name is Kelly Smith. Does it make you nervous to be playing against a professional gambler?"

"No, not at all," Smoke replied.

"It should."

"Really? And why is that?"

"I have been watching you for the last several minutes, Jensen. You are a reckless player. You play with emotion, not with your mind." Smith put fifteen hundred dollars on the table. "I think I should give you a few lessons. But I warn you, they will be expensive."

"I've always heard that a good education is expensive," Smoke said. "But I do seem to have a winning streak going."

"Yes. Well, I'm here to stop that winning streak," Kelly Smith said.

"I do admire a man with confidence," Smoke said. He raked in the cards and started to shuffle them.

"No, don't use those cards."

Smith stuck his hand out to stop Smoke from shuffling the cards. "I'd like to play with a new deck of cards, if you don't mind," Smith said.

"I don't mind at all."

One of the bar girls standing nearby handed Smoke a new deck of cards, and he broke the seal, then dumped them on the table. They were clean and stiff and shining. He pulled out the joker, then began shuffling the deck. The stiff, new pasteboards clicked sharply. His hands moved swiftly, folding the cards in and out until the law of random numbers became king of the table. He shoved the deck across the table.

"Cut?"

Smith cut the deck, then pushed them back. He kept his eyes glued on Smoke's hands.

"Five card stud?" Smoke asked.

"That'll be fine."

Smith won five hundred dollars on the first hand, and a couple of hands later was ahead by a little over a thousand dollars. Smoke was ready to concede that his string of luck had run out. At that time, he was still almost a hundred dollars above what he had started with. He finished his beer.

"Well," Smoke said. "I guess your ambition wasn't misplaced. You've broken my streak. Perhaps I should quit while I have something left."

"You have a lot more money than you are showing on the table, Mr. Jensen," Smith said.

Smoke's eyes narrowed. "What are you talking about?" he asked.

"The whole town knows that you presented a bank draft today that was so large that the bank couldn't cash it. That is right, isn't it?"

"Mister, I figure whatever happens between me and the bank is my business," Smoke said.

"Well, seeing as they're having to raise the money from all the other banks in town, seems to me like it's everybody's business now," Smith said. He looked at the one hundred dollars Smoke had remaining. "What do you say we play one hand of showdown for what you have left on the table?"

Smoke sighed. "All right," he said.

"Let the woman deal," Smith said.

Smoke nodded and handed the cards to the bar girl, who was standing by.

She dealt five cards to each of them, and Smoke took the pot with a pair of fives.

"Again," Smith said.

Within three hands, Smoke was back up to eight hundred dollars.

"You've won three hands in a row. You can't possibly win a fourth," Smith said. "Do you have the guts to bet everything on another hand?"

"You know, Smith," Smoke said as the girl shuffled the deck, "there are only two of us playing at this table. Mathematically, that means the odds are fifty-fifty that I will win."

"So?"

"So I mean, the fact that I have already won three hands does not lessen the odds of me winning again."

Smoke did win with a pair of tens, and Smith threw his cards on the table in disgust. He slid the rest of his money to the center of the table. "I've got another thousand here," he said. "High card."

"All right, high card," Smoke said.

The bar girl fanned out the cards and Smith turned over a queen of hearts. He looked across the table and smiled triumphantly at Smoke.

"I've got you now," he said.

Smoke turned up a king.

"Well, it looks like my luck has returned," he said as he reached for the pile of money.

"You just ran out of luck, mister," Smith said, drawing his pistol and pointing it at Smoke. "Draw your gun."

"You may have noticed that I'm not wearing a gun," Smoke said easily.

"Hell, it don't matter whether you are armed or not. We hang card cheats here in Denver. I'll just shoot you and save the citizens the cost of a hangman."

There was a cold, ominous click of metal, then the barrel of a pistol was pushed against the back of Smith's head.

"Put your gun down."

"What?" Smith asked in a frightened voice. He lowered his pistol and tried to look around, but the gun barrel prevented him from turning his head. Beads of perspiration popped out on his upper lip. "Who are you? What are you gettin' mixed up in this for? This ain't none of your concern."

"My name is Matt. You just threatened to shoot an unarmed man, and that unarmed man is my friend. That makes it my concern. Now, put your pistol on the table, please."

Gingerly, very gingerly, Smith laid his pistol down. Smoke picked Smith's gun up, emptied all the cartridges, and then walked over to the stove, opened the door, and tossed the gun inside.

"Have a nice walk around town, did you, Matt?" Smoke asked as he slammed the door.

"Yes, I did."

"I'm going to cash in the chips. Then I suggest that we take our dinner at the most expensive restaurant in town."

"Good idea," Matt said. He let the hammer down on his pistol and returned it to his holster. It wasn't until after the gun was taken from his head that Smith turned to see who had accosted him. He saw a strongly built youth of seventeen or eighteen, with sun-bleached blond hair and bright blue eyes.

"Why you're—you're just a kid!" Smith sputtered. "You're going to get yourself into trouble playing a man's game. I should've taken you."

Smoke chuckled. "Mr. Smith, have you ever tried to pick up a bob-cat by his back legs? That's exactly what you would have run into if you had tried anything with my partner."

"Really?" Smith said in obvious disbelief. "Well, I guess now we'll never know, will we?"

"And you'd better hope that you never have to find out," Smoke said. "Come on, Matt, let's go."

As Smoke and Matt left the saloon, they were poking money into all their pockets.

"I've never seen so much money," Matt said. "How much did you win tonight?"

"About twenty-five hundred, I think," Smoke replied. He laughed. "And if you think this is a lot of money, wait until tomorrow when we get our payoff at the bank."

* * *

The next day, the entire city of Denver turned out for the arrival of the first train. Most were dressed in their Sunday finest, there to greet the train on what they knew would be a great, historic day. Some were there to take advantage of the gathering, and there were several vendors working the crowd, selling pies, cakes, and candies.

One man had brought his patent medicine wagon up as close to the tracks as he could get it, and he was standing on the back of the wagon, shouting his pitch to the crowd. He was tall and thin, and wearing a black suit that was badly in need of a cleaning. His long, bony finger jabbed at the air as he spoke.

"Yes, ladies and gentlemen, I have come bearing a new miracle drug that will work wonders for all illnesses. If you suffer from ulceration of the kidneys, loss of memory, weak nerves, hot hands, flushing in the body, consumption, torpidity of the liver, hot spells, bearing down feelings, or cancer, this marvelous Extract of Buchu will be your salvation.

"And here is something else this drug will do that no other can. Young, unmarried ladies and gents, do you have an inability to control your own lustful thoughts? Did you know that such impure thoughts often lead to solitary practices against nature? And it is a well-known fact that such sinful practices lead to the diseases of dyspepsia, debility of thought, and insanity. If you are having a difficult time controlling such lascivious thoughts, Extract of Buchu will aid you.

"This miracle drug is available to you for one thin dime, yes, sir, one tenth of one dollar is all it takes to open the doors to health and energy."

"How about women?" someone shouted from the crowd. "If I drink a bottle of that stuff, will it make the women notice me?"

"Mister, you can drink a whole bottle of it if you want to. But if you do, then you had better start carrying a club around because you will need it to beat the women away from you."

The crowd laughed at the medicine man's response.

"Well, if that's the case, give me two bottles," the man replied. "I'll just get a bigger club."

Again, the crowd laughed.

Above the laughter of the crowd could be heard the distant sound of a train whistle.

"There it is!" someone shouted. "That's the train whistle! It's a-comin' down the track!"

Everyone moved toward the track, dangerously close to the brink of disaster as they waited for the train to come into view. Finally, it appeared around a distant curve, the sighting closely followed by the hollow sounds of puffing steam, like the gasps of some fire-breathing, serpentine monster. As if to add to the illusion, glowing sparks were whipped away in the black smoke clouds that billowed up into the bright blue sky.

As the train pounded by, Matt watched the huge driver wheels, nearly as tall as he was, and the white wisps of steam that escaped from the thrusting piston rods. The engine rushed by with sparks flying from the pounding drive wheels as glowing hot embers dripped from its firebox. Then came the cars, flashing by, slowing, and finally grinding to a halt with a shower of sparks.

Even after the train stopped, it was still alive with the rhythmic venting of steam and the popping and snapping of cooling gearboxes as it stood in the station. The crowd of over five thousand people who had gathered to watch this momentous event cheered loudly. The men lifted their hats and the women waved handkerchiefs to mark the start of a new era in Denver.

Matt did not think he had ever seen a more exciting thing in his entire life than the arrival of the first train ever to roll into Denver, Colorado.

After meeting the train, Matt and Smoke went to the bank, where the teller proudly counted out the money. Smoke divided the money while they were still in the bank, giving Matt sixteen thousand and fifty dollars.

"That's a lot of money," Matt said.

"Yes, it is," Smoke agreed. "Most folks don't make that much money in twenty years of work, and here you are, only eighteen, with sixteen thousand dollars in your pocket. What are you going to do with it?"

Matt thought for a moment before he answered. "I'll figure something out," he said.

It was getting late in the evening, and Smoke and Matt were a good ten miles down the road from Denver, when they decided they would start looking for a place to camp for the night. Often, during the ride, Matt had leaned forward to touch the saddlebags that were thrown across his horse. It made him almost dizzy to think that he had so much money. It also made him feel guilty, because he knew this was more money than his father had made in his entire life.

If Matt's father had been able to come up with this much money, they would have never left the farm in Kansas, and Matt would just now be beginning to think of his own future.

Matt had been thinking about his future ever since they left Denver. It wasn't the first time he had considered such a thing. He knew he would not be able to stay with Smoke forever.

But now, with this money, the future was no longer frightening, nor even mysterious to him. He knew exactly what he was going to do.

Matt's thoughts were interrupted when four men, who had been hiding in the bushes, suddenly stepped out into the road in front of them. All four were holding pistols, and the pistols were pointed at Smoke and Matt. The leader of the group was Kelly Smith, the man with whom Smoke had been playing cards the night before.

"You boys want to get down from them horses?" Smith asked.

Slowly, Matt and Smoke dismounted.

"Well, now," Smith said. "You didn't think I was really going to let you get out of town with all that money, did you?"

"What money?" Smoke asked.

"Why, the thirty thousand dollars you got at the bank today," Smith said. "The whole town is talkin' about it."

"Is that a fact?" Smoke asked.

"Oh, yes, it's a fact," Smith said. "You've got that money, plus the money you took from me in the card game last night."

"Well, now, Mr. Smith, if I had known you were going to be that bad of a loser, I'll be damned if I would have played poker with you," Smoke said. "And here you told me you were a professional gambler and all. I guess it just goes to prove that you can't always believe what people say."

Smith laughed, a dry, cackling laugh. "You're a funny man, Jensen," he said. "I'll still be laughin' when I'm in San Francisco, spending your money."

"What makes you think you're going to get my money?"

"Are you blind?" Smith asked. "There's four of us here, and we've got the drop on you."

"Oh, yeah, there is that, isn't there. I mean, you do have the drop on us," Smoke said almost nonchalantly. "By the way, Matt, do you remember that little trick I showed you?"

"I remember," Matt answered.

"Now would be a good time to try it out."

"Now?"

"Now," Smoke replied.

Even before the word was out of his mouth, Smoke and Matt both drew and fired two quick shots each. Kelly Smith and the three men who were with him were dead before they even realized they were in danger.

Matt waited until they were back at Smoke's cabin in the Gore Range before he spoke to Smoke.

"Smoke, I've been thinking," Matt said. "I'm eighteen now and . . ."

"You want to go off on your own," Smoke said, finishing Matt's sentence for him.

Matt nodded. "Yeah," he replied. "Don't get me wrong, it isn't that I don't like it here. You saved my life. More than that, you gave me a life. I've lived here nearly as long as I've ever lived anywhere, and, I reckon, for the rest of my life when I think of home, why, this is the place I'll be thinking of. But—it's just that . . ."

Smoke smiled. "You don't have to explain anything to me, Matt. It wasn't all that long ago that I was eighteen. And I was hell-bent to go out on my own as well. Truth is, if you weren't anxious to go—well, I might just be thinkin' I'd done something wrong in your upbringing."

"I'm glad you understand," Matt said.

"When are you leaving?"

"I thought I'd get started this morning."

Smoke nodded. "Seems about as good a time as any," he said. "Looks like you'll have good traveling weather for the next several days. You'll keep in touch, won't you?"

"I'll have to," he said. "You're all the family I've got."

Smoke nodded, but said nothing.

"Smoke, there's one more thing I want from you," Matt said.

"You can have it."

"You haven't asked what it is."

"It doesn't matter what it is," Smoke said. "If I have it, and you want it, then you can damn sure have it."

"When I first came here, you asked me what my last name was."

"Yeah, I recall."

"I didn't tell you."

"Yeah, I recall that as well."

"The thing is, you never asked me again."

"I figured your last name was your business," Smoke said.

"Only, now it's your business as well."

"What do you mean?"

"That's what I want from you, Smoke. If you don't mind, I'd like to take your name and use it as my own. I'd like the right to call myself Matt Jensen from here on out."

Smoke blinked a few times in surprise, then got up and walked over to look out through the window at the meadow by the cabin, the meadow where he had taught Matt to shoot, and ride, and use a rope and a knife.

"Smoke?" Matt said, addressing Smoke's back. "Smoke, if you don't want me to take your name, well, I'll surely understand. It's just that . . ."

"Matt, I would be honored for you to take my last name," Smoke said.

"You sure you don't mind?"

"Mind? I told you, I'd be honored. In fact, I can't think of anything that would honor me any more than to think of you using my last name."

"Thanks, Smoke. I appreciate that. I really do."

"You're welcome," Smoke replied as he continued to stare through the window. He didn't turn around, because he didn't think it would be good for the kid to see tears in his eyes.

CHAPTER 17

The first thing Matt did after leaving the mountain cabin in the Gore Range was return to Soda Creek. He had not been in the town since he had run away from the Home for Wayward Boys and Girls five years earlier.

The town looked the same to him, and as he rode down the street he even recognized several of the town's inhabitants, though he knew that no one in town would recognize him. He recognized George Tate. Tate owned the feed store, and he was standing out front, supervising the unloading of a wagon. He waved at Andy Morrison, the barber, and saw the confused expression on Morrison's face as he waved back. He chuckled to himself, enjoying the sense of anonymity growing up had given him.

Matt stopped in front of McDougal's Saloon, dismounted, and stepped inside. He had worked in this saloon for the three years he was a resident of the Home, and McDougal had treated him, as he did all his employees, fairly.

Matt glanced toward a table in the right rear corner and, as he expected, there sat McDougal, drinking coffee and working on his books. It was as if Matt had left the day before, as if McDougal had not moved from that very spot in seven years.

"I'll have a beer, Frank," Matt ordered.

The bartender squinted as he looked at Matt. "Do I know you?" he asked.

"We've met, but you've no reason to remember me," Matt replied.

Frank chuckled and nodded. "No, I reckon not. That's the problem with a job like this," he said. "Hundreds of people have come through here over the years. And since there's only one of me, it's a lot easier for them to remember me than it is for me to remember them."

"I understand," Matt said.

Frank brought him a mug of beer and Matt took a swallow, then used the back of his hand to wipe away the foam.

"I'm trying to find someone who used to work here," Matt said. "This was about five years ago."

"Shouldn't be all that hard," Frank said. "Anyone that was workin' for us five years ago is still workin' for us. Except for a couple of the ladies. Flo got married and Jill went back to St. Louis. We've got us some new girls in."

"This was a boy," Matt said. "A young boy, about twelve or thirteen."

Frank nodded. "Oh, you must be talkin' about the orphans," he said.

"Yes."

"How would you know them?"

"I was one of them," Matt said.

Frank smiled broadly and pushed the money back across the bar. "This beer is on me. You must be Matt," he said.

Matt nodded. "That's me."

The smile left Frank's face. "And you'd be askin' about Eddie and Timmy? I reckon you haven't heard."

"Heard what?"

"They're dead," Frank said. "Both of them."

"How did it happen?"

"They drowned," Frank said. "It happened real soon after you left. They was both found drowned in Muddy Creek."

"What were they doing there? It was too cold to swim."

"Most folks think they was killed by Connors and Simon. I know there was bad blood between them two boys and ever'one else in the Home. But the sheriff never could find no evidence that they done it, so there wasn't nothin' he could do about it."

"Do you think Connors and Simon did it?"

"I know they done it," Frank said. "They was both in here drunk one night, and they was laughin' and braggin' as how they had done it and got away with it."

"Did you tell the sheriff?"

"Yeah, I told him," Frank said. "But he said that me just overhearin' 'em talk while they was drunk wouldn't stand up in court."

Matt shook his head sadly. "Damn," he said. "I hadn't heard."

"Well, at least I'm glad to see you survived. Always thought you was a good kid," Frank said. He chuckled. "Never knew you would grow up so big, though. Are you going to stay around town for a while?" Frank asked.

"I'll probably spend the night here tonight, but won't stay any longer than that. I've got some things I need to do. I thank you for the information, Frank," Matt said. "And the beer," he added as he took the last swallow.

"My pleasure, Matt. It was good seeing you again," Frank said.

Leaving the saloon, Matt walked down the street to have supper in Lucy's Café. He had just finished when he saw a young boy come out of the kitchen carrying a tray. The boy began gathering up dishes from the table and he came over to Matt's table.

"Sir, if you are finished with your supper, I'll take your dishes," he said.

"Thanks, I'm finished."

"Uh, the biscuit?" the boy said. "Are you finished with it as well?"

Matt saw the hungry expression in the boy's face as he stared at the remaining biscuit.

"Do you want the biscuit?" Matt asked.

"Yes, sir. I get to eat all the leftover food if I want."

Matt drummed his fingers on the table for a second as he looked at the boy. He didn't know him, but he had seen this same expression in those he had known at the Home. This could have been Timmy or Eddie. It could even have been him.

"What's your name, boy?" Matt asked.

"Jules."

"Jules what?"

Jules shook his head. "They don't let us use last names."

"You're talking about Captain Mumford?"

"Yes, sir. Do you know him?"

"Yes, I know him."

"He's—he's a fine man, sir," Jules said hesitantly, frightened that Matt and Captain Mumford might be friends and allies.

Matt chuckled. "You have a funny idea of a fine man," he said.

Jules laughed as well, but he didn't say anything else. Instead, he went over to one of the other tables and started clearing it. He accidentally knocked one of the plates off the table and it fell in the diner's lap.

"You little son of a bitch!" the man at the table suddenly shouted in anger.

"Oh! I'm sorry, sir!" Jules replied. "I didn't mean to."

The diner stood up and started brushing off his clothes where some food had been spilled.

"Here's a napkin, sir!" Jules said, taking a napkin from the table and trying to hand it to the diner.

The diner pushed Jules away from him so hard that Jules fell on the floor. The diner took off his belt and doubled it.

"I'm going to tan your hide good," he said, drawing back his belt.

It happened so fast that nobody in the café saw it, but one moment the angry diner was raising his belt over his head, and the next, his belt was pinned to the wall, a knife sticking through it. The handle of the knife was still quivering back and forth.

"What the hell!" the diner shouted, looking around. "Who did that?"

"I did," Matt said, standing up and facing him.

The diner pointed at Matt. "Mister, you've just made a very big mistake. You don't have any idea who you are messing with," he said.

"Yeah, I know who you are, Connors. I could never forget anyone as ugly as you."

"What did you say?" Connors sputtered. "Mister, you'd better watch your mouth if you know what is good for you."

Matt shook his head slowly. "You don't want to brace me, Connors," he said calmly.

Connors made a grab for his gun, but because he was wearing no belt, he not only didn't get to his gun, his pants fell down around his ankles, and his pistol clattered to the floor.

"What the hell!" he shouted, reaching down to pull up his pants while everyone else in the café was laughing at him.

While Connors was pulling his pants back up, Matt moved over quickly, then kicked the gun all the way across the floor, where it wound up in the corner.

"I told you you didn't want to brace me," Matt said as he reached up to pull his knife from the belt that had been pinned to the wall. He handed the belt back. "You haven't learned a thing, have you, Connors? You're just as ornery now as you ever were."

"How is it that you know me? Was you in the Home? 'Cause I don't remember you."

"Sure you remember me," Matt said. "I'm the one who stole the ham that you got blamed for."

"You? You're the one that stole it? I thought Eddie and—I mean, I thought someone else stole it."

"Is that why you killed Eddie and Timmy?"

Connors's eyes narrowed to a squint. "I didn't kill nobody," he said.

"Connors," Matt said. "If I hear that you so much as touched one hair on Jules's head, you will answer to me," he said.

"Nobody threatens me," Connors said. "Do you hear me? Nobody threatens me."

"Oh, don't get me wrong, Connors," Matt said. "That wasn't a threat. That was a promise."

CHAPTER 18

The next morning, Matt was awakened by the sounds of morning commerce in Soda Creek. Someone was using an ax and he could hear the thump each time the ax fell.

Thump, thump.

In counterpoint, and sounding on the offbeat of the ax, was the ringing of a blacksmith's hammer.

Thump—ring. Thump—ring.

Next door, one of the clerks of the general store was sweeping the porch, and the scratch of his broom could be clearly heard over the thump and ring of the ax and hammer.

Thump—ring—scratch, scratch. Thump—ring—scratch, scratch.

Finally, adding a coda to the cacophonous symphony, was the squeak of a wagon wheel as it passed down the street of the town.

Thump—ring—scratch, scratch—squeak. Thump—ring—scratch, scratch—squeak.

It was not by mere chance that Matt had come back to Soda Creek. In so doing, he felt as if he was closing one part of his life and starting a new chapter. And as a rite of passage, last night he had been with a woman for the first time. Matt turned his head to see the woman who was lying in bed with him.

She was on her back. Her head was turned away from him, and the bedcovers had slipped down from her left shoulder, exposing her left breast. Matt stared at the nipple, which was lighted by a bar of sunlight that spilled in between the bottom of the window shade and the top of the windowsill.

The woman was lying in such a way that her breast was nearly flat so that the globe of flesh Matt had seen last night—and had thoroughly explored—was now just a gentle curve that was topped by the taut nipple that gleamed in the single shaft of sunlight.

Quietly, and gently enough so that the woman wasn't aware of what he was doing, Matt lifted off the cover, then rolled it all the way down to the bottom of the bed. That action caused her body to be fully revealed so that Matt was able to see everything. He lay with his elbow bent and his head resting on his hand, studying her for a long time.

The woman chuckled. "Have you seen enough, honey?" she asked without turning her head or opening her eyes. "Because I'm getting cold."

"Oh!" Matt said, startled by her response. He had not known she was awake. "I'm sorry." He pulled the cover back over her.

The woman chuckled again. "You don't need to be sorry," she said, turning to look at him. "I'm not a virgin, you know."

Matt smiled. "Neither am I," he said.

"You mean, you are *no longer* a virgin, don't you? Last night was your first time, wasn't it?"

Matt nodded. "Yeah, it was."

The woman shook her head and clucked. "You don't recognize me, do you, Matt?"

Matt stared at her. It couldn't be. This woman looked ten to fifteen years older than he was, not a mere year or two older.

"My God," he said with an expulsion of breath. "Tamara?"

"I wondered when you were going to recognize me," Tamara replied. "Have I changed that much? I recognized you right away."

"No, it's not that, it's just that—well, I never expected to see you—here."

"You mean you didn't expect to see me whorin'," Tamara replied.

Matt didn't answer.

Tamara got out of bed and padded, naked, over to a chair where she had put her clothes the night before.

"What did you expect would happen to the girls at the Home?" she asked as she began dressing. "Mumford had us on the line by the time we were fifteen." She looked up at him and he saw tears sliding down her face. "I told you that. You do remember, don't you, Matt, that I told you that?"

Matt nodded. "Yes," he said. "I remember. I tried to take you with me."

Tamara's expression softened, and she shook her head.

"I know you did, honey. But I guess it just wasn't in the cards."

"If it hadn't been for you, I don't think I would have gotten away that night," Matt said. "You led them away from me and the boat."

"I know I did. And don't think that I didn't think about it a lot of times. I was sure you had died up in the mountains, and I figured that if you had, it would have been my fault."

"As you can see, I didn't die," he said. "And even if I had, it would not have been your fault. Like I said, I thank you for helping me out that night."

"And last night?" Tamara asked, a conspiratorial smile spreading across her face. "How about last night? Do you want to thank me for that as well?"

Matt chuckled and nodded. "Yeah," he said. "I want to thank you for that as well."

"Are you leaving town again?"

"Yes," Matt said. "I—have something to do."

"I know. I remember that you told me a long time ago. You are going to find the people who killed your parents, aren't you?"

"If I can."

"How do you know they are still alive?"

"I know one of them is still alive, because I've seen his name in the paper. It's Clyde Payson."

"Payson?" Tamara said. "Is that who you are looking for?"

"Yes," Matt said. He looked at Tamara with a curious expression on his face. "Tamara, do you know Payson?"

"Not exactly," Tamara said. "But I know where you can find him."

"How do you know that?"

"Men talk, honey," Tamara said. "I don't know, maybe it's a way of showing off, a way of saying they are dangerous, or they know someone who is dangerous. Most of it is just talk, but over the years I've learned how to tell what is true and what isn't."

"And they have told you where Payson is?"

"Sort of," she said. "He's running a town called Gehenna."

"He's running the town? What do you mean he's running it? Is he the mayor? Is he the sheriff?"

"He's both as far as I can determine," Tamara said. "Gehenna is what's called an outlaw town. There is no law there, and the only ones who live there are all wanted by the law. From the talk I've heard, the top outlaw there is Payson."

"Thanks," Matt said.

Tamara shook her head. "Payson is a really bad man. I've seen strong men start shaking with fear just at the mention of his name. I wish you would just ignore him now. Whatever he did has been done, and going after him won't bring your parents back."

"Believe me, Tamara, I know every argument there is as to why I should just forget about this and get on with my life," Matt said. "I know all the arguments because I have used them on myself. But I cannot put this down. I have to find Payson."

"Even if it gets you killed?"

"Even if it gets me killed," Matt said.

"You haven't changed a bit. Matt . . ." Tamara began. Then she looked questioningly at him. "What is your last name, Matt? If you recall, one of the things Mumford did was take our last names away from us. I never knew your last name."

Matt hesitated for just a moment. What name should he tell her? Should he say his birth name, which was Cavanaugh, or the name he intended to use for the rest of his life?

"Jensen," Matt said, making his choice. "My name is Matt Jensen."

"My name is Tamara Peabody." Tamara smiled. "And you may be the only one I've ever told that."

"Well, Tamara Peabody, would you like to have breakfast with me?"

"No, Matt, I can't," Tamara said.

"Why not?"

"I'm a whore, remember? It wouldn't do you to be seen with a whore."

"You're also my friend," Matt said. "I'll be hurt if you turn me down."

Tamara smiled. "All right," she said. "I'll have breakfast with you."

They drew a couple of stares when they went into Lucy's Café, but Lucy greeted them warmly, and that seemed to ease the situation with the rest of the customers. Within a few minutes, nobody was paying any attention to them at all and they were enjoying their breakfast.

Then Jules came up to the table and stood there for a moment until Matt noticed him.

"Good morning, Jules," Matt said, smiling broadly. He handed Jules a couple of biscuits and a couple of pieces of bacon.

"Thank you, no, I've eaten," Jules said. "That's not why I come over to your table."

364 William W. Johnstone

"Oh?"

"The feller you had words with last night? The one you stopped from beatin' me with a belt? He's waitin' for you out in the street."

"Connors is waiting for me?"

Jules nodded. "He aims to kill you," he said.

"I see."

"If you want, you can leave through the back way. He won't see you 'cause the alley is all blocked off."

Matt shook his head. "No, if Connors is throwing a party for me, it would be rude not to show up."

"Matt, no, don't go out there," Tamara said. "I've seen Connors before. He works at the stamp mill, guarding the gold shipments. He's really good with a gun."

"I have to go, Tamara," Matt said as he pulled his pistol and checked the loads. He slipped the pistol back in his holster. "If I don't go out there and face him now, like as not he'll shoot me in the back."

In a town as small as Soda Creek, news of an impending gunfight traveled faster than the telegraph. The street that had been so busy with commerce that it had awakened Matt earlier was now deserted, except for Connors, who stood in the middle of the street about one hundred feet away. Men and women were scurrying down the board-walks, stepping into buildings to get out of the line of fire while taking observers' positions in the doors and windows so as to be able to see everything. Even the horses had been moved off the street, as nervous owners feared they might be hit by a stray bullet.

"I didn't think you'd come out," Connors called.

"Yeah, you would've liked that, wouldn't you?" Matt said. "I would've sneaked out the back, you would look big in front of the rest of the town."

Suddenly, a bullet fried the air just beside his ear, hit the dirt beside him, then skipped off with a high-pitched whine on down the street. The sound of a rifle shot reached him at about the same time, and Matt dropped and rolled to his left, his gun already in his hand. That was when he got a quick glimpse of the rifleman. But it was a quick glance only, as the rifleman ducked behind the Chinese laundry.

By now, Connors had his own pistol out. He fired but missed, his bullet crashing harmlessly into the wooden front stoop of Lucy's Café.

From a prone position on the ground, Matt fired at Connors and hit him in the knee. Connors let out a howl and went down.

The rifleman fired again, this time sending a bullet through the crown of Matt's hat. This time, Matt got a close enough look at him to see that it was Simon.

"Connors! Connors, are you hit?" Simon called.

"Yes!" Connors answered, his voice reflecting the pain of a busted kneecap.

Simon fired again, and the bullet came so close that Matt could feel the concussion of its passing.

Matt was lying out in the open, so he got up and ran across the street, bending low and firing as he went. He dived behind the porch of the barbershop, then rose and saw that he had a perfect shot at Simon, who had moved into position behind a watering trough. He fired, saw Simon drop his rifle into the watering trough, then fall back.

By now, Connors had managed to improve his own position, and he fired again at Matt. His bullet sent splinters of wood into Matt's face.

Matt stared across the street, trying to find an opening for a shot. Then he smiled. Connors had improved his position by getting out of the street and behind a wooden bench in front of a dressmaker's shop. What he didn't realize, though, was that the large mirror in the window of the dressmaker's shop showed his reflection, and from across the street, Matt watched as Connors inched along on his belly to the far end of the bench. Matt took slow and deliberate aim at the end of the bench where he knew Connors's face would appear.

Slowly, Connors peered around the corner of the bench to see where Matt was, and what was going on. Matt cocked his pistol and waited. When enough of Connors's head was exposed to give him a target, Matt squeezed the trigger. The pistol roared and bucked in his hand, and a cloud of smoke billowed up, then floated away. When the cloud cleared, Matt saw Connors lying facedown in the dirt with a pool of blood spreading out from under his head.

CHAPTER 19

Matt was well armed. He carried a throwing knife that he wore on a scabbard that hung just behind his right shoulder, a bowie knife hanging from his belt on his left hip, a .44 double-action Colt on his right hip (though he still kept his .36 Navy Colt stuck down in a saddlebag), and a Winchester .44-40 rifle. He also had a rain slicker, an overcoat, two blankets, two spare shirts, two extra pairs of socks, two pairs of trousers, and two sets of underwear.

But perhaps most significant of everything that he carried was the fifteen thousand dollars Smoke had given him when they divided up. That money was still in its original bank packets, rolled up in oilskin and kept in a secret sleeve on the inside of his saddle blanket.

Matt didn't know the name of the town he was approaching, but it didn't matter. He didn't know today's date, but that didn't matter either. He was looking for Clyde Payson and Garvey Laird, and until he found them, not much else mattered.

Since leaving Soda Creek almost six months ago, he had heard other references to the town of Gehenna, though some referred to it as Purgatory, and others called it Perdition. It was the various names by which it was known that was making the town hard to find.

Of course, the fact that it was a lawless town and a sanctuary for outlaws also made it hard to find. It was on no maps, and many thought it might just be a myth.

Matt was reasonably certain that the town did exist, and he was sure he would locate it. When he did find it, and Payson and Garvey, he knew that the advantage would be all his. He was sure he would recognize them, while they would never connect the six-foot-tall, broad-shouldered, powerful man he had become with the runny-nosed skinny little boy he had been when they encountered him on the trail.

It was mid-morning, and the sun was halfway through its transit to high noon, as Matt approached the town, which was no more than a cluster of buildings clinging to the side of a hill. Shimmering sunlight bounced off the roofs and flashed back from the windows.

This appeared to be a mining community, and a little higher up, above the buildings of the town, zigzagging wooden trestles filigreed the face of the mountain. White wisps of steam escaped from the vents of the press mill, and its cylinder steam pipe boomed loudly, as though the place were under a cannonade. Boiling out of the high smokestack was a large plume of black smoke, its sulfurous odor permeating the entire valley.

Matt's horse, Spirit, realizing that he was near the end of a long journey, picked up the pace slightly as they approached the town.

A kiosk in the middle of the street advertised The Pickax Saloon, and even though it was not yet noon, Matt found the idea of a cool beer appealing. He would have a beer, but not before he had taken care of his horse. Smoke had inculcated that in him a long time ago, not from sentimentality or from affection for the critter, but from practicality—that the health of his horse could mean the difference between surviving and dying.

A few minutes later, with Spirit boarded at the livery, Matt crossed the street and walked down the boardwalk passing a handful of buildings until he came to The Pickax Saloon. A large sign touting the establishment hung over the boardwalk, squeaking an invitation as it rocked in a gentle breeze. Right under the swinging sign was another sign, nailed to the wall alongside the door. This was a big picture of a beer mug, golden yellow at the bottom, white foam at the top. It was actually for those who couldn't read, but it also had the effect of appealing to those who could, for Matt literally licked his dry lips as he passed it on his way inside.

Remembering to enter the saloon the way Smoke had taught him, he pushed through the batwing doors, then stepped to one side and placed his back against the wall as he studied the establishment.

There were eight people in the saloon, the bartender, six men customers, and one woman. Three of the men, wearing coveralls and hats with unlit lanterns, were sitting together at one of the tables. These were obviously miners. The other three men were at a different table. These men were wearing jeans and flannel shirts. They were also wearing cowboy-style hats, and all were wearing pistols with bullet-studded belts. The one woman in the place was sitting in a chair by a piano. The piano was silent and looked as if it had not been played for some time.

The woman, seeing someone new come into the bar, smiled broadly and walked over to meet him. Matt guessed that she was in her early thirties, though her face was older and her eyes were ancient.

"Buy me a drink, mister?" she asked.

"Sure," Matt said.

"My name's Sue," the woman said. "What's yours?"

"Matt."

"You ever been here before, Matt?"

"I don't know."

"You don't know?"

"I don't know where here is," Matt replied honestly.

"Why, this is The Pickax Saloon," Sue said.

"What's the name of the town?" Matt asked.

"The town is called Slick Rock," Sue said.

"No," Matt said.

Sue looked confused by his reply. "No?"

"You asked if I had ever been here before. The answer is no, I've never been to Slick Rock."

Sue laughed.

"How do we get those drinks?"

"Give me the money, I'll get them," Sue offered.

"I want a beer."

Matt sat at one of the tables and waited as Sue walked over to the bar, spoke to the bartender, then stood there for a moment waiting for him to fill her order.

"You come to Slick Rock lookin' for work, mister?" one of the miners called over to him.

"Not at the moment," Matt answered.

"But you are lookin' for somethin', right?"

"Yes, I'm looking for a town."

"Hell, mister, Slick Rock is a town," the miner said. The others laughed.

At that moment, Sue returned carrying a mug of beer and a small glass. It looked like whiskey in the glass, but Matt would have been willing to bet that it was tea. He didn't care; he knew that Sue's job was getting customers to buy drinks. If she could drink tea rather than whiskey, it would keep her sober, and it would be more profitable.

"What's the name of the town you are lookin' for?" one of the miners asked.

"I'm not sure," Matt replied.

Again, the miners laughed. "Well, mister, if you don't even know the name of the town, you are going to have one hell of a time finding it."

"Yeah," Matt answered. "It seems to be working out that way. The thing is I've heard three names for the town. I've heard Gehenna, Purgatory, and Perdition. I just don't know which one is right."

"I've heard of that place," one of the miners said. "From what I hear, it's filled with nothing but bad characters."

"Yes, that's what I'm looking for," Matt replied.

"The town is called Gehenna," the miner said. "But it's an outlaw town. Are you what folks would call an outlaw, mister?"

"I reckon that depends on who is doing the telling," Matt replied.

"Are you a bounty hunter?"

"No."

"Then why would you want to go to a place like that?"

"I've got business with a couple of people I was told might be there," Matt said.

"Who would they be?"

"Clyde Payson and Garvey Laird," Matt said, speaking loudly and clearly.

There was almost an audible gasp in response to the names.

"I've never heard of either one of them," the talkative miner said, the tone of his voice changing drastically.

"Me neither," one of the others said.

"That's funny," Matt said.

"What's funny?"

"When I said the names, a couple of you acted as if you had heard them before."

"Well, whatever, it ain't none of our business," the talkative miner said. "And if you're smart, you'll quit looking for them. They're dangerous characters, both of them."

"Oh? I thought you said you had never heard of either of them."

"I haven't," the miner said. "But if they are hanging out in a place like Gehenna, you don't want to find them."

"I thank you for your concern," Matt said. "But I have a score to settle with the two of them, so I do intend to find them."

Out of the corner of his eye, Matt noticed that the other three men in the saloon got up and left.

"Those three didn't even talk to me," he said to Sue. "They must not be very friendly."

"Don't worry none about them," Sue said. "They're drifters, all three of them. In and out of here all the time. They say they are cowboys, but there ain't nobody ever seen 'em work anywhere. But now me, I can be very friendly, if you know what I mean. I've got a room upstairs just in case you'd like to see how friendly I can be. It wouldn't cost you too much."

Matt looked at her. Tamara was six months ago, and there had been very few others since. Most of the experiences had been temporarily satisfying, but in almost every case it left him with an empty feeling that he couldn't quite explain. He knew that it would probably be like that until he found one woman to settle down with. But he knew also that he would not be fit for any one woman until the thing that drove him was taken care of. Still, the idea of putting down the search, maybe for a short time, did hold some appeal for him.

Sue knew men and could read them the way Matt could read a trail. When she saw the flicker of interest in Matt's eyes, she smiled seductively. The effect of her smile was instantaneous. Now her features weren't quite as hard as he thought, and her eyes were not nearly as old.

"So, how about it?" she asked.

"Oh, I don't know," Matt said. "It seems a little early in the day to . . ."

Sue put her hand on his. "I promise you, you won't be sorry," she said.

There was something in the expression on her face and in the tone of her voice that made Matt think that she was talking about more than just sex.

"All right," he said. He drank the rest of his beer, then wiped his mouth with the back of his hand. "Where do we go?"

"Like I said, I have a room upstairs."

Matt was sitting in a chair, pulling on his boots. Sue was still in bed, with the cover pulled up to her chin.

"If all men were like you, I wouldn't mind this job," Sue said.

"Yeah, I'll bet you say that to everyone," Matt teased.

"No," Sue said seriously. "No, I don't. You are different. You were more . . ."

"Don't say I was more skilled," Matt said, waving his hand. "To tell the truth, I barely knew what I was doing."

"No, I wasn't going to say you were more skilled. I was going to say something that is much better than skill. You have a tenderness about you, a feeling for others. With most men, I'm just here to be ridden, like a horse or something. I'm a tool. But you not only knew that I was here, you acted as if you really cared about what I felt."

"It seemed like the thing to do," Matt replied.

"You have known people like me before, haven't you?"

"You mean other women?"

"No. I mean whores. You have known a whore, not just as a whore, but as a person."

Matt thought of Tamara, and nodded. "Yes," he said.

"Did you love her?"

Matt started to say no, but he hesitated. He was not "in love with" Tamara. But she was a part of his youth, and he couldn't deny that he loved her.

"Yes," Matt said. "I love her."

"I knew it," Sue said, smiling broadly. She reached across the bed to touch him, and as she did so, the sheet fell down, exposing her bare breast. "You are a good man."

"Thanks."

"Mr. Jensen?"

Matt chuckled. "How close do we have to get before you call me Matt?"

"Matt," Sue said. "Do you remember those three men who left the saloon while you were talking with the miners?"

"Yes."

"Look out for them."

"Look out for them?"

"They are from Gehenna, and they know Clyde Payson."

"How do you know?"

"They've been here before," Sue said. "I've heard them talking."

"Do you know where Gehenna is?"

Sue shook her head. "No, I don't, but it can't be too terribly far from here."

"That's what I'm thinking," Matt replied.

"Matt, I mean it when I say be careful of them. You are looking for Payson, which means that all these men would have to do to get on Payson's good side is to kill you."

"I'll be on the lookout," Matt promised. "Thanks for the warning."

"I wish I could talk you into giving up your hunt for Payson. It would be a lot safer."

"I'm sure it would," Matt agreed. "But I'm afraid I can't just put this down."

"I know," Sue said. "But I had to try and talk you out of it. I had to try."

CHAPTER 20

Leaving The Pickax Saloon, Matt walked across the street to have his lunch in the Palace Café. After that, he visited the other saloons in town trying to find out if anyone had any information he could use. He discovered a long time ago that he could get more information in casual conversation than by direct questioning.

Matt had learned a lot about Payson during his search. He'd learned that Payson was a cold-blooded killer. But then, he already knew that because he had witnessed it first-hand. He'd learned also that Payson had built up a network of support, partly because people were afraid of him, and partly because he paid people to protect him.

Matt was standing at the bar in a saloon called the Brown Dirt Cowboy when the sheriff came up to talk to him.

"Would you be Matt Jensen?" the sheriff asked.

"Yes," Matt answered. "But there's no paper on me, Sheriff. If this is about that fracas back in Soda Creek, it was ruled justifiable homicide."

The sheriff smiled. "No, this isn't anything about that. I've got a letter for you. Come on down to my office."

Matt looked confused. "You have a letter for me? That's impossible. Who would know that I'm here? Are you sure it's for me?"

"I guess that depends on whether or not you know a fella named Smoke Jensen," the sheriff replied.

A big smile spread across Matt's face. "What? Yes! Yes, I know him!" he said. "What about him?"

"He's the one who sent you the letter."

"But I don't understand. How did you get the letter?"

"My name is Tate Casey," the sheriff said. "Smoke and I are friends." He stuck his hand out and Matt took it. "He sent the letter to you inside a letter he sent me. In my letter, he said he had a feeling you might show up. Come on down to my office. I'll give it to you."

"Thanks," Matt said.

A deputy was sitting at a desk in the sheriff's office when Matt and Casey went in.

"Johnny, take a round for me, would you?" Casey asked.

"Sure thing, Tate," Johnny answered, getting up and taking his hat down from a peg. There were three jail cells in the back of the building. Only one was occupied and its occupant was on the cot, snoring loudly.

"Who've you got back there?" asked Casey. "Mr. Fitzsimmons?"

"Yes, sir. He was passed out drunk in front of the millinery. He should be wakin' up soon."

"Poor man," Casey said to Matt. "His wife had just bought a new hat and was coming out of the millinery when a runaway team and wagon ran over her, killing her. Fitzsimmons took it hard, and has been a drunk ever since. Two or three times a week, we find him passed out right where his wife was killed."

"And you lock him up?"

"For his own safety," Casey said. "Soon as he sleeps it off, we feed him a meal, then we let him go."

Matt nodded. "Makes sense," he said.

Sheriff Casey opened the middle drawer of his desk, then pulled out an unopened envelope and handed it to Matt.

"Here is your letter, and as you can see, I haven't read it," he said. "Although, technically I could have read it, I suppose, without breakin' any laws, since this was in a letter that was sent to me. But I didn't figure it would be right to read another man's mail."

"Thanks, Sheriff," Matt said as he opened the envelope. "I appreciate that."

Pulling the letter from the envelope, Matt unfolded it and began to read.

Dear Matt,

After you left, I joined up with Preacher again to help him move a herd of half-broken mustangs and Appaloosa. We took them south into the wild country, crossing the Colorado River and keeping west of the Uncompahgre Plateau.

That was when we first picked up the scent. There is no other smell like that of charred flesh, so we had us a notion of what we were about to run into before we actually saw them.

Then we saw them. One man was tied by his ankles, hang-ing from a limb over a fire. His head and shoulders were blackened cooked meat. The bodies of the others were pretty well hacked up, one was tied to the wheel of a wagon. All of them had died hard.

Then we found a young woman hiding in the bushes. Somehow, she'd managed to get away from the Indians. Her name is Nicole, and it turns out that I've taken her for my wife.

Here, Matt looked up in surprise. "I'll be damned," he said. "Smoke has got himself married!"

Sheriff Casey chuckled. "Yeah, he told me that too. Surprised the hell out of me, I have to tell you."

Matt went back to the letter.

Anyhow, the main purpose of this letter was to tell you I got myself married to about the prettiest thing you ever saw. But also, to tell you about Sheriff Casey.

If you are reading this letter, Matt, then I reckon you are sitting in the sheriff's office right now. He's a good man, but I know something about him that not many people do know. I know he used to ride the outlaw trail. Now I tell you this, not to say anything bad about the sheriff, but so you might under-stand that someone like Casey, who has been on the outlaw trail, might be just the man to help you find Payson.

Ask him to tell you what he knows. Say it would be a personal favor to Smoke Jensen. Tell him if he is able to help you, I'll figure that the Spring Hill matter is all squared away. He'll know what you're talking about.

> *Your friend,*
> *Smoke*

Matt folded the letter and put it in his pocket.

"Thanks for giving me the letter," he said.

"Well, I'm glad you came through Slick Rock so I could give it to you. I've had the letter for six weeks or so. I wasn't sure you would show up, but Smoke says you are looking for the people who killed your parents."

"That's right."

"I hope you find them."

"Smoke seems to think you can help," Matt said.

Casey looked surprised. "He thinks I can help find the people who killed your parents? How would I do that?"

"He also said to tell you that if you do help me, the Spring Hill matter would be closed."

"Oh, he said that, did he?"

"Yes. What is the Spring Hill incident?"

Casey ran his hand through his hair and looked at Matt for a long moment. Then he took a deep breath.

"I was young," he said. "About your age, I reckon. I had been raised on a farm back in Missouri and figured there had to be more to life than plowing fields behind a mule. So I came West, and no sooner got here than I met a fella by the name of Amos Meeker.

"Well, sir, it turns out that Amos Meeker was the lead dog of a bunch of what I thought at the time to be really fun people to be with. Like me, they were young, restless, and obviously looking for something more out of life than they were getting. Fact is, I figured we were all riding the same-color horse."

Casey walked over to the stove, where a blue-steel coffeepot sat. Using a folded cloth to protect his hands from the heat, he poured two cups of coffee. He handed one cup to Matt before he continued his story.

"Then one day, they asked me if I would like to come along on a real adventure with them. Here, all this time, I thought we were having real adventures, hunting, fishing, sparking the ladies, that sort of thing. But Meeker scoffed at it, said what we had been doing was nothing. According to Meeker, if I wanted some real adventure, I should come along with them while we robbed a stagecoach."

Casey took a swallow of his coffee and grew silent for a moment.

"So, did you hold up a stagecoach?"

Casey nodded. "Yes, I am ashamed to say that I did. In fact, I reckon we must've hit ten or twelve stagecoaches over the next couple of months. And we were beginning to get pretty well known for it too. To be honest with you, it was sort of exciting. I thought, what was the harm? Nobody was getting hurt, and we always had enough money for whiskey, beer, and women.

"Then came Spring Hill. That was when Meeker decided we were wasting time robbing stagecoaches. He said we should rob a bank

because that was where the real money was. So that's what we did—
or rather, that's what we set out to do."

Casey continued with the story, telling it in such vivid and dramatic detail that it wasn't hard for Matt to believe he was there, watching the drama unfold, rather than listening to it.

There were two tellers and six customers in the bank when Meeker, Casey, and four other would-be bank robbers stepped in with guns drawn.

"Oh, my God! It's a holdup!" one of the tellers shouted in fear.

"That's right, mister, this is a holdup," Meeker said. Meeker waved his gun. "Now, open your safe and give me all the money you have."

The teller shook his head. "No," he said. "I can't do that."

"What do you mean you can't do that?"

"That money doesn't belong to the bank. It belongs to the good people of Spring Hill. I won't give it to you."

Without another word, Meeker shot the teller. There were two women in the bank, an older woman and her eighteen-year-old daughter. They both screamed.

"Now, you," Meeker said, pointing the gun at the other teller. "Are you going to open that safe for us? Or do I have to kill you too?"

The teller was shaking so hard that he could scarcely speak. "No, no, please don't kill me," he pleaded. Then, thinking of a possible way out of his situation, the teller smiled, almost triumphantly.

"You can't kill me," he pointed out. "If you kill me, there won't be anyone left that knows the combination," the teller said. "Then what would you do?"

"You've got a point there," Meeker said, glaring angrily at the teller. Then, inexplicably, he smiled and pointed his gun at the young woman. "But I've got me another idea," Meeker said. "If you don't open that safe in one minute, I'll kill her."

"Meeker, no, I won't let you do it!" Casey shouted, jumping toward him and wrestling for his gun.

"Get away!" Meeker shouted.

The two men struggled over the gun until it discharged. Casey went down with a bullet in his hip.

Casey's attempt to take Meeker's gun failed in its original objective, but had an unexpected effect when it so distracted everyone that two of the male customers in the bank were able to draw their own guns.

"Meeker! Them two has drawed on us!" one of the bank robbers called out in panic.

Guns roared and smoke filled the room as men and women shouted and cursed in fear and anger. When the smoke cleared, three of the bank robbers were lying dead on the floor and a fourth was wounded. In addition, the bank teller, a man named Foster, was dead.

Meeker and the one surviving bank robber had managed to dash out of the bank, and were now galloping away, the sound of their horses' rapid hoofbeats permeating the town.

The robber on the floor, bleeding from a bullet wound in his thigh, was Tate Casey.

Within a matter of moments, several of the town's citizens, having heard the commotion, charged into the bank. Seeing four dead men, one of whom was the teller, the townsmen grew incensed. They pointed to Casey.

"He was one of them!"

"Hang him!" someone shouted.

"I'll get a rope!" another yelled.

"Hold it! Nobody is going to hang anybody!" the older of the two men who had fought the robbers off shouted.

"Mister, you ain't from here, so maybe you don't know. But the teller them robbers killed was one of the best men in this town."

"Mr. Foster taught Sunday school!" another said of the teller.

"I say we hang the bastard!"

There was the deadly click of a pistol being cocked. "And I say that if anyone touches this man, I'll kill him."

"What the hell, mister? Are you one of them?"

"No!" the young woman shouted, pointing to the two armed customers. "These two men ran the robbers off." She pointed to Casey. "And this man saved my life."

"Well, if we ain't goin' to hang this fella, what are we going to do with him?" someone said, pointing to Casey.

"You aren't going to do anything with him. He's coming along with us," the man with the gun said. Then, to Casey, he said, "Do you think you can sit a horse?"

"I think so," Casey answered.

"Then let's go."

The younger of the two men helped Casey to his feet, then, with Casey's arm around his shoulder, started toward the door.

"Hold it. You ain't takin' him out of here!"

"Yes, we are," the older of the two men said. "And if anyone sticks their head out the door to try and stop us, I'll shoot them."

The two men helped Casey out of the bank and onto a horse; then the three of them rode away.

Casey finished the story at the same time he finished with his cup of coffee. He wiped his coffee cup out, then hung it on a nail for future use.

"Here I was, a stagecoach robber and a bank robber, yet those two men took me back to a cabin in the mountains," he said. "And once we got there, why, the older one took the bullet out of my leg with all the skill of a surgeon. They tended me till I was nursed back to health.

"I figured it was all over then. I figured they were going to find someplace to turn me in to the law for the reward, and to tell the truth, I wasn't plannin' on fightin' 'em off. I'd had enough runnin'. I was ready to take my medicine."

"So did they turn you in?" Matt asked.

Casey shook his head. "No, sir, they didn't do nothin' of the sort. What they done was make me promise to leave the outlaw trail. I told 'em that was just what I was plannin' on doin'. So, they let me go, and I've been on the straight and narrow ever since." The sheriff looked pointedly at Matt. "What I've just told you could ruin me," he said. "The only person in town that knows about my past is my wife."

"I think everyone deserves a second chance," Matt said. "Let me guess. The two men were Preacher and Smoke, right?"

Casey nodded. "That's them, all right."

"Have you ever wondered about the young woman? What may have happened to her?" Matt asked.

Casey chuckled. "I don't have to wonder what happened to her. Anytime I get curious, I just go home."

"Go home?"

"Yep. I married her," Casey said with a little chuckle. "I told you that the only one in town who knew about my past was my wife."

"That's quite a story," Matt said.

Casey nodded. "And every word the gospel. All right, Matt, what is it you are wanting to know?"

"I'm looking for the town of Gehenna. Have you ever heard of it?"

"Yeah, I've heard of it."

"Do you know where it is?"

380 William W. Johnstone

"Matt, are you sure you want to go there?"

"Yeah, I do want to go there," Matt insisted. "Do you know where it is?"

"Yes, I know," Casey answered. The sheriff walked over to the wall where a map of Colorado hung.

"It's right here," he said. "On Tabequacha Creek."

"Thanks," Matt said. "I might just be wasting my time, but right now it's all I have to go on."

"You said you are looking for Clyde Payson, right?"

"Yes."

Casey nodded. "Then that's where you need to go. Payson may not be there now, but I know that he has been there. And that's as good a place to start looking for him as any."

Matt felt a charge of excitement. This was the strongest lead he had gotten yet.

"Thanks!" Matt said enthusiastically. He put his empty coffee cup down and started for the door. "And thanks for the coffee," he called back.

"Matt?"

Matt stopped and looked back toward Casey. Casey was standing there with a worried expression on his face.

"I don't have to tell you that Payson is a killer, because you already know that," Matt said. "But I'm not sure you fully understand just what sort of a person he really is. Don't expect to just be able to call him out, because men like Payson don't understand things like honor, or fair play."

"I know," Matt said.

"I'm sure you do," Casey replied. "I just felt like I should tell you anyway."

"I appreciate it," Matt said.

As Matt swung into his saddle, then rode out of town, he thought about Casey's story. Like Matt, Casey's life had been immeasurably affected by Smoke Jensen. Smoke's life had been influenced by Preacher, and Preacher's own life had been shaped by the mountain men who had found him when he was but a boy himself.

Contemplating that gave Matt a sense of continuity. He had lost one family when they were murdered by Payson and his associates. But now, in a very real sense, he felt that he was part of a new family, consisting of Preacher, Smoke, and indirectly, even Casey.

It was a good feeling knowing that he was not alone in the world.

CHAPTER 21

Bud and Fred Pease were brothers. Pug Cooper was their first cousin, and the three were on top of a mesa overlooking the trail by which anyone heading to Gehenna from Slick Rock would have to come. Bud and Fred were lying on their stomachs, keeping an eye on the trail below. Cooper was standing a few feet behind them, relieving himself.

"Ha!" Cooper laughed.

"What are you laughin' at?" Bud asked.

"I just pissed me a grasshopper offen that branch there," Cooper said. "Knocked him clear across that rock."

"Get back over here and help us keep watch. If he comes through before dark, I don't want to miss him," Bud said.

Cooper came back toward the edge of the mesa, still buttoning his pants.

"What makes you think he's comin' anyway?" Cooper asked.

"You heard 'im, same as me'n Fred did," Bud replied. "He said he was lookin' for Payson."

"So what if he is? It ain't none of our concern," Cooper said.

"Yeah? Well, it won't hurt to be gettin' ourselves on Payson's good side," Bud said. "To say nothin' of we'll prob'ly get a reward for killin' this fella."

"If he don't come before nightfall, what're we goin' to do?" Cooper asked.

"Yeah, Bud. If he don't come before nightfall, what are we goin' to do?" Fred repeated.

"We ain't got to worry none about that," Bud answered. "Here he is a'comin' now."

It was too far away to know who was sitting the horse, or even to be able to see the horse. The only thing Bud saw was the golden gleam of a little feather of dust, glowing brightly in the setting sun. Bud didn't need to see the horse or the rider. He knew that this was the man they were waiting for. Nobody else would be coming this way.

"Get ready," Bud said, jacking a round into the chamber of his rifle. "Whenever I give you the word, fire."

The other two jacked rounds into their rifles as well, then Cooper lay down and all three waited for the rider to come into range.

Matt couldn't see them, but he didn't have to. He knew they were there, and he knew they were on top of the mesa. The problem was that the mesa was at least half a mile across, and they could be anywhere on top. There was no way he could get to them without putting himself in their line of fire.

"Well, Spirit, if I can't go to them, I'll just bring them to me," he said, reining to a stop.

"What the hell is he doin'?" Cooper said. "Why don't he come on?"

"I don't know, unless he knows we are here," Bud said.

"How could he know we are here? He doesn't even know about us," Fred said.

Bud stroked his chin. "Some folks just know things," he said.

Cooper raised his rifle to his shoulder. "Well, I'm going to take a shot at him."

"No!" Bud said, pushing Cooper's rifle down. "He's way out of range. You'd just give us away if you shot at him now."

"What do you mean, give us away? I thought you said he already knew about us?"

"He might know, and he might not," Bud said. "But there's no sense in just tellin' him we are here."

"So, what are we going to do? Are we just going to ride on, or what?" Cooper asked.

"I'll be damn," Bud said.

"What? What is it?"

"He's gathering firewood," Bud said. "He's going to camp there for the night."

"Why would he camp there?" Fred asked.

"Why not? There's a creek there. He has water, grass for his horse, dried wood for his fire." Bud chuckled. "I don't know why I didn't think of this in the first place."

"Think of what? Us camping there?"

"No," Bud said. "Us waiting until he camped."

After nightfall, Matt banked the fire so that it would continue to burn, pushing out a little bubble of golden light into the darkness. Then, finding a partial log that was about his size, he spread out his bedroll, draped a blanket over the log, put his hat at the top and his boots at the bottom. Stepping away from it, he looked at his handiwork. From as close as ten feet, it looked exactly like someone sleeping.

That accomplished, Matt slipped away from his encampment, and slid down into a small depression. From there, he had a perfect view of the fire, and the dummy in the bedroll.

He waited.

It was at least an hour before he heard anything.

"Damn it!" someone hissed.

"Shut up! You want to give us away?" another voice said, also in a hiss.

"I just stepped into a cactus, I've got needles in my leg."

"Leave 'em be."

"They hurt."

"Leave 'em be. Wait till we kill this son of a bitch, then you can take all the time you want to pull 'em out."

"Will you two shut up?"

"Has he moved any?"

"No, he's still there, sleeping as sound as a log."

When Matt heard someone say he was sleeping as sound as a *log,* he had to bite his lip to keep from laughing out loud.

The three men stepped into the bubble of light and looked down at the sleeping roll.

"Hey, Bud, there's something funny here," Fred said.

"What do you mean?"

"He ain't movin' or nothin'. Hell, he ain't even breathin'."

"Don't you boys know better than to come into a camp uninvited?" Matt said, standing then.

"What the hell! Shoot! Shoot!" Bud shouted.

Suddenly, the night was lit by muzzle flashes as the three men started shooting at Matt. The three men fanned their pistols, getting off several shots, though they were shooting wildly. Flashes of light continued to illuminate the night as the guns roared and bullets whistled through the darkness.

Matt's return fire was much more deliberate, one shot for each of his adversaries. One shot for each man was all it took, as all three of them went down with fatal bullet wounds. After making certain that all three were dead, Matt pulled them over to one side of the encampment; then he went to sleep.

The next morning, in the light of day, Matt went through the pockets of each of the men. In the pocket of one of them, he found a pencil-drawn map. The map showed the location of the town of Gehenna, verifying the directions given him by Sheriff Casey.

Matt buried the three of them in a shallow grave, backtracked their trail until he found their horses, hobbled on top of the mesa.

"Well, here you are," Matt said. He walked up to the three animals and patted them on the forehead. They seemed grateful for the attention, and nuzzled him.

"It's not your fault your owners were a bunch of no-count bastards," he said as he untied the rope that was hobbling them. He gave the horses swats on their rumps, and all three took off running.

Matt watched them gallop free. He knew that if they stayed in the wild, there was plenty of grass and water for them in the valley. If they wandered into a ranch somewhere, they would be well taken care of. Either way, he had done as much as he could for them. He walked over and rubbed Spirit behind the ear.

"Don't worry about them, Spirit," Matt said. "They'll be fine."

Spirit bobbed his head up and down as if he understood what Matt was telling him.

Matt chuckled, then mounted Spirit to continue his journey, now bolstered by the fact that he had two separate sources that pointed to the same location.

The town was small and flyblown, a dried-up cow plop in the middle of sagebrush and shimmering heat waves. What breeze there was was coming from the south and it felt as if it was coming from the furnace of a locomotive.

Matt stopped to look at the sign, then smiled when he realized that, at long last, he had found the place he had been looking for.

YOU ARE ENTERING

Gehenna
POPULATION UNKNOWN
The Law Ain't Welcome.
If You Got No Business Here,
GET OUT — OR <u>GET SHOT</u>

As Matt rode down the street, he looked around at the town. There was only one street to the town, flanked on either side with a few leaning shacks that were thrown together from rough-hewn lumber, the unpainted wood turning gray and splitting. There was no railroad serving the town, no stagecoach service either. There were no signs of any kind to show that Gehenna was connected to the outside world. The little town may as well have been on the moon. It was a self-contained little community, inbred and festering.

Matt looked at the buildings. There was a rooming house, a livery stable with a smithy's shop to one side, a general store, and a saloon. He did not see any houses, nor was there a school, or a church. There was a saloon.

As he passed the saloon, a woman stepped out on the porch, smiled, and waved at Matt. Matt was surprised to see that the woman was naked from the waist up.

Although Matt had been in several towns throughout the West by now, he had never before been in a town like this. This town differed from all the others because he could see no signs of normal, domestic life here. In addition, the only women he saw were soiled doves, and they moved up and down the street freely, garishly made-up and outlandishly dressed, or in some cases, like the woman he had seen in front of the saloon, nearly undressed. He saw more than one bare breast over the course of his traverse through town.

Without commerce, most towns would be sleepy, almost deserted during the day, coming alive only at night. But though it was only mid-afternoon, Matt could already hear the sounds of revelry. There was only one saloon, but it was more than loud enough to make up for the fact that it stood all alone.

And the sounds were different, not only louder, but more out of control. There was no music, but there were screams, shouts, raucous laughter, and gunfire. Matt didn't know whether the gunshots were being fired in anger, or were part of the overall boisterous condition that prevailed.

The saloon in Gehenna had no name.

"What the hell does it need a name for?" Willie Simpson replied every time he was asked why. "The only thing you need to know is that you can get whiskey and beer here and, seeing as this is the only saloon in town, then it doesn't need a name."

Willie Simpson owned the saloon. He had never owned anything before, but he had managed a few saloons, and though he had no particular criminal past, he had been fired on at least two previous occasions for stealing from his employer.

Despite a past record of cheating his employers, Willie had never been prosecuted and never been put into jail. There had been several close calls, though, and those close calls had closed all the doors to him as far as honest employment was concerned. That being the case, there was nothing left for him but to come to Gehenna and trade with outlaws. What he had thought might be a hand-to-mouth existence proved to be a very profitable operation, cashing in on the misdeeds of others. Outlaws had no choice. They would pay Willie's inflated prices for rotgut whiskey, or they didn't drink.

Gehenna was a robbers' roost, a place of haven for men on the run. Fully three-fourths of the residents of the town were outlaws, and the remaining population made their living by serving the outlaws. Not one person in town was of sterling reputation.

Dismounting in front of the saloon, Matt stepped up on the porch, paused for a moment, then pushed his way inside. Never was the lesson on how to enter a saloon more needed than here. He moved over to the wall and stood there for a moment.

"You son of a bitch! You was holdin' that card out!" someone shouted angrily from one of the tables where a card game was in progress.

"Are you calling me a cheat?"

"Yes, you double-dealing bastard, I'm calling you a cheat!"

The accusation was followed almost immediately by the sound of a gunshot as the man who had been called a cheat drilled the other player through the chest.

The man who did the shooting was wearing a suit and vest, and no holster rig. But he was holding a smoking .41-caliber derringer in his hand. The man who had challenged him was wearing two pistols, neither of which did him any good as both were still in their holsters.

The sudden shooting interrupted the flow of conversation and laughter for but a moment. Then, when everyone realized that the excitement was over, they returned to the business at hand, leaving the dead man sprawled out on the floor.

"You was right to shoot 'im, Pippin," one of the other players said. "You wasn't cheatin'. It's sons of bitches like Miller there who cause trouble for ever'one else. Hell, if they don't know the rules, they got no business comin' to Gehenna."

"Hey, Willie, get us a new bottle of whiskey," Pippin called to the bartender.

Willie put the bottle on the bar. "Annie, take this to him," he said, calling to one of the bar girls.

Annie came over to retrieve the bottle.

"Now, mister, what can I do for you?" Willie asked, running a soiled rag over the bar just in front of where Matt was standing. There was a sour smell to the rag.

"Beer," Matt said.

"Twenty-five cents."

"Damn expensive, isn't it?"

"Find a cheaper beer in town," Willie said, and some of the others laughed.

"I'll take this one," Matt said, putting a quarter on the bar.

Willie drew a mug of beer and set it in front of him.

"You on the run, boy?" one of the men standing at the bar asked.

"Mister, I don't figure that's any of your business," Matt answered.

"Oh, it's my business all right," the man said, turning to face Matt. "You see, there's only two kinds of people come to a place like Gehenna. Those who are on the run, and bounty hunters. Now which are you?"

"I don't know," Matt replied. "I guess it depends on how much you are worth."

"What?" the man at the bar replied, surprised by Matt's answer.

"I could always use a little extra money," Matt said. "If you're worth enough, I might be tempted to do a little bounty hunting."

By now, several others in the bar had overheard Matt and the man at the bar, and they stopped their own conversations to see where this was going.

"Nah," Matt said dismissively. "Somebody like you couldn't be worth more than twenty-five dollars or so. You aren't worth it."

"Ha! He's got your number, Aimes!" someone said, and several others in the bar laughed.

"Why, you snot-nosed punk! I'm going to wipe up the floor with you!" Aimes said, rushing down the bar toward Matt.

Aimes was bigger and heavier than Matt, and figured to use his size and experience. But that same size and experience made him overconfident and as he charged Matt, Matt just stood there until the last second. Then, like a matador avoiding a charging bull, Matt stepped to one side. As Aimes rushed by him, Matt stuck out his foot and tripped Aimes, helping him along by an open-handed blow to the back of Aimes's head.

Aimes went down, crashing into a nearby chair. He got up on his hands and knees, shook his head, then stood up and looked back at Matt. He smiled at him, then raised his fists.

"Sonny, I was just going to play with you a bit," he said. "But now I'm going to hurt you, and I'm going to hurt you really bad."

Aimes rushed toward Matt, trying to catch him with a powerful swing of his right hand. Matt leaned back at the waist, avoiding the blow, then counterpunched with a hard, straight left jab. He scored well, but Aimes shook it off and swung again.

By now, people had come in from the street to watch the fight. Nobody had a favorite, nobody cared who won; they just wanted the entertainment of watching it.

The fight was one-sided in that Matt seemed able to score anytime he wanted, but so far, Aimes was brushing Matt's blows off as if they were totally ineffectual.

Then Matt hit Aimes on the nose, and he felt it go under his hand. The nose began bleeding, but even that didn't stop Aimes. He continued to smile as he swung at Matt, his teeth now red with blood. Aimes finally connected with a punch, and though Matt managed to deflect most of it, it still retained enough force to knock him down.

With a triumphant yell, Aimes picked up a chair and raised it over his head, preparing to crash it down on Matt.

Quickly, Matt rolled out of the way, then kicked out with his right foot, catching Aimes on the side of his knee. With a yell of pain and surprise, Aimes went down, then lay on the floor, groveling and grabbing his knee.

Matt stood up, looked down at him, then walked over to the bar to resume drinking his beer.

"You son of a bitch! I'm going to kill you!" Aimes yelled.

Turning, Matt saw Aimes clawing for his gun. Matt threw the beer mug and hit Aimes right between the eyes. He went out like a light.

"You should'a killed him," Willie said.

"No need to kill him now," Matt said. "I can kill him anytime I want."

CHAPTER 22

Matt recognized Poke Lawson and Syl Richards the moment they came into the saloon. He didn't know their names, but he remembered their faces. Poke and Syl had been with Clyde Payson on the day Payson killed his parents and his sister. He stared at them, holding the stare until Poke became aware.

He looked over at Matt.

"You starin' at me, mister?" Poke asked.

"Yes."

"I don't like bein' stared at."

Matt didn't respond, but neither did he look away.

"Did you hear me? I said I don't like you starin' at me."

Matt still didn't respond.

"You got somethin' stuck in your craw, boy?" Poke asked, growing more frustrated.

"Poke, what's got you all riled?" Syl asked.

"What do you mean what has me riled?" Poke asked. "Look at him, Syl. The son of a bitch just keeps starin' at us."

Now Syl turned away from the bar as well so that both he and Poke were facing Matt.

"Why are you starin' at us?" Syl asked.

"You were with him that day, weren't you?" Matt said. "Both of you were."

"We was with who? Boy, I don't know what the hell you are talking about," Syl said.

"You were with Clyde Payson and Garvey Laird."

"You are gettin' me riled, boy," Poke said. "What about Clyde Payson and Garvey Laird?"

"Do you know where they are?"

"Yeah, I know where they are. What's that to you?"

"I intend to kill them," Matt said. "Both of them."

Both Poke and Syl laughed. "You?" Poke said, pointing at Matt. "You are going to kill Payson and Laird?"

"That's right."

"What makes you think you can kill them?" Syl asked. "Why, you're so young you still got snot runnin' out of your nose."

"How old do you have to be to kill someone?" Matt asked.

"What do you mean how old do you have to be to kill someone?" Poke asked. "That question don't make sense."

"Say you are nine years old," Matt said. "Say you are nine years old and a group of low-life, yellow-bellied bastards come up on your wagon, and they kill your ma, your pa, and your sister."

A hint of recognition began to flicker across the faces of Poke and Syl.

"And say you grab your pa's rifle and get into the rocks, then kill two of the bastards who killed your family. Is nine years old too young to kill?"

"Son of a bitch!" Poke shouted, suddenly realizing what Matt was talking about. "You're that brat!"

"That's right. I'm that brat," Matt confirmed.

Both Poke and Syl made desperate grabs for their guns. Matt waited patiently until Poke and Syl had cleared the holsters with their guns.

Seeing that they had the jump on Matt before he even started his draw, Poke and Syl smiled in triumph.

The smile was short-lived, however, because before they could bring their guns to bear, Matt had his pistol out and fired twice.

The smiles were replaced by looks of shock as the two men realized that they had been shot. Poke tumbled forward, Syl fell backward. Both men were dead before they hit the floor.

Matt held the smoking pistol in his hand for a moment, then looked around the room to see if anyone else was about to challenge him.

"Son of a bitch!" Willie said, pouring himself a whiskey. "I ain't never seen nothin' like that."

"You're as fast as Angus Boone," one of the others said.

"Ain't nobody as fast as Angus Boone," one of the others said.

"I believe this fella is."

"Better not let the Gravedigger hear you saying that."

"Where is Clyde Payson?" Matt asked the bartender.

"I . . . I don't know!" Willie answered. "I admit that he does come in here from time to time, but I ain't seen him in a couple of weeks now."

Matt put his pistol in his holster, then turned his back to the bar and faced the others who were in the saloon. All were wearing looks of amazement over the shooting demonstration they had just seen.

"My name is Matt Jensen and I'm looking for Clyde Payson and Garvey Laird," Matt said.

"Mister, maybe you didn't notice, but we don't welcome the law in Gehenna. And we don't help 'em out none either."

Matt smiled. "I'm not the law," he said. "This is personal."

"Even if we know'd where he was, ain't nobody goin' to be dumb enough to tell you where to find him. I figure if he wants to get his-self found, he'll let you know where he is."

Clem Tyson and Bart Ebersole had seen the whole thing. They were sitting at a table in the back of the room when it started, and Clem started to get involved, but Bart reached out to stop him.

"This here ain't our fight," Bart said. "This is about somethin' that happened before we ever joined up with Payson."

"Yes, but don't we owe . . . ?" Clem began, but Bart interrupted him.

"We don't owe anybody nothin'."

A moment later, seeing the ease with which Matt put down both Poke and Syl, Clem was glad that Bart had stopped him.

"What do we do now?" Clem asked.

"Now we go see Payson and tell him this young punk is after him," Bart replied.

"I thought you said this wasn't our fight."

"If Payson is willin' to pay us to take a hand in it, then it will be our fight," Bart said.

Salcedo

Clyde Payson stuck his hand up under the skirt of a passing bar girl, grabbed the cheek of her butt, and squeezed.

The bar girl squealed, then laughed out loud. "Now, honey, it's not nice to get a girl all hot and bothered like that unless you intend to do something about it," she said.

"Ha, Payson, what do you think? Damn if I don't think she's in love with you," Garvey said.

"She's not in love with me," Payson said. "She's in love with the two dollars it would cost to take her up to her room."

Garvey and a couple of others who were nearby laughed out loud. They were still laughing when Clem Tyson and Bart Ebersole pushed through the front door. The two men came directly for Payson's table.

"Damn, boys, look at you," Payson said. "You look like you been rode hard and put away wet."

"They's someone after you, Payson," Bart said.

Payson laughed. "I expect there's a lot of people after me. There is a reward out, you know." He pointed to Bart and Clem. "Only, it isn't just me. The reward is for you two, Garvey, and Poke and Syl."

Clem shook his head. "It ain't for Poke and Syl," he said.

"What do you mean, it ain't for Poke and Syl? They were in Cedar Creek same as the rest of us."

"This don't have nothin' to do with Cedar Creek," Clem said. "This has somethin' to do with a wagon you'n Poke and Syl come across some years back, afore me'n Bart joined up with you."

Payson shook his head. "A wagon? What wagon? I don't know what you're talkin' about."

"Yeah, well, the man that's lookin' for you knows what he is talkin' about. And Poke and Syl know'd too, just before they was killed."

"Killed? Wait a minute, are you sayin' Poke and Syl are dead?"

"Deader'n a cow turd in the sun," Bart said.

"Who killed them? Did you get a name?"

"Yeah, his name was Jensen. Matt Jensen. And according to what Poke and Syl said just before they was killed, this here fella was at some wagon you all jumped afore me'n Clem joined up with you."

Payson shook his head. "Jensen? Jensen? No, I don't remember jumpin' no one named Jensen."

"From the way they was talkin', this fella was nine years old. He grabbed a rifle and run into the rocks, then killed two of your men."

"Son of a bitch!" Payson said, striking his open palm with a closed fist. "It's the brat! He's still alive! But his name is Cavanaugh. What's he callin' hisself Jensen for?"

"Who knows? Maybe he was adopted and changed his name. Whatever it is, he's alive, and he wants to kill you."

"Oh, he wants to kill me, does he?" Payson replied. He pulled his pistol and rotated the cylinder, checking each chamber. "Well, we'll just see about that."

"He's good, Payson," Bart said.

"Yeah? How good?"

"Fastest I ever seen," Bart said. "Except for maybe Boone."

"He's faster'n Boone," Clem said.

"What makes you say that?" Payson asked.

"Well, for one thing, he waited till both Poke and Syl had their guns drawed before he even started to draw his own gun," Clem said.

"Yeah," Bart said. "This fella just stood there, calm as you please, while Poke and Syl went for their guns. He waited till they had them both drawed before he pulled his own gun."

"Like this," Clem said, using his hand, but without a gun, to demonstrate. "Only it was about three times faster."

"All right, boys, you've made your point. He's fast. What am I supposed to do about it? You think I should run?"

"Might not be a bad idea," Clem said.

"Ain't no way I'm going to run," Payson replied.

"There's something you got to consider," Bart said.

"What's that?"

"This fella has seen you before. He knows what you look like. He could be right up on you before you even know'd you was in danger."

"I've seen him before too," Payson said.

"Yeah, when he was nine years old. I didn't see him then, but I'm pretty sure he don't look the same. As fast as he is, and you not knowin' what he looks like and all, I reckon he can kill you just about anytime he wants."

Payson poured himself a drink. With shaking hands, he lifted the glass to his lips. "Then what the hell am I supposed to do about it?" he asked.

"There is a way," Bart suggested.

Payson tossed the drink down. "What is the way?" he asked.

"You could offer money to anyone who found him for you."

"Well, now, that don't make a hell of a lot of sense, does it? I mean, I don't want the son of a bitch to find me, so why would I pay someone to find him?"

Bart smiled. "Well, not find him exactly. What I meant was, maybe you could pay somebody to kill him for you."

"If he is as fast as you say he is, where'm I goin' to find someone who is willin' to do that?"

"Me'n Clem will do it," Bart said.

"I thought you was tellin' me how fast he is. How are you and Clem goin' to go up against him if he's as fast as you say he is?"

"He is fast," Bart said. "But me'n Clem got an advantage over you, because we know what he looks like. And while he knows what you look like, he don't know us from Adam. He won't be lookin' out for us."

Payson smiled. "Yeah," he said. He nodded. "Yeah, that's right, ain't it? All right, I'll give you hunnert dollars to kill him."

"Apiece," Bart said. "There's two of us."

"No, one hundred dollars for the two of you. How you divide it up between you is up to you."

"A hunnert dollars apiece, or you can handle him yourself," Bart said.

Payson sighed, then ran his hand through his hair. "All right, a hunnert dollars apiece," he said. He pointed his finger at Bart. "But do it quick. I don't like the idea of thinkin' about that son of a bitch lurking around somewhere."

"He'll be dead within the week," Bart promised.

CHAPTER 23

Cobb's Station

Matt rode up to the hitching rail in front of the saloon, dismounted, looped the reins around the hitching rail, and went inside.

The shadowed interior of the saloon gave the illusion of coolness, though it was an illusion only. The air inside was hot, still, and redolent with the sour smells of beer and whiskey and the stench of a dozen sweating, unwashed bodies.

Matt walked over to the bar and put a nickel down.

"Beer," he said.

"You just passin' through?" the bartender asked as he set the beer on the bar.

"Sort of."

"Sort of?"

"I'm lookin' for someone."

"You're lookin' for someone, huh? Are you the law? Or are you a bounty hunter? If you are the law, I'll tell you what I know. If you are a bounty hunter, you'll get no information from me," the bartender said.

Matt shook his head. "I'm not the law or a bounty hunter," he said. "This is personal."

"Who are you lookin' for?"

"I'm looking for two people actually. One named Clyde Payson, the other Garvey Laird."

"I'll be damn," the bartender said. "You're him, aren't you?"

"Him?"

"Matt Jensen," the bartender said. "That would be your name, wouldn't it? Matt Jensen?"

"Yes, it is," Matt said, squinting his eyes. "How do you know my name?"

The bartender chuckled. "Well, hell, Mr. Jensen. You've done got famous, didn't you know that?"

"No, I don't suppose I did know it."

"Well, they ain't here."

"What?"

"Them folks you're lookin' for," the bartender said. "They ain't here."

"Would you know if they were here?"

The bartended nodded. "I reckon I'd know, seein' as they've both been here before. Payson has a scar here." He made a motion across his face with his hand. "And the other'n has half an ear gone."

"That's them."

"The story I've heard is that they kilt your ma and pa and you're out for revenge."

"That's right," Matt said, taking another swallow of his beer.

"Well, like I say, they ain't here now, but I hope you find 'em," the bartender said.

"Thanks."

Another customer stepped up to the bar requiring the bartender's attention, so he stepped way. As he did so, Matt turned his back to the bar and slowly surveyed the interior of the saloon. It was typical of many he had seen. Wide, rough-hewn boards formed the plank floor, and against the wall behind the long, brown-stained bar was a shelf of whiskey bottles, their number doubled by the mirror they stood against. Half a dozen tables, occupied by a dozen or more men, filled the room, and tobacco smoke hovered under the ceiling in a noxious cloud.

"You got anything to eat?" Matt asked when the bartender came back a moment later.

"Ham and taters," the bartender answered.

"Good enough," Matt replied. He nodded toward an empty table. "I'll be over there."

"I'll tell the kitchen," the bartender said.

"Thanks."

As the bartender left to see to his order, Matt moved over to the table to await his food. When he did so, one of the other saloon patrons left, then walked resolutely to another saloon at the far end of the street. There, two men were sitting at a table at the back of the room. They looked up as the man approached their table.

"What are you doing here, Les? Did the cards start running bad for you?"

"Bart, Clem, it's him," Les said.

"Him who?"

"Matt Jensen. He's here in Cobb's Station. He's down at the Horse Shoe."

Bart squinted at Les. "How do you know it's him? What's he look like?"

"He's a big fella, tall, with wide shoulders, narrow at the hip," Les said. "It's him, I tell you."

"You ain't never seen him before. That description could fit dozens of men."

"Maybe. But the barkeep recognized him," Les answered. "He called him out on it, and Jensen didn't deny it."

"Is he still down at the Horse Shoe?"

"He was when I left, and I figure he still is, seein' as he just ordered his supper."

"You think it's him for real?" Clem asked.

"Well, me'n you have both seen him before," Bart said. "If it ain't him for real, we'll know soon enough."

"What are we goin' to do if it is him for real?"

"We're goin' to get ourselves that two hunnert dollars," Bart said.

"The only way we can do that is by killin' him."

"That's the plan," Bart said. "There's three of us, and only one of him."

"Look here, you are the ones who are lookin' for him. Not me," Les said. "All I agreed to do was keep an eye open for him and if I seen him, come let you know. You said you would give me ten dollars. Ain't no way I'm goin' up against this man for ten dollars, even if there is three of us. Which there ain't goin' to be, 'cause I ain't goin' to do it."

"What if we give you fifty dollars?" Bart asked.

"So, what you're sayin' is, you want me to take the same risk as you and Clem, but you'll each get seventy-five dollars and I'll get fifty?"

"Well, yeah, but we are the ones that come up with the idea," Bart said.

"Fifty dollars ain't enough to get myself kilt over. Just give me my ten dollars now and I'm out of it."

"All right, but if it ain't him, you don't get your money," Bart said.

"I want the money now," Les said.

"Why should I give you any money before I know whether or not it is actually Matt Jensen?"

"'Cause if it ain't Matt Jensen, all you got to do is come down here and get your money back," Les said. "On the other hand, if it is him and he kills you, then I won't get my money."

"Yeah, well, I ain't givin' you no money now. So you just better hope we kill him instead of him killin' us," Bart said.

"Yeah? Well, to tell you the truth, I don't have much hope for that," Les said.

"How are we goin' to do it?" Clem asked. "Do you have a plan?"

"Yeah, I have a plan," Bart said. "We're going to call the son of a bitch out."

"Call him out? What are you talkin' about? Ain't no way I'm going to call him out. You seen the way he handled Poke and Syl," Clem said.

"He know'd who Poke and Syl was," Bart said. "And they didn't know who he was. And they was both standin' right together. Only now the shoe is on the other foot. We know who he is, but he don't know who we are. And we ain't goin' to be standin' together."

"Yeah, well, which one of us is goin' to call him out?" Clem asked.

Bart sighed. "It was my idea," he said. "I'll do it."

"You sure you want to do that?" Clem asked. "Go up ag'in him by yourself? You seen what happened to Poke and Syl."

"Oh, don't you worry none about that. I'm callin' him out by myself, but I ain't goin' to fight him by myself. You're goin' to be right there with me, only he ain't goin' to know it," Bart said, smiling.

"Yeah," Clem said. "Yeah, that plan might work."

Matt was halfway through his supper when he saw the two men come into the saloon. He probably wouldn't have paid any attention to them at all, had it not been for their strange behavior. They were obviously together, but as soon as they came in they split up, one going to one end of the bar and the second going to the other end of the bar.

It also seemed to Matt as if they had looked at him longer than mere curiosity about a stranger would dictate. Lessons learned from Smoke had not created in Matt the ability to perceive danger long before it was apparent. It had merely enhanced the natural instinct for survival with which Matt had been born.

To most, the fact that two men came in together, then took up positions at opposite ends of the bar, would mean nothing. But Matt became instantly aware of danger. He moved the chair back from the table and positioned himself so he could watch both men. He watched as each of the men ordered a beer, then stood at the bar, nursing his drink.

After about five minutes, Matt finished his supper. Neither of the men had tried anything, so he was beginning to think that the perceived danger was just his imagination. He walked back up to the middle of the bar and ordered another beer.

"Would you be the fella they call Matt Jensen?" the man at the right end of the bar asked.

Matt almost felt relieved that his instinct had not been a false alarm.

"I am," he replied.

"Well, Mr. Matt Jensen, my name is Bart Ebersole, and I'm callin' you out," the man at the bar said.

With that announcement, there was a sudden repositioning of all the other patrons at the bar, and even in the main part of the saloon, as everyone hurried to get out of the way should shooting begin. Matt noticed, however, that the man at the left end of the bar, the one who had come in with Bart Ebersole, had not left his position.

"Are you sure you want to go through with this, Mr. Ebersole?" Matt asked.

"Oh, yeah, I'm sure," Bart said.

"May I ask why?"

"Yeah, you can ask why. I'm told you are looking for Clyde Payson. Is that right?"

"I am," Matt said. "What does that have to do with you?"

"Let's just say that Payson is my friend, and I wouldn't want to see anything happen to him."

"Mister, if Clyde Payson is your friend, all I can say is you have a piss-poor choice of friends," Matt said.

"Now, Clem!" Bart shouted as he started his draw.

Matt sensed, more than saw, Clem drawing his gun behind him.

For just a moment, Matt was not in a saloon in a festering Western town facing down two armed and determined men. Instead, he was in the little valley alongside Smoke Jensen's mountain cabin, standing between posts that were set fifty yards apart.

There was a tin can on each of the posts, and Smoke Jensen was standing to one side, holding a rock over a pie pan.

"Are you ready?" Smoke asked.

Matt nodded. "I'm ready," he said.

Smoke opened his hand to let the rock fall and Matt drew his pistol. . . .

But Matt wasn't in that peaceful meadow, shooting at tin cans. He was in a saloon, standing between two armed men who wanted to kill him and who had stacked the deck in their favor by positioning themselves to either side of him.

Although it was Bart who shouted the order to draw, Matt sensed that Clem had begun his draw even before the call. Matt whirled to face the man behind him, surprising Clem, who thought that Matt was unaware of him. Matt fired before Clem could get off a shot. Then, as Clem's gun clattered to the floor, and blood began pooling in the hands Clem clasped over his wound, Matt whirled toward Bart. Bart was able to get off a shot, but he missed. Matt did not. Matt's bullet hit Bart right between the eyes and he fell back against the bar, then tumbled forward.

After the final crash of gunfire, there was a long, pregnant moment of absolute silence, broken only by a measured tick-tock, tick-tock from the swinging pendulum of the clock that hung on the back wall by the scarred piano.

"Holy shit," someone said quietly. A few of the others laughed nervously.

Slowly, the patrons started back toward the bar. "This here one is dead," someone said of Bart.

"Yeah, this one too," one who was standing over Clem said.

"Here," the bartender said, sliding some money across the bar.

"What is that for?" Matt asked.

"Your drinks and your supper are free," the bartender said. "Mister, you don't know it, but you just made this place famous. There will be folks comin' from all over to see where Matt Jensen took down two men who were standing on opposite sides of him. You're going to make me a ton of money."

"Thanks," Matt said, pushing the money back. "But I'd rather have some information on where to find Payson."

The bartender paused for a moment, then let out a sigh. "You might try the town of Salcedo," he said. "I heard he was there."

CHAPTER 24

Salcedo

Payson looked at his cards, then pushed a chip into the middle of the table. Not until then did he look up at the man who was standing beside him.

"What did you say your name was?"

"Les. Les Clemmons."

"Well, Les Clemmons, that's quite a tale you're telling me. You say that Bart and Clem are dead and . . ."

"I'm not just saying it. It's true. They are both dead. And they owe me ten dollars."

"Well, now, if they are dead and they owe you ten dollars, it looks like you are going to have a hard time collecting, doesn't it?" Payson called the bet on the table.

"Three aces," Garvey said, turning his cards up, then reaching for the pot.

"Full house, fives over threes," Payson replied, showing his hand as he raked in the pot.

Les cleared his throat. "I thought I might be able to collect the ten dollars from you," he said.

Payson laughed out loud. "Now, what makes you think that?"

"Because I know that Matt Jensen is coming here to look for you."

"And you think I should pay for that information?" Payson asked. "Hell, ever'body who has ever heard of Matt Jensen knows that he is lookin' for me'n Garvey. Why should I pay you for information that I already know?"

"Do you know that he is coming right here to Salcedo?" Les asked.

"No, I didn't know that," Payson answered.

"Do you know what he looks like?"

"No."

"So in other words, he could be right here in this very room, right now, and you wouldn't even know it, would you?"

Even now a new hand was being dealt, and Payson was picking it up one card at a time. He looked up at Les.

"What do you mean? What are you talking about?"

"Just what I said. He could be here right now and you would never know the difference. I could be Matt Jensen."

With that remark, Payson got up from the table so quickly that the chair tumbled over behind him. The sudden movement caught the attention of everyone else in the room, and all looked toward Payson to see him pull his gun.

"No! No! Hold it! Hold it!" Les shouted quickly, frightened that he might have pushed the game too far. "I ain't Matt Jensen!" he said, holding his hands, palms out, in front of him. "I was just tryin' to make a point, is all."

"Yeah? Well, you've got a hell of a way of makin' a point," Payson said angrily. He was still holding the pistol.

"My point is, you don't know what he looks like, and I do," Les said. "I figure that ought to be worth some money to you."

"That's worth nothing to me," Payson said. He put his pistol back in his holster. "But since you know what he looks like, maybe you can do something that will be worth money to me."

"What?"

"Find some way to make the son of a bitch go away," Payson said.

"Make him go away? What do you mean? How am I supposed to do that?"

"I don't care how you do it," Payson said. "Just do it, then come talk to me about money."

"How much money are you willin' to pay?"

"One hundred dollars," Payson said.

Les shook his head. "That ain't enough. You was going to give Bart and Clem two hundred dollars."

"But I didn't."

"That's because they didn't get the job done," Les said. "If I don't get the job done, you don't have to give it to me either. But if I do get the job done, I'm going to want two hundred dollars."

Payson nodded. "All right. Get the job done. It'll be worth two hundred dollars."

Halfway between Cobb's Station and Salcedo was the town of El Gato. One could almost say that El Gato was two towns, one half American, and one half Mexican. The north side of the town was the American side, while the Mexican population was concentrated on the south side.

Ripsawed lumber buildings made up the American town, while in the Mexican section of town, adobe buildings were laid out around a dusty plaza.

Les Clemmons rode into the south side of town, aware that he was being stared at by people who wondered what an Anglo was doing there. He tied his horse off at a hitch rail in front of Rosita's Cantina. A woman's high, clear voice was singing, and that and the accompanying guitar music spilled out through the beaded doorway. Les pushed through the hanging beads, then stepped inside.

He wasn't concerned about being accepted here. He knew that Americans often came to the Mexican side for tequila, or women, or even to eat the spicy Mexican food. Because of that, he raised little attention as he stepped up to the bar and ordered tequila. Pouring salt on his hand, he licked it off, then tossed down the fiery liquid as he examined the patrons of the cantina. He had an idea how he was going to collect the two hundred dollars from Payson, and the idea started here.

A woman, wearing a red dress that was cut so low that her breasts threatened to spill out, came up to him. She was dark and sultry-looking, and she smiled up at him.

"Do you want a woman, Señor? *La mayoria de los anglos que vienen a Rosita's vienen para buscar a una mujer.*"

"Maybe most of the Anglos come looking for women, but I'm looking for men."

The woman got a shocked look on her face. "You don't like women? You like men?"

"What?" Les asked. Then he realized what she was saying. "No! No, it's nothing like that. I need to hire some men to do a job for me."

"What kind of job?"

"I need someone who is very good with a knife. A *cuchillo*," he said, using the Spanish word to make certain she understood.

"I think you want Manuel maybe," the woman said.

"Is Manuel in here?"

"*Sí.*" She pointed. "That is Manuel."

Manuel was standing at the far end of the bar. He was almost a head taller than most of those around him. His hat was pushed back so that Les could see his face. He was standing alone, and the expression on his face gave a hint as to why. He looked like someone who was angry with the world.

Manuel also had a large bowie knife protruding from a sheath that he wore across his chest. Only someone who was very good with a knife would dare to wear it in such a fashion.

"Thanks," Les said. He finished his drink, put it down, then walked over to confront Manuel.

"Manuel?"

"How do you know my name?" Manuel asked.

"How I know your name doesn't matter," Les said. "What matters is the fifty dollars I am willing to pay you, if you are interested."

"*Sí,* I am interested."

"You haven't asked what the job is."

"You will pay fifty dollars?"

"Yes."

"I do not care what the job is, Señor. If you will pay fifty dollars, I will do it."

"We need to find one more person," Les said.

Matt had come into El Gato earlier in the day and, after boarding his horse, spent most of the afternoon in the saloon, playing cards and listening in on conversations for any clues that might help him find Clyde Payson. It was dark when he finally left the saloon and started down the street toward the hotel.

There were no street lamps in this small town, but a full moon and a few dim squares of light splashing through open windows kept the street from being in total darkness. Back in the saloon Matt had just left, the piano player was hard at work, his discordant and cacophonous attempt at music spilling out into the street.

From the shadows of the Mexican quarters on the south side of town, a strumming guitar and a trumpet competed with each other, and though they were playing different songs, they somehow seemed to blend together.

He heard a dog's insistent yap.

A baby's cry joined the mix.

* * *

"That's him," Les whispered to the two Mexicans he had hired.

"That's the gringo you want killed?" Manuel asked.

"Yes."

"Why would a gringo pay me to kill another gringo?"

"Can you do it?"

"*Sí*, it will be easy."

"Then do it. It doesn't matter why."

Matt felt the assassins coming for him before he heard them, and he heard them before he saw them. Two men suddenly jumped from the dark shadows between the buildings, making wide slashes with their knives. But that innate sense that allowed him to perceive danger when there was no other sign had saved his life, for he was moving out of the way at the exact moment the two men were starting their attacks. Otherwise, their knives, swinging in low, vicious arcs, would have disemboweled him.

Despite the quickness of his reaction, however, one of the knives did manage to cut him, and as Matt went down into the dirt, rolling to get away from them, the flashing blade opened up a long wound in his side. The knife was so sharp and wielded so adroitly that Matt barely felt it. He knew, however, that the knife had drawn blood.

One of the assassins moved in quickly, thinking to finish Matt off before he could recover. But Matt twisted around on the ground, then thrust his feet out, catching the assailant in the chest with a powerful kick and driving him back several feet. The second one darted in on the heels of the first, but by now Matt had managed to pull his own knife and he held it out low, with the blade parallel to the ground, letting his attacker impale himself on it.

He heard the attacker grunt in pain and surprise, then give out a long, life-surrendering sigh. Matt twisted the knife in him so that, as the attacker fell, his own weight against the knife opened him up.

"*Mamá de Dios, usted me ha matado, señor,*" the Mexican said, trying to hold his guts in as he collapsed in the dirt. "You have killed me," he repeated in English.

The first attacker, thinking he had the advantage, made another wide, slashing thrust. He was good, skilled and agile, but Matt managed to twist away from him. As he twisted away from his assailant, Matt's knife was not in position to counterthrust, but his left hand was. Matt thrust his left hand out, using stiffened fingers to gouge out both eyes.

"Aiiyee!" the assailant screamed, dropping his knife and reaching up to his face. Mucus and eye matter streamed through his spread fingers, and Matt knew that he had blinded him. This fight was over.

Matt's assailant stood in the middle of the street, screaming in pain and terror.

"*Soy ciego! Soy ciego!*"

By now several of the townspeople, having heard the commotion, had come out into the street to see what was going on. They had watched in awe as Matt defended himself against two attackers.

"What's that Mexican fella sayin'?" one of the onlookers asked.

"He says he is blind."

"I'll be damned."

Across the street, in the darkness afforded by the unlit shadows, Les stood between the apothecary and the leather-goods store. Jacking a round into his rifle, he raised it to his shoulder and aimed at Matt, but before he could pull the trigger, those who had poured into the street crowded around, blocking his target.

"Damn it!" Les said under his breath. "Get out of the way!"

More people arrived, pouring out of other saloons, and even coming from the houses. With a sigh of disgust, Les lowered his rifle.

"I'll give you this, Matt Jensen," he said under his breath. "You are one hard son of a bitch to kill."

Matt felt the nausea beginning to rise. Bile surged to his throat. Light-headed now, he turned and staggered back toward the saloon. He was barely aware of those who had come into the street to watch the fight, barely aware of them moving aside, like the sea parting for Moses, as he walked back to the saloon. Reaching the front of the saloon, he grabbed the overhang pillar for support and pulled himself up onto the plank porch, then pushed in through the door to stand in the brightness. It was not until he was inside, in the bright light, that the severity of his wound could be seen.

One of the bar girls, seeing the bloody apparition standing there, screamed. All conversation came to a halt, and a dead silence hung over the saloon as if it were something palpable. Everyone stared at him, their eyes wide and their mouths open in shock.

Matt stood just inside the doorway, ashen-faced and holding his hand over a wound that spilled bright red blood between his fingers. He looked around the room for just a moment, then with effort, walked over to the bar.

"Whiskey," he ordered.

"Mr. Jensen, you better let a doctor look at that wound you got there," the bartender said. By now Matt's side was drenched with blood from his wound, and the blood was beginning to soak into the wide-plank floor.

"I'll be fine," Matt said. Then his eyes rolled back in his head and he crumpled to the floor, passed out cold.

CHAPTER 25

When Matt awakened, he experienced a moment of confusion as to where he was. But when he moved, a sharp stitch in his side reminded him of what had happened the night before and he reached down to feel the bandage. He was gratified to see that there had been no more bleeding since last night.

Matt looked around at his surroundings. He knew that he was in a hotel room, but he wasn't quite sure how he got there. He didn't know exactly what time it was, but he could tell by the texture of the sunlight streaming in through the window that it was still fairly early in the morning. He also saw his clothes, clean and neatly folded, lying on a chair by the window.

He thought back to last night and remembered the knife fight he had had with the two Mexicans. He didn't know who they were, nor did he know why they had attacked him, though he suspected it might have something to do with Clyde Payson. He had heard that Payson had put out a reward for him, and the incident last night seemed to validate that.

Matt was startled when the door to his room opened. Thinking his gun belt and pistol were hanging from the headboard of the bed, he reached for his weapon.

It wasn't there!

He was about to get out of bed, despite the pain in his side, when the person who opened the door stepped into his room.

It was Tamara!

"Tamara!" he gasped in surprise. "What are you doing here?"

"You're awake!" she said happily.

"Well, yes. It's morning. I normally wake up in the morning," Matt replied. "But you didn't answer my question. What are you doing here?"

"Why, I'm here to take care of you, of course," Tamara answered. "I came as soon as I heard you had been wounded."

The expression on Matt's face reflected his confusion. "How could that be possible?" he asked. "I was just wounded last night."

"Last night?" Tamara said. She laughed. "Silly boy. Do you actually think you were wounded last night?"

"Yes, of course. I had just come out of the saloon when a couple of . . ." Matt stopped in mid-sentence.

Suddenly a jumbled series of scenes began tumbling through Matt's mind.

He recalled the fight.

He remembered going into the saloon.

A worried-looking doctor had cleaned his wound and sewn it shut.

Some men carried him to the hotel room.

Sometime during all this, Tamara showed up, and now, as he thought back on it, he could recall seeing her face many times, worried as she sat on the edge of the bed, looking down at him, sometimes washing his face with a damp cloth, other times stroking his cheek. Sometimes she kissed him.

He looked up at her, and saw that she had been watching him go through the thought process.

"How long have I been here?" Matt asked.

"Ten days."

"Ten days?" Matt gasped. "Have I been out all that time?"

"Not entirely," Tamara said. "You've been in and out of it, and a few times you have even recognized me."

"Really? Have we—uh—have we been together?" Matt asked.

Tamara laughed. "You haven't exactly been in the mood," she said. "Why do you ask? Are you in the mood now?"

"I might be," Matt said.

"Oh, my," Tamara said. "Then I would say you are just about fully recovered."

Tamara walked over to the door, opened it, looked outside, then closed and locked it. When she returned to the bed, she began removing her dress. She lay it neatly on a chair, then stepped out of her petticoat. Next came the camisole, exposing her rather small but well-formed breasts.

"You know, when I first started in this business, the way I was able to get through it was to imagine that the man I was with was you," she said.

"How did that help?" Matt asked. "You remembered me as a twelve-year-old boy."

"Maybe it was my fantasy of what you would become," Tamara said. "And I was right, because look at you now."

Smiling, Tamara started to step out of her bloomers.

Suddenly, there was the tinkling sound of broken glass as something whizzed through the window, followed by a solid "thock," like the sound of a hammer hitting a nail.

Tamara pitched forward, even as a mist of blood was spraying out from the back of her head.

"No!" Matt shouted in a loud, grief-stricken voice.

Across the street from the hotel, on the roof of the hardware store behind the false front, Les saw the woman step into his line of fire just as he pulled the trigger.

"No!" he said, ironically matching Matt.

"Son of a bitch! What did you move for!" Les asked, jacking another round into the rifle. He fired a second time.

Matt heard the second bullet come through the window and slam into the wall behind the bed. This bullet missed him by no more than an inch.

Rolling out of bed, Matt looked around for his pistol, then saw that it was on the chair under his clothes. He crawled over to the chair, pulled his pistol, then crawled to the window.

When Matt looked down onto the street, he saw two men standing in front of the tobacco store. They had obviously heard the shots fired, and were looking up. One was pointing toward the roof of the hardware store.

Yes, he thought. That made sense. The hardware store was directly across the street from the hotel. If someone wanted to shoot into the second floor of the hotel, that would be the best place to shoot from.

At first, Matt saw nothing. Then, something caught his attention on the wall of the feed store that was next to the hardware store. The morning sun was at exactly the right angle to project shadows from the roof of the hardware store, and there he saw the shadow of the shooter.

Using the shadow as a guide, Matt aimed at the false front. He knew that it consisted of thinly cut boards, and he aimed at a point where he calculated the shooter to be. He fired three times in quick succession.

He didn't need the shadow to know he had been successful. He saw the shooter fall off the roof, then land hard on the ground, where he lay without moving. Moving away from the window, he went back into the room to check on Tamara.

There was nothing to check. Tamara was dead.

Salcedo

Clyde Payson threw a whiskey bottle against the wall of the saloon.

"What the hell?" he shouted in anger. "Is he a ghost or something? Is there nobody who can kill him?"

"I can kill him," someone said.

Payson looked toward the door at the man who had just come into the saloon. He was dressed all in black, except for a turquoise and silver band around his short-crowned black hair.

"Boone?" Payson said.

Boone nodded.

"Don't get me wrong. I would welcome anyone killing him. But why do you want to kill him?"

"Because I can," Boone said.

Payson chuckled. "Because you can," he said. He nodded. "Yes, yes, I really believe you can kill him. And if you want to kill him just because you can, well, that's a good enough reason for me."

"And for the one thousand," Boone added.

"What? What one thousand dollars?"

"The thousand dollars you are going to pay me to kill Matt Jensen," Boone said.

"I don't know," Payson said. "One thousand dollars is a lot of money."

"How much is your life worth to you?" Boone asked.

"What do you mean?"

"If I don't kill Matt Jensen, he will kill you. Isn't your life worth one thousand dollars to you?"

"Yes, of course it is. But where am I supposed to get one thousand dollars?" Payson asked.

"That's your problem."

"What if you kill him, and I haven't been able to come up with one thousand dollars?"

"Then it will still be your problem, because I will kill you," Boone said in a matter-of-fact voice.

Payson thought for a moment, then nodded. "All right," he said. "Kill him."

CHAPTER 26

Salcedo

"Yeah, he was here," the bartender told Matt. "Matter of fact, he hung around here for several weeks. But he left a few days ago."

"Do you know where he went?"

"Why should I tell you that?" the bartender replied. "If I tell you where he went and word gets back to Payson that I told you, why, my life wouldn't be worth a plugged nickel."

"It won't make any difference if word gets back to him," Matt said.

"Why would you say that?"

"Because I'm going to kill him."

"So you say. But people have been trying to kill him for a lot of years, and he ain't dead yet," the bartender said.

At that moment a boy, no older than twelve, came into the saloon.

"Here, what you doing here, boy?" the bartender scolded. "This is no place for kids."

"Is there a Mr. Matt Jensen in here?" the boy asked.

"I'm Matt Jensen," Matt said.

"He said if you don't come, he will shoot another one."

"What? Who said that? What do you mean, he will shoot another one?"

"Another kid," the boy said. "Like he shot me," the boy added in a voice that was strained with pain. It wasn't until then that Matt noticed the boy was holding his hand over his arm. Blood was just beginning to ooze through his fingers.

"Quick! Somebody get a doctor," Matt said. He pointed to the bartender. "You, give me a clean towel and a bottle of whiskey."

"What the hell?" the bartender said. "Who did this to you, kid? Who shot you?" the bartender asked as he pulled a clean towel from under the bar.

"Angus Boone shot me," the boy said. Matt was the first one to him, and he sat the boy down in a chair. "Boone is down at the school. Mr. Jensen, he said he was going to shoot someone every ten minutes until you come out into the street to meet him."

"Boone!" someone said. "Did you say Boone shot you?"

"Yes, sir. Angus Boone."

"That's the fella they call the Gravedigger," another said.

The boy looked at Matt. "He's callin' you out, Mr. Jensen. He said he would meet you in the middle of the street."

"You ain't a'goin' to do that, are you, Jensen?" one of the patrons asked. "I mean, this is Angus Boone we are talking 'bout. Nobody is crazy enough to go up against Angus Boone, face-to-face."

"Looks to me like Jensen don't have much choice," the bartender said. "If he don't, Boone will shoot another kid."

"Oh, I doubt that. Not even Boone is that mean."

"Yeah, he is that mean," Matt said as he poured whiskey onto the boy's wound, then wrapped the towel around it. "He shot this boy just to prove that he would do what he said he was going to do. What's your name, son?"

"Cole," the boy answered. "Cole Virdin."

"Cole, you are a brave young man," Matt said. The doctor arrived then, his rapid arrival facilitated by the fact that his office was just next door. He was walking quickly and carrying his bag.

"God in heaven," he said when he saw Cole. "What kind of mad man would shoot a boy?"

"It's Boone, Doc," one of the patrons told him. "Angus Boone. He's down at the school and he says he's goin' to shoot a kid ever' ten minutes unless Matt Jensen meets him on the street."

Matt pulled his pistol and checked all the chambers; then he put his pistol back in his holster.

"You aren't actually going to go out in the street and meet him, are you?" the doctor asked.

"Doesn't look to me as if I have any choice, unless you want to start treating a bunch of kids for gunshot wounds," Matt said. "And he might even kill the next one."

The doctor sighed. "You are right," he said. "I guess you've got to do it."

416 William W. Johnstone

Matt smiled. "I was sort of hoping someone would talk me out of it," he said in an attempt at a joke. No one laughed.

Matt looked back at Cole. "Any of your family still at the school?" he asked.

"Yes, sir, my sister is," Cole answered.

"I hope your sister knows what a brave young man you are," Matt said.

Matt pushed through the batwing doors and walked outside. He started up the street toward the school, which was at the far end of the street from the saloon.

As soon as Matt left the saloon, several other patrons left as well, and they started running up the boardwalks along either side of the street, spreading the word.

"There's going to be a shoot-out!"

"Boone has called Matt Jensen out!"

"Boone and Jensen are meetin' head to head!"

The crowd of onlookers grew larger as Matt walked toward the school, though the spectators were all very careful to stay well back from the street.

"Boone!" Matt shouted. "Angus Boone!"

All eyes were on the school building at the far end of the street.

"Boone, it's Matt Jensen. You asked for me. Here I am!"

The front door of the schoolhouse opened, and Boone stepped out onto the front stoop. He stood there for a moment, then started walking toward Matt.

"Well," Boone said. "I've got to hand it to you, Jensen. I didn't think you would face me."

"You were shooting kids," Matt replied. "I didn't have much choice."

Boone chuckled. "Yeah, I thought that might get your attention."

"I have a question," Matt said.

"Go ahead and ask," Boone replied. "I wouldn't want to see a man die without getting his curiosity satisfied."

"Why?"

"Why what?"

"Why are you calling me out?" Matt asked. "Surely you aren't just trying to satisfy yourself that you are faster than I am."

"That question never crossed my mind," Boone replied. "I know I'm faster than you."

"Then why this?"

"You are looking for a man named Clyde Payson, aren't you?"

"Yes."

"Mr. Payson is paying me one thousand dollars to make sure you go away."

Matt whistled. "A thousand dollars?"

"A thousand dollars," Boone said.

"That's a lot of money. He must be running scared."

"I reckon you could say that he is running scared," Boone said. "You seem pretty determined to kill him. And from what I've heard, you have already taken care of several people he has sent out to stop you."

"That's right."

"And to think that it's all going to come to an end right here on Front Street in the little town of Salcedo," Boone said.

Matt had been watching Boone very closely, all the while monitoring half-a-dozen different things: the tone of his voice, the rhythm of his breathing, the look in his eyes, and the set of his shoulders. As a result, he was aware the instant Boone started his draw.

Matt started his draw at the same instant, and he had his pistol out and the hammer back by the time Boone had his own gun out. Matt pulled the trigger an instant before Boone, hitting Boone in the chest as Boone pulled the trigger on his gun.

Boone's shot went into the dirt. He tried to raise his gun hand for a second shot, but suddenly found that his arm weighed several hundred pounds. He dropped his gun into the dirt, slapped both hands over the wound, then sank to his knees.

"Who would have believed it?" he said aloud. He coughed, and his lips were spattered with blood. "Who would have . . . ?" He fell forward, facedown, into the street.

"Son of a bitch!" someone said loudly. "Did you see that? Son of a bitch!"

Matt stood over Boone's body for a long moment, making certain that he was dead, then kicking Boone's gun away. He returned his pistol to his holster and walked back to the saloon, trailed by half the town. He was followed into the saloon as well; then the tension broke as everyone started shouting at once, ordering drinks and giving eyewitness reports on what they had seen to other eyewitnesses who had seen the same thing.

"Where's the boy?" Matt asked the bartender. "Where's Cole?"

"The doc took him home," the bartender replied.

"Is he going to be all right?"

"The doc said he thought he would be."

"Good."

"I didn't think you could do it," the bartender said. "I seen it all through the window. I sure didn't think you could do it."

The bartender put a beer in front of Matt. "It's on the house," he said.

"Thanks," Matt said, lifting the beer to his lips.

"Dolores Mountains," the bartender said.

"What?"

"You're lookin' for Clyde Payson?"

"Yes."

"He has a cabin up in the Dolores Mountains, about ten miles east of here. Just follow Disappointment Creek until it ends. His cabin is the only one there."

"You are sure he's there?"

The bartender nodded. "Yes, I'm sure," he said. "He and Garvey hired our bouncer as a bodyguard."

"A bodyguard?"

"Yes. He has two bodyguards actually. Ben, who worked here as a bouncer, and a fella by the name of Elmer Gleeson. Gleeson used to be a deputy sheriff till he got hisself fired for stealin'."

"Gleeson sounds like Payson's kind of man," Matt said.

"Yeah, well, Ben ain't no better. I fired Ben for stealin' from drunks."

"I appreciate you telling me where to find him," Matt said.

"If I hadn't seen the way you handled Boone, I never would've told you. But I figure you might just be the kind who could handle Payson and his bodyguards. And if it turns out that you can't, well, just don't let him find out I'm the one who told you."

"He won't find out," Matt promised.

CHAPTER 27

Ben Rogers and Elmer Gleeson were standing at the last bend in the creek when they saw the rider approaching.

"Who's that comin'?" Gleeson asked, cocking the rifle and lifting it to his shoulder.

"No, no, hold your fire," Ben said. "That's Lew. He's bringin' us provisions."

Gleeson nodded and lowered his rifle. They watched Lew as he rode in. He nodded to them, then proceeded on up to the little cabin that was some fifty yards back from where the lookouts were stationed.

Garvey opened the door to the cabin and let Lew in. Payson was lying on one of the bunks with his hands laced behind his head.

"Did you bring whiskey and vittles?" Payson asked.

"Yeah, it's all in this rucksack," Lew said.

"How much?"

"Twenty dollars?"

"Twenty dollars?" Payson said angrily, sitting up quickly. "What do you mean twenty dollars? You can't have more'n five dollars worth of goods in that sack."

"Five dollars in town, twenty dollars out here," Lew said.

"When this is all over, there's goin' to be some settlin' up done," Payson said. "You understand me? There's goin' to be some settlin' up."

"Yeah, I understand you," Lew said.

"What's happenin' with Boone and Jensen?" Payson asked. "Have you heard anything?"

"No."

"You will soon," Payson said.

"And once Boone kills Jensen, we'll be taking care of people who tried to cheat us," Garvey said, glaring at Lew.

"You want the vittles and whiskey or not?" Lew asked.

"I asked you to bring 'em out here, didn't I?"

"Twenty dollars," Lew said again.

"Give him twenty dollars, Garvey," Payson said.

"We ain't got hardly any money left," Garvey complained.

"Give him twenty dollars," Payson said again. "Right now, we got no other choice." He pointed to Lew. "I will remember this," he said.

Lew took the twenty dollars, then remounted and started out of the little valley. Ben and Gleeson waved at him as he passed, and he stopped to speak to them.

"You boys here protecting Payson, are you?" he asked.

"No, we're just out here fishing," Ben answered, and Gleeson chuckled.

"Well, you can tease if you like, but I'd sure as hell never put my life on the line for any son of a bitch like Payson."

"Ha! We're just here to collect the money is all," Gleeson said. "Haven't you heard? Boone is goin' after this Matt Jensen fella. Once Boone gets done with him, our job will be over."

"Once Boone gets done with him, huh?" Lew said. He laughed.

"What is it? What are you laughing about?"

"Matt Jensen killed Boone in a shoot-out this morning."

"What? Impossible! I don't believe it. Who told you that?"

"Nobody told me," Lew said. "I seen it myself. They faced each other on the street, Boone went for his gun first, and Jensen still beat him. Killed him with one shot."

"What the hell? What kind of man is this Matt Jensen?" Ben asked.

"He's not the kind you want to mess with," Lew said. "Especially for some son of a bitch like Payson."

"You know what, Gleeson, he's right," Ben said. "What are we doing out here?"

"We can't leave now, we haven't been paid yet," Gleeson replied.

"What good is the money going to do us if we're dead?" Ben asked. "And even if he don't kill us, he'll kill Payson. How are we going to collect from a dead man?"

Gleeson looked back toward the cabin, then over toward the horses. He nodded. "You're right," he said. "Let's get the hell out of here."

* * *

From his position on a hill, looking down at the head of Disappointment Creek, Matt watched the brief confab between Lew, Ben, and Gleeson. Then he saw Ben and Gleeson go over to their horses, mount them, and ride away with Lew. That left the cabin undefended, except for whoever was inside.

"Jerky and hardtack," Garvey complained. "We paid twenty dollars for jerky and hardtack."

"It'll keep us from starvin' to death," Payson said. "And we won't have to be here much longer. I figure Boone is going to kill Jensen pretty soon now; then it'll all be over."

"What if Jensen kills Boone?"

Payson laughed. "Are you joking? There's not a man alive who could kill Boone."

"Yeah, well, that's good for us now," Garvey said. "But what are we going to do when Boone comes after us wantin' his thousand dollars?"

"I've got a thousand dollars," Payson said.

"What? Where did you get a thousand dollars?"

"You remember the bank we robbed back in Cedar Creek?"

"Yes, of course I remember."

"I held a thousand dollars back from the split."

"What? You mean you cheated the rest of us?" Garvey said angrily.

"Hold on, hold on there!" Payson said, holding up his hand. "I held it back for an emergency," he said. "This is an emergency. If I didn't have the money, Boone would kill us both."

Garvey paused for a moment, then he nodded. "Yeah," he said. "Yeah, I guess you're right."

"Damn right I'm right." Payson took a strip of jerky, then cut it lengthwise into two pieces. "Take this out to Ben and Gleeson."

Nodding, Garvey took the two strips of dried meat, then started up the creek bank toward the bend where the two guards had been posted. When he didn't find them where he expected them to be, he looked around for a moment, then called out to them.

"Ben! Gleeson! I've got your lunch here!" he shouted. "Ben! Gleeson! Where are you? Why aren't you where you are supposed to be?"

"They've run out on you, Garvey!" Matt called.

"What? Who's there?"

Matt stood up on the rock, then looked down at Garvey.

"You know who I am," Matt said. "I've changed a little since the last time you saw me, but you know who I am."

"No!" Garvey shouted in terror. He turned and started running back toward the cabin. "He's here! He's here!" he shouted. "Payson, he's here! Matt Jensen is here!"

Matt climbed down from the hill, then walked, almost casually, toward the cabin. He heard the glass break, then saw a rifle stick out through the window. The rifle barked, and a bullet whizzed by. Matt jumped down behind a rock outcropping.

Matt fired at the cabin a couple of times. Then he followed a ravine that took him around behind the cabin. He heard periodic firing coming from the cabin, and realized that they were still shooting at the rock where he had been.

When he reached the back of the cabin, he crept up to the back door. There were no windows back here, so he knew he couldn't be seen.

"What happened to the son of a bitch?" he heard one voice ask. "Where did he go?"

"He's still behind that rock," the other voice answered.

"How come he ain't showed hisself?"

"He's waitin' for us."

"Yeah? Well, the son of a bitch can wait till hell freezes over. We got enough vittles and water to wait him out."

"We just goin' to stay here?"

"You want to go out, you go out. I'm just going to stay here. Hell, there's two of us, and only one of him. We can take turns sleeping, he can't. We got the advantage."

"Yeah," the other voice said. "Yeah, you're right. We'll just wait him out."

Matt jumped up to grab the eaves that protruded just over the door. Then, using them as the pivot point, he swung out, then back in, bending his legs at the knees as he did so. He thrust his legs forward, and kicked the door open.

"What the hell!" Payson shouted, turning around.

"Drop it!" Matt said, pointing his gun at the two men. "Both of you!"

Payson dropped his gun and Garvey followed suit.

"Now what?" Payson asked. "Are you going to shoot us?"

"I had planned on it," Matt replied. "But shooting you is too good for you. I think I'd rather take you back and watch you hang."

"It's a long way back," Payson said. "Do you expect us to just go along quietly?"

"Whether you go quietly or not, it makes no difference to me," Matt said.

"It makes no difference, huh?" Payson said. "Well, maybe there's something you haven't thought about. You've got to sleep sometime. What makes you think we won't run away?"

"Good question," Matt said.

Suddenly, and totally unexpectedly, Matt fired two shots, hitting each man in the knee. They cried out in shock and pain, and started hobbling around.

"You crazy sonofabitch, you shot us in the knee!" Payson said.

"Yeah, I did," Matt answered calmly. "Let's get going now."

County Courthouse, Cedar Creek, Colorado

"Here ye, hear ye, hear ye! The sentencing is about to be announced. All rise for the Honorable Felix J. Crane, presidin'," the bailiff shouted. "Everybody stand respectful."

The Honorable Felix J. Crane came out of a back room. After taking his seat at the bench, he adjusted the glasses on the end of his nose, then cleared his throat.

"Would the bailiff please bring the accused before the bench?"

The bailiff, who was leaning against the side wall, spat a quid of tobacco into the brass spittoon, then walked over to the table where the defendants, Clyde Payson and Garvey Laird, sat next to their court-appointed lawyer.

"Get up, you two," he growled. "Present yourself before the judge."

Payson and Garvey were handcuffed, and had shackles on their ankles. They limped up to stand, as best they could on busted knees, in front of the judge.

"You two have been tried by a jury of your peers, and found guilty of the murders of Miss Margaret Miller, a beloved teacher of our children, as well as little Holly McGee, one of her students. For these two murders, you are sentenced to hang by your neck until you are dead," Judge Crane said. He cleared his throat, then looked over at Matt Jensen, who was present in the courtroom.

"Mr. Jensen, I regret that we could not find these two despicable creatures guilty of the murder of your family. While I have no doubt as to your veracity, the court has only your account of the incident, and that account is your memory from when you were nine years old. However, though we could not find them guilty for that particular crime, I hope you can find some comfort in knowing that these two men will hang. And they will hang because you have brought them to justice."

"I am satisfied, Your Honor," Matt said. He looked at Payson and Garvey. "You two will be dead," he said. "And dead is dead."

"You go to hell, Matt Jensen!" Payson shouted. "Do you hear me? You go to hell!"

"Silence that man!" Judge Crane said, banging his gavel.

The bailiff signaled two deputies, and they stepped up quickly to gag Payson.

"It is interesting that you would mention hell, Mr. Payson," Judge Crane said. "Because, although I do not have the power to sentence you to hell, I will soon be passing you on to a higher judge who does have that power. And there is no doubt in my mind but that you will suffer eternal torment for the misery you have caused others during your stay on earth.

"This court is adjourned."

As Matt rode away from Cedar Creek, he felt a sense of closing the book on the part of his life that he had shared with his mother, father, and sister.

"Pa," he said, speaking aloud. "I hope you know that I meant no disrespect to you by droppin' your name and takin' up the name of Jensen. Finding the son of a bitch that killed you, Ma, and Cassie gives me some rest now, and I hope it does for you as well."

It was getting colder, and Spirit blew clouds of vapor that drifted away in feathery wisps. Matt headed south. He didn't care much for the cold.

PART THREE
LUKE JENSEN: BOUNTY HUNTER

PROLOGUE

A rifle bullet smacked off the top of the log and sprayed splinters toward Luke Smith's face. He dropped his head quickly so the brim of his battered black hat protected his eyes. A splinter stung his cheek close to his neatly trimmed black mustache.

Luke looked into the sightless, staring eyes of the dead man who lay next to him. "Those amigos of yours are getting closer with their shots, José. Too bad for you that you're not alive to watch them kill me. Reckon you probably would've enjoyed that."

José Cardona didn't say anything. A bullet hole from one of Luke's Remingtons lay in the middle of his forehead, surrounded by powder burns. Most of the back of his head was gone where the slug had exploded out.

More shots rang out from the cabin about a hundred yards away, next to the little creek at the bottom of the slope. The sturdy log structure had been built for defense, with thick walls and numerous loopholes where rifle barrels could be stuck out and fired.

Luke had no idea who had built the cabin. Probably some old fur trapper or prospector. Those mountains in New Mexico Territory had seen their fair share of both.

Currently, it was being used as a hideout for the Solomon Burke gang. Luke had been on the trail of Burke and his bunch for several weeks. There was a $1500 bounty on Burke's head and lesser amounts posted on the half-dozen owlhoots who rode with him. If Luke was able to bring in all of them, it would be a mighty nice payoff for him.

Unfortunately, it didn't look like things were going to work out that way. Luke had tracked the gang to the cabin and had been crouched in the timber up on the hill overlooking the creek, trying to figure out his next move, when someone tackled him from behind, knocking him out into the open. They rolled down the hill together, locked in a desperate struggle, even as the man screeched a warning to the others at the top of his lungs.

The big log, which had also rolled about twenty feet down the hill when it toppled sometime in the past, brought the two men to an abrupt halt as they slammed into it. Luke barely had time to recognize the bandito as Cardona from drawings he had seen on wanted posters when he realized the man was about to bring a knife almost as big as a machete down on his head and split his skull wide open.

Without having to think about what he was doing, Luke palmed out one of his Remingtons, eared back the hammer as he jammed the muzzle against Cardona's forehead, and pulled the trigger.

The point-blank shot blew Cardona away from him, and the dead outlaw flopped onto the ground behind the log. Luke rolled over and started to get up, when a bullet had whipped past his ear. Instinct made him drop belly down behind the log. A second later, more rifles opened up from the cabin and a volley of high-powered slugs smashed into the fallen tree. If it hadn't been there to give him cover, Luke would have been shot to pieces.

As it was, he was pinned down on the slope. The trees above him were too far away. If he stood up and made a dash for them, Burke and the others in the cabin would riddle him with rifle fire. Trying to crawl up there would make him an even easier target. The grass was too short to conceal him.

He was stuck, with a dead man for company and only a matter of time until some of those varmints slipped out of the cabin and circled around to catch him in a crossfire. Luke's craggy face was grim, in spite of the ghost of a smile lurking around his mouth.

In plenty of tight spots during the years he'd spent as a bounty hunter, he had always pulled through somehow. But he had known his luck was bound to run out someday.

After all, he had already cheated certain death once. A man didn't get too many breaks like that.

From time to time, he rose up long enough to throw a couple shots at the cabin, but not really expecting to do any damage—too long range for a handgun. His nature wouldn't let him die without a fight, though. He could put up a better one, if his Winchester wasn't still in the saddle boot strapped to his horse, a good hundred feet upslope. Might as well have been a hundred miles.

"Blast it, José, I must be getting old to let a clumsy galoot like you sneak up on me," Luke said, keeping his eyes on the cabin.

Cardona had been a big, burly man, built along the lines of a black bear. Like all the other men in Solomon Burke's gang, he'd had a reputation for ruthlessness and cruelty. He had killed seven men that Luke knew of during various bank and train robberies, and was probably responsible for more deaths in addition to those. But he wouldn't be killing anybody else.

Luke took some small comfort from that. He tracked down outlaws mostly for the bounties posted on them, and he wasn't going to lie about it to himself or anybody else. It pleased him to know, because of him, men such as Cardona were no longer around to spread suffering and death across the frontier.

More bullets pounded into the log. One tore all the way through it and struck a rock lying on the slope, causing the bullet to whine off in a ricochet and bringing a thoughtful frown to Luke's face. He realized the log had been lying there long enough to be half-rotten in places. He holstered the Remington he was still holding and drew a heavy-bladed knife from its sheath on his left hip. Attacking the log with the blade, he hacked and dug at the soft wood.

It didn't take him long to break through and see what he'd been hoping to see. The log was partially hollow. Luke began enlarging the opening he had made and soon realized the hollow part ran all the way to one end of the log. He could see sunlight shining through it.

It took fifteen minutes of hard work to carve out a big enough hole for him to fit his head and shoulders through. By the time he was finished, sweat was dripping down his face.

He sheathed his knife and looked over at Cardona. "Adios, José. If I see you again, I reckon it'll probably be in hell."

Luke wormed his way through the opening into the hollow log. Down below in the cabin, the outlaws hadn't been able to see what he was doing. He could only hope none of them had snuck around to where they could observe him. If they had, he was as good as dead.

He began shifting his weight back and forth as much as he could in those close confines. He felt insects crawling on him. His nerves twanged, taut as bowstrings. The log began to rock back and forth slightly. Bunching his muscles, he threw himself hard against the wood surrounding him. Over the pounding of his heart, he heard a faint grating sound as the log shifted.

Suddenly, it was rolling.

He let out a startled yell, even though rolling the log down the hill was exactly what he'd been trying to do. Up and down switched places rapidly.

With nothing between the log and the cabin to stop it, the crazy, bouncing, spinning, dizzying ride lasted only a few seconds.

The log crashed into the side of the cabin with a loud cracking sound just as he had counted on. Luke bulled his way out of the broken trunk, pulling both Remingtons from their cross-draw holsters as he did so.

He was on his feet when one of the outlaws appeared in the doorway, unwisely rushing out to see what had happened.

Luke shot him in the chest with the left-hand Remington. The slug drove the owlhoot back, making him fall. His body tangled with the feet of the man behind him. Luke blasted that hombre with the right-hand gun, then pressed himself against the cabin wall and waited. The men inside couldn't bring their guns to bear on him from those loopholes, and the log walls were too thick to shoot through. If anybody tried to rush out through the door, he was in position to gun them down. And, if the door was the only way out, he had them bottled up.

Of course, he couldn't go anywhere, either. But a stalemate was better than being stuck behind that log and his enemies having all the advantage.

As the echoes of the shots rolled away through the mountain valleys, a charged silence settled over the area. Luke thought he heard harsh breathing coming from inside the cabin.

After a few tense minutes, a man called out. "Who are you, mister?"

"Name's Luke Smith." He wasn't giving anything away by replying. They already knew where he was.

"I've heard of you. You're a bounty hunter!"

"Am I talking to Solomon Burke?"

"That's right."

"Who are the two boys I killed in there?"

Burke didn't answer for a moment. "How do you know they're dead?" he finally asked.

"Wasn't time for anything fancy. They're dead, all right."

Again Burke hesitated before saying, "Phil Gaylord and Oscar Montrose."

"José Cardona's dead up on the hillside. I blew his brains out. That's nearly half your bunch gone over the divide, Burke. Why don't you throw your guns out and surrender before I have to kill the rest of you?"

That brought a hoot of derisive laughter from inside.

"Mighty big talk, Smith. You step away from that wall and you'll be full of lead in a hurry. How in blazes are you gonna kill anybody else?"

"I've got my ways." Luke looked along the wall next to him. One of the loopholes, empty now, was within reach.

"We've got food, water, and plenty of ammunition. What do you have?"

"Got a cigar."

"Well, go ahead and smoke it, then," Burke told him. "It'll be the last one you ever do."

Luke kept his left-hand gun trained on the doorway. He pouched the right-hand iron and reached under his coat, bringing out a thin, black cigar. He bit off the end, spit it out, and clamped the cylinder of tobacco between his teeth. Fishing a lucifer from his pocket, he snapped it to life with his thumbnail. He held the flame to the end of the cigar and puffed until it was burning good. "Smell that?"

"Whoo-eee!" Burke mocked. "Smells like you set a wet dog on fire."

"It tastes good, though," Luke said. "I've got something else."

"What might that be?" Burke asked.

Luke took another cylinder from under his coat. Longer and thicker than the cigar, it was wrapped tightly in dark red paper. A short length of fuse dangled from one end. Luke puffed on the cigar until the end was glowing bright red, then held the fuse to it.

"This," he said around the cigar as the fuse began to sputter and spit sparks. He leaned over and shoved the cylinder through the empty loophole. It clattered on the puncheon floor inside the cabin.

One of the other men howled a curse and yelled, "Look out! That's dynamite!"

Luke drew his second gun and swung away from the wall as he extended the revolvers and squared himself up. As the outlaws tumbled through the door, trying to get away before the dynamite exploded, he started firing.

They shot back, of course, even as Luke's lead tore through them and knocked them off their feet. He felt the impact as a bullet struck him, then another. But he stayed upright and the Remingtons in his hands continued to roar.

Solomon Burke, a fox-faced, red-haired man, went down with his guts shot to pieces. Dour, sallow Lane Hutton stumbled and fell as blood from his bullet-torn throat cascaded down the front of his shirt. Young Billy Wells died with half his jaw shot away. Paco Hernandez stayed on his feet the longest and got a final shot off even as he collapsed with blood welling from two holes in his chest.

That last bullet rocked Luke. He swayed and spit out the cigar, but didn't fall. His vision was foggy, because he'd been shot three times or because clouds of powder smoke were swirling around him, he couldn't tell. The Remingtons seemed to weigh a thousand pounds apiece, but he didn't let them droop until he was certain all the outlaws were dead.

Then he couldn't hold the guns up anymore. They slipped from his blood-slick fingers and thudded to the ground at his feet.

I might not live to collect the bounty on these men, but at least they won't hurt anybody else, he thought as he stumbled through the cabin door. The single room inside was dim and shadowy.

The cylinder he had shoved through the loophole lay on the floor near a table. The fuse had burned out harmlessly. The blasting cap on the end was just clay and the "dynamite" was nothing more than a piece of wood with red paper wrapped around it. Luke had used it a number of times before. Outlaws tended to panic when they thought they were about to be blown to kingdom come.

Ignoring the fake dynamite, he stumbled across the room. Sitting on the table was the thing he had hoped to find inside.

It took him a couple tries before he was able to snag the neck of the whiskey bottle and lift it to his mouth. Some of the liquor spilled over his chin and throat, but he got enough of the fiery stuff down his throat to brace himself.

He leaned on the rough-hewn table and tried to take stock of his injuries. He'd been hit low on his left side. There was a lot of blood. A bullet had torn a furrow along his left forearm, too, and blood ran down and dripped from his fingers. The bullet hole high on his chest was starting to make his right arm and shoulder go numb.

He needed to stop the bleeding before he did anything else. With little time before his hands quit working, he pulled the bandanna from around his neck and used his teeth to start a rip in it. He tore it in half and managed to pour some whiskey on the pieces. He pulled up his shirt, felt around until he found the hole in his side, and shoved one wadded up piece of the whiskey-soaked bandanna into the hole.

But that was just where the bullet had gone in. Wincing in pain, he located the exit wound and pushed the other piece of bandanna into it.

That left the hole in his chest. All the gun-thunder had deafened him for a few moments, but his hearing was starting to come back. He listened intently as he breathed, but didn't hear any whistling or sucking sounds. The slug hadn't pierced his lung, he decided. That was good.

The bullet hadn't come out, either. It was still in there somewhere. Not good, he thought. Fumbling, he pulled his knife from its sheath and used the blade to cut a piece from his shirt tail. Lucky he didn't slice off a finger or two in the process. He upended the bottle and poured whiskey right over the wound, then bit back a scream as he crammed the piece of cloth into the hole.

That was all he could do. His muscles refused to work the way he wanted them to. He had to lie down. He took an unsteady step toward one of the bunks built against the side walls. The world suddenly spun crazily around him. The floor seemed to tilt under his feet. His balance deserted him, and he crashed down on the puncheons, sending fresh jolts of pain stabbing through him.

He felt consciousness slipping away from him and knew if he passed out, he probably wouldn't wake up again. He tried to hold on, but a black tide swept over him.

That black surge didn't just wash him away from his primitive surroundings. To his already fevered mind, it seemed to lift him and carry him back, back, a bit of human flotsam swept along by a raging torrent, to an earlier time and a different place. The darkness surrounding him was shot through with red flashes, like artillery shells bursting in the night.

BOOK ONE

BOOK ONE

CHAPTER 1

The bombardment sounded like the worst thunderstorm in the history of the world, but unlike a thunderstorm, it went on and on and on. For long days, that devil Ulysses S. Grant and his Yankee army had squatted outside Richmond, pounding away at the capital city of the Confederacy with their big guns. Half the buildings in town had been reduced to rubble, and untold numbers of Richmond's citizens were dead, killed in the endless barrages.

And still the guns continued to roar.

Rangy, rawboned Luke Jensen felt the floor shake under his feet as shells fell not far from the building where he stood. It had been one of Richmond's genteel mansions, not far from the capital itself, but recently it had been taken over by the government. One particular part of the government, in fact: the Confederate treasury.

Luke was one of eight men summoned tonight for reasons unknown to them. They were waiting in what had been the parlor before the comfortable, overstuffed furniture was shoved aside and replaced by desks and tables.

In the light of a couple smoky lamps, he glanced around at the other men. Some of them he knew, and some he didn't. The faces of all bore the same weary, haggard look, the expression of men who had been at war for too long and suffered too many defeats despite their best efforts.

Luke knew that look all too well. He saw it in the mirror every time he got a chance to shave, which wasn't very often these days.

For nearly four long years, he had worn Confederate gray—ever since the day he had walked away from the hardscrabble farm tucked into the Ozark Mountains of southwestern Missouri and enlisted.

Behind him he'd left his father Emmett and his little brother Kirby, along with his mother and sister.

It had been hard for Luke to leave his family, but he felt it was the right thing to do. Fighting for the Confederacy didn't mean a man held with slavery, although he figured that was what all those ignorant Yankees believed. Luke didn't believe at all in the notion of one man owning another.

At the same time he didn't think it was right for a bunch of Northern politicians in By-God Washington City to be telling Southern folks what they could and couldn't do, especially when it came to secession. The states had joined together voluntarily, back when they'd won their freedom from England. If some of them wanted to say "thanks, but so long" and go their own way, it seemed to Luke they had every right to do so.

Even so, if they'd just kept on wrangling about it in the halls of Congress, Luke, like a lot of other Southerners, would have pretty much ignored it and gone on about his business. But Abraham Lincoln had to go and send the army marching into Virginia, and the battle along the creek called Bull Run was the last straw as far as Luke was concerned. He'd been raised to avoid trouble if he could, but when a Jensen saw something wrong going on, he couldn't just sit back and do nothing.

So he'd been a soldier for four years, fighting against the Northern aggressors, slogging along as an infantryman for a while before his natural talents for tracking, shooting, and fighting got noticed and he was made a scout and a sharpshooter.

He knew three of the men waiting in the parlor with him were the same sort. Remy Duquesne, Dale Cardwell, and Edgar Millgard were good men, and if he was being sent on some sort of mission with them, Luke was fine with that.

The other four had introduced themselves as Keith Stratton, Wiley Potter, Josh Richards, and Ted Casey. Luke hadn't formed an opinion about them based only on their names. He didn't blame them for being close-mouthed, though. He was the same way himself.

Remy fired up a cigar and said in his soft Cajun accent, "Anybody got an idea why they brought us here tonight?"

"Not a clue," Wiley Potter said.

"The treasury department has its office here now," Dale Cardwell pointed out. He smiled. "Maybe they're finally going to pay us all those back wages we haven't seen in months."

That comment drew grim chuckles from several of the men.

Remy said, "I wouldn't count on that, my frien'."

Luke didn't think it was very likely, either. The Confederacy was in bad shape. Financially, militarily, morale-wise . . . everything was cratering, and there didn't seem to be anything anybody could do to stop it. They would fight to the end, of course—there was no question about that—but that end seemed to be getting more and more inevitable.

The front door opened, and footsteps sounded in the foyer. Several gray-clad troopers appeared in the arched entrance to the former parlor. They carried rifles with bayonets fixed to the barrels.

A pair of officers followed the soldiers into the room. Luke and the other men snapped to attention. He recognized one of the officers as a high-ranking general. The other man was the colonel who commanded the regiment in which Luke, Remy, Dale, and Edgar served.

The two men in civilian clothes who came into the room behind the general and the colonel were the real surprise. Luke caught his breath as he recognized the President of the Confederacy, Jefferson Davis, and the Secretary of the Treasury, George Trenholm.

"At ease," the general said.

Luke and the others relaxed, but not much. It was hard to be at ease with the president in the room.

Jefferson Davis gave them a sad, tired smile and said, "Thank you for coming here tonight, gentlemen," as if they'd had a choice in the matter. "I know you'd probably rather be with your comrades in arms, facing the enemy."

Stratton and Potter grimaced slightly and exchanged a quick glance, as if that was the last thing they wanted to be doing.

"I've summoned you because I have a special job for you," Davis went on. "Secretary Trenholm will tell you about it."

Luke had wondered if they were going to be given a special assignment, but he hadn't expected it would come from the president himself. It had to be something of extreme importance. He waited eagerly to hear what the treasury secretary was going to say.

"As you know, Richmond is under siege by the Yankees," the man began rather pompously as he clasped his hands behind his back.

Luke preferred Confederate politicians to Yankees, but they all had a tendency to be windbags, as far as he was concerned.

"Although I hate to say it, it appears that our efforts to defend the city ultimately will prove to be unsuccessful," the secretary continued.

"Are you saying that Richmond's going to fall, sir?" Potter asked.

Trenholm nodded. "I'm afraid so."

"But that doesn't necessarily mean the Confederacy is about to fall as well," Davis put in. "Our glorious nation will persevere. The Yankees may overrun Richmond, but we will establish a new capital elsewhere." He smiled at the treasury secretary. "I'm sorry, I didn't mean to interrupt."

"That's quite all right, Mr. President. No one in this room has more right to speak than you." Trenholm cleared his throat and went on. "Of course, no government can continue to function without funds, so to that end, acting on the orders of President Davis, I have assembled a shipment of gold bullion that is to be spirited out of the city and taken to Georgia to await the arrival of our government. This is most of what we have left in our coffers, gentlemen. I'm not exaggerating when I say the very survival of the Confederacy itself depends on the secure transport of this gold."

Luke wasn't surprised by what he had just heard. For the past few days, rumors had been going around the city that the treasury was going to be cleaned out and the money taken elsewhere so the Yankees wouldn't get their grubby paws on it.

The secretary nodded toward Luke's commanding officer. "Colonel Lancaster will be in charge of the gold's safety."

"You're taking the whole regiment to Georgia, sir?" Dale asked.

The colonel shook his head. "Not at all, Corporal. That would only draw the Yankees' attention to what we're doing." Lancaster paused. "We're entrusting the safety of the bullion—and the future of the Confederacy—to a smaller detail. Eight men, to be exact." He looked around the room. "The eight of you who are gathered here."

CHAPTER 2

Luke had figured that out even before Lancaster said it. The idea seemed obvious. Getting the gold out of Richmond would require speed and stealth, and no one was better at moving fast and quiet than he and his fellow scouts.

It seemed like a mighty big risk, though, turning over a fortune in gold to only eight men. Of course, as long as they were loyal to the Confederacy, it didn't really matter.

"I'll be going along as well," Colonel Lancaster pointed out. "I've been relieved of my command of the regiment and given this task."

"I know you'd rather be with the men you've led in such sterling fashion, Colonel," Jefferson Davis said. "However, we all must make sacrifices for our noble cause."

"Of course, Mr. President," Lancaster said stiffly.

Davis turned back to Luke and the other scouts. "No one is going to order you enlisted men to accept this assignment. If there are any of you who don't want to go along, speak up now, and it won't be held against you. You'll be allowed to return to your units. All we ask is that you say nothing about this. Secrecy is the watchword until the bullion is safely on its way to Georgia."

Luke looked at his friends. Remy shrugged and told Davis, "Mr. President, I don't think any of us are gonna say no to this job."

"That's right," Edgar said. "If this is something that will help the Confederacy, you can count on us, sir."

"I knew that." Davis smiled. "I knew you valiant lads wouldn't let me down, but I felt it was only right to ask. Thank you for justifying my faith in you."

"You can thank us when we get that gold where it's goin', Mr. President," Stratton said.

Luke had been quiet so far, but he asked, "When are we leaving?"

"Tonight," Colonel Lancaster said.

"That soon?" Potter was surprised.

"Do you have a problem with that, Sergeant? Something you need to do here in Richmond before you leave?"

Potter grunted and shook his head. "Permission to speak freely, sir?"

"Go ahead," Lancaster told him.

"Richmond's turned into a hellhole ever since the Yankees showed up on our doorstep, and as far as I'm concerned, the sooner we get out of here, the better."

As if to punctuate his comment, another shell fell somewhere nearby, and the blast shook the house enough that little bits of plaster sifted down from the ceiling.

The general said to Davis, "You should get back to somewhere safer, sir. The colonel and I can handle this."

"Very well, General." Davis turned to the treasury secretary. "Come on, George."

The troopers escorted the two politicians from the room. Once they were gone, Colonel Lancaster said, "The gold is being stored in a warehouse not far from here. It's packed in crates in a couple wagons and covered with canvas so they'll look like supplies."

"No offense, Colonel," Luke said, "but are you sure that's a good idea? With the city cut off like it is, people are starting to get pretty hungry. They're liable to come after food quicker than they would gold."

"How else would you suggest we transport it, Jensen?" the colonel snapped.

Luke shrugged. "I don't know, sir," he admitted. "As scarce as everything is these days, folks are going to be interested no matter what it looks like."

"That's why it's up to us to get the wagons out of the city quickly, and with as little fuss as possible. We have civilian clothes at the warehouse for all of you, as well. Hopefully that'll keep you from drawing too much attention."

Luke didn't know about that, but the idea of getting some fresh duds appealed to him. His gray uniform was worn and ragged and covered with stains from too many nights spent sleeping in the mud.

The black bill of his forage cap was crooked and broken. His shoes were more hole than shoe leather.

His only possessions still in good shape were his Fayetteville rifle and his Griswold and Gunnison revolver, both of which he kept in excellent condition. His life often depended on them.

The general shook hands with all eight of the scouts and wished them luck, then Colonel Lancaster said gruffly, "Let's go. We'll dispense with military formality since we're supposed to be civilians, but don't forget who's in charge here."

Luke didn't think Lancaster was likely to let that happen.

"I don't know about you boys," Ted Casey said with a wide grin, "but I feel like a whole new man in this get-up!"

The civilian clothes they had donned when they reached the warehouse weren't new—some of them even had patches here and there—but they were clean and in much better shape than the uniforms the eight men had been wearing.

Colonel Lancaster, as befitted his rank, was dressed in the only real suit, including a flat-crowned planter's hat. Other than his ramrod-stiff backbone, in those clothes and with his florid face and thick side-whiskers, he might have been mistaken for a plantation owner.

The other men were dressed more like overseers on that hypothetical plantation, in boots, whipcord trousers, linsey-woolsey shirts, and leather vests. They wore an assortment of headgear ranging from broad-brimmed hats to tweed caps.

Luke had snagged one of the hats he thought made him look like a plainsman. Such men rode through the Ozarks from time to time, on their way to or from the vast western frontier, and Luke had always admired them.

His revolver was tucked in the waistband of the trousers. Most enlisted men didn't carry handguns, but since scouts often had to do some close-quarters fighting, they had been issued revolvers along with their rifles. Luke considered himself pretty handy with either weapon, and with a knife, too, for that matter.

He didn't think about it very often, but he had killed quite a few men during his time in the army. It was war, of course. That was what soldiers did. He had killed more than his share up close, though, sneaking up on Yankee pickets and slitting their throats or driving his knife into their backs so the blade penetrated the heart. He had felt the hot gush of enemy blood on his hand, heard the death rattle, and borne the weight of a suddenly limp body that had to be lowered to the ground quietly. He had seen the terrible damage gunshots did to human flesh, especially at close range.

Those memories didn't haunt his sleep, but they were part of him and always would be.

Wiley Potter, Keith Stratton, Ted Casey, and Josh Richards clustered together near one of the wagons. Luke saw them casting furtive glances at the canvas-covered cargo in the back of the vehicle.

"Like dogs lickin' their chops over a big ol' soup bone, eh?" Remy said quietly as he came up beside Luke.

"You can't blame them. I sent some mighty hard looks at those wagons myself. I've never been this close to so much gold." Luke snorted. "Hell, back home I might go as long as a year without seeing as much as a double eagle."

"I suppose I'm more accustomed to it, seeing as I spent a lot of time in the gambling halls in New Orleans. The money always flowed freely there."

"Maybe so," Luke said. "Where I come from, money flows more like quicksand."

Dale asked Lancaster, "Are we going to be riding on the wagons, Colonel?"

"We'll have a driver and a guard on each wagon," Lancaster explained. "The other four of you, plus myself, will be on horseback and serve as outriders."

"Horses sound good," Casey said. "I always hankered to ride something better than an old mule. They turned me down for the cavalry because that was all I had."

"You'll take turns at the jobs, at least starting out. I don't care who does what, though. You can settle that among yourselves."

Dale commented, "I wouldn't mind handling one of the teams. I used to drive a freight wagon before the war."

"So did I," Edgar offered. "I reckon I'll take the other driver's job starting out."

None of the other men volunteered to ride on the wagons as guards. Luke and Remy looked at each other. Luke shrugged, and Remy said, "We'll take the wagons, too, Colonel."

Lancaster nodded. "Fine." He looked to Potter, Stratton, Casey, and Richards. "You men will find your horses in the alley behind the warehouse. Bring them around front and mount up. You can fetch my mount as well." He motioned to the uniformed soldiers who had been waiting in the warehouse, guarding the gold shipment. "Open the doors."

The troopers swung the big double doors back while Luke and his friends climbed onto the wagons. Luke settled down on the seat of the first wagon beside Dale. "Sure you can handle this?"

"Oh, yeah. To tell you the truth, I've never been that comfortable in a saddle."

"I was riding almost before I could walk, at least according to my pa," Luke told him.

The mention of Emmett Jensen put a pensive look on Luke's face. Luke had joined up first, back in '61, but he had suspected his pa wouldn't be able to stay out of the fight for long. Sure enough, Emmett had enlisted, too.

Proving that the world really was a small place, the two of them had run into each other at Chancellorsville, even though they were in different regiments. Hundreds of thousands of troops rampaging around those Virginia woods, and yet father and son had practically bumped heads.

That wasn't the last time, either. Any time their units were any-where near each other, one of them would seek out the other so they could visit in the lull between battles. Neither of them got much news from home, but Emmett was confident his youngest son Kirby was keeping things going on the farm.

"Kirby may be just a boy," Emmett had said during one visit, "but he's got something special inside him. I don't think I've ever seen a boy willing to work harder or more determined to do the right thing."

"He'll have the farm waiting for us when we come back," Luke had said.

"Shoot, he may not even need our help!" Emmett had replied with a grin.

It had been a while since Luke had seen his pa. He hoped Emmett was all right. Both were soldiers, so who knew what might happen. It was a dangerous line of work.

When the wagons rolled out of the warehouse into the darkness, Colonel Lancaster and the other four outriders were waiting on horseback.

"I'll lead the way," Lancaster declared. "I want a rider on each side of the wagons. Keep an eye out behind you as well. We don't want anybody sneaking up on us."

"Did the colonel tell any of us exactly where we're going?" Luke asked Dale as the party set out over the rough, cobblestoned streets.

"Not that I know of," Dale replied.

"I might say something to him about that the first time we stop. He's bound to have a map or something, but if anything happened to him, we wouldn't know where we were supposed to take this"— Luke stopped himself before he said the word *gold*—"cargo."

"Yeah, that's true," Dale agreed. "All we know is that we're headed for Georgia, but Georgia's a pretty big place."

It was pretty far away, too, Luke thought, and almost anything could happen between here and there. He felt the unaccustomed burden of responsibility weighing on his shoulders. He wasn't used to taking care of anybody but himself or maybe two or three of his comrades. He'd never had anything like the fate of the Confederacy riding on his back before.

The city was dark except for the few fires started by exploding artillery shells. The Yankee bombardment continued. It went on almost around the clock. Luke didn't see how the city could hold out much longer.

A shell screamed overhead and landed maybe half a mile behind them, blowing up with a huge explosion. Dale looked back over his shoulder at the pillar of flame rising into the black sky. "What do you think it'd be like if one of those things landed right on top of us?"

"We'll never know," Luke said.

"Because it won't happen?"

"Because if it does, we'll be blown to smithereens before we know what happened."

"You really know how to make a fella feel encouraged, Luke—" Dale stopped short and hauled back on the reins. Colonel Lancaster had come to an abrupt halt in front of the wagon team. Garish, flickering light spilled over the cobblestones as a large number of men, many of them carrying torches, surged around a corner up ahead.

"That looks like trouble," Dale muttered.

Luke was thinking the same thing. He knew mobs made of desperate civilians and deserters had taken to roaming the streets of Richmond. The army was trying to keep things under control, but it was getting more difficult with every passing day as the Yankee siege continued. Already there had been several riots.

And it looked like the two wagons were in the path of another one, as one of the men in the forefront of the mob yelled, "There are some wagons! There might be food in them!"

It was an easy conclusion to jump to. A starving man saw food everywhere.

The man waved his torch forward, and with a full-throated cry sounding like the howl of a wounded animal, the mob surged toward the wagons and riders.

CHAPTER 3

Luke saw Colonel Lancaster look around as if searching for a way out. In the narrow street it would be difficult and time-consuming to turn the wagons around, and there were no alleys nearby down which they could escape.

Fleeing wasn't going to do any good. As close as the mob was, the starving men would be able to overtake the wagons without much trouble.

"Get ready to fight if you have to, Dale," Luke said as he pulled the Griswold and Gunnison revolver from his waistband. He stood up and almost called Lancaster "Colonel," catching himself just in time. He took a breath and shouted, "Mr. Lancaster, get out of the way!"

The army and the Confederate government wanted the bullion shipment kept secret, along with the fact that those with the wagons were soldiers. But the secret would be out if the mob swarmed over the wagons. Although the last thing he wanted was to hurt any of his fellow Southerners, Luke would do whatever was necessary to protect the gold. He hadn't seen any firearms in the crowd, only torches and makeshift clubs. Figuring it was a small risk he raised the revolver.

As Lancaster yanked his horse to the side, out of the line of fire, Luke thumbed back the hammer and squeezed the trigger. The Griswold and Gunnison was a .36 caliber weapon modeled after the Colt Navy and not noted for its accuracy. But the range was short, and he sent the pistol ball slamming into the cobblestones just a few feet in front of the mob's leaders.

They stopped in a hurry.

The other members of the escort lifted rifles or pulled out pistols.

Luke knew hunger could make a man risk a great deal, up to and including his life. He cocked the revolver again and raised the barrel until he was aiming right between the eyes of the man who'd urged the mob into action. He didn't know if the man was one of the leaders or just someone who'd been moved to shout, but he wanted to be certain the man was aware of the danger he was facing.

"You fellas stay right where you are!" Luke warned them. "We'll shoot if we have to, make no mistake about that!"

"You can't kill all of us!" somebody yelled.

Somebody in the back of the crowd, Luke noted. "No, but we can do for half of you. Maybe more than that."

That estimate was good only if every member of the escort emptied his guns and scored a hit with every shot, which was highly unlikely, but the members of the mob probably wouldn't bother to do that ciphering.

"And you'll be the first one to die, mister," Luke went on, addressing the man he'd aimed at. "Is it worth dying for something you can't even eat?"

The man looked scared, but he asked, "What is it? What's in those wagons?"

"Manufacturing equipment," Luke said. He didn't know where that answer came from, but it struck him as a good one. "We're trying to get it out of town while we still can."

"What sort of equipment?"

Luke bit back a curse. The varmint was awfully curious for somebody who had a gun pointed at him. "Leather goods. Tool and die presses."

He wasn't sure that answer even made sense. He didn't know anything about manufacturing, but recalled hearing that phrase once from a fellow who owned a saddle shop.

He figured the stubborn man would want to take a look at the contents of the crate, but before that could happen, somebody else called out, "You don't have any food?"

"Just our own provisions for the trip," Luke answered, putting some sympathy in his voice. "And we're going to be on mighty short rations just like everybody else."

"We might as well let 'em go," another man grumbled. "Can't eat a bunch of damn machinery."

"They've got horses," yet another man said.

"I'll be damned if I'm far enough gone that I'll eat horse meat! Let 'em pass!"

After that bit of discourse, the crowd seemed to be of two minds. Some agreed they ought to let the travelers go, while others were so angered by the fate that had befallen them they wanted to hurt somebody, anybody, for any excuse. It was a delicate balance, and Luke knew it could tip at any second to the side of violence.

He glanced at his companions. They looked tense and ready to fight, but were scared, too. Only fools would not be scared in the face of an angry mob. Luke hoped none of them panicked and got trigger-happy. All it would take was one shot to set off an orgy of killing.

Finally, the man in the lead stepped aside and swung the blazing brand. "All right, go on and get out of here." He raised his voice to the others in the mob. "Get out of the way! Let them pass!"

The men crowded to the sides of the street. As the wagons and riders passed between them it was uncomfortably like running a gauntlet. As the lead wagon rolled by the man with the torch, Luke told him, "You made a wise decision, friend. Good luck to you."

"You're the lucky ones," the man said with bitterness in his voice. "You're getting out of Richmond. Maybe the Yankees will catch you and kill you, but even if they do, it'll be quick. The ones left behind here will be a long time dying."

As he reloaded the expended chamber, Luke had a feeling the man's grim prediction was correct.

The gold escorts didn't encounter any more trouble as they made their way to the city's edge, but Luke knew they were far from being out of danger yet. The Yankees patrolled heavily around Richmond to keep the city's inhabitants bottled up while the artillery bombardment continued.

Colonel Lancaster dropped back alongside the lead wagon and said to Luke, "I appreciate your help with that mob back there, Jensen, but don't forget that I'm in command here. The way you took charge bordered on insubordination."

Well, then, you should've come up with some way to get us out of that mess, Luke thought, *instead of sitting there looking scared and confused.* He kept that opinion to himself, of course. "That's not the way I meant it, Colonel. I was just trying anything to keep those fellas from swarming over us."

"I understand," Lancaster said with a nod. "Just remember in the future that you look to me for your orders."

"Yes, sir."

The colonel rode ahead again, and Dale said quietly, "If we'd waited for him to figure out what to do, we'd all be dead now."

"More than likely," Luke agreed. "The colonel's a good commander out in the field, but I'm not sure he's really cut out for a job like this."

"That's why I'm glad you're with us, Luke. You can think on your feet about as well as anybody I ever saw."

Luke took that compliment in silence. He had never thought of himself as any sort of strategist or tactician. He was just a fellow who wanted to stay alive and was willing to do almost anything to accomplish that goal.

Their route took them north out of the city, which was opposite from where they wanted to go, but Luke understood why. The heaviest concentration of Yankee forces was south of Richmond. The scouts had to take the wagons north, then circle far to the west, well behind Union lines, and make a fast dash southward. It was the long way around, but a direct route just wasn't possible.

Lancaster called a halt. "I want to be out of the city by dawn. The farther away we can get, the better."

"How will we dodge those Yankee patrols?" Stratton asked.

"We'll have to do some good scouting." The colonel nodded toward Luke. "That's why I want one of you men to give Jensen the horse you're riding. I want a mount for Duquesne, too."

"We've done plenty of scoutin', Colonel," Richards protested. "You can send a couple of us."

Lancaster shook his head. "Jensen and Duquesne have served under my command. I know what they can do. You other men were recommended to me, but I haven't seen you in action yet. Now, dismount, a couple of you."

There was some angry muttering, but Richards and Casey swung down from their saddles.

"Keep your eyes open, Dale," Luke said to his friend.

"You bet I will," Dale promised.

Taking his rifle with him, Luke hopped down from the wagon seat. Richards handed him his reins and climbed up to take his place.

Once Luke and Remy were mounted, Lancaster told them, "Follow this road we're on and see if the way is clear up ahead to the bridge about a mile from here. If it is, one of you come back and tell us, and we'll come ahead."

"What if the Yankees have blown up the bridge, Colonel?" Luke asked.

"Then we'll have to find another way," Lancaster replied as if that were the most obvious thing in the world, and Luke supposed it was.

Crossing the river was probably going to be the most difficult part of getting out of Richmond, Luke thought. If the Yankees really wanted to keep the citizens and the Confederate government trapped in the city, the first thing they should have done was destroy all the bridges.

But that would make it more difficult for them to get in and out of the city from the north once Richmond had fallen, so maybe one or two bridges were still standing. In normal times, the small road the Confederates were on was little used and might be overlooked, along with its bridge spanning the river.

Those were anything but normal times, however.

Luke and Remy moved forward, leaving the buildings on the edge of town behind. Trees crowded in on the road from both sides as they rode northward. Although the sky behind them was bright with the orange glow of fires and the flashes of exploding shells from the Yankee barrage, the darkness grew thicker the farther they went. Luke eyed the trees warily. A Yankee cavalry patrol could be hidden in there, and he wouldn't see them until they opened fire.

But he might be able to hear them. He kept his ears open, listening for hoofbeats, the jingle of bit chains, or coughs, and he watched his horse's ears. If the animal smelled other horses, it would prick its ears in the direction of the scent.

Nothing. Only the slow thud of hoofbeats from his and Remy's mounts.

"We're fortunate," the Cajun whispered. "I don't think anybody's out there right now."

"Yeah," Luke breathed, "but I wouldn't count us lucky until we see whether the bridge is there."

The road was fairly straight, with only a few curves in it. They had just ridden around one when a large structure loomed in front of them about two hundred yards away. Luke recognized it as the covered bridge that crossed the James River.

"That's it," Remy said. "It's still there."

Luke grinned in the darkness. "Yeah." His eyes searched the shadows around the bridge, looking for any sign of movement. "Seems to be deserted, too. But we'd better take a closer look before one of us goes back and tells the colonel the path is clear."

"Absolutely." Remy heeled his horse into a slightly faster gait. "Let's go."

Luke started to call out to his friend and tell him to slow down, but Remy was right, they didn't really have any time to waste. As Colonel Lancaster had said, the farther away from Richmond they were by morning, the better. Luke rode after Remy.

They were about fifty feet away from the bridge when a sheet of orange muzzle flame split the night.

CHAPTER 4

Luke's only warning was a sudden toss of his horse's head a split second before the shots rang out, giving him just enough time to duck.

It was a good thing he did. As it passed over his head, he heard the sinister hum of a minié ball.

He pulled the revolver from his waistband—he had five rounds ready—and cocked the gun as he brought it up, turning the cylinder from the empty chamber on which the hammer had rested.

As several men on horseback burst out of the trees just short of the bridge, Luke thumbed off a couple rounds. Even though he couldn't see their uniforms, he knew they had to be Yankee cavalrymen.

More shots blasted as muzzle flames continued to tear orange gashes in the darkness. He pulled hard on the reins to whirl his horse around and flee, but saw something that made him stop short.

A match had flared into life on the bridge. He could think of only one reason why somebody would be striking a lucifer out there.

To light the fuse attached to a keg of blasting powder.

The Yankees hadn't destroyed the bridge yet, but only because they were just getting around to it.

"Cover me, Remy!" Luke yelled, and he did something the Yankees wouldn't have expected in a million years. If he'd had time to think about it, likely he wouldn't have done it.

He charged straight at them.

Luke leaned forward over his horse's neck as he sent the animal lunging toward the cavalrymen. The revolver in his hand roared twice more. He saw one of the troopers topple loosely from the saddle. A glance over his shoulder told Luke his friend had taken cover in the trees at the side of the road and opened up with his revolver. Remy was firing, too.

The Yankees were confused. Instead of fleeing, as they had expected, the two Confederates were putting up a fight. The patrol's charge had broken up, and the horses were milling around in the road.

Luke's horse thundered between a couple Yankees. One of the cavalrymen drew a saber. Silvery moonlight winked off the blade as it started to slash toward Luke. He still had one round in the revolver. Tipping up the barrel, he triggered the gun.

The .36 caliber slug caught the saber-wielding cavalryman in the throat. A fountain of blood, black in the moonlight, sprayed from him as he went backward out of his saddle. Luke flashed past, unharmed.

With no time to reload the revolver, he jammed it back in his waistband. Up ahead, sparks flew in the darkness as the lit fuse burned toward a small keg filled with blasting powder. It would be enough to destroy the bridge. Even if the explosion didn't blow the bridge in two, the fire it was bound to start would finish the job.

The fuse lighter stood in the middle of the bridge, vaguely illuminated by the sputtering glow. Confused by the unexpected fight of the Confederates, he took too long to decide whether to flee or stay. Luke was already on the bridge, his horse's hooves ringing on the planks and echoing from the arched cover.

The Yankee lifted a rifle and fired. The ball whipped past Luke's head.

Luke kicked his feet free of the stirrups and left the saddle in a diving tackle that sent him crashing into the enemy soldier. The collision's impact drove the man backward off his feet.

Luke landed hard, too, knocking the breath out of him. He gasped for air as he scrambled to his knees. The powder keg was about ten feet from him, sitting against the wall on the left-hand side of the bridge. The fuse had only a few inches left to burn.

The Yankee wasn't interested in fighting anymore. He just wanted to get the hell out of there before the powder went off and he was blown to bits. Leaping to his feet, he raced for the north end of the bridge.

Luke threw himself at the keg, snatched it up, and plucked the fuse from it as he rolled over. As he came up again, he flung the keg after the fleeing Yankee.

It landed beside the man and bounced past him. He screamed in sheer terror and stumbled, falling and hitting the ground right at the end of the bridge. He rolled over a couple times and came to a stop with the keg resting on its side a few feet away from him.

Luke heard the swift rataplan of hoofbeats and looked back to see the cavalry patrol had regrouped. They charged toward him. Their revolvers roared as they opened fire.

Luke lunged toward the closest decorative opening in the cover of the bridge as bullets sizzled through the air right behind his back. Down at the far end of the bridge, the Yankee who'd lit the fuse screeched, "Stop shooting! Hold your—"

It was all he got out before one of the wild slugs aimed at Luke struck the powder keg. Luke saw the fierce burst of flames from the explosion out of the corner of his eye as he dived through the opening in the bridge cover.

There wouldn't be enough left of that luckless Yankee to bury.

Luke had problems of his own. He was plunging through empty air toward the black surface of the James River.

He barely had time to drag a breath into his lungs before he struck the chilly water and went under. The river closed over him. He kept sinking for a moment before he was able to right himself.

He wasn't the best swimmer in the world, but he stroked his arms and kicked his feet, fighting his way back to the surface until his head broke out of the water.

While he tried to stay afloat, gun thunder pealed and echoed along the bridge. The Yankees weren't shooting at him, Luke realized. A separate fight was going on under the arched cover. Muzzle flashes were visible through the openings in the walls.

Since nobody seemed to be trying to kill him at the moment, he struggled toward the northern bank, which was closer. By the time he got there, the shooting had stopped and a couple horsemen emerged from under the cover near the site of the blast.

Luke didn't know how he was going to put up a fight. His revolver wasn't loaded, and getting dunked in the river probably had ruined his caps and powder. He still had his knife, but he wasn't in any shape for hand-to-hand combat against overwhelming odds.

The Yankees could just sit there and shoot him while he tried to climb out of the river.

"Luke! Luke, is that you?"

The familiar voice sent a surge of relief through him. "Remy! Down here!"

The Cajun laughed. "Come out of there, you old water rat!"

With river water streaming from his clothes, Luke clambered onto the bank and collapsed. Remy dismounted and went down to help him.

"What happened?" Luke asked as he made it to his feet with Remy's assistance.

"Lancaster and the others heard the shooting and came to see what was going on. You and I had already done enough damage to the Yankees that they were able to wipe out the rest of the patrol."

"Anybody hurt?"

"No, we were lucky. How about you?"

"I reckon I'm all right. Just wet and tired. My ammunition's probably ruined, too."

"Don't worry about that. We'll be able to scavenge plenty of powder and shot from those dead Yankees, not to mention their guns."

"And their horses," Luke suggested. "It won't hurt for us to have some extra mounts."

"Most of the horses have bolted, but we might be able to catch a few."

By the time Luke and Remy reached the road, the wagons had crossed the bridge. They had to steer around the gaping hole in the ground where the keg of blasting powder had gone off, but there was room enough at the side of the road for them to manage that.

Colonel Lancaster said, "From what Corporal Duquesne tells me, if we'd come along a little later this bridge would already be gone. The same would be true if not for your swift action, Jensen. Good job."

"Thank you, sir. And thank you for coming along and taking a hand in the fight."

"When we heard the shots, I should have ordered the drivers to turn the wagons around. We should have gone back and looked for another way out of the city. It really wasn't wise of me to risk our cargo just to see what was happening to the two of you." The colonel shrugged. "But everything seems to have worked out all right. Just don't expect me to keep on pulling your fat out of the fire, Jensen."

"No, sir, I won't." Luke managed to keep the irritation he felt out of his voice. He'd just been following orders when all hell broke loose.

"We'd better move quickly now," Lancaster went on. "There are probably more Yankee patrols in the area. They would have been expecting to hear an explosion, but when their men don't come back, they'll start to wonder what happened. We don't want to be here when they come to find out."

Luke knew that was true. He started looking for his horse and found the animal grazing peacefully on the grass at the side of the road.

He couldn't do anything about his wet clothes except wait for them to dry. That would be miserable, but he could put up with it. He found his hat on the bridge where it had fallen off when he tackled the Yankee.

The Confederates hastily helped themselves to guns and ammunition from their fallen foes. They were trying to catch some of the Yankee cavalry horses when Lancaster said, "No, leave them here."

"It never hurts to have extra mounts, Colonel," Stratton suggested, unknowingly echoing what Luke had said earlier to Remy.

"Those horses have U.S. army brands on them," Lancaster pointed out. "If we're captured, it's unlikely we'll be able to talk ourselves out of a firing squad, but it would be even more difficult if we were in possession of Yankee cavalry mounts."

"The colonel's got a point there," Luke said. "It might be better if we just make do without them."

Nobody put up an argument. A short time later, the group was on the move, following the road into the rugged, wooded countryside of northern Virginia.

Riding on the wagon with Dale again, Luke looked over at Wiley Potter, who rode alongside the vehicle. "Thanks for coming to help me back there."

"Well, sure, Jensen," Potter said. "What else could we do? We're all on the same side, ain't we?"

CHAPTER 5

After the fight at the bridge, the scouts didn't run into any more trouble. A couple times they heard hoofbeats coming along the road and quickly found places where they could pull the wagons off into the trees. Yankee cavalrymen galloped past without even slowing down, never realizing how close the Confederates were.

The riders could only be Yankees. Nobody else would be out and about at night. The people who lived in the area were huddled in their houses and cabins, hoping and praying they wouldn't be slaughtered before morning by the northern invaders.

Luke thought about his ma and Kirby and Janey back on the farm. There had been fighting in Missouri, although not as much as in the east, and widespread bloody raids by guerrilla forces on both sides. He hoped none of the violence had come near the Jensen family farm.

By morning the Confederates were several miles north of Richmond. As the sun came up, Potter and Casey found a cave-like opening under a rugged bluff topped with trees, and Dale and Edgar drove the wagons into it at Colonel Lancaster's command. There was room for the horses under the bluff, too.

"We'll stay here today," the colonel said. "Traveling in daylight is too risky while we're still this close to Richmond. When we swing west and then south we'll be less likely to run into the Yankees, so we can stay on the road more and make better time then."

Based on what he had seen so far, Luke had doubts of Lancaster's ability to be in charge of the mission, but he agreed with the colonel's decision. They were all tired and needed some rest, and it would be better for them to lie low for a while.

They made an unappetizing breakfast of hardtack and salt jowl. No coffee. Luke wasn't sure how long it had been since he'd had real coffee, but it hadn't been any time recently, that was for sure. They took turns sleeping while two men stood guard at all times.

When it was Luke's turn to watch, he was paired with Ted Casey. They hunkered in some brush near the wagons, and the first thing Casey did was reach for a tobacco pouch and papers in his shirt pocket.

Like stopped him with a hand on his arm. "You can't roll a quirly."

"Why not?" Casey asked with a frown.

"Because the smell of tobacco smoke can travel a pretty good distance. The road's only about a quarter mile away. You don't want some smart Yankee coming along, smelling your smoke, and getting curious enough to come over here and take a look around."

Casey let out a disgusted snort, but he shrugged and put away the pouch. "If they was smart, they wouldn't be Yankees."

"They probably think the same thing about us Confederates," Luke pointed out.

"Don't start talkin' about how they just think they're doin' the right thing and how we shouldn't hate 'em because of that."

"They're *not* doing the right thing," Luke said with conviction. "They invaded our homes. Of course we have to fight them. But the ones I really hate are the politicians from both sides who kept prodding and poking at each other until they felt like they had to start a war over something that could have been settled without one."

"What are you talkin' about?" Casey asked.

"Did you know that more than twenty years ago, some congressmen from the South were already talking about ending slavery? Their plan was to get rid of it in stages, so the southern economy wouldn't be ruined in the process. If the northern politicians had just gone along with that idea, by now a lot of the slaves would be free, maybe even all of them, and there wouldn't have been any need for this war. But the Northerners turned it down flat. They'd already started making speeches about how all the slaves had to be freed at once, or they wouldn't go along with it."

Casey gave him a dubious squint. "I never heard nothin' about anything like that. You're makin' it up."

Luke shook his head. "Nope. I read about it in an old newspaper I came across once."

"You know how to read, eh?"

"My ma saw to that. And once I learned, I had a liking for it."

That was true. As a boy and a young man, he had read every book and newspaper he could get his hands on. Unfortunately, in the part of the country where he'd grown up, reading material wasn't all that common.

But some of the settlements had schools, and whenever he could, Luke would ride over to one of them, sneak in, and "borrow" whatever books he could find. He always took them back once he'd finished reading them, so he didn't consider it stealing. He was just doing whatever he had to in order to feed his thirst for knowledge.

One of the few good things about the war, churches across the South had donated Bibles for the troops, so Luke got the chance to read the Good Book from cover to cover, more than once.

Sometimes he came across other books, usually in abandoned houses. He'd nearly always had some sort of volume of prose or poetry tucked away in his gear, and he read them until they fell apart from exposure to the elements.

He didn't have a book with him at the moment, but maybe once they got to Georgia he could scrounge up a few. He had read some plays by an Englishman named Shakespeare, and he had a hankering to read more.

"I don't understand it," Casey said. "I thought those Yankees were so all-fired anxious to have the slaves freed, and now you're tellin' me they turned down a chance to have that happen and went to war instead."

"The politicians in Washington raised a big stink about slavery because they didn't want folks up north thinking too much about the way we were starting to develop more industry here in the South. All those rich men who own factories up there didn't like that. They didn't like the contracts our businessmen were starting to make with businesses in England and other places in Europe, either."

Luke grunted disdainfully, then went on. "The way they saw it, we weren't supposed to do anything except grow the crops. They'd do everything else the country needed and rake in all the money. They stirred up a bunch of well-meaning people who had real doubts about slavery and got them to fight a war over it. But if you want the truth, all you have to do is look around. You don't see any factories still standing in the South, do you?"

Casey frowned as if thinking about the question hurt his head. "It's all about states' rights. That's what we're fightin' for."

At this point, all we're really fighting for is survival, Luke thought. But he said, "It's true the North tried to trample on the rights of our sovereign states, but consider this . . . the Southern businessmen building those factories and making those contracts with the British wanted the money from those things as much as the Northern industrialists didn't want them to have it."

"So what you're sayin' is the politicians and the fellas with a lot of money on both sides have got us fightin' each other because they want to keep rakin' it in?"

Luke shrugged. "Draw your own conclusions, Casey. All I'm saying is the whole situation is a lot more complicated than what most folks think. One side yells about slavery and the other side yells about states' rights, but like nearly everything else in life, most of it always comes back to money."

Casey nodded slowly, as if the implications of what Luke had said were sinking into his brain. After a moment, he said, "You know what we need to do?"

"What's that?"

"We need to get our own hands on some of that money the varmints are fightin' over."

Luke laughed softly. "Men like you and me don't get rich, Casey. It's just not in the cards. And I don't really care. If this war was over tomorrow, I'd go back home and be mighty happy to do it. My family's farm isn't much, but if we have faith and work hard enough, it'll take care of us."

"There's better ways to get rich. Easier ways." And with that, Casey turned his head to stare hard at the wagons.

Luke stiffened as he saw where the man was looking. A harsh note came into his voice. "You can forget about that. That gold belongs to the Confederacy. Thinking otherwise is the same thing as committing treason."

Casey shook his head and said hastily, "You've got me all wrong, Jensen. I'm not thinkin' anything except I'll be glad when our turn at guard duty is over so I can get me some more sleep." He yawned, but Luke wasn't sure if it was genuine. "It was a hard night, and I'm still tired."

"It was a hard night," Luke agreed, thinking about the encounter with the mob in Richmond and then the fight with the Yankee patrol at the bridge.

Casey grinned as he poked a fist against Luke's upper arm.

"Your problem is you got too many thoughts in that head of yours. A man's brain ain't built to work that hard, Jensen. Me, all I think about is whiskey and women and killin' Yankees, and that's plenty."

"I figure it'll be a while before we get any whiskey or women," Luke said, "but it wouldn't surprise me if you get your fill of killing Yankees before this is all over."

CHAPTER 6

After talking to Casey, Luke felt the need for some solitude. He took his rifle, climbed to the top of the bluff hanging over the wagons, and stretched out among the trees so he could gaze around the countryside.

Other than numerous columns of smoke rising in the distance marking the location of Richmond, he couldn't see any signs of the war from where he lay. Here and there, the vegetation was starting to turn green with the approach of spring. A few birds winged through the blue sky.

It would have been a tranquil, beautiful scene if not for the never-ending rumble of artillery, which could be heard even so far from the capital city. The sound of the bombardment was a constant reminder of the ugliness lurking beneath the apparently peaceful surface.

He and his companions were putting that behind them, at least for the moment, Luke reminded himself. He was sure the war would catch up to them again, probably sooner rather than later, but he was going to enjoy the solitude while he could.

Weariness stole over him, begging him to close his eyes. He fought it off, knowing if he gave in to the temptation, he would fall asleep. The possibility of the Yankees sneaking up on the escort on his watch was unacceptable.

To help keep himself awake, he looked down at the brush where Ted Casey still hunkered. He caught a glimpse of the scout through the branches, but only because he knew where the man was. Luke thought it was very unlikely anybody else would spot Casey.

He recalled the way Casey had looked at the wagons while they were talking about getting rich. The memory brought a frown to Luke's face.

As soon as President Davis had explained the details of the mission the night before, Luke had worried about entrusting the safety of so much gold to such a small group of men.

It made sense from a tactical standpoint. Nine men and two wagons could move a lot faster and attract a lot less attention than a company of soldiers.

But if some of those men turned out not to be trustworthy, it could lead to trouble. Luke knew he could trust Remy, Dale, and Edgar, and Colonel Lancaster was completely devoted to the Confederacy. The other four men were unknown quantities. In the long run, how would they react to the temptation of all that bullion?

Of course, they could be wondering the exact same thing about him and his friends, Luke reminded himself. Potter, Stratton, Richards, and Casey certainly hadn't held back when it came to fighting the Yankees at the bridge. They had pitched right in, risking their lives for the cause . . . and also to save him and Remy.

Thinking about the cause made Luke ponder the future. It was pretty obvious the Confederate government couldn't survive without the funds represented by that gold. Even if they made it safely to Georgia with the wagons, and the government set up a new capital there, would it mean anything except the Confederacy would cling to existence by its fingernails for another few weeks?

General William Tecumseh Sherman had already stormed through Georgia, leaving much of it in ruins. Atlanta—what was left of it after the Yankees had burned the city—was in Union hands. Once Richmond fell, as seemed inevitable, Grant could just turn around and march south, and the remnants of the Confederacy would be caught between two overwhelming forces.

The glorious cause, Luke thought bitterly. But despite his own cynicism, he knew he would fight to the end. Jensens didn't give up, even in the face of certain defeat. Sometimes events had a way of taking unexpected turns.

Even so, Luke didn't hold out much hope the mission would really change anything.

He lay on top of the bluff until it was time to wake up Dale for a turn on guard duty. He climbed down, went into the cave-like overhang, and reached under the lead wagon to where Dale had wrapped up in a blanket.

A shaken shoulder brought Dale out of his slumber. "Trouble?" he asked in a groggy voice.

"Nope," Luke told him. "Everything's quiet. But it's your turn to stand guard."

Dale yawned and stretched.

"One thing," Luke went on quietly after glancing around to see that no one was going to overhear. "Keep an eye on Casey, Stratton, Potter, and Richards."

"Why?" Dale asked with a frown.

"I just think it would be a good idea, until we're sure how much we can count on them."

Understanding dawned in Dale's eyes. "All right, Luke. But so far they haven't given us any reason not to trust them."

"Maybe not," Luke said, not wanting to get into the details of his conversation with Casey just yet, "but we want things to stay that way."

Before the sun went down that evening, Edgar Millgard built a small fire under the bluff. The overhang would disperse the smoke enough that it wouldn't be noticed. He cooked more of the salt pork, and they had biscuits with the meat instead of hardtack. "Don't get used to eatin' so fancy," he warned the men with a grin. "We don't have much flour."

They washed the food down with brackish water from their canteens. Josh Richards sighed. "I sure could use a real drink right about now."

"No liquor," Lancaster snapped. "We can't afford to let our guard down, even for a minute."

"Don't worry, Colonel," Richards drawled. "I was just wishin'. We don't have any redeye, anyway." He glanced over at Stratton and winked fast.

Luke barely noticed it, but it made him wonder. A little later, while they were saddling the horses, he pretended not to see Stratton until he bumped into the man.

When Stratton turned with a scowl and said, "Hey, be careful," he was close enough that Luke caught a faint whiff of whiskey on his breath.

"Sorry, Stratton, that was my fault. I wasn't watching what I was doing."

Stratton shrugged. "Well, no harm done. So don't worry about it."

Luke was going to worry about it, though. He was going to worry that either Stratton or Richards—or one of the other two, he supposed—had managed to sneak a bottle or a flask into their gear.

Drinking itself didn't bother Luke. From time to time he liked to have a beer or a shot of corn liquor. But he'd never had the thirst for the stuff some men did, and he agreed with Colonel Lancaster. They didn't need anything to distract them from their mission. They had been given the job of taking the bullion to Georgia, and as soldiers, it was their duty to carry out those orders.

It was just one more reason to keep an eye on the four men, he told himself.

Before they left the camp, Luke went over to Lancaster. "I've been thinking about something, Colonel."

"What's that, Jensen?"

"You seem to be the only one of us who knows exactly where we're going."

Lancaster frowned. "What's your point? I'm the only officer with this detail. The rest of you are just enlisted men. I'm the only one who needs to know."

Luke ignored the man's annoying arrogance. "Begging your pardon, sir, but if anything were to happen to you, we wouldn't know where to deliver the gold. I was thinking that if you had a map or something—"

"So you'd know exactly where to avoid if you tried to abscond with these wagons?" Lancaster broke in.

Luke couldn't stop himself from responding angrily. "Colonel, I never said such a thing. I never even thought it!"

"Well, I can't take any chances. President Davis himself picked me for this mission, and I don't intend to let him, or the Confederacy, down. So you just concern yourself with your own responsibilities, Corporal, and let me worry about everything else."

There was nothing Luke could do except grit his teeth for a second. "Yes, sir, Colonel." He turned and went back to the wagons.

Remy was helping Dale hitch up the team to the lead wagon. He inclined his head toward Lancaster and asked, "What was that about, *mon ami*?"

"Remember we talked about how the colonel is the only one who knows where we're going?" Luke asked.

"Sure."

"Well, I said something to him about it . . . and he wasn't inclined to share the information . . . which he told me in no uncertain terms."

Dale chuckled. "I never minded serving under the colonel in the field. Thought he did a pretty good job, in fact. But put him out here in command of a small group like this and he's sort of a jackass, ain't he?"

"So far," Luke agreed.

"You think he can manage to get all the way to Georgia without getting himself killed?"

"It's not him I'm worried about," Luke said. "I'd just as soon get the rest of us there without us getting killed."

CHAPTER 7

They traveled through the night without encountering any trouble, and after resting the next day Colonel Lancaster announced they would turn and head west for a night before starting south again. "We'll be well clear of Richmond, so we shouldn't run into any trouble."

"We'll be behind Yankee lines," Potter said.

"Yes, but all their attention is focused on Richmond now. As long as we avoid their supply trains and relief columns, we should be fine. I'm relying on you men for that."

Several more days passed without incident. They traveled by day, since they were off the main roads and needed light to see where they were going. Also, they were moving through country where none of them had been before, so they didn't know the terrain. Sometimes they found their way blocked by a ravine or a ridge the wagons couldn't handle, and were forced to backtrack until they found another route.

They were making progress southward, and that was encouraging to Luke. He didn't know how long it would take them to reach Georgia—a couple weeks, more than likely, he thought—but at least they were heading in the right direction finally. He just hoped the Confederacy hadn't collapsed by the time they got there.

In a way, that would be simpler, he mused as he rode ahead of the wagons, scouting with Remy. If the damned war was over, they could just surrender and be done with it. Admitting defeat to the Yankees would be a bitter pill to swallow, but at least they would all be alive.

Of course, in that case the Union would seize the gold. Off it would go to Washington. That bothered Luke, too, but the final fate of the gold was really none of his business.

He suspected Potter, Stratton, Richards, and Casey were all sneaking drinks now and then, but none of them got drunk so he didn't say anything about it. Lancaster seemed oblivious to what was going on, but that was nothing unusual. The colonel was oblivious about a lot of things.

Several times they had to take to the woods and find hiding places when Yankees were in the vicinity. Once they watched from the concealment of trees while a lone supply wagon rolled slowly past, accompanied by a handful of tired-looking blue-clad troopers. In whispers, Stratton and Potter urged Lancaster to let them attack the wagon.

"There's bound to be provisions in there we could use," Potter said.

"And we can kill all them blue bellies before they know what's goin' on," Stratton added.

Lancaster shook his head stubbornly. "We can't risk the shots drawing attention. We'll stay here until they're gone."

Stratton and Potter didn't argue, but Luke saw them looking at the colonel with a mixture of scorn and hatred. He didn't have a very high opinion of Lancaster himself, but those two looked like they wanted to murder him.

The bad feelings he had about the mission grew stronger as they continued heading south. More than a week had passed since they left Richmond when they paused to rest the horses one afternoon and suddenly heard something they hadn't heard in quite a while.

Female voices.

Casey's head came up like a bloodhound catching a scent. "Hear that, fellas? There's womenfolks somewhere close by!"

Luke heard it, all right. Several women, by the sound of it, and they were laughing. The voices were coming from the other side of a thick stand of trees.

"We'd better check that out, Colonel," Stratton said to Lancaster.

"Yeah, there's no tellin' but what they might be spyin' on us," Richards said.

It didn't sound to Luke like the women were spying on them. He thought it would be better to move on as quickly as possible.

But Lancaster nodded. "All right. Three of you go find out who they are and what they're doing here. Jensen, Casey, and Potter, you go."

Luke would have rather gone with a couple of his friends, but he nodded and got his rifle from the wagon. He and Casey and Potter slipped into the woods, moving quickly but quietly.

The stand of trees wasn't very thick. A couple minutes later, the three men came to a creek. A covered wagon was parked on the other side of the stream. A woman perched on the seat with a shotgun across her knees.

"Holy Moses," Casey breathed.

He was looking at six women standing knee-deep in the creek, stripped down to their underthings. They were taking advantage of the creek and the warm afternoon to bathe. The flimsy garments were soaked and clung to their bodies.

"You know what kind of women those are?" Potter asked in a whisper.

Luke knew. It was pretty obvious. They ranged in age from late teens to early thirties, he judged, although soiled doves led such hard lives they often looked older than they really were. Such women always followed the armies. Union, Confederate, it didn't matter. Luke figured such women could have been found with the Greeks outside the walls of Troy. "Must be Yankees around here. Otherwise those women wouldn't be here."

"I don't care about that," Casey said. "I just want to go say howdy to them."

Potter grunted. "I want to do a hell of a lot more than say howdy."

Luke understood. He was as human as the next man, and the sight of all that wet, bare, female flesh made him react just like Potter and Casey. But they had other things to worry about. "We'd better leave them alone. We'd just be asking for trouble if we start bothering with them."

"You're not in charge here, Jensen," Potter snapped.

"No, but the colonel wouldn't want—"

"The hell with the colonel! Come on, Ted."

Before Luke could stop him, Potter straightened, stepped out of the trees, and called, "Howdy there, ladies."

The women in the creek shrieked and giggled in surprise, but the older woman on the wagon seat instantly swung up her shotgun and pointed it across the stream. "Howdy yourself, you damn Rebel. You come a step closer and I'll blast you to hell!"

Potter held up his hands. "Whoa, there, ma'am. I don't mean any harm. I just came along and saw all these beautiful young fillies, and

I had to say hello." As Casey stepped out of the trees, Potter went on. "My friend here feels the same way."

"That's right," Casey said with a broad grin on his face.

Still under cover, Luke saw what was about to happen. "Casey, no!" He started forward, but was too late.

Casey's hand came up with a gun in it. The revolver roared, and across the creek, the woman on the wagon rocked backward as the bullet drove into her. One barrel of the shotgun boomed as her finger jerked on the trigger, but the weapon was angled upward and the load of buckshot went harmlessly into the air.

The woman swayed forward, dropped the shotgun, and pitched off the wagon seat, landing on the creek bank in a limp sprawl. Luke could tell by looking that she was dead.

The screams that came from the whores in the creek weren't playful any longer. The girls were terrified.

Potter drew his gun and said in a loud voice, "Shut up! Nobody's gonna hurt you!" He glared at Casey. "Why the hell did you shoot the old woman?"

"I don't like people pointin' guns at me," Casey said. "Anyway, you heard her call me a Rebel. She was a Yankee madam, nothin' to be worried about."

Even though Luke had seen far, far more than his share of violence over the past four years, the callous way Casey had murdered the woman sickened him. He was about to draw his own gun and cold-cock the varmint from behind when footsteps rushed through the trees toward them. He looked over his shoulder and saw Remy and the other men coming to see what the commotion was about.

"Hold your fire!" Lancaster called, even though no one was shooting. "Damn it, what's going on here?"

As they emerged from the trees, the man all gaped at the women in the creek, who were now huddled together in frightened silence. Even Lancaster stared at them.

Casey holstered his revolver and said coolly, "That old biddy over yonder by the wagon tried to blast us with a shotgun, Colonel. I stopped her."

"I heard those shots," Lancaster said, "and so did any Yankees within a mile of here! Come on. We have to get moving while we still have the chance."

"No offense, Colonel," Casey said, "but I'm not goin' anywhere until I've had a chance to get to know one of those gals a mite better. That one with the yaller hair, I'm thinkin'."

Luke saw how things were shaping up. Stratton and Richards had drifted toward Casey and Potter. Remy, Dale, and Edgar had moved up alongside Luke. Lancaster was in the middle.

The colonel realized it wasn't a very good place to be and stepped back quickly. "I've given you men an order. By God, I expect you to carry it out!"

They were standing on the knife-edge of bad trouble, Luke sensed. He had felt such impending violence in the air many times, and seldom did it end well.

However, something intervened. From the corner of his eye, he saw one of the soiled doves break away from the others. The blonde Casey had mentioned, in fact. She scrambled out of the creek onto the bank and snatched up the shotgun the older woman had dropped.

With their attention focused on each other, none of the other men saw it happening until it was too late. Potter finally noticed the blonde and twisted toward her, his hand clawing for the gun at his waist.

Luke's revolver came out with blinding speed. He leveled the barrel at Potter and drew back the hammer. The sinister metallic sound made Potter freeze.

"Don't do it," Luke warned.

Across the creek, the blonde screamed, "Get out of here, damn you! One barrel of this scattergun's still loaded! I'll cut you all down! I ought to do it anyway, for killin' Maddy!"

Potter's gun was in his hand, already cocked, but it was still pointed at the ground. He looked at Luke through eyes slitted narrow with hate. "You're takin' the side of a bunch of damned whores over your friends?"

"I don't recall you and me being friends, Potter," Luke said. "We just have the same job to do, that's all."

"And that job's in danger the longer we stay here," Lancaster said. "We have to go. Now."

For a second Luke thought Potter was going to lift his gun and pull the trigger, anyway. If he did, the creek bank would erupt in gunfire. They might all die, especially if the blonde cut loose at the men with that shotgun. She very well might do just that, considering the other whores had scrambled out of the creek and taken shelter behind their wagon.

Potter laughed and shook his head. "I'll never figure you out, Jensen." He lowered the hammer of his revolver and stuck the gun back in his waistband. "But I reckon you and the colonel are right. There might be a Yankee patrol gallopin' toward us right now, so we better light a shuck."

"But, Wiley—" Casey began.

"I said we're goin'."

Casey cast a regretful glance at the blonde. Clearly, he might have dared that shotgun to get at her. But too much else was against him at the moment. He nodded. "Yeah, come on, fellas." He pointed a finger across the creek at the blonde and added, "I'll see you again one of these days, darlin'."

"You better hope I don't see you first," she said as her mouth twisted in a snarl.

Luke didn't put his gun away until the men had gone back to the wagons. He saw Potter glancing at him several times as they got ready to move. It was hard to read the man's expression, but Luke knew he had made an enemy.

The outriders mounted up, and the drivers and guards climbed onto the wagons. With no Yankees in sight, they moved out smartly, still heading south.

Remy brought his horse alongside the wagon where Luke and Dale were riding. "The next time those girls see Yankee soldiers, they're gonna tell them about us."

"I expect you're right," Luke said.

"And that blond belle, she be a smart one, Luke. She heard Casey and Potter call the colonel by his rank, and she heard him givin' us orders. She'll figure out that, civilian clothes or not, we're soldiers. Confederate soldiers."

Luke nodded. He knew Remy was right.

And because of what had happened at that creek, he knew their mission had just gotten harder.

CHAPTER 8

The rest of that day, everyone in the group kept looking behind them fairly often, checking their back trail. The same thought was in their minds: one time, they'd look back and see Yankee cavalry chasing them.

It didn't happen, though. By the time they camped that night, they hadn't encountered anyone else.

The next day passed without incident as well, and Luke began to hope if the whores had told somebody about what had happened, the Yankees were too busy to worry about some strange-acting Confederate soldiers dressed in civilian clothing.

They were somewhere in eastern Tennessee, Luke figured, maybe in the Smoky Mountains, and the terrain grew more rugged. The wagons followed narrow, twisting trails running between steep, heavily wooded slopes. Luke watched those mountainsides intently, knowing the dark valleys were perfect for an ambush.

The travelers avoided settlements, but every now and then they passed isolated cabins with small garden patches nearby. The people living there barely subsisted on what little food they could grow, along with any small game they could trap. Obviously, it wasn't much. The people who came out of those rickety cabins to watch them pass were gaunt and hollow-eyed. They looked like it had been months since their bellies were even half full.

The children were the worst, Luke thought. His heart went out to them as they stared up at the wagons and riders with dull, defeated eyes. He wanted to give them something to eat, but he and his companions were already short on rations. His own belly spent a lot of time growling in hunger. The soldiers couldn't do any hunting be-cause of the attention the shots might attract.

They were approaching one such cabin when an old man with a long white beard limped onto the trail to stop them.

Lancaster called, "Get out of the way, old-timer," but the man didn't budge. Dale hauled back on the reins to bring the lead team to a halt before they ran over the old man. Lancaster cast an irritated look over his shoulder, and Luke knew it was because Dale had stopped the wagon without waiting for the colonel's order.

"What do you want, old man?" Lancaster asked.

The man raked gnarled fingers through his long white beard be-fore answering. "I don't know who ye are or where ye be goin', but I want you to take my grandson wi' ye." He turned his head and nod-ded toward the shack, where a skinny boy about twelve years old stood on the leaning porch. He was barefoot and wore only a pair of ragged overalls.

"I'm sorry, we can't do that," Lancaster said.

"If he stays here, he'll starve, sure as shootin'," the old man in-sisted. "The only chance he's got to live is goin' somewheres else, somewheres they have more food."

A harsh laugh came from Potter. "Then he's out of luck, old-timer, because it's like this all over the South. The Yankees have burned and looted and torn down until there's nothing left. The boy might as well stay here and starve instead of starvin' somewhere else."

The old man lifted a trembling hand. "Ye can't mean that. There's got to be some place better. There's got to be a place where folks still have some hope."

"If there is, we haven't seen it," Lancaster said. "I'm sorry, sir, but we have to be moving on. Now, if you'll get out of our way . . ."

In desperation, the old man reached for the halter on the colonel's horse. "Please . . . you got supplies . . ."

"Not enough to share," Lancaster snapped. "Not even enough to last us until we get where we're going." He pulled his horse to the side, out of the old man's reach. "Get out of—"

He didn't say any more. At that moment, a shot boomed and the old man's head jerked as a sizable chunk of it was blown away by a rifle ball. Blood sprayed in the air, turning his white hair pink.

The shot came from just behind them and to the right, Luke judged. While he was turning on the wagon seat to locate the threat, the thought crossed his mind that the shot had been aimed at

Lancaster. When the colonel moved his horse suddenly, it sealed the old man's fate.

More shots roared. Tongues of flame spurted in the trees almost at the edge of the trail. Luke whipped his rifle to his shoulder and fired at one of the muzzle flashes. A man in a dirty blue uniform and black forage cap staggered out from behind a tree, clutching his chest where Luke's bullet had gone. The Yankee soldier collapsed.

The rifle was good for only one shot, and Luke didn't have time to reload. He dropped it at his feet and yanked the revolver from his waistband as he used his other hand to shove Dale off the seat. He followed, diving after his friend.

The bushwhackers seemed to be on the right side of the road. As the Confederates returned the fire, they hurriedly took cover behind the wagons. The saddle mounts bolted down the trail, but that was a problem to worry about later, Luke thought . . . if any of them survived.

Crouching behind the lead wagon, he tried to make his shots count, waiting for a glimpse of blue before he pulled the trigger. Fortunately, the Yankees cooperated. There was no telling where those Union troops were from, but they didn't seem to have much experience at the sort of hill fighting the Southerners did. Nobody grew up in the Ozarks without learning about the dangers of bushwhackers.

Three more men fell to Luke's shots, and the heavy fire from his companions was taking a toll, too. The wagons with their cargo of bullion provided good cover. No bullets could penetrate those crates full of gold bars.

Luke glanced at the other men. They were all on their feet. He couldn't tell if any were wounded, but they were all still in the fight, something that couldn't be said for the Yankees.

The officer in charge of the ambush realized the same thing. He shouted over the sound of gunfire, "We'll overrun them! Charge!"

That was just about the worst thing those Yankees could have done. As they burst out of the woods, yelling and shooting, they were met by a hail of bullets from the wagons.

The first rank went down as lead tore into them, then the second, and the charge disintegrated into a chaotic milling around, turning the soldiers into sitting ducks. A few tried to flee back into the trees, but they were gunned down.

An eerie silence fell as clouds of powder smoke drifted over the trail and around the wagons. Luke risked a look. It appeared all the Yankees were on the ground. A few were writhing around and groaning in pain, but most of them lay in the limp sprawl that signified death.

If there had been enough of them, maybe they could have overrun the wagons and finished off the Confederates with their bayonets. But the attack had fallen short

"Check those men," Lancaster ordered.

Stratton tucked away his pistol and drew a knife. He looked over at Richards and grinned. "Josh and me will take care of it, Colonel."

Richards grinned, too, and pulled out his own knife.

Luke knew they intended to cut the throats of the Yankees who were only wounded. He didn't like the idea of killing defenseless men, but this was war, after all.

A sob made him turn around. The boy who'd been on the porch had come onto the trail, falling to his knees beside the body of his grandfather. He was leaning forward over the corpse, crying.

Luke reloaded his pistol and his rifle, then walked over to the boy and rested a hand on his shoulder. "Come on, son. That won't do any good. Your gramps is gone. I'm sorry."

"The . . . the Yankees came marchin' up a while ago," the youngster managed to say. "They told Grampa that . . . that there would be some wagons comin' along . . . They said they'd been chasin' you for days . . . and wanted him to stop y'all somehow. Grampa didn't want to do it . . . but they said they'd kill us both and burn down our place if he didn't . . . He had to do it, mister. He had to."

"I reckon he did." Luke had already figured out something like that must have happened. "There's no shame in a man doing whatever he has to in order to protect his family. You remember that, son."

"But then they . . . they shot him anyway!"

"I think that was an accident. They were trying to shoot one of us."

"He's dead, though, either way."

There was no denying that. Luke didn't even try to. He couldn't do anything for the boy except squeeze his shoulder again and leave him there to mourn his grandfather.

When he went back over to the wagons, he asked Remy, "Anybody hurt in our bunch?"

"Edgar got nicked on the arm, but Dale's patching it up. The colonel's hat's got a hole in it, so he came mighty close to shakin' hands with the devil. But that's all."

"We were lucky."

Remy nodded. "Very lucky. Maybe the fates, they are smilin' on us for a change."

Luke thought they had been pretty fortunate the whole trip, but he didn't point that out.

Colonel Lancaster said, "I don't know if there are any more Yankees in this area, but if there are, they're bound to have heard this battle. We need to get moving again quickly. Somebody move that old man's body out of the way."

"We could bury him, Colonel," Luke suggested.

Lancaster shook his head. "There's no time for that. Let's go. We'll all ride on the wagons until we catch up to our horses."

Luke thought it was likely the saddle mounts had stopped to graze somewhere along the trail. Once they were away from the sound of shots and the smell of powder smoke, they would have calmed down fairly quickly.

The boy had gone back to the shack and disappeared inside. Luke and Remy picked up the old man's body and carried it carefully off the trail. They had just returned to the wagons and climbed on when the youngster emerged from the cabin carrying an old squirrel rifle.

"You and your damned war!" he cried shrilly. "I hate all of you!" He started to lift the rifle.

Potter's revolver streaked out and blasted. The slug smashed into the boy's frail chest and lifted him off his feet as it drove him backward. Dust puffed up around him as he landed on the ground.

There hadn't been time for the other men to do anything. Lancaster turned to Potter and said in a horrified tone, "You shot that boy!"

"He was about to point a rifle at me," Potter said coolly as he reloaded the expended chamber. "Damned if I was gonna sit here and let him shoot me."

Luke hopped down from the wagon and walked over to pick up the rifle the boy had dropped. The youngster lay a couple feet away, staring sightlessly at the sky. Luke tried not to look at those open, empty eyes.

He checked the rifle and said in disgust, "I don't think this old relic would have even fired! You killed him for nothing, Potter."

Potter's shoulders rose and fell. "I didn't have any way of knowin' that, now did I?"

That was true, Luke supposed. He threw the squirrel rifle aside. The boy and his grandfather lay dead on one side of the road, more than a dozen Yankees on the other. Once again Luke and his companions were surrounded by senseless death.

After all the things he had seen . . . all the things he had *done* . . . he wondered if by the time the war was finally over, he would have any soul left at all.

CHAPTER 9

The gold escort continued south, hoping the Yankees who'd ambushed them were the only ones on their trail. Luke thought it likely the women they'd encountered beside that creek had sent the soldiers after them.

Each day without an ambush or confrontation the Confederates became more aware the Yankees had other things to deal with, like the collapse of the Confederacy. The atmosphere of gloom and despair hung over the landscape like actual clouds. The air smelled of smoke, rotting flesh, and defeat.

It seemed to Luke like a month had passed since they left Richmond, but he knew it hadn't quite been two weeks. "We're getting close to Georgia now," he commented to Dale one day. "Have to be."

"I think you're right," Dale said. "What are you gonna do once we get where we're goin', Luke?"

"I guess that'll be up to the colonel. Maybe he has orders for what we're supposed to do next. If not, I guess I'll stay wherever the new capital is and try to do what I can to help." Luke shook his head. "No point in trying to go back to Richmond, even if we could get there."

"I got a feelin' you're right about that."

The trail entered a long, straight stretch between two mostly bald knobs. Luke frowned at the hills, thinking it would be another good spot for an ambush.

But when the trouble came, it popped up right in front of them through sheer bad luck. A Union cavalry patrol came trotting around a bend in the trail just beyond the knobs.

The Yankees regarded anybody who wasn't wearing the blue as an enemy. Sunlight winked on steel as the officer in charge of the patrol whipped his saber from its scabbard and shouted, "Charge!"

Just like that, the Confederates were in another fight, and there wasn't any good cover on either side of the road.

All they could do was shoot it out.

Luke brought his rifle to his shoulder, drew a bead on the officer leading the charge, and pressed the trigger. The rifle roared and bucked against his shoulder. Through the powder smoke stinging his eyes, he saw the Yankee topple off the galloping horse.

Their commanding officer's death didn't slow down the other cavalrymen. They kept moving forward, blazing away with pistols as they raced toward the wagons and the outriders.

Colonel Lancaster tried to wheel his horse around and gallop back to the cover of the wagons, but he jerked in the saddle as at least one bullet found him. A crimson stain bloomed on the colonel's shirt, as he galloped past the lead wagon.

Dale grunted in pain beside Luke, but he didn't have time to glance over and see how badly his friend was hurt. He had his revolver leveled at the charging Yankees. As he squeezed off his last two rounds, another cavalryman fell, taking his mount down with him. Another horse ran into the fallen animal and upended as well. The trail suddenly became a welter of flailing hooves and swirling dust.

The back of the charge was broken. Only three Yankees remained mounted. They whirled their horses and fled. A few final shots from the Confederates followed to speed them on their way.

Luke turned to Dale and found his friend clutching a bloody left shoulder. "How bad is it?"

"Don't know, but it hurts like hell," Dale replied through clenched teeth. "I'll be all right. See about Remy and Edgar."

Luke twisted on the seat to look back at the other wagon. Remy was reloading and seemed to be all right. He glanced up and gave Luke a brief nod to signify as much. Edgar waved to indicate he was unharmed, too.

Lancaster had galloped past both wagons before coming to a stop. Luke had a feeling the horse had been running blindly, that the colonel was no longer in control. He glanced back to where the horse had stopped. Lancaster was still mounted, sitting hunched over in the saddle.

Casey trotted his horse back to check on the officer. He put a hand on Lancaster's shoulder and leaned over to take a closer look at him. Then he turned and called to the others, "Hey, the colonel's shot to pieces!"

"Get him down from his horse," Luke said, "but be careful with him."

Casey frowned as if he didn't like the idea of Luke giving him orders, but he dismounted and reached up to take hold of Lancaster. Stratton got to them in time to swing down from his saddle and give Casey a hand.

They lowered Lancaster onto his back in the grass at the side of the trail. All the men gathered around him, even the wounded Dale Cardwell.

Lancaster was still alive. His eyes were open, and his mouth moved like he was trying to say something. He couldn't get the words out, though. Nothing came from his mouth except trickles of blood at each corner.

The colonel's shirt was so bloody it was hard to tell for sure, but it looked like the man had been hit at least three times. Clearly, the wounds were bad ones.

Luke figured Lancaster had only minutes to live, if that long. He dropped to a knee beside him. "Colonel, can you hear me? Colonel!"

Lancaster managed to make a sound, but it was just a choked, incoherent moan. From the look in his eyes, he wasn't aware of anything except the pain that filled him.

"Colonel, listen to me!" Luke urged. "We need to know where we're going. Colonel, do you have a map? Can you tell me—"

"He can't tell you nothin', Jensen," Potter said. "He's next thing to dead, can't you see that? We're on our own now."

"Don't say that just yet," Luke snapped. "We can't give up—"

A grotesque rattle came from Lancaster's throat. When Luke looked at the colonel again, he saw that Lancaster's eyes were starting to glaze over.

"Well, he's sure enough dead now," Potter drawled, "and like I said, we're on our own. Question is, what are we gonna do?"

"Go check those Yankees and make sure they're all dead," Luke said as he reached over to close Lancaster's eyes. "Remy, patch up Dale's shoulder."

"*Oui.*"

"Then we'll get moving," Luke went on. "We can't afford to wait around. Three of those troopers got away. They'll go tell other Yankees what happened. We need to get off the trail and find a place to hole up for a while."

He glanced up. No one except Remy, who was tearing pieces off his shirt to bind up the wound in Dale's shoulder, had moved to do what he said. "Blast it, get moving."

"Hold on just a minute, Jensen," Potter said. "I don't recall anybody puttin' you in charge."

"Somebody's got to take over," Luke said. "Or would you rather stand around and argue about it until a whole company of Yankee cavalry shows up?"

Potter thought it over for a couple seconds, then shrugged.

"All right, we'll do what you say . . . for now. But this ain't settled."

Luke didn't expect it to be, but for the moment he would take what he could get. He said to Edgar, "Let's put the colonel's body in one of the wagons."

"Why not leave him where he lays?" Stratton suggested.

"Because I want to search him later and see if he's got any written orders or a map on him."

That answer satisfied the others, and they went about their business. All the fallen Yankees were dead except for a couple, and Casey didn't waste any time slitting their throats. Luke and Edgar carried Lancaster's body over to the second wagon and placed it alongside the crates containing the gold bullion. By that time, the crude job Remy had done of bandaging Dale's wound had stopped the bleeding.

"Somebody tie the colonel's horse behind the second wagon," Luke said. "We'll take it with us."

That done, they followed the trail for another half mile until Luke spotted a narrow path leading off into a thick stretch of woods. He was driving the lead wagon since Dale couldn't handle the team with a wounded arm and drove between the trees, calling back to Remy, "Once we're all off the trail, get a branch and wipe away our tracks as far back as you can."

Remy waved a hand in acknowledgment of the order.

The path was little more than a game trail. Trees and brush crowded in on the wagons from both sides. Branches clawed at the men. Several times the wagons' sideboards scraped against tree trunks, and Luke worried they would get stuck. Finally, they broke out into a small clearing. It was big enough to turn the wagons around and go back out the way they had come in, but it would be a challenge.

When Remy rode in a few minutes later, he said, "Not only did I wipe away our tracks, but I pulled some brush in front of the opening as well. If any Yankees ride by, they may not even notice a gap big enough for the wagons."

Luke nodded his approval. "That was good thinking. Let's get the colonel out of the wagon so I can check his pockets."

"Robbin' the dead?" Potter asked mockingly.

"Checking for a map or orders, like I said before."

"You go right ahead. I ain't fond of handlin' dead men."

Neither was Luke, but he made himself do it. He searched all Lancaster's pockets but didn't find anything except a couple blood-stained letters from the colonel's wife. He didn't read them, tucking them back into Lancaster's pocket. He didn't have any right to intrude on the colonel's private life.

Since that search came up empty, Luke opened Lancaster's saddle-bags next. He was luckier there, finding a leather dispatch case with a folded map inside. As the others gathered around, he spread the map on the ground and studied it. After a second, his finger poked a spot that had been circled. "Copperhead Mountain. That must be where we're going. There's probably a settlement nearby where the government's going to set up." He straightened as he folded the map. "That's where we're going, anyway."

Wiley Potter's voice was flat and hard as he said, "I'm not so sure you're right about that, Jensen."

CHAPTER 10

Luke stiffened. Somehow, he wasn't surprised by what Potter said or the thinly veiled threat in the words. "What are you talking about?"

"All you've got is a map," Potter said. "You don't know that this Copperhead Mountain place is where we're supposed to go."

"It's the only thing in the colonel's belongings that has a destination marked. I think we all know that's what it means."

"Maybe," Stratton said. "But we don't have to go there, now do we?"

"Lancaster's dead," Richards added. "The mission's over."

Luke shook his head. "What makes you think that? Just because we've lost our commanding officer, doesn't mean we don't still have our orders."

"Orders from who? Jeff Davis?" Potter laughed. "The president of a country that may not even exist by now? Hell, Richmond could have fallen the day after we left, for all we know!"

Edgar said, "Even if Richmond fell, the war's still going on. General Lee hasn't surrendered. The way those Yankees keep attacking us proves that."

"Edgar's right," Remy said. "Our responsibility still lies with the Confederacy."

Casey finally put into words what was uppermost in all their minds. He pointed at the wagons and exclaimed, "But there's all that gold just sittin' there!"

It had happened even faster than Luke thought it would. The temptation of that fortune in gold bullion had been there all along, of course. Lancaster's presence and the men's habit of taking orders had held it in check.

But Lancaster was gone, and all Potter, Stratton, Richards, and Casey could think of was how they could be rich men. All they had to do was forget about delivering the gold to Copperhead Mountain, take the wagons, and strike out on their own. If they headed west, they might be able to leave the war behind them. There had been battles between Union and Confederate forces out on the frontier, but not many.

Luke glanced right and left. Remy, Dale, and Edgar stood with him, as he had known they would. They faced the other four men across a short distance. No guns were drawn—yet—but everyone was tense and ready for trouble.

It might not be possible to reason with the others. That much gold had a way of making a man's brain not work as well as it usually did. But Luke was going to try. "Look, you know we're not going to let you take those wagons. That gold belongs to the Confederacy. If we do anything with it except deliver it where we're supposed to, we'll be thieves . . . and traitors."

Potter let out a contemptuous snort. "How can you betray a country that don't exist anymore?" he demanded.

"You don't know that."

"Hell, Jensen, you've got eyes! There's no way Richmond was able to hold out. The streets are probably full of Yankees by now. And if Lee *hasn't* surrendered yet, he's got Grant chasin' him across Virginia. It's only a matter of time until what's left of the army is cornered. Lee's not gonna fight to the death, and you know it. He'll surrender."

Luke suspected Potter was right about that. General Robert E. Lee cared too much about his soldiers to let them be slaughtered to the last man in a futile cause.

But that still didn't change anything. They had their orders.

"Forget it, Potter. From the looks of that map, we're not far from Copperhead Mountain. We can be there in another couple days. And that's where we're going with that gold."

"That's your final word?" Potter asked. Next to him, Casey nervously licked his lips, anxious to grab for his gun. So were Richards and Stratton.

From what Luke had seen of those men, they were probably faster on the draw than Dale and Edgar. He and Remy might be able to match them, but that wasn't good enough. If it came down to a fight, he and his friends would probably die.

Some of the others would die, too, but more than likely one or two of them would survive. Those survivors would be very rich men.

The ones who didn't make it would be dead, and that worry lurked in Wiley Potter's eyes. Potter didn't want to risk his own life to make somebody else rich.

That realization was confirmed a second later when Potter burst out, "Ah, the hell with it!"

"Wait a minute, Wiley," Stratton protested. "What do you mean?"

"I mean I don't feel like dyin' over this," Potter declared.

Casey looked stricken. "The Confederacy don't need that gold," he said with a whining note in his voice. "It oughta be ours!"

"A man can always get rich if he's smart enough," Potter responded. "But not if he's dead!"

Luke didn't relax and let his guard down. He didn't trust Potter, not for a second. It could be some sort of trick. "You'll go on to Copperhead Mountain with us?"

"I didn't say that," Potter replied. "Look, we've fought Yankees over and over again on the way down here. They're probably lookin' for us right now. Our luck's bound to run out sooner or later. I've had enough of this war, Jensen. I'm riding away. The rest of you do whatever you damned well please."

"In other words, you're deserting," Luke said in a hard voice.

Potter surprised him by laughing. "You think I care what you call it? You can't betray a country that doesn't exist, and you can't desert from an army that's probably surrendered by now. All I know is I'm done with it."

"Me, too," Stratton said.

"And me," Richards added.

Casey still looked like he wanted to shoot somebody, but he gave a grudging nod. "Yeah, I'll go along with the others. I reckon bein' alive is the best thing."

"So, Jensen," Potter said. "Is it settled . . . or is it going to be a fight?"

Luke glanced at his companions. Remy shrugged a little. Edgar gave him a tiny nod. Dale just looked like he was in pain from that wounded shoulder.

"Go ahead and get out of here, if that's what you want to do." Luke didn't bother trying to keep the scorn out of his voice.

"We're taking the horses."

"Go ahead. We've got the colonel's horse. Remy can ride it. I'll handle one wagon and Edgar the other."

Potter smirked. "Sounds like you've got it all figured out. You'll be a real hero when you get to Copperhead Mountain with that gold. That is, until the Yankees take it away from you and you see what a waste it all was."

"I'll know that I followed orders, anyway."

"Yeah, that'll buy you a lot." Potter jerked his head at his allies. "Come on. I want to put some distance behind us before any more blue bellies can catch up to us."

"Wiley, are you sure about this?" Stratton asked.

"I'm sure. We'll have other big chances later on. Stick with me, boys, and we'll all be rich sooner or later."

The others still didn't look happy about it, but they followed Potter's lead and mounted up. Potter took a small bag of supplies from one of the wagons and held it up to Luke, raising his eyebrows. Luke nodded for him to take it.

The four men didn't follow the path back toward the road. They struck out across country, soon vanishing in the thick woods.

"Deserters," Edgar said in disgust. "Lousy deserters."

"Maybe worse than that," Remy said. "You don't trust them, do you, Luke?"

"Not one bit. We'll keep our eyes open in case they double back and make a try for the gold."

"So now we have to worry about the Yankees *and* those four," Dale said. "Things don't get any easier, do they?"

Luke shook his head. "Hardly ever."

They buried Colonel Lancaster's body in the woods and stayed hidden in the little clearing all night. Several times Luke heard a lot of hoofbeats in the distance and thought it was likely the Yankees were hunting for them. None of the searchers came close to the wagons, though. Luke wondered if that was because they really hadn't gone very far from the site of the battle with the cavalrymen. The Yankees might have expected them to head on south as quickly as possible.

Nor was there any sign of Potter, Richards, Stratton, and Casey. Luke hoped the four men really had lit a shuck for the frontier. It would certainly make things easier.

By morning, Dale had developed a fever and lay stretched out under one of the wagons.

Luke looked at him, then at the others. "If we move him, we take a chance on him getting worse."

"We could stay here another day," Remy suggested. "Give the Yankees that much more time to get tired of lookin' for us."

That sounded like a pretty good idea to Luke. They continued lying low and took turns wiping Dale's face with a wet cloth to keep him cool as he tossed and muttered. It was all they could do for him.

The fever broke the next night. Dale was still weak, but a lot more coherent the morning after that. As he sipped a little broth Edgar had made from the salt pork, he said, "We gotta get movin' again. That gold needs to get to the new capital."

Luke had his doubts whether that new capital even existed, but on the chance that it did, they had to continue their mission. He nodded. "We'll hitch up the teams."

Dale was able to sit up and ride on the seat of the lead wagon next to Luke. Edgar handled the other wagon while Remy rode ahead to scout their route. He came back to report that the trail was clear.

"Lots of tracks, though, and they're pretty recent," Remy said. "There are still plenty of Yankees in these parts. Might be better if we started travelin' at night again."

"That won't be easy since we don't know exactly how to get where we're going," Luke said. "We've got the colonel's map, though. Maybe we can figure it out."

Late that afternoon, they had to leave the road hurriedly to avoid a cavalry patrol. Luke and Edgar managed to pull the wagons behind a hill before the blue-clad troopers rode past, but it was close.

"You're right," Luke told Remy. "We'll travel at night the rest of the way, starting tonight. We'll stay here and let the horses rest for a few hours, then try to put a few more miles behind us."

They made a cold supper from rations that had dwindled to almost nothing. For days, they had gotten by on about half the food they really needed. Luke's belly felt empty all the time. The trek wouldn't last much longer, he told himself, and then things would be better.

Remy did a little more scouting while it was still light and returned to tell the others, "There's a river about a mile from here. It's shallow, and there's a good ford. We shouldn't have any trouble gettin' across."

"And we can fill up our water barrels and canteens while we're at it," Edgar said.

That sounded like a good plan to Luke. When they had rested for a while and it was good and dark, they started the wagons rolling south again.

The moon hadn't risen yet when they reached the river, but Luke saw stars reflected in its placid surface. Remy rode out in front of the wagons so the others could see how deep the water was. Luke figured it was only about a foot.

"The bottom's good and solid," Remy said. "The only problem is that the bank on the other side is a little steep. It'll be a hard haul for the teams gettin' all that weight up to the top. But I reckon they can do it."

"All right, let's go." Luke slapped the reins against the backs of his team. The big draft horses leaned into their harness. Water splashed around the wheels as the wagon began fording the river.

Luke made the crossing without any problem and started up the grade on the far side as Edgar's wagon rolled out of the water behind him. Remy sat his horse to one side.

Suddenly, what felt like a sledgehammer slammed into Luke, low down on his back. He cried out in agony as the impact drove him forward. Dropping the reins, he slumped over and almost pitched off the seat to land under the hooves of the team. At the last moment he twisted his body and fell to the side, landing with stunning force beside the front wheel.

He had never felt such pain in his life. It swelled and burst into a fiery explosion that seemed as big and hot as the sun. As Luke lay there gasping for breath, he heard shots, heard men cry out. Remy cursed and gasped. Edgar roared in defiance, a bellow that was cut short by a flurry of gunfire.

They had been ambushed. The question was whether the bushwhackers were Yankees . . . or those damned deserting curs, Potter, Stratton, Richards, and Casey.

He got his answer a moment later when hoofbeats sounded close beside his head. Instinctively, he tried to jerk away from them, but his body wouldn't work anymore. All he could do was lie there and twitch.

"I don't hear you giving any orders now, Jensen," a man's harsh voice said.

Wiley Potter. Luke recognized the voice, even though he couldn't respond to it.

He thought his gun was still tucked in his waistband and tried to edge his hand toward it. A gun roared, and mud from the riverbank splattered in his face as the bullet tore into the ground beside his head.

"You're beat, Jensen," Potter said. "You might as well admit it. The other three are dead, and you soon will be. And that gold's goin' with us, just like it was supposed to all along. You stupid idiot, did you really think we were just gonna ride away and leave it?"

Luke was hurting too much to force his thoughts into any coherent order. He shifted a little, and an even more terrible wave of agony made him scream.

"Your back's busted," Potter went on. "That was a hell of a shot I made, if I do say so myself. You're gonna be a long time dyin', Jensen, and I'm going to sit right here on my horse and enjoy every minute of it. So you go ahead and scream. It's music to my ears."

"Wiley, we can't stay here too long." That was Stratton. "We need to take these wagons and get movin'. Why don't you just put a bullet in his head and be done with it?"

Casey laughed. "What fun would that be? I'm with you, Wiley. I want to listen to Jensen scream while he's dyin'."

Luke's mind cleared abruptly. He understood what they'd been saying and forced himself to cut short the agonized cries coming from his tortured throat. He wasn't going to give them the satisfaction.

But his resolve was short-lived, as the pain made him cry out again. Several of the deserters laughed, obviously enjoying Luke's torment.

They weren't going to have much longer to indulge their sadistic glee. A darkness that had nothing to do with night was closing in around Luke, washing over his mind like a black tide. *This is what dying feels like,* he thought in a final moment of clarity.

"He's dead," he heard Wiley Potter say.

That was all. After that, the darkness was complete.

BOOK TWO

CHAPTER 11

When Luke Jensen was ten years old, he fell out of a tree and broke his left arm. It hurt like blazes, and he couldn't hold back the tears as his pa set the bone and splinted the arm.

"No need to cry," Emmett Jensen had said. "That don't make the arm feel any better, does it?"

"Hell yes, it does!" Luke had yelled.

Emmett had laughed too hard to get on to him for cussing. Luke's ma took care of that later, fussing at him until he wished he'd broken his ears instead of his arm.

Luckily, Emmett had set enough broken bones that he knew what he was doing, so his oldest son's arm healed cleanly and Luke didn't suffer any loss of strength or movement in it. He never forgot how bad it hurt when it happened, though.

A couple years later, while getting some wood from the pile next to the back door of the Jensen cabin, he was stung on the right hand by the biggest scorpion he'd ever seen. It felt like somebody had shoved a dull knife through his palm.

The hand swelled up and got almost as red as a beet, and for a while the family worried that he would lose it. Emmett was prepared to cut the hand off if it meant saving Luke's life, but first, he rode up into the hills and brought back an old granny woman who scoured the countryside for plants, made a foul-smelling poultice out of them, and bound it onto Luke's hand.

Within a day the swelling started to go down and the redness went away. By the time a week had passed, the hand was back to normal and Luke couldn't even see the place where the scorpion had stung him.

He remembered what that had felt like, too, and took particular satisfaction in stomping every one of the ugly little varmints he saw after that.

The pain radiating from his back made breaking his arm seem like stubbing his toe. That scorpion sting was nothing more than a mosquito bite. Without a doubt, the current pain was the worst agony Luke had ever experienced in his life.

He wasn't sure how long he lay there, awash in suffering, before he realized the pain meant he wasn't dead.

His pulse hammered an insane rhythm inside his skull. He tried to force his eyes open, but couldn't do it. There wasn't enough strength in him even for a tiny task like that. All he could do was lie there and drag ragged breaths into his body.

After another unknowable length of time, he became aware of light striking his eyelids. He tried again to lift them, and succeeded.

Sunlight lay in a dappled pattern around him. Lying on his stomach on damp ground, his head was turned to the right, his left cheek pressed against the dirt. After a moment, he figured out the sun was shining down on him through some tree branches. Trying to make his brain work provided a welcome distraction from the pain.

He tried to remember how he'd gotten there. At first, everything up until that moment was a blank slate in his mind, but slowly the details began to fill in. He remembered the gold, the journey from Richmond, the friends who had been with him . . .

Then the ambush and Wiley Potter's sneering voice telling him the others were dead and he was dying. In fact, he recalled Potter saying, "He's dead."

Potter had been wrong about that. Luke was too weak to move, but he sure wasn't dead. Not yet, anyway.

Since Potter had been wrong about him, maybe the bushwhacker had been wrong about the others, too. Luke yelled, "Remy! Dale! Edgar! Can any of you hear me?"

It was only when he heard the faint croaking sounds that he realized he wasn't yelling at all. He'd only thought that he was. *He* was the one making those incoherent noises. Finally, after what seemed like another hour, he struggled to get out the name, "R-Remy . . ."

He heard some birds in the distance, the wind stirring the branches in the trees, the tiny lapping sound of the river flowing nearby, but that was all.

He had to get up and look for them. He might still be able to save them.

The gold was gone. Luke knew that. Potter and the other deserters would have taken the wagons with them when they left him for dead, so Luke didn't waste time worrying about that. His only concerns were saving his own life and helping his friends if he could.

He needed to get up and see how badly he was hurt, but one thing at a time, he told himself. First he wanted to look around. He moved his hands enough to dig his fingers into the dirt and brace himself. Then, with a grunt of effort, he lifted his head.

A yell burst from him as even that much movement set off a fresh explosion of pain. He wanted to drop his head, close his eyes, and retreat back into the welcoming darkness.

Instead, he forced his head from side to side in small, jerking motions.

He couldn't hold back a sob as he saw Dale lying on the ground a few yards away. The young man's face was unmarked and his eyes were open, but flies were crawling around on them. He was dead, no doubt about it. His clothes were black with blood where he'd been shot.

Remy and Edgar had fallen in the other direction. Edgar's face was a hideous ruin where several shots had struck him, but Luke recognized his friend's burly build. Remy was disfigured as well, with most of his jaw shot away. The flies were feasting on their spilled blood, as well.

Luke groaned and let his head fall. There was nothing he could do for his friends, after all. Nothing he could do except save himself and maybe go after Potter and the others once the pain in his back got better.

He didn't know how long he lay there, stretched out on the riverbank. The earth turned and the sun moved in the sky, and he was no longer in the shade. When the heat began to bother him, he tried to heave himself up to hands and knees so he could crawl where it was cooler.

The muscles in his arms and shoulders bunched, and the upper part of his body lifted slightly, but that was all. Luke pushed on his hands again to move upward, but was unable to move high enough. He tried to press against the ground with his knees . . . and realized he couldn't *feel* his knees. He couldn't feel any part of his legs.

Horror washed over him. His body seemed to end at his lower back, where the bullet had struck him and the pain was so bad. Below that, however, nothing hurt. His legs might as well not have been there, and for one sickening moment, he believed they weren't. He thought Potter had sawed them off before leaving.

Slowly, Luke moved his right hand next to his hip. Breathing heavily against the pain, he twisted his neck and looked along his body. He couldn't see very well, but caught enough of a glimpse to know his right leg was still there.

He slumped down. The effort had made his heart pound crazily and left him breathless. As he gasped for air, he remembered a farmer back in Missouri named Claude Monroe, who'd been kicked in the back by a rambunctious mule. The accident busted something in Monroe's back, and after that he was never able to walk again. He had lived for a couple years, lying in bed or sometimes lifted into a chair, before he'd taken an old flintlock pistol, carefully loaded and primed it, and blown a hole right through his head.

He wouldn't have to do that, Luke thought as a hysterical laugh worked its way up his parched throat. No, he would die right where he was . . . on the riverbank . . . more than likely. He knew from the terrible thirst gripping him that he'd lost quite a bit of blood, and he might be losing more all the time without being aware of it. The easiest thing in the world would be to just give in to the pain that enveloped him, and wait for death. So easy . . .

There was no dramatic moment, no stirring speech he made to pull himself back from the brink of despair. It was just that after a while he got so thirsty he thought he might as well try to get a drink from the river. He moved his left arm next to his left hip and cautiously looked under his arm to see if his left leg was still there. It was. He pushed and clawed at the ground in an effort to turn himself around.

When he got far enough around, the steep slope worked against him, and before he knew what was happening, he was rolling down toward the water, his useless legs flopping loosely.

So, I'm going to fall in the river and drown in a foot of water. As that thought flashed across Luke's mind he reached out, caught hold of a root growing from one of the trees on the bank, and stopped himself at the edge of the river.

He hung on to the root with one hand while he reached out with the other and cupped it in the stream. When he brought that hand to his mouth, the water he sucked out of his cupped palm was the sweetest he'd ever tasted.

Thirst made him ignore the pain in his back. His movements grew frenzied as he drank. He missed sometimes and splashed water over his face. It felt good.

Then his stomach lurched, and he spewed up all the water he had managed to guzzle down. The spasm made him cry out.

The sickness faded after a few minutes. Luke lay there a little longer and started drinking again, slower.

He kept it down.

When his thirst wasn't so desperate, he twisted around and looked up at the top of the riverbank again. In his condition, the slope seemed impossible for him to climb. He would be better off just staying close to the water, so he could get another drink later.

Making that decision was all he could manage. Closing his eyes, he rested his head against the ground, content to lie there and wait for . . . something.

What he got wasn't good. A short time later, it started to rain.

Luke hadn't noticed the sun going behind the clouds, hadn't been aware the day was growing dark and ominous with the approach of a storm. He had no idea what was happening until thunder suddenly boomed so loud it shook the earth underneath him.

Or was that artillery fire? He had felt the earth move plenty of times in Richmond as the Yankees pounded the city with their big guns.

No, definitely thunder, he thought as several large raindrops pelted the back of his head. In a matter of seconds, a torrent was sluicing down around him.

Luke lifted his head, tilted it back as much as he could, and shouted at the heavens, "Go ahead! Rain on me, damn you! After everything that's already happened to me, how much worse can this be?"

He wasn't sure if he actually bellowed out the words or just thought them, the way he'd thought he was calling his friends' names earlier. But either way, the sentiment was real.

Unfortunately, a few minutes later he realized his situation *could* get worse.

When he looked along the banks, he saw how they were washed out in places. That was why the root he'd grabbed was sticking out of the ground. It meant the river had a tendency to rise when it rained. If the marks on the bank were right, the water could come up higher than the place where he was sprawled.

But how long will it take to do that? he asked himself. *And how much will it have to rain before I'll be in danger?*

He couldn't answer those questions, but it was a downpour, no doubt about that. A real toad-strangler, they'd call it back home. All along the banks, miniature waterfalls were already forming as rain landed higher up and ran down to the river, raising its level drop by drop.

And there were millions of drops.

Luke started laughing again. By all rights, he should have been dead already. How many more times could he manage to dodge the reaper? When was his luck going to run out?

Soon, he thought. Soon.

The water would climb up his body until the current plucked him away from the bank and spun him out into the stream and sucked him under. Tomorrow his lifeless body would wash up somewhere downriver. He could see that grotesque image in his mind, plain as day.

But he wasn't going to give in to that fate without a fight. His father had made it clear to him at an early age that Jensens didn't have any back up in them. Don't go lookin' for trouble, Emmett had told him, but don't ever go runnin' away from it, either. And if the devil finds you, spit in his face.

Luke reached up the bank, dug his hand into the mud, and pulled.

The ground was wet and slick, but he clawed at it stubbornly, grabbed another root, dug in with his elbows, and shoved. He got his body turned so he was facing up the bank again instead of lying sideways on it.

Even if he'd been able to use his legs, it would have been difficult to crawl up that muddy slope. With only his arms to pull himself along, it was sheer torture. The burning pain in his arms and shoulders dominated the misery in his back.

Slowly, inch by agonizing inch, he pulled himself up the riverbank.

After what seemed like hours, when he was too exhausted to go on, he turned his head, looking under his arm, and realized he was only a couple feet higher than when he'd started out. He looked back along his body as best he could.

His feet were already in the water. The river had risen about a foot, and the current was running fast, which meant more and more water was coming down from upstream.

Gritting his teeth, Luke tried to haul himself higher. He made another few inches, maybe half a foot, and his strength deserted him again.

Maybe what he ought to do was try to roll over onto his back, he thought. Then the rain, which was still coming down with blinding force, might drown him before the river rose high enough to do the job.

The problem was, he was too weak to roll over.

Luke laughed. "You got me," he rasped. "I'm done for. Fought all I can fight. I'm sorry, Pa. Wish I could see you again. You and Ma and Janey and Kirby . . . but this is where it ends for me."

His head fell forward. Mud covered his face, clogged his nose, choked him. He coughed and fought free of it, his instincts refusing to let him die. The rain washed some of the muck from his eyes.

And he was able to see the slender fingers reaching down and wrapping around the wrist of his outstretched right hand. Thunder boomed again and lightning flashed.

Luke Jensen blinked in amazement as he rose up as best he could, carefully turned his head, and saw the face of the angel who had reached down from heaven to lift him from earth.

It was funny. He'd always figured when he died, he'd be headed in the other direction.

CHAPTER 12

"Damn it!" the angel yelled.

Confused, Luke blinked rainwater out of his eyes. He'd never gone to prayer meeting all that much, but he didn't remember any preachers he'd ever heard saying anything about angels cussing.

"Come on, mister!" the beautiful vision urged. "You weigh too much for me to lift you by myself. You gotta help me some!"

Understanding sunk slowly into Luke's brain. Despite the pretty face, it was no angel above him but rather a flesh-and-blood girl. She wasn't wearing heavenly robes and didn't have wings, either. She was dressed in tattered overalls, a woolen shirt, and a battered old black hat with rainwater streaming from the brim.

She tugged on his wrist. "Mister, can you hear me? The river's comin' up. If we don't get you off this bank, you're gonna drown."

After fighting on his own for what seemed like an eternity, the sheer fact that someone else was trying to save him filled Luke with gratitude and relief. That feeling was short-lived, though, because he realized she was right. "Can you . . . get help?" he croaked.

"No time!" she said. "This ol' river comes up mighty quick when it rains like this. Goldang it, I told Grampaw I heard somebody yellin' last night!"

"You better . . . fetch him. Has he got . . . a horse or . . . a mule?"

"Yeah, but like I told you, there ain't enough time for that." She dug the heels of her bare feet into the bank and got hold of his wrist with both hands. As she hauled hard on his arm, she said through clenched teeth, "Can't you push . . . with your damned legs?"

Luke couldn't, and he didn't have a chance to explain it. Just then her feet slipped in the mud and she sat down hard as her legs went out from under her. With a startled cry she started sliding down the bank toward him.

She didn't go very far. His head butted her in the stomach and stopped her. Her thighs rested on his shoulders. She put her hands on the ground and pushed herself away from him.

"Dadblast it!" she cried. "Don't you go gettin' any ideas, mister!"

"The only idea I have . . . is not drowning," Luke said. "Let's . . . try again."

The girl scrambled up and took hold of his wrist again. Luke used his other hand to grasp one of the tree roots and pulled. The combined effort was enough to break him free of the sticky mud. He slid upward almost a foot.

"Hang on," Luke told her. "Let me . . . get hold of . . . another root."

She waited until he had a good grip, and then both of them grunted with the strain as they lifted his mostly dead weight. He wound up higher on the bank.

"Here we go," the girl urged. "We're gettin' it now."

They had made some progress, that was true, but Luke didn't know how much longer his strength would last. He was already drawing on reserves he hadn't known he possessed.

The rain was falling harder, turning the riverbank into a swamp. Knowing there was a risk he would slide back down and lose all the ground he had gained, he reached up to grasp another root and pull himself higher with the girl's help.

But the roots were about to run out, he saw with a sinking heart. The top of the bank was only about six feet above him, but it might as well have been six miles. The rest of the slope was nothing but slick mud.

"You've got to hang on here," the girl told him. "I'll go find a branch or something I can reach down to you!"

"You can't hold my weight," Luke said.

"I'll figure out a way. It's our only chance!"

Luke nodded his agreement and got a good grip on the last root. "Okay."

With obvious reluctance even though it was her idea, she let go of his wrist and clambered up the bank, slipping and sliding. When she disappeared over the top, he felt a sharp pang of loss. There was a chance he would never see her again, and for some reason that bothered him as much as the possibility that he was about to die.

He hung on to the root for dear life as the rain continued to pound down on him. The river was making a rumbling sound, and he wondered if the water was already plucking at his legs. He still couldn't feel anything below the waist.

The jagged end of a gnarled tree branch nearly poked him in the face. He looked up and saw the girl lying on top of the bank, extending the branch down toward him. All he could see of her was her head, arms, and shoulders.

"Grab it!" she called. "Pull yourself up!"

Luke let go of the root with one hand and grabbed the branch. "I don't want to pull you over!"

"You won't! I've got it! Now climb, damn it!"

Luke shifted his other hand to the branch. Its rough surface provided a pretty good grip. He looked up at the girl again, and she gave him an encouraging nod.

He didn't see how it was going to work, since she probably didn't weigh even a hundred pounds soaking wet, the way she was at the moment. But he tightened his hands and hauled hard on the branch, and to his surprise, his body followed. Reaching hand over hand, he continued pulling himself up.

When he glanced at the girl, he saw pain etched on her face. Supporting his weight was obviously painful. Not wanting to hurt her any longer, he summoned all his strength and energy and continued climbing up the branch.

When he was finally close enough, she reached out and grabbed his shirt, pulling hard. He added his efforts and surged up and rolled over the top of the bank. He came to a stop on his back and had to push himself onto his side to keep the rainwater from filling his nose and mouth.

"C-careful," she said. "After all that, we d-don't want you to drown now."

Luke blinked water out of his eyes and looked over at her. She still wore the soaked wool shirt, but she had taken off the overalls. The suspenders were tied around the trunk of a tree while one of the legs was tied around her ankle. That was why she'd been hurting, he realized. The strain of his weight had gone through her whole body, passing through her hands on the branch to her shoulders, along her body, and through her ankle.

When he turned his head, he saw the surface of the river racing along about three feet below the edge of the bank. He almost hadn't made it.

This girl, whoever she was, had saved his life.

"Th-thank you," he gasped out.

"Don't thank me yet," she said. "The river could still get out of its banks."

Her hands were scraped raw from the rough bark, he saw as she sat up. Rain washed away the blood seeping from the wounds.

"I'll fetch Grampaw and the wagon," the girl went on. "He's pretty strong for an old fella. We oughta be able to lift you into the wagon." She paused. "Your legs don't work at all, do they?"

Luke shook his head. "No, I can't even feel them. I was . . . shot in the back."

"Last night?"

He nodded wearily.

"Then that was you I heard hollerin'. I wanted to come see, but Grampaw wouldn't let me. He said to let the damn Yanks and the damn fool Rebs shoot each other, that it weren't nothin' to us either way."

Luke didn't know exactly what she meant, but it wasn't the time to discuss it.

The girl untied the overalls from her leg and scrambled to her feet. "You could have the decency to close your eyes, seein' as how I ain't got no pants on and I saved your life and all."

Incredibly, Luke felt himself smiling. "Yes, ma'am." He squeezed his eyes shut. "Could I ask you one more favor?"

"What's that?"

"Tell me your name."

She hesitated, then said, "Emily. Emily Sue Peabody."

"You sound like a good Georgia girl, Emily Sue Peabody."

"I am. Where are you from?"

"Missouri. My family has a farm up in the Ozarks."

"Then you must be a soldier, in spite of what you're wearin'. Otherwise you wouldn't be so far away from home."

"I was a soldier," Luke said. "But not any more."

That was true. The gold was gone, his friends were dead, and he had spent the past day on the razor's edge of death. It wouldn't surprise him one bit if he closed his eyes and opened them again to find himself in Hell.

"What's your name?" Emily asked.

"Luke Jensen."

"Well, I'd say that I'm pleased to meet you, Mr. Jensen, but right now that'd be a plumb lie. Now don't you move . . . Come to think of it, I guess you won't, will you?"

"Not likely."

"I'll be back quick as I can with the wagon. I'd take it kindly if you don't die in the meantime."

"I'll . . . try not to," Luke said as a new wave of exhaustion washed over him. His eyes closed. He heard the swift splashes as Emily hurried away over the wet ground.

Maybe it was his imagination, but he thought it wasn't raining quite as hard. Even if the downpour stopped, it wouldn't mean the danger was over. All the water that had fallen upstream still had to go somewhere. The whole area might flood. If it did, he would be helpless.

I'm pretty much helpless either way, he reminded himself. All he could do was lie there and wait for Emily to come back.

"Emily Sue Peabody," he murmured. It was a pretty name for a pretty girl.

Thinking about her made the pain not quite so bad.

CHAPTER 13

The sound of wagon wheels creaking brought Luke out of his stupor. Rain still fell, but it was definitely not pouring down as hard.

The wheels stopped, and he heard a thud as somebody jumped down from the wagon. Footsteps ran over to him.

"You ain't dead, are you, Mr. Jensen?" Emily asked.

He opened his eyes and lifted his head. "I'm . . . still here," he croaked.

Emily bent down to look at him. "Good." Then she turned her head to call, "He's still alive, Grampaw!"

"I'm glad to hear it," replied a voice cracked with age. "I'd hate to think you dragged me out in this rain for nothin'! My rheumatiz don't like this damp weather at all."

Luke looked past Emily and saw a man with long white hair and a drooping white mustache coming toward them. The years had bent him some, but he was still fairly tall and his shoulders were broad with strength. He reminded Luke of a thick-trunked old oak tree draped with moss.

"Let's roll him onto his back so I can get hold of him under his arms and drag him," the old man suggested.

"We can pick him up and carry him," Emily said. "I'll help you."

"No, the other way will be easier," her grandfather insisted.

"He said he'd been shot in the back. Draggin' him like that's liable to hurt him even worse."

The old man frowned. "You might be right about that," he admitted. "All right, get on that side of him. I can take most of the weight, but you'll have to support some of it."

"I've got it." Emily moved to loop both arms around Luke's right arm in a secure grip.

Her grandfather took Luke's left arm in the same fashion. "All right, you ready? Lift!"

With grunts of effort, they straightened, hauling Luke upright for the first time since the night before. Emily's feet slipped a little in the mud as the strain of his weight hit her, but she managed to keep her balance and didn't lose her grip on him.

"This'd sure be easier if you could walk, mister," the burly old-timer said, "but since you can't . . ."

Half dragging, half carrying him, they started toward the wagon, which Luke saw had a team of four rawboned mules hitched to it. They looked like pretty sorry specimens and the wagon wasn't much better. Every step the old man and Emily took sent pain jolting through him, but he gritted his teeth and didn't cry out. He recalled how he had screamed after Potter shot him, and the memory filled him with shame. He wasn't going to let himself act like that in front of Emily Sue Peabody and her grandfather.

That wasn't the only shame he felt. The knowledge that he had driven right into that ambush, had lost the Confederacy's gold, and gotten his friends killed had started to gnaw at him. He had known good and well there was a chance Wiley Potter and the others would double back and make a try for the bullion. For a couple days he had watched very closely for any signs of an ambush.

But he guessed he'd let his guard down, especially while he was concentrating on getting the wagon up the steep slope of the river-bank. All it had taken was that moment of carelessness, and he had lost everything.

Well, not everything, he corrected himself. He was still alive, even if just barely. Remy, Dale, and Edgar couldn't say that much. The guilt Luke felt because of that ate at his insides all the more.

When they reached the wagon, the old man said, "Mister, you grab on to the sideboard and help hold yourself up whilst Emily puts the tailgate down. Hop to it, girl."

Luke grasped the side of the wagon as tightly as he could. When Emily had the tailgate lowered, they helped him around to it and lowered him face down over the gate. Luke's weight kept him there while they lifted the lower half of his body and shoved him into the wagon bed.

That hurt like hell, too.

"I can see where the bullet tore his shirt," the old-timer commented. "Looks like the rain washed out most of the blood. Maybe it did the same for the wound. If it didn't, he'll likely die of blood poisonin' in a day or two."

"Grampaw!" Emily said.

"Just tellin' you the truth of it," her grandfather said. "I'll wager the fella's already thought of that his own self."

"I . . . have," Luke gasped from where he lay with the side of his face pressed against the rough boards of the wagon bed. "I appreciate you . . . trying to save my life anyway."

"It was the girl's idea," the old man said. "I got no use for either side in this war. Haven't ever since it took my boy and my two grandsons."

That explained the bitter undertone in the old-timer's voice, Luke thought, as well as Emily's comment that her grandfather didn't want to get involved in the Yankees and the Confederates shooting each other. He thought he had already lost enough to the fighting, and he was probably right about that.

Luke didn't consider himself a Confederate anymore, not after the way he'd let down the cause by losing that gold. But it didn't really matter since, as Emily's grandfather had mentioned, he expected to die from his wound in the next few days.

He would worry about guilt when and if he survived.

"Might be a good idea if you was to climb up there with him and hold him as still as you can," the old man told Emily. "It's gonna be a rough ride, and bumpin' around's just gonna hurt him worse."

"You're right." She climbed into the wagon bed and sat down next to Luke. Her grandfather got on the seat and took up the reins, yelling at the mules and slapping them with the lines until they lurched forward into a walk.

The jarring motion sent fresh bursts of agony through Luke's body, just as the old-timer had predicted. His breath hissed between clenched teeth, but again he managed not to yell. Emily lay down beside him and put her arm around his shoulders, hanging on tightly to brace him against the wagon's rocking and bouncing.

He couldn't help being aware of the warmth of her torso pressed to his. If he responded to it, he didn't know it, but somehow it comforted him anyway. Gradually the pain eased a bit.

He didn't know how far it was to their destination or how long it took to get there, but finally the wagon came to a halt.

"We're here," Emily said. "This is our farm."

Luke felt the wagon shift as the old man got down from the seat. A moment later Luke heard the tailgate drop and felt himself moving. He knew the old-timer had taken hold of his feet to drag him out of the wagon, even though he couldn't feel the grip.

The rain had tapered off to a drizzle. It was late in the afternoon and darkness was coming on quickly, earlier than usual because of the overcast. As they lifted him from the wagon, Luke saw a rectangle of yellow light and recognized it as an open doorway. The glow from a lantern spilled out from the room beyond the door.

Emily and her grandfather wrestled him inside.

The old man said, "We better get him outta these wet duds, or he'll catch the grippe for sure. He don't need that on top of ever'thing else. I ought to take a look at that bullet hole in his back, too."

"You think you can help him, Grampaw?"

"You want me to, don't you?"

"Well . . . yeah, if you can."

"One thing I got to know first." The old man hung on to Luke's arm, but moved enough so he could peer into Luke's face. "Are the Yankees gonna come lookin' for you, mister? Is helpin' you gonna get me and my granddaughter killed?"

"The Yankees . . . don't know I exist," Luke whispered.

That might not be exactly true—there might still be patrols searching for eight or nine men with two wagons—but the Yankees would have no interest in a lone man with what was probably a mortal wound in his back. The bodies of Remy, Dale, and Edgar had surely washed downstream, Luke realized, and when they were found, likely they would be miles from there.

He figured Emily and her grandfather would be safe enough having him. If the Yankees had left them alone so far, they'd have no reason to bother them now.

"All right," the old man said. "I hope you're tellin' the truth. I'll hold him up, gal. Get a knife and cut them clothes off him. That'll be the easiest way to do it."

Luke was in too much pain to worry about the girl seeing him naked. Anyway, he'd seen her wearing nothing but that soaked woolen shirt, so he supposed turnabout was fair play, as the old saying went.

He heard the faint sound of a sharp blade cutting through fabric.

His clothes fell away from him. A chill went through him, and he started to shiver.

"Get somethin' and dry him off," the old man said as he struggled to keep Luke upright. "Then we'll put him in my bunk."

Luke felt her drying his torso. When she moved around behind him, he heard her sharp intake of breath. He figured she had spotted the wound low down on his back.

"It don't look too good, Grampaw."

"I wouldn't expect it to. Come on, we need to get him warmed up some."

Emily finished drying him, and they carried him over to a bunk. As they lowered him face first onto it, Luke heard a rustling sound that told him the mattress was stuffed with corn husks.

Even with nothing but a rough blanket covering it, it felt wonderful. He let his face sink into the softness.

His head jerked up a second later as something prodded into the wound in his back. His lips drew back from his teeth in a pained grimace.

"Looks like the bullet's still in there," the old man said. "It'll have to come out, but not now. The hole's already festerin' too much. Fetch me that jug o' corn."

"You don't need to get drunk, Grampaw," Emily said.

He snorted. "I ain't plannin' to drink it. It'll clean out that wound better'n anythin' else we got." ·

After hearing that, Luke knew what to expect. But he groaned anyway, a moment later, when the liquid fire of the corn liquor burned into his back and seemingly all the way through to the core of his being. Something poked into the wound again, probably the old man's fingers, he guessed.

That was confirmed when the old-timer said, "I can feel the bullet. Should be able to get it. But not yet. I'll dig it out in a day or two . . . if he's still alive."

"He'll be alive," Emily said. "I'm gonna see to that."

"Why in Tophet do you care so much whether this varmint lives or dies? You don't even know him."

"I know his name," Emily said softly. "That's enough for now."

The pain eased a little, and Luke let out the breath he had been holding. As the long sigh escaped him, his eyes closed.

Exhaustion caught up to him, crashing down like a hammer, and once again he knew nothing but darkness.

CHAPTER 14

When he woke up the next time, the only light in the room came from a small candle burned down to almost nothing. The dim glow was enough to reveal Emily sitting in an old rocking chair next to the bunk, dozing. Her eyes were closed.

Now that Luke got a better look at her, he saw that his initial impression had been right: she was beautiful. Her face showed lines that sorrow and hard work had put in it already, even though she was only around twenty years old, but that didn't detract from her beauty as far as he was concerned. Her thick dark hair was plaited into a single braid hanging over her left shoulder as she sat in the rocking chair. She had put on a clean shirt and a clean pair of overalls, maybe the only clothes she owned besides the ones she'd been wearing earlier.

Rough snores came from a long, bulky, blanket-wrapped shape in the bunk on the other side of the room. Luke recalled the bunk in which he lay belonged to Emily's grandfather, which meant the old-timer had claimed Emily's bunk while she slept in the chair.

Or maybe she had insisted on sitting up with him, he thought. That was certainly possible.

The pain in his back had receded to a dull throbbing. He felt it with every beat of his heart, but was able to ignore it by focusing his attention on Emily.

Growing aware of his gaze somehow, her eyes opened, the initial flutter of eyelids as delicate as that of a butterfly's wings. She scooted forward in the rocker and leaned toward him. Quietly, she spoke. "You're awake. How do you feel?"

Before Luke could say anything, Emily shook her head. "You don't have to answer that. I'm sure you hurt like hell."

Incredibly, he felt his lips curving in a smile. In a voice that sounded rusty to his ears, he said, "I do."

"Then why are you smilin'?"

"Because I don't think I've . . . ever run across a young woman who . . . talks like you do."

She looked surprised, and Luke saw a pink tinge spreading slowly through her lightly olive skin. She was blushing, he realized.

"You mean the cussin'? I started doin' it for a reason. After . . . after we got word that my pa and my brothers wouldn't be comin' back from the war, I got worried that Grampaw would miss not havin' any other menfolks around, and since one of the things men seem to do a lot is cuss, I figured it might make Grampaw feel better if I was to do it. They all tried to watch their language around me while I was growin' up, what with me bein' the only gal in the place, but I heard enough. I can cuss up a storm when I want to."

"How did that . . . turn out for you?" Luke asked.

"To be honest, it spooked the hell outa Grampaw at first, but once he got used to it, I think he sorta likes it. And I got used to it, too, I reckon, so I don't hardly know I'm doin' it anymore. Sometimes when you're really mad or frustrated, it sure feels good to let loose with a few ripsnorters."

"Yes, I can . . . imagine."

Emily put a hand to her mouth and looked embarrassed again. "As bad as you must hurt, you must really feel like cussin'. You go right ahead if you want to, Mr. Jensen. It won't bother me none."

"That's all right. What I'd really like . . . is for you to call me Luke."

Emily thought it over and nodded. "I reckon I can do that. I've always been taught to be careful around fellas who were slick talkers, because my pa said there was only one thing they wanted, but I guess the shape you're in, I don't have to worry about that, do I?"

"Not hardly," Luke told her. "And even if I . . . wasn't hurt . . . my pa brought me up to be a gentleman."

"I can see that in your eyes," she said softly, nodding. She reached forward and lightly rested her hand on his forehead. "Oh, my Lord! You're burnin' up with fever."

Luke wasn't surprised. He had already known he felt chilled and lightheaded. He supposed the wound in his back had festered and blood poisoning had set in, just like Emily's grandfather had predicted.

"I'll wake Grampaw and see if there's anything he can do for you," she went on.

"There's . . . no need. Just get a wet cloth . . . wipe my face with it . . . That's about all . . . anyone can do for me."

"There's gotta be somethin' else!"

"There's not," Luke told her. "It's pretty much . . . out of our hands now."

He knew that was true. If the fever broke, he might have a chance. If it didn't, he would die. Simple as that.

And it might be better if the fever went ahead and took him, he thought. Emily and her grandfather could bury him and be done with it. They wouldn't have to run even the slight risk of the Yankees finding him and taking action against them.

Better for him, too, because he still couldn't feel his legs or anything below the waist, and he would rather be dead than a cripple. He wouldn't go back to the farm and be a burden to the rest of his family.

Emily got up for a moment and came back with a wet rag. She leaned down and swabbed it over his face. The cool touch felt wonderful.

Sometime while she was doing that, he passed out again. When he woke up, bright sunlight was slanting in through the cabin's open door.

"Huh. You ain't dead after all." That somewhat surprised statement came from Emily's grandfather, who had taken her place in the rocking chair beside the bunk.

Luke licked dry, cracked lips and husked, "I could use . . . something to drink."

"Yeah, you're pretty well wrung out, I expect. I'll fetch you a cup."

The old man came back with a dented tin cup. Luke took a sip of the clear liquid in it and promptly spit it out in an instinctive reaction.

"That's a waste of good corn, son," the old-timer said. "See if you can keep some of it down this time. You're gonna need it."

"What do you . . . mean by that?"

"I mean your fever may have broken for now, but that wound in your back's in bad shape. That Yankee bullet's got to come out if you're gonna have any chance of makin' it."

Two things were wrong with that, Luke thought. It wasn't a Yankee bullet that had laid him low, but rather one fired by a renegade Confederate. And he wasn't sure he wanted to have a chance of making it, not in the condition he was in.

But the hatred of giving up was bred deeply within him. "All right, give me another sip of that shine."

The old man chuckled. "Emily said you was from up in the Missouri Ozarks. I reckon you prob'ly know good corn liquor when you taste it." He held the cup to Luke's lips.

Carefully, Luke sipped the fiery stuff. His stomach rebelled against it, but he managed to keep it down. He drank enough that it affected him immediately and set his head to spinning. "You're going to . . . cut the bullet of me, aren't you?"

The old man nodded gravely. "That's the only thing to do. As soon as Emily gets back from the tradin' post to hold you down, we'll get started."

"Go ahead and . . . do it now," Luke urged. "I can . . . stay still."

"You don't know what you're sayin'. Even with that liquor in you, it's gonna hurt worse 'n anything you ever felt before."

"Look . . . Emily doesn't weigh enough . . . to hold me down . . . if I start bucking around. I'm going to have to . . . control it . . . whether she's here or not."

The old man rubbed his jaw as he frowned in thought. His fingertips rasped on the white stubble. "More than likely you're right about that," he admitted. "Might not make much difference whether the gal's here or not."

"I don't want her . . . to have to see it," Luke said. "Give me . . . a leather strap or something . . . to bite on."

"My razor strop'll do."

"And maybe . . . some more of that moonshine first."

"We can sure do that," the old man said.

A few minutes later, after several more swallows of the potent liquor, Luke's head was spinning even faster. He set his teeth in the leather strap and watched as the old man heated the long blade of a hunting knife in the fireplace until it glowed cherry red.

He carried the knife quickly back over to the bunk. "The wound's scabbed over, but I'll have to open it again so all the pus can get out. You ready?"

"Just . . . get it done," Luke said around the strap. He took a deep breath and closed his eyes.

The old man was right about one thing: it hurt worse than anything Luke had ever experienced. His teeth bore down on the leather and every muscle in his body turned tight and hard as an iron strap . . . every muscle he could still feel, anyway. The mingled stink of burned flesh and corruption filled the room. Luke groaned.

After what seemed like an eternity of torture, the old-timer exclaimed, "I got it!"

Some of the terrible pressure Luke had felt in his back was released. The pain didn't slack off much, but any relief at all was a blessing.

He felt the old man wiping at his back with a rag. "You're bleedin' like a stuck pig, boy, but I reckon that's a good thing. Maybe it'll wash out all the festerin'. If you don't bleed to death first, that is."

The pain continued to recede. Luke's head slumped back to the bunk, and the leather strap slipped out of his mouth as his teeth released their grip on it. His pulse pounded inside his skull, and he breathed harshly and heavily.

"Grampaw, what in hell are you doin'?" That startled cry came from Emily. "My God, there's blood all over the place! You've killed him!"

"Take it easy, gal. He's alive. And I got that bullet outta his back."

"Is that why you sent me to the tradin' post?" she demanded. "So you could start cuttin' on him without me bein' here to stop you?"

"Shoot, I didn't even know he was gonna wake up. His fever broke, but it would've come right back if I didn't get that bullet out. Look there . . . that's healthy blood comin' out of him now. We can go ahead and stop it, and he can start gettin' his strength back."

Emily went closer to the bunk and bent down to peer at Luke's face. He saw her only vaguely through his pain and weariness.

"You mean he's gonna be all right?" she asked.

"I mean he's got a chance now," her grandfather told her.

But the biggest question, Luke thought just as he slipped back into unconsciousness, wasn't whether he would live or not.

The question was whether his legs would work . . . or whether he was going to be a cripple for the rest of his life, however long that was.

CHAPTER 15

The fever didn't come back. When Luke woke again, he was ravenously hungry, but able to eat only a few bites of the stew Emily fed him before it started to sicken him. He kept it down, though.

From talking to Emily, he found out it wasn't the day after she'd rescued him from the riverbank. As a matter of fact, three days had passed since that stormy afternoon.

"You were burnin' up with fever and out of your head most of that time," she told him as she sat in the rocker beside the bunk. "You kept ravin', but I couldn't make much sense out of most of it."

"What did I say? Did I talk about anybody in particular?"

"Oh, your ma and pa, of course. I'd expect that. And somebody named Kirby."

"My little brother," Luke said.

"And Janey."

"My sister."

"And Potter."

It was all Luke could do not to snarl in hatred. "He's not part of my family."

"I hope not, the way you were talkin' about him. Remember how I said I could cuss pretty good? Well, you had me beat all hollow while you were talkin' about that fella Potter."

"He's the man who shot me," Luke said. "He and his friends are deserters and renegades."

"Well, then, you've got good reason to be cussin' him. I figured somebody must've waylaid you and robbed you when I didn't find no horse anywhere thereabouts."

Luke waited a moment, then asked, "Did I talk about anything else?" He wanted to know if he had said anything about the gold while he was out of his head.

"Not really. There were some other names . . . Renny, somethin' like that?"

"Remy," Luke said. "A good friend."

"And Dale and Edgar. Who are they?"

"More friends." Luke didn't offer any further explanation. Their bodies must have been taken by the river before Emily found him, otherwise she would have asked him before now who those dead men were.

Just as well, he thought. He didn't want to tell her about the gold, about the way he had lost it and gotten his friends killed. That was a burden he was going to bear alone.

"Grampaw says it looks like that bullet hole in your back is healin' up better now," Emily went on. "I was sure upset with him when I came in and found that he'd been cuttin' on you, but I reckon he did the right thing."

"What's your grandfather's name?" Luke hadn't heard her call him anything except Grampaw.

"Linus Peabody," she told him.

"A fine name. I'm in his debt . . . and yours."

She shook her head. "You don't owe me nothin'."

"You saved my life. I would have died out there if it wasn't for you."

"It's my Christian duty to help folks in need."

"I wish more people felt like you about that," Luke said. "If they did, we might not have had this war."

"Grampaw says we didn't need to have it anyway. We never had no slaves and didn't want any. He tried to talk my pa and my brothers into not goin' off and fightin', but they said it was their duty because the Yankees had no right to invade us."

"They were right about that. I just wish it had never come to that point."

Emily sighed. "Wishin' don't do folks a lot of good, Mr. Jensen . . . I mean, Luke. If it did, there's a whole heap of things in the world that'd be different."

She was certainly right about that, Luke thought.

Because if wishing did any good, his legs would work again, and so far . . . they didn't.

* * *

It really hasn't been very long yet since my injury, he reminded himself several times that day . . . and the next and the next and the day after that.

By the time a week had passed, Luke's appetite had returned and so had some of his strength. He was able to sit up in the rocking chair with a pillow to cushion his wounded back, as long as Peabody and Emily helped him get there from the bunk.

But he still had no feeling in his legs, and when he sat there and stared at them and willed them to move, nothing happened. The legs remained limp and lifeless.

"I wish I could help you with the chores," Luke said at supper one evening. "You folks saved my life, you're feeding me, and I can't do a blasted thing to repay you."

"Nobody's asked you to repay nothin'," Peabody said.

"I know that, but I want to, anyway."

"Maybe the time will come that you can. You can't never tell."

Another couple days passed. Luke continued to get stronger. Peabody built him a bunk of his own, so he and Emily could return to their own beds. He checked the wound in Luke's back and changed the dressing on it, then proclaimed, "Looks like that hole's just about healed up, son. I got to admit, I didn't think it'd happen that way, but you must be durned near as strong as a mule . . . and stubborn as one, too."

Emily said, "Grampaw!"

But Luke threw back his head and laughed, which was something he hadn't done much of for a long time. "My pa used to say the same thing about me. The stubborn part, anyway. But the real reason I'm not dead is because you and Emily took such good care of me, Mr. Peabody."

"The gal wouldn't have it no other way," the old-timer said, which brought another blush to Emily's face.

Peabody went out to work in the fields, leaving Emily to finish cleaning up after breakfast before she joined him. With just the two of them to take care of the place, they both worked from dawn to dusk most days. They had gotten behind on the chores during the time they'd had to take turns looking after Luke, and knowing that added to his feeling he owed them more than he could ever repay.

A short time after leaving, Peabody hurried back into the cabin just as Emily was finishing up with the dishes. Luke saw instantly that the old-timer was upset about something.

Peabody didn't keep them in the dark about it. "Yankees comin'."

"Oh, dear Lord," Emily said. "How many?"

"Just a dozen or so . . . but that's plenty if they're lookin' for trouble." Peabody frowned at Luke. "You're sure they ain't huntin' you?"

"I don't see how they could be."

An old single-shot rifle Peabody used for hunting game hung on hooks attached to the wall. He took it down and checked its load.

"You don't want to start trouble," Luke warned him. "Not if there are a dozen of them."

"Don't plan on startin' it. But if they force me to it, I'll fight."

Luke thought swiftly. "How close are they?"

"About a quarter mile, I'd say."

"Put the rocker on the porch and help me into it. I'll hold the rifle in my lap, under a blanket."

"They'd be able to see it anyway," Emily said. "I have a better idea." She opened a cabinet and took out the Griswold and Gunnison revolver Luke had brought with him from Richmond.

He didn't know what had happened to his rifle, but the sight of the revolver lifted his spirits a little. Only for a moment, though. He recalled how wet the gun had gotten. "The charges in that are bound to be ruined."

"They were," Emily agreed, "until I cleaned it up and reloaded it."

"Where'd you get ammunition for that gun?"

"Bought it at the tradin' post the other day. I thought we might need it sometime."

Luke hoped that time hadn't come. Even with the revolver, he wouldn't be any match for a dozen Yankee cavalrymen, especially stuck in a rocking chair with useless legs.

But being armed was always better than being defenseless, so he held out his hand for the gun and slipped it into the pocket of the overalls he was wearing. It was a good thing Linus Peabody was a fairly big man. His clothes fit Luke without being too tight.

Peabody dragged the rocking chair onto the cabin's front porch, then he and Emily helped Luke get seated in it. She hurried back into the cabin to grab the blanket from the bunk, which she draped over the lower half of Luke's body.

It was the first time he'd been outside since the day of the storm. The air was warm and smelled good. It was a beautiful spring day.

At least, it would have been if it hadn't been marred by the sight of those Yankee troopers riding toward the cabin.

Peabody came out onto the porch holding the rifle. He said to Emily, "Get back inside, gal. And don't come out no matter what happens."

"You know damn good and well I ain't gonna do that, Grampaw."

"Blast it. For once in your life, do what I tell you!"

Emily looked angry and upset, but she said, "I'll be right inside," and moved back through the door.

Luke put his right hand under the blanket, slipping the revolver out of his pocket and gripping it tightly as he watched the Yankees ride closer. He had to fight down the impulse to yank out the gun and start blazing away at the enemy.

Or are they the enemy anymore? he suddenly asked himself. They were laughing and talking among themselves as they approached the cabin. They certainly didn't seem to be looking for trouble.

The officer in charge of the patrol, a lieutenant judging by his insignia, heeled his horse into a trot and rode ahead of the others. He came up to the cabin with the others trailing behind him and reined in. With a friendly nod, he touched a finger to the brim of his hat. "Good morning, gentlemen. Does one of you own this farm?"

"I do." Peabody's voice was flat and hard.

"Then I'd like to ask your permission to water our horses."

Peabody took one hand off the rifle and jerked a thumb toward the north. "River's about half a mile that way. Plenty of water there."

"Oh," the lieutenant said. "I didn't know that. I'm not that familiar with the area. We're obliged to you for the information. We'll just water our horses at the river."

"That's a good idea." Peabody stood stiffly, both hands tight on the rifle again.

The Yankee officer hesitated, then said, "Sir, you *have* heard the news, haven't you?"

"What news?"

Luke had a hunch he knew what the answer was going to be even before the lieutenant spoke.

"The war's over, sir," the young officer said. "General Lee offered his surrender to General Grant nearly three weeks ago at a place up in Virginia called Appomattox Courthouse."

Luke closed his eyes. He'd been right.

And Potter and the others had been right, too, about the Confederacy collapsing. They hadn't been traitors, after all.

Just murdering, back-shooting rogues.

"The fighting is all over," the lieutenant went on. "There's no need for you and your son to worry, sir. We're all countrymen again."

Peabody didn't correct the man about Luke being his son. He just said, "The river's up yonder."

The lieutenant nodded. "We'll be going, then. Good day to both of you, and thank you again."

The cavalrymen rode around the cabin and headed north. Luke listened to the sound of their hoofbeats fading as Emily came out of the cabin.

"I'm sorry, Luke," she said.

"About the war being over?" He shook his head. "Don't be. I'm not. I knew that was how it was going to turn out. Better to have it end before more good men were killed for no reason."

"Amen to that," Peabody said.

Luke took the revolver from under the blanket and handed it to Emily. "I guess you can put that away again."

"All right." She hesitated, then said, "Luke . . . what are you gonna do now?"

He looked up at her and realized he had no idea.

CHAPTER 16

Luke balanced himself on the crutches, reached into the bag he held, and slung grain onto the ground for the chickens clustering around him. The fowl went after the stuff with their usual frenzied enthusiasm.

He draped the bag's strap over his shoulder, got a good grip on the crutch handles so he could turn himself around, and stumped back toward the cabin.

Emily came out onto the porch before he got there. "I was gonna feed the chickens," she told him with a grin.

"No need," Luke said. "I took care of it."

"There's just no stoppin' you, is there?"

"Not when it's something I can do." He changed course, angling toward the side of the house where the big stump they used for splitting firewood stood. The ax leaned against the stump, handle up.

"What are you fixin' to do now?" Emily asked.

"You said you needed some wood for the stove," Luke explained.

"I didn't say you had to split it!"

"I don't mind." He reached the stump and propped the right-hand crutch against it. With only a small amount of awkwardness, he picked up a piece of wood from the pile beside the stump and set it upright in the middle. Then he took hold of the ax and lifted it one-handed.

"You're gonna miss and cut your leg off one of these days," Emily warned.

"No great loss," Luke said.

"Unless you bleed to death!"

Luke swung the ax above his head and brought it down in a precise stroke, splitting the cordwood perfectly down the middle. He used the ax to brush the two pieces off the stump, leaned the ax against it, and picked up another piece of wood to split.

Emily blew out her breath and shook her head in exasperation. "You are the most stubborn man I ever saw, Luke Jensen."

And that was a good thing, Luke thought, otherwise he'd probably be dead. The wound he had suffered a few months earlier would have killed him.

The late summer sun blazed down, and it didn't take Luke long to work up a sweat. His damp linsey-woolsey shirt clung to his back. He lifted his arm and sleeved beads of perspiration off his face.

When he'd first started shaving himself again, rather than relying on Emily to do it, he'd been shocked at the gaunt, haggard face looking out at him from the mirror. That man looked at least ten years older than he really was, Luke thought.

Since then his features had begun to fill out some, and he thought he looked more like himself. Most of the time, the strain of what he had gone through painted a rather grim expression on his face. When he laughed, though, he didn't feel quite as ugly. *Still ugly, mind you,* he told himself, *just not as much.*

Recently he had stopped shaving his upper lip and let his mustache grow. It gave him a certain amount of dignity, in his opinion, and Emily didn't seem to mind. How she thought about things had taken on a lot of importance during the months he had spent on the Peabody farm.

She came down from the porch to gather up the chunks of wood he had split. "Breakfast is ready. Come on inside and eat."

She didn't have to tell him twice, and she didn't have to help him up the steps. He made it just fine with the crutches.

He had carved them himself, putting quite a bit of time and effort into it. He'd wanted the crutches to be as comfortable as possible, since it looked like he'd be using them for quite a while. Some of the feeling had started to come back into his legs, enough that he could get around a little with the help of the crutches, but he was still pretty helpless. He didn't let himself think too much about how long that might go on. He still held out hope that one day his legs would work again, the way they were supposed to.

Because of that, he'd asked Emily to help him exercise the muscles in them. He knew it wasn't fair to place that extra burden on her, but she didn't object. He had seen what happened to Clyde Monroe back home. Doing nothing after his injury had made him worse. Luke wasn't going to give up like that . . . which led right back to that stubbornness Emily had accused him of.

He fed the chickens and gathered eggs and split wood and hoed the vegetable garden and shucked corn. Anything he could do sitting down or balanced on one crutch, he would do. The work put thick slabs of muscle back on his arms and shoulders and back.

He was damned if he was going to be useless. He would die first.

Emily and her grandfather had both asked him if he wanted to send a letter to his family back in Missouri letting them know he was alive. Luke only had to think about it for a second before he shook his head.

After failing the Confederacy and his friends, he didn't want his pa and Kirby finding out about that. One day, if what he planned came about, he would return home, but not until he had done the job he had set out for himself.

Once his legs worked right again, he was going to track down Potter, Stratton, Richards, and Casey and kill each and every one of them. He knew he probably wouldn't be able to recover the gold they had stolen—there was no Confederacy to return it to, anyway— but at least he could even the score for what they had done to Remy, Dale, and Edgar.

And to him.

Then and only then, when he had reclaimed at least a vestige of his honor, would he return to his family. Until then it was better to let them think he was dead, even though they would mourn him.

It had to be that way. On his darkest nights, he admitted to himself there was a very strong possibility he would never walk normally again, no matter how much he tried. In that case, he would live out his life on the Peabody farm, unless Emily and her grandfather kicked him out.

The way he and Emily had started to feel about each other, he didn't think that was likely.

And yet that thought tortured him, too. Emily might be falling in love with him—Lord knew he'd been in love with her pretty much from the moment he first saw her and mistook her for an angel—but was it fair for him to saddle her with a cripple for a husband? He wasn't even sure he could be a real husband to her, although lately he'd begun to feel some stirrings that told him it might be possible.

Feeling *anything* below the level of the wound in his back was a good sign. The bullet wound was completely healed. A pale, ragged scar was the only sign of it that remained. Luke hadn't seen the scar himself, of course, but Emily had described it for him. He could move around now without feeling even a twinge in his back.

He clumped over to the table Emily had set for three people. Setting one of the crutches aside, he gripped his chair and lowered himself into it.

Emily poured coffee for him and set a plate of flapjacks, bacon, and eggs in front of him. They ate fairly well, because the Peabody farm had escaped most of the damage and destruction inflicted by the Yankees when they rampaged through the area a year earlier.

As she sat down opposite Luke, Emily said, "Grampaw told me he's goin' to town today, if you need anything."

The settlement of Dobieville was about five miles down the road. A trading post was closer to the farm, but Linus Peabody refused to do any business there since a Yankee carpetbagger had taken it over a month earlier when the previous owner had been unable to pay his taxes.

Luke shook his head. "I can't think of anything. Unless he can pick me up a new pair of legs."

Emily frowned across the table at him. "I thought you promised to stop sayin' things like that."

"Sorry," he muttered.

"I know you think you got to walk again, Luke, and I don't blame you for feelin' that way, I really don't. But you don't have to. Not . . . not for me, anyway. It ain't gonna change the way I feel about you."

Suddenly the food in front of him didn't seem so appetizing. He didn't want to have this discussion. Of course, it was his own fault for bringing it up.

He looked at the plate. "We don't need to talk about this. It won't change anything, anyway."

His voice sounded harsher than he intended. He didn't look up at Emily, afraid he would see hurt in her eyes.

"All right," she said. "Let's just eat."

Linus Peabody came in a few minutes later. He'd been in the barn, tending to the mules, the milk cow, and the hogs. If he sensed the tension between Luke and Emily, he had the good sense not to say anything about it as he sat down. "Did Emily tell you I'm goin' to town this mornin', Luke?"

"She did, but there's nothing I need right now."

"I was thinkin' you might want to go with me."

Luke frowned in surprise. "To Dobieville?"

"Yep. Actually, I thought we might all go. Been stuck here on this farm all summer."

Luke glanced at Emily and caught a glimpse of excitement on her face.

She hurriedly covered it up. "I don't need nothin' in town, Grampaw."

"Yes, you do. You need to see somebody 'sides a pair of ugly ol' galoots like me and Luke."

"Neither of you is ugly," she protested.

"There's no point in arguing with the facts," Luke said with a smile. "Neither of us is going to win any prizes for being good-looking, are we, Linus?"

The old-timer cackled. "The judges'd have to be plumb blind if we did!" Peabody nodded. "So it's settled. After we eat, we'll all load up in the wagon and head for town."

CHAPTER 17

Luke had to have some help doing it, but he managed to climb into the back of the wagon. From there he was able to use his arms to pull himself to the front, just behind the seat. Peabody settled down on the seat next to Emily to handle the team.

Despite what the old man had said, Luke had a hunch there was more to this trip into Dobieville than Peabody let on. He didn't press the issue, though, as the wagon rolled across fields and along narrow, tree-shaded country lanes toward the settlement.

It was a good test of how well his back actually had healed. The wagon wasn't in the greatest shape, and its ride was pretty rough, even on level ground. But he didn't feel any pain in his back, and that was encouraging.

The mules didn't get in any hurry. The trip to town took more than an hour. Luke was tired by the time they got there, but he still wasn't hurting.

Dobieville had a wide main street running for several blocks between businesses, along with a couple side streets lined with houses. The steeples of the Baptist and Methodist churches stuck up above the trees on the edge of town. Some of the businesses had been burned when the Yankees came through, but Dobieville had gotten off with less destruction than many Southern settlements.

Several of the businesses that had been burned were being rebuilt, Luke saw as Peabody sent the mules plodding along the street with the wagon rolling slowly behind them. The sounds of hammering and men calling to each other as they worked filled the air.

But Luke sensed something was wrong about what he was hearing, and after a moment he realized what it was. When the workers raised their voices to talk, it wasn't in the slower, softer drawl of Southerners, but rather the hard, brisk tone of folks from up north.

Those were Yankees rebuilding those businesses.

Carpetbaggers.

He had heard Peabody talking about greedy opportunists from up north swarming in all over the South. He saw for himself what was going on. It wasn't just the carpenters. Men in derby hats and gaudy tweed suits and cocky grins strolled along the town's boardwalks, cigars clenched at jaunty angles in their teeth. All Luke had to do was look at them to know they were Yankees.

The true citizens of Dobieville knew it, too. Luke saw the glances filled with resentment, anger, and fear the townsfolk cast toward the newcomers.

Blue-uniformed soldiers lounged here and there. Yankee troopers stood in every block, not necessarily doing anything, but their mere presence was a bitter reminder that the Confederacy had been defeated and the Southern states had been forced back into the union at gunpoint, after the spilling of rivers of blood.

Peabody brought the wagon to a halt in front of Connally's General Store. He turned on the seat and said to Emily, "Go on inside, gal. I'll join you in a minute."

"What about Luke?" she asked.

"I'm all right sitting back here. It's too much trouble for the two of you to help me down and then back up again."

"No, it's not," she argued. "You came to town so you could see something different from the farm."

"And so I can." Luke smiled. "I can see just fine from right where I am."

"Oh, all right." Emily climbed down from the wagon. "But if you change your mind, we can get you out of there and you can use your crutches."

"I know," Luke assured her.

She still looked a little puzzled, but she went on into the general store. Peabody sighed and turned more on the seat to say quietly, "I wanted a chance to talk to you while Emily ain't around, Luke."

"I thought that might be the case. What's wrong, Linus?"

Peabody let out a disgusted snort. "What's wrong? Just look around you, son!"

"You're talking about all the Yankees?"

"Soldiers and carpetbaggers alike. They've moved in like a swarm of locusts!"

"What did you expect? We lost the war. They can do whatever they want now."

"They could treat us with some respect," Peabody said as fierce anger edged into his voice. "Instead they've just bulled their way in, run folks off, took over businesses . . . What you're lookin' at, son, is the beginnin' of something that may turn out to be even worse 'n the war itself."

"I don't see how that could be possible."

"You just hide and watch," Peabody said. "Them Yankees got the idea they can waltz in, grab what they want for themselves, and grind the rest of the South into dust under their heels. And they'll laugh at us while they're doin' it."

That was probably right, Luke thought. That was exactly what the carpetbaggers intended to do, and they had the Yankee troops to back them up on it. "Why did you want to show me this?"

"Because there's gonna come a time when we may have to fight for what's ours. So far the Yankees ain't come anywhere near the farm, but one of these days they're liable to. And I don't intend to just let 'em take it away from me."

"You didn't support the war," Luke said. "They should leave you alone."

Peabody waved a gnarled hand. "This ain't about the war anymore. It's about greed, pure and simple, and the chance for a bunch of no-good skunks to grab what ain't theirs."

"And you want to know if I'll stand with you against them?" Luke couldn't keep the dry, acid tone out of his voice.

"I'm just sayin' you may have to make a choice," Peabody snapped. "Legs or no legs."

Luke sighed and nodded. "You're right, Linus. I'm sorry. I appreciate you bringing me to town today and showing me what we may be facing. It's always best to know when trouble's coming."

"That's what I thought."

"And as for whether or not I'll be with you when that trouble comes . . . you ought to know the answer to that. You saved my life, you and Emily . . ."

"I know how you feel about her, too," Peabody said. "I've seen the way she's started lookin' at you lately. I ain't sayin' that I like it—"

"I'm not exactly the man you had in mind for your granddaughter. I know that."

"Maybe not, but you're a good man, Luke." Peabody clapped a hand on Luke's shoulder and squeezed. "I know that, too." He wrapped the team's reins around the brake lever. "Now, I'm gonna go and help Emily pick up a few supplies. Sure you'll be all right out here?"

Luke nodded. "I'll be all right."

"Okay." Peabody jumped down from the wagon and went inside the store.

Luke looked around at the bustling settlement. If it hadn't been for the presence of the Yankees, he would have said Dobieville was well on its way to recovering from the war already.

Unfortunately, under the surface, the truth was that Dobieville was well on its way to being gutted by the carpetbaggers.

Peabody was worried their greedy reach would extend outside the settlement, Luke mused. The old-timer was probably right about that. Even though the prospect worried Luke, too, he didn't see what an old man, a girl, and a cripple could do to stop the arrogant outsiders who now held power in the South.

Peabody wanted to fight if the carpetbaggers came for his property, and he wanted Luke to fight with him. If it came down to that, Luke knew he wouldn't turn his back on the two people who had saved his life. But if that happened, there was a very good chance he and Peabody would wind up dead, leaving Emily alone and defenseless . . .

Or else she would take up arms, and the Yankees would kill her, too.

Maybe the best thing to do, Luke thought suddenly, would be to pack up and leave at the first sign of any Yankees trying to take over the farm. It would mean running from trouble, which stuck in his craw worse than anything. Peabody would probably feel the same, but it might be the only way to save their lives.

The frontier was a big place, with lots of room for folks to settle and start new lives. Luke thought maybe he could even swallow his pride and return home to the Ozarks, taking Emily and her grandfather along with him.

He took a deep breath. No use getting ahead of himself. At the moment, things were all right. Maybe they'd be lucky and it would stay like that.

As he mused, a couple Yankee soldiers came along the boardwalk toward the general store. They stopped and propped their shoulders against one of the posts holding up the awning in front of the store. One of the troopers, a wiry little man with dark hair, glanced at Luke and then looked away, obviously uninterested in him.

The taller, brawnier soldier, with bushy side-whiskers and a thatch of straw-colored hair sticking out from under his forage cap, fastened a cool, appraising stare on Luke.

Keeping an eye on them without drawing attention to himself, Luke tried to ignore them.

A short time later, Emily and her grandfather came out of the store. She was carrying a crate of supplies, while Peabody had a bag of flour slung over his shoulder. As they moved to place the supplies in the back of the wagon, the big trooper straightened from his casual pose.

"Hey, Reb"—he directed the harsh words at Luke—"what kind of man sits by and lets a girl and an old geezer do all the work?"

Peabody turned toward the soldier and snapped, "Who you callin' an old geezer, sonny?"

Emily put a hand on her grandfather's arm and asked the soldier, "Just leave us alone, why don't you?"

"I wasn't talking to either of you." The Yankee soldier pointed at Luke. "I was talking to that big strapping specimen of Southern manhood." A grin stretched across his rough-hewn face. "But I guess he's like the rest of those Johnny Rebs . . . just a lazy coward."

Emily forgot about being reasonable. Even as Luke started to say, "No—", she put herself in the trooper's face. "Shut your mouth, you big, stupid, Yankee tyrant."

The man's eyes widened in surprise. He brought his hand up to slap her and growled, "You foul-mouthed little Rebel slut! I'll—"

Luke grabbed the crutch from the wagon bed beside him and drove the tip of it into the soldier's midsection as hard as he could. He put plenty of the strength in his arms and shoulders behind the punch.

The trooper cried out in pain and stumbled back a step, tripping on a loose board in the porch. He sat down hard, gasping for breath, the blow had been so strong.

His companion acted swiftly, unsnapping the holster at his waist and pulling out a revolver. He eared back the hammer as he raised the gun and pointed it at Luke's face.

CHAPTER 18

L uke knew in that instant how close he was to dying. He had re-acted instinctively when Emily was threatened, and it looked like that reaction was going to cost him his life.

But before the little Yankee could pull the trigger, a voice asked sharply, "What's going on here?"

The soldier's gaze darted past the wagon toward a man who had come along the street from the other direction. The short Yankee hesitated, licking his lips. "This Reb just attacked Private Packard, Mr. Wolford."

The newcomer strode past the wagon to confront the soldiers. "It looked to me more like he was defending this young woman. Packard was about to strike her, wasn't he?"

"Beggin' your pardon, sir, but you didn't hear what she called him."

"Nor do I care," Wolford replied. "A man who acts like he's going to hit a lady deserves whatever he gets. And I'm confident Colonel Morrison would agree with me." He used the walking stick he carried to point at the bigger soldier. "Now put that gun away, help Private Packard to his feet, and both of you move along."

The little trooper took a deep breath, obviously reluctant to fol-low the civilian's orders. But Luke could tell he was afraid not to do what Wolford said. After a couple seconds the soldier holstered his revolver and turned to extend a hand to his companion. "Come on, Packard. We got things to do."

Packard had gotten his breath back, but his face was pale. Anger made twin spots of red glow on his cheeks. He brushed aside the other soldier's hand and climbed to his feet on his own.

"This ain't any of your business, Wolford—"

"Come on," the smaller soldier urged. "Let it go." He got hold of Packard's sleeve and tried to drag him away.

Packard didn't want to, that much was clear. He glared darkly at Luke, who saw a promise in the man's eyes that the skirmish wasn't over. But the soldier turned and stalked off along the boardwalk, his shorter compatriot hurrying to keep up with him.

Wolford turned to Luke, Emily, and Peabody and smiled ingratiatingly. "I'm sorry about that unpleasantness. Unfortunately, too many soldiers haven't gotten it through their heads yet that the war is over." He put out a hand to Peabody. "Vincent Wolford."

The man's accent marked him as being from somewhere in New England. He was about forty, with a lean face, dark hair, and thick, salt-and-pepper side-whiskers. His suit was a subdued blue, and he wore a black beaver hat.

Wolford wasn't just a carpetbagger, Luke thought. He was a *boss* carpetbagger.

Peabody hesitated, clearly not wanting to shake hands with any Yankee, but Wolford had kept the little soldier from shooting Luke. After a moment, he took Wolford's hand and clasped it briefly. "Linus Peabody."

"It's a pleasure to meet you, Mr. Peabody." Wolford smiled at Emily. "And this is your granddaughter, I expect? I can see the resemblance."

"My name's Emily. I ain't much on shakin' hands with Yankees, though."

Wolford smiled. "That's all right, Miss Peabody. A perfectly understandable attitude, considering all the upheavals that have taken place. Believe me, I know what you're going through."

Luke didn't believe that for a second. Wolford had the smooth look of a man who had always been rich and gotten whatever he wanted.

"Or perhaps it's not Miss Peabody," Wolford went on as he turned to Luke. "Are you the lady's husband, sir?"

"That's Luke—"

"Luke Smith. I'm a friend of the family, that's all."

"I see." Wolford glanced at Luke's legs and the crutch still in his hand. "You were wounded in the war?"

"That's right."

"A terrible shame."

Luke was aware that Emily and her grandfather were looking at him curiously, no doubt wondering why he had given Wolford a false name. Without much thought, it had popped out of his mouth. He'd been brooding a lot lately—about the stolen gold and the deaths of his friends—and hated to think the name Jensen would ever be linked to such a shameful failure. That probably had something to do with it.

And the fact he instinctively didn't trust Vincent Wolford.

"Colonel Morrison, the commander of the troops in this area, is a good friend of mine," Wolford went on. "I'll have a word with him and ask if he could order his men to treat the citizens with a bit more respect. After all, we're all partners now in rebuilding the South. If we're going to work together, we should get along, shouldn't we?"

"We don't want trouble with anybody," Peabody said, which didn't really answer Wolford's rhetorical question.

"Of course not." The man smiled and lifted a hand to the brim of his beaver hat. "Well, good day to you folks."

As Wolford strolled away, Peabody climbed quickly to the wagon seat and told Emily, "Get on the wagon, girl. We're gettin' outta here."

The old-timer turned the vehicle around and got the mules headed back toward the farm. Peabody muttered under his breath about how they shouldn't have come to Dobieville today in the first place.

Emily turned around to lean over the back of the seat. "You shouldn't have got mixed up in that, Luke. That big, dumb Yankee never would've been able to hit me. I'm too fast for the likes of him."

Luke shifted on the wagon bed. "Maybe so, but it's bad enough I had to sit by while you and Linus loaded the supplies. You can't expect me to do nothing while that soldier attacked you."

"You almost got yourself killed, that's what you did."

Luke couldn't argue with that.

"If that slick-talkin' Yankee carpetbagger hadn't come along, that mean little varmint would've blowed your head off."

"More than likely," Luke admitted with a sigh.

"And what was that business about callin' yourself *Smith*?" Peabody asked. "Have you been lyin' to us all along, son? Are you some sort of criminal on the run from the law?"

"No," Luke answered without hesitation. "Absolutely not. I may not have told you quite everything, Linus, but I give you my word, nobody's looking for me, lawman or otherwise."

Peabody nodded. "Reckon I can accept that. Just like I can accept it's your business what you call yourself."

"Well, it may take me some gettin' used to, after callin' you Jensen all this time." Emily paused. "Just don't get yourself killed on account of me, Luke Smith or Jensen or whatever the hell name you want to use."

Luke laughed. "I'll certainly try not to."

When they got back to the farm, Emily and her grandfather helped Luke down from the wagon before they unloaded the supplies. He stood at the back of the vehicle on his crutches and said, "If you want to drape that flour sack over my shoulder, Linus, I might be able to carry it in."

"There ain't no need of that," Peabody said. "You don't have to prove anything to us, Luke."

"That's right." Emily turned away from the tailgate with the crate in her hands. "You already do plenty to help out around—

Oh!" she cried out as the heavy crate slipped from her grasp and fell on Luke's right foot.

Luke took a sharp breath.

"Hell and damnation!" Emily exclaimed. "Oh, Luke, I'm so sorry! I didn't mean to drop that on you. It must've—"

He smiled as she stopped short in what she was saying. "Must have hurt? Only a little. That's one thing I don't have to worry about."

Looking flustered, Emily picked up the crate. "Well, when we get inside, I want to take a look at your foot anyway. You could be hurt and not even know it."

"I suppose you're right," Luke said.

A few minutes later, he was sitting in the rocking chair. Emily knelt in front of him and took off his boot and sock. There was a red mark on the top of his foot where the crate had landed, but no blood. Emily poked around on the spot.

Luke blinked.

"Doesn't feel like any bones are broken." Without looking up, she pulled his sock back onto the foot. "You were lucky."

"That's me. Lucky Luke Smith."

Emily snorted.

After they ate a hasty midday meal, Emily and Peabody went out to work in the fields, leaving Luke sitting in the rocker. When he was sure they were gone, he put his hands on his thighs and squeezed as hard as he could, working the muscles. He had succeeded in covering up his reaction so Emily and her grandfather hadn't noticed it, but it had hurt like blazes when that crate fell on his foot, the most sensation he had felt in one of his feet for a long time. And it had been repeated when Emily poked at the site of the injury.

It excited him as no pain ever had.

He stared at his legs, willing them with every fiber of his being to move, but all he could summon up were a few twitches.

He slumped back in the rocking chair, suddenly breathless and exhausted. *That might be the most my legs will ever move,* he told himself. But his heart soared inside him, anyway. For the first time in months he had real hope again.

Hope that someday he might be able to have the things he most wanted . . .

Emily.

And vengeance.

CHAPTER 19

Over the next few days, Luke struggled against the impatience he felt as he looked for another sign that his legs might be improving. Any time he was alone at the cabin, he moved them as much as he could, sometimes unconsciously straining his other muscles until he was breathing hard and sweat popped out on his face. He rubbed his legs and then pounded on them in frustration when they failed to respond as much as he wanted them to.

One day he lifted himself out of the chair with his crutches, then let them fall to the sides in the hope he could force himself to stand.

He fell on his face.

And struggled hard to push himself up with the crutches to get back in the chair.

He didn't give up. He worked at it every day and would continue as long as it took.

He didn't say a word about his efforts to Emily or her grandfather. If he failed—again—he didn't want them to know about it. There would be time enough later to fill them in if he was successful in learning to walk again.

Emily continued to exercise the muscles in his legs, massaging and working them back and forth.

Several days after his fall she noticed a change. "It may be my imagination, Luke, but it seems to me like your legs are getting stronger rather than weaker."

"Really? Well, that's good, isn't it?"

"Yeah, real good. I knew it was just a matter of time before you started healin' up."

He thought she was just trying to be encouraging, but maybe she was more right than she knew. Whenever Emily and her grandfather weren't around and Luke was on his crutches, he let more of the weight of his body rest on his legs.

At first they had buckled, but as the days went on he was able to stiffen them and partially support himself more than he could before. He still didn't say anything to Emily or her grandfather. Hope and resolve filled him, but he was wary.

One evening while Emily was inside cleaning up after supper, Luke sat in the rocker on the porch and the old man sat on the steps. Peabody filled his pipe and lit it, then said quietly enough that Emily wouldn't overhear, "I spotted some fellas on horseback watchin' the place today."

Luke tensed, hearing the worry in the old-timer's voice. "Soldiers?"

"Nope. Civilians. I didn't get a very good look at 'em, but I could tell that much."

"What do you reckon they wanted?"

Peabody shook his head. "Don't know, but Bud Harkness come by today and talked to me. Bud's got the next farm over. He says there's some problem with the taxes and he might lose his place."

"Didn't he pay them?"

"He did . . . but the judge the Yankees put in charge of such things says that Bud didn't pay enough. It's a blamed lie . . . but he's a judge."

"What's this fellow Harkness going to do?" Luke asked.

"What *can* he do? He can stay and fight, or he can leave." Peabody puffed on the pipe for a second or two in silence, then went on. "Bud's got five kids and another on the way. He can't afford to get himself killed."

"So he's going to pack up and leave?"

"I expect so. That's the smart thing to do."

"If they're after his place . . ."

"This one's next in line," Peabody said, his voice heavy. "That's who I think was watchin' us today. Somebody who works for the varmint who's got his eye on this place."

"You happen to know who that is?"

Peabody turned his head to look at Luke in the fading light.

"Wolford."

The answer didn't surprise Luke. Vincent Wolford had stepped in to help them that day in Dobieville when they'd had the trouble with the soldiers, but he had seen through the man's slick façade to the predator underneath. Weighing his words carefully, Luke said, "Maybe Harkness has the right idea. There's Emily to think of—"

"You mean you think we should run, too?" Peabody snapped. "That ain't the way you sounded the last time we talked about this, son."

"I know. I just don't want anything bad to happen to Emily."

"You think I do? But you got to remember this . . . gettin' her to leave wouldn't be easy. This land . . . well, look at it this way. When her pa and her brothers went off to fight, they figured they were doin' it to protect our home. This land. Emily still sees it the same way. She'll feel like she has to defend it, too, just like they did."

Luke understood that. He felt the same way about the Jensen farm in Missouri. So would his pa and Kirby.

There was no good answer. None at all.

Emily appeared in the doorway behind them, drying her hands on a cloth. "What are the two of you talkin' about so serious-like?"

"Who says we're talkin' serious?" her grandfather said. "I was just tellin' Luke a joke."

"I didn't hear anybody laughin'."

"That's because I ain't got to the funny part yet." Peabody turned to Luke. "So then the farmer says, 'You're all mixed up, mister. That there's my prize hog.'" He slapped a hand on his thigh and hooted with laughter.

Luke threw back his head and laughed, too, even though on the inside he had seldom felt grimmer.

Using the crutches, Luke lifted himself from the chair and stood beside the table. He took a deep breath and let go of the crutches, allowing them to fall to the sides like he had done before. As they thumped on the floor, he stood with his hands spread, trying to balance himself.

He didn't fall immediately. He felt the weight on his legs, felt the muscles struggling to support him. But they began to give out, and he had to slap his palms down on the table to hold himself up. Even that was progress, he thought as his pulse pounded in his head. He hadn't collapsed. Yes, he was leaning on the table, but he was still standing.

A footstep sounded on the porch.

Luke turned his head toward the door, and as he did so, his legs folded up underneath him. He tried to catch himself on the table, but wound up lying on the floor between the chair and the table.

Emily came in and saw him there. "Damn it all to—" She stopped herself. She had been trying to stop cursing so much lately.

He thought maybe she had decided it wasn't ladylike . . . as if acting more like a lady might have become more important to her.

She rushed over to him and bent to take hold of him. "Lord have mercy, Luke, what happened? How did you manage to fall?"

"Don't worry about that," he snapped, furious at himself for letting her distract him. "Just help me up."

He saw the quick flash of hurt in her eyes and wished he could call back the sharp words, but they were already out there. He couldn't do a thing about them except add in a softer tone, "Please, Emily."

As she lifted him, he reached up and grabbed hold of the table. With it to support him, she was able to get him back into the chair.

"I'll pick up your crutches."

He held out a hand to stop her. "I can get them. Thank you."

She looked at him with a slight frown. "Were you trying to walk, Luke? I've told you, I don't care about that, not for me. I want it for you, but it's not going to make any difference how I feel—"

"Of course it makes a difference. It's bound to." Luke frowned at her.

"No," she said as she leaned closer to him. "I swear to you, it doesn't. I'll prove it to you."

Before he could stop her, she lowered herself onto his lap, her arms clasped around his neck, and her mouth pressed hungrily to his.

Luke bit back a groan of mingled despair and desire. His arms went around her. She was such a little bit of a thing, yet the curves of her body were those of a woman. Her lips worked urgently against his, their taste sweet and hot.

As he held her and kissed her, he felt something, no doubt about that.

She did too. Pulling back slightly, her eyes widened. He was about to apologize, but a pleased glow sprang to life in her eyes. "See, Luke," she whispered. "I told you it didn't matter."

She kissed him again, then slid out of his arms and stood up.

"Grampaw might be comin' in any time, so we'll save our sparkin' for later."

Luke nodded. After everything Linus Peabody had done for him, he didn't want to offend the old-timer.

Peabody hurried in a short time later, all right, as Emily had predicted. He wore a worried expression on his face, and it quickly became obvious the last thing on his mind was who was sparking his granddaughter. "There's a buggy and some riders comin'." He reached for the rifle hanging on the wall near the door.

"Yankee soldiers again?" Emily asked, her body tensing as she stood next to the stove where she had started supper.

Peabody shook his head as he checked to make sure the rifle was loaded.

"Nope. It's that fella Wolford, and unless I miss my guess, the men he's got with him are hired guns."

CHAPTER 20

"Get my revolver," Luke told Emily.

"What're you thinkin' about doin'?" She looked at her grand-father. "What are the both of you thinkin' about doin'?"

"Nothin' we don't have to," Peabody told her. "Could be Wolford just wants to talk. If he does, I'll listen to him. Won't do him any good, but I'll listen."

"Is this about the folks who have been losin' their farms to the carpetbaggers?"

Peabody frowned. "You know about that?"

"How the hell could I *not* know about it?" Emily blurted out. "It's the only thing folks all over this part of the country are talkin' about!"

"I need my revolver," Luke said again. He was trying to stay calm, but the same tense feelings he had experienced before every battle were going through him. He might soon be fighting for his life, and the lives of Emily and her grandfather as well.

But that wasn't exactly likely, he told himself, not just yet, anyway. From what Peabody had said about Wolford's attempt to take over Bud Harkness's farm, the carpetbagger was using quasi-legal means in his land grabs, relying on corrupt judges and what passed for the law under Yankee occupation.

Wolford would have hired guns in reserve, though, and if he couldn't get what he wanted peacefully, he would use force to take it. Luke had no doubt about that.

He looked intently at Emily until she sighed and went to the cabinet where the Griswold and Gunnison revolver was kept. She took it out and brought it over to Luke. "I can use this gun."

He held out his hand. "You need to stay inside."

A quick flash of anger lit up her eyes. "Luke—"

"Luke's right," Peabody said. "You stay in the house, girl, like you did when the Yankees came."

"Men!" she said in exasperation. "You're the most stubborn critters on God's green earth!"

Luke stuck the revolver in the pocket of his overalls and grasped his crutches. "That's because we're raised by women to be that way." With a smile, he lifted himself to his feet.

She still looked mad, but rested a hand on his arm for a second. "Don't start trouble with them."

"I don't intend to start trouble with anybody," Luke assured her. He didn't say anything about finishing it, if things came down to that. He looked out through the door Peabody had left open. "Here they come."

"Be careful," Emily whispered to Luke. "We just . . ."

She didn't finish, but he knew what she meant. They had just admitted how they felt about each other. She didn't want him going and getting himself killed.

Luke didn't want that, either. He nodded to show her he understood as much.

Peabody went out onto the porch. Luke followed him, moving fairly easily on the crutches. He wished he could have walked out there bold as brass, but that was something for the future if his legs continued to improve.

With a clatter of hoofbeats and wheels, Vincent Wolford drove his buggy up to the cabin and brought the vehicle to a halt, reining in the two fine black horses pulling it. Luke found himself wondering who those horses used to belong to, and how Wolford had gotten his hands on them. He was willing to bet the carpetbagger hadn't bought them fair and square.

Three men on horseback accompanied Wolford. As they reined in, Luke studied them. Back home he had seen Jayhawkers from Kansas on several occasions, and these men reminded him of those ruthless guerrillas.

One wore a derby and a flashy eastern suit. He was big, with broad shoulders and a rough-hewn face dominated by a rusty handlebar mustache. His hands were huge, with knobby knuckles broken more than once in various brawls. He wasn't carrying a gun that was visible, but Luke figured there was probably a revolver in a shoulder holster under that tweed coat.

The other two riders were dressed more like frontiersmen in boots, work clothes, and broad-brimmed hats. They wore their guns out in the open, carrying holstered pistols on their hips. They had rugged, hard-planed faces and cold eyes.

Luke knew all three men were probably killers, paid by Vincent Wolford to enforce his will and help him take what he wanted. They would be fast on the draw. If Linus Peabody raised his rifle, one or more of the gunmen would drill him before he got a shot off.

Luke was pretty handy with a gun, but knew he wasn't a match for those three. Not with the Griswold and Gunnison stuck in his pocket. If he had a regular gun rig and a pair of revolvers, he might manage to down a couple, maybe all three, but they would get lead in him, too.

It wasn't going to come to that. He couldn't allow the carpetbaggers to kill him and Peabody, leaving Emily at their mercy.

"Take it easy," he said under his breath to Peabody. "Stay calm."

The old man nodded, but the tense way he stood and the urgency with which he gripped the rifle told a different story. He was ready to fight. He *wanted* to fight.

Luke levered himself forward on his crutches, putting himself between Peabody and the buggy. He nodded to Wolford. "Howdy. What brings you out here from town?"

"Mr. Smith, isn't it?" Wolford asked with that phony smile of his, without getting down from the buggy. "I came to speak with Mr. Peabody there. I have a business proposition for him."

Peabody moved up even with Luke. "I ain't interested in doin' business with the likes of you."

"You should hear me out," Wolford said. "That's just a smart rule of thumb. Always listen to the other fellow's proposal. You never know when he might offer something you want."

Peabody glared darkly at the visitors, but after a moment he nodded. "I'll listen. I don't reckon it's very likely you got anything I want, though."

"You might be surprised. What I'm proposing, Mr. Peabody, is that I take this farm off your hands for a very reasonable price."

"Why in blazes would I want to sell?" Peabody snapped.

"Well, the market for cotton, tobacco, and other crops is very depressed right now. You can't hope to make very much for them."

"We'll get by," the old man said.

"Yes, perhaps, but you can do even better somewhere else. I hear people are having phenomenal success migrating to the frontier. There are millions of acres out there just ripe for the taking."

"This is my home. I've lived on this land all my life, and my pa lived here before me. I intend to stay until the Good Lord calls me home."

Wolford's smile didn't budge, but Luke thought he saw impatience growing in the man's eyes.

"You can do that," Wolford said, "but you'd still be wise to sell out to me. If you don't want to leave, you can always stay and work the land on shares."

"Why in the Sam Hill would I want to do that?"

"You wouldn't have all the worries of dealing with the new government. I'd handle all that. You could just work the land the way you always have."

"While you rake in all the profits?" Peabody asked.

"Not all of it. You'd still get by, as you put it." Wolford's voice finally hardened as he went on. "You don't seem to understand, Mr. Peabody, that things have changed around here. It's not the same as it was before the war, and it never will be again. Different people are running things now. I happen to be well acquainted with Colonel Morrison and Judge Blevins, and although I may be speaking out of turn here, I know they're going through all the records and uncovering a number of cases where insufficient taxes were paid on properties in this area."

"You mean you're gonna grab folks' land by claimin' they owe taxes they really don't," Peabody said.

The big eastern tough in the derby glared and edged his horse forward. "Don't you talk to Mr. Wolford like that, you old Rebel," he warned.

Wolford lifted a hand. "Take it easy, Joe. I'm sure Mr. Peabody didn't mean to cast any aspersions."

"What I'll cast is you offa my land," Peabody said. "I paid my taxes, and can't nobody say otherwise!"

"Yes, but you paid them to the Confederates who were in charge here at the time." Wolford shook his head as if he were genuinely regretful. "There's no way of knowing where all that money went, but it isn't in the county's coffers like it's supposed to be. Unfortunately, in order to fund the new government, a new taxation schedule will have to be put in place—"

"Why don't you call it what it is?" Peabody broke in. "Stealin', plain and simple!"

"I'm just trying to help." Wolford leaned over slightly on the buggy seat to look past Luke and Peabody. "Isn't that your grand-daughter I see just inside the door?" He raised a hand to his hat. "Good day to you, Miss Peabody. You're looking as lovely as ever."

"You leave Emily outta this—" Peabody began, but she stepped onto the porch and confronted Wolford and his gunmen, too.

"We don't want your so-called help, mister." Her eyes blazed with fury.

She counseled restraint, Luke thought, but her emotions got the better of her and she couldn't practice what she preached.

"You'd better turn that buggy around and get off our land, right now!"

"Or what? An old man and a cripple will run us off?" The gunman leaned over in his saddle and spat. "I don't think so."

"Please, Howell, there's no need for unpleasantness." Wolford smiled at Emily again. "I think if you'd just give me a chance, Miss Peabody, you and I could be good friends. If you were to help per-suade your grandfather to be reasonable, why, I can see all sorts of benefits in it for you. A girl as beautiful as you should have some of the finer things in life, the sort of things a man like me could give you—"

"So I could be some sort of backwoods harlot for you?" Emily turned toward her grandfather and reached for the rifle. "Gimme that gun."

Luke saw the three hired killers grow tense in their saddles and knew the situation was teetering perilously close to violence. Under the circumstances, the outcome of that wouldn't be good for him and his friends.

He moved between the Peabodys and the unwelcome visitors and said in a loud, hard voice, "That's enough."

"Do you speak for these people, Mr. Smith?" Wolford asked with a sneer.

"I speak for myself, and this is what I've got to say, Wolford." Luke looked right into the man's eyes. He didn't like taking his attention off the others, but knew they wouldn't act unless Wolford ordered them to. "If there's trouble here today, you'll be sorry. I'll see to that personally."

"That's mighty big talk for a man on crutches." The eastern tough called Joe sneered.

Luke let go of the right-hand crutch, letting it fall behind him, and moved his hand so it wasn't far from the butt of the revolver sticking out of his pocket. "I only need one to balance on," he told Wolford, making it clear as he could. If any gunplay broke out, Luke was going to draw that revolver and kill Wolford, no matter what else happened. He might die, and Emily and her grandfather probably would, too, but Wolford would die first.

Luke was going to see to that.

Reading the deadly message in Luke's steady gaze, fear flared in the carpetbagger's eyes. An instant later, it was replaced by smoldering anger.

But the fear was still there, underneath, and Luke knew it.

"All right," Wolford snapped. "I was just trying to be generous. I thought perhaps we could consider ourselves friends and neighbors, Mr. Peabody. But if you'd rather this . . . this unreconstructed Rebel speak for you—"

"Smith's right," Peabody said. "We've heard enough. You and your boys need to git."

Wolford lifted the reins. "We'll be going, then. Perhaps I was wrong, Mr. Peabody. Perhaps you won't lose your farm"—he paused—"but don't count on it."

With that, he turned the team and sent the buggy rolling away from the cabin. The three gunmen lingered a moment, giving Luke hard, murderous stares before they wheeled their horses and followed Wolford.

"I ain't countin' on nothin'," Peabody said, "except that this trouble ain't over."

Luke knew the old-timer was right about that.

CHAPTER 21

Wolford had been so angry when he drove away Luke wouldn't have been surprised if problems started cropping up right away. But several days passed with no sign of the carpetbagger or his hired guns.

Linus Peabody reported the Harkness family on the neighboring farm had packed up and moved away, abandoning the place because they couldn't pay the exorbitant taxes being demanded by the Reconstruction government. Another worried neighbor had come by the farm and told Peabody about it, adding that the sheriff was going to auction off the Harkness farm in Dobieville on Saturday.

Luke knew Vincent Wolford would win that auction at a rock-bottom price. And he would probably get some of the money back from the sheriff and the judge in the form of a kickback.

The idea of Emily going out to work in the fields with her grandfather worried Luke. If Wolford's gunnies showed up, intent on causing trouble, Peabody wouldn't be able to protect her. In his current condition, Luke couldn't watch over them, so he made up his mind the best thing for him to do was improve as much and as quickly as he could.

With that determination goading him on, he worked with his legs for long hours each day while Emily and her grandfather were gone. He put more and more weight on his own muscles, forcing them to move and carry him, not just support him.

Back and forth across the cabin's main room he shuffled endlessly, using the crutches. Eventually he was able to take a step, then several steps, without touching the floor with the crutches, although he held them ready to catch himself if he fell.

Those efforts made his legs ache almost intolerably, but he welcomed the pain, even embraced it. To have his legs hurt was so much better than to have them feel nothing at all.

By the time a week had passed since Wolford and his gunmen had shown up at the farm, Luke was able to take actual steps as he walked across the room, no longer sliding his feet in a shuffling manner. He left the crutches behind and walked on his own, something that had seemed utterly impossible a few months ago. His gait was slow and halting, to be sure, and he told himself with a wry smile that he was a long way from being able to dance a jig, but he was getting there.

He was getting there, all right, and it was the best pain he had ever felt, although he sometimes had to bite his lip to keep from crying out when Emily massaged his legs.

It wasn't long before she noticed the change in his legs. "These muscles are definitely harder and stronger than they were. You're gonna walk again one of these days, Luke. You just wait and see."

"Thanks to you, I am," he told her. Without the way she had kept him going through his darkest days and nights, and without the determination his fear for her safety gave him, he might not have ever walked again. Soon he was going to be ready to reveal his secret to her.

A little later, when Peabody caught a moment alone with him, the old-timer said, "I spotted them fellas who work for Wolford watchin' the place again today."

Luke hated to hear that, but he wasn't surprised. He had known better than to hope Wolford would give up on getting his hands on the farm. Even worse was knowing the man wanted to get his hands on Emily. He had hinted as much when he visited the farm, and Luke had seen the unmistakable lust in the carpetbagger's eyes when Wolford looked at her.

"Why don't I start going out to the fields with you and Emily during the day?" Luke had discarded that idea a week earlier but was beginning to think it might work.

"On your crutches?" Peabody asked with a frown.

"No, you can help me climb into the wagon, and I'll sit up there and keep an eye on things while you're working. We can take along the rifle and my revolver. I can handle a gun just fine."

Peabody scratched his stubbly jaw and shrugged. "That ain't a bad idea."

The next day they put it into practice, even though Emily was insistent on knowing why Luke was coming with them.

"Wolford's men have been watchin' us again," Peabody admitted.

"Oh, them? Shoot, I saw them before. They don't scare me."

"Well, they scare me, and they ought to scare you, too," Peabody insisted. "They're bad men, and the fella they work for is even worse. We got trouble on the horizon."

It was even closer than they suspected.

With help from Peabody and Emily, Luke climbed to the wagon seat and they went out to the fields. He wished he could help them harvest the late summer corn crop. Unfortunately, his legs weren't yet steady enough. Instead, he scanned the surrounding countryside for any sign of Wolford's men without spotting them.

The sound of shots made Emily cry out in alarm and Luke twist around on the seat to peer toward the cabin.

The shots continued from that direction as Emily and Peabody dropped what they were doing and ran to the wagon. Peabody scrambled up to the seat and jerked the reins loose from the brake lever while Emily practically threw herself into the back. Even the normally stubborn mules sensed something was wrong. They broke into a run as Peabody headed them toward the cabin.

Breathing hard, Emily leaned over the back of the seat between the two men. "What are they doin'?" she asked anxiously. "What's all that shootin' about?"

"We'll know in a minute." Luke gripped the rifle tightly. It was only a single-shot weapon, but the revolver in his pocket was fully loaded.

The shooting stopped before they came in sight of the cabin. As they did, Luke caught a glimpse of several riders galloping away from the place. They were already too far off for him to make out any details, but he was willing to bet they were the three hired guns who worked for Vincent Wolford.

"No!" Emily cried as her grandfather wheeled the wagon into the open area between the cabin and the barn. Limp, bloody bundles of feathers were scattered around on the ground. The chickens had been blasted to pieces. In the pen over by the barn, the hogs lay motionless in the mud.

Emily leaped out of the wagon and ran into the barn. When she came back a moment later, tears were running down her cheeks. "They killed the milk cow, too. Looks like they just shot everything that moved."

"Why in blazes would they do that?" Peabody asked furiously. "It aggravates the hell out of me, but losin' those animals ain't enough to ruin the farm."

"This is just the opening gambit," Luke said. "Think of it as a warning. Wolford wants to let you know it'll get a lot worse if you don't give him what he wants."

"Never! I'm goin' to town and swearin' out a complaint against the varmints! The sheriff's got to do somethin'. He's supposed to uphold the law around here."

"The sheriff works for Wolford and that judge of his and the rest of the Yankees," Emily said bitterly. "He's not gonna do anything, Grampaw."

"We don't know that. If nobody ever speaks up, nothin' will change around here!"

The old-timer was right about that, Luke supposed. But like Emily, he didn't think complaining to the law would do any good. They would never know if they didn't try, though. "We'll all go to Dobieville. Maybe round up some of your friends and neighbors who've had trouble with the carpetbaggers and take them with you. If more people are speaking up, the men in charge will have a harder time ignoring them."

Peabody nodded. "That's a good idea."

"Not as good an idea as goin' to town and shootin' that snake Wolford for tellin' his men to do this," Emily said.

It might come to that, Luke thought, *but we have to try reason first . . . then bullets.*

Peabody spent the rest of the day visiting his neighbors and putting together a delegation to complain to the sheriff in Dobieville. The killing of his livestock wasn't the first such outrage in the area. Barns had burned down mysteriously, crops had been trampled on dark nights, wells had been fouled, and cattle had been run off.

Nor would that harassment stop, Luke thought. In fact, he expected it to escalate into outright violence in fairly short order. Wolford and the other carpetbaggers were not patient men.

The farmers rendezvoused outside of town and rode in on mules and in wagons and buggies. Some of them walked. A few had brought their wives and children with them, something Luke thought probably wasn't wise. A group about forty strong converged on the sheriff's office.

Their arrival in town stirred up enough of a commotion that the lawman heard them coming. He stepped out onto the porch of his office to wait for them. He was a middle-aged man with thinning brown hair and a mustache. A gun belt was strapped around his waist, and he carried a shotgun in addition to the holstered revolver.

"Fella's name is Royce Wilkes," Peabody explained to Luke as they approached in the wagon. "Used to be a deputy here, but he was too fond of corn liquor. The old sheriff ran him off. When the war was over, the Yankees put him back in office and gave him the sheriff's job. He's local, but he's in the back pocket of them no-good carpet-baggers."

Wilkes had the shotgun cradled in his left arm. He held up his right hand for silence and called, "All right, what the devil's goin' on here?"

Everyone in the group turned to look at Linus Peabody. He had talked them into coming, and they regarded him as their spokesman.

"Sheriff, we're all here to lodge complaints against Vincent Wolford and those fellas who work for him," Peabody said. "I beg pardon of the ladies in earshot of my voice, but Wolford's men have been raisin' hell hereabouts, and it's gotta stop."

"You know for a fact that what you're sayin' is true, Linus?" Wilkes asked.

"I do," Peabody replied with a forceful nod. "They came out to my place yesterday and shot all my chickens and hogs and my milk cow. We seen 'em ridin' off after they done it."

Luke and Emily nodded. In reality the riders had been too far away for a positive identification, but there was no question in Luke's mind that Wolford's men were responsible.

"Well, that's a mighty serious charge," Wilkes said.

Another man in the crowd said, "That ain't all they've done. My barn burned down last week, and I know good and well somebody set that fire. I rode into town and told you all about it, Royce."

"You did," Wilkes said, "but you also told me you didn't see who done it."

"It had to be Wolford's men! You know that!"

"I'm a lawman," Wilkes boasted, his chest puffing out pompously. "I got to have proof. And somebody thinkin' they saw something ain't proof."

"Are you callin' us liars?" Peabody demanded.

"I'm sayin' maybe you were mistaken."

Luke suggested, "Why don't you at least ask Wolford about it? See

554 William W. Johnstone

if he can account for the whereabouts of his men yesterday when Mr. Peabody's livestock was being slaughtered."

Wilkes shook his head stubbornly. "I ain't gonna bother an important man like Mr. Wolford—"

"It's no bother," a new voice said.

Everyone swung around to look. The crowd parted, and Vincent Wolford himself sauntered up to the porch.

"I heard there was a gathering of some sort and decided to come see for myself what it was about," Wolford went on. "I'd be glad to answer any questions you have for me, Sheriff."

"I don't have any questions," Wilkes said.

"I do," Peabody snapped. "Did you send your men to kill my livestock, mister?"

Wolford gave a solemn shake of his head. "Of course not, Mr. Peabody. Why in the world would I do a thing like that?"

"To try to run me off so you can grab my land!"

"I wanted to make you a fair offer for your land, but you wouldn't even consider it," Wolford said. "As far as I'm concerned, our business is over."

"Where were your men yesterday morning?" Luke asked.

"Burnett, Howell, and Prentice?" Wolford shrugged. "I'm not sure. I don't keep track of their whereabouts every hour of the day. As long as they do the jobs I give them, that's all I really care about."

"Did you give them any jobs yesterday?"

"As a matter of fact, I didn't." Wolford smiled. "I didn't even speak to them. So you see, even if there was anything to these ludicrous accusations—and I assure you, there isn't—I can't be held responsible for them."

Wilkes nodded. "Looks like that clears it all up. Sorry to bother you, Mr. Wolford."

"Oh, it's no bother, Sheriff, I assure you. All I want to do is carry on my business and get along with my neighbors."

Wilkes turned back to the farmers. "You've said your piece, now it's time for all of you to go back home and stop botherin' folks."

"Are you runnin' us out of town?" Peabody asked. "Don't we still have a right to go where we please?"

"No, you don't," Wilkes snapped. "Gatherin' up in mobs like this is against the law. So if you don't break it up and leave, it'll be my duty to arrest you . . . and I'll get the soldiers to help me, if I need to."

"You'd better do what he says, Linus," Luke told the old-timer.

"You mean let them get away with it?" Emily asked.

"Getting arrested isn't going to help anything."

Peabody scowled darkly, but he said, "All right, we'll go. But this ain't over, Sheriff. We'll get justice somehow."

"You step out of line and you'll be sorry," Wilkes warned.

With a lot of angry muttering, the crowd turned to leave town. As the wagon rolled past the last buildings, Emily said, "Like I told you, nothin's gonna change."

"At least Wolford knows we're on to him," Peabody said. "He's the one who's really to blame for everything."

"And all he's gonna do is laugh at us," Emily said as her shoulders slumped in despair.

If that's all that happens, Luke thought, *then they might be lucky.* Wolford's smooth façade had never budged, but he had to be angry that the farmers had banded together to complain about his tactics. Luke wouldn't be at all surprised if he decided to teach them a lesson.

And if he did, it would be a painful one. Luke was sure of that.

CHAPTER 22

Emily was cool toward Luke on the ride back to the farm and for the rest of the day. He wasn't sure why she was upset with him, unless it was because he had talked her grandfather out of setting off a showdown in town. Maybe she didn't understand he didn't want anything to happen to her . . . or maybe she did, and that just made her angrier.

Whatever the reason, she didn't have much to say to him around her grandfather, and they didn't get a chance to talk alone. Luke turned in knowing nothing was settled and the situation was likely to get worse before it got better . . . if it ever did.

Sometime during the night he came awake instantly, smelling smoke. It was too strong to be coming from the fireplace or the stove. He sat up. No lights burned inside the cabin, but a flickering red glow came through the cracks around the front door and through the thin curtains hung over the windows.

The barn was on fire. It was the only explanation that made sense.

And he knew it hadn't caught fire by itself.

"Emily!" he shouted. "Linus! Wake up!"

Peabody bolted from his bunk. Emily bolted from hers and cried out in alarm. "Something's on fire!"

"The barn!" With his nightshirt flapping around his legs, Peabody grabbed the rifle from the chair where he had placed it to be handy and headed for the door.

When he flung it open, the garish red light from the blazing barn spilled into the cabin. He rushed outside with Emily right behind him.

Still struggling to get out of his bunk, Luke swung his legs to the floor and stood up, using the back of a nearby chair for support. He picked up his revolver off the chair and grabbed one of his crutches propped against the wall next to the head of his bunk.

Hoofbeats pounded outside. Someone shouted, and Peabody's rifle cracked.

"No, no," Luke panted as he hurried toward the door as fast as he could. He knew without having to think about it what had happened. To get back at Peabody for trying to organize the farmers against him, Wolford had sent his men to the farm to set fire to the barn.

And those killers were still out there, where they threatened Emily and her grandfather. That thought made Luke's blood run cold.

As he reached the porch, he heard Emily scream, "Grampaw!" In the garish light of the fire, Luke saw a man on horseback nearly run down Linus Peabody. The old-timer threw himself out of the way just in time, losing his balance and sprawling on the ground. The rider wheeled his horse around and pointed a gun at Peabody as Emily ran toward her grandfather.

She leaped to shield him as the rider pulled the trigger. Luke fired at the same instant. Flame spat from the barrel of his revolver. The impact of the bullet jarred the man on the horse, knocking him forward.

"Emily!" Peabody cried out. "Oh, my God, Emily!"

Luke suddenly realized he was off the porch and didn't think about what he did next as he cast the single crutch aside and broke into a stumbling run toward Emily and Peabody. The nightmarish glare of the fire revealed Emily's body lying stretched on the ground while her grandfather hovered over her.

Hoofbeats thundered again as two more riders lunged out of the jagged shadows cast by the firelight. The newcomers seemed intent on trampling them. Still stumbling, Luke raised the revolver and thumbed off two more shots. He didn't know if he hit either of the attackers, but they veered sharply away.

The man he'd wounded yelled, "I'm hit! We gotta get out of here!"

Luke recognized the eastern accent of the tough named Joe Burnett. The other two had to be Howell and Prentice. One of them snapped a couple shots at him, coming close enough for him to hear the bullets whine past his head, as the other grabbed the dangling reins of Burnett's horse and all three gunmen fled.

Pain flared through Luke's legs, but they continued to support him. Peabody looked up at him as he reached the old man's side, but he didn't seem to notice Luke was standing and moving around without the aid of the crutches.

"Emily's hurt!" Peabody cried. "When that no-good shot at me, she got in the way of the bullet!"

"How bad is it? Where's she hit?" Luke figured if he knelt down, he wouldn't be able to get back up again, so he made his voice urgent in an attempt to get through the fear and confusion that gripped Peabody.

It seemed to work, because the old-timer looked down, gently grasped Emily's shoulders, and rolled her onto her back. Luke caught a glimpse of blood on her nightclothes, but the stain appeared to be a small one, at least so far.

"I . . . I don't think she's hurt too bad," Peabody said after a moment. "Looks like the bullet just nicked her side."

Emily groaned.

"She's comin' to." Peabody continued to watch his granddaughter.

Luke watched and listened for any sign of the gunmen doubling back. In the firelight, the three of them made good targets, he thought.

Not seeing further danger, he turned his attention back to Emily and Peabody. "You'll need to pick her up and get her back in the cabin. Can you clean that wound and put a dressing on it?"

"Yeah, I reckon I can." Amazement crept into Peabody's voice as he went on. "Luke, you're standin' up on your own! And you ran across there a minute ago! I saw you with my own eyes."

"Don't worry about that. Just take care of Emily."

"I will. What are you gonna do?"

"Something that somebody should have done before now," Luke said.

He didn't know how long his legs would keep working. It had taken the threat to Emily and her grandfather for them to move like they had a few minutes earlier. The mixture of fear, desperation, and rage had burned through him like the fire that was consuming the barn, a cleansing fire that forced muscles and nerves to work again the way they were supposed to. His movements were rusty and a little clumsy, but he could get around again, and didn't want to waste the opportunity.

Peabody was still strong, and Emily was a slip of a girl. He had no trouble picking her up and carrying her back into the cabin.

Luke followed. While Peabody tended to Emily, he got dressed, reloaded the Griswold and Gunnison, and went back outside. His face was impassive in the firelight despite the pain shooting through his legs with every step. The rest of those nerves were waking up again after their long sleep, he thought. If they kept working for a while longer, it would be enough.

He pocketed his revolver and walked over to the spot where he had wounded Joe Burnett. The man's revolver, a Colt Navy, lay on the ground where Burnett had dropped it. Luke picked up the gun, hefting it in his hand, and realized his ammunition would fit it. Both weapons would be fully loaded when he headed for town.

He frowned. How was he going to get there? The luckless mules had been in the barn, and so had the wagon. His legs were finally working again, but he couldn't walk all the way to Dobieville.

Shouts and hoofbeats made him swing around and raise both guns. The man riding up to the farm reined in sharply and threw his hands in the air. "Whoa!" he exclaimed. "Hold your fire, mister! I'm a friend!"

Luke recognized the newcomer as one of the men who had gone into town with them that morning. He thought for a second and recalled the man's name. "You're Thad Franklin, right?"

"Yeah." The man dismounted. "My place is a couple miles east of here. I saw the light from the fire and knew somethin' had to be wrong. Thought I'd better come see if I could help." He shook his head. "It's too late to save that barn, though."

"Maybe you and the others can help Linus rebuild," Luke suggested.

"Is he hurt? How about Emily?"

Luke jerked his head toward the cabin. "They're in there. Emily was wounded by the varmints who set the barn on fire, but I think she's going to be all right."

"There'll be more folks showin' up soon, I reckon. People always come to help when they see a fire."

"You can help right now," Luke said. "Give me your horse."

"My horse? What? Say, you're the fella who can't walk!" Franklin looked Luke up and down in confusion. "But you're standin' up now."

Luke lifted the Colt Navy and pointed it at Franklin, saying coldly, "I need your horse. I'll get it back to you, if I can. If I can't, you'll find it in Dobieville."

"Careful with that gun, mister! What're you gonna do?" Franklin's eyes widened as he realized the answer to his own question. "You're goin' after the men who did this?"

Luke used his free hand to take the reins out of Franklin's fingers. "Sorry, but it's got to be done." He got his left foot in the stirrup and swung up into the saddle, clenching his jaw at the pain caused by mounting.

"You're crazy," Franklin said. "You can't fight those carpetbaggers. There are too many of 'em, and they got the Yankee army on their side!"

"I don't plan to fight all of them, just one in particular and the men he sent to do this."

"They'll kill you!"

"Probably. But I plan on sending them to hell ahead of me."

CHAPTER 23

Still burning brightly, the fire cast an orange glow into the sky be-hind Luke as he rode toward Dobieville. Being on a horse again felt good.

Despite his concern for Emily, he felt more alive than he had in a long time.

He hadn't had a chance to reload the Navy after all. Checking the gun's cylinder, he found that Burnett had fired only one round. The other five chambers were loaded. He had eleven shots.

It would have to be enough.

Regret gnawed at him. He hadn't taken the time to say good-bye to Emily and her grandfather. He knew they would have tried to talk him out of forcing a showdown with Wolford. Luke didn't trust him-self not to give in to Emily's pleading and stay at the farm with her.

If he had stayed, things would continue to get worse. He didn't know if they would actually improve once Wolford was dead, but at least if the carpetbagger and his gunmen were gone they wouldn't be able to threaten anyone else.

The raiders had come very close to killing Emily, and that knowl-edge filled Luke with a rage overpowering every other emotion. Somebody had to take a stand against their evil.

He was the man.

Simple as that.

Luke had a good sense of direction and was able to find the settle-ment without any trouble. When he saw its lights, he reined in for a moment, thinking of the situation and what he should do next.

The three gunmen weren't that far ahead of him. He figured the first thing they would do was report to Wolford, so there was a good chance he could find them together. It would certainly make things easier if all four of his enemies were in one place.

That notion turned his thoughts to Potter, Stratton, Richards, and Casey. He'd had four enemies to deal with that fateful night, too, and it hadn't turned out well. But he'd been taken by surprise, even though he shouldn't have been, and tonight he'd be the one doing the surprising.

He shook his head and turned his thoughts back to the situation at hand. Wolford owned the North Georgia Land Company. Luke had heard talk about it and had seen the sign on a building in town, earlier, when the group of farmers came to talk to the sheriff. He nodded. It was the first place he would look for his quarry.

He used his heels to get the horse moving again. Dobieville was quiet. No reason for it not to be, Luke supposed. The citizens didn't know what had happened out at the Peabody farm. They would hear about it by morning. As he rode down the deserted streets they were blissfully ignorant.

That was about to change.

The saloons were open, and a light still burned in the general store, but most of the businesses along Main Street were dark, including the building that housed Wolford's office. It appeared to be locked up for the night.

A faint glow in the alley behind the place told a different story. Luke looked along the side of the building, saw that glow, and knew one of the windows in the rear was lit up.

He dismounted and his legs sagged for a second, forcing him to grab the saddle horn and hold himself up. He straightened and looped the reins around the hitch rack in front.

Hoping his muscles wouldn't betray him at the worst possible moment, he drew both revolvers from his pockets and started down the narrow passage beside the building. His gait was awkward as he kept his legs rigid, but they got him where he was going.

Reaching the rear corner of the building, he edged around it carefully and saw the lighted window. It was raised a few inches to let in the night air.

As quietly as possible, he moved closer to hear what was being said inside.

". . . doctor," a man said harshly. "This bullet's gotta come out of me."

"If we fetch the doctor, there'll be questions about how you managed to get shot, Joe." That was Wolford's voice. "I'd rather not deal with the potential embarrassment."

"So you're just gonna let me die?" Burnett's voice was drawn thin with pain.

"Of course not. Harve can dig the bullet out, can't you, Harve?"

One of the other gunmen answered, "I reckon I can give it a try." He didn't sound too confident about it.

"And I have a bottle of whiskey right here," Wolford went on. "Take a nice healthy slug, Joe, and then Harve can clean the wound with it, too."

"I don't know about this." Burnett was clearly reluctant to trust his fate to the medical skills of his fellow hired gun.

"You're being well paid to take risks," Wolford snapped, losing his patience. "And you didn't even manage to kill the old man like I told you to."

"That's not my fault," Burnett replied, a whine creeping in his tone. "I told you, boss, the girl jumped right in front of my gun just as I pulled the trigger."

"Yes, well, if she's dead, that's going to be very regrettable . . . for her and for you. I mean to have her, along with her grandfather's farm."

Luke's hands tightened on the guns, wanting to burst in there and start shooting. But it wasn't quite the right moment yet. He needed to wait just a little longer.

"Here's the whiskey," Wolford said.

Luke heard the glugging sound as the wounded man took a healthy swallow of the liquor.

Wolford went on, "You can lie down here on my desk, Joe. Thurman, you hold him down while Harve removes that bullet."

Murmurs of agreement came from the men.

Luke waited as he listened to them moving around.

Burnett let out a yelp. "Damn it, boss, at least give me somethin' to bite down on!"

"All right—"

Now, Luke thought.

While they were all gathered around the desk with their attention focused on the crude surgery he took a couple steps and rammed his shoulder against the building's back door. The flimsy lock gave under the impact and the door flew open.

Luke stumbled over the threshold, catching his balance as he brought up the guns in his hands. "Hold it!" he yelled. "Nobody move!"

They ignored the command and moved, all right. Luke had figured they would. But he had given them a chance to surrender, so his conscience was clear.

One of the gunmen—he still didn't know which one was Prentice and which one was Howell—whirled away from the desk and tried to claw out the gun holstered on his hip. Luke shot him in the face with the Griswold and Gunnison. The .36 caliber slug destroyed the man's nose and plowed into his brain, driving him backward over the desk, where he fell on top of the wounded Burnett.

The second gunman cleared leather, but before he could raise his gun, let alone get off a shot, a slug from the Colt Navy in Luke's left hand ripped into his throat. The man spun around in a half turn, blood from severed arteries spraying across the expensive rug on the floor of Wolford's private office.

Roaring in rage, Burnett shoved the dead man off himself and plucked the man's Colt from its holster. Even wounded, he had the strength to lunge up off the desk.

Luke fired both guns into Burnett's chest. The double impact lifted the big easterner off his feet and dumped him onto the desk again.

A pocket pistol went off with a small popping sound, and Luke felt something lance into his left shoulder. It wasn't much worse than a bee sting, but he knew he'd just been shot. He knew, as well, Wolford had shot him, because the other three men in the room were already dead.

Wolford fired again as he darted for the door leading into the front part of the building. Luke ducked, which gave the carpetbagger time to flee from the private office. As Luke straightened, he fired again and stomped into the bigger, darkened room after Wolford.

Wolford's gun went off again. Luke spotted the little tongue of flame from the muzzle as he heard the slug whine past his ear. He snapped a shot in return. Wolford cried out.

With Luke pursuing him inexorably, Wolford didn't have time to unlock the front door. He took the only way out, throwing himself against the front window. Glass shattered and sprayed as he burst through it and sprawled on the boardwalk outside.

Luke kept moving. His legs hadn't betrayed him so far, and miraculously, he was still alive. His quick reflexes and speed with a gun had saved him, but the job wasn't done yet.

He stepped through the broken window onto the boardwalk as Wolford tried to scramble away. Wolford screamed for help.

"Should've thought of that before you sent those men out to the Peabody farm tonight," Luke told him.

"You . . . you can't be doing this!" Wolford gasped as he scrambled to his feet. "You can't even walk!"

"Seems that I can." Luke shot the carpetbagger's left leg out from under him, the bullet shattering the kneecap into a million pieces. "But you can't."

Wolford collapsed and clutched his bleeding, ruined knee as he screamed. Luke aimed carefully, since the man was writhing around, and blasted apart Wolford's other knee.

"Drop that gun!" a man yelled over Wolford's shrieks of agony. "Drop it right now!"

Luke glanced over and saw a hatless, nightshirt-wearing Sheriff Royce Wilkes pointing a shotgun at him.

Luke lined the Griswold and Gunnison's barrel on Wolford's forehead and eared back the hammer. His thumb was all that kept it from falling. "You can blast me to hell, Sheriff, but you can't pull those triggers fast enough to keep me from killing Wolford."

The carpetbagger realized how close he was to death, and screamed, "Don't shoot him, Sheriff! Don't shoot him!"

Wilkes held off, but the slight tremor of the shotgun's twin barrels showed how much he wanted to pull the triggers. "Listen here, mister, you'd better put that gun down. Otherwise you'll die here."

"So will this murderer," Luke said, "and I think I'm just fine with it if that's what it takes to rid the world of him."

"I . . . I never murdered anybody!" Wolford gasped. "Oh, God! Somebody help me!"

"You're beyond help from God or anybody else," Luke growled. "And you paid those gunmen of yours to go out to the Peabody farm, burn down the barn, and murder Linus Peabody. I heard you say that yourself, just a few minutes ago."

"Why . . . why would I . . ." Wolford couldn't go on. He lay whimpering in pain.

"Because with her grandfather dead, you thought Emily would have no choice but to turn to you," Luke continued. "You thought I didn't represent any threat. You were wrong on both counts. Even if you'd killed Linus and me, Emily would have wound up cutting out your heart. Trust me on that, Wolford."

"You . . . you're crazy."

"Am I? Sheriff Wilkes, why don't you ask Mr. Wolford if he sent his men to kill Linus Peabody?"

The shotgun was still trembling in Wilkes' hands, but it seemed to be from fear. "I don't want any part of this. I'm supposed to enforce the law—"

"Then arrest Vincent Wolford. Arrest him for murder and see to it he's tried, convicted, and hanged. And if you do that, then maybe, just maybe, there's still some hope for this country after all."

"Mr. Wolford?" Wilkes said, clearly uncertain what he should do.

"What does it matter?" Wolford suddenly cried. "Of course I sent my men to get rid of that stubborn old geezer! He's just a Rebel! We beat them! We won! We can do anything we want to them!"

"There's still supposed to be some law—"

"Not for Rebels!"

"We're still Americans," Luke pointed out. "Isn't that one of the so-called reasons you Yankees fought the war in the first place?"

Wolford let out a shriek of rage and hatred and pushed himself up from the boardwalk with his left hand. His right flung up the little pistol. "Go to hell!" he screeched.

"You first." Luke lifted his thumb. The revolver roared and bucked in his hand, and the bullet smacked into Wolford's forehead, hammering the back of his skull down on the planks. The gun fell out of Wolford's hand, unfired.

Luke expected to feel a double load of buckshot smash into him, ending his life.

Instead, he realized that other than the echoes of his shot dying away, the street was quiet.

He looked over at Wilkes. The sheriff had lowered the shotgun. Maybe it had something to do with the crowd of townspeople surrounding him. They had been drawn by the shots and the screaming, and probably had heard Wolford's confession. It was possible a lot of them didn't like the way Wilkes had been doing the Yankees' bidding. He had to be worried the crowd would turn on him, if he shot Luke.

"The . . . the soldiers will be coming from their camp," Wilkes stammered out.

"When they get here, you can tell them some criminals have been executed," Luke said.

"There was no trial—"

"More than they deserved. Wolford got to speak his piece." Luke nodded at the crowd. "All these people heard it."

"There's gonna be warrants sworn out on you—"

"Fine." Luke tucked the Colt Navy away, but kept the Griswold and Gunnison in his hand as he stepped down carefully from the board-walk. The horse he had ridden into town was only a few steps away. It looked like he wasn't going to be able to return the mount to Thad Franklin after all. If he could, later on he would send some money to the man to pay for the horse.

"I thought you couldn't walk," Wilkes remarked.

"It seems that I can," Luke said again.

"Old Peabody and his granddaughter . . ."

"They're all right. Emily was wounded, but I don't think it's bad."

"Then Wolford's men didn't murder anybody after all."

"Not for lack of trying," Luke said. "And there's no telling what other crimes they're guilty of, or how many men they've killed."

"You're the killer," Wilkes said, his voice shaking. "A cold-blooded killer!"

"In that case, Sheriff," Luke said quietly, "I think you'd do well to stay out of my way." He put his foot in the stirrup and swung up onto the borrowed horse. Or stolen horse, if you wanted to look at it that way, he thought.

Part of him couldn't believe he was still alive, or his legs were still working. But that was the case, and he had learned to deal with things the way they were, not the way he wished they could be.

Wilkes was right. The law would probably come after him. He could never go back to the Peabody farm. It would bring down more trouble on their heads, trouble they didn't need.

One thing had to be left perfectly clear before he rode away. Raising his voice so he addressed the townspeople as much as the sheriff, he said, "Emily Peabody and her grandfather had nothing to do with what happened here tonight! I did it on my own, and the law has no reason to bother them for this or anything else! I'm counting on the good people of this community to make sure that's under-stood! *I* did this!"

"We don't even know your name, mister," one of the townies called out.

"It's Smith. Luke Smith."

With that, Luke jammed his heels into the horse's flanks. People scrambled to get out of his way as he galloped out of the settlement. The darkness at the edge of town swallowed him.

It swallowed Luke Smith . . . because Luke Jensen was dead. He had died the night the Confederate gold was stolen. His ma and pa, Kirby, and Janey would never know he was a failure and a fugitive.

The swift rataplan of hoofbeats in the night faded and then was gone.

BOOK THREE

CHAPTER 24

1870

An icy wind clawed at Luke through the sheepskin coat he wore as he brought his horse to a stop in front of the squat roadhouse. Settlers' homes and most businesses on the almost treeless Kansas plains were built of sod because it was too expensive to have lumber freighted in. Any grass on the thatched roofs was dead. It was late autumn.

He was glad he'd found the place perched on the bank of a narrow creek with ice forming along its edges. No other human habitation was in sight for miles around on the open plains. At least he'd have somewhere to spend the night out of the frigid weather.

His legs sometimes gave him trouble when it was cold. Usually he got around just fine, as if he'd never been injured, although it had taken months to regain his full strength. The wound in his shoulder was minor and had healed quickly, but his legs had given him trouble for a long time. Every so often the old ache was there, deep in his muscles, and it was worse when the temperature dropped.

Other old aches bothered him more, like the knowledge that he had failed the Confederacy and his friends, and the fact that he had ridden away without saying good-bye to Emily.

At least he knew she and her grandfather were all right.

A few months after leaving Georgia, he'd been tending bar in a little East Texas town when none other than Sheriff Royce Wilkes had walked into the saloon where Luke worked. Former Sheriff Royce Wilkes was more accurate, because as it turned out, Wilkes had been run out of town, just like when he'd been a deputy.

Luke dismounted and tied his horse at the rack with half a dozen others. He glanced at the gray sky. Sleet or snow would probably fall later, but for now there was just the cold wind and the fading light. He shuttered in the cold, remembering that long ago meeting with Wilkes.

As he came up to the bar, his eyes widened in shock as he recognized Luke. "Smith!" His hand dropped toward the gun on his hip.

Luke reached under the bar and rested his hand on the stock of the sawed-off shotgun the owner kept on a shelf there. "I wouldn't do that, Sheriff. There's a Greener pointing at you under here."

Wilkes moved his hand well away from his gun and muttered, "Sorry. And I ain't a sheriff no more. Haven't been since not long after you left Dobieville."

"What happened?"

Wilkes' mouth twisted bitterly. "Everybody in the damned county raised hell with Judge Blevins and Colonel Morrison about how Wolford tried to have Linus Peabody killed. That old man's well-liked around those parts. Morrison and the judge tried to brush it off. Blevins swore out a warrant for your arrest on murder charges. But I said I wasn't gonna go after you, so they booted me from the job."

"That's a shame," Luke said. "A man shouldn't lose his job for doing the right thing . . . for once."

"You don't know what it was like back there when the Yankees came in." Wilkes scowled and shrugged. "Or I reckon maybe you do, since you were there. Anyway, the Yankees didn't want me anymore, and the townsfolk didn't have any use for me to start with, so I thought I might as well come on out here to the frontier and see what I was missin'. So far it ain't been a hell of a lot."

Luke asked, "Do you know how Emily is?"

"She was fine when I left. She wasn't hurt bad that night. In fact, she started lettin' Thad Franklin's boy Jess start courtin' her."

Luke drew in a breath. Hearing that hurt, but at the same time he was glad Emily wasn't sitting around and pining away. He wasn't worth her being unhappy.

"What about those murder warrants?"

Wilkes shrugged again. "They're still in effect, I guess, but nobody's gettin' in any hurry to serve them. I reckon there's a good chance that if you stay out of Georgia, nobody's even gonna bother lookin' for you."

Luke hoped that was true. He had spent the first three months looking over his shoulder, even as he worked his way west, taking whatever odd jobs he could find.

"I see you're still up and walkin' around," Wilkes went on.

"Yeah, my legs are a lot better."

"You're a lucky man. How about a beer?"

Luke nodded and reached for a mug. "I can do that."

Wilkes had his drink and left. Luke was relieved, knowing Emily was all right. Maybe she would marry the Franklin boy and settle down to have a long, happy life, Yankees or no Yankees.

It was still on Luke's mind when he left the saloon that night and started back to the shabby little room he rented a block away.

The soft scrape of a footstep behind him was all the warning he had . . . or needed. As he twisted, his hand streaked to the Colt Navy tucked in his waistband. He never went anywhere without being armed. One of his revolvers was always in easy reach, even when he was sleeping.

The gun came out with blinding speed. The muzzle flash from the other man's gun bloomed n the darkness. Luke's revolver crashed. A man cried out and reeled from the mouth of the alley Luke had just passed, collapsing in the muddy street.

He knew, even before he snapped a lucifer to life with his thumbnail, the man he'd just killed was Royce Wilkes. He'd been nursing a grudge against Luke ever since leaving Georgia, and when fate had brought the two of them together again, the moment was inevitable.

And it was a damned shame, Luke thought. Back in Dobieville, Wilkes had acted like a real lawman for a moment, but ultimately, doing the right thing had brought him to a violent end.

The former sheriff was responsible for bushwhacking him, though, so Luke wasn't going to lose any sleep over killing the man. Nor was he going to stay around. He didn't need the attention or the trouble. Before anyone came to see what the shooting was about, he hustled to his room, rounded up what little gear he had, got his horse from the shed behind the boarding house, and lit a shuck, heading west again.

In the years since, he had continued to drift, never staying in one place for too long. He had driven a freight wagon, worked as a shotgun guard on a stagecoach run, tended bar, and even worked as a clerk in a store more than once, although he hated that job. Sometimes he sat in on a poker game and usually came out ahead. He had made enough money to send some back to Thad Franklin for the horse, a mount he had traded in on a better one in San Antonio. He owned a decent saddle, a Winchester rifle, and a gun belt and holster in which he carried the Colt Navy. He kept the Griswold and Gunnison either in his saddlebags or tucked in his waistband. He picked up books wherever he could find them and spent most of his nights reading.

It wasn't much of a life, but it was what he had.

The vague idea of going to Denver had struck him, and the way he lived, he didn't spend much time thinking about what he was doing next. He just did it. So he'd set out across Kansas, not figuring on the late autumn storm that was sweeping down across the plains from Canada. He might have to hole up at the roadhouse for a while before continuing his endless journey.

The first thing that struck him as he stepped inside the sod building was the silence. He'd expected some talk and raucous laughter from the patrons, maybe the clatter of coins tossed onto a table as somebody anted up in a poker game, or the clink of a whiskey bottle against a glass.

Instead, once he swung the door closed behind him and cut off the long, hard sigh of the wind, he didn't hear anything.

Then the sound of harsh breathing came to his ears.

The low-ceilinged, windowless room was lit only by a couple dim and flaring lamps, and the air was thick with smoke and shadows. Luke's eyes adjusted quickly to the gloom, and took in the scene before him.

A couple young men who looked like they might be cowboys up from Texas sat at one of the crude, rough-hewn tables scattered around on the hard-packed dirt floor. Another man in an overcoat with a flashy but well-worn suit underneath it sat alone at another table. Luke pegged him as a gambler.

Three men in shaggy, buffalo hide coats had a woman pinned up against the bar, which consisted of planks laid across several whiskey barrels. Long-haired and unshaven, they were about as shaggy as the buffalo that had provided their coats. They turned their heads to glare at Luke.

A few feet away, on the other side of the bar, a skinny, bald-headed man stood, looking nervous. He probably owned the place, Luke thought.

The young cowboys looked a little scared, too. The gambler's face was impassive, but that didn't mean much. Tinhorns made their living by not letting their faces give anything away.

To the room at large, Luke said in a mild voice, "Don't mind me. I'm just looking for a place to get out of that blue norther that's blowing in."

One of the hardcases shrugged and started to turn away, and Luke thought that was the end of it. But the woman said, "I know you."

Luke hadn't gotten a good look at her. He'd seen enough soiled doves in his travels, taking what comfort he could from them when he had to. She tried to step out of the half circle of men around her, and the lamplight hit her face, revealing the curly blond hair, the face that was still pretty despite the hard lines settling in around the eyes and mouth, and the little dark beauty mark near the corner of that mouth.

Luke stiffened. He remembered her, too. It was hard for him to forget somebody who had pointed a shotgun at him. The most vivid memory was of her standing in a shallow creek in wet, skimpy undergarments, but it was followed closely by the mental image of her threatening him and his companions with that scattergun. "Tennessee. Or maybe Georgia."

Before the woman could respond, one of the hardcases put a grimy hand on her chest and shoved her back against the bar. "Mind your own business, mister," he snarled.

"Oh, I intend to," Luke said. "But I'd appreciate it if you wouldn't treat the lady quite so rough, friend."

The blonde said, "They're gonna do a lot worse than that." Her voice rose a little as she tried to control the fear she obviously felt. "They're going to kill us all, once they're through having their fun. These are the Gammon brothers."

The name didn't mean anything to Luke, but he said, "I see."

One of the hardcases said, "Hey, Cooter, you think this fella could be that U.S. marshal who's been on our trail?"

"I don't know, Ben." The man squinted across the room at Luke. "But it don't really matter, does it?"

As soon as the hardcase said that, Luke knew the woman was right. The three of them planned to kill everybody and loot the place before they rode off. They'd probably keep the blonde alive the longest, figuring she could help keep them warm until the storm blew over.

Luke didn't take his eyes off the outlaws, but he asked the cowboys, "You fellas from Texas taking a hand in this?"

"Mister, all we got are rifles, and they're outside on our horses," one of the young punchers said.

"We just came in for a drink," the other added miserably. "Now we'd just like to get out of here alive."

"How about you, Ace?" Luke asked the gambler.

"The deck was stacked against me . . . until now."

The hardcase who had spoken first yelped, "Hellfire, Cooter, they're gonna draw on us!"

Luke told the Texans, "You boys hit the floor *now!*"

CHAPTER 25

Moving fast but not rushing, Luke palmed the Colt smoothly from its holster. At the same time, his left hand twisted at the wrist, grasped the butt of the Griswold and Gunnison sticking up from his waistband, and pulled that gun, too.

He wished the blonde wasn't standing right by the bar where a stray bullet could hit her, but most of the time a man couldn't choose the fights that came to him. All he could do was try to stay alive.

The outlaws swept aside the long buffalo coats and grabbed for their guns. They were fast, but Luke was faster. They had just cleared leather when his guns began to roar.

He shot the one called Ben first, triggering the Colt twice and slamming the slugs into the man's body, hoping two shots would be enough to put the big man down.

The bullets slammed Ben back against the bar and knocked some of the planks loose. Luke fired his left-hand gun at Cooter and saw the man stagger.

To Luke's left, the gambler's pistol cracked, but the third outlaw had his gun leveled and jerked the trigger twice, sending return shots at the tinhorn.

Luke pivoted and used the Griswold and Gunnison on the third brother while he sent two more slugs from the Colt into Cooter's slumping form. The third man was hit, but he still stood tall and straight and fired at Luke, who felt the hot breath of the bullet as it whipped past his ear.

Something flashed in the lamplight, and the third Gammon brother made a gurgling, gasping sound. Bright red blood flooded from his neck, which the blonde had opened almost from ear to ear with a single backhanded swipe of the straight razor she held in her hand. The man dropped his gun and pawed at his neck, but there was nothing he could do to stop the bleeding. He collapsed onto his knees and then pitched forward on his face to lie motionless as a crimson puddle formed on the dirt floor beneath his head.

Cooter and Ben were both down. So was the gambler, and so were the two cowboys, although they lifted frightened faces to look around as the shooting ended. Luke saw the proprietor peeking out from behind one of the whiskey barrels where he had taken cover.

Luke said to the blonde, "Why don't you step away from those men, ma'am, so I can make sure they're dead?"

"The one I cut is, you can count on that. Looks like just about all the blood he had in him has leaked out."

"It never hurts to make sure." Luke approached the fallen outlaws with both hands still filled with revolvers and toed them over onto their backs. In all three cases, sightless eyes stared up emptily at the low ceiling.

"Told you," the blonde said.

One of the cowboys had gotten up to check on the gambler. "This fella's hurt bad."

Luke tucked away the Griswold and Gunnison but kept the Colt in his other hand as he went over and knelt beside the gambler. The man's white shirt was dark with blood under his once-fancy vest.

"Sorry," Luke said.

"D-don't be," the gambler managed to say. "I knew it was . . . a game of chance . . . when I took cards . . . It's just the way they were . . ." He wasn't able to finish as his eyes went glassy.

"That's right," Luke said, even though the tinhorn couldn't hear him anymore. "It's just the way they were dealt." He looked up at the blonde. "You know his name?"

"I don't have any earthly idea. He just rode in a while ago, like the rest of you. Those cowboys were first, then him, then the Gammons. Then you."

Luke stood up, reloaded the Navy, and introduced himself. "Luke Smith."

"I'm called Marcy."

"Pleased to make your acquaintance . . . again." He noticed the razor she had used to cut the throat of the third Gammon brother was nowhere to be seen. She'd probably slipped it back into a hidden pocket in her dress. "I take it these are some of the local bad men?"

"They're bad, all right. They've robbed, raped, and murdered their way across half of Kansas and Nebraska."

"Then the world's better off with them dead."

"I reckon. The world really would've been better off if they'd been put in gunnysacks and drowned when they were babies."

Luke couldn't help smiling. "A bit bloodthirsty, aren't you?"

"Men like that deserve it," Marcy said, prodding one of the bodies with the toe of her boot.

Luke turned to the Texas cowhands. "How about giving me a hand dragging them out?"

The proprietor spoke up from behind the bar. "As cold as it is, there's liable to be wolves around tonight. If you put the bodies out-side—"

"Then these three will finally serve a purpose in nature, won't they?" Luke looked at the gambler. "We'll put this fellow in the shed where the wolves can't get at him. Maybe the ground won't be frozen too hard in the morning to dig a grave."

The proprietor told Luke his money wasn't any good as long as he was there. Since Luke's funds were running a little low, he didn't argue, and enjoyed the beer, the bowl of stew, and the chunk of hard bread the man brought to his table once the bodies of the dead men had been tended to.

Marcy came over and sat down at the table with him, bringing a glass of whiskey with her. "What happened to those fellas who were with you the last time I saw you?"

"Four of them are dead," Luke said. "I don't know about the other four."

He had kept his eyes and ears open while he was drifting, hoping he might run across something or somebody who could put him on the trail of Potter and the others, but so far he hadn't had any luck. He had no idea where to start searching, so he asked questions about them and waited and hoped. "You haven't seen any of the others since then, have you?"

She shook her head. "You're the first one, Luke."

He swallowed some of the beer from his mug and smiled. "I ap-preciate you not shooting me that day."

"Don't think I didn't think about it," she said solemnly. Then a faint smile tugged at her lips, too.

"You're about as hardboiled as a lady can be, aren't you?"

"Who the hell said I'm a lady? And do you know any other way for a woman to survive out here? We've got to be tougher than all you men. We just can't let you see it."

Luke grinned and lifted his beer. "To toughness."

She clinked her glass against his and nodded. "To toughness."

After they drank, he said, "What happened to the other women who were with you that day?"

"Turnabout's fair play on that question, eh?" She shrugged. "Damned if I know. Some of them are dead, and the others are scattered. Just like your friends, I reckon."

"The ones who are left alive aren't my friends," Luke said, his smile disappearing.

Marcy regarded him shrewdly for a moment and then nodded. "It's like that, is it?"

"It is."

"Well, then, I don't know whether to hope you find them or not."

"Why's that?" Luke asked.

"Because there's four of them and one of you, and I hate to see any man I let into my bed without payin' get himself killed."

Luke's eyebrows rose a little. "You're going to let me into your bed without paying?"

"Let me finish this drink"—Marcy lifted her glass—"and then we'll see."

Luke and Marcy spent the night in one of the small rooms partitioned off at the back of the roadhouse. Wrapped up in blankets and each other, they stayed warm enough despite the icy wind howling outside.

When Luke woke up in the morning, she was gone, but he smelled coffee brewing and hoped he would find her in the main room. He sat up and dressed quickly. Pushing the curtain aside, he stepped out of the tiny room and saw Marcy standing at the stove fully dressed with a blanket wrapped around her shoulders. Even inside the roadhouse, it was cold.

She looked up at him and smiled. "How do you feel?"

"Not bad." As he walked over to her his gait was a little awkward. His muscles had stiffened up some while he was asleep.

She noticed, and asked, "Something wrong?"

"Just an old injury. Nothing to worry about."

She nodded. "Yeah, I know all about those old injuries. The world's got a way of knockin' folks around, doesn't it?"

"It sure does," Luke agreed.

"Well, sit down somewhere. Coffee will be ready soon, and then I'll whip up some breakfast."

"You're the cook here, too?"

"That's right." Her smile was wry. "I have lots of different jobs."

While Luke was sitting there, the two young cowboys came in from outside. They had spent the night at the roadhouse, too, and Luke figured they'd been out to check on the horses, all of which had been put in the shed behind the building along with the body of the gambler.

"Mornin', Mr. Smith," one of the youngsters greeted him. "Got something here for you." He lifted a gun belt with double holsters. The walnut grip of a revolver stuck up from each holster.

"We took 'em off one of those Gammon brothers when we dragged the carcasses outside last night," the other puncher explained. "Didn't see any point in armin' the wolves that were gonna drag 'em off."

"I see." Luke took the gun belt from the first cowboy. The holsters were reversed for a cross draw. He slid one of the guns from leather and recognized it as a Remington. *Fine weapon*, he thought. "What about the other two brothers?"

The cowboys grinned and pulled back their coats to reveal that they had taken the gun belts from those bodies, too.

"Those looked like the best guns, so we figured you deserved to have them, Mr. Smith. And the horses, too, if you want 'em."

"I'll take one horse as an extra mount," Luke said. "You fellows can get some good use out of the other two, I expect."

The punchers exchanged grins.

"We sure can," one of them said. "We was just about broke last night, 'cept for our saddles and our hosses. Now we got good guns and extra mounts. Reckon we're plumb rich!"

Luke wasn't sure he had ever been as young and carefree as those two Texas cowboys. If he had been, he couldn't remember it.

Marcy came over with the coffeepot. "You two sit down," she told the punchers. "Breakfast will be ready in a little bit."

They were all eating a short time later when the door opened again. Luke glanced up and saw a bulky figure silhouetted against the gray light of the overcast day. The first things he noticed were the rifle in the man's hand and the tin star pinned to his coat. He recognized it as a United States marshal's badge.

The man wore a thick sheepskin coat and had a broad-brimmed brown hat pulled down tight on his head so the wind wouldn't blow it away. His face was red, either from the cold, a close acquaintance with whiskey or both, and a close-cropped blond beard stuck out on his cheeks and chin.

Luke took a deep breath. He was still wanted on murder charges back in Georgia.

CHAPTER 26

"Good morning," the man said as he came into the roadhouse and swung the door closed behind him. "Mighty chilly out there to go with the dusting of snow."

"We have coffee if you want it, Marshal," Marcy said. "And grub."

The lawman slapped gloved hands together to warm them and grinned. "That sounds fine, ma'am. Nothing like hot food and drink to warm a man up."

Marcy stood and motioned with her head toward one of the empty tables. "Have a seat. I'll get you a cup and a plate."

"Much obliged."

The marshal went over to the table, set his rifle on it, pulled off his gloves, and dropped his hat next to them. He smiled at Luke and the two cowboys. "Morning, gents."

The punchers muttered greetings, but Luke said, "Good morning, Marshal."

"Deputy Marshal," the lawman corrected him. "Name's Jasper Thornapple."

When a man introduced himself, it was only polite to return the favor, and despite the rough environments in which he spent his life, Luke had come to pride himself on his manners. "I'm Luke Smith."

Thornapple didn't seem to recognize the name, but that didn't mean anything. Maybe he was just good at covering up his reactions.

"Teddy Young," one of the cowboys said.

"Burt Tuttle," the other puncher added.

"Pleased to meet you," Thornapple said.

Marcy set a cup of steaming coffee in front of Thornapple. "What brings you out here in the middle of nowhere, Marshal?"

Thornapple nodded his thanks for the coffee. "Well, I'm trailing some men."

Luke wasn't surprised by the answer.

"Cooter, Ben, and Carl Gammon. Reckon you've probably heard of them," the marshal added.

"I sure have." Marcy went back and sat down next to Luke.

"Or rather, I should say I *was* trailing them," Thornapple went on. "Came across a wolf pack about a mile east of here, having themselves a feast in a dry wash. There wasn't much left of the fellas they'd been after, but I'm pretty sure one of them was Cooter Gammon. He had a streak of white in his hair hard to miss. Since there were two men about the same size with him, I feel confident my boss can close the books on the Gammon brothers."

"Bad luck for them, being caught by a pack of wolves like that," Luke commented.

Thornapple took a sip of his coffee and nodded. "Especially when those wolves were carrying guns," he said with a shrewd smile.

The two cowboys couldn't stop themselves from flinching guiltily. Luke's face was like stone, though. "What do you mean by that?"

"I mean one of those skulls had a bullet hole smack-dab in the middle of its face. Somebody shot that Gammon brother before the wolves got at him. A well-deserved fate, I might add." Thornapple took another sip of coffee. "You folks have anything you want to tell me? Bear in mind I'm a federal lawman who doesn't cotton to being lied to."

"Mr. Smith didn't have any choice!" one of the punchers burst out. "He didn't have any choice at all. Those Gammons were worse 'n hydrophobia skunks. They were gonna kill us all!"

As soon as the words stopped tumbling out of the youngster's mouth, he turned a stricken face to Luke. "I'm sorry, Mr. Smith. I shouldn't 've said nothin'—"

Luke lifted a hand to stop the apology. "That's all right. I have a feeling Marshal Thornapple already had a pretty good idea what happened. He strikes me as a man who's been to see the elephant."

"There and back again," Thornapple agreed with a smile. "You killed all three of them, Mr. Smith?"

"Two of them, anyway, and I contributed to the third."

"I cut his throat," Marcy put in. "He probably would have died anyway, but I didn't see any harm in hurrying him along to hell."

"Nor would I, ma'am," Thornapple said. "In that case, I suppose the two of you will have to come to some sort of equitable arrangement concerning the division of the reward money."

"Reward money!"

"That's right, ma'am. Each of the Gammons had a thousand dollar bounty on his head."

Marcy leaned back in her chair, her eyes wide with amazement. "Three thousand dollars!"

"That's right. Come with me to Wichita, and I'll authorize payment. You can collect from the bank there."

Marcy looked over at Luke. "My God, we're rich! I never saw three thousand dollars in my life!"

Luke hesitated to say anything. He didn't fully trust Thornapple. Maybe the lawman was trying to trick him into going along to Wichita, where he would promptly place him under arrest.

Giving it more thought, that didn't seem likely. Luke could tell by looking at Thornapple the badge-toter had plenty of bark on him. If Thornapple wanted to make an arrest, he'd just do it instead of trying some fancy trick.

More than likely, Thornapple had never seen any of the wanted posters charging Luke with murder that had circulated back in Georgia.

"There's just one thing," Luke said slowly. "I'm not a bounty hunter."

"You killed three men with a price on their heads," Thornapple offered. "It's not like you have to file papers ahead of time or anything. That money is yours by rights, Mr. Smith."

Marcy looked even more excited. "We've got to do it, Luke. We've got to claim that reward."

He understood then how much it meant to her. She had spent her life struggling just to get by, enduring hardship and degradation. The tough times were starting to take a real toll on her.

Yet there was still a spark of dignity inside her, and a sense of determination that might allow her to make something better of her life if she just got the chance. The bounty money could give her that chance.

"All right," Luke finally agreed. "We'll go to Wichita with the marshal."

She threw her arms around his neck. "Thank you, Luke! You don't know what this means to me."

It meant he had inadvertently done something good for somebody. That wasn't enough to make up for past failures . . . but it was a start.

Thornapple nodded toward the holstered Remingtons and coiled shell belt still laying on the table where Luke and Marcy sat. "Nice looking guns. Whose are they?"

"They're mine." Luke reached out and pulled a gun out of the holster. *One more bit of bounty for killing the Gammon brothers,* he thought.

They split the reward money down the middle, fifteen hundred apiece. Marcy didn't think that was fair. She wanted to take five hundred for her part and give the rest to Luke, but he refused and insisted she take half.

They set aside an equal amount from each share, and got a room in the finest hotel in Wichita. For a week they ate in the best restaurants the town had to offer, drank champagne they had sent up from one of the saloons, and spent long hours together in bed.

After that week, pleasant though it was, Luke was so restless he couldn't stand it anymore.

He left the room early one morning while Marcy was still sleeping and walked to the livery stable where he was keeping his horses. He had just thrown his saddle on one of the animals when a voice asked, "Going somewhere, Mr. Smith?"

Luke looked around to see Marshal Jasper Thornapple standing in the open double doors of the livery barn with his shoulder propped casually against one of the jambs.

"Thought I might take a ride," Luke answered, assuming as casual an attitude as Thornapple.

"Did you tell the young lady good-bye?"

"Who said I wasn't coming back?"

Thornapple chuckled. "I've seen plenty of fiddlefoots in my time, Smith. Hell, I've been one. I know the look of a man who feels the call of distant trails."

Luke shrugged. "Marcy and I aren't really the sort for sentimental farewells."

"I have a hunch you might be wrong about how she feels . . . but it's none of my business, is it?"

"No, it's not."

"That's right, my business is hunting down lawbreakers. That line of work has given me a healthy curiosity about the people I meet."

Luke turned a little so he could move faster if he needed to reach for the Remingtons. He had started wearing the cross-draw rig, and wished he'd had more time to practice getting those irons out in a hurry. "Out here on the frontier, curiosity's generally considered to be not that healthy," he commented.

"Maybe not, but it's my job. So I sent some wires and did some checking. I wasn't surprised to find out that Luke Smith is a pretty common name."

"Lots of Smiths around," Luke said, his voice tight.

"The only one I came across that might be of some interest to a man like me was from Georgia. He was wanted for killing a land speculator and some hired guns about five years ago. *Was* wanted, Smith. That's important. The charges were dropped last year."

Luke's heart suddenly slugged hard in his chest. He wanted to believe what Thornapple was telling him, but it didn't seem possible it could be true. He managed to ask, "Why would they drop the charges in a case like that?"

"Because once the Reconstruction government was forced to let go of some of its power, the facts of the case came out. Turns out the land speculator was nothing but a carpetbagging thief, and evidence indicated he'd had men killed in order to grab their land. That particular Luke Smith can go back to Georgia without having to worry about the law anymore."

Luke drew in a deep breath. "That's a lucky break . . . for him."

The excitement he'd felt for a second had vanished. There was nothing waiting for him back in Georgia. Emily was probably married to Jess Franklin and raising a couple kids. Even if she wasn't, she wouldn't want to see him again. Not after he'd ridden off that night and never come back.

"I just thought you might be interested in hearing about that before you rode off," Thornapple went on. "Which way do you plan to head? West . . . or east?"

"I set out to go to Denver a while back," Luke said. "I suppose I still will."

Thornapple straightened and nodded. "Have a safe journey, then." He turned to head out of the livery.

Something occurred to Luke. "Marshal."

Thornapple stopped and turned back to Luke. "Yes?"

"Can I ask you if you've heard of some other men? While in your line of work, I mean."

Thornapple's brawny shoulders rose and fell. "Sure, go ahead."

"Wiley Potter. Keith Stratton. Josh Richards. Ted Casey."

For a long moment, Thornapple frowned in thought. Then he shook his head. "None of those names ring a bell, Smith. Should they?"

"I don't know. Thought it was possible."

"Well, I haven't heard of them. Sorry."

"That's all right. I'll catch up to them one of these days."

Thornapple lingered. "What do you plan to do with yourself?"

Luke thought about it for a second, then grunted. "Seems like there's good money in bounty hunting."

"Well . . . there's money in it. Some wouldn't call it good. Some folks call it blood money. And going after it is a good way to get yourself killed." Thornapple shrugged again. "But you saw that for yourself. Not every owlhoot has a price on his head as big as the bounties on the Gammon brothers. But some are even bigger."

"That's what I thought." Luke tightened the cinch on his saddle. "I'll be seeing you, Marshal."

"I wouldn't be a bit surprised," Thornapple said.

Luke didn't wave or even look back as he rode out of Wichita. He hoped Marcy was still asleep, snug and warm in that hotel room bed, dreaming of the new life she could make for herself with her share of the money. He hoped that when she woke up and found him gone, she wouldn't hate him.

But either way, he was going.

CHAPTER 27

Blood money, Thornapple had called it, and that turned out to be true.

As the years passed, Luke Smith saw a veritable lake of blood.

From the Rio Grande to the Canadian border, from New Orleans and the Mississippi River delta to San Francisco, Luke roamed, always on the trail of men with a price on their heads. Whether the bounty was big or small didn't really matter. Kill enough penny-ante owlhoots, as long as somebody was willing to pay for the carcasses, and the money added up.

Sometimes there were big kills, too, high-dollar rewards netting Luke enough cash that he wouldn't have to track down any more outlaws for a while if he didn't want to.

But what else was he going to do?

The face looking out at him from the mirror when he shaved became craggier, more weathered. The ordeal he had suffered at the end of the Civil War made him look older than his years, and the life he lived after that certainly didn't make him appear any younger. Those deep-set eyes had seen too much death and suffering to ever be innocent again.

His only consolation was the men he killed had it coming. They were robbers, rapists, arsonists, murderers.

He wasn't arrogant enough to consider himself some sort of avenging angel delivering justice. If he was working for any higher power, it was Lucifer, reaping more souls to be plunged, screaming, into the depths of Hades.

Luckily, there were a few moments of humanity here and there, or he might have gone insane.

Deadwood, 1877

The gold rush that had caused the town to spring into existence a year earlier had dwindled away as mining syndicates and corporations moved in and, for the most part, replaced the individual prospectors who had sunk shafts in the sides of the gulches all around the settlement. It still had its rough edges, though, and enough vice to attract men from all over, including those on the run from the law.

Luke rode in on the trail of a man named Robert Fescoe, who had killed a bank teller during a robbery down in Yankton. Fescoe was reported to be heading west , and Luke hoped the fugitive paused long enough in Deadwood to get drunk and find himself a whore.

Those two things didn't sound that bad to Luke, either, although he wasn't one to indulge his baser appetites indiscriminately. However, a man couldn't just sit and read during all his spare time.

He stopped at a livery stable, and as he turned his horse over to the hostler, he asked, "Have you seen a tall, skinny fellow with a half-moon-shaped scar on his chin?" Luke was grateful for the outlaw's scar because it made him easy to describe.

The hostler frowned in thought and shook his head. "Can't say as I have, mister."

"He would have ridden in within the last day or two," Luke added.

"Nope. Sorry."

"Is this the only livery stable in town?"

The hostler chuckled. "I wish it was. I'd make a lot more money that way. No, there are three or four more. Maybe the hombre you're lookin' for left his hoss at one of them."

"Maybe so." Luke flipped a five-dollar gold piece to the man, who caught it deftly. "That ought to cover my bill for a while . . . and buy your discretion if you happen to see the man I'm looking for."

"If you mean I won't say nothin' to him about you lookin' for him, you're danged right about that. I'll even come see if I can find you."

"I'd be much obliged," Luke told him. "Meanwhile, what's the best place in town to get a drink?"

The hostler scratched his beard-stubbled jaw. "Well, there's the Bella Union. It's pretty nice. Or the Gem, which ain't as nice, but their whiskey is good and they got some fine whores. Folks tend to get shot there from time to time, though."

"An all-too-common occurrence."

"Or there's a new place you could try. It's called the Buffalo Butt."

Luke had to laugh. "What a name for a saloon!"

"Yeah, I don't know why the gal who owns it decided to call it that. *She* don't look like a buffalo's hind end, I can tell you that for dang sure. She's one of the prettiest gals in Deadwood, I'd say."

"Well, that certainly sounds intriguing. I'll give it a try." Luke lifted a hand in farewell and left the livery stable.

It didn't take him long to find the Buffalo Butt Saloon. Despite the crude name, it appeared to be a well-furnished and successful establishment, sitting at an intersection with its bat-winged entrance right at the corner so it was easily visible from both streets.

Luke pushed the batwings aside and stepped in with his usual caution. A man in his line of work never knew when he might run into an old enemy, although most of the men Luke tried to take into custody put up a fight and wound up dead.

A long mahogany bar ran down the left side of the room, with gambling layouts to the right and tables in between. At the far end of the room was an open area where people could dance and a small stage for performers, which was empty at the moment. Men sat at about half the tables, drinking, and the bar was pretty busy, too, although there were plenty of open spots. A couple poker games were going on, and the click and clatter of a roulette wheel mixed with the sounds of talk and laughter. Luke liked the looks of the Buffalo Butt, inelegant moniker and all.

A staircase next to the stage led up to the second floor. If the place was like most saloons, the girls who worked downstairs delivering drinks also worked upstairs delivering something else. Luke glanced at the women moving around the room. Unlike some saloon girls, they were fully dressed in nice gowns cut low enough to reveal the swells of their breasts. Luke might have tried to single out one of them for his attentions later, but a man at a nearby table tilted his head back to look up and said, "Lord have mercy, who's that?"

Luke instinctively followed the direction of the man's gaze. His breath caught in his throat and he stiffened as he saw a woman standing at the railing on the second floor balcony, looking down at the room. She wore a dark red dress tight enough to reveal her splendid figure, and a thick mass of curly blond hair spilled around her shoulders.

Luke knew her instantly. Marcy hadn't changed much in the seven years since he'd ridden away from Wichita, leaving her in that hotel room.

He saw her suddenly clutch the railing and knew she had recognized him, too. He started toward the stairs, weaving among the tables, as she came along the balcony. He went up the stairs as she came down, and they met halfway, embracing with a desperate urgency as their mouths met.

"Aw, hell!" That disappointed exclamation came from the man who Luke had heard speak when he entered the saloon. "Looks like she's already took."

Luke and Marcy kissed for a long moment, and Luke felt the dull emotional pain that dogged his steps flow out of him. The unexpected reunion was like being plunged into a clean, icy mountain stream.

Then Marcy pulled back a little, lifted her hand, and pressed the barrel of a derringer against the side of his head. "Damn you, Luke Smith. I ought to put a bullet in your brain."

Most of the time, if somebody pointed a gun at him, he reacted violently. He suppressed that urge and smiled instead. "You'd probably be justified. I knew you'd be upset that I left you in Wichita. On the other hand, you appear to be doing well for yourself."

He remembered what the liveryman had said about the owner of the Buffalo Butt being one of the prettiest women in Deadwood. Wherever Marcy was, she would fall into the category. "This is your saloon, isn't it?"

"What if it is?"

"You wouldn't be the owner of a successful business if you hadn't gotten a start from your half of that reward money, would you?"

She let out a snort. "That shows what you know. I used that money to buy an interest in a whorehouse in Wichita. Then it burned down and I lost everything. I had to start over. But by then I'd learned I was pretty good at running things. It took me a while, but I'm doing all right again."

"I'm glad to hear it," Luke said. "Now, if you're not going to pull the trigger on that popgun, I'd appreciate it if you took it away from my head. It might go off by accident."

"I don't do *anything* by accident."

As Marcy lowered the derringer and let its hammer down carefully, Luke became aware the saloon had gone deathly quiet. He supposed someone had noticed her holding a gun to his head and pointed it out, and as the news spread, everyone stopped what they were doing to watch.

Marcy kissed Luke again, and someone let out a cheer, breaking the silence. Customers returned to their drinking and gambling, filling the saloon with noise once more.

Marcy took Luke by the hand and led him upstairs so they could get reacquainted properly.

That evening, Luke sat with Marcy at her private table in the rear corner of the saloon's main room. One of her bartenders had brought supper over from the dining room of the Grand Central Hotel. It was the best food in the Black Hills, she had explained, and Luke had to admit she was probably right. The roast beef was as good as any he'd had in a long time.

As they ate, washing down the food with sips of fine wine, they talked about everything that had happened since they'd seen each other last.

"I don't have much to tell," Luke told her. "I'm a bounty hunter, have been ever since that run-in with the Gammon brothers."

"I know. I've heard talk about you from time to time. You have quite a reputation." Marcy smiled. "Did you know I named this place after the Gammons?"

"I wondered how come you called it the Buffalo Butt."

"In those buffalo coats, they were as ugly and smelly as buffalo rumps."

"I can't disagree with that," Luke said.

"Even though I didn't want to admit it to you this afternoon, I reckon that was when my life started to change for the better. So I felt like I ought to commemorate the occasion."

Luke thought about it and decided the name was appropriate after all. He lifted his wineglass. "To the good that can come from ugly, inelegant things."

"I'll drink to that." Marcy clinked her glass against his, and he thought her eyes had a meaningful, mischievous twinkle in them as she looked at him.

He *was* ugly and inelegant, he thought. He had so much blood on his hands he could never wash it off, even if he tried.

But he had done some good in his life, too. He had saved Emily and her grandfather from Vincent Wolford. If the carpetbagger had lived, he wouldn't have stopped going after them until he got what he wanted.

And Luke had helped Marcy escape a life that would have eventually killed her if she hadn't gotten out of it. Some people might consider owning a saloon in a frontier town like Deadwood to be pretty disreputable, but those folks just didn't know how low people really could sink. Marcy was better off. He was sure of it.

"What are you going to do now?" she asked.

"I thought I'd have another glass of this surprisingly good wine," he replied with a smile.

"No, I mean with your life. Blast it, Luke, you know that."

He poured the wine and set the bottle aside. "I'll keep doing what I've been doing. I don't see any reason to change now. I'm not sure I *could* change, even if I wanted to."

"I did," Marcy said.

"You wanted to."

"Wouldn't you like to have a normal life? Maybe a business? Like . . . half interest in a saloon?"

He saw the hope in her eyes and knew it would be kinder to dash it right away, rather than letting it linger and grow. He shook his head. "I'm not going to settle down. I can't. Now that I know you're here, I might try to drift this way more often—"

"Don't put yourself out on my account." Her expression turned cold, like a blue norther blowing down across the plains.

"You don't understand. I can't be who you want me to be, Marcy, but knowing that I have a friend somewhere . . . well, it might make those cold nights out on the prairie a little easier to bear."

She wasn't going to give in easily. "I'll think about it." Her voice and body remained stiff with disappointment and anger.

Luke lifted his glass to her. "That's all I can ask."

She came to him that night seemingly as passionate as ever, but he sensed she was holding something back. His declaration that he would be riding on had changed whatever had been between them.

And how could it fail to do so? he asked himself, regretting it had happened.

Later, as Luke was dozing off with Marcy's head pillowed on his shoulder, he heard her whisper, "If you run out on me in the morning without saying good-bye again, I'll hunt you down and kill you."

He laughed softly and promised, "I'll be here."

He was sound asleep when his instincts took over and warned him. Maybe it was the faint creak of a floorboard, but whatever the reason, his eyes snapped open and caught a flicker of movement in the shadows of the room.

Reacting with the speed that had saved his life many times, Luke shoved a startled Marcy out of bed and rolled the other way. With a boom like a crash of thunder, a shotgun went off, twin gouts of flame erupting from its barrels.

Luke snatched up the Remington he had left lying on a chair right beside the bed and thumbed two shots just above the muzzle flash from the scattergun. Momentarily deaf from the shotgun's roar, he couldn't hear if his target cried out or dropped the weapon.

Keeping himself low to the ground, he crept forward. After only a couple steps, Luke tripped on something and stumbled. He put his left hand out to catch himself and it landed on something hot and sticky. He pulled it back and lashed out with the revolver, thudding against something soft.

"Get a light on," Luke told Marcy, hoping none of the buckshot had winged her.

A lucifer flared to life. He squinted against the glare, his eyes adjusting as she lit a lamp on the table beside the bed. Light filled the room and revealed Luke kneeling beside a gaunt man with a scar shaped like a half-moon on his chin. The would-be killer's chest was a bloody mess from the two slugs that had torn through it.

"Who is he?" Marcy asked. "Do you know him?"

Luke heard the question, indicating his hearing had come back. He shook his head. "We never met, but I know who he is. His name's Fescoe. I've been on his trail for a while. Somebody must have told him I was in town looking for him, so he asked around until he figured out where he could find me. Thought he'd get me off his trail permanently."

Luke was going to have a talk with that liveryman, who had obviously double-crossed him.

Marcy put her hands on her hips. "My bed's ruined from that shotgun blast, and he's getting blood on the rug, too."

Luke stood up. "I'll send you money for the damages once I've gotten the reward. I'll have to ride back down to Yankton to collect."

"But you won't be coming back?"

"Not for a while. Not after this."

"I've seen men die before, you know. I've even had them try to kill me."

"Death doesn't follow you around, though. Not like it does with me."

Marcy sighed as one of the bartenders pounded on the door and called out to see if she was all right.

"I can't decide if you're the best man I know, Luke Smith, or just a sorry SOB."

Luke walked to the chair by the side of the bed and slipped the Remington back into the holster. "It's a good question. I don't know the answer myself."

CHAPTER 28

Even though his visit to Deadwood had a more bittersweet ending than he would have preferred, Luke took some good memories away from there. He knew Marcy was not only still alive but thriving, and that eased one of the worries he had carried around with him for years. He made himself a promise to drift up to the Black Hills every now and then to visit her and hoped the next time they met, she would still be glad to see him.

The next year, in the summer of 1878, he was in Santa Fe when he saw another familiar face across a crowded cantina. He picked up his mug of beer and made his way across the room until he reached the table where a thick-bodied man with graying fair hair and beard sat nursing a glass of tequila.

"Hello, Marshal," Luke said to Jasper Thornapple.

The two of them had crossed trails several times over the years. Luke had turned over to Thornapple a few fugitives he'd captured and sometimes it was sheer coincidence how they met. The frontier, for all its vastness, could sometimes seem like a small place.

The lawman looked up with a pleased smile. "Luke! I was hoping I'd run into you again one of these days. I've got some news for you." Thornapple gestured for Luke to have a seat at the table. "Heard about it from another deputy marshal."

Luke settled down into the chair. "What kind of news?"

"Remember a long time ago, the first time we met up in Kansas, you asked me about four men?"

Luke stiffened. "You mean Potter, Stratton, Richards, and Casey?"

"Those are the ones. You never found them, did you?"

Luke frowned but didn't say anything. His mind was too full of bitter memories. He had looked for the four men who had betrayed him, betrayed their country, murdered his friends, nearly killed him, and stolen the gold. As much as he roamed, as many people as he met during his travels, he had thought it was inevitable that he would pick up their trail.

But instead he had run into stone wall after stone wall. Nobody knew the men he was looking for. Maybe they were all dead already, he often told himself, but never really believed that. It was as if fate had conspired with those four no-good deserters to keep them safe from his vengeance.

Finally, in a quiet voice, he told Thornapple, "No, I never found them. To tell you the truth, after a while I quit looking so hard." He looked at the marshal, his pulse quickening. "Do you know where they are?"

"I do," Thornapple said, then dashed Luke's hopes. "They're in the ground. They're all dead, Luke."

A strange feeling washed through Luke. It wasn't disappointment, really, or even relief, but rather an odd, hollow mixture of the two. He wanted them dead, but he took no real satisfaction from knowing that they were.

"What happened to them?" he asked Thornapple, although he didn't really care.

"They were killed up in Idaho Territory a while back, at a settlement called Bury. The name turned out to be fitting. They started the town and ran everything in the area. Ran roughshod over everybody in those parts, too. A gunfighter calling himself Buck West rode in and raised hell. Wound up killing all of them. Turns out that wasn't really West's name at all. He was really a fella named Smoke Jensen."

The surprise Luke had felt at hearing his enemies were dead was nothing compared to the shock that went through him upon hearing his family name. It had been so long since he'd used the name Jensen it seemed like he had always been Luke Smith.

Despite that, he had never forgotten his family. Sometimes it was hard to remember what his ma and pa had looked like. They might both be dead. Probably were. And Janey and Kirby would be grown. He might pass them on the street and never know them.

But who in blazes was Smoke Jensen?

Luke shook his head. "I haven't heard of him."

"No reason you would have," Thornapple said. "There were wanted posters out on him for a while, especially while he was calling him-self Buck West, but from what I hear there are no charges against him now."

"Did you ever see him?"

Thornapple shook his head. "Nope. Supposed to be a big, sandy-haired fella who's really fast with his guns. He'd have to be, because from what I've heard, not only did he kill those men you were look-ing for, but he and some old mountain man friends of his wiped out a small army of hired killers who worked for Potter and the others, too. It was a full-fledged war up there."

Kirby had ash-blond hair, Luke recalled. If he'd grown big enough, he might fit the description of Smoke Jensen. But why in the world would he have taken that name?

Why not? That wry thought crossed Luke's mind. I *took a differ-ent name, and for a good reason, didn't I? Maybe Kirby did, too.*

"You know where he is now?"

"Jensen?" Thornapple shook his head. "No idea. The way I heard it, he rode away from Bury with some good-looking gal he met up there, and they never came back. Do you want to find him?"

"I thought I might look him up. Thank him for doing my job for me."

"I had a feeling you had a score to settle with those hombres you asked about," Thornapple said. "Well, it's done, so you can forget about it now."

"I suppose so." Luke drank down the rest of his beer and set the empty mug on the table. Inside he felt as empty as that mug.

He continued to ride, drifting from one place to another. Over time that feeling faded. Glad Potter and the others were dead, Luke would have liked to have been the one to pull the trigger and send them to hell, but nobody ever said life was fair. Justice had caught up to them, and he had to be satisfied with that. He had other killers to hunt down and bring in. But as he went about it, he kept his ears open and learned everything he could about the man called Smoke Jensen.

Smoke was said to be fast with a gun, mighty fast. Maybe the slick-est on the draw in the entire West. Luke heard stories about some of the battles Smoke had had with a wide assortment of outlaws and cold-blooded killers, and Smoke always emerged triumphant.

But those who had met him, without fail, said Smoke Jensen was no arrogant, vicious gunman, but rather a stalwart friend, a decent man, and a loving husband to his wife Sally. They had a successful ranch somewhere in Colorado called Sugarloaf, and judging by all the stories Luke heard about the man, Smoke wanted to live a peaceful life and never went out looking for trouble.

He sure didn't back down from it, though, and just about the worst mistake anybody could ever make was to threaten one of Smoke's friends or relatives. That was a mighty quick way to wind up dead.

Yes, Smoke Jensen sounded like the sort of man Luke would be proud to know, but despite what he had told Thornapple, he never made any attempt to find Jensen. Maybe the famous gunfighter really was his little brother Kirby, or maybe he wasn't, but either way, he figured Smoke wouldn't want a bloody-handed bounty hunter showing up on his doorstep claiming to be kinfolk. Luke felt sure if any of his family had even thought about him during the long years since the end of the Civil War, they must have assumed he was dead.

Because of that, whenever Luke was in Colorado, he was always careful to steer well clear of the Sugarloaf Ranch and the nearby town of Big Rock, the same way that he had never returned to the Ozarks of southwestern Missouri. It was entirely possible there weren't any Jensens left back there, but he didn't want to take that chance.

It was better for Luke Jensen to just stay dead.

He was in northern New Mexico Territory, in the town of Raton, with the Sangre de Cristo Mountains and Raton Pass looming to the north, when he heard a rumor that Solomon Burke and his gang had been spotted in the area.

Luke had been trailing Burke for a couple weeks, so he took a keen interest in what he heard and finally located the old-timer who was the source of the rumor. He bought the man a drink in the High Hat Saloon and asked him about Burke.

The garrulous old man was glad to talk. "I seen 'em while I was out huntin' one day. I got me some diggin's up there, so I keep a pretty close eye on all the comin's and goin's thereabouts."

Luke didn't figure the old-timer's mining claim amounted to much, but that wouldn't stop him from being fiercely protective of it.

"I heard riders comin' and took cover in some trees," the wizened, bearded oldster continued. "Seen 'em ride right past me, no more 'n fifty yards away. I seen ree-ward dodgers on Burke with his picture on 'em before, so I recognized him right away. Had a couple o' big Mexicans with him, so I figured they had to be Hernandez and Cardona. I've heard mighty bad stories about them two. Don't know who all the other hombres were, but they was prob'ly Burke's regular bunch of owlhoots."

Luke didn't doubt that. "Could you tell where they were going?"

The old prospector hesitated, licking his lips, and Luke signaled for the bartender to bring another round. That got the old-timer talking again.

"I don't know for sure, no, but they rode on outta the valley where my diggin's are and over the pass into the next valley. They's an old abandoned cabin over there they could be usin' as a hideout, right on the banks of Bluejay Creek. I can tell you how to get there"—a shrewd look appeared on the man's whiskery face—"And I will, if you swear to give me a cut of the bounty you collect on 'em."

"How do you know I'm a bounty hunter?" Luke wanted to know.

"Well, you don't really look like a star packer, and I can't think of nobody else who'd be trailin' a bunch of hydrophobia skunks like Solomon Burke and his gang. Gimme your word you'll cut me in?"

Luke nodded his agreement and then added, "If I come back alive, that is."

"Yeah, it's kind of a sucker bet on my part, ain't it? But here's how to get to that cabin . . ."

Luke had followed the old-timer's directions. The valley was a two-day ride from Raton. He thought he was still in New Mexico Territory, but up in the high country it was difficult to be sure. He might have crossed over into Colorado without realizing it.

Colorado . . . the place where Smoke Jensen lived. It wouldn't take but a few days to reach Big Rock, Luke mused as he trailed the Burke gang. He might be able to get a look at Smoke without having to introduce himself. Would he recognize his own brother, if that's who Smoke turned out to be?

That question still lurked in the back of Luke's mind as he dismounted and crept forward through some trees to spy on the old cabin where he thought the outlaws might be hiding.

Then bad luck cropped up again, as José Cardona, out hunting or taking a leak or just looking around, stumbled on him, tackled him, and tried to kill him. Nothing could ever just be easy. Not for Luke Smith.

He'd wiped out the gang, but he'd taken three bullets in return. His efforts to patch himself up hadn't done much good. He wound up passing out and crashing to the floor in the cabin.

Just like fifteen years earlier, when he'd been left for dead on the banks of a shallow river in Georgia, as blackness claimed Luke he was sure he would never wake up again, that it was the end.

BOOK FOUR

CHAPTER 29

Luke winced a little as light struck his eyelids. He turned his head away and felt something soft and smooth against his cheek. *A pillow? Light?*

He was alive. Like the other times over the years when he had come awake after being convinced he was going to die, he struggled to grasp the concept that he wasn't dead after all. Once again, his stubbornness had somehow kept him breathing . . . although he was sure he'd had help, too. Someone had found him in that cabin after he'd passed out from losing so much blood.

Wondering where he was and how much time had passed, he tried to open his eyes, but the light was too bright. *Sunlight,* he thought, but it didn't seem like he was outside. He didn't feel any wind. Moving his hands, he felt crisp fabric. He was lying on a mattress covered with clean sheets. So . . . he was in a bed, inside a house somewhere, and the sun was shining on him through a window.

Keeping his eyes closed, he turned his head back and heard a sweet sound that puzzled him. It reminded him of the music of a mountain stream.

It was music, all right, he realized. What he heard was a woman humming softly to herself.

His tongue felt twice as big as it should have as he licked his dry, rough lips. He had to swallow a couple times before his throat loosened enough for him to speak. All he could manage was to rasp, "H-hello . . . ?"

"Oh, my!" the woman exclaimed.

Luke heard the rapid patter of her footsteps as she crossed the room. The mattress shifted a little, and he figured she had rested a hand there as she leaned over him. Even through his closed eyes he felt the light change as she came between him and the light, so he tried opening them again.

For the second time in his life, he found himself looking up at what seemed to be an angel. This woman was older than Emily Peabody had been, but she had the same sweet, dark-haired beauty.

She smiled. "You're all right. You've been wounded, but you're going to be just fine. You're among friends."

"F-friends?" Luke repeated, his voice weak. "I don't . . . have any friends."

That wasn't strictly true. He considered Jasper Thornapple to be a friend, and Marcy, too, of course. But Thornapple was nowhere around, as far as Luke knew, and he was a long way from Deadwood.

"You're wrong," the woman told him, still smiling. "Anybody who's in trouble has friends here." She straightened. "You just lie there and rest. I'll go tell Smoke you're awake."

Once again Luke felt a shock go through him. As the woman turned away she moved out of the sunlight, causing him to flinch as the brilliant rays fell on him again. But he was able to say, "Wait . . . Did you say . . . Smoke?"

She paused, still smiling down at him, although it was hard for him to see her with the light filling his eyes.

"That's right. Smoke Jensen. He's my husband. I'm Sally Jensen. You're on the Sugarloaf Ranch, near Big Rock, Colorado."

That was loco, Luke thought. Smoke Jensen's place was days away from where he'd fought that battle with Solomon Burke and the rest of those outlaws. How in the world had he gotten to the Sugarloaf?

Someone had brought him, of course, he realized as he forced his brain to work and struggled to put his thoughts in order. But why had they brought him to the ranch of a man who might well be one of his relatives? How had they known?

"I'll be right back." Sally hurried out of the room, leaving a very confused Luke lying there.

He continued wrestling with his thoughts. He must have been unconscious for days since he was far north of where he'd been the last time he knew where he was.

Slowly, he became aware of something tight around his torso, and moved his hand to his chest. Someone had wrapped bandages around him. He moved his hand upward and discovered his shoulder was bandaged, too, and so was his arm. The wounds he'd received during the shootout had been tended to.

With a sigh, he tuned into his wounds. They ached, but not too bad. With the instincts of a man who lived somewhat like a wild animal, Luke knew he wasn't going to die from his injuries after all. For that, he could thank whoever had come along and found him in that old cabin.

Footsteps sounded in the hallway outside the room. Sally came back in, followed by a tall man with very broad shoulders. She stepped over and pulled the curtains over the window, shielding Luke's eyes from the bright light. "I'm sorry, I should have thought to close these before I left. The sun must be blinding you."

Luke was looking at the man who stood next to the bed, but cleared his throat and managed to squeak out a few words. "That's all right. The sun was warm. Felt good."

The man's face was too rugged to call handsome, although it was the sort of face women usually found attractive. The strong features were topped by close-cropped, ash-blond hair. In him, Luke saw both his mother and his father, the resemblance vivid enough to almost take his breath away.

He knew he was looking at his brother. He almost said Kirby's name, but stopped himself in time.

The man gave him a friendly smile. "Welcome to the Sugarloaf. Sally was afraid we were going to lose you, but I took one look at her and told her not to worry. I know a stubborn varmint when I see one."

"He ought to," Sally put in. "He sees one looking back at him from the mirror every morning."

The man chuckled. "I'm Smoke Jensen. This is my ranch."

"L-Luke. Luke Smith."

"Pleased to meet you. We'll shake and howdy later, when you're feeling better. Right now you need some rest, Mr. Smith. You lost a lot of blood. Stubborn or not, it's a miracle you survived the trip up here from the Sangre de Cristos."

"How . . . how did I . . ."

"How'd you get here?" Smoke asked. "An old prospector heard a bunch of shooting and decided to go investigate."

The old-timer had been trying to protect his potential payoff, Luke thought.

"He had a couple friends visiting him at the time," Smoke went on, "a pair of old mountain men. They all went looking and found you still alive in a cabin with a bunch of dead men outside. It must have been quite a battle."

Luke managed to nod slightly. "It was," he whispered.

"Anyway, you'd been shot up and were running a fever. You were out of your head and did a lot of ranting and raving while they were taking care of you. You mentioned my name several times, and those mountain men knew who I was. I have a lot of friends among those old-timers. They figured I might know you, and when they thought you were strong enough, they decided to bring you up here." Smoke paused and gave Luke an intent look. "*Do* we know each other, Mr. Smith?"

Luke forced himself to shake his head. "S-sorry. Never saw you before." Those words practically broke his heart. He knew he was looking at his own flesh and blood.

Nearly twenty years had passed since he'd seen his little brother, and he couldn't even acknowledge that. Kirby—Smoke—had built a fine life for himself. Why ruin that by admitting the shot-up stranger was really his disreputable, bounty-hunting failure of a brother?

Smoke frowned. "Then why were you talking about me while you were feverish?"

"Hell . . . I don't know. Like you said . . . I was out of my head. Maybe I heard somebody else talking about you . . . before I got shot. I know the name . . . You're some sort of . . . gunfighter."

"That's a reputation I never set out to get." Smoke's face settled into grim lines.

The moment passed quickly, and he smiled again. "Well, I suppose it doesn't really matter. What's important is that you're safe here, and your wounds are starting to heal. Now that you're awake again, you can concentrate on resting and getting better."

"Why would you . . . go to so much trouble for me?" Luke asked. "For a . . . stranger?"

Sally answered his question. "Nobody who needs help is a stranger on the Sugarloaf, Mr. Smith. That's just the way we are around here."

"I can't . . . pay you."

Smoke's face hardened again. "You don't know Sally and me, so we'll let that pass. Are you hungry?"

Luke suddenly realized he was ravenous. It had probably been quite a while since he'd had any solid food. "Yeah. I could . . . sure eat."

"I have a pot of stew on the stove downstairs," Sally said. "I'll bring some up to you, although it'll be mostly broth starting out."

"That sounds . . . mighty good, ma'am. I'm . . . obliged to you." Luke looked at Smoke. "And to you."

"*De nada,*" Smoke said, then before he could go on, somebody knocked on the open door.

Luke cut his eyes in that direction and saw a tall, gangling cowboy standing in the doorway, holding a battered black hat in one hand.

Smoke looked toward the doorway and asked, "What is it, Pearlie?"

"Hate to bother you, Smoke, but Cal just rode in and told me somebody caved in a bunch of boulders on the Fortuna Ridge water-hole. Covered it up completely. We'll have to move the cows on that range, since they won't have any water."

"Could it have been a natural rockslide?" Smoke asked with a troubled frown.

"Didn't sound like it from what Cal said. He told me he rode up to the top of the ridge and found a place where a bunch of horses stopped this mornin'. He figured some of Baxter's men dabbed their loops on one of them boulders and used their horses to start it rollin'. That's all it would've took. But you can ride up there and take a look for yourself, if you want."

Smoke shook his head. "I trust Cal's opinion. He's a good hand, even if he is pretty young. But there's no way of knowing it was Baxter's men who ruined the waterhole."

"We don't know they were the hombres who took them potshots at us the other day, or ran off that jag of cattle, but who else could it be? You got any other enemies around here right now?"

"Simeon Baxter claims he just wants to be neighbors with us."

Pearlie let out a disgusted snort, then glanced at Sally. "Sorry for almost sayin' what I almost just said," he apologized.

"Don't worry about it," Sally told him with a smile. "I was probably thinking the same thing about Simeon Baxter. All I had to do was look at the man to know he can't be trusted . . . and I think you know that, too, Smoke. You just want to give him the benefit of the doubt."

"Yeah, well, that's starting to wear a little thin," Smoke admitted. "Pearlie, tell the boys to saddle up. We're going to take a ride over to the Baxter spread."

"Now you're talkin'," Pearlie said with undisguised enthusiasm. "I'll tell 'em to oil up their smoke poles, too."

"We're not going to ride in shooting."

"No, but we may have to ride out that way."

Smoke didn't dispute that speculation.

Luke saw the worried glance Sally directed in her husband's direction as Pearlie hurried away down the corridor.

"Is this going to turn into another range war, Smoke?" she asked.

"I hope not. I've had my fill of those, and I know you have, too. But I'm not going to let Simeon Baxter bull his way in and take over. You know me better than that."

"Yes. I do."

"And you wouldn't want me to be like that, anyway." Smoke went to her and kissed the thick dark hair on top of her head.

"No, I don't suppose I would," she agreed. "But I wish you'd be careful, anyway."

"Always," Smoke said with a grin. He hugged her and then hurried out after Pearlie.

"Sounds like . . . you folks have some trouble around here," Luke acknowledged.

"It's nothing for you to worry about, Mr. Smith," she assured him. "Just some range hog who moved in recently. He's got the loco idea in his head that he can bully Smoke Jensen."

"Sounds like . . . a pretty foolish thing to do."

"It is." Sally sighed. "I just hope this isn't the time Smoke's luck finally changes."

"It's not . . . luck." Luke knew it was the Jensen blood. The sheer determination to do the right thing and stand up for yourself. He had failed in that respect so long ago, and he'd been trying to make up for it ever since. He could take another step on the long road back . . . if he could strap on his guns and stand beside his brother as Smoke faced down this trouble.

But that wasn't possible, at least not at the moment. Luke had lost too much blood, been unconscious for too long, grown too weak. All he could do was lie there and regain his strength.

When he was stronger, he could offer to help Smoke with his troubles. He wouldn't have to reveal who he really was. He'd just be a grateful stranger returning a favor.

Time enough for that later. He could barely keep his eyes open.

Sally recognized his weariness. "I'll bring you some of that stew later, Mr. Smith. I think you need to rest a bit more before you eat."

"Maybe . . ." Luke murmured, trying to fight off the exhaustion threatening to wash over him. Realizing he couldn't, he gave in and let it claim him.

His last thought was that he wasn't passing out. It wasn't unconsciousness, it was good honest sleep. Healing sleep—just what he needed.

And when he woke up next time, he would be that much closer to being able to help his brother.

CHAPTER 30

The stew Sally Jensen brought up to him tasted as good as it smelled, Luke discovered after the delicious aroma roused him from his slumber. It seemed to possess some magical power, as well, he decided, because after one bowl of it, he felt strength coursing back into his body.

She sat in a chair beside his bed and fed him, and when the bowl was empty, Luke asked, "Did your husband get back from talking to that fellow Baxter?"

Sally had been smiling and cheerful when she came into the room, but a shadow passed over her face at his question. Luke didn't like that he had caused her distress, but he needed to know what was going on.

"They talked," Sally said. "Baxter denied having anything to do with the trouble we've been having. From the way Smoke sounded, it was pretty tense between them for a few minutes, but there was no shooting."

"That's good. Range wars usually don't work out well for either side."

"I know that. Sometimes you have to stand up and fight for what's yours, though. I know that, too."

Luke couldn't argue with her. Earlier, the exact same thought had crossed his mind. He said carefully, "I've heard stories about your husband, Mrs. Jensen. I would think a man would have to be pretty foolish to come in and try to hog Smoke Jensen's range."

"Some men are so arrogant they think they can have whatever they want," she replied with a shrug. "Baxter has plenty on his payroll who are fast with their guns. Smoke just has our ranch hands, although Pearlie had a reputation as a gunman, too, before he gave that up to be Sugarloaf's foreman."

"How did Smoke leave it with Baxter?"

"With a warning that nothing else had better happen."

Luke thought that was unlikely. He knew what Sally meant about the arrogance of some men driving them on, even when the smart thing to do would be to back off. He counted on the outlaws he hunted having the same attitude. They could usually be goaded into doing something stupid that would give him a chance to bring them down.

Sally changed the subject, saying she wanted to check the dressings on Luke's wounds. He let her do so, feeling a little bit embarrassed about having his sister-in-law poking around his body. She didn't know they were related, and he didn't tell her.

"Everything looks fine," she announced when she was finished. "Those old mountain men who found you probably had plenty of experience patching up bullet wounds. They took good care of you and put you on the road to recovery."

"How long do you think it'll be before I'm up and around?"

"Not long," she assured him. "It's mostly just a matter of getting your strength back." Sally hesitated. "I noticed a terrible scar on your back . . ."

"An old war wound," Luke said, trying not to sound too curt but making it clear he didn't want to talk about it.

"Smoke was too young for the war, but just barely. His father and brother fought in it, though."

Luke's interest quickened. "Did they make it through?"

"His father did . . . but he was killed not long afterward by some men responsible for the death of Smoke's brother Luke during the war." She cocked her head to the side as she looked down at him. "You have the same name as him."

Luke suddenly worried that he had probed too much. "There are plenty of men around named Luke."

"Of course there are."

Even though he knew he probably shouldn't, he risked another question. "What happened to those men? The ones responsible for the deaths of Smoke's pa and brother?"

"Smoke found them."

The flat sound of Sally's answer told Luke all he needed to know. Jasper Thornapple's information had been correct. Smoke had settled that long-standing score.

Only it was worse than Luke had ever known. From what Sally had just said, Potter and the others were responsible for the death of his father as well. The confirmation that Emmett Jensen was dead, and had died violently at the hands of trash like that, was like a knife inside Luke for a second.

"Good riddance, I'd say," he forced out.

"Yes, indeed," Sally agreed. She brightened. "You get some more rest now. Let that stew do its work."

"I'll do that," Luke promised. He leaned his head back against the pillows and closed his eyes. He owed a debt to Smoke Jensen for killing those four no-good thieves. He would find a way to pay that debt, he promised himself.

Even if it had to be as Luke Smith.

A couple nights later, Smoke brought him a cup of coffee and a plate of bear sign. Luke was glad to see him. After being unconscious for so long, once he began to get his strength back he wasn't nearly as sleepy.

"Need me to break pieces off this and feed 'em to you?" Smoke asked as he settled down in the chair beside the bed.

"I think I can handle a pastry." Luke sat up, moved the pillows behind him, and then proved it by taking one of the doughnuts off the plate.

"You sound like a cultured man, Smith."

Luke managed not to laugh. "Far from it. I just have a taste for reading. I suppose I've picked up a few things from that. Most of my life has been spent about as far from what people would consider culture as you can imagine."

"I have some books downstairs. Would you like me to bring a few of them up here for you?"

"That would be very much appreciated," Luke said.

"In the meantime, you can tell me about all those dead men scattered around the place where my friends found you."

Luke smiled. "You've been wanting to ask me about that ever since I woke up, haven't you?"

"That old prospector said they were outlaws. Somebody named

Solomon Burke and his gang. Supposed to be pretty bad hombres. Did you kill all of them by yourself?"

"Seemed like the thing to do, especially since they were trying to kill me at the time."

"If they were using that place for a hideout, that means they didn't ambush you. It was the other way around, wasn't it?"

"I was hunting them, yes," Luke admitted with a nod. "I was after the bounty on them." He had to laugh. "I'll bet that old pelican claimed it for himself, though."

"I wouldn't be surprised," Smoke said. "So you're a bounty hunter."

"That's right."

"There was a time I had a price on my head." Smoke shrugged. "But I suppose a fella's got to do whatever is necessary for him to get by."

"I don't blame you for not being fond of the idea of having a bounty hunter under your roof. For what it's worth, all the men I've gone after were bad sorts, the kind of men who really need to be behind bars or six feet under."

"As far as you know," Smoke said.

Luke inclined his head in acknowledgment of that point. "I believe I'm right, but no one knows everything about the other people in this world."

"That's true. For example, you strike me as the sort of man who has secrets of his own, Smith."

Luke didn't like the turn in the conversation. "You already know all that's worth knowing about me, Jensen."

It sounded odd to him, saying his own name like that.

"I'm not sure," Smoke said. "There's something about you . . . something I can't put my finger on. I feel like I ought to know you. Are you sure we've never met?"

"Positive." Luke hoped he kept the tension out of his voice. "I know who you are, but I never heard the name Smoke Jensen until a couple years ago." That was true, as far as it went.

Smoke made a face. "I never asked for a reputation as a gun-fighter. I just wanted to be left alone. But then I found out some men had done my family wrong—skunks who had to be dealt with—and I set out to do it. I'd already met an old mountain man named Preacher. He taught me how to handle a gun. Taught me everything worth knowing that my pa hadn't already taught me. Along the way I got married to a fine woman, even had a son, but some other evil lowlifes took that family away from me. I met a young fella named Matt Cavanaugh and took him under my wing the way Preacher did with me. Matt's the same as my brother now, even goes by the name Matt Jensen. Then Sally came along—" Smoke stopped and shook his head.

"I don't know why I started going on about all of that. You're not interested in my checkered past, as they say in the dime novels. But it might be boring enough to help you sleep."

"I wasn't bored," Luke said honestly. In fact, he had a hard time keeping the emotion out of his voice. Hearing about his brother's life stirred up a lot of feelings inside him. He wished he had gone home after the war, that he had been at Kirby's side when trouble came to call. Things might have turned out completely different.

But he hadn't been able to return. He'd been a wanted fugitive, and didn't know Kirby—Smoke—had gone through the same sort of ordeal for a while.

All that was behind them. Luke couldn't think of a single reason why he couldn't tell Smoke who he really was.

And suddenly that was exactly what he wanted to do.

I've been a damned fool all these years, he told himself.

As soon as Thornapple told him the gunfighter named Smoke Jensen had killed Potter, Stratton, Richards, and Casey, Luke should have gone looking for him and found out the truth. That blasted prideful stubbornness of his had stolen two more years out of his life, two years he could have spent with his brother . . . or at least knowing he had a brother.

The coffee and the bear sign were forgotten. Luke wasn't sure exactly how he would go about it, but it was long past time for the truth to come out.

And it might have, if fate hadn't chosen that moment for the sudden, harsh sound of gunfire to fill the night.

CHAPTER 31

Smoke was on his feet instantly, blowing out the lamp on the bedside table and stepping to the window to flick back the curtain so he could look out without being silhouetted. "Masked raiders shooting up the place," he snapped, dropping the curtain.

Luke opened his mouth to say he wanted to help, but it was too late. Smoke was through the doorway and gone, leaving Luke sitting in the bed listening to the sounds of battle as gunmen attacked his brother's ranch.

Not while I can do anything about it, by God, Luke thought as resolve stiffened his muscles. Especially since his revolvers were within reach.

Earlier, he had asked Sally where his guns were. She'd tried to tell him not to worry about that, but he had persisted, learning his gun belt and the twin Remingtons were in a wardrobe at the side of the room, along with his clothes. His Winchester was downstairs.

He didn't think he could handle stairs, but he could get to his revolvers. He pushed the covers aside, swung his legs out of bed, and stood up.

A wave of dizziness swept through him. He fought it off as his eyes adjusted to the moonlight filtering through the curtains. Tightly bandaged as he was, he found he could move around without his wounds hurting too much. Wearing only those bandages and the bottom half of a pair of long underwear, he made his way to the wardrobe and opened it.

It had been too long, he thought as his hands closed around the smooth walnut grips of the guns. For a decade and a half, the weapons he carried had been the closest friends he had. That might not be true anymore—he had a brother again—but it still felt mighty good to heft the Remingtons as he turned around and walked back to the open window.

The night breezes were tainted with the acrid bite of powder smoke as Luke thrust the curtains aside and looked out. Riders with bandannas tied over their faces galloped through the open area between the ranch house and the bunkhouse. The guns in their hands spat flame and lead as they sent shots in both directions.

Return fire came from the Sugarloaf's defenders, but they were heavily outnumbered. Luke figured there were at least thirty raiders in the yard.

He could improve the odds a little, he thought as he thrust the right-hand Remington out the window, drew a bead on one of the riders, and fired. The masked man rocked back in his saddle and had to drop his gun and grab the saddle horn to keep from toppling off his mount.

One low-down sacker out of the fight, Luke told himself. He eared back the Remington's hammer and shifted his aim to another of the masked men.

He got off several rounds, dropping a couple more men, before the raiders noticed the shots coming from the second floor window of the ranch house. A few twisted in their saddles and flung their guns up to fire in that direction. Luke was forced to reel back from the window as glass shattered and bullets whipped through the opening.

He waited until the barrage stopped and then moved forward again, kneeling at the window so the wall gave him some cover. It looked thick enough to stop most bullets.

Still galloping back and forth, the raiders continued their barrage, but the deadly accurate fire of the defenders was starting to take a toll. Luke added to it by triggering both revolvers and spraying bullets among the marauders. Gun-thunder rolled from the Remingtons.

The masked killers finally had enough. The one who seemed to be in command wheeled his horse and yelled, "Let's get out of here!"

Those still mounted—some badly wounded—followed him as he galloped off into the darkness, leaving seven or eight bodies scattered on the ground.

Luke didn't stand up immediately. He didn't want to catch a final wild slug thrown through the shattered window.

Also, he was tired. When he was sure they were all gone, he placed his left-hand gun on the floor and used that hand to brace himself as he leaned forward and drew in several deep breaths. The bandages around his midsection prevented him from breathing too deeply, but he did the best he could.

The door opened behind him. Sally Jensen stood in the doorway, wearing a nightdress and a coat slung around her shoulders. "Mr. Smith! Are you all right?"

Luke looked back over his shoulder at her, noticing immediately the rifle in her hands. He figured she had been right in the middle of the fight downstairs. "I'm fine."

Feeling a little stronger, he picked up the gun and pushed himself to his feet.

"Smoke said he thought he heard shots coming from up here. You really shouldn't have gotten out of bed."

"After all you folks have done for me, I wasn't going to just lie there while you were under attack," Luke argued. "That's not the way I'm built."

Sally smiled. "I know. We haven't been acquainted for long, Mr. Smith, but you remind me a little of my husband. He can't turn his back on a fight, either."

It was the Jensen blood, Luke thought, but he couldn't say that. Instead he asked, "Was anybody hurt?"

Sally's smile was replaced by a look of grim anger. "We're fine in here, but Smoke's gone out to the bunkhouse to see about the men. I'm worried some of them were wounded."

Luke became uncomfortably aware that he was standing in his underwear with a pair of empty guns in his hands. He wasn't sure which of those things bothered him more. He didn't think the masked raiders would double back and launch another attack, but the possibility couldn't be ruled out entirely. First things first, he decided. "I'd better reload. Just in case."

"No, what you'd better do is get back in that bed and let me check your dressings. I want to make sure none of your wounds have broken open again."

Luke thought about it for a second, then chuckled. "I always try not to argue with a woman, especially one holding a loaded rifle."

"That's a good policy," Sally told him, smiling again.

He was back in bed and she had taken a look at his bandages, determining that none of the wounds were bleeding again by the time

Smoke came into the room with a Colt in his hand. Sally turned toward him with a worried frown on her face.

"Two men were killed," Smoke reported. "Steve Rankin and Charlie Moss."

Sally cringed. "Oh, no. What about the wounded?"

"A bullet busted Phil Weston's arm. Other than that just some nicks and scratches." Smoke's face was set in hard, bleak lines. "But they killed two men who rode for me, and I'm not going to let Baxter get away with that."

"You don't know they were Baxter's men," Sally maintained.

"Yes, I do. I took a look at the bodies of the men they left behind. I remember seeing all of them at Baxter's place when I was over there a couple days ago."

"Then you can go tell Monte about it and let the law handle this," Sally suggested.

Smoke shook his head. "I'll send a rider to Big Rock tomorrow to tell Monte what happened, but Pearlie, the rest of the men, and I will be heading for Baxter's ranch."

Sally opened her mouth, and for a second Luke thought she was going to argue with her husband. But then she nodded. "You're right, Smoke. We need to stomp our own snakes."

Smoke grunted. "Damn right we do." His expression eased a little as he looked at Luke. "Are you all right, Smith?"

Luke nodded. "I'm fine."

"You were burning some powder up here, weren't you? I heard the shots."

Luke grinned. "Like I told your wife, I owe you folks too much to sit by and do nothing. If you'll let me borrow a horse, I'll ride over to Baxter's with you in the morning for the showdown."

"Oh, now, I don't think that would be a good idea at all," Sally protested. "You're not in good enough shape to ride yet, Mr. Smith."

"I agree with Sally," Smoke added. "But I appreciate the offer. I'm obliged to you for taking a hand tonight, too. You're probably responsible for some of those men we downed."

Luke knew he was, but didn't say anything. He'd never been one to boast.

Smoke went on. "You just keep recuperating. I'll handle Baxter."

Luke nodded. "All right." He looked at Sally. "I'd be obliged, though, if you'd bring my gun belt over here. I sure don't like having empty guns." He smiled. "Gives a man the fantods."

* * *

Pearlie, Calvin Woods, and the rest of the Sugarloaf hands were so upset about the deaths of their friends that they had wanted to charge over to Simeon Baxter's ranch right away and settle the score. But Smoke had decided to wait for daylight, thinking Baxter might have an ambush set up for them.

He mentioned that reasoning to Luke early the next morning, before dawn actually, when he stopped by Luke's room.

"That's good thinking," Luke agreed. "I've ridden into more ambushes than I should have, just because I was too eager or too careless. Gunfighting is almost as much about thinking as it is about shooting."

"You sound like a man speaking from bitter experience," Smoke commented.

"Is there any other kind?"

Smoke hefted the rifle he had carried into the room. "I brought your Winchester up. I don't expect you to need it, but I thought you might feel better having it close at hand."

Luke smiled. "Thanks. You'd better not put it on the bed, though. Mrs. Jensen wouldn't like it if you got gun oil on her sheets."

"Wouldn't be the first time," Smoke said with a grin as he placed the rifle on the floor next to the bed. He didn't look like a man who was about to ride off and fight a battle to the death with a ruthless enemy. But like Luke, life on the frontier had taught Smoke how to live in the moment.

"Still wish I was going with you," Luke said.

"I know that." Smoke stuck out a hand. "And I appreciate it."

They shook. Again, Luke wished he could tell Smoke who he really was, but he had decided that could wait. Smoke already had enough on his mind without the shock of finding out the brother he had thought to be dead for the past fifteen years was really alive.

"Sally will be up with some breakfast in a little bit." Smoke lifted a hand in farewell and left the room.

Luke looked at the holstered revolvers and coiled shell belt on the table beside the bed, then pushed the covers back and swung his feet to the floor. He stood up, feeling a lot steadier than he had the night before. Getting back into action seemed to have had a bracing effect on him.

With the approach of dawn, the sky outside was lighter. He went over to the wardrobe, opened it, and could see his clothes hanging on hooks inside the wardrobe. As he pulled on the black shirt and buttoned it up he realized it was clean. Sally had cleaned and patched his clothes. He took the black trousers off the hook, braced himself with one hand on the wardrobe and hung the pants as low as possible with his other hand. Gingerly, he put one leg, then the other into the pants and pulled them up around his hips.

He picked up his boots and clean socks from the floor of the wardrobe and carried them to the chair. Carefully, he lowered himself down. Taking a big breath, he crossed one leg over the other and pulled on a sock. He grimaced. One sock, and he needed to rest before crossing the other leg and pulling on the other sock. It had taken more effort than he had anticipated. After another moment or two, he stood and stuck his feet into his boots. It wasn't easy, but he managed without doing any damage to his wounds.

Being dressed made him feel even better, but he wasn't *fully* dressed yet, he thought with a wry smile as he turned toward the bedside table. He picked up the cross-draw rig and buckled it on.

A footstep sounded at the doorway. "What in the world are you doing, Mr. Smith?" Sally stood with her hands on her hips.

Luke turned toward her. "I was thinking I might come downstairs for breakfast for a change."

"I'm not sure that's wise."

"I've got to get up and start moving around again sometime. The sooner I do, the sooner I'll get better."

She gave him a stern look for a moment, then shook her head and laughed. "I've seen Smoke act exactly the same way, and arguing with him never did any good, either. I swear, if I didn't know better—" She stopped short, and a puzzled frown came over her face.

To keep her from thinking too much, Luke said hurriedly, "If you'd just pick up that rifle and hand it to me . . . I'm not sure I'm ready to do a lot of bending yet."

"All right." She went over to the bed, picked up the Winchester, and gave it to him. "You want your hat, too? It's in the wardrobe."

"A gentleman doesn't wear his hat indoors. I know I may not look like one, but I strive for a certain standard of civilized behavior."

"No offense, Mr. Smith, but you're an odd man."

"So I've been told."

Keeping the rifle in one hand and the other on the wall for support, Luke followed Sally down the stairs. As they reached the kitchen, he heard the sound of numerous horses leaving the ranch.

Her face tightened at the sound. Smoke and the other men were riding off for the showdown with Simeon Baxter and his hired gunmen. She knew her husband was going into danger, but what woman ever truly got used to it?

Sally brought Luke a cup of coffee and a plate of flapjacks, bacon, and eggs, and he dug in with gusto. His appetite had come back as strong as ever, and Sally's good cooking had already put some meat back on his bones.

As he ate, he asked, "Did Smoke get any sleep last night?"

"Not much," Sally admitted. "He was upset about the men who were killed. He was up early this morning, well before dawn, digging graves for them in the little graveyard we have here on the ranch. Pearlie went out to help him, but Smoke would have done it by himself."

"He's a good man," Luke said.

"The best I've ever met, by far," Sally agreed. "And I thank God every day that the two of us found each other."

Luke would have liked to think he had something to do with the way Smoke had turned out, but that wasn't likely. Kirby had been only twelve years old when Luke went off to war, so he hadn't had much chance to mold the boy into the man he had grown up to be. Their father had more to do with that, along with the old mountain man called Preacher. Luke hoped to hear a lot more about him before his visit to the Sugarloaf was over.

And it was only a visit, no doubt about that. Even if he told Smoke the truth and Smoke invited him to stay at the ranch, Luke knew that wasn't going to happen. Smoke sure as hell didn't owe him a home, and after all the years of drifting, Luke didn't think he was even capable of settling down.

After breakfast, he said, "I think I'll go sit out on the front porch for a while, and take the rifle with me. I believe the sun might be good for me."

"You're probably right. I'll clean up in here, and then I might come out and join you." Sally paused, then added, "I'm really curious about something, Luke . . . but we can talk about that later."

He frowned as he made his way to the porch. He had an idea what Sally wanted to talk about, and it wasn't a conversation he wanted to have just yet. Not until he'd discussed it with Smoke, anyway.

She might not give him any choice, though, he thought as he carefully sat down in one of the rocking chairs on the porch and slowly cocked his right ankle on his left knee. After the way she had taken care of him, he didn't think he could bring himself to lie to her.

His head was so full of those thoughts he almost didn't notice the wink of sunlight on something metal in the trees about two hundred yards away from the ranch house. But his instincts still worked and shouted a warning to him. He hadn't stayed alive by ignoring what his gut told him.

He threw himself forward, landing on the porch on his knees, just as a rifle cracked in the distance. He felt the wind-rip of a bullet passing close beside his ear.

CHAPTER 32

Two hundred yards was too far for a handgun, so Luke drew his rifle and fired a shot in the direction of the hidden rifleman, aiming high so the bullet would carry a little farther. Ignoring the pain lancing through his side, he rolled toward the doorway as another shot blasted. He didn't want the wound on his side to break open and start bleeding again, but that pain was better than being a sitting duck.

The slug struck the rocking chair he'd been sitting in, and a chunk of wood flew off the back of it.

"Mr. Smith!" Sally cried as she jerked the door open. "Luke!"

He dived at her, tackling her around the knees and taking her down as a bullet plowed into the door. They scrambled farther into the house, and Luke kicked the door closed behind them.

"Luke!" Sally gasped. "I heard shots! What—"

A rumble of hoofbeats sounded outside, and Luke knew Smoke had miscalculated . . . and so had he. Neither had realized Baxter's attack on the ranch the night before was just a feint. Baxter had counted on some of his men being killed, and on Smoke recognizing them. He'd been trying to goad Smoke into rushing over to the neighboring spread and taking most, if not all, of the Sugarloaf crew with him.

"It's Baxter," Luke told Sally in a taut, grim voice. "He's come for you. He figures with you as his prisoner, Smoke won't have any choice but to do what Baxter tells him."

"Men have tried that before," Sally informed him. "Smoke killed them. He'll kill Baxter."

"More than likely," Luke agreed as the rush of hoofbeats came to a stop outside the house. "If I don't kill him first." He jerked his head toward the stairs. "Get up there. I'll stop them."

"You're one man against two dozen, and you're wounded!" Sally protested. "You can't—"

"Go!" Luke told her as he climbed to his feet. He didn't have anything to lose, making him more dangerous than any number of men Baxter could muster.

Sally didn't understand that. She stood up beside him, and suddenly threw her arms around him and came up on her toes to brush a kiss across his gaunt cheek. "Luke," she whispered, "I don't know how it's possible, but I think I know—"

"Just go," he cut in, "while you still can."

A man shouted orders outside. The gunnies knew Baxter wanted Sally alive, but they also knew at least one man with a gun was inside. Luke figured they wouldn't come in shooting for fear of hurting her, but they would rush the place, counting on the force of numbers to overwhelm any opposition.

Sally squeezed his arm and turned to run to the stairs. As she started up, Luke faced the door, squaring himself to the opening and bracing his feet. He had both guns drawn and pointed at the doorway, waiting grimly to start their thunderous song.

He didn't have long to wait. Something crashed against the door and it flew open. Hard-faced men with guns in their hands rushed into the room, and at the sight of the tall, lean man dressed in black waiting for them, they raised the weapons to open fire.

They were too late. The revolvers in Luke's hands were already spouting flaming death.

As it always did at such moments, everything else faded away for Luke. The world receded until there was nothing left in the universe except him and the men he was trying to kill . . . the men who were trying to kill him. The roar of guns was like the bellow of great primordial beasts, the clouds of powder smoke rolling through the room like the eruption of ancient volcanoes, and the blood flowing the bright crimson of man like going all the way back to the dawn of time.

Luke didn't feel the smash of bullets like he expected. He was still on his feet and fighting, and that was all that mattered to him. Men fell before his guns like wheat before a scythe.

Vaguely, he became aware of shots pealing out from other places.

There seemed to be a battle going on *outside* the ranch house, as well as a rifle blasting somewhere close by.

Suddenly, as the hammers of both Remingtons clicked on empty chambers, only one enemy faced him, a tall, burly man with a rough-hewn face and silver hair under a black Stetson. The man's clothes were better and more expensive than those of the others, and Luke had a hunch he was facing Simeon Baxter.

That was confirmed a second later when the man pointed a fancy, nickel-plated revolver at Luke and yelled, "I don't know who you are, you lousy interloper, but you've ruined all my plans! Now you're gonna die, you and that skirt both!"

Luke glanced over and realized Sally was standing beside him, holding the Winchester. "I'm empty. You?"

"Me, too." But she was smiling, unafraid.

Luke realized why when a powerful voice bellowed from outside, "Baxter!"

The would-be cattle baron whirled around. A shot blasted from his gun, soaring harmlessly into the air, and was answered by a pair of crashing reports from a Colt. The bullets drove Baxter through the doorway and spilled him onto his back, almost at the feet of Luke and Sally. He writhed in pain, pawing at his chest with blood welling through his fingers, and ended up on his side looking up at Luke. "Who . . . who are you?" he gasped.

Smoke appeared in the doorway. "His name's Luke Jensen. He's my brother."

Baxter's head sagged back, an ugly rattle came from his throat, and he died.

Normally the first thing Luke did when he held empty guns was reload them, but he was just too tired. He slid both guns back into their holsters and looked himself over, expecting to see more blood on his clothes. It was a shock to realize he didn't seem to be hit. With all the lead that had been flying around the room, he didn't see how it was possible, but he didn't feel any new pains, just a dull ache in his side from that old wound.

Smoke pouched his iron and rushed across the room to draw Sally into his arms. He cupped a hand behind her head and kissed her. "Are you all right?" he asked when he lifted his mouth from hers a moment later.

"I'm fine . . . thanks to Luke. Smoke, he's—"

"My brother. I know. I can't figure out how it's possible, but there's no doubt in my mind." With his arms still around Sally, Smoke turned his head to look at Luke. "All I had to do was see him standing there with the dead men he'd killed defending you heaped at his feet, and I knew." He shifted so that he could hold out a hand to Luke. "Welcome home . . . brother."

Luke didn't hesitate. Reaching out, he clasped his brother's hand.

Pearlie and the other hands had dragged the corpses out of the living room and dumped sand on the floor to soak up the blood. Cleaning it all up was going to take awhile.

In the kitchen, Smoke filled Sally and Luke in on what had happened after he left the ranch. "I figured out what Baxter was up to when we were about halfway to his ranch. We turned around and got back here as fast as we could, with me kicking myself for being a damned fool the whole way."

"You were upset about your men being killed last night," Luke said. "It's understandable you wanted to have a showdown with Baxter."

"And that's what he was counting on." Smoke shook his head. "I'm just glad we got back in time."

"So am I," Luke said with a wry smile. "I didn't have enough bullets to kill all of Baxter's men."

"Maybe not, but from the sound of it I expected to find a small army trying to fight them off inside the house, not just the two of you."

"Luke did most of it." Sally gave credit where credit was due. "I never saw anybody handle guns like that, Smoke . . . well, nobody but you, that is."

"It's a skill that seems to run in the family." Smoke took a sip of his coffee and fixed Luke with an intent look across the table. "I heard you were killed fighting Yankees in the wilderness, and then told later you were murdered by those varmints who stole that shipment of Confederate gold. What's the real story, Luke?"

"I suppose if anyone has a right to hear it, it's you." Luke looked away. "Some of it's not too pretty, though."

"I want to know anyway."

"Of course."

For the next half hour, Luke told them everything that had happened since that fateful night in Richmond with the Yankee artillery pounding away at the city. He didn't leave out anything. When he was finished, he glanced at Sally and saw tears shining in her eyes.

"You considered yourself a failure because those terrible men ambushed you?" She wiped at a tear.

"They stole the gold I was supposed to protect. They killed my friends."

"And they nearly killed you! My God, Luke, that wasn't your fault. You could have gone back home to your family."

He shrugged. "I saw it differently." He knew from the look in Smoke's eyes that his brother understood.

"That wasn't all. I was wanted for murder in Georgia."

"Well, that just wasn't right," Sally declared. "You were only trying to protect that girl and her grandfather."

"Yes, but I figured I'd caused enough trouble for them."

"*You* didn't cause the trouble." Sally was starting to sound a little exasperated with him. "You saved them from it!" She blew out her breath and shook her head. "You stiff-necked Jensen boys! Matt's the same way, and he's not even a blood relative. You all think you have to be perfect and that you can never let anybody down."

"Well, that's something to aspire to, isn't it?" Smoke asked with a faint smile.

"Maybe . . . but it's not human." Sally took Smoke's hand, then reached across the table and clasped Luke's hand, too. "At least the two of you are back together, after all these years. Now I understand why you seemed so familiar to me, Luke. Even though you and Smoke don't look that much alike, I was seeing him in you. I knew there was something special about you all along."

"That's nice to hear," he told her as he squeezed her hand.

"And you have a home again at last," Sally added.

Luke didn't say anything. Glancing at Smoke, he saw the knowledge in his brother's eyes and realized Smoke knew he wasn't going to stay on permanently. Luke could never adjust to that sort of life. The wanderlust was just too strong in him.

Anyway, he still had outlaws to hunt down.

But not right away.

At that moment, he was content to sit in a quiet kitchen with his family and know that, while the place would never be his home, it was as close to one as he would ever come.

EPILOGUE

Three weeks later, on a cool morning with streamers of fog hanging around the mountain peaks in the distance, Luke saddled the fine horse Smoke had insisted was his and led the animal out of the barn, leading a pack horse behind him. He had thought he might be able to slip away from the ranch without anybody noticing until he was gone, but he supposed that was too much to hope for.

Smoke stood waiting for him. "You don't have to go, you know."

"Yeah, I do." Luke checked the cinches one more time. "I've been talking to Monte Carson, and he tells me that Badger McCoy was spotted up in Laramie a few days ago."

Monte Carson was the local sheriff in Big Rock, and he had a whole desk drawer full of wanted posters he had let Luke look through.

"Badger McCoy," Smoke repeated.

"Train robber. The reward's only eight hundred dollars, but I have a hunch I can get more out of the railroad if I'm able to recover some of the loot McCoy's stolen, too."

"So you're bound and determined to go on risking your life hunting down fugitives?"

"It's what I do," Luke said. If anybody could understand that, it was Smoke.

After a moment, Smoke nodded. "Sally won't be happy you didn't tell her good-bye."

Luke shook his head. "Not good at that."

"I know. I'll try to explain it to her. And I'll tell her you promised to come back. You will, won't you? I want you to meet Preacher and Matt."

"I'd like that." Luke put out his hand. "Next time."

"Next time," Smoke agreed as he shook hands.

Luke swung up into the saddle, but before he could ride away, Smoke went on, "There's one more thing."

"What's that?"

"Forget about calling yourself Luke Smith. You've got a name. You should use it."

Luke frowned. "You really want people to know me as Luke Jensen? A bounty hunter?"

"You're a good man and you're my brother." Smoke looked up at Luke. "That's all I care about. Jensen's a proud name, and I think you should wear it."

Luke thought about it for a moment and then nodded. "All right. If that's what you want, I can do that."

"Good. So long, Luke."

Lifting a hand in farewell, Luke turned his horses and rode out of the ranch yard.

"Don't forget!" Smoke called after him. "You always have a home here if you want it!"

Luke waved, but didn't look back as he rode north. *Home*, he thought. He hadn't had one of those for a long, long time. The idea would take some getting used to.

But it was a pretty thing to think about. It surely was.